"FULL OF SLAMBANG ACTION"

Publishers Weekly

"How delicious it is . . . events, spies, frighteners, and zaniness begin from page one and mount in liveliness and suspense to the end. Characters are splendid, sky-high improbable, but always rooted in simple truth. Description of both scenes and happenings is wonderfully skillful."

The London Times

"Peter Dickinson upstages almost everyone around with his distinctively different, stylish and literate entertainments and just one word will do—*exceptional.*"

Kirkus Reviews

Other Avon Books by
Peter Dickinson

THE POISON ORACLE 33308 $1.50

PETER
DICKINSON
THE LIVELY DEAD

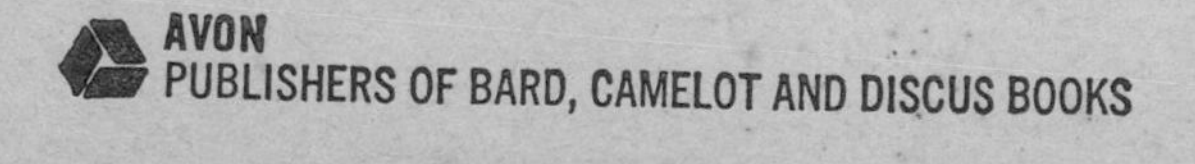
AVON
PUBLISHERS OF BARD, CAMELOT AND DISCUS BOOKS

Originally published in Great Britain by Hodder and Stoughton Limited.

AVON BOOKS
A division of
The Hearst Corporation
959 Eighth Avenue
New York, New York 10019

Published by arrangement with Pantheon Books.
Library of Congress Catalog Card Number: 74-25226
ISBN: 0-380-01706-7

First Avon Printing, August, 1977

Printed in the U.S.A.

THE LIVELY DEAD

1

BENDING TO ADJUST THE CLAW of her crowbar against a joist, Lydia saw the man's feet. The Building Inspector from the Borough Council, she thought, come about that beam and high time too. She didn't turn round because it amuses most men to see a woman struggling with a man's work, and consequently it amused Lydia to startle them. She heaved firmly on the crowbar and relished the mandrake-screech as the nails came up that vital first quarter-inch.

Then she worked along the board, using the crowbar in her right hand and the claw-hammer in her left. It came out more cleanly than some. If it wasn't infected she could use it again. She flipped it over on its back above the cavity and worked along it with the hammer, banging the nails half-way out so that she could turn it over once more and claw them free. A male workman would have let them fall into the cavity, but Lydia collected them in an old coffee-tin, not because they were any use but because she didn't like the idea of bent and rusty nails littered below her floor. When at last she looked up, pretending to notice him for the first time, she found it was not a bloke from the Council but a gentleman from the Government–little Mr Obb, currently Minister of Maritime Affairs, waiting there dapper and sad.

"I interrupt, I fear," he said.

"I'm in a bit of a hurry," said Lydia. "If I don't get the floor back down before I fetch Dickie he'll insist on exploring the whole cavity, and get stuck probably and filthy certainly. I don't really mind him getting dirty, except that it's not too easy to clean him up again at the moment."

Mr Obb smiled, but even that was sad. He was a small, freckled, shiny old man with very pale eyes. The dust and the dank odour from the cavity and the dreary light from the bare bulb seemed like a stage atmosphere, created to enhance his central melancholy. Bloody hell, thought Lydia. He wants me to do something.

"It is not nice to be stuck under floors," he said. "I have hidden for five weeks in much such a place, under a cabin in the woods. The ground was marshy so that my clothes rotted off my limbs. Only I did not rot."

"Is something the matter, Mr Obb?"

"Yes, yes. The duplicator will not function."

As Lydia rose from her knees echoes of that first "bloody hell" diminished down the tunnels of her resentment. But it probably wouldn't take ten minutes, and it might be useful to see what sort of a mess the Government were making of their rooms since Mrs Newbury had died.

"OK, I'll see what I can do," she said, beginning to peel off the rubber gloves and kick off her wellingtons at the same time.

"Have I behaved carelessly, coming down here in ordinary clothes?" asked Mr Obb.

"It's all right," said Lydia, slipping her feet into her Scholl sandals. "There's a lot of mumbo-jumbo about dry rot—the spores are all over the place anyway, so it doesn't make much difference if you spread a few more around. What matters is leaving infected timber about. I wear these things to keep myself in decent nick. Shall I go first?"

The Government occupied the top two floors of the five-storey house in Devon Crescent, W.11, of which Lydia was the landlord. They had their own brass plate and bell at the front door, and again at the inner door at the bottom of the flight up to the fourth floor. By the time they reached this point Mr Obb was gasping with the climb, so that Lydia knew that despite her hurry she'd have to stop and let him rest. Poor old boy, she thought; he'd already been something in the Livonian Government when the Russians had taken over the Baltic States in 1940; say he'd been fortyish then, he must be well over seventy now. But even a septuagenarian male face has to be saved, if possible. She nodded towards Mrs Newbury's door, on the right of the landing.

"Have you found a new cleaner yet?" she asked. "You'll miss Mrs N."

"We are interviewing candidates," said Mr Obb, a little distantly, as if wishing to imply that the engagement of a charlady was an Internal and not a Maritime Affair.

"It won't be the same, I'm afraid," said Lydia. "She was very fond of you."

"A good servant. To such people one has obligations."

Again, despite the panting, Lydia heard a tone of mild reproof, as if Mr Obb didn't admit the relationship of "fondness" between master and servant. Silly old driveller, she thought, but her impatience with him was suddenly exorcised by his sweet smile.

"We have made all arrangements for the funeral," he said.

"Yes, I know. It's very kind of you."

"It will be in the Liv fashion. The coffin comes here to-day, at noon."

"Back here!" Lydia claimed to be squeamish not about death itself but about the trappings and fuss of burial.

"That is our fashion. I understand that she had no kin except this daughter who is in prison, so it is for us to sit and watch with the body while the Long Candle burns and the soul goes to God. Then to-morrow is the burial. You will attend?"

Lydia shrugged. It was the last thing she wished to do, but she was grateful to the old man for taking all this on. Almost her first thought when she was coming out of the shock of Mrs Newbury's death had been that she'd have to find the cash to give her even a half-decent funeral, such as she'd longed for, and that would mean cutting down on the plasterer's wages and doing some of the plastering herself, which would have been infuriating as Lydia knew she couldn't do it up to professional standards. And then Mr Obb had taken over. So she could hardly refuse to attend the dreary ceremony.

"Of course I'll come," she said. "And I'll ring up the prison and see if they'll let the daughter out."

"Excellent," said Mr Obb after a slight pause. "I understand she is very beautiful."

Panting no longer he fished a key out of his waistcoat, opened the door and led the way up.

Lydia had never discovered whether all Livonians were mechanical morons, or whether it was just a coincidence that the members of the Government were. Their Gestetner was a servant almost as old as Mrs Newbury and no less faithful, but they treated it without respect. One small error and they panicked, twiddling knobs at random and when that failed applying extra ink to the rollers. The gaunt, grey widows who did their typing would not go near the machine. Lydia, soon after she had bought the house, had come in on one of these scenes of grimy desperation and had sorted things out for them. Since then they had tended to come down about once a month to ask for help.

This time heaps of crumpled paper lay around, streaked with great black lines round the edges. General Busch was standing by the window, tense as a weightlifter, as though making up his mind to throw up the sash and leap to oblivion. Count Linden was kneeling amid the mess, apparently praying. Lydia cleaned up the roller, reset the spacers and eased the stencil smooth. As she adjusted the pile of paper in the rack she saw what was wrong.

"This isn't duplicating paper," she said. "You can't use this."

Mr Obb translated. General Busch swung round from the window with his great slab of a face frowning and his pale eyes glaring at Lydia. He spoke in Livonian.

"The Prime Minister insists that we use that paper," said Mr Obb. "It is high quality paper, for respect. Aakisen is dead."

"Dead!" said Lydia.

"The President of the Livonian Republic is dead," said Mr Obb. "It will be in your newspapers to-morrow, if you can make the duplicator function. The Muscovites have never admitted that they captured him, but we knew. And now further news has reached us. He died two months ago at a camp in Sredne Vilyuysk in Siberia. Only now can we announce this horrible murder to the world. But we must use dignified paper."

"I'm sorry," said Lydia.

She thought of Mrs Newbury and her horror of a pauper's funeral. She thought of these old men, hearing that their national hero, their Churchill-figure, was dead at last, but still finding time and reserves of decency to see that their servant was buried with respect.

"OK," she said, sighing. "I'll see what I can do."

Each sheet needed to be fed individually into the machine. The ink supply had to be exactly right, because the paper was barely absorbent. For the same reason each sheet had to be separately lifted clear and draped somewhere to dry. At first Lydia wasted two sheets in three, but two hours later she had got the ratio down to one in three, and then the job was done. She was dead beat, far more than if she had spent the morning heaving up floor-boards.

"We are truly grateful," said Mr Obb, shirt-sleeved and streaked with ink, but smiling still.

"Varotnisho!" shouted General Busch.

Count Linden, lean and wispy and grey as a mouse's belly, hobbled next door and came back with a heavy decanter and four small tumbler-shaped glasses. The liquid was paler than cider. Lydia sniffed her tot with curiosity and caution, and found it smelt like a milder version of the solvent used in her dry-rot fungicide.

"Aakisen!" snapped General Busch, making the name sound like a snuff-taker's sneeze.

"Aakisen," said the other three, Lydia a little late. The men downed their tots at a gulp. Lydia sipped. As her eyes unblurred she saw swimmingly before her the last sheet she had printed.

AAKU AAKISEN DEAD

President of Livonia, Hero and Patriot,
dies in secret Siberian Labour Camp.
After seventy-six years of fighting and suffering for his country, the great Aaku Aakisen is dead at last.
The hero who, from his marshy hide-out among the Baltic lakes, for nine years defied the might of Stalin's armies, and who since 1955 . . .

Lydia didn't want to know any of that. It was over. She sipped again at her glass and found that she relished the stuff, fiery but smooth, with a strange, clean, piny flavour.

"I'm afraid I can't drink it at a gulp like you do," she said.

"Good, good," said Count Linden. "That is for men and peasant-women. A lady takes only little sips. I regret that we have no smaller glass."

Hell, thought Lydia, watching the little grey creep serve out another whack to the men, next time I'll get it down in one, and I bloody well won't choke either.

"What is it?" she asked.

"Vodka," said Mr Obb.

"But I thought . . ."

"Muscovite vodka is a liquid designed to make swine drunk without effort," explained Count Linden. "This is the vodka of the Livs. *Varosh,* we call it. It is distilled like vodka, but flavoured with hazel nuts and pine cones and some herbs. Of course . . ."

"Leh dillidyat immish!" snarled General Busch, raising his glass.

"Lady Lydia Timms," echoed Mr Obb and Count Linden.

Lydia's own glass was half-way to her mouth before she grasped what they'd said. She felt the tide of blushing race up her neck and encrimson her face. The General, smacking his fat grey lips over his empty glass, bellowed with laughter.

Lydia sipped quickly at her drink to hide her shame and fury, gulped and spluttered but managed to control the explosion without doing the nose-trick.

"We are truly most grateful," she heard Mr Obb saying. "Now we will come and assist you with your flooring."

"No, no!" she gasped, thinking of these old men heaving at crowbars, smashing the boards into unusable splinters, falling between joists and breaking ankles. "It's quite all right. I . . ."

A bell rang.

"The bottom door," said Count Linden.

Lydia slipped round the Gestetner and was at the door before any of them had moved.

"I'm going down anyway," she said, brisk as a March wind. "I'll let them in. If it's anything I can't cope with I'll ring your bell three times. OK? Thank you very much for the *varosh.*"

Escape from them made her feel remarkably happy. Or was it the booze? Or some gland switching itself on at random? The wooden soles of her sandals made a lively tap-dance on the stairs. Mrs Pumice's baby was awake and starting to whimper. That's what, thought Lydia, when I've finished with this dreary fungus I'll have another baby. Right. That's settled. She was humming *Pin-Ball Wizard* by the time she opened the door.

The man on the doorstep was dressed all in black.

"At least somebody's happy," he said, and before she could answer turned and waved like a butler summoning a train of footmen. Four other men appeared round the privet hedge, carrying a coffin on their shoulders.

"Know where she goes, Miss?" said the first man. "I was expecting one of them old gents."

"That's all right," said Lydia. "I know where they want it."

Going back up the stairs at the pace of the mourners her sandals sounded like drum-taps.

Mrs. Newbury's room had been shifted round. The bed was against one wall, leaving space in the middle for a trestle table draped with the pink and gold flag of the Livonian Republic. The dressing-table which had once been covered with a hundred hideous knick-knacks was now something like an altar. One enormous coloured candle stood on the floor by the trestle.

"Hello," said the undertaker. "Full military honours! OK, lads, table seems firm. Down. To you a bit, Dave. Fine. Tell the old gents. I'll be on the doorstep to-morrow morning, ten o'clock sharp. Ta ta. We can let ourselves out."

"I'm coming down, as a matter of fact," said Lydia. Some of her suppressed shock and disgust must have crept into her voice and come out as aristocratic chill, because the undertaker's demeanour became noticeably servile as they trooped downstairs. Lydia liked this even less than his previous slightly camp parody of grief, but knew that any attempt to sort out the brief relationship would end in mess.

Down in the basement she fitted the planks back over the cavity and tapped a couple of nails into any that were short enough for Dickie to scrabble up. Then she felt she might as well have lunch, so she went into the front room, which at the moment was the Timmses' bedroom, nursery, living-room, kitchen, workshop and study, and boiled herself a couple of eggs. She had picked up the local Trotskyite rag, *Get Notted*, on her way back from taking Dickie to school, so she was able to perch by the window and dip fingers of brown toast into the egg-yolk while she read a series of flailing attacks on the police, the courts, the Borough Council and the private landlords. There was a writer called Tony Bland who seemed to have a particular gift for the plausible but destructive detail. Food and fervour combined to cheer her spirits, overlaying the gloom of the wasted morning and the coming of the coffin and General Busch's boorish gallantry.

After lunch she rang the prison and pecked away for half an hour at the bleak shell of authority, trying to find a cranny through which she could send her message about the funeral to the human core within. Then there was still an hour before it would be time to fetch Dickie, not enough to do the floor-cavity; nor was there any point in starting on any of the minor jobs in the back room until she'd got the big beam out and seen how far the rot had spread. It would be madness to start mucking around in Dickie's bedroom or here, dismally decayed though both rooms were. Lydia roamed round, stared for a minute at the bedraggled back garden, where the unpruned rose-bed, fuzzy with dead willow-herb, spread itself in gawky gestures. She hated gardening. OK, she thought, I'll go out.

She washed her face in the egg-water, brushed the dust

and cobwebs out of her straight, coarse, blue-black hair, dug her sheepskin coat out of one of the polythene sacks in which all their clothes were stored at the moment, and let herself out of the basement door.

The spy was standing on the doorstep, sheltering from the faint February drizzle which had begun during lunch. Lydia caught him by surprise, and he her, so neither of them had a story ready. Lydia tended to be sorry for the spies who sometimes hung about Devon Crescent to watch the Government's futile comings and goings; it didn't matter whether they came from Our Side or Their Side; to her they were simply victims of authority, detailed to come and waste a stretch of their own lives.

However a protocol had been established. Richard Timms had begun it, pointing out that if you spoke to a spy as though you had detected his trade he had to report it, and might get punished; the polite thing was to behave and talk as though he had a perfect right to be hanging about, and was engaged on some other business than spying. As some of the spies were probably not spies anyway, this system was doubly good sense.

Lydia's own fictional gift was weak, unlike her husband's, so she preferred to think out a charade beforehand if she knew she was going to meet one of the men. So now she simply looked at him, stammering. He raised his shabby hat. The memory of the horrid rose-bed inspired her.

"Oh," she said, "are you the bloke who was going to come and see about doing the garden for a bit?"

"Uh," said the man. The grunt sounded almost affirmative. Lydia glimpsed a vista of tidy organisation, the rose-bed dug out, the leaves swept up, Mrs Schelling's endless complaints about her back avoided, the spy himself provided with an acceptable mask—but she drew back from the brink. She liked to think things through before she took action.

"I'm afraid I've got to go out now," she said. "Could you come back, let's think, I'll be busy to-morrow morning, and the next day—the day after that? In the morning?"

"Uh," said the man, standing out of her way.

"That's fine," said Lydia and ran up the steps.

She felt full of warmth and inner life. She knew that the sheepskin coat didn't suit her, making her already pudgy figure seem square as a brick. Ages ago, before Dickie was born, one of her half-sister Lalage's blokes had made a family film at Christmas and had shown it to a roomful of people. A lot of it, of course, had been of Lalage looking languorous, but there'd been one long middle-distance take of Lydia walking down a path beside a yew hedge, wearing a heavily padded anorak. The whole room had laughed, including Lydia herself. So now she knew exactly what she looked like as she clip-clopped past the sugar-icing façades of the other Devon Crescent houses—a sort of square leather parcel-thing, with her sturdy legs strutting jerkily below and her aggressive little head, pink-cheeked, black-browed, poking out at the top. She didn't mind. She was herself, Lydia Timms. That's what she *was* like. You could say that the trouble with the sheepskin coat was that it suited her too well.

She went to Minwick's and bought a couple of hacksaw blades and resisted the temptation of a brutal blue wrench which would have been just the job when it came to cope with back-room sink, but at four pounds sixty was simply a luxury, when she could do the job with the tools she had already. Then she went to the hire shop and checked that the Acrow hoists were coming to-morrow afternoon. She came out knowing from the man's manner that they were, but wouldn't have been if she hadn't checked. At the library she looked in vain for something to read to a seven-year-old dyslexic boy who had an obsession with warfare; she also checked the travel shelves to see whether there were any new books on Russia (there were) and whether any of the travellers had thought Livonia worth more than the usual Intourist paragraph (they hadn't).

Finally she picked Dickie up from his remedial tutor, took him to Holland Park for a machine-gun battle with his cronies in the adventure playground, and home for tea.

She was still cheerful.

2

EVEN AT WEEK-ENDS Lydia and Richard Timms didn't speak much to each other during the day, and their week-day evenings, once Dickie was in bed, would have appeared to a stranger very gruff and chilly. If something simply had to be discussed they would talk it over rather formally, like a two-man committe. But mostly after supper Richard worked at his law-books while Lydia made careful diagrams for tomorrow's carpentry, or drew look-and-say pictures of tanks, Greek hoplites, Crecy archers and atomic submarines, or–if she felt suddenly escapist–worked on her plan of the fantasy car she was going to build as soon as Richard was earning real money and the dry rot was vanquished. They had no television and seldom listened to the radio.

But once the lights were out they were both slow droppers-off, and since Richard's breakdown had got into the habit of talking for an hour in the dark, sometimes in each other's arms for a while and then holding hands, but more often simply lying side by side on their backs. When they had to spend a night apart Lydia missed this hour horribly and found it difficult to go to sleep at all. She wondered, those times, whether–supposing Richard took a girl to his hotel room (unlikely)–he simply lay on his back in the dark and talked to *her*. That would have made Lydia more jealous than if he'd attended the sort of orgies at which Procne Newbury had earned her living before she went to jail.

"Dead?" said Richard. "Yes, I suppose it's about time."

"What do you mean? You usually say he doesn't exist."

"Um."

"Then he can't be dead. I mean . . . Don't be flip about it, darling. I can't imagine why, but a care."

"Sorry. What I think I meant is that they'd have to kill him off some time–it'd look a bit fishy if they were still putting out propaganda about the great national hero imprisoned by the wicked Bolsheviks when he was officially a hundred and twenty. They must have slipped a year or two in any case. He can't have been only seventy-six."

"It said seventy-six years of fighting. He couldn't have begun till he was . . . how old?"

"Say twelve. Eighty-eight. Pretty long-lived for a labour camp."

"He existed once."

"Of course. You know, I think he was probably pretty well always a figurehead—that's why they made him President in the first place. Then he stayed behind with the Resistance, and I should think the Russians got him about 1946, tidying up after the war. The people here would simply hope, and go on putting out propaganda stories about him and his Hereward-the-Wake stunt in the marshes. But when the Cold War began to thaw, and Amnesty got going, and so on, they decided that they'd get more mileage out of making him a prisoner of conscience, or whatever they call it, so they announced that news had come that he was in Siberia. But even that couldn't last for ever. Now's a good time to bump him off."

"Why now?"

"Oh, well, they must be getting pretty jumpy now Sir Alec's gone from the FO. He'd invested a lot of face in the Baltic States, right back to before the war, so even with all this détente going on he'd have stood by them. The Kremlin boys never give up. At some point quite soon there'll be something we want, and they'll ask for a quid pro quo, and that might be closing down the Baltic legations in London and recognising Russia's de jure sovereignty—we'd do it, too, if they offered us enough. So all the old men can hope is to up the price by throwing Aakisen into the fight. If people believe he's just been starved to death in a labour camp, it'll make it that bit harder for us to go along with the Russians."

"It makes me sick. If a thing's wrong in the first place, it can't suddenly become right just because we've got a new Foreign Secretary."

"There aren't any rights in that world—only a choice between wrongs."

"I hope it was true—Aakisen, I mean."

"I rather approve of the old boys, fighting their war with men who are dead already and can't be killed any more."

"They brought back Mrs N to-day."

The tenants were none of Richard's business and he had seen very little of Mrs Newbury. He simply accepted the news with a grunt, and it was some seconds before he really took in what Lydia had said.

"Back?" he said.

"The Government are being very funny about her. They've laid out her room like a military chapel, and they're going to stand sentry over it all night."

Richard chuckled.

"I nearly took Dickie up to see," said Lydia.

"Good God! Isn't that carrying his obsessions a bit far?"

"Oh, it wasn't for the soldier bit. It's just I've read you ought to get kids used to the meaning of death. I'm not keeping hamsters."

"Darling, I don't think it's a very good idea."

"I only thought about it. He didn't really like Mrs N. She used to make him kiss her."

"Ugh. That makes it worse. Furry corpse stiffening in its cage, I can see the point. Ogress shut away in box, nightmares. She'd be lifting the lid and coming for him."

Most of Lydia's own nightmares ran at the level of attending grand dinners and discovering she was still wearing her rubber gloves. Only occasionally did she wander into a darker world, and even then it seemed to be someone else who ran, hopeless, from . . . waking, she could not even remember what, only the terror.

"I think I've got a gardener," she said.

"That's housekeeping."

"I think I can scrape up three hours a week. And I was talking to Mr. Tevell at 76, and he hates gardening too. And 87's a jungle—I don't know the people there but I can go and ask. And Jack Stoddart would far rather spend time on that stupid boat of his. And it wouldn't matter if this bloke didn't know anything about gardening because Mrs Schelling would love to boss him about and I know she's looking for somebody because her back is getting so bad."

"Where on earth did you find a man with so much time? What does *he* say?"

"He said 'Uh' twice. I bumped into him in the doorway. He's the latest spy."

"Darling!"

"I can't see why it shouldn't work. And it would give the poor sod something *real* to do."

"I can see you're going to make it work. I love you. You spend half your days fighting social systems and the other half constructing new ones. You're the Lenin of W.11."

Lydia didn't feel like wandering down the old track, endlessly fascinating to Richard, that explored the thicket of her own personality. She didn't find it a very interesting place.

"I wonder how you get references from a spy," she said.

"Supposing he is one."

"Who else could he be, hanging around in the basement door? Oh, bloody hell! You don't think he was the Building Inspector?"

"Inspectors are more garrulous than that."

"Damn! If it wasn't him, he didn't come. I bet he comes when I'm at the funeral."

3

Mr Obb, wearing a black frock coat and a black tie, came down to fetch Lydia. His pale eyes widened slightly at the sight of her.

"I'm sorry," she lied. "I haven't got anything blacker than this."

It was a dark blue trouser-suit, ideal for wearing at windy gravesides. Its sharp-edged, soldierly cut looked well on Lydia, emphasising her competence and energy, mitigating her pudginess.

"We will provide a sash," said Mr Obb.

"Thank you."

(The last time Lydia had worn a black sash was outside South Africa House.)

Almost a dozen frock-coated men waited in the hall. Two or three were surprisingly young. At a nod from General Busch they marched out down the steps and peeled off into the glossy black cars of the cortege.

"Have you met Mr Paul Vaklins?" said Mr Obb. "Lady Timms."

Lydia, already shrinking into herself, reducing her world-awareness against the coming dreary charade, took a second to realise that she was being introduced to one of the young men, whom she vaguely recognised. His large, muscular body was topped by a head which seemed slightly too small and not quite adult, as though the years had never properly smoothed out the crumpled skin of childbirth. Apart from that he would have been very handsome, with his short blond hair and pale blue eyes. He half-bowed.

"We've encountered each other a couple of times on the stairs," he said. "I have the honour to escort you, Lady Timms. My car's down here."

He led her to a vast, bright yellow monster, Italian coach-work on an American chassis by the look of it. The door he held for her seemed as big as the whole side of a Mini.

"I'll stay a bit back," he said as the big engine sucked the car away behind the black Daimlers. "She's not quite the thing for a funeral. I hope you don't mind."

"I prefer it," said Lydia. "I love cars. In a year or two I'm going to build one for myself."

One like this?"

"No, almost the exact opposite, as a matter of fact. Small and square, with a very tight lock. Sixty m.p.g. Nothing to rust. My husband says it will be a hundred-mile-an-hour shopping basket."

She cocked her head and listened to the engine.

"Sixteen cylinders?" she asked.

"That's right–it's a bit ridiculous, isn't it? I tell myself it's a symbol of exile. I don't have a home, I have a car."

Lydia warmed to him, not simply because he accepted without a smile the notion that a woman could build her own car. His hands on the steering were stubby and short-fingered and he drove with no fuss at all, although the pace of the cortege came tiresomely at a point where his automatic transmission couldn't quite make up its mind between ratios. At traffic lights the car sidled close up behind the last of the Daimlers.

"Did you ever meet Aakisen?" said Lydia.

He seemed faintly startled, turning to stare at her with ice-blue Livonian eyes. Then he laughed.

"Yes, I see," he said. "You're being a bit subtle, but you may be right. Because we can't bury Aakisen properly we're acting out our mourning by giving a grand funeral to this woman? But no, I never met him. In fact I never heard his name until I came to England. Officially in Russia he didn't exist."

"Oh . . . I didn't realise . . . I mean you speak English so well."

"Better than I speak Liv, to be honest. Russian is my first language and English my second. Liv is a nursery language I've had to re-learn. I got out in the aftermath of the Krushchev regime. But my old colleagues, they stick to their bad accents as a means of sticking to their identities. I think if you shouted at Busch in English that the house was on fire he would run down the stairs."

"I'd like to be there. It sometimes irritates me, I'm afraid, though I'm not much good at languages myself. Is that why they're such mechanical nits, too?"

"Uh?"

"I have to keep running up and mending the Gestetner for them. If you're going to be about at all, I'll show you and you can do it."

"I don't know. I would say that their mechanical incompetence was a bourgeois class thing, a bit like the way Chinese Mandarins grew their nails long to demonstrate that they did no manual work. So gentlemen and intellectuals prefer to show that they do not belong to the mechanic classes. But as for being at Devon Crescent . . . it's not the ideal moment to ask, but have you any plans for Mrs Newbury's room?"

"For you?"

"If possible. There's going to be a Government reshuffle, now Aakisen is dead. Busch will be President and Obb Prime Minister, and I will take over Maritime Affairs. After all, I own the ship."

"I thought there was more than one."

"Yes, there are six, but I own the new one."

"How on earth did you get a new one?"

Lydia knew that some of the Government's money came from the tiny merchant fleet that happened to be out of Livonia when the Russians had come. But by now all of them must surely be much-patched old dodderers.

"Willi Brandt gave it to me, in effect, as a result of his Ostpolitik. It was a highly complex transaction which freed certain assets frozen in East Germany but belonging to me through my grandmother who was a West German. It would take a lawyer to explain how these assets came to me not as cash but in the form of a 6,000-ton Stralsund-built coaster. Do I drive in? Will the car mar the atmosphere of grief? Agh, it is too cold to walk."

In the car-park he helped her to adjust the black sash, again with unfussy efficiency, so much so that he surprised her by standing back when he had finished and saying, "No need to be ashamed of it. It goes with your uniform. The sash of the Order of Aakisen."

She smiled meaninglessly, not even sure whether it was a joke. He took her arm and led her along a muddy gravel driveway behind the old men, bareheaded now, who were following the flower-strewn hearse. The path became worse and worse, puddled, and churned here and there by tyres. Grey grave-stones flanked it, hugger-mugger, the grass between them coarse and spiritless as that on an over-used recreation field. They crossed another driveway, and here the grass was not even mown, but a rank fawn mat criss-crossed with the purple arching stems of brambles. Some of the grave-stones leaned crooked and many of their inscriptions were illegible; but slowly, as the tangle and decay grew worse, the jutting monuments became grander; at another crossway sat the first carved angel; ivy seethed around her knees and sent tentacles up to fondle her shoulders; she looked posed, intentional, as if the wilderness and ruin were proper to her. Beyond that the procession trudged through an area of mausoleums, wilder and more entangled still, though here and there some great-niece of the last deceased had kept the family tomb tended; pillars stood askew, gothic vaults had been patched with corrugated iron, buddleia seedlings sprouted from pediments. In places between these shanty-like monuments a fresh grave had been dug and filled and was marked with a modern headstone or a white wooden stake bearing only a number; the effect was like that of a Victorian suburb of large houses, plots of whose gardens are now sold as sites for neat new bungalows. At just such a site the cortege halted.

The undertaker's men hefted the coffin out. A train drummed past on the other side of the boundary wall, and by the time its noise faded the priest's ghastly mumble had begun.

Lydia was so withdrawn into herself, snail-like, against being touched by any of this dreary celebration that it took her some time to notice that four of the party had not come from Devon Crescent. Her attention was first caught by two men in short fawn coats who were acting in a non-mourning fashion, prancing and posing—who were in fact taking photographs. Lydia thought this excessive as an act of piety for a Government burying its charlady, until she saw that the photographers were aiming their cameras at two women on the far side of the grave, a tall pale girl also (to Lydia's relicf) wearing trousers and a nondescript older woman in a dark blue coat. There was a touch of the old-fashioned nanny about this second woman, but the girl didn't look the type to have belonged to the nannied classes; her face was working, without tears, until she noticed the photographers and steadied herself. Then her features settled and she became Procne Newbury.

Lydia had never met Mrs Newbury's famous daughter, though she had been forced many times to look through the collection of press cuttings of the trial. Before that Mrs Newbury had often talked of herself as a sadly wronged mother, but when Procne had rocketed into notoriety she had been filled with pride and pleasure, as though it had been she who had lit the touch-paper. For Lydia this encounter by the graveside was like the thud of the stick falling.

As soon as the coffin had been lowered and the earth had rattled onto its lid Lydia slipped round the blind side of the crowd and walked straight up to Procne.

"Hello," she said. "I'm Lydia Timms. Your mother had a room in my house."

"Eff off," whispered Procne.

The nanny surged round from her far side.

"No talking to the prisoner, if you please," she said.

One tenet of Lydia's anti-authority creed was that underlings are victims too. She turned sympathetically to the warder.

"I thought Miss Newbury would like to hear about how her mother got on during the last few months," she said. "I saw quite a bit of her."

A policeman, hitherto unnoticed, loomed into the periphery of Lydia's vision.

"You can't do that here," said the warder. "If the prisoner wants a visit you'll have to arrange it through welfare."

At a nudge from her elbow Procne turned away and the two of them moved off towards a dark car which had been waiting further along the driveway. The policeman stayed where he was, watchful, as if suspecting the Livonian Government in Exile of being a cover organisation for a group bent on rescuing tarts from prison. One of the photographers blocked Lydia's view.

"I'd better have your name," he said. "They might want the one with you in it."

He had a trival beard and looked as though he hated mankind.

"Timms, L."

"Miss or Mrs?"

"Neither."

He was making an Oh-God face when Lydia heard a shout of "I'd like a visit, please, Miss." She stood clear and saw Procne climbing into the car. She waved to show she'd understood. Two more policemen emerged from behind tombs and climbed in also. Lydia smiled, thinking how thrilled Mrs Newbury would have been to know that her daughter had come to her funeral so grandly escorted.

"A very important prisoner," said Mr Vaklins at her elbow.

"Oh, I suppose there might have been a mob of sight-seers," said Lydia. "There are always people who will stand around for hours just to goggle at someone like that for a few minutes. Heavens, what wreaths! She'd have loved that."

They were hideous, piled in sheaves along the bank of artificial grass which covered the mound of sticky yellow clay from the grave. One or two seemed to be unconventional in shape, until Lydia realised that they were representations of the Viking horn which was the crest of the Livonian Republic. Now that the mummery was over Lydia almost smiled again—they seemed such absurdly appropriate ornaments for the tomb of an old battle-axe who had died drunk.

4

"You will give me to a hospital, won't you? Promise. None of this rubbish about the family vault. Honestly, I'd rather be turned into pet-food."

"I'll think about it, darling. Would you haunt me if I didn't? You'd make a very bad ghost–not your style at all."

"I'm serious."

"I know you are. When you're serious your voice drops and you speak very slowly, as though I'd suddenly gone soft in the head. But I can't take it seriously–I mean, if you think like you do, what does it matter what's done to you afterwards? The dead have a duty towards the living. Anyway, I want a great big marble slab on the wall of the church at Duxbury with eighteenth-century lettering–early eighteenth-century, please–enumerating my virtues and palliating my vices, and finishing with a bit of verse in Latin embodying a metaphysical conceit about . . ."

"Richard."

Beside her in the dark she felt the faint, almost Pavlonian response of tension in his muscles. She sighed to herself, remembering the time before his breakdown when they'd both merely thought it funny that that was his reaction to her use of his Christian name.

"It's all right," she said. "I'm not going to ask you to think about anything you don't want to. Just let's talk about something else. I shouldn't have started it."

"You don't think you ought to talk it out, if it's bothering you?"

"No. Listen, about Mrs N's room, have you any views?"

"What was she paying?"

"One pound fifty. She was controlled. I daresay I could have gone to the rent people and squeezed it up a bit, but I hadn't the heart. Now this Vaklins bloke wants it."

"Ask twelve."

"That's not the point. I mean, there's hundreds of people

who need it more than he does. If I could find some old biddy . . ."

"And ask one fifty?"

"No, she'd have to be able to afford four, somehow. I'd like her to come from somewhere round here, too."

"How much are they asking for the new flats at forty-six?"

"Forty for the basements, Mrs Tevell said, but that's not the point. They oughtn't to have been made into that sort of flat–it was monstrous. It was a typical Dice and Dottridge transaction."

"But they're estate agents. They aren't allowed to own property."

"Don't you believe it, darling. They're everywhere. They used a holding company. But don't you remember the Hoods who used to live there? That old man with the racing pigeons –his wife who used to scamper out with a carrot for the rag-and-bone man's horse?"

"Vaguely. They had a daughter in Canada."

"That's right. Dice and Dottridge gave them a silly little lump sum to move out and found them a high-rise flat in Acton. Mr Hood's dead. She's in a home."

"Poor old ducks. But the world's changing, Liz–you can't stop it."

"I *can*."

She slid her hand down his arm and twisted her fingers into his. She knew that he would let her do what she wanted, and wouldn't complain, even if it meant tap-water and scrag-end stews for months. So it was only fair to try to do things in a way which he too thought was reasonable.

"Suppose Mr Hood would have died anyway," she said, "and Mrs Hood gone into that home. Even so they must have had a time–eighteen months, two years–when they were completely miserable. If they'd been able to stay here, where they knew people . . ."

He squeezed her hand and chuckled.

"I love you," he said. "How are you going to phrase your ad for the new tenant? How are you going to screen the applicants for worthiness? Pay the rag-and-bone man to drive past and watch whether they reach for the carrots?"

Lydia was already worried about that. She hated the idea of using her power as a property-owner to discriminate between the needs of two or more people–it would be like choosing a puppy in a pet-shop window.

"Suppose I don't let Mrs N's room at all," she said. "Just keep it as a memorial to her?"

"No! Shut up! Listen. I get that beam out to-morrow. The dry-rot people come next week, and the damp-course people the week after. When they'd gone I was going to finish those rooms, move us in there and do these two. But suppose I simply get the beam back in—I've still got the floors to check, too—and then leave it and do Mrs N's room. I'll have to move the sink, but I can put a proper cooker in there if I don't tell the Council. Then I can persuade Mrs Pumice to move up. She's always behind with her rent because Don—Mr Pumice—is a swine about the maintenance, and if he's not here she doesn't need that extra room. Leave Doctor Ng where he is. The Pelletiers' tenancy runs out next month, and from one or two things she's said I know she's dead scared about what I'm going to ask for the new agreement, and with Stan married they don't need that little back room; so I think they'll be happy to go up into Mrs Pumice's and pay what they're paying now. That clears the first floor for the Evanses. I can put a bath and loo into Stan's old room, which'll mean they'll have their own bathroom and be all on one floor, and I know they won't mind paying a bit more for that. The men said the dry rot wasn't too bad in those two ground floor rooms, so we can move up to the ground floor . . ."

"We'll have it all to ourselves?"

"That's right. We'll need it. As soon as I've got the basement really nice and self-contained and bringing in some income I want to start having a baby."

"Oh . . . what sex?"

She rolled on her side to kick him, but either he misinterpreted her movement or his reactions were more dextrous than sometimes; at any rate the kick missed and his legs tangled round hers as his arm slid under her neck. The Timmses didn't make love one quarter as often as the sex-pundits say decent people should; Lydia liked it when things went right, but they didn't always, and quite often this was her fault. It wasn't that she resented her role, but she could never be sure when they began whether she was going to be able to melt herself into it. To-night, half-way through a first quite promising kiss, something fizzed inside her mind and spat out a gritty little thought; she knew it would be useless to go on until she'd said it aloud, so she eased her mouth free.

"It all depends on not finding any more horrors anywhere else," she said.

5

THE BIG BEAM in the back room, after a first few minutes of total obstinacy, came out with less trouble than Lydia had expected, as though it were tired of supporting the whole garden façade and were glad of a rest. Cataracts of fine mortar dust fell continuously along most of its length as Lydia levered it inchmeal onto the cradle of scaffolding she had built. The room smoked with the ancient, pinky-grey powder, but she'd known it would be like that so she was wearing a smog-mask over her nose and mouth. Four or five bricks came loose, making the beginnings of a ragged arch, but the Acrow hoists supported the ceiling so well that not a crack showed.

The beam must have weighed three hundredweight. At the tricky instant when it was balanced half on the brickwork and half on the cradle, a man coughed in the room behind her. No doubt he'd done it just to call attention to his presence, but once he'd started he was unable to stop; at each gasp his lungs sucked in fresh supplies of dust to aggravate the next spasm.

"Sorry," called Lydia, unable to look round. "I had to start without you. Why don't you wait in the passage till the dust clears. I'll be out in a couple of minutes."

But the man stayed where he was, gradually mastering his gullet once the beam was clear of the wall and ceased to drag out mortar as it came. The coughs diminished on a surprisingly deep note, like the retreating grumble of a thunderstorm. As soon as she was sure that the beam was firmly on the cradle Lydia turned.

He loomed through the dust-cloud, an enormous Indian in a linen suit, black shirt and yellow tie and turban. He was holding a bright pink handkerchief to his face.

"You are the man from the Council?" asked Lydia.

He grunted.

"I couldn't wait, you see," she said. "I wasn't sure that

you'd be coming at all, and I had to get on. It's quite safe, if you want to come and check. The joists above run north-and-south so the hoists take the weight there, and the wall really bears on the concrete lintel on the outside. Look, you can see clearly now."

He stepped prissily over and peered into the smoking cavity with bloodshot, bulbous eyes.

"All right?" said Lydia, suddenly anxious at his long silence.

"I know nothing about such matters," he said. "If it falls, that is God's will."

His eyes swivelled towards her, as if cueing her for the Amen. She could see the white all the way round each iris.

"I thought you said you were the man from the Council."

"I am the man from a Council. A man from the Council. Let's get out of here."

Lydia had already promised herself a cup of coffee as soon as she got the beam clear, so she led the way to the front room.

"You'll have to sit on the bed," she said as she put the kettle on. "We're living all in one room at the moment, while I get the rest of the basement sorted out. If you aren't from the Borough Council, who are you?"

She spoke sharply, because she resented this man who had materialised like a genie out of the smoke, first misleading her and then somehow taking charge of the situation, as if he had the right.

"I came to tell you about Bob Roberts. My name is Ambrose."

"Mine's Lydia," said Lydia, who approved strongly of instant first-name terms.

"Ah, in that case mine is Jack Ambrose. I will have hot milk, please. I must keep up my strength for my work."

Again Lydia had that sense of sleight-of-mind, as though he were deliberately strewing conclusions around for her to jump to. Despite the turban he didn't look or sound like an Indian. He had the feel of a ham actor, a heavy, one of those would-be giants of the stage who make up for their total lack of skill by imposing their own personality on the material. Mr Ambrose had a personality to impose, at least. She looked at him, full face. He looked back, unsmiling but bland. Powdered with the pale mortar-dust he might have been made of milk chocolate the whole way through. He wore several signet rings on each hand, like knuckle-dusters.

But there was plenty of milk, so she fetched it out of the fridge and put some in a saucepan.

"And who's Mr Roberts?" she said.

"A friend. You spoke to him about your garden."

"Oh, yes! I asked if he could come back to-morrow morning, but it was a bit vague, so I didn't really . . ."

"Of course. Bob is a good gardener. What is your proposal?"

"Well, I don't know how much time he's got. There isn't more to do here than would take a man one morning a week. But I know several of my neighbours would like a gardener too, so if he wanted more time than that . . ."

"Money?"

"The rate round here is eighty pence an hour, but if he's really a skilled gardener . . . I couldn't afford more than three pounds a week, in any case."

He didn't answer, but turned away and stood with his back to her, running his mailed fingers up and down the folds of his neck-muscles. The kettle screamed. Lydia switched off the gas, poured water on the coffee-powder, added a little cold milk and lifted the mug to her lips, only to find that she was still wearing her face-mask. This irritated her more than anything, because it was not like her to make such a mistake. It was Mr Ambrose's fault. He lay like an iron bar, thrown by hooligans across the smooth track of the morning. What's more, she damn near let his milk boil over too.

"Here you are," she snapped. "What's the problem? If he's a good gardener he can get twice that amount almost anywhere, so you needn't worry about turning me down."

"Ah, thank you for the milk," said Mr Ambrose, swinging round. "I will help myself to sugar, please. My strength, you know. The problem, Lydia, is our friend Bob. He has had, well, a certain amount of difficulty in recent years."

"Been inside, you mean," said Lydia. "I don't mind, provided it's not for molesting kids. I've got a small son. Otherwise I'd be glad to help."

"Ah, a social conscience," said Mr Ambrose, stirring his eighth spoonful of sugar into his milk. He sounded faintly mocking.

"Yes," said Lydia.

"Bob is a bit inadequate, it is true," said Mr Ambrose, after a pause. "He needs help and support. But he is honest, and a good gardener. That is all. He will be here on Monday morning at nine. I will leave it to you to make arrangements with your neighbours."

He sucked the scalding milk down in two gulps, smacked his lips and put the mug on the draining board.

"Eighty pence an hour, OK," he said. "Try to arrange five mornings a week. Bob will be here on Monday. Routine, routine. Good-bye. Thank you for the milk."

Huge though he was he seemed to glide away and had reached the door and gone before Lydia realised that the interview was over. She heard him climb the stairs, light-footed, three at a time.

She sat on the kitchen stool, becoming herself again, sipping slowly at her coffee and at first deliberately trying not to think about her own reactions to Mr Ambrose. This proved impossible, so as the coffee sank in the mug she settled down to organising her anger into parcels which she could cope with. Part of the problem was the shame of disliking a coloured man so strongly and instantly. Richard maintained that even in the most saintly and unprejudiced of mankind there is a sociological id, a demon of racial spite, which the sociological ego controls and represses. For the first time Lydia was afraid that he might be right. She asked herself whether, supposing he had been a white man but otherwise the same—as gross, as off-hand, as masterful—she would have treated him just the same. No—she would have counter-attacked, demanded to know what his interest was, refused him milk, even. (Milk? Why did she resent that so?)

But would she? Or would she have given in just as easily? Was her anger really no more than spite at being told what to do, having arrangements made for her, in her own house, by a man? Furthermore the man was somebody she ought in theory to approve of, helping the inadequate to find a place of comfort among the grinding cogs and trundling levers of the social system. Perhaps benevolence towards the underdog tends to balance out into insolence towards the comfortable, which the comfortable must tolerate and respect. A saint is entitled to his own bad breath, surely.

Coffee finished, Lydia rose with a sigh, tied her mask on again and went back to work. Most of the visible dust had settled, but minute particles still prickled in the air. She plugged in her inspection lamp and studied the beam, inch by inch. A little woodworm had attacked one corner, but she could find no trace of rot anywhere along it, nor in the cavity from which it came. All it needed was a good double dose of protective fluid and a blitz on the woodworm, and then it could simply go back. Thirty pounds saved! Three days gained!

She should have been singing, but as she cleaned up the dust, sprayed on the fluid and mixed a little cement to re-point the brickwork of the cavity, the ghost of Mr Ambrose seemed to stand behind her shoulder, ready to cough again.

6

THE BEAM CAME OUT on Thursday. Friday was spent getting it back and making good. Early on Saturday morning Richard sat up in bed, stretched and said "Let's go somewhere."

"If you make the arrangements," muttered Lydia, purring back into the nest of warmth in which she'd woken.

The week-end turned into an absurd little idyll, most of it spent plodding round a patch of Hampshire, among untarred lanes and across fields, while Richard and Dickie refought the Battle of Cheriton Wood from the strangely confused accounts of the Civil War diarists. It was brisk but not bitter weather, with a pale blue sky, snowdrops in the hedgerows, birds singing and hopping, pudgy lambs nuzzling at ewes' udders, and the noon sun strong enough to make summer seem quite near. The hired car didn't break down, the fisherman's inn on the Itchen contained no fishermen, and though it was fairly crowded with raucous near-gentry on Saturday night the Timmses went to bed early and treated the noise as though it had been sea-surge against cliffs under a hotel window. They lay talking for a long time, weary and fond, about nothing that concerns us.

7

THE SPY WAS RAPPING at the basement door when Lydia got back from taking Dickie to school. Approached from the other side, with the light full on him, he looked quite different, smaller, older—less, in fact, like a spy.

"You're Mr Roberts," said Lydia, running down the basement steps. "I'm sorry if I'm late."

"I don't know you're late," he said.

"Now, she said, "I've talked to some of my neighbours, and I think we can find you something to do every morning, Monday to Friday. We've all got the same lay-out, a bit of garden in front, mostly paved, and a bigger bit at the back. Mine's in an awful state, I'm afraid, because I don't like gardening and I've been throwing all sorts of building rubbish out and burning it. Come and have a look."

She led him through the basement and up into the litter and mire of the back garden. Mrs Pelletier was hanging her washing out. As usual, Mr Pelletier seemed to have got through twelve shirts in the week.

"I've tried to keep the rose-bed clear," said Lydia, "but the roses don't look very happy to me."

The spy shook his head, fingered a weary leaflet, poked his toe-cap into the slimy earth and grunted.

"I don't much care for roses anyway," said Lydia. "Look, I think the best thing, for a start, would be if I took you round to the other houses and introduced you. Then, if there's any time after that, you could make a start on my front garden. I don't think there's any point doing anything back here till I've finished the worst of my building."

"Best get that finished," he said.

Mrs Tevell was in, and garrulous. Mrs Schelling insisted on hobbling all round her domain, discussing every shrub. June Stoddart was having coffee and needed somebody to moan to about the loneliness and uselessness of wives. So it was nearly eleven when Lydia got home. That left her time before lunch to find the spy some tools, ring the prison to check that her visit to Procne was still in order, and give the back-room beam its final dosing of chemicals. It also meant that she had to pay the spy two pounds forty for an hour's work, but at least he had got a lot done in that hour–in fact it was extraordinary how spruce and lively the front garden now looked, with all the leaves and sweet-papers gone, and the wistaria pruned, and the black, winter-smeared soil raked and aerated. Despite the expense Lydia ate her lunch with a feeling of triumph at having made another step towards civilisation, and only a faint regret that Mr Roberts wasn't a spy. That really would have been using the system to beat the system. She was still a little worried by her inability to be certain whether he was the same man that she'd first met, but even if he wasn't that probably only meant that Mr Ambrose had sent along a different lame dog, a bloke who actually knew a buddleia from a buttercup. It would be typical of Mr Ambrose's dictatorial style not to tell her what he was doing.

Once upon a time, when criminals were still deported to Australia, they used to be kept waiting for shipment in the idiot squalor of the hulks. They were a suppuration, which eventually even our thick-skinned society noticed, and slapped a poultice on, and called it cured. Procne's prison had been part of the poultice, built on the south-eastern outskirts of London, not far from the main-line railway. Unfortunately the railway had attracted a suburb of fair-sized respectable houses, whose developers were distressed by the notion that house-buyers might wish to pay less for property so close to a prison, as though crime were a sort of marsh-fever that might seep out and infect the honest bourgeois. The balance was redressed by the prison architects, who made the prison look thoroughly, even grandly respectable—a close replica of the Château de Chambord, in fact. The gate-tower still looks stunning against the western sky as you walk up the dreary (and now quite unrespectable) avenue of Croydon Road.

Lydia hated the tower, and was not remotely interested in its history. Her clothes and skin seemed to melt into a hard, protective carapace as she waited at the gate for the warder to open to her knock; and waited again in the drab octagonal room where other visitors sat and smoked, all tense with the nearness of Authority; and waited finally in a pink, oppressive barrel-vaulted cell while a welfare officer went to fetch

Procne Newbury. The cell had been converted to an office, and contained a couple of chairs and a desk. Lists of names were Sellotaped to one wall and a Mucha poster of a dreamy pale woman, all gold, to another. There was a telephone and an overflowing ash-tray. But despite these signs of a live occupant, to Lydia it might have been an alcove in Richard's family vault. All that weight of sooty brick, all the weight of that other edifice whose bricks are warders and policemen and judges and Home Secretaries and respectable people, towered above her as a monstrous burial-mound. But Lydia didn't feel that she was buried as a body is buried. She was more like the bulb of a bluebell in a town garden over which paving-stones have been laid, but still the leaves find their way out to the light, heaving aside if necessary the crushing hundredweights of stone.

Outside little bell-like noises went to and fro as officers passed, all carrying their own bunch of keys. Lydia had brought cigarettes, knowing that that was expected; she herself smoked seldom, but she thought it would seem more natural, less Lady-Bountiful, if she already had an opened packet when Procne came, so she lit one and sucked the smoke in with shuddering relief. At last footsteps stopped at the cell door and keys jingled with a purpose. The Welfare Officer held the door open for Procne, who came rather hesitantly in.

"Will half an hour be enough?" asked the Welfare Officer, breezy and friendly but not waiting for an answer. The door closed and was locked. Lydia found that she was standing and smiling too, unnaturally, with a patch of tense muscle in either cheek. Procne looked back at her, cow-eyed, emotionless. They stayed like that for some time. Procne was six inches taller than Lydia; she wore her hair dyed silvery blonde, in a semi-afro frizz; except for her eyes her features were small, and her face was slightly flat, its skin very soft and coloured, partly with make-up and partly by nature, like a sentimental pastel of a child. A minute before all Lydia's thoughts and emotions had been a complex of angers and theories about the oppression-machine which surrounded her; now she was flooded with absurd longing and resentment, almost with jealousy. Procne's life was smashed, her future a foreseeable vista of shoddy notoriety and shoddy let-downs. Lydia's was still full of drive and promise and, even, love. But to be so beautiful! Impossible not to believe that it made everything else worth while.

"Wh-which chair would you like?" she said at last.

"I don't mind," said Procne in a dull voice.

They settled. Procne took a cigarette and lit it awkwardly. Slowly the strange mood seeped away.

"My name's Lydia—Lydia Timms. I came to tell you about your mother."

"I spose so. You butch?"

"No. At least I don't think so. I've never tried. Are you?"

Procne shrugged.

"Sorry, what did you say your name was?" she said.

"Lydia. Or Liz."

"Lydia and Procne. Jesus, some parents want their heads looked at. Mine wasn't Mum's fault, not really. She wanted to call me Suez, but the parson wouldn't have it. She near as hit him, right there by the font, she told me. She was after something real unusual, see. Not some bleeding saint, neither. That's how they come to Procne. Dad always said it sounded like a bloody health-food."

"I never knew your father."

Procne nodded. She sat uncomfortably in her chair with the arm she wasn't using for smoking held stiffly across her stomach, as though in an invisible sling.

"But I got to know your mother pretty well these last few years," said Lydia. "I remember the first time I met her . . ."

It was a relief to be able to put into words what she had felt, but never till now formulated, about Mrs Newbury, what had made the old rogue, with her sharp-featured decisive head and slack, floppy, shambling body, so intricate, so amazing. There are some people, worthy and cultured, whose characters can be discussed and agreed on in five minutes; others will occupy a party of close friends all through a wet week-end, and Mrs Newbury was one of those. Quite soon Procne took her arm out of the imaginary sling, leaned forward, began to gesture agreement, and then started on her own store of childhood study. Mrs Newbury had been a houseful, a street of people, a world . . . Suddenly Lydia saw how proper it was that this estranged daughter should have wept so at her mother's funeral.

"Not that we got on, not really," Procne said. "She was always at me, never satisfied, trying to live my life, plans, plans, plans. My first bloke—not counting boys at school, acourse, I was only a kid then—he found me a lovely flat near Marble Arch, colour TV, the lot. Mum was ever so cross and snarky. Wasn't me setting up professional—he had to pay the rent somehow, didn't he?—but cos Mum hadn't found him for me herself. In the end it come so she'd just phone me up Thursdays and we'd have a long chat, and I didn't even go round, Christmas, with a present. She never come and visit me here, mind. Did she read all about my trial?"

"Oh yes—she kept a scrapbook. I'm afraid she rather revelled in it."

"Well, that's Mum—you can't hold it against her. In fact I'm glad she had her bit of fun. No fun for me, mind, shut away like this."

"I think it's absolutely disgraceful. All those time-serving hypocrites who'd have been queueing up to meet you if they'd had the chance, working out their stupid little repressions by smashing you to bits. I couldn't even read about it, I was so angry."

"D'you really think so, Liz? I know some judges what go with girls, but mine wasn't like that. I saw a picture of him in the papers with his family in front of his house. Two lovely daughters he had. Honest, I don't think he was like that."

"I didn't mean . . . oh, I'm sure you're right. I get a bit het up about the things we do to each other, sometimes. Your mother used to tell me . . ."

"How much rent she pay you?"

"One pound fifty. I hope it wasn't too much. It was what she was paying when we bought the house."

"Je-sus! You're another wants her head looked at! I always sent her ten quid a week to help with the rent."

Lydia laughed. It was so typical of Mrs Newbury—not that she'd ever had the feel of real poverty about her and had often said that old-age pensioners had nothing to grumble about and ought to be more grateful for what the Government did for them.

"Are you sure she got it?" she asked.

"All I know is that time I couldn't spare it . . ."

Suddenly Procne seemed to shrink back into the stolid, dull, institutionalized self she had been before they started talking about Mrs Newbury. She even glanced at the door, as if expecting to see an eye peering in through the peep-hole.

"What's the matter?" said Lydia.

Procne looked at her troubled.

"All right," she said, "I better tell you. I got to tell somebody, or I'll do my nut. You know I was saying about my bloke what found me that flat? Gavin's his name. We was doing OK, but he fancied himself as a businessman and he wanted to expand—get a few more girls on his books, all that. *I* didn't mind. Trouble was, he had big ideas but he didn't have the organisation, and after a bit he run into a mob what did. They done him proper—he's in Morocco, last I heard. It come at a bad time for me—I was due an abortion—it's not as nice as it says in the papers, really—so one thing and another the mob didn't realise at first I was—you know—valuable. So I was short, and Mum was getting at me, and I met this lordship at a party. He's quite famous but he's ever so forgetful, always leaving things in my flat, like, and sending his chauffeur round for them after. I just knew he wouldn't notice if I took a couple of his cheques, like, and he didn't. I wasn't greedy—just enough for Mum for a few weeks, and buy me a new trouser suit. Well, after that the mob cottoned on to what I was worth—it's funny, another lordship what works in the City told me it's just like that when one company does a take-over on another, they take a bit of time to sort out what they bought. Anyway the mob set me up proper again, and put in a bloke, Chris, to look after me and that, and I thought well this is a bit of OK. Chris is nice, and he can act posh, and he was too scared of the mob to beat me up the way Gavin sometimes done, but he was just like Gavin one way—he had ideas. When I told him about them cheques he said "We'll try a bit more of that." He worked it out that if we was careful whose cheques we borrowed—you know, blokes what wouldn't like to come out about their funny tastes, and that—we'd be OK. Only it didn't work out. We was ever so stupid, really. One thing, it was a mercy the police copped us before the mob found out. That would *not* have been funny."

Carried away by the vigour of her story-telling, Procne only came back in the last few words to remembering her fear of "the mob". Even then she only saw one part of the ugliness of it all, and didn't seem to realise that "the mob" was really only another section of the oppression-machine—the crudely stamped reverse of the medal whose obverse is Justice, elegantly engraved.

"They sound pretty frightening," said Lydia. "Could they really be spying on us here, though?"

"Not in here—we're off the wing. But I shouldn't be surprised they knew you was coming. I got a message from Chris. He's in Parkhurst, and first week he was there he had his face slashed and a couple of ribs broken. They'll leave him alone now . . . Cheer up, Liz, don't you worry–you'll never meet up with them."

"I hope not, but that isn't what bothers me. I hate being part of a society in which that sort of thing is allowed to exist."

"Nothing you can do about it, so why worry? What was we on about? Oh, yes, I was telling you about the cheques. Point is, Mum begun it."

"I don't think she realised."

"Course not, but she wouldn't of minded. Given her a kick, more like, thinking I done it for her sake. I wonder what she done with all that money."

"She may have spent it. She wasn't old enough to draw her pension, was she?"

"No, but there was Dad's from the railway, and what she was getting cleaning for them foreign gentlemen–she was ever so funny about them, sometimes. Used to tell me on the phone, all their little secrets–no, if she was only paying one fifty rent she wouldn't have no cause to spend what I was sending her."

"I don't know. Vodka costs getting on for . . ."

"Vodka! Mum never touched a drop! Never!"

"Oh. I didn't realise you didn't know. I'm so sorry. At the inquest . . ."

"You ever seen her drinking? Or drunk?

"As a matter of fact, no."

"There you are then. You can't keep it quiet, not in a lodging house like what you keep."

"We were all very surprised, but the evidence at the inquest semed clear. She was in pretty good condition, the pathologist said, but there was quite a lot of alcohol in her blood stream. She seemed to have been climbing up on her table to do something to her curtains, and she fell and hit her head on a brass fender. One of my other tenants, Mrs Pumice, went up next morning to ask your mother to mind her baby and found her lying there, still in the clothes she'd been wearing the night before. There was a bottle of Smirnoff on the mantelpiece and four empties in the cupboard. They all had her fingerprints on."

"Empties!"

"That's right."

"Never!"

"But . . ."

"Listen, Liz, when my Dad was drinking, the trouble Mum

went to to get the empties out of the house! She got a funny little basket on wheels and took the washing out to the public laundry in it, what she'd always used to do at home. She tucked the empties into the washing, see, and went to the laundry the long way round so as she could put the bottles into people's dustbins what wasn't her neighbours. Always."

"Even so, I suppose she might have been saving a batch up to get rid of. And . . ."

"Hey! You find out where she was buying the stuff?"

"I don't think the question came up. If you like I could . . ."

Procne, without asking, helped herself to another cigarette and lit it with shaking fingers. Her face seemed to have gone pale and textureless.

"Tisn't true," she said suddenly.

"I'm afraid it seems to be."

"No, it's only *evidence*. Evidence doesn't have to be true. I got sent down fair enough, seeing I done what they said I did. But you should of heard some of the evidence, both sides. I know. And I know Mum had a horror of drink, an absolute horror. My Dad was a bastard drunk—near as killed me when I was five. *I* drink. I've been to a party Friday night and next thing I know it's Tuesday and I don't know who I've been with or what I've done. That's what come between me and Mum, more than anything; she was always at me to pack it in, but it's my life, isn't it? Supposing she's been on the bottle, she'd have been a bit more friendly like, wouldn't she?"

"I don't know. Perhaps she only started drinking after you'd come here. We don't drink anything much at the moment because we haven't got any spare cash, so she didn't get at me. She did tell me about your father hurting you, and talked about the wickedness of drink in general—but you know, she did it with a sort of relish, slightly like a reformed drunk at a temperance meeting."

"Yes, that's Mum. It was all a play to her, wasn't it, with her acting all the best parts, too!"

Procne's laugh was surprisingly loud, but seemed to Lydia a completely natural sound, an expression of pure enjoyment of the instant, which the dreary hours coming before and after could never infect or alter. Most educated people have had a sheltered upbringing, because shelter makes the educator's task easier. Procne had not. For the past six years she had led a life which many people nowadays would consider sophisticated, that is to say a life in close contact with violence, drama, risk and passion. You might have thought that by now she would be mature and knowledgeable, pickled in the brine of life. But she was naive, ignorant and unenquiring about the nature of the society that had used and crushed her. In fact she was not even aware that she had been crushed. Even here, in the heart of the burial mound, she fizzed like a child.

Lydia felt for her a strangely powerful flow of attraction and sympathy. In her own bustling life she had often fought with all her energy for odd underdogs and misfits; but these earlier episodes suddenly now seemed to her callow, sacrifices to her own conscience, Pharisaic in their rectitude and egoism. Procne was different. It seemed to Lydia of enormous importance, comparable almost to the love and protection she owed Richard and Dickie, that an area of freedom should be found in which Procne could live and expand and fulfil her enormous potential for happiness.

"All right," she said. "I'll tell you what I'll do. I'll try and find out where your mother was buying the drink. We ought to know. My father's a surgeon and knows a lot of medical people—I'll see if he can find out whether there was anything in the medical evidence that didn't come out at the inquest. And I'll try and find whether anyone knows anything about what she did with the money. I suppose that's the most important, because if there's any left it would be useful to have you come out."

"Ooh, yes," said Procne, evidently thinking of this point for the first time. "That would be ever so useful. Only, if she made a will. . ."

"I doubt it. She had a thing about lawyers. My husband is training to become a barrister, and she was always at me about it, suggesting other things he ought to do. She said lawyers were worse than criminals, all out to cheat you. I can't see her making a will."

"That's only Mum. Soon as she wanted a bloke she'd of gone and found one. One time, a bit after I set up with Gavin, she was on about making a will just to leave me out of it—course I only laughed. Never thought I'd need the money."

"OK, I'll see if I can find out about that too. She might have told Mrs Pumice."

"And the booze," said Procne earnestly. "Don't forget about the booze. That's screwy, Liz, I promise you. Anyway, vodka! I mean, suppose she'd started drinking, it'd of been Scotch. Or gin. Can't you just see what she'd of said about vodka? Foreign muck! Don't know where it's been or what they've put in it! Dead men's feet! Sniff!"

Both voice and sniff were so accurate that the ghost of Mrs Newbury floated vividly through Lydia's mind and the hair on her nape prickled. They laughed together, and the conversation was still effortlessly flowing out of the suddenly opened spring of their friendship when the Welfare Officer came back.

"Thank you for coming," said Procne, rather formal in this new presence.

"I've loved it," said Lydia. "Thank you, too. Shall I see if they'll let me come again?"

"Ooh, would you? That'd bc great!"

8

THE PATTERN, by which men came unnoticed into a room where Lydia was working, continued. They seldom offered to help, though.

"Can I help?" said a voice.

Lydia poked her head up between the joists. Mr Vaklins was standing by the door, wearing a dark mauve suit and an egg-yellow polo-necked jersey.

"You'd ruin that snappy get-up," she said.

"I have overalls in the car. What are you doing?"

"Just checking for dry rot under here. It's come in from next door, along that wall, and got into that cupboard. The question is how far it's spread. I've had that beam out and back, and it's OK, and so far I can't see anything under here, so we may be just in time. Did you come to ask about the room?"

"To see you and ask about the room."

"Oh . . . well . . . it's a bit difficult . . . I can't really make up my mind yet . . ."

"No hurry. I suppose the rent would be somewhere round twenty pounds a week?"

"Twenty! You could get somewhere much nicer for that!"

"Not a room in the same house as my work. You see, being a Minister is not a full-time job, so I would run my own business from here also. I've been using my flat as an office, and I've got used to sleeping above the shop, you know. You wouldn't mind if I put a telephone in?"

"Of course not," said Lydia, torn by the thought of the extra rent, and wine for Richard at supper, and a bike for Dickie, and a powder sander. "Hell . . . you see, the trouble is I've been sort of planning to use Mrs N's room to sort the tenancies out a bit. People have grown into this house all higgledy-piggledy, and now I think I could work it so that everybody lived on their own floor, with their own bathrooms and so on."

"Yes, I see . . . Are you going to have that wainscot off? Shall I do it?"

"You can't. Those sockets are live. Some nit seems to have done some private wiring, years ago, and as far as I can make out they come off the supply to the top two floors, so I can't switch them off without putting the Government out of action."

He shrugged, nodded and picked his way out.

It was almost pleasant to be back again in the dank, rank cavity beneath the joists; the problems here were at least inanimate (though sometimes it is hard to believe that the dry-rot fungus does not have a primitive, malevolent will of its own). Lit by the inspection-lamp the cavity was dreary but not gruesome; it smelt of town gas and mouse-droppings and the faint, sweetish, fallen-leaf reek of one of the wet-rots, whose brownish mycelium fanned out, pretty as sea-weed, along the party wall. The creak of footsteps came when Lydia was some distance away from her entrance-hole. By the time she had huddled her way back Mr Vaklins, in clean white overalls, was kneeling by the wall unscrewing one of the live sockets.

"Don't be a bloody fool," she snapped.

He turned, smiling, and spread out a hand which wore a heavy-duty rubber glove. Sulkily Lydia climbed out of the hole and stood by his shoulder, lighting his work with her inspection-lamp like a dutiful little woman, tense to cope if he made a mistake. He knew exactly what he was doing, though; his movements were quick, firm and deft. He'd brought his own little kit of electrical tools, which Lydia at once longed for in the way some women long for jewels; they seemed to her beautiful, neat and glistening in their wash-leather roll.

"Forgive me," he said, moving to the second socket. "I'm always inquisitive, especially about my hosts, the English. I don't quite understand why you're doing this—I mean doing it all yourself, crawling under floorboards, bashing away at plaster. I know some of your tenants only pay you a pittance, but the Livonians pay an economic rent, and your husband goes out to work. I'd have thought you could afford to hire men to do the worst of it."

Lydia approved of his asking so directly—it was what she would have done herself. That made her uncomfortable about having to hedge her answer; but Richard's breakdown was still no one's business but the Timmses'.

"Well," she said, "I do like to do things myself. That's partly because I enjoy it, and partly because it makes me feel a parasite if I buy someone else's time to do a job which I could perfectly well do myself. I mean, I'm not much good at plastering, so I'm happy to hire a plasterer–that's an art. But it makes me sick when I read–oh, there was a bloke in the *New Statesman* last year complaining in one breath about the exploitation of the working classes and the next that he couldn't find anyone to fix his slates at a reasonable price. *Anybody* can fix slates. But in fact you're wrong about Richard–he's not earning at the moment–he's studying law."

"Ah," said Mr Vaklins, apparently perfectly satisfied. But Lydia, having got that far, thought she owed both him and Richard more.

"He was a soldier when I married him. I hated the idea, but you know, one's in love, and besides his family had always been soldiers, and so on. I thought I could stick it out, but I couldn't. He did a stint as military attaché in a couple of places, but I couldn't even stand that. So he jacked it in."

"That must have been a wrench."

"Yes . . . well, we looked around and decided that he'd make a good lawyer. I wasn't going to have him doing some dreary job all day and then doing night school. Besides, he'd done it all for my sake, so now I thought it was up to me to support him. I didn't want to go out to work because of Dickie–that's our son–he's seven now. But my mother left me just enough money to buy this place–we got it cheap because of all the sitting tenants–and that's how I became a landlady. It suits me."

"It appears to, certainly. You wouldn't make a happy parasite."

His movements slowed. Rather thoughtfully he wrapped the last length of insulation tape round the earth wire, making a neat finish so that the end of the cable looked like the bandaged stub of an elfin limb. He rose slowly and gazed discontentedly at the results.

"I don't know if I shall stay in England," he said. "It is so full of parasites. Every society must have a few, I suppose, but in a way England has become like this house of yours, full of weak places and rots and moulds. Your tenants, my Government, we live here as though the house would go on just as before—and in England there isn't someone like you to repair the structure. They just slap on a bit of paint, blue or pink, over the worst bits. But you know, Lydia, when you've done you'll still have an old house, always in need of repair."

"You've got to do what you can," said Lydia.

"That is the rule?" (His voice sounded more foreign once he got away from small talk.)

"I don't know about rules. But if you let things go you never forgive yourself. Look, Paul, I haven't been quite honest about that room. It *would* suit me if I could get Mrs Pumice to move up there, and the rest of the tenants to sort themselves out. But . . . about parasites . . . I hate the idea of being one. I hate the idea of exploiting people just because my mother happened to leave me enough money to buy this house. I've never turned anyone out, and I keep the rents as low as I can, and even if all the tenants suddenly cleared out I wouldn't dream of converting to a lot of expensive flats for Biba people. I like tenants who have some sort of right to live here."

"Can we just rip this off, or must we be careful?"

"I'll get my crowbar."

As soon as she'd levered a gap big enough for him to get his fingers down he ripped the wainscot away as if it had been cardboard. Lydia crawled along with her inspection lamp. The fan of wet-rot had sent a tendril up this far but there seemed to be no sign at all of that faint, grey, cobwebby network which is the first wave of a dry-rot invasion.

"Great," she said. "It seems all clear. The damp-course men can do it the same time they do the front room. I'd been dreading what I'd find along here."

"What now?"

"Oh. Well, I've just got time to finish inspecting underneath before I go and fetch Dickie from school."

"May I take you? I'm at a loose end. Honestly."

She was about to refuse, out of a habit of independence, when she realised how enormously Dickie would enjoy a ride in that car. Carless, he longed for cars as petless children long for imagined furry friends.

"That would be marvellous," she said. "It gives me ten minutes extra, too. Can we leave at twelve fifteen?"

"I'll be there."

His smile and nod—even his stance—made it a relief for

her to slither into her musty catacomb and work off her embarrassment by scrabbling into dark nooks. The last conceivable thing she wanted was a dashing, rich, handsome, *helpful* admirer.

9

WITH BABIES Lydia let herself go. When she had been pregnant with Dickie, in Germany, she had read all the how-to-be-a-mother books she could find–in much the same spirit, Richard had said, as she'd have read all the manuals before deciding to buy a new car. She'd been alarmed by all the advice about a baby's need for fondling and for the stimulus and reassurance of touch, because she's felt this to be contrary to her own nature. So (again to Richard's amusement) she'd borrowed neighbouring babies to practise on, and had found that she had been wrong about her own nature, or perhaps about Nature. She had liked–loved–the touching and fondling.

Then Dickie had turned out an awkward baby, all elbows, and curiously cunning at folding a floppy little leg the wrong way; a wriggler, almost from the instant of birth. This might have been a factor inherited from either parent; or it might have been something to do with the insecurity caused by the slowly forming crisis that would take Richard out of the army; or even by the child perceiving before either parent the first signs of Richard's breakdown. Anyway, he'd never been fun to hold.

But Lydia still allowed herself to go soft with other people's babies; if challenged she'd have argued that it must be dangerous to suppress such a strong impulse in herself, but Mrs Pumice wasn't the type to raise questions like that. She was simply glad to have her baby held.

Trevor Pumice cannot have been the Health Visitor's delight; his skin had a yellowish tinge and he was about two pounds overweight. He was still very bald at an age when Dickie had sprouted a handsome thatch. Though not yet teething he dribbled. But he fitted his head into the hollow by Lydia's collar-bone, allowed one gross little hand to slide across the fullness of her breast and fell instantly asleep.

Mrs Pumice, also yellow-skinned and overweight, smiled

and lit a fresh cigarette from the stub of her old one. She had had her seventeenth birthday a week after Trevor was born.

"Crying half the night again," she said. "Now he'll sleep all day and wake up in time to cry all night."

"Poor you," said Lydia. "Dickie was hell at that age, too. It's the most tiring thing in the world."

"It's not being tired I mind, only it's so dead boring. But I'm glad you come. I was meaning to ask, will it be all right about the rent for a few days?"

"Is Mr Pumice out of work again?"

"I don't think so. I haven't heard nothing, and I expect I'd of heard if it was that. You see, it'd be a bit of an excuse for him getting so far behind with my payments, wouldn't it?"

"Oh dear. I suppose it's all right, Mrs Pumice. I won't turn you out, or anything, I mean. But I really can't afford to let you get tremendously behind. Look, I'm going to put a proper cooker into Mrs Newbury's room, and paint and paper it. When that's done, I wonder whether you'd like to move up there; it's less than half the rent, and you can have the pick of the furniture out of both sets of rooms, if you want."

Mrs Pumice's round, spiritless face went blanker still, but the look in her pale brown eyes hardened. Lydia didn't resent this–it was natural that somebody already so cheated by life as Mrs Pumice should regard any proposal at all as the start of yet another confidence trick. She gave her time to think by wiping away Trevor's steady, frothy dribble. The baby stirred, stretched and snuggled back. Lydia smiled at him.

"I'm going to have another of my own as soon as I can get a bit more sorted out," she said.

"That what you want me to move up to Ma Newbury's for?"

(Mrs Newbury, after her break with Procne, had tended to treat Mrs Pumice as a surrogate daughter. Mrs Pumice had resented this but had also in a way welcomed it, as even resentment was better than nothing at all in the vacuum of her life.)

"Not really," said Lydia. "I simply want to sort things out."

She explained carefully just how. Mrs Pumice's frown deepened.

"But what'll I do when Don comes back?" she burst out, clearly not having listened to half of what Lydia was saying. Don's return was a piece of future myth, in the sense that the arrival of Apollo at Delphi is a piece of past myth, and of much the same order of credibility. It was safe to promise almost anything against that event.

"With luck I'll have the basement ready by then," said Lydia.

"Oooh, well . . ." (Another thought slowly penetrated.) "If I'm saving that lot of rent I could trade in my TV for colour."

Lydia achieved a smile. Mrs. Pumice already smoked the rent she'd be saving, plus the rent she owed. This was no moment to start the old argument about having part of Don's wages attached; Mrs Pumice simply said you couldn't expect a man to put up with that kind of treatment. It was better to move the conversation elsewhere.

"Did Mrs Newbury give you any papers to look after?" Lydia asked.

"Not really," said Mrs Pumice, still thinking about colour TV.

"You see, I was talking to her daughter last week . . ."

"Were you? Honest?"

In a flash the whole atmosphere changed. The dreary room seemed to withdraw its weight of boredom as Mrs Pumice leaned forward, greedy-eyed. A tinge of health glowed in her cheeks. Her lips, half open, glistened.

"Yes, I went to explain about her mother's death."

"In prison!"

"That's right. I liked her. I think she's been very unfairly treated."

"Brought it on herself, Ma Newbury said. Ruined by drink, she said."

"That reminds me—did you have any idea that Mrs Newbury was drinking so much herself?"

"Cunning old bitch—you could of knocked me down with a feather. But what about Procne?"

"Oh . . . I told her I'd find out whether her mother had left her anything, or made a will. I thought perhaps you . . ."

"She was *making* a will. I mean, she was on about me not being able to sign it, cos I was under eighteen. I never seen it. Nothing to leave, had she? Drunk it all."

"I don't know. I just said I'd find out. When was this?"

"Ooh . . . bit before Christmas. She was on about how

ungrateful Procne was, and what a nice lady Princess Anne was. I don't know as she actually got it written out proper, but if she did I bet she got it signed all right. She might of burnt it after, perhaps, so as she could get a thrill out of being that noble and forgiving . . ."

It was a measure of the vigour of Mrs Newbury's personality, her heroic scale, that even the totally self-absorbed Mrs Pumice was able to sketch a vivid outline of how she might have behaved.

"I don't suppose there's much point in searching her room," said Lydia. "The police must have done that."

"Him!" said Mrs Pumice. "Down here for cuppas half the time, on about what a hard life it was. But Procne . . . She OK? How's she doing her hair now? What's it like in there?"

"Inside? It's exactly my idea of hell. It's a system designed to grind you down."

Lydia was about to expand on the society-induced apathy and loneliness of prison life when she saw that it wouldn't seem much different from the life Mrs Pumice herself lived. So she notched up a resolution to find excuses for visiting her tenant more often and switched to a description of Procne's coiffure.

"She really is beautiful," she added. "The photographs don't give you any idea."

"Oh, I seen her."

"I thought she'd never come here."

"No, Ma Newbury got it into her head to go to court one day and drug me along. I seen her then."

"She didn't tell me."

"Well, she loved a bit of a secret, didn't she? Fact, she made me promise not to tell. But then, being her, she got talking with some bloke and the next thing I knew we was in the papers. Look, I nicked the picture out of her collection —something to show Don when he comes back, see?"

She lumbered out of her chair and fetched from a collection of papers jammed behind a biscuit tin a clipping from the *Sun*, already yellow and brittle. Mrs Pumice, in the left foreground, might have been any bun-faced gawper. Mrs Newbury, in the centre, was herself even to the exact angle of her snapping-turtle head as it poked from her awful fur tippet. Over to the right, a bit further off, stood a very large, solemn Indian. It took Lydia a while even to notice him, and a while more to realise that he was Mr Jack Ambrose.

She was startled until she saw that the coincidence wasn't

all that strange. A man whose job is to help the inadequate must quite often find himself hanging around the courts. Still, the sight of him there, and the tenuous connection to Procne, depressed her. But what mattered was the good likeness of Mrs Newbury.

"May I borrow this for a couple of days?" she said. "I'll let you have it back."

"OK," said Mrs Pumice, wholly uninquisitive. "My, Trev fancies you, don't he? You wouldn't like to keep him?"

Her joky tone only half hid the wistfulness behind the question. Lydia was not conscious of any movement in herself, but the baby seemed to sense her inner rejection, waking into a whine. Carefully she petted him back to oblivion.

"I fancy him too," she said. "I'd love to look after him sometimes if you want to get out."

"Would you really? That'd be great!"

Those were exactly the words Procne had used, in the heart of *her* prison. Lydia was shocked at the difference in her own reactions—her eagerness to go back to Holloway, her grudging acceptance of a duty to take Trevor over and let Mrs Pumice escape for a few hours.

"Yes, I'd love to," said said. "Any time."

10

"I'M A BIT DRUNK," said Richard, drowsily. "One bottle of plonk, only. What was that in aid of?"

"I can explain everything," wheedled Lydia.

"The trouble is we've got out of the habit. Do you remember that restaurant in Salzburg where we knocked back four bottles after *Rosenkavelier?* I can't remember much about the opera, but the hangover remains vivid. You don't suffer at all."

"You drank twice as much as I did. One of the things I really like about the way we live now is not having to go to any more operas."

"I've got twice your mass, so I ought to be able to absorb twice as much alcohol. What was it in aid of to-night? Celebration of moving in here?"

"Not really—at least I hadn't thought of that. It's funny about fresh plaster. It's got a sort of white smell, even in the dark."

"Hyperaesthesia, they call it. Where do you strike next?"

"Mrs Newbury's. I'm pretty sure Mrs Pumice will move up, and that means Paul can't have it."

"I thought you like him."

"I do. When he's serious, and when he's doing things. But . . . anyway, whether I like him doesn't matter."

"Umm. What was the wine in aid of, then?"

"Nothing. I just felt I had to buy it because the bloke in the off licence was so helpful. It's that one at the bottom of Addison Avenue."

"Aren't there some nearer than that? At least four, I make it. Helpful about what, anyway?"

"Oh, recognising Mrs Newbury. Mrs Pumice lent me a photo of her. The bloke said she went there every week to pick up an order. You remember her old red shopping bag with the black rim? It turns out she had two of those, and she'd take one of them back every Tuesday morning, full of empties, and he'd have the other one ready and hand it over —six bottles of vodka and one of brandy. She gave him the money and took the change and went. She never said a word. He told me he'd inherited the system from the bloke who was there before him, and he didn't even know her name. If there was someone in the shop she'd walk past and come back when it was empty. He didn't even know she was dead. He'd still got the last order waiting—he showed me. And he never asked why I wanted to know, or anything, so I felt I had to buy something. I liked it, actually."

"So did I. When I'm a judge we'll have a couple every night, unless we're going to the opera. What does vodka cost?"

"Three oh nine. I looked."

"Plus the brandy. Over twenty quid a week. Where the hell was she getting it from?"

"Well, Procne was sending her ten quid a week. Richard?"

He tensed at his name, but only a little. Perhaps the wine helped. For a moment Lydia wondered whether that had been her subconscious motive in buying it.

"Ung?" he said, wary.

"What's going to happen to Procne?"

"The *News of the World* will pay two thousand quid for her life story in six instalments. There might be another thousand from a book. After that, if she's got any sense she'll emigrate."

"Don't be a bloody man of the world. What will *happen* to her?"

"Sorry . . . I hadn't got it that you minded . . . wheeee! You want her to come here?"

"What do you think?"

"Provided she doesn't bring her work home . . . damn! Sorry. That's the wine. What do I think? My first thought is you're nuts—only I know you're not. So . . . ummmm . . ."

"You see, darling, I've read again and again that when you come out of jail or a mental home or something like that . . ."

"The army . . ."

"Shut up or I'll bite you. The point is you've got to have something to do, somewhere to live, and a community to live in which accepts and supports you. Otherwise you simply go back and do whatever you did again. I think I'm probably the only person she knows who doesn't belong to her old world. I mean, if she wants to go back there, that's her decision. But we could at least offer her a choice. I think we ought to. Darling?"

"Ung . . . if you put it like that . . . I don't know . . . all the empties were vodka? No brandy?"

Richard's technique for not thinking about what bothered him was to think about something else. He did it quite deliberately. Sometimes Lydia had woken in the small hours to hear him murmuring lists of names—every man who had served in some company with him, all the cricket teams at his prep school.

"She'd probably dumped those," she said.

"You went to her room quite a bit, didn't you?"

"Why?"

"Vodka doesn't smell. Brandy does. Besides, six bottles a week of hard liquor—even Jack Arbuthnott didn't quite reach that level. Where the hell was she getting twenty-five quid a week? Six quid from the Government, say six from her pension, ten from Procne . . . you know, that ten from Procne sounds a little bit like blackmail. Perhaps there was someone else."

"Only too likely," sighed Lydia. "She had a Mafia outlook on life. Or she might have been nicking the Government's stamp money. She was awful. I miss her."

"Umm . . . suppose you decided to let Procne come, you could say to this Vaklins chap that he could have the room till then. Honestly, Liz, you could do with the cash."

"I know. But I really do want to take the chance to move the tenants into more sensible rooms. Besides . . ."

"Does he bother you? Am I going to have to unpack my hunting whip? I wonder where the hell it is."

"Yes, he bothers me, but not like that. I mean, at first I thought it was like that, you know the 'I'm a man and you're a woman so it's my nature to admire and court you and your nature to pretend not to like it but eventually succumb with gladness' bit. But I think that's only a manner, a sort of foreign politeness. There's something else—I don't quite know what."

Richard chuckled in the dark and squeezed her hand.

"Just a bit too eager to please," he said. "Perhaps if you gave him the room he might slack off a bit."

"I don't know."

"Or you could find him an outside interest."

"I'm sure he's got plenty. He really is very handsome in

a slightly gnomish way. I get an occasional urge to scribble a moustache on his face."

"Umm. What's Lalage up to?"

"Last I heard she's walked out of her job. I don't keep up with her love life."

"It's worth a try. Let's have a beano. I'm beginning to feel a bit hermit-like."

"I'll ask her when I see her."

"Great. That's fixed."

After that the conversation became spasmodic. Between whiles Lydia cast up mental minutes of the meeting. It had been agreed that if when the upheavals were over a room became available Paul should be offered it until Procne needed it, but that Procne could come if she wanted to. But as Richard had given more than Lydia to reach this compromise, she'd compensate by setting up a proper dinner party for him, with the family silver gleaming in the candlelight and all the other bloody trimmings.

11

It was just bad luck that the day Lydia wanted to start on Mrs Newbury's room was Dickie's half term. She was planning bus-routes for a round trip taking in The Army Museum, the Imperial War Museum, Apsley House and the Armoury at the Tower when Mrs Pumice knocked at the door and came in without waiting for an answer. She was wearing flared orange trousers, a purple jersey and a cap to match the trousers. Her baby whined on her arm.

"Oh, I'm ever so sorry," she said. "I got to go out. It's ever so urgent. I was hoping you could look after Trev for a couple of hours. He's got a bit of a grizzle, like, but you're ever so good with him."

It was the first time she had asked. It was impossible to refuse. So Lydia smiled and took the child; with minimal thanks Mrs Pumice was gone, eager and excited, as if she were dashing to meet a lover who was waiting for her somewhere in the snapping February wind.

"It isn't fair," said Dickie. "It's my half term."

"I'm sorry darling. I'll just see if I can get him to sleep, then we can go and throw furniture about in Mrs Newbury's room. We might even find treasure."

Trevor refused to sleep. His whine wasn't anything burpable, and didn't seem to be a teething noise, it was just an expression of generalised vague discontent, much like his mother's normal view of the world. Dickie tried to interest him in being a besieged army in a fortress of furniture, but that didn't work either. In the end Lydia humped him, still whining, up to Mrs Pumice's room, where she changed him and dumped him in a carricot. This she carried up the next flight and deposited on the landing outside the Government's front door, as though he were a bastard they'd jointly fathered. Dickie fought a heroic retreat up the stairs behind her, dying gloriously three times on the way.

"OK," said Lydia, "we'll start by looking for treasure."

Dickie enjoyed that. He rooted unsystematically among the drawers, hurling around Mrs Newbury's incredible musty old garments, until he came across a huge whale-boned corset which he decided could be worn upside down as a breastplate. Strapped into this he held the bed against an attacking army while Lydia put the clothes back and searched anywhere he hadn't rifled. There was no sign of money or will. Outside the door Trevor's whine at last stilled into sleep.

"Now, darling," said Lydia, "the next thing is to get all the furniture over here. Then we can roll the carpet up. Do you want a ride?"

The bed became a tank. A brief engagement with a panzer division was fought. Lydia was practised in using her slight weight efficiently, but she'd forgotten how Mrs Newbury had managed to accumulate all the heaviest furniture in the house. In particular there was a vast satinwood wardrobe against the inner wall, which could wait for the moment but would have to come to pieces before she could shift it. While Dickie bounced untiring on the bed she hoicked the tacks out of the carpet and began to roll it up, away from the window. As she worked she became vaguely conscious of a smell–not gas, not Mrs Newbury (who had generated her own strong odour of tea and shampoo and chocolate biscuits), not that reek of age and poverty which had filled the house when she'd first bought it, none of the rots she knew. She had a moment of sick despair about the rots, until she realised that what she was remembering was not the odour of any fungus but of the solvent that carried the fungicides.

When she'd rolled the carpet a few feet she slipped tuppence under the far end, then rose and walked round the room, sniffing. The strange smell seemed strongest in the corner by the wardrobe.

"Are you smelling for treasure?" said Dickie.

"I don't know. Come here and see what you think."

At once he was on hands and knees beside her, sniffing like a snuff-addict, rump taut.

"Dead man's chest," he said in a puzzled voice.

(One of Richard's family traditions was that children with colds must have their chests rubbed with Vick. During the process the adult who was rubbing had to sing the pirates' catch from *Treasure Island*. This mightn't help the child to get better, but it was the Right Thing to Do.)

"Yes, it does smell a bit like that," said Lydia. "It seems stronger higher up. Oh, look!"

The satin in the corner of the ceiling was not very noticeable, but Lydia was reasonably sure it was new. She pulled the table over, stood on it and reached up. The patch was sticky to the touch, and whatever it was had dribbled a little way down the corner where the walls met; the smell on her fingertips was resinous but not really chemical. Could even a weeping fungus weep such tears? As far as she could remember the room directly above was the one in which the Government filed their documents, chiefly evidence for claims for compensation against Soviet Russia when freedom and democracy once again dawned in Livonia.

She would have liked to go and investigate, but could hardly walk in on the Government with Trevor whining on her shoulder and Dickie winkling out machine-gun nests behind her.

"Come and help me with the carpet, darling," she said. "It's getting a bit heavy for me alone. You push at that end."

Dickie got down and heaved against the roll with such verve that it trundled forward all askew and he tumbled after it, missing the planted tuppence. Still he was thrilled when Lydia pointed it out and went back to the bed to bounce, holding it high over his head and whooping at each bounce. Outside on the landing the baby joined in. The door opened.

"Sorry," said Paul Vaklins. "I've woken someone's child. Can I help?"

"I can manage, except for that wardrobe," said Lydia. "It comes to bits. I'd like to get it over there. Oh, damn that bloody kid!"

"Me?" asked Dickie, very interested.

"Of course not, darling. Sorry, Paul. Look, that sort of cornice thing lifts off . . ."

The wardrobe was like a vast Chinese puzzle, separate shapes self-locked to each other. The cornice was light enough, but the first section of actual hanging-space seemed to weigh several hundredweight.

"Whew!" said Lydia, as they settled it down by the window. "Thanks. I couldn't have done that alone."

"I'm glad to hear it. You sometimes give the impression that you can do anything. Hello!"

Paul had strolled back to where the other half of the wardrobe stood, tall but proportionless, displaying a cobwebby interface. The end section of the pedestal had fallen out sideways. Paul bent and picked up a large brown envelope, to which a smaller white envelope had been taped.

"It appears to be for you," he said in an amused voice.
"Treasure!" shouted Dickie.
"Family letters or something, I should think," said Lydia dryly. "Drat that kid, I'll have to go and change him. Let's get this other bit across, then I can manage."
"Can I open the treasure?" asked Dickie.
"No, darling," said Lydia. Her hand shook as she took the envelope from Paul and put it on the mantelpiece. As they hefted the other half of the wardrobe across she collected her wits. The feel of the envelope had certainly been that it held banknotes; there was no reason to be panicky and secretive; all she need feel was excitement at Procne's good fortune. On the other hand, there was no sense in telling the world.
"I must cope with that poor child," she said as she carried the pedestal across. "Dickie, will you be all right here for a bit?"
"I want to see the treasure," said Dickie.
"You stay here with me and I'll tell you a story," said Paul.
"A battle?" asked Dickie.
"There used to be some pretty scary witches in Livonia."
"A battle," said Dickie. "I'll make the sand table. Here."
He jumped off the bed and hoicked its cover into a range of mountains.
"I'm sorry," said Lydia. "His grandfather is a nut on military history. You don't have to do it, honestly, Paul."
"No, that's fine," said Paul. "I was in a sort of battle once. I'll tell you how Aaku Aakisen ambushed the Russian slave-train and rescued the prisoners. OK?
"That's marvellous," said Lydia. "You don't know what you've let yourself in for, though. I'll be about five minutes."
She snatched the envelope off the mantelpiece, ran out and whisked the carricot down the stairs with such acceleration that Trevor was startled out of his whine. She grabbed the pot out of Mrs Pumice's room, rushed him down to the basement and plonked him down on it. His whine modulated into a wail, but she ignored him.
The money was in five-pound notes, in labelled bundles of £200. There were five of these and a thinner one containing £165. Just under twelve hundred quid. The envelope contained one piece of lined writing-paper covered with Mrs Newbury's large and spiky script. It said:

I, Doris Newbury, of 11 Devon Crescent, London W.11, being in my right mind and all that, undo all my other wills, not that I have made any as I remember, and leave this money and everything else I got to Lydia Timms, Lady Timms that is, for her boy Dickie to have when he grows up, and I do NOT leave anything to my own daughter Procne, that's been a pain in the neck to me no matter how I've tried. Signed by me Doris Newbury on the 12th of Jan, being in my right mind like I said.

She had signed with vigour, but had not asked anyone to witness the will.

Lydia read it again, sighing.

"Silly old bitch," she said, out loud.

She held the paper over her sink to burn it. Trevor stopped whining to stare in astonishment at the creeping flame, vivid in the gloom of the basement. When the paper was ashes Lydia broke them up smaller, turned on the cold tap and eased them down the drain. As she carried Trevor, clean and dry but still grizzling, back up the stairs, her shoulder bag containing twelve hundred pounds bounced menacingly against her other hip.

"Slowly the slave-train stopped," Paul was saying. "Wheeee, ssshhhh."

"Tonkatonkatonkatonktonktonk," added Dickie, always the perfectionist where stage effects were concerned.

Three pens tied with thread lay end to end in a valley on the white bedcover. The valley was blocked by a tumbled heap of paper pellets. Paul and Dickie craned over the scene, like the Gods above Troy.

"Now," said Paul, "old Aaku wanted the Russians to think that the avalanche was an accident until all the guards were out of the train and he'd blocked the line behind—otherwise they'd just reverse out. From the hillside he watched the soldiers climb out. Their uniforms looked black against the snow . . ."

Lydia crept out and rang the bell of the Government's inner door. After a long wait Mr Obb opened it. He smiled with pleasure when he saw her, then stared doubtfully at the baby. The baby stopped whining and stared back. Their faces had a lot in common, blankness, baldness and an innocent bleariness of eye.

"I'm sorry to bother you," said Lydia. "I've just started to redecorate Mrs Newbury's room, and I've found a place where something has leaked down from above. I don't know whether it comes from outside or from that room where you keep your files. Can I come and look?

Mr Obb shrugged. For a moment Lydia thought he was going to refuse, but he smiled again and held the door open. Trevor, on being taken into an unfamiliar part of the house, snuggled closer against her side but stayed silent, as though instinctively aware of protocol. The filing room was a fair size, the same as Mrs Newbury's but with a lower ceiling and smaller window. It was so crammed with filing cabinets that it seemed claustrophobic. A narrow alleyway led straight from the door between two ranks of cabinets, all at least five feet high and piled on top with bundles of documents, completely screening the corner where the leak had come through. At the end of this alley Lydia found another rank of cabinets backed onto the one she had just passed, and another faced that, and another backed onto that, facing the far wall. But here there was a change–instead of a final rank lining the wall she found four large barrels and two big plastic dustbins. Until she had almost reached them the dusty dry odour of old documents had obscured this other smell, but now it was unmistakably the same as that of the leak below. She stood and stared, petting the baby absent-mindedly.

"What on earth . . ." she began.

"Oh, oh," said Mr Obb in a worried voice, "I had not thought. Of course, of course, Yes."

"I don't get it."

"This is where we make our *varosh*–our vodka."

"You aren't running a still, for heaven's sake?"

"Still? Ah, distillation. No, no, no. We, tsk, tsk, tsk, infuse, yes?"

"Are all these things full, Mr Obb?"

As she reached her free hand towards the lid of the nearer bin Mr Obb seized her elbow, squeaking with alarm.

"No, no, no! Not to touch, please! *Varosh* is most infectable!"

"I'm sorry," said Lydia, withdrawing. "I was worried about the weight. I hadn't realised how much you kept in here. I don't know whether the joists will stand it. This is an old house, you know."

Mr Obb stood back, stroking his bald head and looking vaguely relieved, as though the collapse of the floor were a minor problem compared with the invasion of his booze by some bug.

"We have kept all these things here for many years," he said.

"Well, let's hope it's OK. I'll ring up the Building Centre and see whether they have any standards for the strength of floors supporting filing cabinets. You've got rows–eight in a row, forty. What about the barrels?"

"Oh, ah. Linden would know. Yes. Two barrels and one bin are always full. Sometimes the third barrel."

Lydia measured them with her eye. About forty gallons in the barrels and twenty in the bins. If it had been water, that would make a bit over half a ton. Say a couple of hundredweight each for the cabinets. Another four tons. Say five in all, minimum. It ought to be just about OK, provided the joists were sound. She nodded.

"OK," she said. "Now, do you know how much got spilt? I've got to have some idea how long it's going to keep coming through."

Mr Obb made vague gestures with his hands, a poor method of indicating liquid volume.

"Perhaps two litres, perhaps three," he said at last. "We had an old man, a servant, who made excellent *varosh,* very skilled, very careful. But then he died . . ."

"In this house?"

"No, no," said Mr Obb, suddenly vehement again. "*Not* in this house. But . . . yes, Count Linden and I were changing the liquor from one stage to the next when Linden dropped the jug. It is a fault of education. To be not clever with one's hands is a mark of the intellectual–in Linden's case of the aristocrat, of course. How could old Linden have known that the day would come when his heir must make his own *varosh*? Tsk, tsk."

It was impossible to dislike Mr Obb, even when he burbled class-ridden nonsense like this. In fact he seemed naively eager to placate Lydia's wrath at the spillage, as ingratiating as a savage who has committed some venial murder and is trying to explain his harmlessness and goodwill to a District Officer–a comparison out of another world which no longer exists and so can now also have its iniquities smiled at. Mr Obb mimed shame, and eagerness to please, and promises that he and Count Linden would never again throw sticky liquors around. Trevor Pumice gazed at him with a look of mild distrust.

"I expect it will be all right," said Lydia. "If it keeps coming through I can line that bit with foil before I paper."

"We will pay, of course."

It's hard to guess why Lydia's mind, occupied by the practical problem of stopping strong drink from penetrating a fresh-painted ceiling, should have at that moment made a lateral leap.

"You top the bins up with vodka and brandy," she said. "Mrs Newbury used to buy it for you."

"Yes, yes," agreed Mr Obb. "You see, we are spied on, all of the time. We must be most careful to do nothing that will make bad propaganda. We must not allow the Muscovites to say in Livonia that we spend government income on *varosh*. We do not, of course. We spend our own money."

Lydia would have like to ask for more details, but was afraid that if she did so he would put two and two together and find out that Mrs Newbury had been cheating them. As soon as she took a step away from the barrels he scuttered to the door and held it open for her. Down the corridor she could hear General Busch's rasping voice, speaking German behind a closed door.

"Political matters," said Mr Obb, relaxing. "A man from *Der Spiegel* is interviewing Busch about the death of Aakisen. The tragedy has created great interest on the continent."

"Heavens!" said Lydia. "I must rush. Poor Paul Vaklins is still telling Dickie about how Aakisen stopped the slave-train."

"Not Aakisen," said Mr Obb. "That was an episode in the Estonian resistance–a good story, however. Quite true."

"Let's hope Dickie doesn't find out. He disapproves strongly of fiction–it's his grandfather's fault. I'll let you know whether the Building Centre people think that floor's safe. Oh, can you remember exactly when you spilt the stuff?"

"Indeed," said Mr Obb. "It was the night before the funeral. Linden was tired with his vigil by the coffin–that is how he dropped the jug."

"Thanks," said Lydia. "I'll let myself out. Sorry to have bothered you."

"Delighted, delighted," said Mr Obb, his relief at getting rid of her so obvious that Lydia ran down the stairs wondering what on earth the old men were up to that they were so anxious to hide. Probably some piece of Baltic politics, so mummified that it no longer mattered to anybody except themselves.

A Mig howled over Mrs Newbury's bed. Paul did the jet-scream and Dickie the guns.

"Wheeeeeeeeeeee."

"Tack attack attack attack attack tack."

It curved away over a coarsely darned hill-ridge.

"The prisoners ran between the pine trees," said Paul. "The bullets made lines across the snow like the tracks of a running deer. They threw white splinters from the pine-trunks. Women screamed. A man carried his dead son up the hill, but the bullets caught him and he himself fell dead across the body. The smoke from the wrecked train was like a war-signal, calling to the Russian garrisons. The prisoners wanted to scatter, to hide, to crouch down in the snow, to go back and surrender. But Aaku was their sheepdog, old Aaku with his sticky-out ears. He kept them fleeing in one bunch, all up the hill where the trees were thickest. Fresh groups of his men waited to help the prisoners and to pin down the pursuit. See, now, here is the hill-crest, where the sledges were waiting, and rough little ponies. They pile the women and the wounded on and race down the far slope. Night comes soon in our winters. It is dusk when they reach the frozen river. All along the ice the explosives are set. They cross, and . . ."

His fingers made explosions on the dust sheet.

"Boom! Boom! Boom!" yelled Dickie.

"So now the river was a defence line, and beyond it lay the wild forest and the marshes which Aaku knew like no man else. A few planes came over, dropping bombs at random . . ."

"Kerrump, kerrump."

" . . . but they had no target and did no harm."

Even Lydia's imagination was unwillingly stirred, more by the idea of freedom than by the old hopeless heroisms. She waited for Dickie's inevitable question.

"Is it true, please?"

"Quite true," said Paul, "It was just like that. I was there."

Lydia was faintly irritated by the truthful ring of what she knew to be a lie, and then by the amused glance Paul flashed at her.

"Dickie is a good demonstration of Lysenkoist theory," he said. "The military urge has become hereditable."

"Rubbish," snapped Lydia. "He's been indoctrinated, and by a civilian sawbones at that. Sorry–I didn't mean to sound churlish. He's loved it, haven't you, darling?"

Dickie grunted his thanks, already absorbed in the process of re-settling the paper avalanche on its hillside so that he could fight the whole battle over again. Trevor stirred on Lydia's shoulder and burped so suddenly and violently that he shocked himself into a howl. Like a mother seal rushing to the sound of her pup's voice Mrs Pumice came bowling into the room, looking almost dizzy with happiness.

"Hello!" she cried. "My, you've been busy. Have you been a good boy then, sweetie?"

Trevor's wail rose. Mrs Pumice snatched him from Lydia's arms and made a great but ineffective show of loving him.

"I must go now," said Paul, picking up the pens, and did so before Lydia could thank him. Dickie looked sulky at the disappearance of his train, but in a second or two he had replaced it with an imaginary one which puffed, inaudible through Trevor's crying, between the snow-sprinkled pines.

"I'm glad you found me up here," shouted Lydia. "I wanted to consult you about colour schemes in here."

"It's all right," yelled Mrs Pumice. "I haven't got to move. "I've got my back rent, *and* a month in advance."

She dumped Trevor onto the bed, ruining the Livonian landscape. He rolled onto his stomach and crawled towards the scene of the battle, whining. A Mig came over, whining on a different note, and strafed him vigorously. Mrs Pumice took her rent book and a sheaf of money out of her shoulder-bag.

"Five weeks back is twenty-two fifty," she said, "and four in advance is eighteen. That's forty fifty, right?"

She counted the money out in five-pound notes.

"You've found treasure too?" said Dickie. "I found treasure, Mum found treasure, you found treasure. Tack attack attack attack tack."

"You found Ma Newbury's will?" said Mrs Pumice, bright and gossipy. "Was there any money with it? I bet there was."

"Dickie found tuppence under the carpet and I found some family papers of Mrs Newbury's. There isn't a will," said Lydia.

She tried to speak with less coldness than she felt but the tone came out obviously false, and that made her produce one of her classic blushes, scarlet from scalp to collar-bone. Mrs Pumice evidently felt the rebuff, for she answered with sudden aggressiveness.

"You never asked me where my money come from," she said. "Don sent it, more than what he owed."

"That's great."

"So now I haven't got to move. You can't *make* me, can you? It might mean he wants to come back after all, see?"

She stared at Lydia as if challenging her to say it was a lie. Mrs Newbury had used exactly that look to support her more outrageous fibs.

"Well, that's fine," said Lydia. "We'll just leave everybody where they are for the moment, and Mr Vaklins can move into this room, which he wants to do."

"Ooh, that'll be nice," said Mrs Pumice. "Have you seen his car? It's smashing! Well, I'll be seeing you. Tirra, Dickie."

She snatched her child out of Livonia and left. Dickie restored his battlefield to coherence and started the ambush again. Lydia went gloomily back to work, reshaping her ideas as she did so. OK, leave everybody in their existing rooms. If Paul would pay twelve for this one there'd be no need to ask the Pellettiers for any more. Allow another six weeks to get the basement into decent nick, why, she could have started her baby months ago and she'd still have been all right. Some clouds do have silver linings.

12

IN THE UNWILLING MARCH SUNSHINE Dickie and Lydia stood under the porch of the white plaster wedding-cake which was 109 Hyde Park Gardens. First Sundays in the month were always the same: she woke with a vague reluctance which increased by midday to a depresion which made lunch seem completely insipid; Dickie, on the other hand, lived in a mounting tornado of activity and excitement; now they both stood under the porch, Dickie skipping from foot to foot even while he pressed the bell, and Lydia feeling as usual like a dark little mouse whose weight on the step would snap the trap shut and cage her for ever.

"Who is it?" crackled Lalage's voice from the speaker by the column of bell pushes.

"The men come to hoover the elephant," cackled Dickie (a new joke, concocted by him and Richard during last night's bed-time session).

"She's been getting a bit dusty," said Lalage. "We're thinking of buying a non-stick elephant. Have you anything in that line?"

"Only non-stick hippo . . . hippo . . ."

Dickie broke down before he could finish the word.

"Well, bring one up," said Lalage. "Don't bust the lift, though."

The door buzzed and opened. In the lift Dickie bounced and thrilled, mercifully unable to sense Lydia's inner shrinking. Lalage was holding the flat door open and he hurtled through it, yelling "Boom, Boom, Kiss me Hardy, Boom, Boom."

"Boom, boom," answered Father's voice from the old nursery. Even in those two syllables Lydia sensed that he was the kindly old scholar this visit. Dickie hurtled through the nursery door.

"Men!" yawned Lalage. "How are you, darling. You look marvellous. I've got a new job."

"That's great," said Lydia, relaxing. It was going to be an easy visit, with plenty to talk about and both Father and Lalage in bearable roles. By the time she'd hung her coat on her own peg in the passage Lalage was on the sofa in the drawing room, sprawling luxuriously among the cushions. Lydia settled into her usual small, hardish, constricting chair, opened the sewing-box beside it and took out the tapestry stool-cover that had already seen her through two years of first-Sundays-in-the-month.

"What's the job?"

"London correspondent of a New York glossy business mag. Six thousand a year plus three thousand expenses."

"That sounds perfect."

"Can't you be a *bit* jealous, darling, just to put the cream on my cake."

"But I couldn't begin to do a job like that, let alone like doing it. It's the same as that stupid question about which past age would you prefer to live in. I live now, and that's part of me being me. To live then I'd have to be someone else. To do your job I'd have to be someone else. I'm me, I like it."

Lydia threaded her needle with mauve silk and began to stitch in another line of background between the two stunted chaffinches which were the main feature of the design. It really was becoming gratifyingly hideous. Lalage stretched on the sofa, thinking about money, sensual as Danae under her storm of gold. Lydia stopped stitching and mentally compared her half-sister's prettiness with Procne Newbury's beauty. Lalage's complexion was almost as good, and was set off by her glossy black hair. Her features were small and well-formed too; but there was something deficient in the soft, clear oval of her face, an absence of character, not because Lalage lacked character but because she didn't allow it to appear on the surface to spoil the pretty image. Whereas Procne *was* her own beauty, all through.

"Have you got anything I can wear at a big embassy reception?" asked Lydia.

"Jesus! Which embassy?"

"Russia."

"I'm not lending you my best new Cardin to get all ripped up when you're chucked out. What's it about this time? Exit visas for Jews?"

Lydia laughed.

"I did wonder whether I oughtn't to," she said. "But I've

promised Richard I'll behave. I'll promise you too, if you like."

"Then why are you going at all? You?"

"Oh, it's perfectly stupid. Richard has a friend called George Dunakhov–I like him too–he's like somebody in a Chekhov farce–we knew him when we were at the embassy in Buda and now he's in London and he's got us invited to a big cultural do. In fact I threw the envelope away without opening it, because I thought it was an ad for some shoe-shop or something, but then I fished it out of the waste-paper basket because I needed a bit of card to draw a diagram for a rather thick electrician, and there was this absurd invitation, with a note from George, and at that moment he rang up to check I'd got it. I hadn't time to think of an excuse, and anyway Richard's a bit starved of that sort of function. So what have you got I can wear?"

"Let's go and try a few things on," said Lalage.

They spent almost an hour doing that, while the gunfire of Trafalgar thundered in the nursery and faint whiffs of gunpowder crept under the door to mix with the boudoir odours of Lalage's room.

Tea went very well. Afterwards Dickie decided to watch TV and let Lydia enjoy the privilege of clearing up the battle of Trafalgar. Father, with his characteristic fussy precision, put away his beautifully painted little Airfix models while Lydia swept up the remains of expendable paper ships (Father was very proud of his exploding *Bucentaur*), tidied away the fans which provided the prevailing winds, hoovered the canvas sea and finally rolled it up to expose the old, familiar-stained brown nursery carpet.

"I want a bit of help," she said abruptly.

"Cash?" said Father, sickeningly understanding. "I'm fairly flush just now."

This was recognised family code, and meant that he wasn't spending every penny he earned on some girl with a taste for Ferraris, Krug and the Bahamas.

"No, we're doing OK, thanks," said Lydia. "I've got a new tenant who's paying more for one room than some of them are for four. I want some advice, really."

"Good God!"

"I want to know something about a particular post mortem . . ."

"Which hospital?"

"St Ursula's."

"Might be able to help. I know Crichton-Powell there. What's up?"

"You remember about the old woman who died in my house? The evidence at the inquest was pretty straightforward–she had a lot of alcohol in her bloodstream and she'd been climbing up on a table to do something to the curtains when she fell and hit her head on the corner of the fender. I want to know whether there's any way of telling how long she'd been drinking for, and also whether there was any other possible interpretation of the evidence."

"Umm–this sounds a bit paranoid, my dear."

"It's not for me. I'm visiting her daughter in prison, and she's absolutely convinced that her mother would never have touched alcohol. I want to get her to accept the facts before *she* becomes paranoid. There's another thing–the old lady left a bit of money behind, and I think there's a chance she'd been cheating her employers out of the booze. It would suit me if she'd only just begun drinking, because that would mean that they hadn't much claim on the money and it could all go to the girl."

"Umm. I do a stint at St Ursula's on Tuesdays. I can't guarantee to bump into Chrichton-Powell, but I'll probably do so before next month. What are the details–name, address and date ought to be enough."

"Mrs Daphne Newbury, my address, died on the night of the 31st of January."

Father was half-way through writing this into his little black pocket-book when his good-samaritan face slipped, creased and became inquisitive and roguish as he turned to stare at her.

"Not little Procne's Mamma?" he said.

"That's right," she snapped.

He pursed his lips, head cocked, speculative. Lydia swallowed.

"Did you know her?" she said.

"We had quite a bit of fun together, once, but then she moved out of my class. How is she?"

"Prison is hell. You can't ask how people in hell are, especially if you helped put them there. But I hope she's going to come and live at Devon Crescent when she gets out."

It was a momentary comfort to see him shocked. It may be amusing, even delightful, for randy old cynics to consort with harlots, but it is certainly improper for the daughters of the cynics to invite harlots into their houses.

"You asked me for some advice, my girl," he said. "I'm going to give you some. Steer clear of Procne Newbury."

"I like her."

"Perhaps. In my experience Procne has no moral sense at all."

"Balls!"

"But I have heard it argued that the question whether she has any moral sense is subsumed into the large question whether she has sense of any kind. She's not merely impulsive—she's an embodied impulse."

"You simply can't judge somebody like that by the way somebody like you knows them."

"Perhaps. I told you she'd moved out of my class. That was only partly true. What really put me off was that she moved in with a group of people I find very frightening indeed. Genuine, hard, violent criminals. There are some men who get an extra kick out of that sort of thing. Not me."

"She didn't move in with them, she was taken over by them. And how's she ever going to get away from them if there's nowhere for her to go to and no one else she knows?"

"Well, I've said my piece."

"OK. Now shut up!"

He sighed and stopped. Grey-hairs-with-sorrow-to-the-grave. Lydia sensed the old appalling useless rage beginning to thresh round and round inside her, battering against the walls of her being like the dying king cobra in *Rikki-tikki-tavi.* At the crisis moment Dickie hurtled into the room brandishing his grandfather's best ebony walking stick.

"Have at you, fat varlet!" he cried, and thwacked his grandfather on the knee.

"Toothache!" he yelled.

"It's been *The Three Musketeers* on the box," said Lalage from the door. "Sometimes he makes me realise how much I've missed, being a girl. I've often longed to do that. Are you all right, darling?"

"By God, I've lost my leg!" gritted Father.

"So you have, by God!" squealed Dickie. "Stand up, Guards! Hard pounding, gentlemen—we'll see who can pound hardest. Boom! Boom!"

He fell on one knee and began to load the walking-stick with an invisible ram-rod. Father lowered himself into a chair and rubbed his knee-cap. Lalage leaned against the door-post, laughing soundlessly with all her teeth showing.

Lydia stood by the window, completely left out, unable even to enjoy Dickie's whirling happiness. Dickie himself in the act of spitting a musket-ball down the barrel of the walking-stick suddenly remembered the other battlefield and reverted to D'Artagnan.

"My turn," said Father, holding out his hand for the lunging stick. "The defeated army needs its crutch to hobble home on."

"Cut it off? Boiling tar?" asked Dickie.

"May not be necessary," said father. "On the other hand, next time you come I might be wearing a peg leg. Time for you to go, isn't it? I'll find out about your old lady, my dear."

"Thanks," said Lydia.

"Goodness, I enjoyed that," said Lalage. "Don't forget the dress, darling–I really ought to give it you, it suits you so well. Look, if I come and collect it some time next week I can see how you're getting on with your upheavals."

The last wash of rage receded. Lydia remembered Richard's idiotic suggestion.

"Come and have supper," she said. "I'll give you a ring. I've got a handsome young ship-owner I'd like you to meet."

It was foolishly gratifying to watch Lalage's eyes widen.

13

Lydia's second visit to the prison was rather different from the first. It had taken considerable persistence to persuade the authorities to let her come at all, as she was neither a relation nor a technically acceptable visitor. She had kept her cool, recognising that the problem was not official bloody-mindedness, or even lack of goodwill, but just the blind intransigence of the system. However, as Procne had no other visitors, and as Lydia persisted until even the system dimly recognised that she wasn't going to go away, here she was again, waiting in the crowded octagonal room by the gate, feeling almost an old hand.

But the wait was longer than before, and then she was taken not to the pink cell but to a larger room which contained a number of long tables with chairs on either side—something like a library reading-room without any books. Most of the places were occupied by other visitors and other prisoners. Two prison officers invigilated the scene. The room was full of muttering which, even though the words were inaudible, seemed to move in stilted rhythms.

Procne was already waiting, wearing a neutral-coloured overall. She was obviously the prettiest girl in the room (though there was one thin, tiny-headed black girl who might have collected a few votes) but Lydia didn't feel this time as though she was in the presence of something amazing, a different order of creation from all the other people she knew.

"Hi," said Lydia. "How's things?"

"Hi, Liz. Good of you to come."

"I had a bit of trouble persuading them. If you want me to go on coming you've got to ask. You look as though it's been getting you down a bit."

"Get anyone down. I been sleeping badly."

"Is that worry?"

"Nothing to worry about in here, have I? No, it's just

being shut up like this you might as well be dead. Being asleep and being dead's not much different, really. So I don't need the sleep, see?"

"Are you eating OK?"

"Not so bad. But the food! It's not disgusting, like, only it's dead boring, always the same. I used to eat a lot of scampi. First thing I'll do when I get out is to go and buy myself a bloody great plate of scampi."

She fell silent. The mild animation which the imagined taste had raised waned from her features.

"You'll be able to afford it," said Lydia. "I found the money your mother left."

"Did you really? That's great!"

"It's a bit over a thousand pounds."

"Great! Hey, are you sure she meant it for me?"

"There's nothing to show she didn't. I put it in the Post Office in my name, because that seemed easiest, but you can have it as soon as you want."

"You haven't told anyone, have you?" said Procne in a whisper.

"No, of course not. Why?"

"Perhaps if the police found out they'd want it back, pay for them cheques."

"Oh, I don't think so. It was your mother's money, not yours."

"It come from me. Besides . . ."

Her eyes flicked to either side and when she spoke again her voice was even lower.

"That mob I was telling you about, they wouldn't like it. If I got a bit put by, they might think I was trying to get shot of them, see? They keep an eye on what their best girls are doing. There was one of them at my trial, most days."

"I had an idea about all that, Procne. Would you like a room in my house when you come out? The rent's quite low."

"I don't know about that."

"You see, there's two things. They're much more likely to let you out of here, early I mean, on parole, if you've got somewhere to go to—I mean a room of your own, and friends who they think are honest, and a job, and so on."

"Well, I haven't got a job, have I? There's only one thing I can do."

"Rubbish. You'd make a marvellous model, and you could use some of your mother's money to pay for a course. I think

I could easily set up a job for you if you wanted—I mean a proper job you'd be really interested in doing . . ."

"I don't know."

"Well, think about it . . . look, I'm not trying to tell you what to do—that's your own business. Only I don't want you to feel that you've got to go back to living the way you did because that's all there is for you to do. If you want to, that's fine. But if you want to try something else, I think I could help."

"It's been my own fault, really. Just it always seems the easiest thing, so I string along. Then when this mob . . . Honest, Liz, you'd better keep out of it. You don't know them."

"I can cope. They've got where they are because people are scared to stand up to them. Somebody's got to, some time. I'm in a better position than most. The important thing is that you should have the choice open to you."

"Sometimes it's best not to have no choice, then it isn't your fault, see?"

"Well, there's plenty of time . . . damn! what a stupid thing to say. I found out about the vodka."

"Bet she wasn't drinking none."

Lydia explained about the *varosh*, and the regular order at the off-licence. Procne shook her head.

"Never!" she said. "Oh, she'd have nicked the booze and not turned a hair, provided she'd got someone she could flog it to. But empties in her room, never! I told you last time about what she did with Dad's empties?"

"Yes, you did. I had one possible idea—suppose your mother sometimes found a little in the bottom of one of the bottles—the old men are pretty clumsy with it—they spilt a whole jugful last month. Don't you think she might have started to collect those dregs . . ."

"Pity to waste that," said Procne. The imitation of her mother's voice was so accurate that Lydia was side-tracked.

"Can you do that with other people?" she asked. "I mean could you do me?"

"I'd have to have a bit of practice. I got one la-di-da voice I do, but it ain't quite right for you. My dear girls, I have come here to-day to talk to you about the joys of crochet-work."

"Oh dear. I hope that's not me."

"Course not. You got a way of biting your words off short, specially when you're angry. Snip snap, that's that, anyone else want a thorough dusting over? No, that's not it, it's only the top bit, not all that happiness you got inside you. Your husband's a lucky man, Liz."

"I gave him a nervous breakdown three years ago—or at least I helped to give it him."

"Don't you believe it—he'd of had it worse with anyone else."

"I'm sorry. I don't normally tell people. What were we talking about?"

"Oh, me doing voices. I'll have a bit of practice at yours—I can do all the screws, and the governors—passes the time, see?"

"I think it's marvellous. I'm sure you could use it, too. But I meant before that—suppose your mother had collected about a bottle, and she suddenly felt depressed, or ill. Suppose she persuaded herself that the vodka counted as medicine . . ."

Procne shook her head.

"No, Mum weren't never ill," she said. "You'd of had to lay her out before you could make her touch a drop. Why, weddings she always used to take her own Thermos of tea to toast the bride in."

"Well, what do you think happened?"

"Someone done her in," whispered Procne.

"Why should they?"

"Find that money, of course. Or perhaps . . . yes, look, Liz, she was ever so nosey. I told you we used to have a long chat on the phone, Thursdays, and I told her how I was doing and all? Well, I don't remember but I expect I told her quite a bit about the mob what I was working for. Suppose she thought she might try a bit of blackmail? They wouldn't of stood for that, but she wouldn't of known. They'd rub her out, easy as winking, wouldn't they?"

Lydia decided to go along with the fantasy. Procne evidently had all her mother's relish for melodrama, and there was no point in spoiling her fun by raising any of the obvious practical objections.

"You'd better not tell anyone, Procne," she said. "I mean, if you're right, you don't want to get it into the grapevine."

"Or I'll tell you what," said Procne, ignoring her. "Them old gentlemen, they got something hid up there. There's rooms they wouldn't never let her into."

"I've been into all their rooms," said Lydia.

"But you're not nosey, like what she was. They got *secrets.*"

"Yes, I suppose so," said Lydia, sighing mentally at those mummified Baltic intrigues. "Anyway, I'll see if I can find out some more. I'll remind my bloody father . . ."

"Why don't you get along with him, Liz? You sound worse than what I was with Mum. What's your mother like?"

"She died when I was eight. I think she killed herself but I've never had the guts to find out. She divorced my father when I was four."

"That's why . . . you and your Dad, I mean?"

"We've always fought. It was worst when Richard decided to leave the army. But we get along now in a sort of way, like most people. Anyway, I'll remind him to find out about that autopsy. The trouble is, with a house like mine it's only too easy for a stranger to get in and out."

"There you are then. Only you be careful too, Liz. Don't go nosing around. It isn't worth it. Tell me about your little boy."

Dickie lasted them until the half hour was up. In a few last gabbled sentences they made arrangements for another visit and Procne promised to think about whether she wanted a room at Devon Crescent. Lydia walked to the tube, buffeted by the dusty gusts of a dry spring wind and depressed by the knowledge of the odds against her bringing off what she wanted to achieve for Procne. But by the time she was sitting in the clanging train she was already so busy with plans for reducing the odds that she was humming loud enough to make the bloke sitting opposite her keep glancing at her over his paper.

14

IT WAS IMPOSSIBLE not to think of Mr Roberts as 'The Spy' still. There was something about him that kept the absurd charade alive, and actually made Lydia slightly jumpy when he came in for morning coffee, in case she should accidentally say something which let on that he had a two-fold existence, if only in her mind. The trouble was that it wasn't pure charade—there were several silly little details which kept making links with the real world, not strong enough to bear the weight of any deduction, but teasingly there. He was too good a gardener, and too hard a worker, for one thing. It was quite unnatural that a casual labourer, engaged by impulse, should be such a treasure. He was a stock little man in his late fifties, with a rather soft and completely humorless pale face, but Lydia was still genuinely not certain that he was the same man she'd bumped into in the basement doorway. She had quite a strong mental picture of that other man —taller and thinner with heavy eyebrows—but again she wasn't wholly sure that this wasn't her imagination. Finally there was his conversation. He had, or affected, a peasant-like reserve. When Lydia said anything, however provocative, he would appear to think about it in silence for several seconds. Then he would agree with her, usually repeating her words in a flat, unplaceable accent. Often she wasn't even certain that he understood what he was saying. The style of assent was almost theatrically sage, but sometimes she felt it was a technique for preserving his own privacy as an urban solitary; sometimes for concealing his real trade as a spy; and sometimes just an instinctive method of disguising stupidity.

At his second visit he had asked quite a lot of questions about the other occupants of the house, what their families were and how long they'd been there, but had shown no interest at all in the Government—in fact he had almost ostentatiously avoided talking about them. Yet another thing was that Mrs Tevell had told Lydia that he was a frightful old gossip, though that may have been only her way of describing a good listener. At any rate, he made Lydia nervous.

On a soft Monday morning in the third week of March they stood side by side at the top of the steps leading up into the back garden from the basement. Their mugs steamed in their hands. Birds trilled, buds glistened in the precocious and deceitful sunlight. The fresh-dug earth in front of them, though, seemed to smell still of winter, clammy and chill.

"I can't tell you how glad I am to see the last of those roses, Mr Roberts," said Lydia. "I hated them. They had a few mangy flowers in summer and looked hideous for the rest of the year."

"Weren't much good," agreed Mr Roberts.

"What shall we do with the bushes? The dustmen are a bit bolshie about collecting rubbish, especially if it's got thorns on."

"Well, yes, there's thorns," admitted Mr Roberts.

"Are they too wet to burn?"

"They're wet enough."

"Anyway, let's try. I've got some bits of spare timber you could use to start a bonfire—I kept them to show the dry-rot people, but they weren't interested. And I'll find you a couple of planks to put down by the wall there, so that Mrs Pelletier can get at her washing-line."

"Ah."

"It seems a pity to get a good fire going just for a few old rose bushes. I wonder whether there's anything worth burning at Mrs Tevell's or any of the others. We could get rid of it all in one go."

"Ah."

This grunt seemed even more non-committal than the last. Did it go against his training as a spy to admit that he kept reserves of garden rubbish elsewhere? Did he regard his dealings with his other employers' rubbish as a private matter? Was he simply too thick to grasp the advantages of a communal bonfire? Lydia stared at the neat patch where the roses had been, suddenly oppressed by the knowledge that now she'd have to decide what to put into it. One half of her longed for flagstones, trouble-free tubs of annuals, a tree for summer shade; the other half wanted jungle, wildness and freedom in the urban barracks.

"Would a passion-flower grow here, Mr Roberts?"

"Passion-flower. Ah."

"I don't mean in the bed–I mean up the back of the house."

He turned and stared up at the white façade, so much less regular, but somehow more pleasing, than the front. Lydia followed his gaze. There was a smear all down the clean Snocem from one of the drain-pipes–Mrs Evans had blocked her sink outlet again. Bloody woman. It was really quite extraordinary that somebody who could turn herself out so neatly and behave, socially, with such precise decorum, should fail to grasp that a mixture of tea-leaves, potato-peelings and grease was bound to block a sink outlet.

Higher up a head craned out of a window gazing down at the garden, motionless, a live gargoyle. It was Count Linden, but he didn't answer Lydia's wave. The spy appeared not to notice him.

"Ah, a passion flower," he said. "That'll grow all right. Right old nuisance you'll find it, too. *And* you'll have to restrict its roots, or you won't get no flowers."

"Restrict its roots?" said Lydia, changing roles so that she echoed what he said.

"Ah," said the spy. "Squash 'em in tight. That's right."

It was only in the spy-fantasy that he seemed to be speaking about Count Linden, and thinking of little Livonia. It would be the season of thaw in the Baltic republics now, the time (Mr Obb had once said) when the whole world seemed new and beautiful, full of beginnings.

"I'll think about it," said Lydia.

He made a very effective bonfire, got the roses burning, fetched hedge clippings and Michaelmas daisy stalks from other gardens, swept up every leaf in the back garden (in London new drifts of leaf-fall seem to accumulate all winter) and burnt them too. Not once, as ordinary gardeners do, did he stop working to gaze into the smoking pile, as if searching in the twirling white streams for portents and omens. Before he went he shovelled the hot ashes onto the rose-bed, forked them around and raked them in.

If you thought of him as a gardener he was a jewel, Lydia agreed with her neighbours. But if you thought of him as a spy his efficiency was frightening. When he had gone the rosebed had the look of a patch sown with salt, deliberately, so that nothing should ever grow there.

15

"CAPTAIN SIR RICHARD TIMMS and Lady Timms," bawled the bloke. As always at this moment Lydia blushed, not with shyness but with shame at the ridiculous tag which an accident of love had wished on her. The Russian Ambassador and his wife both looked as though they had been deliberately bred to conform to a new module of humanity, perhaps designed to colonise a planet with greater gravity than earth's, as they were stocky and extraordinarily short-necked. The Ambassador took Lydia's hand and bent as if to kiss it, but then seemed to recoil from such a revision of Marxist-Leninist etiquette and compromised with a pudgy, lingering squeeze. Lydia had a sudden lust to kick him on the knee-cap and see what happened, but that would have been impossible in the ridiculous crimson tube which Lalage had coaxed her into wearing.

She and Richard passed on, took glasses of champagne from a tray, and drifted into the muttering throng. The atmosphere was familiar from diplomatic days. It always reminded Lydia of the congregation in a church before a big posh wedding, crowds of people who know each other well and long to give glad cries and swap family scandal, but are forced by the semi-sanctity of the occasion into small gestures and whispered talk. Then George Dunakhov barged between two groups of silvery First Secretaries like a tank coming out of a birch wood. He buffeted Richard on the shoulder and hugged Lydia so firmly to his unyielding chest that she felt that she would be branded for the rest of her life with a vertical row of little red stars where the buttons of his uniform dug into her

"Hoi, hoi," he bellowed. "Now I see it is worth I come to England!"

He was drunk already.

"George will never stay the course, unless there's a war," Richard had once said. "Suddenly they'll get tired of him, and then, puff. If there's a war he'll do well—he's a bloody good tank commander."

But here he was still beating the system somehow. Lydia would have liked him for that alone. He let go of her, but grabbed her hand and towed her at high speed through the crowd to a table by the wall. Naturally he'd already set himself up with the necessities of life—two bottles of champagne, spare glasses and a smiling huge-bosomed blonde in a green dress. With exaggerated gestures, like a pimp in a baroque comedy, George introduced her. Her name was Natya, plus one of those impossibly amnemonic Russian surnames. She preferred to speak French.

Before they'd settled a tall, dark-skinned young man strolled up and found himself sucked into the tornado of George's hospitality. His name was Nikolai Diarghi. He worked at the Embassy and spoke perfect English.

George immediately began to tell the blonde a shooting story, remotely based on something that had actually happened to him and Richard in Hungary. In the middle of a train of surreal improbabilities he would stop and ask Richard to confirm some small irrelevant detail, as if taking up an everyday parcel at a little way-side halt, before steaming on through the landscape of his fantasy.

"Do you find much shooting in England, Lady Timms?" said Mr Diarghi, deliberately drawing her out of George's audience.

"We don't live that sort of life nowadays. Richard is reading for the bar and I look after a large house and a small boy."

"A small boy? Ah, I wonder if you can help me. I am preparing a report on the British nursery education system. Of course I have access to all sorts of official views, but it is hard for me to make contact with ordinary mothers of small children. Do you have any views on the subject?"

Poor man. It was as if Moses had struck the rock and out gushed Niagara. Lydia's views on nursery education were precise and vehement. For six months in the previous year she had been one of an action group who were trying to coax or force the ILEA into opening a new nursery school in her area, and had resigned when she discovered that most of her colleagues really wanted it as a convenience for the Lady Timmses of W.11 and not as a life-line for the Mrs Pumices. She was still talking when the flunkey bawled for silence. The Ambassador made an oily little speech of welcome. Everybody started to move towards another room.

"I didn't realise we were going to be fed," said Lydia.

"Oh, yes," said Mr Diarghi. "Excuse me. Dunakhov will know where you sit. I'd like to carry on with our conversation, so I'll just nip ahead and see if I can fiddle the seating plan."

It was a vast, slow meal, with speeches and toasts between the courses. The object of the reception was to celebrate a big cultural-exchange deal between the two countries, and the British speakers–politicians, diplomats, art administrators–seemed to Lydia even suaver and more hypocritical than the Russians. Only one knighted actor even faintly hinted at the lives that might be crushed, the truth that might be poisoned in order that the garden of Russian culture should bloom as its owners wished. His speech was especially well received, being neatly within the limits of polite protest and thus serving as the token conscience of authority. But for her promise to Richard Lydia would have thrown her plate at the purring sir. Instead, when talk and eating restarted, she loosed her rage on poor George.

He smiled, shrugged and began another of his stories. Lydia was already a bit irritated with him, because she'd decided that the real reason for their being there was that George wanted to show off his baronet to his blonde. When she swung away from him in mid sentence Mr Diarghi neatly fielded her diatribe.

"Yes," he said when she ran out of breath. "Have you been in Bombay, or any place where there are many beggars?"

"No."

"It is horrible, but it is also a parable. Along the streets where the rich men go they line the paving, like soldiers guarding a state visit. Each has his own pitch, and each has his own hideous defect–he is blind, she has a withered arm, that child has no legs, that old man a great sore that suppurates. No, I am not changing the subject. My point is that the idea, in that context, of a healthy beggar is a contradiction in terms. In the present context of the world–the stage we have reached in the historical process–the idea of a government that does not crush some individuals is a contradiction in terms. They all must do it, and in that case it is clearly more satisfactory to have a government that knows who it is crushing, and why."

"I don't think I accept any of that," said Lydia, too earnest to eat. "I don't accept that governments have to crush people. Suppose they do, though, I don't accept that it's better for them to be aware of what they're doing, because that sanctions the repression and makes it officially OK. And even if it were better, it's still vital that people shouldn't accept it. Once you start shrugging your shoulders whenever somebody gets trampled on, then the stupid government engine begins to think that no one minds. *It* had no feelings, you see. So it tramples where it likes. Look, as a Marxist you're supposed to be working towards a perfect government, so it matters even more that you should have the imperfections shown up, by people like me, if there's no one else to do it."

Mr Diarghi nodded but said nothing.

"How long would *I* survive in Russia?" she asked.

"If you started throwing plates at distinguished speakers at official functions?"

"I wouldn't get asked again, but what else?"

"Well, you would survive your natural span, of course, but perhaps if you disturbed the ideas of too many people it might be necessary to restrain you. But remember, if you think that an injustice, that you have to balance it against the far greater injustice of the millions of people in capitalist countries whose lives the system makes ugly and stunted, but who would be allowed to thrive under our system."

"By restrain me you mean send me to a lunatic asylum, or to a labour camp?"

"If necessary."

"Are you seriously telling me that I'd live to a ripe old age in Siberia?"

"Most people do—in fact some remain active to an extraordinary old age—Aaku Aakisen is a good example."

Lydia was about to argue when the plates were cleared and a Russian rose to reply to the actor with a speech so inept and boring that it seemed to dim even the chandeliers. Lydia could sense the dust settling on distinguished pates, the infection of dullness creeping, like one of the Devon Crescent fungi, from mind to mind. George was not the only guest snoring. When at last the man sat down to a round of muffled clapping she found that she no longer had any gusto for a political set-to.

"I didn't know that you acknowledged Aakisen's existence," she said.

"Oh yes. His name came to mind because I've just read a

report of his death in a CIA propaganda sheet, but it's surprising that you've heard of him. The attempt to make propaganda with his death was very ineptly handled."

"Oh dear. All that effort wasted. I printed his obituary notice for the Livonian, er, Consulate. They live on the top two floors of my house. I'm their landlady, and I'm the only person who seems able to manage their duplicating machine. In fact there's a bloke baby-sitting for me at the moment who probably told my son a bed-time story about Aakisen."

"What a coincidence that I should mention him! How do you reconcile your views on authority with your giving shelter to a so-called Government in exile?"

"Oh, they were there when I bought the house. Anyway, I don't think much of any governments, but at least I prefer ones which have been chosen by the people they govern. I rather like the Livs—they're a lot of harmless old dreamers, kind and sad."

"Their dreams are nightmares, Lady Timms. The so-called Balkan Republics have had a difficult history, but it is a mistake to treat them all as one. I personally admire and respect the Estonians, for instance, even the ones who have come into exile. But I do not care for the Livs. Listen, you have three old men in your house, I think. Busch, Linden and . . . I've forgotten his name."

"Mr Obb."

"Obb. A quiet man, I believe, a survivor. He would be living in Livonia still if he had not collaborated a little too freely with the Nazis, but otherwise I know nothing against him. Busch and Linden, though . . . During the war of 1919-20 (which, by the way, is still the root cause of Russian suspicion of the motives of the European powers) Busch led a cavalry regiment. There was a period when our Revolutionary Army was in retreat, under attack from the so-called White Russians, together with French and British troops and units from the Balkan States. Where Busch's regiment came, they killed every Russian they found, man, woman and child. Some they tortured first. This was on his personal orders."

"But . . ."

"Let me finish. There has always been a strong German influence in the Baltic States. Most of the great landowners were Germans by origin and allegiance. For instance, Linden's family owned larger estates than many of your English dukes, in a country one tenth of the size. The people who lived on his land were worse protected even than our Russian serfs. His grandfather had powers of life and death—not legal powers, but he exercised them. That is the Livonia Linden fought for . . . no, he wasn't a soldier, but during the Nazi invasion he was a very active collaborator. He took charge of a programme to export all Livonian Jews to Germany, to the extermination camps. He also organised a squad of internal terrorists, on the Nazi side, to eliminate difficult citizens—they had many little techniques. It was quite noticeable, for instance, that a number of Linden's political opponents died very suddenly from what appeared to be heart stoppages. He was extremely zealous. Even if all the stories you read in your British papers were true, Lady Timms, we Russians have done nothing to the Jews remotely comparable to the actions of this man you now have living under your roof."

Somebody had put a many-coloured hill of ice-cream in front of Lydia. Nuggets of scented chocolate were buried in its slopes. She took a vague spoonful and licked at it. It seemed to have no taste at all. She suddenly remembered Count Linden leaning from the back of her own house, staring down at the patch of fresh-dug earth. In her memory, for a moment, he became visibly a monster—almost fanged, almost bat-winged—before she shook herself and asserted that it had been a pretty March morning and Linden no more than a grey old man leaning out of a window. The ice-cream acquired flavour.

"You mustn't think I'm just making propaganda," said Mr Diarghi. "You'll find an account of Busch's activities in a report by Colonel Tallents, in volume three of the *British Foreign Policy Documents*, 1919-39, First Series. And several times shortly after the war there were questions about Linden in your House of Commons. I can send you the Hansard references if you want to look them up."

Still Lydia said nothing.

"I'm sorry," said Mr Diarghi, smiling. "This isn't really dinner-party conversation."

"It's all right," said Lydia. "I mean, I'd much rather talk about things like this than the weather. OK, send me those references—though I wouldn't accept them as proof. There's always a bunch of MPs who'll ask any kind of question at all if they think it'll embarrass the government—they don't have to be in your pay for that."

"You'll be hard to convince of anything you don't want to believe."

"So's everyone, and quite right too," snapped Lydia. "Sorry–don't let's get onto that–it's just another of my hobby-horses–I mean, you have to trust your emotions a bit about anything that matters–where were we? Oh, yes, it doesn't make any difference to me if everything you say about my Livs is true. The only possible way to behave is to take people as they are now–they're part of your life and you're part of theirs, and you've got to accept that. It doesn't matter what they were or what they've done. Obviously, there are a few people who've got to be restrained, prevented from repeating anti-social sorts of behaviour, but they're far fewer than any of our societies makes out. And . . . well, for instance, what Israel did to Eichmann was by any standards vile. It didn't matter by then what *he'd* done. That had been vile too, but it was over, finished, unalterable."

Mr Diarghi shook his head.

"You are what I was taught at school to call a Utopian," he said. "Pragmatically I can't see that it would be possible to organise anything but a small group of like-minded people on your beliefs. We are all prisoners of what has happened and what has been done, by ourselves, by our enemies, by our friends. For instance, your late Foreign Secretary maintained a very consistent line for over thirty years about the Baltic States. He invested a great deal of face in their independence. While he was in office it was technically impossible for us to come to any kind of agreement about our *de jure* sovereignty over the areas. Even now there are difficulties. For instance, the Americans pay these Consulates interest on the gold reserves which they hold for them, and this contributes marginally to the British balance of payments. It seems to us that the British Government, thirty years ago, contrived a bribe to itself, and is now trapped by having taken it so long. And so on. You could trace through six hundred years the causes that have brought your old men to live in your two top floors."

"Yes, but most of the causes don't matter any more. And what you told me about Busch and Linden would only matter if there was any chance of their going back to Livonia to form a Government. Then it would at least matter that the voters knew about it . . ."

"It's already well-known in Livonia."

"I bet it isn't known to be true. I've got a friend who went on a lecture tour in Poland, talking to senior schools about the economics of developing countries. One of his lectures had a bit to do with Vietnam—this was before the Americans pulled out—and he gave a fairly factual account of how the war was fought—napalm on villages, defoliation, all that—and he noticed that the kids always smiled at that point. One day he managed to get alone with some of them and ask why. 'Oh,' they said, 'we know you've got to tell a few lies like that or they wouldn't let you in.' "

"Poles," said Mr Diarghi. "Even when you deal straight with them they still manage to cheat themselves."

"Tell me about Aakisen," said Lydia. "What's the truth? Richard says he was probably caught or killed just after the war, and my friends kept him alive for propaganda purposes. I don't know why I should care, but I've got an obsessive sort of feeling that it matters."

Mr Diarghi hesitated.

"I was only quoting the Livonian propaganda as an example," he said. "It may be true, and if it is that would be possible to ascertain from labour camp records. But if Aakisen died, or disappeared—which he may have chosen to do deliberately—then I don't see how anybody can ever be sure. Lady Timms, I have been a little indiscreet in some of the things I have said. I'd prefer not to be quoted, especially to your Livs. This is not my subject, not my area of responsibility. I'm most grateful to you for your help about nursery education, though, and I may well be in touch with you again."

Poor sod, thought Lydia. As soon as he lets his hair down he gets frightened. What a system!

"OK," she said. "I've enjoyed this do a lot more than I expected. Except . . . oh, God, not another one!"

The plates had been cleared again and an English diplomat rose to make a speech of skilled elegance and emptiness. George was woken from his snooze by the applause, and seemed to be at least half sober now. In fact he became attentive and amusing, while Mr Diarghi talked to the woman on his far side. At one moment Richard caught Lydia's eye with a glance of despair; he had the blonde to himself; she laughed, smiled, leaned forward as if offering him some object for inspection on the jutting ledge of her decolletage, reached with smooth bare arms for grapes . . . poor Richard. The act made him almost comically jumpy. He kept raising his right hand to run it through his thinning gingery hair, then failing to complete the movement.

"George," whispered Lydia. "Be a dear and rescue my husband."

George glanced to his right like an anarchist conspirator in a cartoon. His face became immensely serious. He picked up a napkin, folded it into a big triangle, and with a movement of great deftness draped it across the blonde's upper slopes and tied the points behind her neck. She looked at him in momentary astonishment. He put on a parson's face and said something in heavily nasalised Russian. She pealed with laughter like a harlot in a bar near closing-time, a false, hysteric whoop. Richard's relief was so obvious that Lydia and a couple on the far side of the table laughed too. Stirred by this instant of real pleasure amid the desert hours a middle European rose and proposed a toast whose gist seemed to be that cultural exchanges should consist mainly of nudes, which he called nekkid vimmin. He was drunk, and presumably not on the official list of speakers, but several Englishmen were sufficiently far gone to start shouting "Hear, hear," in plummy voices, which George and other irresponsible foreigners parodied with gusto. Lydia tingled with delight at the way, even here, at an event which had been deliberately sealed and sterilised to prevent any such thing happening, life somehow thrust its green blade through.

Mr Diarghi drove them home at nearly two in the morning, but (thank heavens) refused to come in for a nightcap. Paul Vaklins was sitting at the kitchen table soldering a join in a hairy-looking bit of apparatus.

"Welcome to the Resistance Group," he said. "Dickie and I have been building a secret transmitter."

He pressed a key and produced a quick burst of morse.

"It's quite a short-range," he said. "I've fitted suppressors so that it won't interfere with anyone's TV. I'll fix a tape-recorder my end, so that he can get answers to his messages."

"Will he be able to cope with Morse?" said Richard. "He's not really reading yet."

"He might, though," said Lydia. "His reading problem seems to be mainly a visual block."

"He made a damn good start this evening," said Paul. "He's as keen as mustard."

"I think it's a marvelous idea," said Lydia. "It might be

a real way round his problem, especially if I've got to learn Morse along with him."

"The spy sat on the mat," said Richard.

They all laughed, said good-night and went to bed.

16

"A VERY CURIOUS BEANO," said Richard meditatively. "A very rum occasion indeed."

When you are used, as the Timmses were, to going to bed well before midnight your metabolism seems to slow down when it recognises the time, even though you are still wide awake. Then your bed, when you at last slide into it, seems extra cold. The Timmses did not own an electric blanket and Richard hated hot-water bottles, so now they lay extra close, for warmth. Lydia could feel the tension all along his limbs, though she herself felt happy and relaxed.

"I enjoyed myself after all," she said. "Apart from those ghastly speeches. That Diarghi bloke–well, I suppose anyone who listens to me and takes me seriously seems brainy to me –he told me rather a nasty thing about the Government, though."

"Which Government?"

"Ours. I mean our own. I mean this one here. I mean the Livonians."

She explained about the Livonian atrocities.

"Umm," he said. "That's curious too. Hell, suppose it's true, does it bother you? You're the one who has to cope with them."

"We argued about that, too. I told him it didn't, but it does. I know it oughtn't to, but I can't help it."

"Umm. How did you get onto the subject?"

"I can't remember. We started talking about nursery education, because he's writing a report on that, and then–oh, yes, it was after that actor's speech, we got onto personal freedom and how long people who got sent to Siberia lived, and he produced Aakisen as an example. He knew quite a bit about the Livs, too."

"Umm."

"Don't keep saying 'Umm' like that, as though it all meant

something. Tell me about George's blonde. She looked a toughie, I thought."

"Bang on. That's what she is, if I've got the right girl. Do you remember Jake Seidlitz?"

"Darling, she can't be that girl."

"I don't know. I saw the photographs, and she's just like."

"You never showed me the photographs."

"They were part of a secret film some ass made to warn British businessmen what to expect in Moscow. They'd blacked out Jake's face, but everybody knew. And I saw an FO dossier on her a bit later, when she'd got promoted and was running her own show in East Berlin–same line of business, but with some other girls and a couple of lads to cater for different tastes–so what the hell's she doing as a cultural attaché in London?"

"And throwing her charms around so freely in front of you? Perhaps she was simply keeping in practice. I thought she was just George's girl and he'd got us asked to show her what nobby friends he had. I was pretty disgusted with him at one point."

"Turn but a stone and start a snob. George . . . now there's another thing . . . how sloshed was he?"

"About half-gone to begin with, and three-quarters by the fish. Only about a quarter at the end–those speeches were pretty sobering."

"Umm. You know he's supposed to be in Damascus, training Syrians in tank tactics? I got it out of him. He'd only been there a couple of months, too. And at a kulturfest! George! How much did your chap actually know about nursery education?"

"I did the talking. He kept his end up."

"More than that? Sensible questions?"

"Yes, but not many. Why?"

"Umm. Look, it's probably only glands, or the Law of Real Property maddening me with dullness . . . but when that woman kept brandishing her bust at me . . . and George goes to sleep and wakes up at just the right moments . . . and you're sat next to a chap who starts by triggering you off on one of your hobby-horses . . ."

"Mixed metaphor."

"No, you start hobby-horse races with a popgun. On your sticks, get set, pop . . . and then he drags Aakisen in and he knows all about Livs and he tells you horror stories . . . Diarghi's a Georgian name, I think . . ."

"At least he pretty well admitted Aakisen did die in Siberia."

"Umm."

"Come off it, darling. You never really believed in FCPs, even when we lived in that world."

(Most of the Timmses' diplomatic stint had been done at a time when the Foreign Office had been riddled with red scares, and junior staffs had explained all crises—shortage of tonic-water, the Ambassador's daughter's pony going down with equine flu, and so on—as Fiendish Communist Plots.)

"You get trapped by your past, don't you? Now it's impossible for us to believe that anything that happens could conceivably be engineered by the Russians, even though we've got an anti-communist government run from our house. My notion was it might be a bit of a probing operation, George brought over from Syria to get us to the party at all, bloke told off to get you going on schools and then slip in a few horror stories about the Livs, girl imported to see whether there's any leverage to be got from me . . . she'll have to put in a nil return, poor thing."

"You've just got more refined tastes than she's usually asked to cater for. Kiss me?"

"Not just now, thanks."

"I feel all soft and gooey."

"Well I feel like an overwound alarm-clock in a badly assembled time bomb."

"I could kill that woman."

"Oh, it isn't her. I mean, if it is, that's all happening in cupboards I never open. I just feel that we've got about as much on our plate as we can cope with, you in particular, and if somebody starts mucking you up just now I shall go round the bend again."

"But why should they? Why us? Why now?"

"When does the Government's lease run out?"

"First of October, this year."

"I wonder if they know . . . they might. Suppose they either blackmailed me or horrified you into deciding not to renew the lease, that'd mean that the Government would have to try and set up elsewhere, and that might mean the FO had to reconsider the whole question of their diplomatic status. Now old Alec's no longer Foreign Secretary, it'd be a good time for the Russians to put a bit of pressure on. They might even try to show that the Government's been up to some sort of dirty work . . . currency fiddling or something . . . I expect they're working on that already . . ."

"Seriously?"

"Yes. No. It's probably only my imagination. I wish I hadn't got those bloody exams coming up–I never used to have exam nerves . . ."

"But you know it all, darling. You can do it easily."

"Provided I don't go to pieces. Hell!"

Clearly it was a moment to switch the talk back to the FCP.

"But George," said Lydia. "He wouldn't let himself be used, just like that, would he? Bait? He's our friend."

"Darling, if you think about it honestly you'll see that you've got two sorts of friends, ones you like and ones you trust. Sometimes they overlap, not always. I like old George very much, but I'm quite sure he'd slit our throats if he needed to."

This business about liking and trusting was an old argument, so safe in Richard's present state. She let him ramble through a list of all the people they knew, putting them into one category or the other, a soothing game.

"It's more marked with you," he said. "It's natural to feel you can trust people from your own caste, but you don't approve of your own caste, so you tend not to like them."

"Balls. Anyway, I think you're wrong about George. He's not part of an FCP, or if he is he hasn't been told. I suppose there's just a chance you might be right about the rest of it –it *was* a bit odd, in some ways . . ."

"About ten to one against, I'd say."

"Do you think I ought to warn Mr Obb?"

"Umm. You actually want them to stay? What Diarghi told you is probably true–he sounds too bright to tell you fibs you could check."

"Of course I do. I mean, even if I'd been wanting to get them out before, I'd dig my heels in if I thought we were being pushed around by the bloody Kremlin, whatever they'd done, almost. Damn. The idea makes me so angry I'm beginning to become ungooey."

Richard laughed but still didn't really relax. They lay and talked almost till dawn.

17

THE DINNER-PARTY for Lalage went very well at first. Lydia often felt that the only mystery in cooking is why so many cook-book-writers, however inspirational, are quite unable to string together a series of clear and unambiguous sentences. She relied on half a dozen books which understood that a recipe is no more than an assembly instruction; with these she found she could produce good meals with no sweat. Taking the whole day off from building operations she shopped; got the silver out of the bank; improvised a table out of two tea-chests, a door and a sheet of hardboard; pinned up about thirty of Dickie's gaudy battle-pictures to cover the patched and mottled walls of the back room; and there, by the time Dickie came back from school, was a dining-room where yesterday had been a desert. He was thrilled with his art gallery and spent the hours until his bed-time touching in a few more explosions and dead bodies and dive-bombers.

The wine was no problem, because Richard had inherited some, which he kept with a wine-merchant in the City and refused to sell, though somebody had once told Lydia it would fetch twenty quid a bottle. As she wasn't allowed to convert it into floor-boards or stair-carpets she got a certain kick out of simply knocking the stuff back; to drink it like that was an acceptable sort of revenge on a society that had got its values so crazy as to price a bottle of plonk higher than a week's social security payments.

Richard put Dickie to bed. They now had a night-time ritual which involved an adventure behind enemy lines and the use of Paul's Morse transmitter to get the vital message through; it had barely finished its last sleepy beep when Lalage arrived carrying a box of chocolates as big as a tombstone. The other guests were a married couple who lectured in anthropology at London University, Paul Vaklins, and a strange pair, unmarried, who lived in a basement across the road and sent a small girl who didn't seem to be their own child to Dickie's school. They ran an ornamental leather stall in the Portobello Road and turned up for the party wearing identical caftans. Another oddness about them was that they were both devoted workers for the local Tories. Lydia had only asked them on impulse, the morning she'd rung up the Russian embassy and learnt that George had already been posted back to Damascus, but they made a good mix, and the party went well and easily until Lydia, coming back from the kitchen with Richard's favourite pudding (which was a mound of sweetened cream cheese piled with pears soaked in claret) noticed that an extra guest had arrived.

He announced himself as a softness in the shadows, half-seen disturbing shapes in Dickie's dim-lit pictures, a shimmer in the candle-flames, a mutter under the talk, a vapour creeping from the wine. He was Eros.

When Lalage had been only fourteen she had first stolen one of Lydia's blokes, a rather thick lock forward called Pete, just to show that she could. She'd done the same several times since, usually letting the poor sod down with a bump as soon as she'd thoroughly spoilt things. She'd even tried Richard once, but to the best of Lydia's belief had got nowhere. So, though the purpose of the party had been to interest Paul and Lalage in each other, when it happened—happened like that, with an intense flow of invisible energies between them, strong enough to disrupt the talk and make the male anthropologist knock his wine-glass over—the memory of all those old insults rose against Lydia's teeth like vomit. She pressed her lips hard together and spooned the pears out in angry dollops. When she saw Richard, oblivious, smiling at something the female caftan-wearer was telling him she almost slung his pear and cheese in his face.

After that the evening became thoroughly sour for a while, and was made no better when they moved next door for coffee by Paul's attempt to behave decently and accept the re-shuffle of talking-partners. But Lalage broke that up and it was a relief when she suddenly sprang a migraine, too agonising for it to be safe for her to drive herself. Paul gravely accepted the charade and took her home.

"That's quite a large car," said Richard as they watched the tail-lights fade. "I wonder if they'll wait to reach a bed."

Lydia kicked him as hard as she could on the shin.

"Hi! What was that for?"

"I didn't think you'd even noticed. The bloody little bitch!"

"But I thought that was the object of the exercise."

"And she's left that bloody dress behind."

"And her car. Cheer up, she'll get a parking ticket in the morning. That'll be something."

Lydia laughed, found and squeezed his hand and allowed herself to be led back to talk genteelly to the other guests till midnight.

18

THE PAINT-BRUSH was beautifully loaded, fat with white gloss but not dripping, when the telephone rang. Lydia cursed.

It had been mid-morning before she'd got down to what she thought of as proper work. The first two hours had been spent in returning the "dining-room" to a bare-board state in which she could work at it, and this she'd done grudgingly, with an unusual sense of resentment that Richard should get out of it by going off to his crammers, and another layer of resentment that she'd let herself in for entertaining according to the mores of a life-style which she detested. During her coffee-break she had sat sniffing the odourless steam and wondering whether she was getting flu, or had eaten a dubious mussel, or was enduring for the first time in her life a real hangover. Just to suggest these possibilities was to dismiss them, and at the same time to force herself to admit that her bile and spleen were caused by Lalage. The physical symptoms—dusty tongue, half headache, dreariness in the blood—were the result of a bad night's sleep, itself the result of undigested fury. The mental symptom was self-disgust, trying to masquerade as self-righteousness.

So, though there was still plenty of clearing-up to be done she had settled down after her coffee-break to a job she normally enjoyed, laying a smoothly professional layer of gloss paint onto a skirtingboard. It was going well—paint just the right thickness, brush not losing any hairs, her own hand steady and precise—when the telephone rang. I know who that is, she thought. She was right.

"I'm sorry," said the husky but childish voice.

For the moment Lydia was unable to speak.

"Is that you, Liz?"

"Yes."

"I'm sorry. I really am. I behaved unspeakably."

"It doesn't matter."

"Yes it does. Honestly, I just couldn't help myself."

"I know."

"You're a saint. *You* don't go about behaving unspeakably because you can't help yourself."

"Yes I do. I can't help myself . . . if you were here, I'd hit you, hard."

"Oh, darling! But . . ."

"Forget it. It's all ancient history."

"I didn't realise that you . . ."

"Now listen. I'm not cross with you. I'm furious."

"But . . ."

"Shut up! I'm not cross with you for hitting it off with Paul, because that's what I wanted, roughly. I'm not cross with you for spoiling the party, because you didn't, it was OK after you left, and anyway that sort of party is stupid. But I am furious with you because I can't help it. That's all. Thank you for ringing. You've left your dress and your car behind. I'll be in this evening if you want to come and pick them up."

"Hang on. There's two other things."

"Yes?"

"You probably won't be very pleased about this either, but I felt so awful that I've bought you a tree."

"A *what*?"

"It isn't a very big one—I mean it won't grow into a spreading oak or anything. It's very pretty. I saw one in a friend's garden and it has delicious little whitey-pink flowers most of the winter. Prunus subhirtella autumnalis. I thought you might put it where the roses came out, and pavement underneath . . . Liz, I'll cancel it if you don't want it. I just thought . . ."

"No, it's all right. I mean, thanks, darling, that'll be lovely, it's just what I wanted. I expect. I didn't know what to do with that bit, so it's nice to have my mind made up for me."

"Oh, super! You wouldn't like two? I mean, a pair? I mean . . . oh, pull yourself together, woman! I've been so worried. I didn't know what to *say*."

"Say it with trees."

"Oh, Liz, you are a saint! Shall I order another one?"

"One will be masses, thanks. What was the other thing? I've got a wet paint-brush."

"Oh, I'm sorry . . . I didn't know . . . yes, of course I did, because there's always something like that. Er, it's about Paul, I'm afraid."

"Yes."

"What do you know about him?"

"He's my new tenant. He's a Livonian exile, and now he's Minister of Maritime Affairs in the Government. He's got his own ship, and he seems to be pretty rich. But he likes to do things for himself. He's very efficient with his hands."

Lalage giggled.

"Anything else?" hissed Lydia.

"Oh, God, I *am* putting my foot in it. I haven't fallen for anyone that way for absolute years. Him too, I think. We're the same kind of animal. Usually I like to see my blokes crawl a bit, sometimes . . . but . . . I suppose it's because we're both utterly selfish, so at least we've got that to respect each other for . . . you can be honest with somebody like that . . ."

"Dickie adores him," said Lydia. She knew there was no point in setting up prickly zarebas of anger and envy—they'd only have to come down again.

"That's what I wanted to ask you about," said Lalage, surprisingly. "Not just Dickie—all of you. Did you know Paul's absolutely obsessed by you? I don't mean just you, Liz, as a potential mark, I mean the set-up. He's like an anthropologist who wants to know all about a tribe."

"What did you tell him?" It looked as though the zarebas were going to have to go up after all.

"I told him to mind his own business. I was pretty shirty at first, because I thought it meant he'd only fallen for me because he couldn't have you—I mean, someone like that you're a sort of challenge to, aren't you? Then I saw it wasn't that, so I told him things anyone could find out, like Dad being a surgeon and marrying twice, and Richard having been in the army, and you being a bit of a left-wing nut. I let him look over the hedge, but I didn't ask him into your garden."

"I expect that's all right."

"Yes, but . . ."

"Well?"

"Look, Liz, this is pure hunch. But there's something going on."

"What on earth do you mean?"

"I don't know."

"What kind of something, Lal? Do you mean he's using

his ship to smuggle heroin, or something like that?"

"I don't think so. I don't think you're in it, though. I'm not even sure he is. Of course as soon as I got to the office I started to find out all I could about him. His ship's OK, and he's set up a nice steady two-way series of contracts between London and Helsinki. There's enough loot there to support his life-style. But . . . look, he's not really the same sort as your old men in your Government, is he? What's he doing there?"

"He's a Liv. The Russians chucked a lot of people out. They don't all have to be the same as each other."

"I know, but . . . one idea I had was he might be involved in some sort of currency juggling, using your old men as a front. I can't quite see how it would work, if it's roubles—there's no profit in getting roubles out, only getting dollars in, and then the profit's in Russia—perhaps it's something to do with old Czarist bonds, or there might be an unredeemed Livonian loan or something. Would you mind, Liz?"

"Mind? Oh, I see. I don't really want my old men taken for a ride, but otherwise I'm all for it. The more rats there are in the capitalist system, the sooner it'll fall apart."

"Squeak, squeak."

"Any rats that get fat will be collected and cooked by recipes in the Little Red Cookbook."

"I think you're marvelous, darling. Do take care. I don't believe in much except my own comfort, but while you and Richard are OK I know there are higher things in life. Bye, darling."

Lydia went back to her painting. She was glad Lalage had called, not because it had really settled anything but because her own fury had somehow unknotted itself during the last few minutes and ravelled smoothly away to nothing. At least I haven't got rats, she thought. Only rots which, checked in one place, could still put out creeping grey strands, invisible behind paper and plaster, to reach and infect fresh timber, so that all the work had to be done again. That's what the world's really like, she thought. Rats? Rats!

19

—. .—. .— —. .— snickered the key. Lydia lifted down from the shelf the stopwatch she had used for rallying before she ever met Richard. Dickie crouched in the corner behind a pile of cardboard boxes, waiting for the answer to his call sign.

After a brief pause the metallic note beeped .— —. . . .— three times. She pressed the starter knob. Paul had recorded quite a long message and seemed to be going slightly faster; trying to read the letters in her head she got lost almost at once, so she returned to modifying the back suspension of her dream car. When the Morse ended she pressed the stop button and slid her sketches under the armchair. From the hiding-place a pigeon crooned.

"All clear," said Lydia. "A patrol came past five minutes ago. I gave the corporal a slice of fruit cake."

Dickie's head poked up like a gopher's from its burrow. He even sniffed the air for danger. Then on tip-toe he crept across the room and slid a sheet of paper onto Lydia's lap. The lines of dots and dashes were far neater than any writing he had ever done.

"Couldn't you write the letters underneath, darling?" coaxed Lydia. "I'm only an ignorant cobbler's wife. You can't expect me to read Morse."

"I'll read it," he whispered. His lips puckered to shape each letter but he didn't say them aloud until he had wrestled a word clear.

"Ammo . . . train . . . at . . . pass . . . 0300 . . . what's huh rrr sss?"

"Hours. It's a short way of spelling it. That means three o'clock in the morning. I'll be in bed, fast asleep."

"I'll be up in the pass with Aaku, of course."

He picked his way through the message, making three mistakes and twice needing help with words that didn't pronounce themselves easily—Dickie was receiving at just under five words a minute now, when a month before he had been taking a sulky minute to drag one word out of ordinary letters. The Morse Code, by reaching his mind through his ear, had somehow by-passed whatever was causing the blockage between mind and eye. Even the dots and dashes on the paper were representations of sounds, and he seemed able to use them because of that. The next stage was to persuade him that letters were really much the same.

Lydia, miming secrecy and caution, fetched from its hiding-place behind the bookshelf an old fountain pen.

"Number Eight brought that this morning," she said.

Forgetting to go to his secret radio Dickie lay on the floor, unscrewing the cap of the pen and teased out the cylinder of paper that Lydia had hidden there. He was painfully turning the letters into dots and dashes when the phone rang.

"May I speak to Lady Timms?"

"That's me."

"Ah, good. This is Diarghi, from the Russian Embassy. How are you?"

"Fine, thanks. You never sent me those references. I was beginning to wonder . . ."

"Exactly. Well, I have an apology to make. Baltic affairs are not my subject, and I'm afraid I relied too much on memory. When I came to check the references, I discovered that I'd made a mistake. What I told you about Busch is approximately correct, but I'd confused Linden with another man."

"Oh! Are you sure?"

"Yes, why?"

"Well, our Central Library has a run of Hansards, and when I was taking some books back I thought I'd see if I couldn't find something, and I did."

"It was the same name, and he was a minister in the Livonian Government in exile."

"Of course, of course—that is how I came to make the mistake. I have since consulted our specialist on the area, and I find that the Lindens are a large clan. Naturally, after the publicity, the man I was telling you about faded into the background. I believe he died in Canada."

"I see. Well, thank you for letting me know. I wasn't going to do anything about it, as a matter of fact."

There was a pause. Dickie's key beeped his call-sign. Mr Diarghi coughed.

"We have a crossed line, I think," he said.
"What? No. No that's OK. It's just my son using a Morse key."
"Ah."
No wonder he sounded relieved. It's bad enough having to ring up British citizens and tell them that you've been feeding them mistaken propaganda, but the sudden intrusion of a burst of amateur Morse into your conversation must produce a real chill of alarm.
"Well, there it is," he said rather abruptly. "I hope my misinformation hasn't caused you any distress. I'd very much like to meet you again when I have made further progress with my report."
A few polite half-promises on both sides, and he rang off.
The Morse key beeped on. Lydia blessed Paul in her heart. It was a typically male piece of behavior to devise such a fully-functioning toy, and to explain in total seriousness that a real spy can't expect to have his messages answered at once, supposing they get through at all. Upstairs the patient tape, triggered by the call sign, would be taking down Lydia's contribution to the bloody farce of this imaginary war, and quite soon Richard would come home and play the part of the stupid Russian police, angrily searching the basement and shouting threats and commands, but never, somehow, finding the secret hide-out.

20

"ALL RIGHT," said Lydia, "I'll get a taxi. It's as urgent as that?"

"Yes," said Richard's voice, very strained.

"OK, I'll come at once."

"Trouble?" asked Lalage as she put down the receiver.

"Yes, I don't know what. Can I leave Dickie here? I'll ring you up when I've sorted things out."

"Lovely—it doesn't matter how long. There's a stack of food and Dad's longing to read him *Greenmantle* . . . Oh, hell! Dad's got some gen for you about a corpse or something."

"Bother. That'll have to wait. With any luck I'll be back in a couple of hours."

"No hurry. I was going out with Paul, but he'll be quite happy to stay here and play war-games with the other fellows, God rot their masculine guts. Sure you don't want me to come with you?"

"No thanks. See you."

She was in luck. A taxi was putting down a very shaky old man two doors along the street, so when the fumbling fingers had at last counted out the tiny tip she was able to jump in, sit back on the tatty mock leather, and fret. What the hell could be happening at Devon Crescent that Richard needed her to cope with, and that he couldn't explain on the telephone? He sounded as though there'd been someone in the room with him, too. Was it some blood-curdling quarrel between tenants? Had Don Pumice come home half-crazed? Had the joists under the Government's store room given way? And killed Paul Vaklins? That would account for Richard's reticence, if he'd known Lalage might be listening. If that floor had collapsed, what about the one below? If Mrs Pumice were in, and baby Trevor, and the Evanses on the floor below that, each fall adding its weight and impact . . .

The streets were all sleepy with Sunday, and the taxi buzzed rapidly through like a bluebottle in an empty kitchen. As it swung into Devon Crescent the curve of the buildings hid Number Eleven, but Lydia crouched forward with the fare and tip hot in her palm, straining to see what columns of smoke or dust were streaming from which smashed windows. Then, when her house came into view, she saw the whole façade was as calm as a tomb.

Nearer, she saw that something was up. A small crowd was gathered round her gate, and several loiterers stood on the opposite pavement, staring. The taxi drew up behind a double-parked car, but she didn't notice that it was a police car until she'd paid her fare. A uniformed constable stopped her at the front gate.

"Keep back, *if* you please," he said.

"I live here. This is my house."

"If you'll have a word with the officer at the front door there. Him in the grey hat."

Drugs? Stan Pelletier back from university with pockets full of pot? Or Mrs Pumice–she'd come very suddenly into a windfall. Or the Government in some crooked deal, as Lalage had hinted? Again that might account for Richard . . .

The policeman at the door gave her no clue. He simply nodded and led her into Mrs Pelletier's back room, dark with the enormous pieces of mahogany furniture that had come with the house. Richard was there, very grey and twitchy, sitting on the edge of the big bed. Lydia ran across to him.

"Are you all right, darling? What's up?"

He looked up, made an effort and knew her. He smiled.

"Ah, you made it. That was quick."

"What's going on darling? Please!"

He shook his head. Somebody coughed. Lydia swung round and saw a tall, glossily tanned young man with curly hair and long side-burns.

"Gentleman's a bit shook up, I'm afraid, ma'am. The Superintendent won't be long now, I expect."

"I must know what's going on. Where is he?"

"Now, ma'am . . ."

"Are you seriously going to try to stop me going where I like in my own house? You haven't any authority to do so. In fact, as far as I'm concerned you haven't any authority to be here at all. Now, where is this Superintendent?"

The man's tan didn't actually pale, but it lost some of its

lustre. He was hesitating about standing out of her way when Lydia heard voices and footsteps coming up the back stairs from the basement or the garden door. The policeman coughed again, reclothed himself in authority with the surreptitious speed of a man tucking his shirttail into his trousers in a public place, and opened the door.

A slim, dreary-looking man entered, grey haired, grey-lipped, solemn as a verger. Behind him came a much bigger man with a round, red, shiny face; he looked like a bather in a Donald McGill postcard.

"Are you the Superintendent?" said Lydia.

"Superintendent Austen, CID," said the grey man. "This is Sergeant Eissmann. You are, er, Lady Timms?"

"That's right. Now, could you please tell me what's going on?"

He didn't answer but crossed to the window.

"If you'd come here a moment, Lady Timms," he said.

Lydia hesitated, then joined him. The garden had changed. When Lydia had left it after lunch it had been a stodgy rectangle of raked earth, crossed in one place by the paved path and in another by the planks the spy had put down so that Mrs Pelletier could reach her washing-line. Now there were a lot more planks, a huge mound of earth, and four or five men standing about. One of them was kneeling down just beyond the mound and another was taking photographs of something there. Further away two more seemed to be laying out a sort of tent.

"What the hell's going on?" said Lydia.

"Now, madam," said Superintendent Austen in the voice of a shop-walker trying to soothe a fierce customer, "can you tell me exactly when that patch of earth out there was last dug over? It appears to be quite recently."

"Why? What's happened?"

"We'll come to that later. I asked you . . ."

"We'll come to it now. What's happening? Why are you here?"

"If you please, madam . . ."

"Unless you give me a reasonable explanation of your presence I shall ask you to leave my house."

Richard groaned. Lydia went and sat beside him and gripped his limp hand.

"It's all right, darling," she said gently. "There's no reason why I should tell him anything until he's satisfied me that he's got some sort of right to know."

Sergeant Eissmann sucked in his breath.
"Sir Richard asked us to come," said Superintendent Austen. His tone of voice hadn't altered, but two little bunches of muscle had appeared just below his cheek-bones.
"That's all right," said Lydia, taking care not to snap at him because she didn't want to upset Richard any more. "But as you can see my husband is in a state of shock, and I need to know why. In fact the garden was thoroughly dug over the Monday before last, a fortnight ago. Now will you tell me what's happening?"
"A fortnight ago," said the Superintendent in a musing voice. Sergeant Eissmann had a notebook out and wrote a few words. Lydia discovered that she was squeezing Richard's hand so hard that she must be hurting him. She willed herself calm.
"Superintendent," she said, "whatever you're doing you're doing it in a very stupid way, exactly calculated to get minimum help from me."
"I am conducting an investigation into what looks like a case of murder," said the Superintendent.
"Murder! Who?"
"I dug up a hand," whispered Richard. "It came out of the clay. It was like a fungus."
(That wasn't so bad, if he could talk about it. For the first time since she'd come into the room Lydia felt that she could relax her protection slightly. But . . . a hand!)
"We do not yet know who," said the Superintendent. "An elderly woman. My men have only just finished clearing the earth from the body."
"Do you want me to see if I know her?" said Lydia. "Is she . . . recognisable?"
"Not so bad," said Sergeant Eissmann, beaming. "I've seen much worse."
"I was planting the tree," whispered Richard. Lydia squeezed his hand again and stood up.
"I won't be long, darling," she said.
"An identification would certainly be of value," said Superintendent Austen, "but I would prefer . . ."
"Let's get it over," said Lydia. "Can somebody please stay with my husband?"
"You take her down, Dave," said the Superintendent.
Sergeant Eissmann hummed a dreary humn-tune as he followed her down the stairs to the basement. As she was opening the garden door he said, "If I was you ma'am, I'd ease up

on the super a bit. You won't get much change out of him, whatever you say."

Lydia smiled tightly at him. She realised now that it was her antipathy to the Superintendent that had trapped her into marching off like this to peer into the eyes of death. She began to feel very withdrawn into herself, very screwed-up. Outside she discovered that, although there was plenty of daylight left, the air seemed drab, as if it were already dusk. A chill came out of the darkening sky, a chill rose from the raw earth. Sergeant Eissmann's hand steadied her across the boards and round the neat-piled mound. Lalage's tree, its roots still wrapped in sacking, lay to one side.

Just beyond the mound was a rectangular hole. The photographer had fixed a floodlight to shine on its lip, and his assistant was adjusting a white cardboard arrow to point at something under its glare.

"Borrow your light a mo so that the lady can see what's what?" said Sergeant Eissmann.

"Jesus Christ, how d'you expect me . . ." muttered the photographer, but he swung the lamp over and made it glare down into the hole. Lydia stepped forward on the greasy plank.

The woman lay there, wrapped in a curious tube of coarse raw cotton or cheap canvas; it was torn on one side where Richard's spade had sliced down; a bony hand showed. Somebody had cut the top end of the tube with greater care and folded the flaps back to make a sort of high-winged collar through which the head poked out. The cheeks and forehead were streaked with yellow clay and the sparse hair was full of the stuff. Between the streaks the flesh seemed bruised and wrinkled, like a fungus as Richard had said, or like the hand of a child who has stayed too long in the bath. The eyes, mercifully, were closed, but the mouth below the bony little nose hung open in an everlasting snore. The woman looked diseased, leprous under the fierce light, but there was no mistaking her.

"It's Mrs Newbury!" Lydia gasped. "But we buried her! Weeks ago! Why did you plant it there? She got out of her box! You said she would! Getting out and coming for him! Getting out and coming for him!"

Her voice was no longer her own but an animal shriek. The laughter followed it, rising up her throat like vomit. Each hooting gasp seemed to end in a muscular contraction which could only be released by another series of shrieks. Inside this ghastly, melodramatic creature the real Lydia waited, appalled, unable to interfere. She was quite conscious of how Sergeant Eissmann took the creature by the elbow and led it away across the planks and into a dark place, and there was Richard coming down the stairs to hold her close while the shrieking creature appeased itself and the fit died out in shudders and whimpers.

"I'm sorry," she mumbled. "I don't know why I did that. I'm all right now."

"That bloody man," said Richard. "He shouldn't have let you . . ."

Her lungs sucked in breath for a new bout of hysteria, but she clenched her teeth and hands and willed her body into decency.

"It must have been worse for you, darling," she said.

"I'm getting over it, I think. Can you tackle the stairs?"

They were still holding hands like lovers in a tulip garden when they reached the Pelletiers' back room. Superintendent Austen looked no different, as uninterested in what had happened as if Lydia had merely left the room to put on a kettle for coffee. But Sergeant Eissmann fetched her a chair.

"Now," said the Superintendent, "I believe that you can clear up the identification."

"It's Mrs Newbury," said Lydia.

"No!" said Richard.

"Please, sir," said the Superintendent. "Yes, madam?"

"She was one of my tenants. She died of a fall in her room at the end of January. I went to the inquest and then to the funeral, at Kensal Green. We buried her. I tell you, we buried her!"

"Take it easy, madam. We will go into that later. You are quite certain of this identification?"

"Yes. In fact Mrs Pumice has got a photograph of her. She lives on the second floor, left-hand side as you come up the stairs."

"Dave," said the Superintendent. Sergeant Eissmann rose and left.

"Now, I'd like to return to the question of when the garden was dug, and why, and by whom. A fortnight ago, you say?"

"That's right. I and several of my neighbours employ a casual labourer called Mr Roberts to do our gardens. It was a complete mess, with only a few scrubby old roses, so I asked him to dig it right through."

"What do you mean when you say it was a mess?"

"Oh, I've been doing a lot of repairs to the house, and throwing out timber and things, and burning everything I could. But in fact it hadn't been a *garden* for several years."

"So you mightn't have noticed if somebody had buried the body in there earlier?"

Lydia rose and walked to the window. The photographer and his helpers were still mopping and mowing around the grave like students of the black arts.

"Oh yes, I think I would," she said. "That bit was usually fairly clear. But surely you can tell by the state of the soil whether the grave was dug before or after Mr Roberts worked it over."

"That's as may be," said the Superintendent. Lydia felt her antipathy rising again—he seemed to be just the sort of official she most detested, giving nothing, secretive for secrecy's sake, a servant of the system, indifferent to the individual people whom the system chumbled about. Sergeant Eissmann came back looking cheerier than ever and gave him the newspaper cutting. The Superintendent gazed at it, rubbing his chin.

"Take a dekko at the caption," said Sergeant Eissmann.

At once the Superintendent's eyebrows rose and his lips pursed into a soundless, prurient whistle.

"Do you know if the deceased was the mother of a woman called Procne Newbury?" he asked.

"That's right," said Lydia, grudgingly.

"We've got one reporter here already," said Sergeant Eissmann. "I guess we'll have the lot along in half an hour."

"Can't be helped," said the Superintendent, looking not at all displeased. "Now, madam, refresh my memory. You say this Mrs Newbury died longer ago than the Monday before last."

Carefully, picking her words so that she herself gave nothing away either, Lydia went through the story from the discovery of Mrs Newbury dead in her room until her funeral.

"So you identified her for the coroner's court?" said the Superintendent at one point.

"That's right."

"Well, now, I don't want to distress you, but can you remember whether her skin was then in a normal condition?"

"Normal?"

"You must have seen that the skin is now in a very peculiar state, wrinkled and . . ."

"Don't go on! No, it was quite normal. A bit pale. She

always had rather a flushed complexion when she was alive, but that may have been because she was usually het up about something. There was a bit of blood and a bruise on her temple. I thought that . . . out there . . . that was just being in the ground . . ."

The Superintendent shook his head, keeping to himself yet another secret not to be revealed to the common herd. Lydia went on.

"I see," he said when she'd finished. "Now is there any possibility of Mrs Newbury having had a twin sister?"

"Not that I know of. In fact she once told me that she was an only child."

"Can you tell me the circumstances of that conversation?"

"It isn't relevant."

"Allow me to judge that."

"No, thanks."

Lydia felt that there was no reason why she should recount the whole history of Mrs Newbury's long campaign to persuade her to have a few brothers and sisters for Dickie. He stared at her, glanced at Sergeant Eissmann's notebook and shrugged.

"Well then, can you let me know the name and address of the undertakers responsible for the funeral at Kensal Green?"

"I'm afraid not. I don't know. The Government arranged all that."

"The Government!"

"I'm sorry. The top two floors of this house are let to the Livonian Consulate. Livonia used to be the smallest of the Baltic republics before the Russians took over, and this is really the Livonian Government in Exile. We call them the Government. Mrs Newbury was their cleaner and they arranged rather a grand funeral for her . . . they'll be very put out about this. Oh, dear. Sunday. Mr Obb has a flat up there, and he was the one who fixed it. He might . . ."

"By the way, they've got diplomatic immunity," said Richard in a perfectly normal voice. Lydia almost laughed aloud with pleasure and relief to hear him talking like that, and making such a typically Richardy point, too. It had the effect of tilting Lydia's world back onto its proper axis; what had happened ceased to be nightmare and became a real event, sudden and horrible but copable-with. Priorities emerged.

"When can you move the body?" she said. "I don't want to bring our son home till it's gone."

The Superintendent ignored her. Back out of the nightmare Lydia perceived now that he was a man who had reached that crucial level in the hierarchy where he could cope with his own job, but only just. Faced with immune diplomats and twice-buried but unmurdered bodies of the mothers of famous harlots and small boys needing to come home, his mind slid away to areas he understood.

"Just go and see whether we've got any reporters, Dave," he said.

"OK, OK," said Sergeant Eissmann.

"Would you like me to take you up and introduce you to Mr Obb, if he's there?" said Richard. "I've been a diplomat, so I know the ropes."

Typically, Superintendent Austen accepted the suggestion almost with eagerness, because it came from a man. While they were out of the room Lydia telephoned Lalage, told her what had happened, and asked her to bring Dickie round in an hour. As soon as she put the receiver down the phone rang again. It was a reporter from the *Sun*, asking her to confirm the news. She cut him off without answering. The machine rang again, and this time she simply left the receiver off. Within five minutes somebody had persuaded the engineers to start the howler. Lydia unscrewed the earpiece and slid the diaphragm clear–she reckoned that it would need a lot of influence to get an engineer out to Devon Crescent on a Sunday evening, and at least the police could deal with any reporters who came to the door.

A bit later Superintendent Austen came down again, to ask for the key to what was now Paul Vaklin's room. Lydia refused to let him have it without Paul's permission. That meant reassembling the phone and ringing up Lalage again. Paul was there and said he'd come straight round. That in turn meant another fight with Austen about whether the body could now be taken away, so that Paul could bring Dickie with him. Austen was still refusing when Sergeant Eissmann came in to say that the job had already been done, and did the Superintendent want to be present at the autopsy. Without waiting for permission, Lydia fixed up with Paul and dismantled the phone again. By the time she'd done that the policemen were going out of the door.

"By the way," she called, "Mr Roberts–the gardener–will be here to-morrow morning. Do you want to see him?"

"Instructions will be left with the officer on duty at the door," snapped the Superintendent, and stalked away, the model of petty dignity.

Lydia smiled to herself as she poured water into the kettle.

"I think you might give him a bit more rope, darling," said Richard. His voice sounded tired but normal.

"Are you all right, darling?" she said.

"I'm fine. It was a shock, and I thought I was cracking up again, but then you turned up, and that was better, and as soon as you said it was Mrs Newbury that was all right."

"Why on earth . . ."

"Not knowing was what hit me."

"But we buried her!"

"You buried somebody else. The Government had the coffin brought home, and all that rigmarole, because they'd got somebody else to bury. Or possibly something else—documents, gold—no, that would be too heavy—oh, it doesn't matter. Now it's their look-out."

"I wonder if you're right. How did you get on with them?"

"It was Obb—very polite, very concerned, very stiff. Not saying anything. Oh, yes, we got the undertaker's name out of him, that's all. Poor old Austen, with Obb giving him the brush-off upstairs and you kicking him in the teeth down here. Do go a bit easy on him, darling."

"But . . ."

"What's the point? He'll get what he wants in the end, and you only make an enemy of him."

"OK, I'll try to be polite, but . . . I mean, Paul's key! He simply wasn't entitled to it. I *couldn't* have given it to him!"

"I suppose so. What's for supper? Shall I peel the spuds?"

Ten minutes later Lalage brought Dickie down to the basement. He was in a state of frenzied thrill at the presence of so many policemen, and though Lydia had drawn the curtains he somehow managed to spot the tent that now covered the hole in the garden. Richard told him firmly that it was all a secret, and he spent the hour till his bed-time sending a long message about it up to Paul. No answer came.

21

SHE TOLD DICKIE NEXT MORNING, as she was walking with him to his play-group—it was holidays now, but half-a-dozen mums worked a rota system with their kids. There had still been a policeman on the door, and one or two loiterers, and a depressed man taking photographs of anybody who went in or out.

"Why's he doing that?" asked Dickie. "Are we famous?"

"Not yet, thank heavens," said Lydia. "Do you remember Mrs Newbury?"

"She's dead."

"That's right. Well, there seems to have been a mistake about her funeral. I don't know how it happened, but she got buried in our garden, instead of in the cemetery, and the police want to find out why. That's all."

"But the man took a picture of *us*."

"Well, you see, this sort of mistake doesn't happen very often—in fact it's very rare—so I suppose some people might think it's interesting enough to put in a newspaper."

"Will there be a picture of us?"

"I don't think so. They always take far more pictures than they can possibly use, just in case."

"Like a football. Derek's father does that. He takes hundreds of pictures, and only sometimes it's a goal."

"Yes, just like that."

And that was that. All over. No fuss, no spores to float through the darkness inside his little skull, settle in some recess and grow slowly into nightmare. Children have a marvellous ability to treat everything that happens as if it were normal. On her way back to Devon Crescent Lydia determined to do the same herself. To-day would be an ordinary day. She planned to wallpaper the back room and she'd do just that. Great. April began to sparkle along the roof-tops, to glisten in the gutters, to twinkle from passing cars. Her own sudden cheerfulness seemed to bounce like the sunlight off people and objects. The policeman at the door grinned at her as she passed.

"Have you seen Mr Roberts, that's the gardener?" she said.

"No ma'am. The super's been asking for him too."

"Bother. Perhaps he's decided to do a turn at one of the other houses. If anyone wants me I'll be downstairs, in the back room."

"Very good."

She mixed Polycell, got the trestle out, fetched the steps and her big scissors and measured and cut the first strip. She was slithering paste onto it when she heard men's voices, and feet on the bare stairs. To-day is an ordinary day, she told herself. I'll be patient with the bastards.

"Good morning, Superintendent," she said, still slapping away with the brush. "Do you want me?"

"If you can spare the time, madam."

"That's all right, provided you don't mind if I go on working. You'll find a couple of chairs in the kitchen, Sergeant, if you'd like to sit down. I'm afraid Mr Roberts hasn't turned up."

"So I am told," said Austen, in a dry voice.

"He's a bit of a hermit. Perhaps he was frightened off by the people at the gate. It might be worth seeing whether he's gone to any of the other gardens instead."

She rattled off the numbers of the relevant houses. Sergeant Eissmann left to instruct some underling and Austen himself fetched the chairs. Lydia folded the bottom third of her paper up on itself, picked up the two top corners and climbed the steps by the wall. Her plumb-line hung tremorless against the mottled plaster. The sergeant came back as she was easing the top eighteen inches smooth.

"It's all right," she said. "I can talk while I'm doing this."

"Wish I had a wife or two like you," said Sergeant Eissmann.

"Now, madam," said Austen, "first I want to check a detail about the funeral. The undertaker tells me that when he brought the coffin back here on the night of the fifth of February the room was prepared for some kind of wake. Is that correct?"

"Yes. It wasn't exactly a wake. I told you that Mrs Newbury did the cleaning for the Livonian Consulate. She'd done it for a long time. Mr Obb told me that they wanted to bury her properly—rather grandly, in fact—to show their appreciation. One of their national customs is that they sit up with the body all night before the funeral."

"I see. Did you go into the room while the coffin was there?"

Satisfied with the hang of her paper Lydia peeled the bottom section down and began to ease the wrinkles out to the sides.

"I showed the men where to put it when they came," she said. "But after that . . . I don't even know whether the Livs did watch all night—it's just that Mr Obb said they would."

"I see. Now, madam, the body was buried approximately three feet down. If your husband had not started to dig a hole for the tree there it wouldn't have been found, being below the normal level of cultivation. The question is, who knew that he would plant the tree just there? Have you mentioned this to anyone?"

"No," said Lydia, easing the top of her strip clear so that she could cut it true to the ceiling. "Nobody knew. We hadn't actually decided. I rather thought I'd like it in the middle, where the rosebed had been, but he thought that would darken this window too much. I left it to him when I went out."

"Was that what you were referring to when you said 'Why did you plant it there?' "

"Did I? When did I say that?"

She had the top of the paper fitted now and began to come down the steps, feeling curiously shivery.

"When you were by the hole, madam. Apparently you said, or rather shouted, 'Why did you plant it there?' Also something about coming out of a box."

"It's Mrs Newbury," said Sergeant Eissmann, reading from his notebook in a drab, heavy voice. "But we buried her. Weeks ago. Why did you plant it there? She got out of her box. You said she would. Getting out and coming for him (twice)."

It seemed lucky that she had reached the bottom of the steps, and there they were, to sit on, carefully, feeling for them in case she collapsed in the suddenly darkened room. She put her head in her hands.

"Did I say that? I don't remember. Sorry."

"Take it easy," said Sergeant Eissmann.

"I'm sorry, I really don't remember anything that happened out there, except that I recognised Mrs Newbury and then I had hysterics. Read it again."

"Have a smoke first?" suggested the Sergeant.

As she reached gratefully for the packet she saw Austen's eyes gazing at her with intense, withdrawn interest. Eissmann was smiling, but his eyes had the same look. Eissmann, nice man, she thought as she lit up. Austen, nasty man. The usual team. Bastards. Anger steadied her, so that she could listen without emotion to the words she was supposed to have spoken.

"Yes, I see," she said. "The bit about where my husband planted the tree is obvious. The other part is all to do with a conversation we had the day they brought the body back. You're supposed to let small children acquire some experience of death, and I discussed with my husband whether I shouldn't take Dickie into the room where the coffin was. He quite rightfully told me it was a bad idea, as Dickie used to be rather afraid of Mrs Newbury, so he might have nightmares about her getting out of the box and coming for him."

She looked up. Eissmann was still smiling his trained smile, but there was a new expression on Austen's face.

"You seriously mean to tell me," he said, "that you were proposing to take a kiddie into a room with a coffin in it, to let him look?"

Voice and feature were those one might see on the face of a respectable Borough Councillor who has just been told that some blue film is a superlative expression of artistic freedom.

"We only talked about it," said Lydia. "Whether I would have done it is my own affair. It only concerns you because it explains what you say I said in the garden."

Austen resumed his clinical mask with a speed that reminded Lydia of her father. He paused to let Eissmann finish taking a note of what she'd said. Lydia found herself irritated by this process, an irrational disgust caused partly by Austen's own persona and partly by dislike at having her words taken down and filed away—particularly words screamed involuntarily by that other Lydia who usually slept the days away in secret and only stirred about once a month to drift and then scramble through a nightmare. To ease her tension she got off the steps and marked and trimmed the lower end of her strip. She was smoothing it back when Austen coughed for her attention.

"Now," he said in a back-to-business voice, "may I ask

you to look at a few photographs for us? We want to see whether you can identify a man."

"Of course."

"I must warn you that the man is dead."

"Oh."

"Tisn't that horrible," said Eissmann. "A bit peculiar, only, but not bloody or anything."

"OK. Will this take long? I do want to get the papering done before my son comes back. He's an absolute devil with glue."

"If you'll look at the pictures I don't think we'll need to bother you again for a while."

"OK." Lydia took an uncomforting suck at her fag and stubbed it out.

The prints were large and shiny. At first Lydia thought that she was looking at a bit of mildly experimental portrait sculpture, then she saw that the thing was not puddled plaster but flesh. It was a sunken-cheeked, bald old man. His eyes were shut. His ears were large, thin and very protruding, his mouth wide and sharply turned down at the corners. You could imagine him sitting on a park bench, wearing a shabby overcoat and leaning forward over his walking-stick, trying to suck the sunlight into his veins to enrich the thin, sad blood. Only if you had seen him sitting like that you would have immediately looked away, rather than stare at the strange ailment that affected all his skin, innumerable seams and puckering which did not follow the natural creaselines that one sometimes sees on old men's faces, but wandered and crossed at random.

"It's the same as Mrs Newbury!" she said.

"Only he'd been in it longer," said Sergeant Eissmann.

"In what?"

The Superintendent managed to look as though he alone knew. The Sergeant simply shrugged.

"Some kind of alcohol," he said. "The lab say he's never going to rot now, he's been soaking in it that long."

Lydia looked at the other photographs. Some were in profile and two showed the whole body, naked and unwounded, but all pocked and puddled with the same patterning as the face.

"How tall was he?" she asked.

"Little fellow," said the Sergeant. "They'd put in a couple of polythene bags, full of sand, to bring it up to the weight when the old lady was in it."

"I'm afraid I've never seen him before," said Lydia. "You mean they buried him instead of Mrs Newbury?"

"Seems so," said the Sergeant.

Lydia gazed steadily at the long-imagined, but (now she saw it) totally strange face. What had brought him to this end?

"Was he . . . I mean, did he die naturally?" she asked.

"Cancer of the liver," said the Sergeant. "Rather him than me."

"Now, let's get this straight," said the Superintendent. "You say you have no idea who this man was, nor how he came to be buried instead of Mrs Newbury?"

Lydia hated lying, but her antipathy to him let her do so now almost with pleasure.

"No," she said, briskly. "Is that all?"

"That's all . . . for the moment," he answered. He managed to load the pause with reservations, but Sergeant Eissmann winked as they left. At last their footsteps faded.

Lydia measured and hung a second strip of paper before she allowed herself to think about the interview, and then the image on the top of her mind turned out to be that of the strangely wrinkled corpse of a little old man, buried in secret so far from home. Aaku Aakisen, leader of the Livonian Resistance. Little Aaku with his sticky-out ears. *We had an old man, a servant, who made excellent varosh, very skilled, very careful. But then he died* . . . What do you do, when all the time he's supposed to be attracting propaganda values to your cause by living on in the icy, licy hell of Siberia? Obviously, you preserve his body by popping it into a barrel of strong alcohol. There it stays . . . how long? Years. Then (for the random mercy of God sends an occasional blessing even to the forgotten Livs) Mrs Newbury dies, and the opportunity arises to give the national hero a grand burial, if under an assumed name and sex, but better than lying soaking in *varosh*. Mrs Newbury takes up that sinister duty. Yes, they'd needed to pack the coffin with a couple of sandbags to make up the extra weight, which meant, presumably, that there had been extra volume also. Mrs Newbury had displaced more *varosh* than old Aaku, so the liquor had overflowed, run down between the floorboards and made a strange sticky patch on the ceiling below. Lydia had actually stretched out her hand towards the very bin . . . *Not to touch, please*! *Varosh is most infectable*! Ugh. Yes, Mrs Newbury had still been huddled in there, in the amniotic booze, because it had been days later when Lydia had stood in the garden with the spy and seen Count Linden staring down at that convenient patch of fresh-dug earth in which Mrs Newbury could be buried hugger-mugger. When? Why, the night of the Russian Embassy reception, because the only way out to the garden was through the basement, which meant that the Timmses had to be out of the way. So Paul knew. Of course he did. In the car, going to the cemetery, Lydia had mentioned Aakisen out of the blue and Paul had been startled. Then, very quickly, he had come up with the plausible pretence that she'd thought that the Livs were burying Aakisen by proxy. But he'd known it was the hero himself.

Slopping a brushful of paste onto the third strip of paper Lydia decided that the one person who had a right to know the truth was Procne, who had wept there, beside a stranger's grave. Anyway, she'd love it–that was drama, in the Newbury style.

In fact there'd been two heroes, Aaku and Mrs Newbury, but she'd been real and solid till her last evening, whereas he'd been made into a sort of ghost long before he died, only his name any use, and his ability to make good *varosh*. His duty had been to become a legend. All that had mattered was the lies that could be told about him, first the imaginary escapades and then the imaginary sufferings. Bloody old men! The worst of it was that they'd become so immersed in their own falsehoods that they'd needed to carry them to the sentimental end of that awful funeral. Really it would have been more honourable to tuck Aakisen away in the rose-bed. But that would have denied them the last chance to summon a lump into their scrawny old throats. Bastards!

However . . . this strip of paper seemed almost to float itself into place, confirming like an omen the rightness of Lydia's choice. All governments, to her, were abominable, but not equally so. She didn't care whether there was any logic in her instinct to support the tiny and defunct government upstairs against the vast and far-reaching neo-Stalinist engine in the Kremlin. She simply knew that their smallness made them incapable of more than little lies and minor mischiefs, whereas in Russia there were probably ten thousand Aakus and a million Mrs Newburys. Perhaps she would mull the problem through with Richard one night; he liked large and abstract questions (think first, fight afterwards, the soldier's art) though Richard himself preferred trains of thought that didn't rattle towards the trenches of action. But Lydia's main mode of thought *was* action. Her dealings with Superintendent Austen confirmed her belief that the government of Britain was only marginally better than that of Russia, because an historical accident had left the individual citizen with a little more power against it; but the police state was there, waiting to be released into domination, like a djinn in a bottle.

So, slowly, her anger with the old Livs and Paul settled into an almost pleasurable displeasure with them. They had behaved disgustingly, but that was the nature of governments, and at least their crimes had been crimes against the dead. To embarrass them would be to help the Kremlin. Her choice to say nothing had stood the test of action.

The papering continued to go well; but no old house has a true right-angle anywhere in it; in every corner each wall meets its neighbour on a slight skew, so that if you simply run the strips on round it you find that what was a vertical on the first wall has become a slant on the second. Lydia was sliding in a neat gusset to turn the corner towards the door when big feet banged on the stairs and a uniformed policeman bounced into the room, a large young man, excited as a puppy.

"Oh," he said. "Sorry. Seen the super?"

"Upstairs," said Lydia. "Were you the chap who was looking for Mr Roberts, the gardener."

"Not me, ma'am, but I hear there's no sign of him."

"Damn," said Lydia. She hadn't particularly wanted him to do anything, but his absence was disturbing, a symptom of disorder setting in in an area where she thought she had created order.

"Seeing you," said the policeman and charged off like a schoolboy looking for Mum to tell her that he's down to play for the under-twelves on Saturday. His overt excitement reminded Lydia of something that she had barely noticed, but had somehow registered, during her interview with Austen. He had been excited too, and so had Eissmann. But Aaku had died of cancer, and Mrs Newbury of a fall—there was only this complicated and unnecessary mess to be cleared up, and where was the excitement in that?

Next time feet rattled on the stairs she was on the ladder, measuring for the strip that would have to run down beside the door and half-way across the top of it.

"Hang on," she called. "I'm on the ladder just inside. I'll

be about a minute. Why don't you put the kettle on for some coffee?"

There was no answer. When she took the ladder away Austen and Eissmann heaved into the room with solemn tread. Even though her head was full of figures Lydia could sense that their mood had changed.

"Now, madam . . ." began the Superintendent.

"Wait a sec. Just let me write my measurements down."

He sighed, but said nothing.

"OK," she said, picking up her scissors.

"Now madam, I am saying this because I don't want any misunderstandings and difficulties later. With a more co-operative citizen there'd be no need for me to become this formal at this stage, but I want you to understand that a serious crime had been committed and it is part of my duty to question you. You are not obliged to say anything unless you wish to do so, but what you say may be put into writing and given in evidence."

"Seriously?"

"This is a serious matter."

"Christ!"

"Now . . ."

"Wait a minute."

Lydia took the scissors off her fingers slowly, as if she were peeling off a glove. Her first thought was to wish that she owned a tape-recorder. As a next best she chose a piece of wallpaper from her heap of scrap, put it on the mantelpiece and wrote at the top "Memo of interrogation of L.T. by Superintendent Austen, Monday April 3rd, Sergeant Eissmann also present."

"OK," she said.

Austen walked over to see what she had written.

"That's quite unnecessary," he said.

"I hope so."

"Well, if you wish . . . My first question is whether you have any knowledge of a sum of money left in her room by Mrs Newbury."

Lydia dropped her pencil. As she scrabbled for it, she wondered how a policeman puts into his notebook, as evidence, an obvious and appalling start of surprise.

"I'm afraid I can't answer that," she said, still on her knees. Austen waited for her to rise.

"When you say you can't answer, do you mean simply that you don't know?" he said.

"I can't answer that either."

He waited again. Sergeant Eissmann was quicker at taking down notes than Lydia.

"Well," said Austen at last, "do you have any knowledge of a will left by the late Mrs Newbury?"

"Same answer," she said, not looking up from her scribbling.

"Let me make this quite clear, Lady Timms. You are not saying that you know nothing about the will or the money? You are saying that you are not prepared to answer questions about them."

"No I'm not. I'm saying I can't."

"But you admit that the will and the money exist, or existed."

"I can't answer that, either."

This time his pause lasted longer than it took Lydia to write down her note.

"You realise, Lady Timms," he said at last, "that in view of your refusal to answer two simple questions I have every justification for asking you to accompany me to the police station for further questioning?"

"And I have every justification in refusing to come. You have to arrest me, formally, before you can make me come, and after that I have an absolute right to refuse to answer questions and to demand to see a solicitor. That's right, isn't it?"

"That is part of the Judges' Rules, yes."

"Judges' Rules, hell. That's part of the law, isn't it?"

"If you say so."

"Well, do you really want to go through all that? I'm afraid it wouldn't get you any further, because those are questions I literally can't answer, no matter how much you banged away at them. If you want to arrest me, I'll come, of course. I imagine you'd give me time to make arrangements for my son to be looked after."

She had no idea whether the threat was real, or whether the mention of Dickie changed his mind (not necessarily out of human kindness, for there were still a couple of photographers hanging about and Dickie was an extremely photogenic kid). She could sense his hesitation as she scribbled.

"You misunderstand me," he said. "I was only trying to point out to you how suspicious your refusal to answer these questions might seem. A serious crime has been committed, and . . ."

"Has it?" said Lydia. "You don't know whether any money or will existed. Perhaps it's only gossip. If they did exist, perhaps they haven't been nicked. Otherwise there's only this stupid business of somebody putting bodies in the wrong place. That's not really a *serious* crime, is it?"

"Some might think so, Lady Timms. But you will have to take my word for it that a crime which even you would recognise as serious has been committed."

"Oh . . . OK . . . well . . ."

"And you still refuse to answer the two questions I asked you?"

"I *can't*, I tell you! Damn! I've forgotten to write any of this down."

"Take a copy from mine, ma'am," suggested Sergeant Eissmann.

"What crime, anyway?" said Lydia.

"I am not obliged to tell you that," said Austen.

"All right," said Lydia. "Look, I've accepted your word that it matters. Will you accept mine that I've got a perfectly good reason for not being able to answer those two questions? I'm sure there's lots of others I could answer.

The moment she'd said it it sounded stupid.

"I think we'll leave it at that for the moment, Lady Timms. I have other enquiries I can make elsewhere. I think it's a great pity that your husband is not here, and I advise you very strongly to talk this matter over when he returns."

"OK."

"Shall I initial your notes of our conversation?"

"Oh . . . thanks."

It was astonishing, when they'd gone, that the L-shaped strip of paper that Lydia cut from the measurements she'd scribbled down ten minutes before fitted. One might have expected the world to be a slightly different shape, after all that.

22

It was irritating not to have finished the papering, but a relief to be out of the house. Lydia was experiencing all over again the oppression and despair that had settled on her when she had first discovered the dry rot, a feeling of half-mysterious forces working against her, which were also somehow her fault, so that if she noticed the symptoms sooner, or traced the trouble to its cause the moment she had noticed them, then coping with it would have been cheap and simple, instead of a long, grimy and costly struggle. As she walked along the Crescent the mood began to lift; a gang of small girls were playing hopscotch; male pigeons were pouting at coyly circling females; the green of the new leaves in the privet hedges was a strong as fresh paint, not yet dusty with urban summer. She began to look forward to her lunch, a proper lunch, since Dickie was at home, grilled bacon and peas and . . .

"Hi, Lydia," said a deep voice. For a moment it seemed to come from nowhere, then she saw that the large white car by the kerb wasn't parked there, but had Mr Ambrose in the driving seat. His big head, made bigger by a gold turban, leaned out of the window. He was wearing dark glasses.

"Spare me a minute, sweetie?" he said.

"I'm afraid I can't. I've got to fetch my son."

"Ah, come on," he said, patting the seat beside him. "Let the little bastard wait. He's got to learn some time."

"Sorry," said Lydia. "Is Mr Roberts OK? He didn't come this morning."

"You've got trouble. Bob doesn't like trouble."

"It isn't anything serious."

The arched eyebrows rose clear of the dark lenses.

"You've got plenty of trouble, Lydia," he said. "I want to talk to you about that."

"I'm afraid I haven't got time, and in any case it's none of your business."

"Everything that happens round here is my business, sweetie. I hear you've been seeing my little friend Procne."

"That's none of your business either."

"You'd better stop seeing Procne, Lydia. It's not the sort of friendship that will do either of you any good."

There was something wholly infuriating about his manner, his largeness, his calm slouch at the driving-wheel, his apparent assumption of omniscience, his possessive attitude to Procne–even, in the sparkling April noon, his darkness which seemed to challenge her to say something unforgivably racialist about him, which he would then forgive. But before Lydia could decide whether to walk on on without answering or to tell him once again to mind his own business, his manner changed. He had been shaking his huge head slowly to and fro, as if to emphasise the unwisdom of Lydia's relationship with Procne, but suddenly he froze, frowned at his wing mirror, started his car and drove away without another word.

Lydia simply stood staring, then swung round to see what he had noticed in the mirror. There seemed to be nothing, except a nondescript young man in a tan jacket admiring Mrs Tevell's daffodils. She walked on, disturbed more by her dislike of Mr Ambrose than by anything he had said. It was, after all, perfectly natural, if Mr Ambrose's job was criminal rehabilitation, that he should know Procne–a coincidence, but not an impossible one. It was also natural that he should resent the intrusion of an amateur. Lydia even approved, in theory, of his eccentric approach to his job; anything was better than to be just one of the precedent-following, rule-worshipping workers in the official hive, the *them* of *us and them*. But that didn't make it easy to like him. He was a bully, and somehow bullies for the right are more objectionable than bullies for the wrong.

It was just the bad luck of the young man in the tan jacket that Dickie dropped his cardboard Spitfire in the gutter in such a way that as he darted back for it Lydia spun around to check that he wasn't rushing into the road. The young man, unprepared, hesitated much too obviously before turning into the nearest shop which (again unluckily) was an undertaker's. No doubt you could have thought of explanations for it all, including his sudden decision to make an enquiry about a funeral in a jacket like that, but Lydia didn't bother. He was following her.

It was as though a hunter, after a long, blank day in which juicy game had appeared frequently over his sights only to move into cover before he could squeeze the trigger, came towards evening on a sitting target, a half-grown rabbit, perhaps, which he'd normally have let scuttle away but now in his frustration he blasted to bits with both barrels. Lydia's anger, too, had found a target. She astonished Dickie by dragging him into a stationer's and buying him a usually forbidden *Wizard*. It enraged her still more that the man was so incompetent at his job. Now he was actually standing on the pavement outside, wondering where she'd got to. If the police are going to intrude on your privacy by following you on your most harmless errands, they might at least do it with competence. Lydia ran her mind over the opening shots of her onslaught, then walked briskly out and touched his elbow.

"Are you looking for me?" she said.

He turned. His hand rose as if to remove the hat he wasn't wearing. His eyes widened and his mouth opened as if to stammer the beginning of a denial. Then he spoilt the whole campaign by smiling.

"Ah, L-lady T-t-timms," he said. "I w-w-wonder if I c-c-could have a few w-w-words with you."

"I want to know who ordered you to follow me here."

"N-no one did. It was my own i-i-idea. B-but when I saw you t-t-talking to Jones I thought I'd better w-w-wait a bit."

He was a bit under six foot, blond and pink and very slight. He looked as though he ought to have grown a footling pale moustache to demonstrate a minimal masculinity, but he hadn't. His hair was cut quite short. His stammer was natural.

"Aren't you one of Superintendent Austen's men?" she said.

He shook his head.

"Then why the hell are you following me about?"

"I w-wanted to talk to you away from the p-police. It's about Jones."

"I don't know anybody called Jones."

"That c-can't be true, if you think about it. Besides, I saw you t-talking to him. The big Indian in the w-white car."

"His name's Jack Ambrose."

"Sorry. Yes, it's that, too. And A-ambrose Jones. Do you know what his job is?"

"Something to do with criminal rehabilitation, I believe. He works for a Council of some sort."

"I d-don't know what they call themselves now. I suppose it is a s-sort of rehabilitation—but it isn't like that at all, Lady Timms. Jones is a f-f-frightener."

"A what!"

"A frightener. His job is to frighten people. M-mostly it's to make them leave their homes, so that his mob can t-take them over, but sometimes he frightens minor p-pimps and such, and takes their girls off them."

Procne, thought Lydia, shrinking into herself. *They done him proper—he's in Morocco, last I heard.* She was scared but not terrified. This was the moment which all her life she'd known might leap out at her, the point when she'd have to fight, as a soldier does. Her mind flashed to the weak places in her defences—Dickie, lying on his belly on the pavement lost in a ludricrous strip about a phantom tank; Richard—how much to tell him? When? After yesterday . . .

"Who are you?" she said suddenly.

"Me? My n-name's Tony Bland."

"Oh . . . you write for *Get Notted*?"

"That's me."

"In that case . . . hell, you'd better come home, if you've got time. I'll give you some lunch. Come on, darling, bacon and crisps. Have you been reading the balloons?"

"Sometimes," drawled Dickie, still drowning in the dream. As he crawled to his feet Lydia saw that he'd been lying across a patch of dried dog-piss. It didn't seem to matter just now.

Tony Bland's stammer turned out to be mostly shyness, but partly (Lydia began to suspect) a protective device, a demonstration of harmlessness and ineffectualness, which might even be quite useful for a young man whose purpose was to sieze capitalism by the ankles, stand it on its head and shake the money out of its pockets.

"What do you think of *G-get Notted?*" he asked as Lydia was turning the bacon on the grill.

"I nearly always buy it, but I don't always agree with it. I like what it stands for in principle, but quite often I get angry about the way it sets about things. Last year I was involved in an effort to get a decent nursery school in this area.

Your lot quite rightly wanted it further north–in fact I resigned from our committee about that very thing . . ."

"I know. That's why I c-came to you. You see . . ."

"Let me finish. You did several stories on it, and they nearly always got something badly wrong."

"We've g-got a very small staff," he said.

"Yes, but that wasn't the trouble. The real problem was that you couldn't distinguish between truth and propaganda."

He cut a dainty square of bacon, piled a little mashed potato onto it and decorated it with three peas, so that it looked like a cocktail canape. He put the load prissily into his small mouth, and didn't answer until he had chewed and swallowed it.

"In most cases there isn't any d-difference," he said.

"I know that argument, and I dislike it. But even if you allow it this wasn't one of those cases. I think it might just have been possible to get a school going, in the right place, with enough money behind it, if that's what we'd all been working for. But you didn't seem to mind whether there was a school or not, provided you could throw enough muck in the Council's face. The Council stinks, and perhaps we wouldn't have got the school anyway, but it wasn't up to you to decide that."

She waited for him to answer, but he simply went through his bacon-cutting ritual and nodded as though he'd heard all this before and had learnt to be patietnt about it.

"So you see," she said, "I'm going to be cagey about what you say about Mr. Ambrose. That's all."

Dickie, eating his lunch in his cardboard hide-out, made a curious wheezing explosion. Tony jumped, but Lydia knew the sound well.

"It's all right," she said. "He's just seen a joke with his mouth full of crisps. Don't worry–he'll sweep up. He's very fussy about his own territory, like a badger. Look, if what you say is true, why did Mr. Ambrose take such trouble to provide me with a gardener?"

"How did it happen?"

She explained the absurd half-fantasy about the spy.

"That t-ties in," he said. "There was an old woman died here, wasn't there–Procne Newbury's mother? And now there's this business about bodies being switched. And I hear s-something about missing money–that's not got into the nationals yet."

"Yes, but . . ."

"Procne w-worked for Jones's mob. The old woman died from natural causes?"

"She fell off a table when she was drunk. It all came out at the inquest."

"Yes . . . I wonder if you could f-fake that. Never mind. The mob had a reason for being interested in this house, you see. That b-body-switching business doesn't sound their style—too fancy. But perhaps they heard about it, perhaps they knew about the money, perhaps they s-simply wanted to check up, on principle. But whatever it was, they'd enough reason to send a bloke to do a preliminary scout round. You b-bumped into this bloke, and talked to him about gardening. That g-gave them an opening for their usual operation—Jones came round to check, and you offered him just what he w-wanted—a job for one of his men in half a dozen houses."

"It wasn't the same bloke! I *knew* it wasn't! They found an ex-con who knew about gardening and sent him along! But . . . you mean he was supposed to find out which houses were worth burgling?

"They might try that, as a side-line, but their main interest is housing. They w-work it like this. They find a street which suits them and they put somebody into it for a couple of months . . ."

"What do you mean, into it?"

"It varies. One c-case I heard about, they twisted the milkman's arm—showed him a fiddle, trapped him into working it and then threatened to show him up. They p-paid him a bit of cash, too. Sometimes they take a room. It doesn't really matter, provided they can get a toe-hold. You see, their theory is that there's always a few weak points in any community, and if you can find them out you can exploit them. That's w-where the frightener comes in. The sickening thing is how mean they are. They're rich, but they'd rather scare an old couple out of their home than b-buy them out. Usually it's a bit of both. And once they've g-got their men into a couple of houses they can d-do what they like. Up in G-golborne ward they emptied one street in ten months, f-flat."

"It wouldn't be like that here. Quite a lot of these houses are owned by—it sounds awful to say this—people who'd know how to fight that sort of thing. You know, people with money and education, people the police would listen to."

"I d-don't know. They've got big ideas. But they might play it differently here. They might g-go almost legal. You're right on the edge of the p-posh area in Devon Crescent. If they c-could find a few places which owners were thinking of selling, and then just b-bring down the tone of the Crescent a bit, so that it became p-part of the p-poor area, they c-could start to buy up below the market price, and then there might be a bit of a panic, and perhaps they'd pick up some more houses. Then they c-could take their heavies out, and smarten it all up, and sell off, or l-let off, at a big profit. One of the things I'd like to p-prove is that they've got a working agreement with Dice and Dottridge . . ."

"The estate agents?"

"Right. I'm p-pretty certain they have, but if I could prove it that would really shake things up."

He paused, looking almost wistful at the thought of dragging into the open this juicy big slug of a scandal. Dickie came crawling out of his hide-out, still somehow managing to gaze at his comic with one hand and shuffle his plate along the floor with the other. He rose to his feet and moved like a sleep-walker to the sink.

"Honestly, darling," said Lydia. "I think you've been looking at that long enough for now."

"No, I haven't."

"Please, darling. If you stop now and read it again after tea, you'll enjoy it much more then."

"Can I have an apple."

"Of course."

"All right. I'll go and practise my code."

He let go of the comic so slowly that there might have been half-set glue on it, still running in sticky strands out to his fingers after he'd let go. But he didn't seem to sulk at all. Lydia felt a rush of enormous affection as she watched his round rump wriggle into his hide-out. When she turned back to Tony she found he'd picked up the comic and was reading it with serious absorption.

"Hey!" she said.

"G-great stuff," he said, looking up. "My parents wouldn't let me b-buy them."

"Quite right," said Lydia. "I don't usually. "They're mental pollution."

"They're an alternative universe."

"Seriously?"

"Seriously."

"All right, I'll think about it. But stop reading it now, damn you. I want to know what to do about Mr Ambrose. Do you mind that noise?"

. – . . – . – beeped the buzzer as Dickie began to work at random round the letters. Sometimes he kept it up for an hour at a time. Lydia found it restful, like the song of a metal bird.

"N-no," said Tony. "That's fine. D-did your g-gardener ask you questions all the time?"

"No. As a matter of fact he was a remarkably silent bloke."

"Oh. That's not so good."

"On the other hand, Mrs Tevell told me that he was a tremendous gossip. She never stops talking herself, so I thought she just meant that he was a good listener. But perhaps . . ."

"That's b-better. I know the t-type. Just what he'd want. Look interested, egg her on a bit with the odd question, and she'd t-tell him everything she knew."

"So he didn't need to ask me anything?"

Tony frowned.

"I d-don't think that's it. I think it's more likely he'd b-been told to keep his mouth shut here. What did Jones w-want?"

"I don't know. He said he wanted to talk to me. He said I was in trouble. But he raced off when he saw you."

"I w-wish he h-hadn't seen me. The ch-chap who was on the job before me g-got a very nasty beating up. And the p-police don't want to know, because we've made quite a bit of t-trouble for them since we started."

"Yes, I read about that. You were right all along the line there, I thought."

"G-good."

"What do you think I'd better do now?"

"I d-don't know what you'd *better* do. I know what I'd l-like you to do."

"What?"

"I think he'll c-come back. N-not while the police are here, l-later. I'd like to get a t-tape-recording of what he says."

"Why should he come here? I have to go out sometimes. And I haven't got a tape-recorder."

"He'll c-come here, because he likes to g-get at people in their own homes. It m-makes them feel they aren't safe anywhere. If he t-tackles them outside, they feel they've still got somewhere to run to. We'll lend you a recorder. Do you know how they work? I've got a friend who can fix it all up for you. You've got to be able to set it going without him seeing."

"Hell," said Lydia. "Let me think."

Dickie's nonsense message to nowhere filled the room still. Tony cut up and ate the chilly remains of his lunch, apparently without noticing how unpalatable it had become. His neatness and sensual apathy depressed Lydia. These people, she thought, my natural allies–do I want them in power if that's how they are? Suppose Mr Ambrose were an official in some left-wing group, a frightener for urban guerrillas, would Tony turn one wispy hair? No. But he's not, and he's got to be fought, at some point, by someone. She realised that it was unlikely that anyone would ever be better placed to fight him than she was, herself, now. His earlier victims had been unprepared, without influence, without allies. She was none of these things.

"How did you hear this rumour about money?" she said. "I don't think it's true, but how did you hear it?"

Tony shook his head, knowing but not revealing, just like Austen.

"You've got a friend in the police, haven't you?" she said.

He shrugged.

"Oh, for God's sake!" she said. "I'm not going to get him into trouble. The point is that the Superintendent in charge of this body-swapping business has got it into his head that something serious is going on. I think he's nuts, but if he's right then I think Mr Ambrose must be the bloke he's looking for, so really I ought to tell him about him . . ."

"I'd much rather you d-didn't. He'll ju-just fade away and I'll have to start again."

He sounded quite plaintive about it. No question of his seeing any problems but his own.

"Well, I've got to reserve the right to tell him if I need to. In fact it goes against the grain to tell him one bloody thing. But what I can't afford is for him to find out that I knew who Mr Ambrose really is, without my having told him, and I was afraid your friend in the police . . ."

"N-no, that's OK. What does he mean, *serious*?"

"I wish I knew."

Tony masticated a last, slow mouthful.

"Well?" he said.

"OK," said Lydia slowly. "I don't think there's much chance of it coming off, but I suppose I've got to give it a try."

23

THEY SPENT THE AFTERNOON in Holland Park, Dickie ceaselessly gunning down his mates under the salad-coloured leaves of the adventure playground while Lydia sat on a bench and tried to read her new *Autocar*. There was one dark-haired little Roscius who died a thousand deaths, all spectacular, crumpling into a bullet-riddled heap at one moment and at the next picked off by a sniper as he teetered along a wooden walk-way six feet from the ground. Two pig-tailed girls banged and died with the best of them, but it was noticeable that only the kinder-hearted boys bothered to gun them down. So even at that age men were almost as prejudiced as Father about the feminine role. Lydia made a deliberate effort and dragged her mind away from Mrs Newbury, and Aaku, and Austen, and Mr Ambrose. She took out a pencil and on a blank bit of an advertisement for sparking-plugs wrote "Resolutions: If it's a girl." But the list wouldn't materialise. The dark, cloudy bulk of Mr Ambrose edged continually between her and her imaginary daughter; the ghost of Mrs Newbury gibbered in ancient admonitions, and Superintendent Austen coughed a warning dry cough. That was real. He was walking along the path by the bamboos and when he saw that she had noticed him he raised his hat and walked on. Lydia scribbled out the words she had written. The daughter would have to wait.

When they got home the telephone was ringing.

"Liz?" said Lalage's voice, urgent.

"Yes, darling."

"How are you?"

"Fine. I spent the morning paper-hanging and arguing with the fuzz, and this afternoon I've been watching Dickie shoot his friends. What's up?"

"Oh . . . I just wanted to check . . . I mean, I didn't want to spring this on you if you were feeling . . ."

"Do get on with it. I'm OK."

"Well . . . do you remember I told you Dad had some gen for you about the corpse?"

"That's right. I want to know about that."

"Wait. He's just rung up in an absolute fury."

"Why on earth?"

"Well, he can't see it's not your fault."

"What isn't, for God's sake? Lal!"

"Sorry. I'd forgotten he could get like that. I mean, it's been years. Last time was when Richard left the army . . ."

"I *know* that. Do pull yourself together, darling. Or else tell him to ring me."

"He can't. He's operating on someone's bum. I hope his hand's not quivering still. He wouldn't anyway."

"I can't stand this. I'm going to ring off."

"No. Wait. You asked him to find out whether there was anything odd about the autopsy on Mrs Newbury. Right? He did that. He was waiting to tell you yesterday. Answer, rather huffily, of course not, all above board. Brain haemorrhage caused by fall when drunk. But now they've come round and hauled him out of the theatre and asked why he wanted to know. Tremendous kerfuffle. High horses everywhere. The point is that it *wasn't* all above board. Got it? They'd missed something."

Lydia felt her body gasp, almost as though that were what politeness demanded, while her mind accepted the news. Procne had foretold it, had been right where the world was wrong. It would have been, Lydia now vaguely felt, disloyal to her to be surprised.

"What?" she said.

"They did find something."

"I meant what did they find?"

"Dad said something about a kaffir trick. He was almost incoherent."

"Why didn't he ring *me*?"

"Can't you see, darling? He wants to keep his hands clean. You've made him . . . oh, I expect they'll hush it up, anyway. But he's lost face, and he probably lied to them, and now . . ."

"Does he think that I . . ."

"I don't know *what* he thinks. When he's calmed down a bit . . . Is it serious, Liz? Really?"

"It might be."

"But who on earth?"

"The trouble with this house is that anyone can go in and out."

"Mrs Newbury sounds like a born blackmailer, too."

"Yes."

"At least you're in the clear. And Richard. They can't . . . Liz! They can't, can they?"

"Father seems to think they might, doesn't he? You might remind him that I only wanted to know about the autopsy so as to be able to guess how long Mrs N had been on the bottle."

"Oh. Yes. He got that, before this other thing. No time at all is the answer. The bloke who did the job decided that that was why all the alcohol had been absorbed into her blood-stream, and why she got so drunk and fell off the table."

"Only now it looks as if she didn't."

"Oh, God! What did he mean by a kaffir trick, Liz? It rings a faint bell."

"Don't you remember–it was one of his favourite toughen-em-up no-nightmare stories, about witch doctors creeping into huts in the dark and sliding a fine spike into the spinal column? No blood, no wound."

"Oh, Liz, you're so practical. Trust you to remember something like that. I bet you could do it, too."

"Lal!"

"Oh, God! Sorry. Of course I don't . . ."

"You'd better stop talking, darling. Think about money. That'll have a calming effect. Thank you for warning me. Bye."

She put the receiver down to find Dickie standing close beside her, frowning.

"Grandfather told me that, about the spike, too," he said. "What I want to know is where."

"Africa, he used to say. But I don't think it happens any more."

"I meant where on me?"

"Oh. Didn't he show you?"

She remembered the surgeon's fingers, precise as a machine, feeling along the vertebrae. She remembered her own clenched jaw, her violent stillness, determined not to shiver or wriggle, being even then sure that that was what he'd really wanted.

"There wasn't time," said Dickie. "It was Rorke's Drift. Show me."

He stripped his jersey and T-shirt up in a single movement and waited. Lydia counted along the spine, numbering off the hidden beads down the necklace of bone, wondering whether a run-of-the-mill autopsy–with the cause of death so obvious–could be expected to spot this tiny extra wound, and the severed nerves that would carry no more the traffic.

"There," she said, pressing gently. He shivered and wriggled quickly into his clothes. The touch of his body seemed to have restored her blance, so much so that she longed to pick him up and hold him tight on her lap. But he wandered off to the bread-bin, cut himself an erratic slice and spread it thickly with peanut butter. Lydia made coffee, drank it and then slung together a bacon and potato pie for supper. She thought as she worked. OK, I must accept it. Mrs Newbury had been killed. By whom? The case against Lydia Timms. Lydia Timms had been friendly with the deceased, enough to be trusted. She might therefore have known about the hoard of money. She had taken that money and put it into a Post Office account, under her own name. She had destroyed the will of the deceased. She had known and understood the technique of the so-called kaffir trick. She was in severe financial straits, caused by fresh discoveries of dry rot in her house. Furthermore, with the decease of the deceased, the room of the deceased would cease to be leased under a controlled tenancy–a new tenant, a handsome young businessman, lover of the said Lydia Timms's half-sister, and no doubt of the said Lydia Timms on the side, would pay ten times the amount that the deceased had. Furthermore, the said Lydia Timms had concealed from the police several material facts, and had refused to answer certain material questions, and had added one lie. Furthermore . . .

But Lydia's mind wandered down the by-way of working out whether she could in fact have killed Mrs Newbury, without help, in the way it seemed to have been done. You would have to lay her out–no, first, surely, you would have to trick her into drinking a little vodka, then lay her out, then, while the heart was still working, inject more alcohol into her blood-stream, then fake the fall from the table to cover the bruises of the laying-out, then bash her head hard against the fender, and finally do the kaffir trick. She couldn't have done it alone. She didn't know how to lay a person out, for certain, without the use of drugs which would show up in an autopsy; nor was she strong enough to manhandle that sack of a body. As in life so in death, you couldn't get any leverage on Mrs Newbury.

Rolling out the pastry–a brisk and cheerful operation, most days–Lydia reluctantly dragged her mind round to Mr Ambrose. If Mrs Newbury had been murdered, presumably he was the murderer, for some motive to do with Procne. There was no evidence yet for this, but it was the only thing that made sense. So obviously, Superintendent Austen ought to be told about Mr Ambrose. Equally obviously, Lydia wasn't going to tell him. She numbered off her reasons, knowing as she did so that she was only putting up bulwarks round a decision that had been made at a deeper level than reason. First, she didn't want the link with Procne brought to light; second, if Austen had to find out, it would be far better for him to do so from somebody other than Lydia–if she went running to him with the news, he might well think that she was simply trying to drag a red herring across her own trail; third, and most important, it wasn't the murder that mattered, it wasn't Mr Ambrose who was the enemy. The really vital thing, in the long run, was to try to bring into the open the activities of the people he was working for, right back to Dice and Dottridge, if possible. They were the real creators of misery and injustice; they were the people who had moved the Hoods out of Number Forty-six, and broken up the pigeon loft–and had done the same, often with trickery and violence, to thousands of other harmless people, all in the sacred name of property. They were the enemy. Though Tony's plan had only a slim chance of success, Lydia was determined that it mustn't be she who spoilt it. And if it did come off there would be a by-product. Superintendent Austen could hardly refrain from transferring his suspicions to Mr Ambrose, without Lydia having to tell him anything.

Dickie was spending a quiet morning as a submarine waiting to ambush a passing battleship, so Lydia sat down and wrote a careful account of everything that she had done and decided, and her reasons. Then she put it in an envelope and dated the flap and wrote a note to Mr Muxbury, Richard's family solicitor, asking him to certify the date and keep the envelope unopened. Poor Mr Muxbury, lover of trusts and entailments and contingent heirs, dreader of anything to do with the criminal law! If only he knew . . .

The feet on the stairs were heavy but shambling. When Lydia opened the door she found Mrs Pumice outside, with

Trevor on one arm and the other carrying a battered suit-case. It took her an instant to realise that if Mrs Pumice had decided to quit she would have left her luggage in the hall.

"Bloke brought this for you," said Mrs Pumice. "Lord, it's heavy."

"Oh, thank you," said Lydia, taking it. "I expect it's some books I wanted."

"Can I come in?" said Mrs Pumice. "I sort of got to . . ."

Her voice trailed into hesitation. She looked very nervous and miserable.

"Come and have a cup of coffee," said Lydia. "Shall I take Trevor for a bit?"

But Mrs Pumice clung to him and came very timidly into the room, as though expecting, somehow, to be punished for being there at all. She jumped violently when Dickie torpedoed her. Lydia took her arm and settled her into Richard's big arm-chair. Trevor, despite his suety appearance, was sensitive to his mother's mood and looked on the verge of wailing.

"What's the matter, Mrs Pumice? I hope the police haven't been pestering you. You mustn't let them. They haven't any right."

That only seemed to make it worse.

"Oh, oh," sobbed Mrs Pumice. "You been so kind to me and I went and told 'em."

"Told them?"

"Oh, oh, if it had been anyone except Princess Anne! She's so lovely. You oughtn't to have took it. Old Ma Newbury really loved that wedding, she did!"

"Honestly . . ." said Lydia.

"Oh, oh," said Mrs Pumice.

"Boom!" said Dickie.

"Shut up, Dickie," said Lydia.

She settled herself on the arm of the chair and put her arm round the throbbing shoulders. Dickie emerged from under the table, flat on his stomach, and using only his toes propelled himself to his cardboard cave. Trevor watched him with suspicious eyes.

"Listen," said Lydia. "As far as I know Mrs Newbury didn't leave anything to Princess Anne. I can't tell you exactly what she did leave, because it isn't my secret, but I promise you I haven't taken anything, and you haven't done any harm, really you haven't."

But still Mrs Pumice sobbed. Lydia found her impatience

at such feebleness tinged with envy. To be able to cry so easily, for so little. To be able to collapse in tears, and refuse to cope, and let the tide of the world drift you wherever it willed, instead of having to swim all the time against its hidden and unpredictable currents. It was a gift, of a kind.

"Oh, oh," sobbed Mrs Pumice, "then I'm worse than what you are. Oh, oh."

24

THE SUITCASE contained an absurdly large tape-recorder, sensitive no doubt, and capable of recording a good couple of hours of incriminating talk, but impossible to hide in the Timmses' sparsely furnished room. In the end Lydia put it under the floor-boards, with the microphone in an empty tin of scourer standing quite plausibly below the sink. She thoroughly enjoyed constructing a trigger mechanism to set the thing going, with a rat-trap lashed to the recorder-box and set so that its arm, when the trap was sprung, came down across the "Start" and "Record" buttons; she padded the buttons up with foam rubber, so that the arm of the trap could get at them and at the same time not make too loud a click. After some thought she decided that the best way for her to spring the trap was by some definite action, rather than trying to do it unobtrusively. So she led a length of black button-thread up from the bait-points of the trap, between two floor-boards, and fastened it to the flex of the telephone so that a jerk on the instrument was enough to release the arm. She reasoned that it was entirely plausible that she, when threatened, should attempt to use the telephone. If Mr Ambrose let her she could jerk it herself. If he prevented her, the struggle would be enough.

That was about all she did enjoy over the next few days. Superintendent Austen questioned her every day for a week. He took to arriving unannounced, almost sliding into the room as if hoping to catch her in some incriminating posture, actually counting the missing money, or reading the missing will. She didn't see him outside the house again—perhaps the momentary glimpse in Holland Park had been a coincidence—but she did spot the curly-haired young man with the side-burns a couple of times. He was much better at his job than Tony, so she got no chance to accuse him. In any case, she reasoned, it wouldn't be a bad thing to have him about just in case the frightener, Mr Ambrose, attempted something in the open.

The interviews with Superintendent Austen became a sort of ritual, with the same questions and responses. Lydia didn't make the old mistake of elaborating, either on her lie or the truth. Superintendent Austen didn't think of any new questions, but on the third morning there was a variation in the ritual. Once more he had asked her about the money and the will, once more she had told him she couldn't answer, once more he had asked whether she had discussed the matter with her husband, once more she had told him to mind his own business. Then he said "Lady Timms, I have no need, I am sure, to tell you how severely the law treats any attempt to interfere with witnesses."

"What on earth do you mean?"

"I mean what I say. I must advise you in the strongest terms not to attempt to interfere with witnesses."

"Heavens! You don't mean Mrs Pumice?"

It was not in the Superintendent's nature to admit even that.

"I'll make a statement about that, if you like," said Lydia. "Ready, Sergeant? Mrs Pumice came to see me, apparently to apologise for telling you about a will and some money that Mrs Newbury was supposed to have left and I was supposed to have stolen. I told her I hadn't stolen anything. That's all. Now, listen to me–Mrs Pumice is very young and she hasn't had much luck in her life. You've got to leave her alone. She simply isn't up to hours and hours of interrogation. If you try that she'll get scared and run away, and then she's bound to get into trouble."

"She has nothing to be afraid of," said Superintendent Austen.

"People like Mrs Pumice have everything to be afraid of. Oh, you make me mad, the way you can't see it!"

"If you would tell me the truth about these other matters there would be no need for me to question Mrs Pumice."

"Can I have that in writing?"

"What?"

"Your threat to subject Mrs Pumice to endless questioning in the hope of making me change my mind."

"I made no such threat."

"Well, that was what it sounded like."

He hesitated, shrugged and retreated into the old ritual.

That was almost enjoyable, but the rest of the periods of

interrogation were merely dull, dull with the added tension of Lydia having to stay fully aware throughout them in case some variation of phrase might trap her into a casual admission. Too fidgety to begin a major job, she settled to the finicky and boring business of stripping antique layers of paint off the banisters, and finding that the wood underneath was too battered to be worth button-polishing and would all have to be stopped and repainted. That meant hours in gawky postures on the stairs, apologising every time one of the tenants wanted to get past with an armful of shopping or a pram.

Spring turned chilly, and the draught up the stairs made the job beastlier yet. Usually Lydia disliked having to stop and chat when she was working, but it was pleasant when Mr Obb came slowly up and stood watching.

"I wonder whether that was once Livonian pine," he said. "We had quite a good trade in timber, once."

"I don't imagine you can tell," said Lydia, peering at the straight march of grain over the bobbles and flutings. "Do you know, I read somewhere that at one time in the last century pine—deal, we call it—was so fashionable that it became more expensive than oak."

"We have good oak woods also. Just now they will be all yellow with their little flowers. My father used to say that winter was a prison for the earth, locking it in walls of frost. But in spring it broke free and was happy. You do not know what spring is like, because you have never known a real winter. You do not know how the world smells, so fresh, so young, in spring."

"Do you know—you can't smell it now because of this foul stripper I'm using—but I noticed the other day when I was sanding a bit that you could still smell that it was pinewood, after eighty years. It smelt a bit like your *varosh*, in fact."

"Ah, you have not tasted real *varosh*. The stuff we drink here is *ersatz*."

"I liked it."

"One day, again I shall taste true *varosh* . . . Lady Timms, I must discuss with you some time our lease. It runs out in October, I believe."

"That's right. I hope you're staying. But I'm afraid rents have gone up a lot in the last few years. I think perhaps we'd better get some independent person to arbitrate a fair rent."

"Oh, the rent we can manage, but would it be possible for

us to occupy more rooms? If we could perhaps incorporate Mr Vaklins' room, and . . ."

His sad, pale eyes flashed queryingly to Dr Ng's never-open door.

"I don't know about that," said Lydia. "I've made one attempt to shuffle the tenants round, and they dug their heels in. But if there are any vacancies before October of course I'll think about it."

"You are very good, very good," said Mr Obb. "I must go. Very good, very good."

He smiled with extreme sweetness and went murmuring up the stairs. Lydia felt even more dismal as she returned to her dreary chore.

But worst of all was not being able to be frank with Richard. She was quite sure that she was right not to tell him about Mr Ambrose. He had his Bar Examinations in five weeks and was already intensely nervous about them. How could he hope to do decent work if he was worrying all the time about what might be happening to her at home? And though he might respect her decision not to explain to the police about Mr Ambrose, it was impossible that he would agree with it. So she couldn't tell him, but all the time she felt the lie inside her, corrupting her, growing bigger, slowly rotting, strand by strand, the web of love that held them together.

For instance, when they lay talking in the dark she found herself growing tense and wary as the conversation edged towards the secret. When Richard had found Mrs Newbury's body the shock had been like a mental wound, tearing open the half-healed tissues and letting him see again the raw, repulsive innards of his breakdown, three years ago. Now the wound had closed once more, leaving only a sort of itch which he liked to tease as he relaxed.

"I had lunch with Tommy Norris to-day," he said one night.

"Oh? What's he doing? How did you run into him?"

"He's still at the FO, Department 14."

"Isn't that counter-intelligence?"

"Not exactly. They work with counter-intelligence a lot, because their main job's keeping an eye on what foreign embassies in London actually do with their time. I met him on the tube, but I think he rather arranged for it to happen."

"Oh. What did he want?"

(The first twist of the tension-screw.)

"Just checking up, I think. They seem to want minimum fuss. He didn't tell me anything, much, but . . . you know . . ."

"All right, he didn't say anything but he allowed you to gather. What?"

"Umm. Put it like this. I think there's a bit of a power struggle going on in the FO. Alec Home wasn't the only one who had a lot of face invested in the Baltic States. I'm pretty certain Tommy knew it was Aakisen in the box—by the way, he let on that Obb pulled a fast one there. Apparently when there's a wake the undertakers have a duty to satisfy themselves that they've got the right body in the box before the funeral, but Obb told them that Mrs Newbury's room was Diplomatic ground, so it didn't apply . . ."

"It will be soon, if I let it. I don't mean let it, I mean let it."

She could sense his smile in the dark. He had always enjoyed her tendency to stray into all the homophonous quags which bestrew the meadows of our language.

"Dr Ng's leaving," she said. "He came and saw me this morning when I was doing the stairs, dressed in his best white suit and taking those yellow gloves on and off the whole time. He was terribly nervous. He must have thought I wasn't going to let him go."

"I'll miss him. Why's he going?"

In fact nobody ever saw Dr Ng. He wasn't a real doctor, but had been sitting various medical examinations without success for the last twelve years, so they gave him a courtesy title. Richard had a strong fellow feeling for him, as another late-come student.

"He's come into money. He wants more room, so that he can bring his family over."

"That makes two."

"What?"

"Two lots of tenants who've come into money. Mrs Pumice."

"She doesn't count. Don sent it."

"Umm. How did Dr Ng get into the conversation?"

"If I let the Government have his room they could move their door to the top of the stairs and include that and Paul's room in their territory."

"What makes you think they'd want to?"

"Something Mr Obb said yesterday. I met him on the

stairs. At least doing banisters means I see a bit of the tenants. It's a bloody job."

"You're marvellous. I'll do some at the week-end, if you can find a place where bad workmanship won't show. What did Obb say?"

"Well . . . he started talking about what Livonia's like at this time of year, very strange and a bit weepy. Then all of a sudden he said that when the new lease was agreed they could do with a bit more room. It's only a year since they were talking about looking for somewhere smaller."

"Umm. So they've come into money too. I don't like it."

(Another twist.)

"What do you mean?"

"I don't know. Has it struck you that Mrs N's fingerprints would have been on those bottles anyway, if she brought them home? But if they were empties the Government had used, then Linden's would be on top of hers?"

"I know. What's that got to do with Dr Ng's room?"

"I don't know. It's just the way Tommy was nosing about. You don't think . . . this is quite mad. Suppose they wanted to expand, and wanted to bury Aakisen . . . that's two motives for bumping off Mrs Newbury."

"Oh, rubbish!"

"Your friend Diarghi told you that Linden had all sorts of little ways of making people die from apparently natural causes. And didn't Lal say she thought there was something going on, to do with Paul?"

"Honestly, darling, they're such incompetents. I was thinking only the other day how I'd have tackled it, if it had been me, and I decided I couldn't."

"Paul's pretty handy. I've decided I don't care for him, you know."

"Darling, this is nonsense. I mean, Lal was talking about currency fiddling, though she couldn't see how it would work . . . are they all in it? Do you need extra rooms to fiddle roubles? It's all much too fancy. The world isn't like that. You'll tell me next it's an FCP."

"Umm. Somebody killed her."

"Well, I think Procne must have told her something in one of those telephone calls, and she must have tried to use it for blackmail purposes, and that was that."

"Have you told Austen?"

"I can't. And in any case I won't. I'm not sane about that man."

"Perhaps I'd better."
"No!"
"What's up, Liz?"
By will-power she resisted the tightening screw, disciplining her limbs muscle by muscle into slackness.
"Sorry," she said. "Cramp."
"You must eat more salt."
"That's just the sort of pseudo-science you learnt from your nanny."
Richard loved reminiscing about his nursery, and did so now, apparently without a thought that they had only a few moments back been talking about a murder done under their own roof and still not solved. Or perhaps he was using his old technique to put the notion out of his mind. At any rate, Lydia was glad to lie half-listening to him and half-trying, in fits and starts, to make more coherent sense of her growing certainty that Mr Ambrose had come to "frighten" Mrs Newbury and had finished by killing her. She was sure that coherent, practical thought would fit in the missing elements, the empties, the alcohol in the bloodstream, and so on. But her thoughts wouldn't cohere. She kept dipping in and out of dreams, all irrelevant. It wasn't until she was truly asleep that she dreamed anything that she could remember next morning: she was hacking plaster off a wall when, between stroke and stroke, the untouched plaster bulged and fell away, and the brickwork crumbled outwards leaving a smoking orifice out of which Mr Ambrose stalked, on tip-toe like a dancer, all covered with strands of grey mycelium which twitched like tentacles and reach towards her own flesh. The dream woke her, and she heard by his breathing that Richard was also awake.
"Nightmare," she said, reaching for his hand.
"Yes," he said, mysteriously, pulling her close, whether for his comfort or hers she couldn't tell.

25

HE CAME NOT AS A MONSTER from behind the wall, nor as a voice in the telephone saying that Dickie would never come home unless . . . but standing on the front doorstep in a green turban, pressing the bell, looking solemn and respectable like a charity collector for an already prosperous Maharishi. It was mid afternoon. Dickie was home from school. Superintendent Austen hadn't visited the house for a couple of days. Lydia's impulse to slam the door was very strong.

"Oh, hello," she said. "Where's Mr Roberts? We've missed him. I hope he's coming back."

"I have tried to repersuade him," said Mr Ambrose gravely, "but when he learnt that you had refused to talk to me he was most hurt. I've been a very good friend to him, you know."

"I'm sorry–I really didn't have time that day."

"You have time now."

"Well, I suppose so," she answered, though it hadn't been a question. "Shall we go downstairs?"

She had hardly time to stand aside as he pranced over the threshold. He was already at the top of the stairs by the time she had shut the door.

"Mind your head," she sang out. Mr Ambrose was tall enough to give the warning some point, but really it was only part of Dickie's spy-game, a code-word meaning "Take cover". With most visitors Dickie would have scuttled into hiding at the first footfall on the stairs, but Mr Ambrose seemed to float down with no noise at all. At the bottom he turned the wrong way and strode into the chaos of what was now Lydia's workshop and timber-store. She took that as a good omen; it was the kind of unsettling trick that he deliberately worked on other people. Only he didn't seem to mind.

"Sorry," she said, holding open the right door. "We've

switched it all round since you were last here."

"You have sold your bed?" he asked, standing in the doorway and peering around.

"No. We've got a separate bedroom now."

"You are luckier than most of my friends, Lydia."

"Yes, I know. Milk?"

"Hot. A large cup."

"I'll put it on. The big chair's more comfortable than it looks."

"You have it then. I'll sit here."

While Lydia lit the gas and put the saucepan on he picked up an upright chair and flicked it over to the shelf by the telephone. Slowly, hitching up his trousers with great delicacy so as not to spoil the creases, he settled onto it. It was a performance, a demonstration. He was master and could choose his own ground and take his time about it, picking in the end a place that commanded both the door and the telephone, cutting her off from the world. Lydia perched herself on the arm of Richard's chair. Mr Ambrose said nothing, but looked round the room as though he were memorizing its contents for a game of Pelmanism.

"I think you were trying to warn me about something," said Lydia at last.

"No."

"Oh. You said I had trouble. I'm sure you did."

"That is your own affair, Lydia. You told me so, and I believed you. How can I do my work if I do not believe people?"

"What exactly is your work?"

(It was a nuisance to have reached this stage without having had a chance to trip the rat-trap, but the opportunity to ask so bluntly might not come again.)

"Ah," said Mr Ambrose in episcopal tones, "I could tell you that that is *my* own affair, but it is not, because my work is helping other people, advising other people."

"You mean like the Probation Service?"

"Sometimes I work with the Probation Service."

"Who actually employs you? Are you part of the Borough Council?"

"I work for a private charity, the Citizen's Council Trust. We call it the Council. We prefer to work without publicity, so you will not have heard of us. We specialise in housing problems."

"Are you a registered charity?"

"Why do you ask, Lydia? I am not begging for a subscription."

Tense though she was, some body-clock clicked. Lydia dashed for the cooker and caught the milk just as it rose. She blew on it to break the uprush, poured it out and carried it across to him. As she did so she felt him watching her, felt the pressure of his personality focussed tightly upon her, building up moral dominance. His many-ringed fingers gripped the hot mug without flinching. The rings had sharp outlines on the fat, dark flesh; a sideways flap of the hand would rip a face open in half a dozen places, but Lydia was sure he didn't often need to do that. The feel of the man was enough; there was this switch or stop marked THREAT, which he could pull and at once the threat boomed out of him, without his needing to do or say anything.

"Hang on a moment," she said. "I have got to make a phone call. My sister will be going out later, and I can't put it off."

"Yes you can, Lydia. Your sister must wait."

"She can't. I told you she's going out."

"Then she will wait longer."

"Really, Mr Ambrose . . ."

"Do not use that voice to me. I have taken the trouble to come here to tell you something of importance. I find it intolerable that you should prefer to chatter to your sister."

Lydia hesitated an instant too long. If she had moved at once for the door she could have got there, but the knowledge that Dickie was still hidden in the room, and the determination to trip the rat-trap made her dither, although she knew that the encounter was now out of her control. She had a half-notion that if she made for the door Mr Ambrose, impeded by his mug, would move into her path and thus give her a chance to grab at the phone. So she walked deliberately in that direction. But he was far faster than she'd bargained for. Before she'd taken a couple of steps he had put his mug on the shelf by the telephone, risen, lunged and caught her by the elbow. A flick of his wrist spun her against him with her shoulder in his chest. His stance seemed as solid as a cast-iron pillar, though he was resting all his weight on one leg while the other locked round hers. One hand gripped both her fore-arms behind her back. The hold was gentle but completely firm, like that of a vet examining a wounded bird. Close to, she discovered he used scent. He smelt of wild honey, not strongly but piercingly. The whiff of it seemed to reach in to her, all along her veins.

"Let me go," she said. She didn't expect him to, of course, but she instinctively felt that he wanted her to struggle, to scream. So the best thing was to enter, so to speak, a formal protest. The wild-honey scent frightened her more than his touch and his strength. It suggested an element of irrational savagery; but the rest was just an act, a demonstration. She could cope with that.

With a slow movement like a caress he slid his free hand across her breasts, down her ribs, till it reached her own hand. Carefully he began to bend her third finger backwards until all the tendons were fully stretched.

"Stop it," she said quietly.

He smiled, gave the finger a well-judged extra tweak which made pain twang up to her elbow, then without waiting for her reaction tossed her into the armchair. She'd put good casters on it, so it slid smoothly back under the impetus of her body until it fetched up against Dickie's hide-out. She fancied she could hear his breathing.

"You don't work for a charity at all," she said, scooting the chair back towards the middle of the room. "You're just some sort of hired bully."

"In my work I sometimes need to restrain hysterics. It is a melancholy business."

"I don't believe you."

"You're a fool, Lydia. You think you can buck the system. You've got a very nice set-up here, nice hubby, nice kid, nice tenants. Why should you want to spoil all that?"

Lydia said nothing. Mr Ambrose moved back to his chair, sat, leaned forward and put his ringed fingers together, like a prissy clergyman explaining some point of doctrine.

"It is my experience," he said, "that citizens who misbehave do not get away with it. They are not directly punished, but the good Lord strikes them down in their pride and obstinacy when they least expect it. I remember a young man who started to tell lies about some of my friends, and shortly afterwards he became involved in a fight in a bar and was very severely hurt. I can remember many such cases. A busybody interferes in the life of an unfortunate young woman, and shortly afterwards her own son is knocked down by a car in the street. I have seen it happen many times."

"If you want to make threats you'd much better make them openly."

"To the trained mind that is a hysterical remark. You are too intelligent to become the victim of a persecution complex, Lydia."

"Balls. Your job is to scare people. You put Mr Roberts in to see whether it was worth trying to scare the owners out of some of these houses. You probably decided it wasn't because we'd be able to fight you and that might bring into the open some of the other schemes which your bosses are involved in. Did you have anything to do with Mrs Newbury's death?"

"That old bag?"

He mismanaged the note of surprise, pausing too long before he answered.

"Mrs Newbury didn't die by accident," said Lydia. "And Mr Roberts was a different man from the bloke I first asked about gardening. I believe that Mrs Newbury's daughter worked for your lot, and she used to phone Mrs Newbury once a week for a long chat. She probably told Mrs Newbury a lot of things which you'd rather didn't get out, and if she did Mrs Newbury might easily have tried to use them. I think that first bloke was doing a clumsy sort of recce. Whether you killed Mrs Newbury or not, you'd need to know what was going on."

Mr Ambrose modulated his surprise into a dismissive laugh, not bothering to make his amusement sound genuine. He shook his head, then leaned forward, suddenly earnest.

"We have good friends in the police force, Lydia," he said. "I hear the old bag left a number of papers which you purloined."

"You hear wrong."

"Lydia, Lydia, some of the things you have said about me suggest that you have been listening to lies, or reading lies. But it is true that poor little Procne used to phone the old bag, and Procne is a great liar. I need to know what she told the old bag, and what the old bag wrote down. There was some money, too, wasn't there? That belongs to my friends. Where is it?"

Despite her vulnerability and her failure to reach the telephone Lydia felt that she still had some control over the situation—rather more, in fact, than when Mr Ambrose had worn his facetious mask of charity. She'd actually gained ground. The memory of the wild-honey scent began to recede. And if Mr Ambrose felt as earnest as this about the imaginary blackmail material, it became increasingly plausible that he, or someone else in his organisation, had earlier eliminated the blackmailer.

"Your friends in the police haven't kept you up to date," she said. "I believe that the witness who told them about Mrs Newbury leaving something has now decided she made a mistake."

"The power of landlords over tenants is very great."

"Nonsense," said Lydia, stung to be equated with the type of landlord Mr Ambrose worked for. "In any case, suppose there had been some money, I would have thought it belonged to Mrs Newbury's daughter."

"Ah, our mutual friend, little Procne," he said. "I wanted to talk to you about her. That is the purpose of my visit. When I spoke to you, and you were too busy to sit with me in my car, I did not then know that you had stolen this money of ours. I was merely concerned to point out what damage you might do—would *certainly* do—both to her and your own family by . . . Ah, Lydia, Lydia, you took this money so that you could give it to little Procne when she is released. A sentimental theft. I see."

He sat for a few seconds moving the tips of his fingers against each other and clicking his tongue quietly.

"I hate butch women," he said. "I think I must teach you a lesson."

He reached for his untouched mug of milk and looked at it.

"Skin," he sneered. He poured the milk out on the carpet. "And a cracked mug. Unhygienic."

He put his thumbs into the mug—Dickie's old mug with a steam threshing machine as the design—and pulled it apart. He dropped the pieces in the mess of milk.

"What on earth do you think you're doing?" said Lydia, rising.

He leaped up, grabbing his own chair so that for an instant Lydia thought he was going to hit her with it. But he simply thrust her back into the armchair and stood over her, legs wide. She opened her mouth to yell.

"You scream for help," he said, "and I break your neck. You need some new furniture, Lydia. This old stuff is no good."

He plucked a leg out of the chair and tossed it away, disgustedly. Then with no visible effort he broke the back of the chair across his knee.

. . . — — — . . . sang the metal bird. . . . — — — . . .

"Stop it! Stop it! Stop it!" yelled Lydia, crazily hoping to drown the sound.

Mr Ambrose stepped back, nostrils flaring, then dashed at the pile of boxes, tearing them violently from each other and leaving Dickie naked to the world with his hand poised over the key. Even in her fear for him Lydia shared the shock of his finding himself in a world where the brutal enemy did discover the hero's hide-out. She jumped up, tense to bite and claw. Mr Ambrose snatched Dickie up by the scruff of his T-shirt and said "Catch". The chunky little body caught her square in the chest but she managed to clutch it as she fell and convert her fall into a sprawl back across the arm-chair. By the time she had struggled into a sitting position Mr Ambrose was back between her and the door, looking at the transmitter. He dropped it and put his foot on it as if it had been a beetle. The key scrunched sideways. Dickie gasped. The wild-honey smell was very strong.

"I was wondering where the little bastard had got to," said Mr Ambrose. "Now that's better. You sit quiet, Lydia, or I'll pull one of his ears off. Now, listen to this. You go to the police after, you make any complaint, and my friends will get to him. I've got one particular young friend who is very interested in teaching little boys a bit of a lesson. You get it? Where'd you find these pans. They're trash."

Lydia was particularly proud of her cooking pans because none had cost more than tenpence. She'd picked them up over the years off junk stalls, and even out of skips. She'd straightened dents, found lids that fitted, rivetted handles firm, scoured all shiny. They were part of her personality, far more cherished than any row of matching copper-bottomed pans at eight quid a go could have been. Mr Ambrose snatched one off the shelf, twisted its handle free, bcnt one side inwards and crumpled the rest together almost as though it had been foil. Think, Lydia muttered to herself. Think. She felt Dickie stir in her arms as the catatonic tension of fear became the willed tension before action. Mr Ambrose pulled the saucepan shelf off the wall—with something of an effort, Lydia was glad to see, because she'd fixed it.

"Pretend to be a bit frightened," she whispered to Dickie under the cover of the clattering pans. "Don't move till I tell you."

No other useful thought would come. She reminded herself that this was a demonstration only, and the sensible thing was to appear to be impressed by it, otherwise he would merely escalate the violence. He kicked a lid across the room, snapped a couple of plastic plates in two, then paused, looking round the room, faintly baffled. He pulled out the sink drawer and tipped its contents on the floor.

"Trash," he said, sounding now disappointed as well as disgusted.

Suddenly Lydia saw his problem. His technique depended on material possessions. The poorest family, living in the lousiest basement, still own things that they value, the half-paid-up telly, the wedding album, Gran's basket of china fruit. You make a token mess, smash a few worthless objects to prove your ruthlessness, then you pick up this treasure, this particular central icon which will make your victim scream "Not that!" But the Timmses had no icons. There were no material hostages.

"Trash," muttered Mr Ambrose again. He stood in the middle of the room, moving his lower lip up over his upper lip and then sucking it down again. Lydia was just wondering why there had been no mess of this kind in Mrs Newbury's room when he suddenly stirred.

"Come here, you little bastard," he said.

"Don't move, Dickie," said Lydia, holding him tight, but beginning to wriggle herself sideways so that she could spring free.

"Come here, I told you," said Mr Ambrose.

"If you touch him you'll get at least six years," said Lydia.

"Leaving the country next week," said Mr Ambrose. "You won't have woken up. Come here, bastard."

Lydia twisted, spilling Dickie into the recesses of the chair, and half rose, shunting the chair back as she did so. Mr Ambrose moved slowly this time, smiling. This was what he had been manoeuvring for, a situation where she should attack him and he could punish her, slowly. Her whole object was to see that it happened in such a way that Dickie had a chance to escape. She didn't notice the door opening.

"Can I help?" said Paul. "I heard your SOS, Dickie."

Mr Ambrose stood still and glanced over his shoulder.

"Out," he said.

Lydia snatched Dickie out of the chair and dragged him behind it. Paul raised her eyebrows at her.

"Please could you go and telephone . . ." she began.

Mr Ambrose moved, springing at Paul like a cat at a bird. As he did so his right hand came flailing round, the rings on it glistening. Lydia seemed to see a collision of bodies but couldn't interpret it because it happened so fast, and because she was trying to work round, taking with her Dickie and the slithery barricade of the chair, to where her kitchen knives hung on their magnetic rack. The house shook with a deep quiver, like the thud of a bomb. But Paul was on his feet, apparently untouched, backing into the middle of the room. Mr Ambrose was turning in the doorway, shaking his head. Somehow he had managed to miss Paul and had cannoned into the door-post.

"Stay in the corner," said Paul. "I'll deal with this nigger."

Lydia did as she was told, taking the chair with her, poised to ram it into Mr Ambrose's path if she got the chance. Mr Ambrose stood by the door as if planning his tactics. With a swiping gesture he swept the telephone off its shelf, ripping the cord from the wall. The snap of the trap seemed only part of the larger racket. He tossed the machine, uncaring, into a corner then began to move slowly, legs well apart, towards Paul. Paul backed away a bit more, watching him. Lydia sidled with Dickie and the chair towards the inner wall.

"Stay where you are," said Mr Ambrose. "Stay where you are."

His deep, gentle voice had acquired a sing-song note, almost like that of a medium in trance.

He feinted a couple of attacks, then moved in with a rush, but this time his left-handed swipe was also a feint; as Paul ducked from it he seemed to duck into Mr Ambrose's other fist as it came looping round in a low arc; but there was no smack of impact as Paul continued his movement and swivelled it to his left while his right arm, flung out at first seemingly for balance, blurred into a whip-like slash. By this time his whole body was close to the floor, twisting so that its energies all culminated in the karate blow that caught Mr Ambrose behind his right knee as Paul flowed away to his own left. The movement was dance-like, formal, and as Paul turned he struck a pose which, though poised and springy, had an artificial and theatrical quality like that of a performer finishing a turn in a ritual dance. And the two thin streaks of blood where the rings had grazed his cheek gave his white face the look of a dancer's mask.

Mr Ambrose had grunted when his blow had missed and the grunt had become a sort of snort when Paul hit his knee. He almost tumbled, clutched at the sink for support, then turned.

"You're thick, nigger," said Paul.

Mr Ambrose lurched towards him, but as soon as he put his weight on his right leg he halted. His head swung away from Paul and glared for an instant at Lydia. Then he was rushing towards her, clumsy now, but still very fast.

"Door, Dickie!" she shouted. "Run!"

She threw all her weight on the chair, whooshing it forwards. Mr Ambrose side-stepped but was no longer nimble enough. The seat of the chair caught him just below knee-level and he tumbled thuddingly forwards, grabbing as he fell. Her own impetus behind the chair carried her into his grasp. The huge hand closed on her fore-arm, locked, twisted. She shouted with pain and tried to drag away, but was forced to her knees beside the chair, with her shoulder-joint also twanging with agony. The chair jolted under an impact. Something gave in her shoulder, but then she was loose. She stood up, sobbing and blind with pain, shaking her head.

By the time the mists cleared the two men were locked together on the ground with Mr Ambrose underneath and gripping Paul round the shoulders with one arm. Lydia checked that Dickie was clear of the room, then ran for the knife-holder.

Her best big knife was a French one, with a dull triangular blade and a black wood handle. As she snatched it down she knew it was no use. She couldn't do it. She could not, even in hot blood, choose her spot on the brown flesh and drive the sharp blade home. She looked over her shoulder, hoping that Paul was winnning, but he wasn't. Mr Ambrose was still on his back. Paul had some sort of lock on his legs and had forced his left arm into a spread-eagled position. Mr Ambrose's turban had fallen off, revealing a bald scalp puckered with scars from some old beating-up. Without it he seemed not mysterious at all, no longer the swami of violence, not even Indian, just thug.

Now the whole fight was concentrated into small, shuddering spasms as Mr Ambrose strove to hug Paul's body down towards his own, which would break Paul's leverage on the arm he held. Paul needed his own left arm to force himself back against the gross muscles, but he was losing the fight. Both of them were gasping for breath. A grunt from Mr Ambrose broke the spell.

Lydia dropped the knife and snatched from the shelf beside the holder her blue flour-bin. She took the lid off, ran forward and tilted the flour over Mr Ambrose's face.

There were five pounds of wholemeal flour in the bin. She poured carefully, making sure the first cataract filled the open mouth, then concentrating on the nose and eyes as the big head threshed from side to side. Mr Ambrose began to choke, sending up white puffs of fine flour like the momentary eruptions of a volcano. When his mouth opened to choke Lydia poured more flour into it.

"Stand clear," snapped Paul.

She backed off. He convulsed and broke free, but instantly darted in again, seized a flapping wrist and with a violent jerk flipped Mr Ambrose clean over onto his face. As he leaped in to straddle the back his hand closed round the blubber-protected neck, felt, shifted, tightened. A thumb sank deep but precisely into a fold below the lobeless ear. Mr Ambrose bucked once, feebly, then lay still. Paul seemed to be counting to himself. At last he relaxed his grip and stood up. The blood from the two gashes in his cheek had streamed down his face and smeared his jersey.

"Have you killed him?" whispered Lydia.

Paul shook his head. He laughed in excited triumph.

"Perhaps you have," he said. "That's something they never taught us."

He sounded even faintly hysterical.

"Are you all right?" said Lydia. "Your cheek's a mess. Here's a clean cloth. I'd better go up to your room and ring the police. He bust my phone."

Paul stood, panting still with triumph. Suddenly he seemed to collect himself. He took the cloth from her and dabbed musingly at his cheek, thinking hard.

"Yes," he said. "I don't think you can keep the police out. That would look very strange. Got any cord? He'll come to in a minute."

Lydia always kept spare sash-cord. They used some to lash Mr Ambrose's arms and legs and then to strain the two sets of lashings together. While they were at it Mr Ambrose gasped and choked, then vomited hugely over the carpet. Paul dragged him clear of the mess.

"He'll do," he said. "Here's my key."

Dickie was waiting by the door of the hall, holding Mrs Pelletier's hand. They had the front door open and seemed ready to make a dash for it. Mrs Pumice was peering down from the hall landing with Trevor in her arms.

"It's all right," said Lydia. "We've managed to get him quiet. Thank you for looking after Dickie."

"He's been looking after me, more like," said Mrs Pelletier and burst into tears.

"Come up to Mrs Pumice's," said Lydia. "She'll make us all a cup of tea while I phone for the police. You come with me, Dickie."

She shook the two women off outside Mrs Pumice's rooms and went on up with Dickie to Paul's. She hadn't been in since he'd taken it, but she found it almost unaltered. Paul had imported no furniture of his own apart from a big hi-fi system. The ghost of Mrs Newbury seemed still to breathe from the room despite the new wallpaper. Lydia was astonished to find that she couldn't lift the phone to her mouth with her right hand, and that made her realise for the first time how much her shoulder was still hurting, and that in turn made her furious with the police at Sirdar Road when they were slow at grasping that there was any real urgency in the situation. At last the desk sergeant said "All right, madam, we'll have a couple of men round there as soon as poss."

"At once," snapped Lydia.

"Oh, very good, madam."

When she put the phone down she saw Dickie standing by the hi-fi control panel.

"Don't touch, darling."

"But it's supposed to be going. Always. I think it's this one."

He jabbed at one of the buttons.

"Get me a doctor," said Mr Ambrose's voice, thick and grunting, "I got that stuff in my lungs."

"Bother, that's the wrong one," said Dickie, pressing another. "That's right. They're going round now."

The tapes revolved in silence. Lydia stared at them, half hypnotised, half in a daze with the pain in her shoulder. She sat on the edge of Paul's bed and pulled Dickie against her with her good arm. Something was wrong, she felt. Paul had come down because of Dickie's SOS, in Morse. Her brain didn't begin to clear until she remembered that other set of tapes revolving in the musty dark beneath her own floorboards. In the silence a bell rang. She got up and pressed the stop button.

"Come on, darling," she said. "That's probably the police." It felt very strange to be running down stairs actually to welcome them.

26

THE OFFICES OF *Get Notted* were decorated in an amazing green and purple swirling design and smelt of dust, Nescafé and pot. A very dirty girl in the outer office was talking to a smart young negro but stopped the moment Lydia came in and stared at her as though she were an enemy.

"I think Tony's expecting me," Lydia said.

"Through there," said the girl, pointing.

Tony was in a tiny room which might have been a lavatory when the house had been a house instead of a bit of urban blight. He was typing very fast with two fingers.

"G-got something?" he said. "I'm s-sorry. It was m-much nastier than I expected. What happened."

"He dislocated my shoulder," said Lydia. "It'll be all right. I don't think I've got anything much use to you, but I want to listen to something and I can't at home. I hope you've got a spare machine."

She took the tape cannister out of her sling and put it on the table.

"Can d-do," said Tony. "What happened, though?"

"I'll tell you after I've heard this. It depends what's on it. It didn't really start until after most of the talking was over, but I've made some notes about that. OK?"

While Tony fetched and fixed the machine she sat brooding, going over for the tenth time every inch of the living-room in her night-and-day search for the hidden microphone. No new thought came, only the old anger and disgust making it impossible for her to think coherently. In her mind the microphone had become another fungus, creeping into her privacy, rotting her love and trust. Sometimes, if she closed her eyes and tried to relax, she saw against her eyelids a mycelium web of intricate wiring, fruiting all over with electronic sporophores. With another part of her mind she began to be afraid that the obsession might herald a breakdown of her own hitherto solid personality.

At last Tony pressed the "Play" button. There was a crash, then another as the telephone hit the wall. A short, shuffling pause. "Stay where you are," sang Mr Ambrose's voice, trance-toned. "Stay where you are."

"That's him," said Lydia.

"Ps-psychopath?" asked Tony.

The first flurry of thuds and grunts took less than fifteen seconds. Paul jeered briefly. More thuds. Lydia screamed to Dickie to run and now heard, for the first time, his footsteps going, but drowned suddenly by her own yelp of pain. Then more uninterpretable drummings and suddenly, and strangely ghastly even if you didn't know what it was, the sound of Mr Ambrose choking on flour. Proper voices began again, hers and Paul's, both almost in whispers. Then came Paul's Rupert-of-Hentzau laugh.

"That's something they never taught us."

"Who t-taught who?" said Tony.

"I don't know. Shh. We're coming to where I left the room . . . That's tying him up . . . and that's him being sick . . . now!"

But for a long time there was a silence, broken only by a few scratchings. Paul said, "Lie still, Jones," a couple of times.

"How did he know the n-name was Jones?" said Tony.

"I didn't tell him."

She waited, dreary with disappointment.

"Get me a doctor," said Mr Ambrose's voice, thick and grunting. "I got that stuff in my lungs."

"Nothing the prison doctor can't cope with," said Paul's voice.

"Now listen to me, Jones. You're going to go quietly and you're going to plead guilty."

"Bollocks to you, pansy-face," said Mr Ambrose.

"You are a very stupid man, Jones. Have you not asked yourself how there comes to be a man in this house able to deal with you?"

"I'd have got you if that bitch hadn't . . ."

"Shut up and listen. You belong to a little organisation which controls a few streets, and you think you're a king. Now you've run into a much bigger organisation. Much bigger. When your bosses learn about it, do you know what they'll do? They'll pull out. They'll know they can't fight us. They'll tear your guts out if you try."

"Bollocks."

"Jones, we have only recently become aware of you. Listen, you fool. We've had nine days since we learnt of your existence, and already my friends have photocopies of every file in that back room above the Organic Traveller Restaurant. You see? You understand what that means?"

Even through the scourer tin the grunt was audibly one of surprise.

"We know what happened at the Durley Bridge murder, Jones."

Silence.

"I think you have no previous convictions, Jones."

"That's right."

"Good. So you will plead guilty. You will explain that you are obsessed by this girl, Procne Newbury. You will say you resented Lady Timms's friendship with her, and lost your temper. You will get a short sentence, or possibly even a suspended sentence. OK?"

Grunt.

"In either case neither you nor your organisation will make the slightest move against Lady Timms or her family. You will move out of this street. You won't . . . that's the police. I'm going to untie you. You'll go quietly. You'll say you don't know what came over you. Right?"

"OK. I get the message. Thanks."

Feet on the stairs. Paul's voice saying "It's all right, he's coming round . . ."

"That's all," said Lydia. "You don't want to listen to me cleaning up the mess, do you?"

She snapped the machine off. The space round her seemed very small and drab. It wasn't just Tony's office, it was the space round her own life, and Richard's, and Dickie's. She felt very tired of fighting the oppressors, the corrupters, the enemies of freedom and love.

"G-God!" said Tony. "Who was the other bloke?"

She shook her head.

"Leave him alone," she said. "He's out of your league. I'm afraid there wasn't much there for you. I'm sorry. Do you know that restaurant?"

"Kn-know it! Best nut curry in t-t-ten miles!"

"I thought you weren't interested in food."

He almost strangled himself with sudden shyness as the

question of his own likes and dislikes was thus dragged to the surface. Lydia could only gather that she had been right, but that for semi-ideological reasons he felt a duty to be enthusiastic about certain vegetarian restaurants. They played the tape through again to let him recover himself.

"What's Durley Bridge?" she asked.

"Miscarriage of j-justice. Years ago. Wrong man hanged. They were still hanging 'em then."

"Do you want to do anything about it?"

"I d-don't know. It's slightly crank territory. Why?"

"Well, if there'd still been someone in prison, we'd have had to. But I'm very frightened of Mr Ambrose now. I'd like to think that somebody still had some sort of hold on him."

"This other bloke?"

"Leave him to me. I've got to go now, Tony. I've got to collect Dickie. Listen, when you do what you're going to do. whatever it is, you'll remember it's got people in it, won't you? People like me and Mrs Pumice and Procne Newbury. Sorry, I know that sounds rude. It's just I sometimes think that you get carried away and forget."

"N-not much chance of forgetting about you. Or P-P-P-Procne. D-different reasons, of course."

"Glad to hear it. Bye."

That evening Lydia sat in her chair. Richard was reading a dismal-looking volume on company law, an aspect of his studies that normally infuriated her, because she wasn't quite able to envisage an industrial society that could be run without it, though its detailed provisions seemed to her almost exclusively immoral. But to-night all her furies were concentrated on her search for the microphone. She had even drawn a careful grid of the room, to search through square by square, because anger had warped all the mental grids she had made.

Dickie came crawling from his improved hide-out behind the bookcase and in complete silence collected a spoon, a clothes-peg, a wooden skewer and two wooden play bricks. He sat on the floor with them, frowning and moving them about. Lydia went back to her grid. Click. Click-click. Click. Click-click-click. Click.

"Bother," said Dickie as his improvised Morse key fell to bits. "I wanted to practise."

"What's the matter, Liz?" said Richard. "You look as

though you'd just won an Aston Martin off a cornflake packet."

"Try using a big elastic band round the skewer and under the block and over the other end of the skewer," said Lydia. "Then you won't need the clothes peg. Can we have a drink, darling? And stop reading that horrible book and tell me I'm a nitwit."

"I can't do that without hearing the evidence."

"Let's have a drink, anyway."

"OK."

"Well," he said. "What about that evidence?"

Lydia was lying on the wrong side of the bed, because of her shoulder. It seemed very odd to be holding the wrong hand. Otherwise she felt marvellously relaxed, simply from having decided that there was no microphone in here, either.

"Darling, you won't laugh at me?" she said.

"I don't know until I see what you say. Sometimes I can't help it. You make me laugh. It's one of the reasons I love you."

"Pig. Do you think I'm really a lesbian?"

He didn't try very hard. She kicked him as he lay snorting.

"Damn you, I'm serious," she said.

"I know you are. It was just the surprise. You didn't give me a chance. You might have led up to it tactfully. If you'd given me a thousand guesses about what I wasn't allowed to laugh at, I'd still have . . . stop kicking me! I'm sure it's bad for your shoulder."

"It is, but it's worth it."

"All right, all right. My face is straight as the equator."

"That's only straight if you look at it sideways. Am I a lesbian?"

"Explain a bit more."

"I've had Austen here again, twice."

"How's he taking things?"

"Not very kindly. I mean, if you're baffled already, it must be a kind of insult to be confronted with fresh bafflements."

"So he accuses you of being a lesbian?"

"Not yet. But he's got on to the connection between Mr Ambrose and Procne, and he knows I've been to see Procne, and I've been wondering what sort of story Mr Ambrose is going to tell. I mean, all the evidence I've got is that he pretended that he was some sort of social worker and told me to stop seeing Procne. If he says he did it out of jealousy . . ."

"This is all very much up in the air, for you, Liz. It's the kind of thing I spend my days fretting about."

"No. It's practical. I mean, it's almost like a piece of machinery."

"Umm. What does Austen think?"

"I don't know. I think he still really wants to prove that Paul and I got together to kill Mrs N, because I wanted the money and he's my lover. That's why I redecorated the room as soon as I could, to cover fingerprints or something."

"Umm. How far could Ambrose take his story? Could he say that you attacked him out of sexual jealousy and that's what caused the mess in the room?"

"It won't wash. I made them fingerprint some of the things he'd smashed, and the telephone and so on."

"You are the original wonder-woman. Anyone else would have been running about screaming or filling themselves up with sedatives."

"I came damn near it."

"That's what's marvellous . . . but why are you bothered about this other thing? I mean it's . . ."

"Being crypto-butch?"

"What do *you* think, Liz. That's what matters."

"What do I *feel,* you mean? I don't think I feel . . . damn . . . you see, I suppose I keep my feelings so battened down that anything like that would come out all changed . . . but it was the first question Procne asked, Richie."

"What you're saying," said Richard in the finicky, thin voice he used for arguing out intimate teasers, "is that Procne–partly because she's a natural animal and partly because she's had a lot of experience–might instantly perceive in you a strand of which you are unaware. Perhaps Ambrose might see the same thing. You feel that this would account for your apparently low sex-drive and your obsession with Procne and your dislike of your father and your passion for doing what most people think of as masculine jobs at least as well as a man can. You are, of course, mainly worried about whether your desire to help Procne and your liking for her are based on this hidden drive. It is the secrecy and uncontrollability of the drive that frighten you. You wouldn't think it at all disreputable of someone else to be a lesbian, or of yourself, if you chose it consciously. But you are alarmed about the possibility of something inside you rebelling against your conscious choices."

"I hadn't thought it out as far as that. I expect you're right. Shall we talk about something else?"

"Not until I've told you I think it's all balls."

"But you don't *know*."

"Look, I do know some things. I've been through some experiences most people have missed out on. I've watched myself falling to bits and then being pieced together again. I know what's at the centre of my world. It's not one great abominable serpent stirring in its dreams that makes the surface heave and erupt. It's hundreds, thousands, of smaller creatures. They're all right, most of them, provided you let them bide where they were created to be. In their natural dark they are beautiful. So . . . Entia non simplificienda praeter naturam."

"Gentlemen don't talk Latin in bed. What does it mean?"

"Look how much it leaves out, the, er Ambrose hypothesis. Here's this girl who's a perfect symbol of all the things you really care about, an archetypal spoilt life. You've got a Pavlov reaction to that sort of thing. And, look, you aren't going to tell me that your fondness for that frightful old harridan Mrs Newbury was crypto-butch? You managed to like her a lot, in spite of everything, and naturally you transferred some of that to Procne . . . has Austen been to see her?"

"I think so. He went before, soon after we found the body, but she won't have told him anything. She'd just clam up, or lie. This time I think he asked her about me. Anyway he asked me about her, quite a bit, and why I wanted to visit her, and so on. He asked me the usual old questions about the will and the money, but he's getting very half-hearted about that, so I don't think she told him what I'd done."

"Pity. I wish she would. That'd take him off your back . . . Liz?"

"M?"

"Come a bit closer, if you can without hurting yourself. If I go threshing about I'll do your shoulder in, but I want to talk to you."

Moving carefully she achieved a position of surprising comfort, curled along his side with her head on his chest. He stroked her hair gently.

"You don't have to go on looking after me," he said.

"What do you mean?"

"I'm OK. I can take my share again."

"Of course you can. You do."

"Liar. Listen. I knew you were up to something, those days before Ambrose came. I knew it was important and you were scared. I decided quite consciously I wouldn't interfere —of course if I'd realised quite what you were up to, I *would* have, but . . . can you see that not interfering, going along, trusting, all that was much more of a strain than it would have been to ask? A year ago I couldn't have done it. Do you follow me that far?"

"Yes."

"Well, then, don't you think you ought to tell me what you're up to now? Lie still. Take it easy. That's better. Now . . ."

She told him, slowly, in a whisper. It took a lot of persuasion to make him let her go ahead with it.

27

"SORRY," said Lydia. "The Post Office engineer's just been to mend the phone and I wanted to try it out. Would you like a cup of coffee?"

"Indeed I would," said Paul. "I'll bring Dickie's transmitter down. I've patched it up."

"Oh, you *are* kind. He's out with a friend, but he'll be thrilled when he comes back."

No mucking about this time with fancy trip-cords. Lydia pulled the thread with her own fingers and heard the rat-trap snap. Then she put the kettle on. She was spooning Nescafé into mugs when his head poked round the door. The stitches down his cheek looked like two rows of little black ants.

"There," he said, putting the transmitter on the table. "It wasn't too bad, because I made it tough enough for a kid to knock about in the first place."

The kettle hummed to the boil.

"I thought it stood up remarkably well," said Lydia, pouring out the water and handing him his mug. "The other half was still working, wasn't it?"

He took the mug without a tremor and sat down, smiling.

"I'm sorry," he said. "I hope you'll forgive me. Do you want me to explain?"

"If you can. Where is it?"

He took from his pocket a delightful multiple tool which with a twist and a click became a small screwdriver. He undid two screws and swivelled the toy sideways on its base. The object that nestled in the cavity didn't look like a microphone at all.

"Is it transmitting now?" said Lydia.

"I hope so."

"Surely when Dickie pressed the key . . ."

"Yes, that was a mistake. I devised a beautifully efficient jamming system for my own transmitter."

Point one. If he was telling the truth, he hadn't heard the part of the conversation with Tony about her own bugging system. Curiously this slight gain made Lydia suddenly more tense. He seemed aware of the change.

"You *are* angry," he said. "I'm sorry. You see . . ."

"Switch that thing off first."

His eyebrows flickered up above his pale eyes. He tapped his teeth a couple of times with the screwdriver, then used it to disconnect the microphone.

"That's better," said Lydia. "Well?"

"Does Lalage talk to you about me?"

"Not much. We don't."

"I see . . . well . . . I'm sorry, this is rather embarrassing, because it's going to sound like a declaration of love, but it isn't."

"My heart is already possessed by Another."

He laughed and relaxed, or seemed to.

"I know," he said, "that's part of it. I asked about Lalage because she is often cross with me for talking about you so much. I have allowed myself to become somewhat obsessed with you . . ."

"Oh, that's rubbish."

"No, really, it's true. I mean . . ."

He gestured with absurd and theatrical penitence towards the little transmitter.

"Tell me something, since we're talking about truth," she said. "You remember you told Dickie a story about ambushing a slave-train? Were you really there?"

"Yes. Why?"

"But that happened in Estonia. It was nothing to do with Aakisen at all."

"I changed a few details. If I'd known Dickie then like I do now, I wouldn't have."

"I don't think you're a Liv at all."

"I am, Lydia."

"I think you were one of the guards."

"I'm too young. I was a child, on that train."

He looked broodingly at the little tool in his hands, clicked and twisted it and produced instead of the screwdriver blade a fine steel spike, with which he started to clean his nails, though it was not well adapted for the job.

"I *am* a Liv," he said quietly. "I was a small child when my father died in a political upheaval. My mother took me to Estonia, but she too had been a political activist, so later, at a time of . . . I was taught to call it 'normalisation' . . . she and I were included among dissident elements who were to be removed from Estonia to another part of Russia, for our own good and the good of Estonia. So that was how I came to watch the attack on the train. I saw it between the the slats of a cattle truck. They didn't attack our truck, because they were only interested in rescuing certain elements of their own organisation. Both sides were equally incompetent. Several people in my truck were wounded or killed by bullets from the partisans. On the other hand, the train was booby-trapped with explosives so that we could all be blown up if we were ambushed, but this the guards refused to do. I doubt whether many of those who escaped survived their exposure in the marshes. Some of us, it's true, also died of exposure during the journey, but not nearly so many, and when we reached our destination my mother was given work and I was allowed to live with her. I was also given an education, a very sound one. When my mother died, quite normally, of a brain tumour which would have happened under any political system, I was almost grown up. You see? I could not tell it like that to a child."

Lydia sipped her coffee and thought. Paul seemed to want to talk; she had expected to find him much more guarded and wary.

"About your education," she said. "You said something when I poured the flour into Mr Ambrose's mouth. You said 'That's something they never taught us.' Who were 'they'? What were you?"

He smiled at her and shook his head.

"Well, then," she said. "How did your father die? Did Count Linden kill him? Or have him killed?"

The smile seeped away.

"With a spike like that? Between the vertebrae?"

"You are being stupid, Lydia."

"I need to know. It's all right–I'm quite safe, I think. I've taken precautions. They'd work, I think."

"If you took them, they would. Of course."

"Well?"

"But you are still being stupid."

"What did you say to Mr Ambrose while I was out of the room?"

"Very little."

"You didn't promise him anything or threaten him with anything?"

"I told him to leave you alone."

"And then as soon as you get the chance you suggested to me that we should play down what he'd done, in our statements."

"I said I would, provided he agreed to leave you alone."

"And you think he'd stick to his side of it."

"He'd better."

"Paul . . ."

"No, it's my turn. I want to know what's on your mind. You've got some sort of theory, and you want me to confirm it. So you are trying to lead me into saying things which . . . I don't know. Wouldn't it be easier if you told me what you are worrying about and I told you whether you were right or wrong?"

"I'd rather you just answered my questions."

He shook his head, smiling again, but wary now.

"OK," said Lydia, after a pause. "I'll tell you some of the things that are worrying me. Mrs Newbury had a horror of drink, and a horror of empty bottles; and there ought to have been more fingerprints than just hers on the bottles. Then there was that night you made the transmitter and we went to the Russian Embassy—a man called Mr Diarghi told me some stuff about Count Linden and General Busch; afterwards Richard and I decided it was a rather obvious attempt to get me to refuse the renew the lease for the Consulate here, but then Mr Diarghi rang up to tell me he'd got his facts wrong. But he hadn't. I looked them up. Then you've been trained in unarmed combat, and you've got a natural entrée into the Liv set-up here because you own a ship rather mysteriously released by East Germany. Then there was Mrs Pumice's money—she dressed up to go and collect it, and she looked wildly excited, and she was obviously lying about where it came from—Don would never send her more than enough—and it meant that she didn't have to move rooms so you could have Mrs Newbury's room. And only a few days ago she came and told me (but she wasn't at all coherent) that she'd behaved badly about something to do with money in a way which she imagined had let me down. I believe she meant she'd taken that money from you and pretended it came from Don. Then there was Dr Ng coming to tell me that he'd come into money too, and wanted to leave, and he seemed pretty nervous about something. And Mr Obb had been talking to me the day before about renewing the lease, and hinting that he'd like to expand into Dr Ng's room; and he was also in a rather funny state, very nostalgic about Livonia and saying that he'd soon be tasting real *varosh* again, which he could only do if he went back to Livonia. And then there's this stupid business of putting a mike in here. I can't believe your explanation for that, I'm afraid . . ."

"It's true, Lydia."

". . . and then, when you were alone with Mr Ambrose you told him something quite different from what you said just now. Dickie switched your machine on and I heard."

"Not different," said Paul, accepting the half-lie. "Just more elaborate. I wanted to convince him that he'd suffer if he caused trouble."

"And you did that by telling him about the Organic Traveller Restaurant. That had to be true to be any good. How could you have known about it unless the rest of what you said was true?"

Paul hesitated between a frown and a smile, neither very convincing. His sigh was more real.

"I cannot see a pattern in these details," he said. "What is your theory?"

"Look, Paul, I'm not trying to find a victim. I don't believe in punishment. I think you killed Mrs Newbury and I think it was a wicked thing to do, but it's over now. If I could prove it, I'd still only want to use it if you started to mess around with the lives of the other people living in this house. That was your real reason for putting a microphone in here–you knew I discussed with Richard what I was going to do, and you needed to know everything about what the tenants were up to, and my plans for them, because I was in the process of moving everybody round to cope with the dry rot so there were all sorts of possibilities for intervening and gradually taking over the whole house, provided you knew in time. The sickening thing is that it's exactly the same technique that Mr Ambrose's organisation used when they wanted to take over a street. But all that's over now too, and the police seem to be easing up as well. It is over, isn't it, Paul? You haven't been working on Mrs Evans, for instance? I noticed she seems suddenly a bit shy of meeting me."

Paul stretched and almost yawned.

"And you still don't believe I'm fascinated by you," he said. "In the camp where we were taken by that train there was an old man with one leg, a cook. He'd been sent there from the South, almost into India. He used to tell us kids stories about the heroes of his tribe, little chiefs who had fought their big neighbours to hold onto their freedom, little kings with their own little courts who, for the sake of a few valleys, would hold off the armies of two empires which were trying to crush them from either side. And all this was five hundred years or more ago, but their names were still alive on the lips of an old cook sitting by a stove in Siberia. You are like one of those old heroes, Lydia. You have shown me something. I was taught that your view of the world was, at best, a mean type of self-deception, and now I know it is a noble type of self-deception. But even you, Lydia . . . can you explain to me the moral difference between the Russians using physical force to move people to a place which is more convenient for everybody, and you using economic force to move Mrs Pumice to a room which is more convenient for everybody?"

"Mrs Pumice matters to me as a person. I wouldn't have moved her against her will."

"But it was against her will, Lydia. As soon as she was presented with an adequate weapon, in this case a countervailing economic force, she refused to go. Those petty kings I was telling you about, they were admirable men, heroes, their names bring a brightness to the eyes of old men and children, but historically speaking all they achieved was to prolong for a couple of generations the miseries of their people."

"Talk about now, damn you!"

He gave a little silent snort of laughter and shook his head. His eyes too had a brightness in them. He was, Lydia suddenly saw, getting a kick out of the situation. She tried to make allowances for what she knew to be her own imperceptiveness about other people, and her tendency to think of them in types—the downtrodden, the oppressor, the insular housewife—perhaps, she realised, it was Mrs Newbury's blatancy of personality, breaking this barrier, that had made her seem so valuable to Lydia. But Paul . . . hitherto she had been thinking of him as the honed tip of a big machine for subduing people, and for killing those who couldn't be subdued. Now she saw there was something else, all sorts of complexities, and that his absurd romantic babble about dead princes wasn't merely a tease, though with part of his mind he was undoubtedly teasing her.

"You don't understand at all, do you?" he said.

"I understand that you're being exploited just as much as the rest of us," she said. "Only you think you aren't."

At last she had surprised him. It was as if a wrestler, poised and balanced, had felt something squirm under his foot.

"Somebody your side wanted a bloody great cock-up," said Lydia. "They decided you were the man to produce it. I wouldn't be at all surprised either if somebody in our own FO had guessed what was going on, and was just allowing you enough rope to hang yourself. There's plenty of that sort of bastard about."

"Now it's my turn not to understand at all."

"Think about it. You were sent here with instructions to infiltrate the Liv Consulate, which you did. This probably started as a minor operation, because it must have been preparing for several years, but when we expelled all those Russian agents it suddenly became more important, because it offered you the opportunity to create a fresh base . . ."

"Lydia, you are being absurd. You cannot seriously believe that if I were a Russian agent I would have jeopardised my task by an unnecessary killing. I say that since you seem to think . . ."

"You didn't even blink when I suggested first time that you'd killed her. And yes . . ."

"But there are plenty of large empty houses in London."

"Not with diplomatic immunity there aren't. When we expelled those Russians we expelled part of a big machine, which needed to work in a single establishment and was geared to having diplomatic immunity. Bosses like the ones you work for can't ever be quite happy about letting agents loose on their own in a capitalist society. Look how you love that car of yours. They must have thought this was a unique opportunity, with an agent already here and ready to start work."

"But don't you see, that would be risking this carefully planted agent?"

"I know. There are two things about that. The first is that I'm sure the original purpose in getting you here at all was to work to discredit the Livs, and if possible all the Baltic Consulates, with the British Government. Mr Diarghi was still working on that, as you learnt that first night you used the microphone—we were still sleeping in here then. When they decided on this new plan they said to themselves that they'd do it in such a way that if it went wrong it could always be blamed on the Livs. That's why you had to kill Mrs Newbury in just that way, so that if the murder was discovered it would turn out to be one of the ways in which Count Linden used to dispose of people. That's quite well known—there were even questions asked about it in Parliament. His motive would have been to provide a funeral for Aakisen. One thing puzzled me for a long time—the Russians must have known for ages that Aakisen was here, so why didn't they say who it was when his body was found? That would have completely discredited the Livs, even if they couldn't make the murder stick. Great national hero, supposed to be fighting and suffering behind the Iron Curtain, actually pottering around in Kensington making booze for a gang of ex-Nazis."

"Well, why?"

"Because this other scheme looked like coming off. I bet it was a near thing, but they let you go ahead in the end. They probably told themselves that even if they set up a spy nest here it would be blown in a few years but there would still be this bonus—the British would be pretty well bound to close the Consulate down then, and perhaps the other Baltic Consulates as well."

Paul shook his head.

"Too tricky," he said.

"Exactly," said Lydia. "But you were the agent. I said there were two reasons for the risk. I very much doubt whether you had permission from your bosses to kill Mrs Newbury. Under the new scheme you were supposed simply to infiltrate the Consulate, buy Obb if possible, and then expand by offering me more rent than my existing tenants were paying, buying them out where necessary. But you like risks. For instance even I could see that you enjoyed the idea of fighting Mr Ambrose . . ."

"It amuses me that you still call him Mr," said Paul. He did sound genuinely amused, too, as he twiddled the deadly little spike between finger and thumb. Perhaps he was enjoying this fight also—same arena, different opponent.

"I'm grateful to you for getting me out of that," said Lydia. "Even though I know you had to fight him. You couldn't have his crowd muscling in on your schemes. But what I was saying is that I think you enjoy risks—you actually need them. You have a romantic view of yourself. Perhaps you told yourself that it would be satisfying to have Count Linden falsely convicted of a murder done by the same means as the murder of your father. Revenge is a horribly romantic idea . . ."

"Horribly?"

"I think so. What you were saying just before about me being like a medieval prince–you meant that as a compliment, but it isn't one. I'm not like that and I don't want to be like that. But I think it is how you see yourself . . ."

"If so, we are the same kind of person. Because you *are* like that, Lydia."

"No we're not! You think you can use people. You don't think about them as people, individuals. There's just you and the rest of the world. Look how you used Mrs Newbury, just as if she'd been a handy piece of timber, one of those planks which are exactly the right shape for the job you have in hand . . . What you don't seem to realise, Paul, is that you're being used in exactly the same way . . ."

"But according to your theory I am acting beyond my instructions."

"That's right. But I bet there's somebody–somebody quite high up in the system–who guessed you would. I know the type. You get them on committees. They're professionals. They don't say much, they just cover their own position and let you go along into disaster. In my case it's usually because they like to see amateurs making a mess of things; but in yours it's because there's a lot of high-ups in your organisation who are bitterly opposed to the whole idea of détente between Russia and the West, and are perfectly happy to engineer a bloody great security row to try to spoil things, provided it doesn't endanger their own position . . . I bet you can guess just who it was, too."

He shook his head, still smiling, but his eyes were angry. Perhaps he really did want her admiration; he didn't mind her thinking of him as cruel and treacherous, but he did mind that she should think he could be used, like a tool, without free will.

"It is funny," he said. "I've always thought of you as a practical person, yet here you are indulging in this enormous fantasy, and it isn't even coherent. I'd expect you to make your fantasies work, at least; but here I am, in your fantasy, threshing around and causing chaos; and yet at the same time things were going very well according to another part of the fantasy. It was only by accident that Richard dug up Mrs Newbury's body."

"That must have been a shock."

"It was. I thought Busch was going to have a heart stoppage."

"But I think she would have got out somehow."

His eyebrows rose in apparently genuine surprise that she should admit to this pocket of blatant fantasy.

"I don't mean physically," she said. "But there are some people you can't ever quite bury, and she was one of those. I wish I thought Aakisen was another."

"This is an absurd situation. It is like a sort of French farce for moral philosophers. We both demand that the world shall breed heroes. You choose that terrible old woman to be yours. I choose you to be mine. Then you accuse me of killing your hero."

"But that's real. You did, didn't you? You brought her down the empty bottles, wiped clean of fingerprints, so that only hers would be on them. Count Linden makes the *varosh,* so taking his fingerprints off might throw suspicion on him. I don't know how you tricked her into drinking some vodka but I know how you laid her out, because I saw you do it to Mr Ambrose. Then you injected more alcohol into her blood stream while she was still alive. Then you killed her the way Linden used, with that spike. And last of all you faked the fall to cover any bruises. Bodies can bruise quite badly after death. I know that. Am I right?"

He looked at her, head cocked on one side, then sighed.

"Let us pursue the fantasy. Let us suppose I did. What then?"

"Don't let's start on that yet."

"No, that's what matters. You said so yourself. Everything else is over and done with, like my father's death. It doesn't matter any more."

"I didn't mean exactly that."

"That's exactly what you said, in effect," said Paul. He had left his head cocked in its teasing attitude, but she could hear in the dryness of his voice that he was only barely controlling some emotion, grief or anger.

"Let us suppose all your fantasy is true," he said. "Let us consider what the consequences are of your discovery. There would have to be some sort of bargain, for your silence. You would not expect an organisation which has invested time and effort and prestige into setting up the system you've imagined–you wouldn't expect them now simply to shrug and go away and not trouble you any more."

"No," said Lydia slowly. "I've thought about that. Organisations aren't machines, though. They consist of people, and people do have free will. I can't see any reason why you shouldn't simply stop working for them . . ."

"Defect?"

"Not if it means working for our side instead, in the same way. We're just as bad. But I'm sure you must have arranged some escape-routes for yourself—escapes from this whole world. If you took one of those, that'd be enough. All I'd need is proof that it was you who'd killed Mrs Newbury, and I'd only use it if somebody else was accused of killing her."

"Then you'd be an accessory after the fact."

"I've got to risk something, haven't I?"

At last he uncocked his head and leaned forward with the bright little spike dangling loose in his hand.

"Doesn't it strike you," he said, "that an organisation such as the one in your fantasy might consist of people who choose to work for it, of their own free will?"

"Yes, I'd thought of that too. In that case I'd still need proof, and I'd still only use it if I or my family or my tenants were threatened by your lot, or again if someone else were accused."

"Have you considered what would happen if my supposed organisation simply withdrew our protection from you, and informed Ambrose?"

"Yes. I'd have to find ways of fighting them off."

"You would lose."

"Still, I'd have to try."

"Suppose, in exchange for your silence and their continued protection this organisation were to accept a renewed lease for the Liv Consulate, including the floor where my room is?"

"No."

"Perhaps they might also be able to arrange protection for Miss Newbury when she comes to live here."

"No!"

"Why the emphasis?"

"You would want to use her. She'd become a tool, a thing, a prisoner again!"

"Lydia, where is the tape-recorder?"

He caught her completely off balance. She felt the blush encrimson her neck and face.

"I have realised almost since we started talking that there must be one," he said. "I think I understand you very well, Lydia. You like to achieve everything by yourself, without help. It is inconceivable that you would arrange for police witnesses."

He sat back, but seemed now not at all relaxed. There was something about the movement of his fingers, playing delicately but restlessly along the line of stitches on his cheek that reinforced Lydia's perception of sharp emotions reacting inside him, like chemicals in a retort—the old anger for the death of his father perhaps, and the stress of facing her and the deeper stress of facing the nature of his own actions, desire for her admiration, fear of his own masters—at any rate, she sensed, the reaction was coming to its climax. Perhaps it was not too late to persuade him to take one of the escape routes. At least she ought to try. The first essential, then, was to show that she trusted him.

"I'm sorry," she said. "You do see? I had to have a hostage. I can't get at the machine but I can switch off the mike."

She rose, crossed the room and kneeled by the sink. It was slightly tiresome having only one good hand to ease the mike out of the scourer can.

"Ingenious," he said, so close above her head that she jerked with surprise. "You even have holes in the lid to admit the sound. Do you mind if I check?"

She held the mike so that he could see her thumb sliding the switch into the "Off" position.

"Ah, the machine is under the floor, of course," he said.

"That's right. I . . ."

His hands closed round her neck. She jerked backwards, uselessly. Fury filled her, not at him but at the system that was making him do this, and all the wasted lives, including now her own. She threshed, consciously trying to make it hard for him to find the pressure point, consciously trying to mark her own body so that the struggle would show. Another Lydia, somewhere, longed to be still, to accept, to float into undreaming dark, but she was still writhing against his hard legs and the sink supports and the slithering linoleum when that dark came. In the last instant the hands round her neck, strong and precise, turned into her father's.

28

Procne's eyes were round as a baby's with horror and delight. Emotion made her seem yet more fragile and new-created, just as the first flush of growth in one warm March week draws out delicate-looking petals which ought to be completely tender but are, in fact, kitted out by evolution to stand the tortures of the equinox. In this mood she was very obviously the daughter of her mother.

"Je-sus!" she whispered. "You sure you're OK? I mean, you aren't used to it."

All round them the conversations with other prisoners created privacy.

"I was pretty stiff for a couple of days," admitted Lydia, not a little smug at her sudden entry into the great sisterhood of battered women. "My shoulder's not quite right yet, but otherwise I'm fine. Better than ever, in fact. I almost feel as if I'd been to a health farm and got toned up."

"I know what you mean. Sometimes a bashing does that to you, and sometimes it don't. But d'you think he'd actually have finished you off?"

"I don't know. That's one of the things that's been making me furious. I've been trying to see him but they won't let me. They say it's because it's security, but really it's that bloody little man Austen, getting his own back for my not telling him about who the man in the coffin was, and your money, and Mr Ambrose . . ."

"Lucky the police come just then. You ought to count your blessings, Liz."

"Lucky, my foot! They'd been watching me for weeks, following me about. I'd even spotted them a couple of times. And they'd got two men in Mrs Evans's spare room—I'd noticed she was looking a bit nervous—I think that's what made me crossest of all, them frightening one of my own tenants into hiding them so that they could catch me and Paul making love, or discussing how we'd murdered your mother, or something, and tiptoeing down and standing outside my door to eavesdrop . . ."

"But honest, Liz, you're lucky they did, or they wouldn't of been there to rush in and haul him off of you. I don't see how you can't see it!"

Lydia laughed.

"That's what Richard says," she said. "*His* chief interest—no, that's not fair, I mean his chief interest after he'd got over worrying about me—is whether the Russians will try to exchange Paul . . ."

"They can't! Not after he's been done for murder!"

"I don't know whether the police can make that stick," said Lydia. "And if they don't there's not much else he can be charged with."

"Bashing you, but—don't tell me—you're not going to bring charges. Honest, Liz, you're just as stupid as the rest of us."

"I expect so. I mean, what's the point? If they don't charge him with murder or something else they'll deport him. That clears him out of *our* lives . . ."

"You'll be sorry, won't you? You liked him?"

"I liked his company. I hated the things he did. And I can't keep them separate. Richard says he has a psychopathic personality. Richard knew quite a lot of spies at one time, and he says four-fifths of them were nut cases. What worries me is that sometimes I'm afraid Dickie's going to grow up like Paul—he lives such a fantasy life. He's inconsolable, poor little brat . . ."

"You didn't tell him!"

"Richard did, as much as he could understand. I shirked it. I was so frightened he'd feel it was my fault, and never forgive me. You see, he'd only just had this other shock of seeing Mr Ambrose beat me up and Paul coming and rescuing me . . ."

Procne frowned, suffering Dickie's lost illusions, his betraying hero. Her sympathy was easy, perhaps even facile, but for the moment it filled her being. Lydia waited for it to seep away, not wanting to mar in any way the news she had been saving up for towards the end of her visit.

"Do you know a vegetarian restaurant called The Organic Traveller?" she said at last.

"I been there," said Procne, suddenly very cautious.

"Well, rather a curious thing happened. While I was talking to Paul I mentioned the name, so it was on my tape which the police took. Besides, they may have heard it when they were listening outside the door. Mr Ambrose's organisation kept their records above the restaurant—I don't know whether you knew?"

Procne shook her head, still wary.

"Well there must have been a leak from the police station, because the organisation started moving their files out. But earlier I'd told a friend of mine about this restaurant, and he works for a local Marxist group . . ."

"Honest, Liz, your friends!"

"He's all right, I think. Listen. He'd been keeping an eye on the place. He didn't explain quite how it happened. I think he'd been planning to fake up a race riot in the restaurant and then hope somehow to get upstairs, but when the van was almost loaded he took his chance—his lot are very efficient—they had a couple of hundred blacks and whites battling up and down in the street—it was all in the papers next day, including that some of the rioters stole a van belonging to a local businessman. My friend's lot are infiltrated by the police of course, so they didn't have very long, but they managed to photocopy a lot of the documents and send them to the *Sunday Times* and the Minister of the Environment and the Director of Public Prosecutions and people like that."

Procne looked appalled.

"Nothing about me!" she whispered. "Not all over again!"

"My friend brought me your file. Some of the others wanted to keep it, but he wouldn't let them even copy it. He's a better bloke than I thought. I burnt it. I hope you don't mind."

"Mind! Me mind! Liz, that's the greatest thing that ever happened! Say, you didn't read it, did you?"

"No. I should have, perhaps, in case there was anything in it that would have been useful to you, but . . . you know, Richard's got about ninety-nine theories about friendship, and one of them is that you've got to accept the face people show you, and not keep looking for faces they don't want you to see. So . . ."

"I only got just the one face," said Procne. "I don't know what you mean, really. This is me."

She looked at Lydia, earnest and puzzled, but also somehow as though she were looking at her own face in a mirror, deciding on the day's make-up. Lydia looked back, thinking that perhaps it was true, perhaps that was the secret of her extraordinary appeal. They both smiled together.

"You know, I feel extraordinarily peaceful," said Lydia. "I feel as though I'd spent the past few weeks walking down a narrow passage whose walls kept getting closer and closer together, all those people trying to lean on me and use me. But now I'm out in the open again."

"Yes, you look like a cat what's . . . oh, Liz, does that mean you've started your baby? My, you can blush, can't you?"

"Hell! The answer is I don't know. I hope so. I've missed a period and I'm pretty regular usually, but it might have been the shock of getting myself strangled and all that."

"Well, where there's hope there's life, like Mum used to say. D'you remember how she used to get that sort of thing inside out?"

"She once told me that wild horses on bended knees wouldn't drag her into some store or other."

"Selfridge's, I bet. She had a thing about Selfridge's, going back to . . ."

They talked, until it was time for Lydia to leave, about that rather awful, rather ordinary old woman who had had so much life in her that even now the memory of her seemed more solid and immediate than any meeting with some living citizen.

"That's what I can't forgive Paul," said Lydia. "Just using her like that, snuffing her out, not knowing what he was doing."

"Don't you worry," said Procne. "He did her a good turn, I been thinking. I mean, where she is now, if she knows it'll be a big thrill, won't it, being a murder victim; even up there there's not a lot of them can say that. And if she don't know, it's no skin off *her* nose, is it? She'd had a smashing life, her way. I mean there wasn't much to it, but she made it smashing, didn't she?"

"Yes. I suppose that's what matters."

"Course it is."

Praise

by *New York Times*

"This book starts ou
Marie Force is
will be on my must-read list in the future."
—Dee Dailey, reviewer, *The Romance Studio* on *Fatal Affair*

"This is a suspense that never stops.
Add it to your book list today."
—*NightOwlRomance.com* (Top pick)

"Marie Force's second novel in the Fatal series is an outstanding romantic suspense in its own right; that it follows the fantastic first installment only sweetens the read."
—*RT Book Reviews* (4.5 stars) on *Fatal Justice*

"The author makes the reader part of the action, effortlessly weaving the world of politics and murder in which the characters come alive on the pages. The plot was addictive and scandalous with so many family secrets... Drama, passion, suspense—*Fatal Affair* has it all!"
—*Book Junkie*

"Force's skill is also evident in the way that she develops the characters, from the murdered and mutilated senator to the detective and chief of staff who are trying to solve the case. The heroine, Sam, is especially complex and her secrets add depth to this mystery."
—*RT Book Reviews* (4.5 stars) on *Fatal Affair*

Also available from Marie Force and Carina Press

FATAL AFFAIR
FATAL JUSTICE
FATAL DESTINY
FATAL FLAW
FATAL DECEPTION
FATAL MISTAKE
FATAL JEOPARDY

And watch for FATAL SCANDAL coming January 2015 from Marie Force and Carina Press.

MARIE FORCE

FATAL CONSEQUENCES

INCLUDES THE BONUS NOVELLA *FATAL DESTINY*

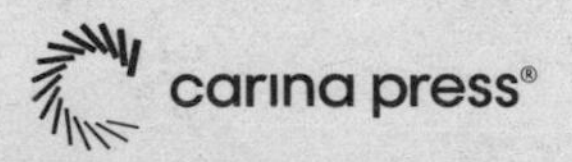

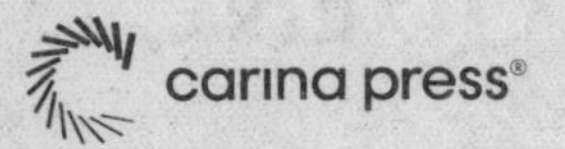

Recycling programs for this product may not exist in your area.

ISBN-13: 978-0-373-00223-8

This edition published by arrangement with Harlequin Books S.A.

www.CarinaPress.com

Printed in U.S.A.

CONTENTS

Acknowledgments

First and foremost to my family: Dan, Emily and Jake, who accommodate my writing and ignore my manic mumblings, and my dad, who follows all the ups and downs. My mates in the Lair: Kendra, Cindy, Cheryl and Linda, you keep me sane and laughing—thank you! Thanks to all my buddies on Facebook who cheered me on as I wrote this book—the first one I've written to deadline—your support and encouragement made a big difference. To Mitchell Waldman, thank you for the help with child custody legalities. Christopher Burnette astutely answered questions on forensics and lab test timing. Newport, RI Police Lt. Russell Hayes is my go-to guy for all things police-related, and he's always there with an answer that gives me ideas for new directions. Thank you, Russ! I spent a memorable evening scouting wedding locations in Washington with my friends Christina Camara and Julie Cupp, as well as my cousin, Steven Lopes. Thanks, guys, it was fun playing pretend, and I'm delighted with what we decided on for Sam and Nick. I'm thrilled—and lucky—to have three beta readers who love Sam and Nick as much as I do: Alyson Hackett, Ronlyn Howe and Kara Conrad. You ladies are the best and I can't thank you enough for the astute comments and insight. My editor, Jessica Schulte, has been the guiding hand behind this series, and I appreciate all the TLC she has shown to Sam, Nick and me. To everyone at Carina Press and Harlequin, your support of the Fatal Series means the world to me. I can't thank you all enough.

FATAL CONSEQUENCES

For my daughter, Emily: Happy Sweet Sixteen.
You had me at hello.

ONE

"I'LL BET THERE was less red at the St. Valentine's Day Massacre," Lt. Sam Holland said as she stood in the doorway to the Fraternal Order of Police Hall and surveyed the scene before her.

"Wow." Senator Nick Cappuano took a long look around the big room. "*Wow.*"

Sam's sister Tracy joined them. "Oh. My. God. Celia and her friends went freaking *nuts* with the hearts and flowers."

Every square inch of the large room was decorated with red flowers, balloons and streamers.

"I've seen murders that were less bloody than this reception," Sam said.

"It is her first wedding," Nick reminded them. "She has the right to go all out."

Sam wondered if he'd expect his first wedding to be as elaborate. She'd been there, done that and had no desire to do it again. But for him…Well, for him she'd do just about anything. However, she was drawing the line at hearts and flowers. She had a reputation to uphold.

"Holy shit," Sam's sister Angela said when she joined them. "Check out the ice sculpture. Jesus."

"Cupid, not Jesus," Nick said, smiling at the horror on the sisters' faces. "Be nice, you guys. Celia is so excited."

"I had no idea she had this in her." Sam battled her way through the streamers and balloon ribbons to get to the bar. She needed a drink, and she needed it now.

"You'd be well advised to keep her far, *far* away from your wedding," Tracy said.

"No kidding." Sam downed a glass of pinot grigio and gestured for another. "How much of this do you suppose Dad knew about?"

"None of it," Angela said, smirking.

"He's a smart man," Nick said, "so I'm sure he told her to do whatever she wanted."

"Is that what a smart man does?" Sam asked, raising an eyebrow.

"Not *this* smart man. If I did that, we'd end up with beer and peanuts at O'Leary's."

"And that would be bad how exactly?"

Nick bent to kiss her. "We can do better."

Before Sam could tell him she didn't want to do better than O'Leary's, they were interrupted by the arrival of the bride and groom. Sam couldn't deny that her father and his new wife radiated happiness. How could Sam begrudge the woman who had married her paralyzed father the reception of her dreams? Her own wedding, Sam vowed silently, would be as low-key as she could possibly make it. In fact, eloping was starting to look *really* good to her.

DRESSED IN RED satin bridesmaid gowns, Celia's new stepdaughters stood faithfully by her side while she cut the heart-shaped red velvet cake and fed a piece to her groom. They endured the speeches and the toasts and smiled for no fewer than a thousand photographs. The ultimate insult, however, still awaited them.

"She can't make us," Tracy said when the DJ asked the sisters, their husbands and fiancé to come to the dance floor.

"Dad can make us," Angela said. "He still has that *look*. You know the one I mean."

"I've never wanted to be called to a murder scene more than I do right now," Sam said through gritted teeth.

"Ladies," Nick said with that charming smile he'd been using all day to manage them, "it's one dance, and then you're done."

"I know I speak for my sisters when I tell you to shut up and stop defending Valentine's Day Bridezilla," Sam said.

Nick laughed at the dismay on their faces as the first notes of Bette Midler's "The Rose" filled the room.

"I'm going to puke in my shoes," Angela muttered. Three-and-a-half months pregnant with her second child, she'd been green for weeks.

"Those are *my* Jimmy Choos," Sam reminded her, "and if you puke on them, I'll kill you."

Angela scowled at her. "Would you rather I puked on those?" She nodded to the Manolos that Nick had bought Sam to wear the night they got engaged.

Sam glanced down at the precious shoes. "Don't even think about it."

"Mine are from Payless," Tracy said. "Puke away."

Nick took Sam's hand as Angela's husband Spencer and Tracy's husband Mike did the same with their reluctant wives. The guys made for a dashing trio in the tuxedos they'd worn as Skip's groomsmen.

Across the room, Sam's partner, Detective Freddie Cruz, Detective Tommy "Gonzo" Gonzales and some of her other detectives were sharing a laugh that was—no doubt—at her expense. She'd think of some way to punish them on their next shift. It didn't escape her notice that Freddie had brought his girlfriend Elin Svendsen or that Gonzo was there with Nick's chief of staff Christina

Billings. Sam didn't approve of either relationship, but no one had bothered to ask her opinion.

When she realized Nick wasn't going to let her escape the mandatory dance, Sam gave up the fight. Besides, being pressed against his muscular chest was one of her favorite places to be, so she may as well enjoy this obligatory moment.

At six foot four, he was one of the few people in her life who towered over her. Those broad shoulders, the chocolate-brown hair that curled at the ends, amazing hazel eyes, smooth olive-toned skin…Sam had never known a sexier guy. And that mouth, *whoa.* Speaking of sexy…

"There," Nick said, apparently sensing her capitulation. "Isn't that better?"

"I'm still mad at you."

"You can punish me later." Bringing his lips in close to her ear, he added, "All night long."

Sam smiled at his softly spoken words. She didn't want to because he was making her dance to the cheesiest, most clichéd song her stepmother could've possibly chosen. But let's face it, she was slow dancing with Nick, and that definitely went a long way toward making things all better.

Nick's lovely chest ruined the moment by vibrating against her cheek.

"Ignore it," he said of the BlackBerry he'd stashed in his chest pocket. "No phones today."

"You won't hear me arguing." They still hadn't managed a full day off together in the nearly two months since they'd reconnected after U.S. Senator John O'Connor's murder just before Christmas. Six years after a memorable one-night stand, they'd picked up right where they'd left off. Nick had since been tapped to complete the last year of John's term in the Senate and was now in the midst of the campaign to win the seat on his own in November. They'd looked forward to this day off for weeks and had big plans for a romantic early Valentine's Day celebration after the wedding.

Nick's phone buzzed again. "Ignore," he said more forcefully this time.

"What if it's your dad or there's some sort of disaster in Virginia? You can't just ignore it."

"Yes, I can." With all the campaigning he'd been doing lately, she knew he needed the day off even more than she did but if there was one thing Sam couldn't stand, it was a ringing phone.

"*Nick.*"

"*Sam.*"

She worked her hand into his jacket to retrieve the buzzing phone. "Henry Lightfeather," she read off the screen. Even she recognized the name of the senior senator from Arizona.

"Work." Nick tightened his arms around her. "He can wait until Monday."

"He's called twice."

"He can *wait.*"

"There's a voice mail message. Aren't you curious?"

"Okay, it's official—you're an even bigger workaholic than I am."

"Not possible. Hey, he sent a text—'Call me, Nick. 911.'"

Nick stopped dancing and took the phone from her. "Now you've gone and done it," he said with a scowl.

"Done what?"

"If you had ignored it, I never would've seen that text. Now I have no choice but to call him."

She grinned at him. "At least we can escape this nightmare dance before the seed becomes a rose."

Phone pressed to his ear, Nick stalked off the dance floor. Halfway across the room, he stopped, turned and signaled to Sam.

Curious, she walked over to join him.

"He's actually looking for you, Lieutenant." Nick handed the phone to Sam and went to have a word with Skip and Celia.

"Senator," Sam said. "This is Sam Holland. What can I do for you?"

"I need you to come here," Lightfeather said. He sounded rattled and undone. "Right now. I think she might be dead. I need you. Just you. No other cops."

"Who's dead?"

"Regina." His voice broke. "Beautiful Regina."

"How can you tell she's dead?"

"There's so much blood, and she's cold."

"Where are you, Senator?"

He rattled off an address in Columbia Heights, a culturally diverse neighborhood located in the city's northwestern corner.

"I'm on my way. Don't touch her. Don't touch anything. Do you understand?"

"Yes," he said, his voice breaking. "Hurry."

After a quick trip to Nick's house so Sam could exchange the red satin bridesmaid monstrosity for jeans, Nick drove her from Capitol Hill to Columbia Heights. As he dodged the black BMW through traffic, Sam wondered when he'd started driving like a cop and how she'd failed to notice.

"What do you know about him?" she asked.

"He's a friend—one of the first to welcome me to the Senate, the first to tell me what I really needed to know, the first to offer his help."

"And?"

"And what?"

"What else do you know that you're not sure you should tell me in light of current events?"

"There are times when it's terribly annoying that you know me so well."

"Likewise. Now start talking."

He glanced over at her. "I think he might be living in his office."

"Why do you say that?"

"I've seen him there at odd hours in sweats and T-shirts. He showers in the gym, but I've never seen him work out."

"If you're there at odd hours, why can't he be?"

"It doesn't seem like he's actually working, you know? I hadn't really given it all that much thought, to be honest, until right now."

"Why would he be living in his office?"

"A lot of people in Congress struggle to support two places—one in their home state and another here. As we both know, it's not cheap to live around here, and despite what people think, not everyone in politics is independently wealthy."

"Does he have a family?"

"A wife back in Sedona and five children, all adopted, a few of them special-needs."

"That could be why he doesn't have the money for an apartment in Washington."

"Wouldn't surprise me."

"He sounds like a nice guy."

"He is."

"So what's he doing with a dead woman in Columbia Heights?"

"I have no idea."

Covered in blood, Henry waited for them on the landing outside Regina's third-floor apartment. Sam took a quick inventory of the senator: medium build, dark complexion, jet-black hair and eyes. He was younger than he appeared on television—late forties, early fifties at most.

"Hurry," he said when he saw them coming. "This way." Henry grabbed Sam's arm and all but dragged her into a shabby apartment. She let him lead her only because he was Nick's friend. Anyone else would have a broken hand by now. "In the bedroom."

Regina lay naked on the floor in two pools of blood, one by her head, and the other between her legs. Her throat had been slit from ear to ear. She had long dark hair, a slender build, small but firm breasts and smooth skin that was marred only by a few stretch marks on her belly, indication that she'd probably birthed at least one child or lost a tremendous amount of weight. Based on her slender body, Sam was betting on the baby. She judged the victim to be in her mid-thirties and was able to see past all the blood to determine she'd been quite beautiful.

When Nick saw the bloody scene, he gasped but at least he didn't seem faint as he had at previous crime scenes. The more time he spent with her, the more used to such things he seemed to become. Sam wasn't sure if that was a good or bad thing.

Next to Sam, Henry broke down as he stared at the dead woman.

"How do you know her, Senator?" Sam asked Henry.

He was crying so hard he couldn't reply.

"She works for the company that cleans the Capitol," Nick said, his tone flat with shock. Sam had heard that tone far too often after the murders of Nick's friends John O'Connor and Julian Sinclair.

"Did you know her?" Sam asked Nick.

"I've seen her around."

She sensed there was more to it than that, but she decided to wait until they were alone to grill him further. To Henry, she said, "Senator, I need to call this in."

"I have to go," he said, panicked. "I can't be here when the police come."

"I'm afraid you'll have to stay, sir. You're a material witness at the very least." She glanced at his blood-covered dress shirt and then up at his dark eyes.

"At the very least? What does that mean?"

Well aware of the power this man yielded on Capitol Hill, Sam swallowed hard. "I have no way to know whether or not you're responsible for this without investigating further."

Outrage mixed with grief as Henry stared at her. "I called you because I thought you could help me! We have to find the person who did this to her!" He looked imploringly at Nick. "Tell her. You know me, Nick. You know I couldn't have done something like this!"

To his credit, Nick said nothing.

"I can't believe this! *You actually think I could've done this to her?*" He swiped ferociously at the tears cascading down his face.

She fixed her eyes on his bloodstained shirt. "I need to rule you out as a suspect. You can either help or hinder that process, but either way, you're not going anywhere, Senator. Do you understand?"

"Yeah," he said bitterly. "I get it."

"I'd like you both to move to the hallway." After they stepped out of the room, Sam reached for her cell phone. "This is Lieutenant Holland. I need to report a homicide in Columbia Heights."

TWO

"I'D PLACE TIME of death at around five o'clock," said Dr. Lindsey McNamara, chief medical examiner. Due to the senator's possible involvement, Sam had requested Lindsey be called to the scene. Once again they had a powder keg of a case on their hands, and Sam was leaving nothing to chance.

She glanced at her watch. It was now nine o'clock, and a long night lay ahead of them—not at all the romantic evening she and Nick had planned. Sam experienced a pang of remorse. They had so little time together that she hated to sacrifice a minute of it. But when she glanced at Regina Argueta de Castro on the floor, she was reminded that some things were more important.

"Sexually assaulted," Lindsey said as she turned the body. Bruises marked her back and buttocks. "He was rough with her, the poor thing."

Lindsey's empathetic nature was another reason Sam wanted her on the case. Regina would get far more compassion from Lindsey than she would from some of the deputy medical examiners.

While Lindsey completed her initial investigation, Sam took more photos before turning things over to the crime scene detectives who would sift through every item in the sparsely furnished apartment. Sam instructed the responding patrol officers to knock on neighboring doors to see if anyone had heard a disturbance coming from apartment 3B earlier in the evening.

When she was done giving orders, she joined Nick and Henry in the hallway. Nick leaned against the wall while Henry sat on the floor, holding his head in his hands. His shoulders were stooped with exhaustion and grief. Sam glanced at Nick, taking comfort in his steady presence. Whatever needed to be done, he'd be right there with her. For a woman who'd been so fiercely independent most of her life, she was still amazed by how much she'd come to depend on him in such a short time together.

"Senator," she said to Henry. "I have some questions for you, and I'd like to conduct the interview downtown."

He glanced up at her, his face filled with despair. "Am I under arrest?"

"Not at this time. However, we need to clear up a few things and until we do, we'll need to retain you."

"Do I need a lawyer?"

"That's entirely up to you, but I'd recommend that you cooperate as much as possible at this point so we can figure out what happened to Regina. I have the authority to retain you for twenty-four hours without charging you. In that time, I'm required to produce enough evidence to charge you with a crime. If I fail to do that, I'll release you. Do you understand?"

Nodding, he ran a trembling hand through his silky dark hair. "I want to find the person who did this to her." He glanced up at Sam. "Will it be all over the media that you're retaining me?

"We'll do our best to keep it quiet for now, but I can only do so much. It's a safe bet that the media will catch wind of your involvement. Even if we don't file charges, you found the woman who cleans your office dead in her apartment."

Sam looked at Nick. His handsome face was set in an unreadable expression, but she had no doubt he was reliving the worst day of his life—when he'd found his boss and best friend dead in his apartment.

Releasing a resigned sigh, Henry stood up. "Would it be possible to call my wife? I have to talk to her before this is all over the news."

"I'll need to take a statement from you first, but after that I'll see what I can do."

Out of deference to his position and friendship with Nick, Sam didn't cuff Lightfeather, even though she rarely transported anyone without handcuffs. Once they had Henry settled in the backseat of the car, Nick rested his hand on Sam's arm to stop her.

She looked up to find him looking troubled. "What is it?"

"It may be nothing."

"Or it may be everything. Just tell me, and I'll figure out which it is."

"I think they might've been involved."

"Why do you say that?"

"Remember I told you I'd seen him in his office, looking relaxed and very casual at odd hours?"

Sam nodded.

"One time, recently, she was there with him. I stopped by his office on my way out late one night. The two of them were having a glass of wine. She was wearing the cleaning crew uniform, but she was sitting on his sofa with her feet up. They seemed to be having a grand old time. When I came in, she got this really guilty look on her face and darted out of there like I'd caught them naked or something."

"What did he say?"

"He shrugged it off and said she looked like she needed a drink."

"Did he look like he'd been caught doing something he shouldn't be doing?"

Nick thought about that for a minute and then shook his head. "He was his usual cool, collected self."

"So why do you think they were involved?"

"I only saw them unguarded for a minute, but there was something going on—something more than a glass of wine. I'm sure of it."

"I might need you to make a formal statement about what you saw that night. Would you be willing?"

He winced. "Could we wait and see if you need it?"

Sam studied that handsome, earnest face she loved so much. He'd been through the wringer lately with two close friends murdered in the scope of weeks. She'd do anything she could to spare him more pain. "Yeah, we can do that. Want me to drop you off at home before I go to HQ? Could be a long night."

"I'll hang with you in case you need me."

Sam smiled. "I always need you."

"That's why I'm sticking with you." He stole a quick kiss and laughed at her reaction. She hated his public displays of affection, especially when other cops were around, which of course was why he loved to do it.

"Give me a minute to report in to Malone." She drew her cell phone from her coat pocket. The frigid air stole the breath from her lungs as she paced the sidewalk and waited for her mentor, Detective Captain Malone, to pick up.

"Lieutenant," he said, sounding slightly buzzed. "What had you hightailing it out of your father's wedding so quickly?"

"A little thing called murder."

She could picture him sitting up straighter at that news. "What've you got?"

Sam relayed what she knew thus far and told him she had taken the senator into custody but had not arrested him.

"What's in the water lately? All these powerful people involved in murders."

"I wish I knew. It's gonna be another hot one."

"At least this one doesn't involve your personal life."

"Well," Sam said, grimacing. "It could. Lightfeather is a friend of Nick's."

"Of course he is," Malone said.

Sam laughed. "Who isn't, right?"

"No kidding. The guy's nothing if not well connected. Want me to send over some of the A-team?"

"Nah, I didn't call them because I knew they'd been partying all day. Let them have their night off. I'll do what I can tonight, and then we'll hit it hard in the morning."

"Sounds good. I'll let them know they have a curfew."

"I'm sure they'll appreciate that. How's the groom holding up?"

"His new wife took him home about an hour ago. He was starting to get a little tired, but it was a good day for him. Nice to see him so happy."

"Yeah." After all her father had been through with her mother leaving him for another man and then the shooting that had left him a quadriplegic, Sam couldn't agree more.

"You and Cruz are still working the angle on the stuff you found in Reese's house, right?"

"We're trying." Every time they had a lead in her father's two-year-old unsolved shooting, they hit a new roadblock. "We're having trouble tracking down the guy who rented the house before Reese. We can't find the landlord so we can't even get a name. The neighbors claim to not remember who lived there before Reese. We think they're stonewalling us for some reason."

"Don't give up," Malone said. "If you keep asking the questions, eventually you'll get an answer."

"I sure hope you're right." After Clarence Reese murdered his family, detectives had uncovered newspaper clippings and photographs related to Skip Holland's shooting. Reese had claimed the box of clippings belonged to the former tenant who had never come back to get some of the things he'd left behind. Now, if they could just figure out *who* the former tenant was. Sam couldn't bear the frustration of being unable to solve the most important case of her career. It didn't help that one high-profile murder case after another sucked up all the time she wanted to be spending on her father's case.

"Keep me posted on the senator and the dead woman."

"I'm going to retain him at least until the morning to confirm his alibi, so you might want to let the chief know that the senior senator from Arizona will be our guest in the city jail for the evening."

Malone snickered at her choice of words. "Will do."

DETECTIVE FREDDIE CRUZ helped his girlfriend Elin Svendsen into his dilapidated Mustang and caught a glimpse of long, muscular leg as she settled herself into the seat. Imagining that long leg wrapped around him had his cock surging with anticipation. But then he remembered his mother, sick at home with the flu, and decided to go by and check on her before he attended to more pressing concerns.

The instant he slid into the driver's seat Elin's tongue was in his mouth and her hand was cupping his balls. Freddie wrapped his arm around her and gave into the carnal kiss for several heated minutes. She had him on the verge of a fast and embarrassing release when he once again thought of his sick mother.

Moaning with frustration, he pulled himself free of Elin's embrace. "I have to go by my mother's before we go home."

"Why?" Her fingers trailed up and down his inner thigh, and he grabbed her hand before she could reach her destination. "We were just there before the wedding."

"That was hours ago, and she's really sick."

Elin's face twisted into a petulant pout. "Doesn't she have any friends who can check on her?"

"Sure she does, but she only has one son."

"Who is a total mama's boy."

"Guilty as charged. She did everything in the world for me all my life, and there's nothing I wouldn't do for her. You'd better get used to that." The animosity between his mother and Elin had escalated over the last few weeks, which was the only black spot on an otherwise satisfying time in Freddie's life. After holding true to a vow of celibacy for twenty-nine long years, he was enjoying the hell out of his first sexual relationship—except for the fact that his beloved mother hated his new girlfriend and did very little to hide her contempt.

When he'd picked up Elin earlier and gotten his first glimpse of a black dress cut low enough that the cupid tattoo on her left breast was visible, he knew he would be the envy of all his cop friends at Skip's wedding. Sure enough, he'd gotten lots of nudges and winks from the guys who'd barely tried to hide the fact that they were lusting after *his* girl. Freddie loved that she was his and his alone. If only he could convince his mother to give Elin a chance. That was the only thing standing between him and true happiness. Well, that and the fact that his partner Sam could barely tolerate Elin, either. Two of the most important women in his life didn't much care for the third one, and their disapproval was taking something away from his enjoyment of the relationship. How he wished he could be the type of guy who could tell his mother and Sam to piss off, but that was *so* not him. It mattered that they disapproved, and he hated himself for letting it get to him.

He pulled up in front of his mother's apartment building, located just a few miles from his own place.

"Leave it running," Elin said. "Since she was so pleasant earlier, I'll wait here this time."

Freddie leaned over to kiss her. "I'll be quick."

"You'd better be. I'm losing the mood."

Freddie laughed. "When have you ever lost the mood?"

"If you don't hurry up, you might find out."

"I'm going. Lock the doors." He waited until he heard the click of the doors locking before he jogged into his mother's building. Since it was quicker than waiting for the elevator, he ran up the four flights, taking the stairs two at a time. His still-recovering shoulder made a small protest at the rapid movement. Freddie ignored it but wondered just how long it took for a bullet wound to fully heal.

Using his key, he let himself into his mother's neat, cheerful apartment. He found her propped up in bed sipping a cup of tea.

"Hi there." Even though her voice was heavy with illness, she still managed to work up a smile for her only child. "I didn't expect to see you again tonight."

"I couldn't go home without making sure you're doing okay."

"You're such a good boy."

He sat next to her on the bed and leaned over to kiss

her warm forehead. In her early fifties, Juliette Cruz was still a beautiful woman. "I'm told I'm a mama's boy."

Juliette's expression hardened. "By your *girlfriend*, no doubt."

Freddie shrugged. "It's not like it isn't true."

"It's never been an issue before."

"Still isn't."

His mother put down her tea and reached for his hand. "She's all wrong for you, Freddie."

"So you've said. A few times now, in fact."

"I just don't get what you see in her."

He laughed. "Really? You don't? The other guys at the wedding had no trouble getting what I see in her."

His mother frowned. "You've never been one to let your head be turned by a pretty face and a killer body. There's a hard edge to her that I don't care for."

"I know you don't, Mom. Believe me, I know."

"I hope you're being careful...about protecting yourself."

He stared at her, incredulous. "Are we *really* having this conversation? I'm twenty-nine years old!"

"Don't think you're fooling me, Frederico Cruz."

"I would never presume to fool you." He brought their joined hands to his lips and kissed the back of hers. "Don't worry about me. I'm a big boy, and I can take care of myself."

"You *think* you can. You have no experience whatsoever in dealing with people like her."

Okay, that hurt. Was she forgetting what he did for a living? He released her hand, stood up and fought for control of his temper. She had given him everything, had sacrificed everything for him and he had no doubt her concerns were coming from a place of unconditional love.

But he was a grown man—a mama's boy all the way—but a grown man nonetheless.

"I'm glad you're feeling well enough to lecture me, Mom, but I like her, and I'm asking you to let me make my own decisions. This guilt trip you're laying on me is making me crazy. You haven't even given her a chance, and you've already decided you don't like her. That's not how you brought me up, and I have to say I'm kind of disappointed you're acting this way toward a friend of mine—a really nice girl who you haven't bothered to get to know before judging her."

Juliette's face flushed with uncharacteristic chagrin.

"Don't hate her just because you're pissed I broke the vow," he said softly. "That's what this is really about, and you know it."

She looked up at him, her expression pained. "That's part of it. I won't lie to you. I'm disappointed in that."

Raised a devout Christian, he had taken a vow of celibacy at fifteen and stuck to it for fourteen long years—until he met Elin during the O'Connor investigation.

"Okay so we're both disappointed. It would mean a lot to me if you would give her a chance. That's all I'm asking."

Juliette studied him. "I'll try."

"Thank you," Freddie said. At this point, he'd take whatever she was willing to give toward keeping the peace. "Call me if you feel worse during the night."

"I'll be fine. Don't worry."

"I'll always worry." He bent to kiss her forehead one last time. "That's what makes me a good mama's boy."

"You're a very good boy, Freddie. Don't let anyone tell you otherwise."

"I won't. Sleep well."

"You, too."

From the doorway, Freddie flashed a rakish grin and winked. "I hope I don't sleep *too* well."

She threw a pillow at him and just missed his head.

He tossed it back and blew her one last kiss. Laughing at how he'd managed—for once—to get the last word with her, he locked her in and hurried back to Elin.

THREE

"I WISH YOU'D tell me what's been bothering you all day," Christina said.

From the driver's seat, Metro Detective Tommy "Gonzo" Gonzales glanced over at her and then returned his eyes to the road.

Christina sighed with dismay. Since they met at Sam and Nick's New Year's Eve promotion party, she'd never seen this closed off, unreachable side of Tommy. She'd heard rumors that he'd been quite the player in the past and couldn't help but wonder if he was growing tired of their monogamous relationship. That thought saddened her. Here, finally, was a guy she connected with not only in bed, but everywhere else, too. She didn't want it to be over between them. Not yet.

She took a deep breath and swallowed all her hard-won self-esteem. "Did I do something to upset you?"

He reached for her hand. The warmth of his skin against hers filled her with a sense of rightness she hadn't experienced before. "It's nothing to do with you. I promise."

Christina laced her fingers through his, enveloping his hand between both of hers. "Is something wrong at work?"

"No."

"Then what?"

Even though she could see he wanted to tell her, he maintained the stony silence that had marked their day.

Frustrated and confused, Christina turned to look out at the winter night passing by as he drove her home.

They pulled up outside her town house in the swanky Georgetown neighborhood a short time later. Tommy killed the engine and stared at the windshield.

Christina reluctantly released his hand. "I guess I'll see you when I see you." One thing she'd learned over the last six weeks was that dating a cop was nothing if not unpredictable.

"Wait," he said.

Something in the way he said the single word tugged at her heart. He sounded so tormented that she wanted nothing more than to ease his pain. "What is it, Tommy? You can talk to me. Whatever it is, we'll figure it out."

He released a pained chuckle. "I hope you mean that."

"You know I do." She took his hand again. "Come in with me. Tell me what's got you so upset."

He got out of the car and followed her into the house, keeping his hand on her elbow the whole way in case they encountered ice on the sidewalk. It was just that kind of gesture that had endeared him to her from the very beginning. Underneath his suave, sexy Cuban exterior was a true gentleman.

They hung their coats on the brass stand inside the door. "Can I get you anything? A drink maybe?"

"Yeah," he said, dropping onto the sofa. "That'd be good."

She fixed him a glass of the scotch she now kept on hand for him and brought it to him.

"Nothing for you?"

Christina shook her head. She was too wound up for a drink that would no doubt go straight to her head after all the champagne she'd consumed at the wedding.

He held out his arm to invite her to sit closer to him.

Christina scooted over and rested her head on his chest, breathing him in as his arm tightened around her.

His lips found her forehead, and she was filled with relief. Whatever had him so troubled seemed to have nothing to do with her.

"I'm sorry I've been such a jerk all day."

"You weren't a jerk. You were quiet, which isn't like you." She tilted her head so she could look up at him as he sipped the scotch.

"You know me so well."

"Sometimes I feel like I don't know you at all, but I want to. I want to know you."

He tilted her chin up and brushed his lips over hers, a teasing promise of the delights to come if he could find a way to tell her what had him so burdened.

"You're good for me, Christina. You make me want to be a better man than I've been in the past."

She reached up to caress the stubble on his jaw. He was so insanely sexy that sometimes she had to pinch herself to believe she was really with a guy like him. All her years of unrequited love for the late Senator John O'Connor seemed like a bad dream since she met Tommy. "Tell me."

He put down the glass and ran his free hand through his dark hair. "Last night, I got a text from a woman I went out with a couple of times. It was a year or so ago. I haven't seen her since."

"Does she want you back?" *Who could blame her?*

"Not exactly. She wanted to tell me about my son."

Christina's breath caught in her lungs. She sat up so she could see him. "You have a son."

"That's what she says, although I'm not sure I believe her. Who knows if he's mine or not?"

"You slept with her?"

He seemed ashamed to nod in agreement. "A couple of times, but I used condoms. You know how I am about that."

"Condoms fail."

"She said the same thing. She swears to God he's mine. All day today I've been trying to figure out what I should do."

Christina slipped into chief of staff mode. "The first thing you do is confirm he's really yours. Demand a DNA test."

"What if she won't do it?"

"I assume she's interested in financial support for the child."

"She didn't come right out and say that, but the implication was clear."

"If she wants your money, you're perfectly within your rights to require proof the child is actually yours."

"You're right, and that's what I'll do tomorrow." He looked down at the floor and then back at her. "What does this mean for us?"

"What does what mean?"

"I'd understand if this was too much for you. We haven't been together that long—"

Christina placed her hands on his face and kissed the words right off his lips. "We've been together just long enough that your problem is my problem, and we'll figure it out together."

"Really?" His expression was so rife with relief that Christina would've laughed if the situation hadn't been so serious. And here she had worried all day that he'd had enough of her.

"Really." She ran her fingers through his hair and guided his mouth back to hers. Running her tongue gently over his bottom lip, she coaxed him into participating in the kiss.

A groan rumbled through him as his arms tightened around her. "I thought you'd be so pissed. I was afraid to tell you."

"It happened a year ago. It's got nothing to do with me or us."

"And if I do have a son?"

"Then I guess we'll have to get a couple of cribs—one for your place and one for mine."

He shifted her under him on the sofa and looked down at her, his eyes hot with desire and relief. Even though he was so much bigger than her, he never handled her with anything other than total gentleness.

"I hate that you tortured yourself this way all day." She massaged the tension from his neck and shoulders. "Next time something is bothering you, will you just tell me so we can figure it out rather than stewing in silence?"

"I'm not used to having someone to work things out with."

"Well now you do, so you'd better get used to it."

He flashed the sexy, dimpled smile that got him anything he wanted from her. "I love it when you get all bossy with me."

"Is that so?" she asked with the coy grin that usually had the same effect on him.

"You know it is."

Bringing his head down close to her lips, she whispered a two-word order in his ear.

His eyes widened with shock and then heated with passion. His lips came down hard on hers, and as she wrapped her arms around him, Christina wanted to weep with relief and joy that he had confided in her. Then his lips found her neck at the same instant his fingers closed around her nipple, and she ceased to think at all.

LINDSEY MCNAMARA JOINED Sam outside the interrogation room.

"What've you got?" Sam asked the pretty, redheaded medical examiner.

"Nothing new quite yet. As soon as we're done here, I'll get started on the autopsy."

"I'm going to talk him into giving up a DNA sample. You've got the kit with you?"

Lindsey held up the long swab used to collect a buccal sample. "Ready."

Sam glanced at her watch. Ten-thirty. Nick was watching from observation, and she still hoped they could salvage a bit of their romantic evening. "Let's get this done."

Inside the room, Senator Lightfeather startled out of his daze when the two women entered. "Senator, this is Chief Medical Examiner Dr. Lindsey McNamara. May I have your permission to record this interview?"

He nodded and waved his hand in agreement.

"Before we begin, I need to advise you of your rights in this matter." Sam ran through the Miranda warning. "Do you understand your rights as I have explained them?"

"Yes," he said, sounding broken and despondent.

"I want to be clear. We can charge you at any time with failing to immediately report Regina's murder to proper authorities. Calling your colleague whose fiancée happens to be a cop smacks of you trying to cover your own ass. However, if you cooperate with our investigation, I'll speak to the assistant U.S. attorney about waiving those charges. Do you understand?"

Lightfeather granted her a small nod. "I get it."

Sam pushed a piece of paper she'd prepared earlier across the table. "We'd like your consent to obtain a sample of your DNA."

He looked up at her, shocked by the request. "For what purpose?"

"To determine what, if any, contact you had with the victim."

"Can't I just tell you what contact I had with her?"

"We'd like you to do both."

Glancing from Sam to Lindsey and then back to Sam, he reached for the pen in his shirt pocket and scrawled his signature on the form before pushing it back across the table to Sam.

She nodded to Lindsey who explained the procedure before she swabbed the inside of the senator's cheek.

"Thanks, Dr. McNamara," Sam said. "Please ask Detective McBride to step in." They'd decided before that three officers entering the room together would've been one too many. The last thing Sam wanted was for the senator to shut down and lawyer up before she could figure out what he knew about their victim and what had happened to her.

Detective Jeannie McBride entered the room, and Sam introduced her to the senator. "If you could, Senator, can you tell us how you know Regina Argueta de Castro?"

"As Senator Cappuano mentioned earlier, she works for the company that cleans the Hart Senate Office Building."

Sam noticed that he still spoke of Regina in the present tense, as if he had yet to accept her death. "And you met her how long ago?"

"Two years. Maybe a little more." He took a moment to gather his thoughts. "I work late a lot of nights, and she'd come in to clean. We'd get talking, and over time I guess you could say we became friends."

"What did a United States senator have in common with a cleaning lady?" Sam asked.

His lips curved into a smile that didn't reach his eyes. "More than you'd think. We were both living away from our families, missing our kids, working hard to provide a better life for them. We understood each other."

"Where are her children?"

"Guatemala. They live there with her mother. Roberto is seven and Isabella is five. She was hoping to bring them here someday. She talked all the time about how happy she'd be once they were together again." A tear traveled unchecked down his cheek. "I'd like to be the one to tell them she's gone."

"I'll see what I can arrange in the morning."

"I have the number in my office."

"I can't help but wonder why you'd have the number to the Guatemalan cleaning lady's family."

The senator's face hardened into a difficult-to-read expression. "She gave it to me. In case something ever happened to her."

"Was she concerned about her safety?

"Not that she ever said, but something was troubling her. The last few weeks, she'd been different, as if the weight of the world rested on her fragile shoulders. Even more so than usual."

"Can you think of anyone who might've wanted to harm her?"

"She was briefly married when she first came to this country, but she never told me his name or anything about him. I got the sense their breakup was acrimonious."

"Did she mention feeling threatened by him or anything like that?"

"Not that she ever said to me."

Sam made a note to check into Regina's brief marriage. "Were you romantically involved with her, Senator?"

New tears tumbled down his face. He brushed them away with the back of his trembling hand. "I never meant for it to happen. I swear to you. I love my wife and my children, but sometimes it just gets so lonely being away from them for weeks on end. Regina understood what that was like. We were friends for a long time before anything ever happened."

"What exactly happened?"

His shoulders hunched with defeat, as if it was registering all at once that his entire life was about to unravel. "It was her daughter's birthday. She was sad to be missing it. I gave her my international cell phone so she could call home, and she was so happy and thankful after speaking with her kids. We had a glass of wine and sat together on the sofa. We were talking about Isabella, about all the little moments we were both missing with our children—moments that could never be recaptured. It was all very innocent. Until I kissed her." He broke down into wretched sobs that shook his entire body. "I never meant..."

Sam gave him a few minutes to compose himself.

"It was just supposed to be comfort between friends," he said.

"But it was more than that?"

He nodded. "We made love right there in my office where anyone could've discovered us. I never even stopped to lock the door. Afterward, I couldn't believe I'd let that happen. The chances I had taken with my family, my office, with Regina, my dearest friend. I've never before been unfaithful to my wife. I was literally sick with guilt."

"So it didn't happen again?"

The senator released a long rattling breath. "We were both so shocked by how carried away we'd been that we steered clear of each other. Another woman cleaned my office, and I didn't see Regina for many weeks."

"And how long ago was this?"

"Three months."

"Did you eventually see her again?"

"Her immigration status was in question. She had applied for a green card when she was married, but apparently the marriage was deemed suspect and the application was denied. Her work visa was running out, and she came to me to ask if there was anything I could do to help her. She'd applied for permanent residency on her own, but her application had been denied. The only way she could properly support her family was to stay in the United States, and it was important to her that she be here legally. She was getting quite desperate as the expiration date approached."

"Were you able to help her?"

"I made a few phone calls, but I had to be careful since she wasn't one of my constituents. We were able to get her a three-month extension, and I put in a good word for her with the Immigration and Naturalization Service. I asked them to reconsider her application. That was all I could do without arousing suspicion."

"And did she appreciate your help?"

"Very much so."

"Did you rekindle your romantic relationship?"

A look of sheer torture came over his face. "You have to understand. . . my family is everything to me, but when

I was with Regina, it was like I became someone else. I couldn't resist her."

"How many times were you intimate with her?"

"Too many."

"Ten? Twenty? Thirty? More?"

"Thirty or more, I guess. We were together just about every day for the last month."

"Where did these liaisons occur?"

"Most of the time at her apartment, but a few more times in my office—with the door locked."

"Why not your apartment?"

"With a wife and five kids in Sedona, I can't exactly afford a place here too," he said, seeming embarrassed. "I sleep on the sofa in my office."

Nick's hunch had been spot-on. "Was she involved with anyone else?"

Lightfeather's eyes widened. "Of course not. She wasn't promiscuous."

"You're sure of that?"

"Yes, I'm sure!"

"When was the last time you were intimate with Regina?"

"Earlier today. I was over there for lunch and we made love afterward. I was there for a couple of hours before I left to do some work in my office. I tried to call her a little while later on the cell phone I'd given her. When she didn't answer, I became concerned and went back to her apartment. There was so much blood. At first I couldn't figure out what was wrong, and then, when I saw her on the floor…I started screaming for help but no one came. That's when I called Nick. I didn't know what else to do."

"You could've called 911."

He looked right at her. "I'm a married United States senator who just found his mistress murdered in her apartment. If you were me, would you call 911 or would you call your friend whose fiancée is a homicide detective?"

"So you weren't so upset about your dead lover that you didn't take a moment to think about your family and your career before calling for help for her?"

He slapped a hand on the table, startling her. "I was horrified that someone had harmed this beautiful, sweet woman, and I wanted the best cop in this city to find out who did this to her. She was, *and is*, my first thought."

Something about the way he said that triggered a new realization for Sam. "You were in love with her."

"Yes," he said, breaking down again. "God help me, but I was in love with her, and I have no idea how I'll ever live without her."

FOUR

"GET OVER TO the Capitol and get me a security guard, a junior staffer, *anyone* who can put Senator Lightfeather in that building late this afternoon," Sam said to Detective McBride. "That place is crawling with cameras, so get me video on his movements all day yesterday and fill in the timeline on the murder board. I also want Regina's cell phone dumped and while you're at it, dump Lightfeather's too."

"You got it, LT," Jeannie said, gesturing to her partner, Detective Will Tyrone.

After they left the pit, Sam returned to her office and ran her hand through hair still sticky from the product the stylist had loaded it with before the wedding. She glanced at her desk and did a double take at how neat and orderly it was.

Nick approached her from behind, resting his hands on her shoulders and massaging the tense spots. He knew exactly where her stress collected, and it was all Sam could do to remain standing as his talented fingers hit all the right places. "It's getting late, babe."

"Did you clean up my desk again?"

"Maybe."

"It's a sickness. You have a sickness."

"Guilty as charged." He laughed softly and planted a kiss on her neck. Desire rippled through her. She was so easy where he was concerned, and he knew it. "What's up with Henry?"

The facts of the case ran through her mind like a silent movie. "Until I get Lindsey's report, I'm at a standstill."

"Then let's go home."

Back in the day, Sam would've waited all night—if necessary—for the autopsy report and lab results. Now, though, she had a good reason to go home. She looked up at him. "Sorry for letting work invade our day off. Maybe one of these days we'll succeed in actually scoring a full day off."

"We can dream."

She let him help her into her coat and lead her from the office. "I know you really needed the break."

"Not your fault, and besides, I did get a day off from campaigning, so it's all good."

"We missed out on our early Valentine's Day," she said once they were in the car.

He reached for her hand, laced his fingers through hers. "Every day with you is Valentine's Day."

Sam smiled at him. "Even if we end up on different sides on this case?"

"We may not always agree, Sam, but we're always on the same side."

She relaxed into the heated leather seat and enjoyed the companionable silence. That was one of her favorite things about her relationship with Nick. Even in the quiet spaces between words, she was always in tune with him. In the past, when she'd been unhappily married to a manipulative man who wanted to control her every thought, she'd often been lonely even when he was sitting next to her on the sofa or lying next to her in bed. She had never once felt that way with Nick.

"What're you thinking about over there?" he asked.

"I'm thinking about us."

"What about us?"

"Could I ask you something and will you tell me the truth?"

He glanced at her. "Of course you can and of course I will."

"When we're together, do you ever feel lonely?"

"Lonely?" He released a short laugh. "That is one thing I never feel when I'm with you."

"Good," Sam said, relieved. "That's good."

Nick parallel parked on Ninth Street, killed the engine and turned to face her, reaching out to caress her cheek. "What's that all about?"

"Sometimes, well…a lot of the time when I was with Peter, I remember being lonely even when he was right there with me. I was thinking that I've never felt that way with you, and I was hoping you hadn't either."

"I've never felt that way, and I'm glad you haven't." He reached for her, and she leaned into his embrace. "If you're ever lonely, will you tell me?"

She nodded. "Will you?"

"I promise."

"I doubt it'll ever be an issue between us. Everything about this is different."

"Yes," he said, kissing her. "It is. Come on, let's go in."

Inside, Nick hung their coats in the closet.

"Would've been quicker to toss them on the sofa," Sam said. She loved goading him about his anal-retentive neatness.

"That's not where they go." He followed her upstairs and took advantage of the opportunity to smack her on the ass.

Sam laughed and took off running, knowing he'd give chase. He caught up to her in the bedroom, and they tumbled onto the bed. "You can run," he said, attempting a menacing look, "but you cannot hide."

"Wanna bet?"

"Mmm," he said, capturing her mouth for a deep, sensual kiss.

Sam pressed against the tight hold he had on her hands. "Let me go. I want to touch you."

Nick released her hands and removed her sweater.

Sam shivered from the cool air hitting her warm skin.

"Are you cold?" he asked.

"No." She freed the onyx studs from his tuxedo shirt, dropped them into a pile on the bed and pushed the shirt off his broad shoulders. "Too many clothes," she said, tugging at his undershirt.

Nick laughed and pulled it over his head. "Better?"

Sam ran her hands over his muscular chest. "Much."

He gathered her into a tight embrace and rocked against her.

She caressed his back. "What?"

Releasing a long deep breath, Nick pressed his lips to her neck. "Marry me, Samantha."

"I believe I've already agreed to that. Remember the Rose Garden?"

He raised his head to meet her eyes. "Soon. I don't want to wait."

She reached up to run her fingers through his hair. "I thought you wanted a nice wedding."

"We can't have a nice wedding soon?"

"How soon are we talking?"

"I don't know. A month?"

Sam laughed. "Weren't you there earlier when I was plunged into another complicated case? How do you expect me to plan a wedding and contend with that at the same time?"

"I'll plan it. Leave everything to me."

As much as she'd love to turn the whole thing over to

him, their wedding was too important for her to be totally removed from the planning. "I thought we'd plan it together."

"Is that what you want?"

"I figured that's what *you'd* want."

"I want to be married. That's all I care about."

"That's not what you said the other night when my sisters were grilling you about what kind of wedding you wanted. You said you want the bells and whistles. What changed?"

He framed her face with his hands and leaned in to kiss her.

"Nick? What is it? Why the sudden urgency?"

"It's just…listening to Henry talk about Regina. I could relate to how he felt about her. I can't imagine what he must be going through."

"You're awfully certain he's not responsible for her murder."

"You heard him, Sam." Nick kissed her nose, both cheeks and then her lips. "He was in love with her. He doesn't know how he'll live without her. I understand how he feels."

She curled her legs around his. "Nothing's going to happen to me. There's no need to rush our wedding. You're only going to do this once, right?"

"That's the plan."

"Then you ought to do it right. The way you want it."

"What about what you want?"

"I already had that. This time can be all about what you want."

"No, babe," he said, shaking his head. "This time has to be all about what *we* want."

The idea of planning another elaborate wedding made Sam feel slightly ill. She'd do it for him, but she'd much rather call in a justice of the peace and be done with it. "What I want right now," she said with a saucy grin, "has nothing to do with cakes or flowers." She reached between them to free his belt and unzip his pants.

Nick gasped when she curled her hand around his erection. He gripped her hand and held her still. "I'll make you a deal."

"Why do we need a deal? In case you haven't noticed, I'm a sure thing."

He laughed and then moaned when she stroked him. "Do you want to hear my deal or not?"

"All right." She released her hold on him. "Shoot."

Bending over her, he pressed his lips to her belly and then turned those potent eyes up to meet hers. "If I can make you come three times in the next half hour, you'll let me set a date—any date I want.

Sam raised an eyebrow. "And if you can't?"

"I'll wait for you to set the date."

"You won't mention it again?"

"Not until you do."

She *never* came three times. Ever. "Okay. You're on. Do your best work."

His smile was nothing short of predatory as he kissed his way down her body.

Twenty-eight minutes later, Sam hovered on the brink of a third orgasm as Nick pumped into her from behind. Determined to hold it off, she jolted when he reached around to coax her. Damn it, she was powerless against that combination, and he knew it. Lesson learned: Never make a deal with the guy who knows you better than anyone. His fingers moved urgently over her most sensitive place as he went deep again, sending her tripping over the edge into yet another climax.

This time, he joined her. They fell into a heaving pile

on the bed. He kissed her back and then her shoulder. His lips brushed against her ear.

"March 26."

SAM'S FIRST THOUGHT the next morning wasn't of the murder she needed to investigate. No, her first thought was of the deal she'd made with the devil himself. How would she ever manage to plan a wedding while in the midst of another complex investigation? And during his campaign. She sighed. Then she remembered how he'd gotten his new house put together in just under a week, in time to entertain his Supreme Court nominee friend. If anyone could pull off a classy wedding in just over a month's time, her fiancé could.

She glanced over at him, asleep with one arm thrown over his head. The sprinkle of whiskers on his usually smooth jaw only made him more appealing to her. At the end of one crazy month and a half, he'd be her husband and they'd have the rest of their lives together. Surely she could get through whatever she had to in the next few weeks to have forever with him. Right?

He shifted onto his side and reached for her in his sleep.

Smiling, Sam snuggled into him. No, she never felt lonely anymore. Even when he was asleep, he was still right here with her and he truly loved her. Of that, she had no doubt at all.

He tightened his hold on her. "What're you thinking about?" he mumbled.

"Our wedding." She shifted onto her back so she could see him. "What do you want me to do?"

"Dresses for you and your sisters, flowers and the cake." He still hadn't opened his eyes. "I'll take care of everything else."

"I've finally figured out how you get so much done. You work while you're asleep. That's the only possible explanation."

He chuckled softly. "I wish." His knee bumped her leg. "You need to get going."

"I know." Before she got up, she turned into his embrace and breathed in his warm, clean scent. "After I close this one, we're taking a day off. I don't care what we have to do, but we're getting our day."

"March 26." He finally opened his eyes as he kissed her. "We'll take that day off for sure—and the whole week after. The Senate goes into recess until mid-April."

"Won't you need to campaign?"

"I'll let Christina know I'm unavailable that week. I'll be on my honeymoon."

"And where will that be?"

"I haven't decided yet. Where do you want to go?"

"Anywhere that isn't the District of Columbia." Sam looked up at him. "You know, March 26 is only three months since we got back together."

His eyebrow arched. "Do you need more time to be sure you're doing the right thing?"

Sam thought of the six years she'd spent missing him after one unforgettable night together. "No."

His fingers spooled through her hair. "Neither do I. So we're on? March 26?"

"Yes," she said, kissing him. "We're on."

"WELL, THAT'S A first." Sam closed her cell phone and put it in the back pocket of her jeans.

"What is?" Nick asked as he stood before the bedroom mirror to knot his tie.

"Gonzo called in sick the day after we caught a hot case."

Nick turned to her. "That's odd. Christina called, too. She was supposed to go to Richmond with me today, but she said something came up."

Sam scowled. "They're probably lolling about in bed while we're giving up yet another Sunday to work."

"Or maybe they're actually sick."

"Hungover is more like it. He was putting away the scotch yesterday."

Nick came over to her and kissed her forehead. "We were all drinking. Don't be too hard on him."

"It's just not like him."

"He'd probably say it's not like you to hang out at home longer than necessary so you could have breakfast with your fiancé when you've got a body chilling in the morgue."

Sam replied with another scowl.

Nick laughed and cuffed her chin. "I'm just saying. People change. Life happens. And no one, not even you and me, can work all the time."

"We have been lately."

"A week off, coming soon. Can you take the full week?"

"I have like eight weeks of vacation built up, so it shouldn't be a problem."

"Just make sure you remember to ask."

She rolled her eyes at him even as the thought of an entire week alone with him made her heart race with anticipation. "Yes, dear. So what's up in Richmond today?"

"A rally at VCU," he said, referring to Virginia Commonwealth University, "a visit to one of the state homes for kids and then a fund-raising dinner. I won't be home until late."

She went up on tiptoes to kiss him. "Me, too, so I'll catch you when I catch you."

When she started to draw back from him, he brought her in for a better kiss. “Mmm,” he said several minutes later. “That oughta hold me until you catch me.”

Smiling, she patted his freshly-shaven face and kissed him again. “See ya.”

“Hey.”

Sam turned back to him.

“Be careful today.”

“Always am.”

FIVE

"ARE YOU SURE it's a good idea to just show up without calling first?" Gonzo asked Christina. He eyed the nondescript white town house that might—or might not—house his son.

"I'm sure. This way she doesn't have time to pull any crap. She's not expecting you, so you gain the upper hand."

He glanced over at her. Even after a nearly sleepless night, she looked fresh-faced and polished. Sometimes he still wondered what the heck a classy woman like her saw in a rough-around-the-edges guy like him. "This is why you're so good at your job."

"It's called strategy," she said, smiling at the compliment. "You gotta have one." She leaned over to kiss the dimple in his chin that she'd once told him was ridiculously sexy. "Remember, you're just going to tell her you want to see the baby and talk about what you can do to help out. Keep it all friendly. We'll let the lawyer get into the DNA business with her. It'll be better if that doesn't come from you."

"Okay." He took a deep, fortifying breath. "Here goes nothing."

Christina squeezed his arm. "It'll be fine. You haven't done anything wrong, Tommy. Just remember that."

Grateful for her calming presence, he nodded and reached for the door handle. At the last second, he stopped and turned to her. "Come with me."

"I thought we decided it would be better if I waited here."

"I don't care what we decided. I want you with me when I see him for the first time. It wasn't like I had a long relationship with her. How can she be put out if I have someone else now?"

"Are you sure?"

"Yeah. I'll feel better if you're there with me," he said, startled to realize it was true. He always felt better when she was around.

"Then let's go."

On the front stoop, Gonzo rang the bell. Would he know right away that the child was his? Would he be able to love a child he hadn't even known about? What if he couldn't love the baby, even if he *was* his?

The door swung open, and Lori gasped when she saw him. Her brown hair looked like it hadn't been washed in days and her oversized red T-shirt was stained with what might've been breast milk. Gonzo tried to recall what he'd once seen in her, but she had changed so much he barely recognized her.

She pushed open the storm door. "Tommy? What're you doing here?"

He swallowed hard. "I've come to see my son."

Lori's gaze shifted from him to Christina and then back to him.

"This is my, um, girlfriend, Christina." He was surprised he didn't choke on a word he usually went out of his way to avoid. "Christina, this is Lori."

The two women sized each other up for a long, long moment. Finally, Christina said, "Nice to meet you."

The sound of a baby wailing from inside ended the awkward moment. "Come in." Lori gestured them into a space cluttered with baby paraphernalia and piles of dirty clothes.

Gonzo eyed the overflowing ashtray on the coffee table with dismay. The place reeked of smoke.

"I'll just, um, go get him," Lori said, darting from the room.

When they were alone, Christina reached for his hand.

"How does he breathe in here?" Gonzo whispered.

"I was wondering the same thing."

When they heard Lori's footsteps on the stairs, Gonzo released Christina's hand.

She came into the room carrying the baby. The first thing he noticed was the baby's dark hair. Not that he knew much about babies, but he seemed to have a lot of hair. Gonzo's nephew Joey had been born with a similar head of hair. His stomach dropped as Lori handed the baby to him.

Gonzo and Christina gasped at the prominent dimple in the baby's chin.

He stared down at the puckered little face and fell instantly in love. Big eyes stared up at him, open and trusting, and it was all Gonzo could do not to weep. The immediate tidal wave of love that surged through him left him defenseless in its wake.

Christina's hand landed on his back, and he glanced over at her to find that she, too, was overwhelmed.

"What's his name?" Gonzo asked.

"I haven't named him yet."

Startled, Gonzo looked up at her. "But he's a couple of months old!"

"Believe me, I know how old he is."

"You have to give him a name."

"So that's how this is going to go? You come into *my* home and start telling me how to raise *my* kid?"

"You called me, Lori. I never would've known about him if you hadn't called. Did you expect me to just go on with my life and act like I'd never heard about him?"

"Don't try to pretend you have any interest in him."

"Of course I'm interested in him. He's my son."

"Look, it's really nice of you to come all the way over here to see him, but the only thing I need from you is some money for diapers and day care. I don't expect anything else."

"I want more than that."

The front door swung open, bringing a blast of cold air and startling the baby. He began to wail.

Even though he had next to no experience with babies, Gonzo patted his back.

"I'll take him," Lori said, reaching for him.

"I don't mind that he's crying," Gonzo said.

"The lady wants her baby back," a deep voice said from the foyer.

Gonzo glanced over to find a giant of a man glaring at him. He had a red bandana tied around his long hair and tattoos on his neck and arms.

"Take it easy, Rex," Lori said. "He's a cop."

"Doesn't give him the right to hold onto your kid when you want him back."

"He's my kid too," Gonzo said, using his best cop glare on the guy.

Rex's eyes widened with surprise. "That so?"

Lori nodded.

Rex glowered at her.

"You really need to go now," she said to Gonzo. This time when she reached for the baby he let her take him.

"I'll go," Gonzo said. "But I'll be back. Soon." With one last look at his son, Gonzo ushered Christina out the front door. Once they were outside, he took a deep gulping breath of fresh air. The stench of cigarette smoke clung to their coats. "She hasn't even given him a name," he said, filled with despair.

Christina pulled her cell phone from her coat pocket.

"Who are you calling?" Gonzo asked.

"Nick's lawyer friend Andy. He specializes in family law."

"I should probably check with Sam. She might not appreciate me calling on a friend of Nick's without asking her first."

"I'm sure Sam would want you to do everything you could to take care of your son."

He hoped Christina was right. "How could she not even care enough about him to give him a name?"

Christina squeezed his arm. "Don't worry. We're going to take care of him, okay?"

Gonzo nodded. His entire world had been turned upside down by one tiny dimpled chin, and he was grateful for her cool competence.

"GIVE ME SOMETHING, give me anything," Sam said to Dr. McNamara. Regina Argueta de Castro lay on the table under the glare of fluorescent lights.

"Twelve weeks pregnant," Lindsey said.

"Well, that's interesting. How soon until you know if the fetus's DNA matches Senator Lightfeather's?"

"A couple of days. I'm running it now."

"Anything else?"

"I got a partial print off the bruises on her buttocks. I ran it through AFIS," she said, referring to the Automated Fingerprint Identification System. "But no hits. Also, I found semen from two different men in her vagina."

"Of course there were two," Sam said, frustrated that

her slam-dunk case against Senator Lightfeather seemed to be falling apart. "Let me know what the DNA shows."

"Will do. So how're the wedding plans coming?"

"Fine. I guess." Her stomach clenched when she thought of the wedding she'd agreed to in six short weeks.

"A proposal in the White House Rose Garden." Lindsey sighed. "So romantic."

"He does have his moments," Sam conceded. "Get me some info, Doc."

"I'm on it."

Sam left the morgue and headed for the pit where she found Freddie popping pills. "Are you hungover too?"

He startled and looked up at her, a guilty expression marking his handsome face. "What? No. Are you?"

"Not me. Gonzo. Called in sick today."

"He wasn't drinking that much because he had to work today."

"So what's your excuse?"

"I have a headache, if you must know. And it's not from drinking. I didn't sleep very well."

"Spare me the gories." Sam was surprised when he didn't fire back with the usual retort. "What's the matter?"

"Nothing." He reached for some papers on his desk. "I've got McBride's report from last night. She spoke with several security people at the Capitol who reported seeing Senator Lightfeather there yesterday afternoon into the early evening. One of them reported seeing him leaving around six, and he seemed to be in a rush."

Just as he'd said, Sam thought. "We've got a DNA match to his semen, but there was a second guy. Lindsey's running it."

"McBride reported that they 'interrogated the lock'

on his office door and his key card swipes matched up with his timeline."

"Let's get him back into interrogation to cross the Ts before we let him go."

"You got it, boss. One other thing. We've had several calls from the media asking for confirmation that we're holding Lightfeather in connection with the murder of a member of the Capitol cleaning staff."

"No comment for now."

"That's what I figured you'd say."

Sam nodded. "Go get him."

"On my way."

Sam watched him go, noting the slight hunch to his shoulders. Yes, something was definitely troubling her partner. Before the day was over, she'd get it out of him.

A few minutes later, she joined Freddie and the senator in one of the interrogation rooms. Lightfeather's night in jail seemed to have diminished him.

"Were you aware that Regina was pregnant?" Sam asked.

Lightfeather's hands trembled. "Yes."

"Was it yours?"

He nodded.

"You're certain of that?"

"Of course I am."

"You're *sure* she wasn't seeing anyone else?"

"We were together most nights, so I can't imagine how she'd have time for anyone else."

"Didn't she work nights cleaning the Capitol?"

"Five nights a week, four to midnight."

"You said you were together 'most nights.' What did she do on the nights she didn't spend with you?"

"I'm not sure. She never said."

"Did you ask?"

He nodded. "It was a…a bone of contention between us."

"Did she have girlfriends? Anyone she would've confided in?"

"She was quite friendly with several women she worked with, but I'm not sure what she confided in them. I'm confident she told no one about our relationship. She knew what was at stake."

"For you or for her?"

"For both of us. She couldn't risk losing her job."

"What about what was at risk for you?"

"Obviously, she was well aware of that too."

"Was she pressuring you for more? She's carrying your child, facing possible deportation. I imagine she was quite desperate for some safety and security."

"She knew I'd take care of her and the baby, but she wasn't pressuring me. She was painfully aware of my marital status."

"How were you planning to take care of her and the baby when you didn't have enough money to get an apartment in Washington?"

Lightfeather's slumped in his chair. "I was going to do whatever I could for her."

"Which wouldn't have been much, am I right?"

He shrugged.

"She had to be feeling quite desperate. Another mouth to feed, day care, diapers. How would she swing all that when she was supporting her family back home?"

"We didn't talk a lot about that. We were going to work something out. I told her not to worry. I'd find the money. Somehow."

Freddie gestured to Sam, and she nodded to him.

"Senator," he said. "Are you familiar with the term 'anchor baby'?"

Lightfeather sat up straighter in his chair. "I am."

"I'm not," Sam said. "Enlighten me."

"When babies are born to illegal immigrants, they 'anchor' their mothers to the United States because the 14th Amendment grants automatic citizenship to anyone born in this country," Lightfeather said.

"Ahhh," Sam said, seeing where Freddie was going with this. Proud of his initiative, she waved her hand to give him the floor.

"Seeing as Regina's immigration status was in question, I'm wondering if her pregnancy was planned or not."

"It was most definitely *not* planned."

"How does that happen? I have to assume you both knew how to prevent an unwanted pregnancy."

The senator's hands, Sam noted, were trembling.

"We think it happened that first time. In my office."

"You didn't use protection?" Freddie asked.

"She said she was on the pill and I believed her."

"But she wasn't?"

"She was. I saw them later in her purse."

"Did she take them?"

"She swore she did. When she first discovered she was pregnant, she was furious that the pills hadn't worked."

"Or," Sam said, "they'd worked exactly as she'd intended."

Lightfeather's dark eyes narrowed. "What're you insinuating?"

"That you might've been duped, Senator. Seduced by a woman who knew *exactly* what she was doing when she allowed a United States senator to impregnate her."

"How dare you say such a thing about her? We were in love! Once I assured her I'd do everything I could to care for her and the baby, she was overjoyed about her pregnancy."

"She was overjoyed to be having a baby in the U.S. of A.," Sam said. "That it was the child of a high-ranking official was a bonus."

"I can't believe you'd say such a thing about a lovely woman who was brutally murdered. You don't care about her at all. I never should've called you."

Sam smacked her hand on the table, which startled him. "Don't tell me who and what I care about. I'll find out who killed her, and I'll make sure her killer pays for what he did to her."

Lightfeather broke down. "I'm sorry. I know you will. I'm just…I still can't believe this has happened." He turned tear-filled eyes up at Sam. "May I please call my wife? I can't have her hearing about this through the media."

Sam glanced at Freddie. "She may have already heard it. We've received numerous calls today from reporters who know we have you in custody."

The senator moaned and dropped his head into his hands.

"Detective, please arrange for an outside line for Senator Lightfeather," Sam said to Freddie.

"Yes, Lieutenant."

Sam stood up. "We'll give you a minute to make your call. Please be aware that we will be monitoring the call."

Freddie brought in a phone and plugged it into a jack. Handing the receiver to the senator, he hit the button to get an outside line.

Sam and Freddie left him alone and stepped into the observation room where they found Captain Malone and Chief Farnsworth waiting for them.

"What've you got, Lieutenant?" Farnsworth asked.

"Not enough to charge him," she said, frustrated. "Let's listen in for a minute."

"Annette," Lightfeather said, his head resting on his free hand. "Something has happened." He began to weep as he told his wife about his involvement with Regina. "I need you to come. Can you come?" He listened for a moment. "I know, honey, but I really need you. I've made a terrible mistake."

Sam wondered if he meant that. From what she'd seen, he'd hardly considered his affair with Regina a mistake. Part of her wanted to call Annette Lightfeather and tell her to stay put in Arizona. Sam hated when political wives stood by their scumbag husbands after they'd embroiled their families in scandal.

As the conversation ended, Sam deduced that Annette would arrive in Washington before the end of the day. She turned to the chief. "I'm going to release him with orders to stay in the city until we close the case. Even though he's got motive galore, his alibi for the time of death is tight." To Freddie, she said, "Tell me more about this anchor baby thing."

"I remember reading about it in the paper last year. The numbers were quite startling—something like 8 or 9 percent of all babies born in the U.S. in 2008 were anchor babies. There's been a lot of talk about repealing the 14th Amendment to close the loophole in the immigration laws."

"Didn't they just pass a new immigration bill?" Sam asked, thinking of the O'Connor-Martin bill that Nick had worked so hard on as John O'Connor's chief of staff. Ensuring passage of his friend's bill had been Nick's first order of business as a senator.

"Yes," Freddie said, "but it didn't address this issue."

Sam made a mental note to read up on the amendment and to get Nick's thoughts on the anchor baby issue. "It's time to start digging into Regina's life," she said.

"Agreed," Malone said.

"Go ahead and spring the senator," Farnsworth said. "But dig into his life too. He certainly had motive."

"We're on it," Sam said. "Cruz, let's have him make the call to Regina's family before we release him."

"One thing, L.T.," Freddie said, "McBride let me know that she's getting stonewalled by the cell phone company. They're not willing to release records for Regina or especially Lightfeather without subpoenas."

"McBride told them she'd been murdered?"

Freddie nodded. "The direct quote was something like, 'We're not giving you the private cell records of a United States senator without a subpoena. We don't care what he's suspected of.' Don't forget—her cell was in his name. He got it for her and paid for it, so they're both listed as his."

"Well, then get them the subpoenas. I want that data ASAP."

"You got it," Freddie said on his way out.

"I don't get these powerful guys who risk everything and think they're never going to get caught," Malone said.

"I don't get the passive political wives who stand by their men," Sam said. "If my husband cheated on me, there's no way he'd get me to stand meekly by him while he tried to explain away his failings." She watched as the two men exchanged amused glances. "What?"

"Given this some significant thought, huh?" Farnsworth said.

"Hardly," Sam said with a snort. "My future husband knows if he ever cheats on me I'd shoot him before I'd *ever* stand by his side like the humiliated little wife."

The two men laughed.

"You think I'm kidding?" Sam asked.

"Oh, we know you mean it," Malone said, making a

poor attempt at a serious expression. "Poor Nick. Someone really ought to warn him."

"No one needs to warn him," Farnsworth said. "He knows he's got the best of the best at home. Why would he ever look elsewhere?"

Embarrassed by the compliment, Sam smiled at the man she'd called Uncle Joe as a child. "Thank you for that."

"I only speak the truth." He headed for the door with Malone following him. "Keep us in the loop."

"I will." When she was alone, Sam got to work on her murder board, beginning at the left side with photos from the crime scene. She made a column for information about Lightfeather.

Freddie returned to the room. "Um, boss, we have a small problem."

"What's that?"

"The building is surrounded by press. They know we've got Lightfeather here, and they're clamoring for the story."

Sam thought for a second. "Here's what we're going to do."

SIX

NICK SLID INTO the back of the sedan and quickly shut the door. "Jesus," he said to his driver, Tony. "That was insane."

Tony chuckled. "You're more popular than ever, Senator. Never seen anything like the numbers you're drawing on the stump."

"Senator O'Connor had similar turnouts."

"Not like this he didn't." He glanced into the rearview mirror. "Ready for your next stop?"

"Yes." Nick rested his head back against the seat. "Thanks." He watched the VCU campus roll past. "What do you suppose it is, Tony?"

"Sir?"

"That brings them out in such numbers."

Once again, Tony laughed. "You're young, handsome, full of hope, humble. People relate to you and your story."

"Senator O'Connor was all those things too."

"He didn't have the same...what's the word I'm looking for? Charisma."

"It's because I took his place after he died."

"You'd be selling yourself short if you think it's just that. There's something about you they've connected with."

"Yeah, my love life. They're all connected to that."

"Doesn't hurt," Tony said, smiling into the mirror. "It's a combination of all those things. You were the right guy at the right time."

"I guess." Nick pondered what Tony had said. He'd known the man a long time as he'd been John's driver for years. Living as close as he did to the state he represented, Nick—and John before him—relied on Tony to get him around to campaign stops that were within driving distance.

He usually made use of the time in the car to work. Today, he was using the time to think. More than one hundred thousand people had shown up for the VCU rally, which was four times the number they'd expected. Despite the cold, the numbers had forced the rally outdoors to Monroe Park.

"I hear they've got four thousand on the waiting list for tonight's fund-raiser," Tony said. "The money is rolling in."

Millions had flooded into his campaign since he'd declared his candidacy. "It's an embarrassment of riches," Nick said.

"Enjoy it while it lasts. You'll do something to screw it up eventually."

Nick cracked up at the dryly spoken comment. "Gee, thanks."

"I'm just razzing ya. You've got the golden touch, Senator. You can ride the wave all the way to Pennsylvania Avenue at this rate."

The Democratic National Committee had already expressed an interest in running him in the primary in three years. President Nelson had started out strong, but his numbers had fallen off in recent months, and the party was considering its options should their incumbent choose not to seek a second term. Nick couldn't believe his name was even in the mix. He'd only been in the Senate for a month and a half and was in the midst of his first campaign. The notion of running for president was almost laughable—until he remembered the sea of people at the rally chanting his name and clamoring for a handshake or autograph. This whole thing was still unreal to him. His best friend and boss had been murdered by the twenty-year-old son John kept hidden from even his closest friend. Despite all the doors John's death had opened for Nick, he'd gladly give it all up to have his friend back.

Tony pulled up to the curb outside a nondescript red brick building in downtown Richmond. "Here ya are, Senator."

This stop had not been on his official schedule for the day, and Nick was relieved to note that his traveling band of reporters had not followed him here. "See you in a bit," he said to Tony on the way out of the car.

Inside, Irene Littlefield, director of the state home for children, greeted him. She'd appealed to his office for help in ensuring the continuation of a crucial federal grant that helped to fund the program. Nick figured her to be in her early sixties. "Senator," she said, shaking his hand, "it's such an honor to have you here. The children have been looking forward to your visit."

"It's great to be here. I've heard wonderful things about your program."

"That's nice of you to say. We do what we can with the resources made available to us. Let me introduce you to the children."

"That'd be great." He followed her through sterile-looking hallways in what used to be a VCU dormitory to a homey-looking common area filled with sofas, a big-screen TV, games and books. About thirty scrubbed and polished children waited patiently to say hello. Over the next half hour, Nick visited with each of them and marveled at their excellent manners and enthusiasm.

"We've asked Scotty to give you a tour of the facility," Mrs. Littlefield said after each of the children had had a chance to visit with Nick. She had her hands on the shoulders of a boy who was maybe eleven or twelve. His dark hair looked like it had been brushed into submission for the occasion. He wore a smart-looking navy sweater with khaki pants.

He flashed a mischievous grin. "I've been here the longest, so I got the short straw."

Nick laughed. "I'll try not to ask too many questions."

Scotty smiled at him. "Right this way, Senator."

As Nick followed him through the hallways, Scotty kept up a steady stream of chatter, pointing out the kitchen and dining room and discussing the food, which apparently ranged from fabulous to gross, depending on the chef's mood.

"What's your favorite meal?" Nick asked him.

"Spaghetti," Scotty said without hesitation.

"Ahhh, a man after my own heart."

"That's your favorite too?"

"Sure is. A good Italian boy like me has to get his pasta fix at least once a week."

"I don't know if I'm Italian, but I'd eat spaghetti every day if I could."

Nick felt a pull of compassion for the boy. "What are some of your other favorite things?"

"Baseball," Scotty said without hesitation.

"What team?"

"The Red Sox."

"Get out of here," Nick said, laughing. "You're just saying that to impress me."

"I am not! I've always loved the Sox."

"I grew up just north of Boston. I've been a Sox fan all my life."

Scotty's eyes got very big. "Have you been to Fenway Park?"

"Many times." He didn't add that he'd been twenty-four the first time he could afford to attend a game at the fabled ballpark.

"Oh, you're so lucky! I'd give anything to go there and sit in the Monster seats. I've read every book I could find on the Red Sox and Fenway Park. Did you see the movie *Fever Pitch*? It's my favorite."

Nick wished he could wave a magic wand and be sitting atop the Green Monster wall in Fenway Park with Scotty and a couple of Fenway Franks. "I loved that movie. I'm sure you'll get to Fenway someday."

"As soon as I have any money, that's the first place I'll go."

"How did you become a fan?"

"My grandfather was from Boston. He talked about the Red Sox all the time. Ted Williams was his favorite player. Did you ever see him play?"

Nick winced. "How old do you think I am, man?"

"Oh, sorry."

Nick mussed his hair. "Don't be sorry. I was just kidding. Is your grandfather still alive?"

Scotty shook his head. "He had a heart attack when I was six. A month later, my mom OD'ed. That's how I ended up here." He ushered Nick into his small room. "But it's not so bad."

Nick's heart broke when he imagined the horror of six-year-old Scotty losing his grandfather and then his mother. "You don't have any other family?"

"Nope. My mom had sisters but they were estringed."

"You mean estranged?"

"Yeah, that's it. They didn't talk to her because of her drug problems."

"What about your dad?"

"Never knew him." He rifled through some things on the desk. "Check this out—a Dustin Pedroia rookie card."

Nick examined the cellophane-sealed baseball card. "Wow. Look at that. You should take really good care of it. I bet it'll be worth big money someday."

"That's what Mr. Sanchez said. He was my math teacher last year. He's a Feds fan," Scotty said, referring to the Washington Federals. "He took me to a game when the Feds played the Sox in interleague play. It was my first time to a real ballpark, and I got to see the Sox. Best day of my life."

"I went to one of those games."

"The one I went to, the Sox won three to two."

"That's the one I was at!"

"Hey, that's cool."

Nick sat on the bed and looked around at the sparse room. "You need some posters for your walls. Who's your favorite player? I'll send you one."

"That's really nice of you, but we aren't allowed to hang stuff on our walls. The custodian says the tape takes the paint off."

Nick's scowl made the boy laugh.

"Rules are rules," Scotty said with a shrug.

"If we were breaking the rules for a minute, who would you want on your wall?"

"That's easy—Big Papi. He's the *bomb*."

Nick smiled. "His *bat* is the bomb."

"That's why I love him." Scotty sat next to Nick on the bed. "So you're really a senator?"

Even though it was still hard to believe sometimes, Nick said, "I really am."

"Isn't that kind of a boring job?"

Nick hooted with laughter. “It can be. You have to do a *lot* of reading.”

Scotty’s face screwed up with distaste. “I wouldn’t like that. I *hate* to read.”

“I used to hate it too, but now it’s easier. Do you play any sports?”

“Just baseball with some of the other kids here. There’s no money for Little League or anything like that.”

Nick ached listening to his easy acceptance of the hand life had dealt him. Talking with Scotty brought back memories of his own lonely childhood, spent with a grandmother who’d never missed the opportunity to remind him that there were other things she’d rather be doing than raising her son’s child.

“Do you play any sports?” Scotty asked.

“Just some pickup basketball here and there at the gym. I used to play a lot of hockey. I was pretty good at that.”

“I’d *love* to play hockey, but it’s really expensive.”

“Yeah, it can be.” Nick recalled how grateful he’d been the year his father sent enough money for him to play. “So this seems like a nice place to live.”

“It’s okay. One of the kids in my class at school is in foster care, and he has to move a lot. I wouldn’t like that.”

“You probably have more of a chance of being adopted here.”

“Nah, everyone wants babies. They go fast. The rest of us have each other. It’s kind of like having thirty brothers and sisters to fight with.”

He was so matter-of-fact that Nick realized the child had stopped hoping anything would ever change.

Mrs. Littlefield appeared at the door. “I guess you can see why we call Scotty ‘The Mayor,’ Senator,” she said with a smile. “He’s never met a stranger.”

"He's an excellent tour guide," Nick said, earning a grin from the boy. "The next time the Sox come to Baltimore or Washington, what'd you say I get us a couple of tickets to a game?"

Scotty's eyes widened. "For real?"

"Sure. I'd love to take in a game with another Sox fan."

"But how would I get there?"

"You let me worry about that. You just take care of doing really well in school, okay?"

"Okay! Thank you!"

Nick stood up and shook hands with the boy. "It was great to meet you, Scotty."

"You too, Senator. Thanks for coming to see us."

"It was my pleasure." It had been, Nick realized, the most pleasant half hour he'd spent at work since he took the oath of office. With one last smile for the boy, Nick followed Mrs. Littlefield from the room. "What a delightful kid."

"He's the heart and soul of this place. The other kids follow him around like the Pied Piper. I don't know what we'd ever do without him."

"There's really no chance of him being adopted?"

Mrs. Littlefield sighed. "Unfortunately, the older he gets the less likely it becomes. But not to worry, we'll take good care of him until he comes of age."

"And then what? Who'll take care of him then?"

"I'm afraid I don't understand, Senator. He'll be an adult."

"I apologize for my tone. It's just that I was thrust out on my own at eighteen and found the world to be a rather harsh place for an 'adult.'"

"I understand what you mean, and I can assure you that Scotty will have plenty of adults to call on should he encounter any difficulties. My staff and I are quite fond of him."

"I have something I'd like to send him. Would it be possible to get his last name and the address here?"

She wrote the information on the back of her business card and handed it to him. "Here you go."

"Thank you."

They reached the front door and Nick shook her hand. "I appreciate your time today, Mrs. Littlefield. I'll have a chat with the people overseeing your grant and see what we can do about getting it renewed."

"We'll appreciate anything you can do, Senator."

"I'll be in touch," Nick said on his way out.

Tony held the car door open for him. Once inside the car, Nick looked back at the building. From an upstairs window, Scotty watched him leave. Nick glanced down at the business card in his hand. Scotty Dunlap. He reached for his BlackBerry and got busy ordering a David "Big Papi" Ortiz jersey.

SEVEN

SAM HIT THE speaker button and punched in the phone number for Regina's mother in Guatemala. Calling victims' families was the thing she hated most about her job, so she was relieved to turn the task over to Senator Lightfeather. Freddie, who spoke Spanish, was prepared to take notes on the exchange.

A woman answered the phone with a cheerful, "*Hola*."

Appearing frozen, Lightfeather stared at the phone. Sam had no doubt that this phone call was even harder for him than the one he'd made earlier to his wife. "Senator?" she said softly.

He startled, seeming to realize all at once that everyone was waiting for him.

"*Hola*?" the woman said again.

"Señora Argueta?" he said, his voice rough with emotion. "*Yo estoy Senator Lightfeather*."

Sam's limited Spanish allowed her to deduce that Mrs. Argueta recognized the senator's name and knew he was a friend of her daughter's.

He spoke softly for another moment before the woman on the other end released a wail of despair.

Sam's stomach clenched. How anyone survived receiving the news that their child had been murdered she'd never know. These moments were the only time she was ever grateful to be childless.

Tears cascaded down the senator's tanned face. He

brushed them away as he continued to speak softly to the woman on the phone.

Sam glanced at Freddie's notes. Promising to arrange to have the body sent home as soon as he can, Freddie had written. Promising to continue helping her and Regina's children. No mention of the baby she'd been expecting.

Lightfeather concluded the phone call and rested his head on his folded arms. His shoulders shook with sobs.

Sam signaled to Freddie that they should give him a moment. Freddie followed her from the room.

"Hard to watch," Freddie muttered.

"Yeah."

"No question he genuinely loved her."

"Or had himself convinced that he did," Sam said.

"True. How do you want to get him out of here?"

"Take him out through the morgue. Check him into a hotel so we can keep tabs on him. Put a couple of officers on the door and let them know his wife will be joining him later today."

"Got it. What about the media?"

"I'll handle them." Sam left him to deal with the senator and returned to her office to find her nemesis, Lt. Stahl, waiting for her. "What do you want?"

"Nice to see you too, Lieutenant," Stahl said with a smarmy smile.

"I'm busy."

"Ahhh, yes, another homicide involving your 'boyfriend.' Quite a track record he has lately."

"He has nothing to do with this, nor did he have anything to do with John O'Connor's murder or Julian Sinclair's, as you well know. And P.S., he's my *fiancé*."

"Your *fiancé* knew all the victims."

"And that proves what, exactly?"

"That being an acquaintance of his can be bad for your health," Stahl said, laughing at his own joke.

"You aren't threatening me—again—are you, Lieutenant?"

"So touchy. Such a woman that way."

As usual in his presence, Sam held back the urge to smash her fist into his fat face. "As delightful as this conversation has been, I have work to do. If the rat squad isn't keeping you busy enough, Lieutenant, I'm sure Captain Malone can find something for you to do with your copious free time."

His jowls jiggled as he scowled at her. "Heard an interesting rumor today."

"Good for you."

"About your ex."

That got Sam's attention. "What about him?"

"That the case against him isn't as airtight as you thought it was."

She pushed her hands into her pockets to keep from punching him. "That case is airtight. I saw to it myself."

"Not all of it you didn't." On his way out the door, he said, "Have a nice day, Lieutenant."

Hands trembling, Sam reached for the phone to call Malone. "What do you know about Peter?"

The question was greeted with silence, which sent her heart into a wild gallop. "Tell me. Right now."

Under normal circumstances, she'd never speak so forcefully to her superior officer. But anything having to do with Peter tossed all the usual rules out the window.

"His attorney has requested a suppression hearing to determine whether the evidence gathered from his apartment is fruit of the poisonous tree."

The term turned her blood to ice. If the bomb-making evidence Freddie, Gonzo and Arnold had found in Peter's apartment had been gathered improperly, their entire case against him would be in jeopardy.

"We have his print on one of the bombs," Sam reminded Malone. "The one he strapped to Nick's car. The one that didn't detonate."

"It's a partial print, Sam. Not enough to hang the case on. We need the stuff from his apartment."

The very idea of Peter being set free after he'd tried to murder her and Nick made her sick.

"Don't panic yet," Malone said. "His attorney still has to convince the judge."

"What's the lawyer basing the challenge on?"

"That they kicked in Peter's door without any evidence linking him to the bombing other than your suspicion."

"But he did it!"

"We all know he did it, Sam. It's just the timeline of how we confirmed it that's under examination. They should've waited for the warrant before they busted into the apartment."

"They had reason to believe that he had bomb-making materials in there! Were they supposed to wait until he blew up the entire building before they acted?"

"They were running on adrenaline and emotion after you were nearly killed."

Sam sank into her desk chair. "He cannot be released. He just can't be."

"We'll fight it. Try not to worry."

"You're worried. I can hear it in your voice."

"The chain of events concerns me. It has all along."

Sam released a low moan. "Oh, *God.* Oh my God."

"We have media out front clamoring for information about Lightfeather. Do you want me to handle them?"

"No," Sam said, pulling herself together. "I'll do it."

"We're doing everything we can to keep him where he belongs, Sam."

"I'm counting on that. Keep me posted?"

"I will."

She hung up the phone and tried to breathe through the pain circulating in her gut. Since Nick's doctor friend Harry had ordered her to give up soda, her stomach troubles had been dramatically better. Hearing that Peter might be released from prison, however, brought the pain back in fierce waves. Sam forced herself to breathe—in through the nose, out through the mouth. Repeat.

A few minutes later, she stood up on shaking legs and reached for her coat. She had a job to do, and not even the threat of her malicious ex-husband being released from jail could keep her from doing what needed to be done on Regina's behalf. The dead woman's family was counting on Sam for answers, and she would get them what they needed no matter what might be happening in her own life.

Fueled by determination to do what needed to be done, Sam headed for the lobby.

Chief Farnsworth flagged her down before she could head outside. "Lieutenant." His warm gray eyes studied her with concern.

"Chief."

"You've heard the news about Gibson."

"Lieutenant Stahl took great pleasure in clueing me in."

"Sorry. I was on my way to talk to you about it when I got waylaid. Are you all right?"

She nodded. "I'm working the de Castro case. Doing what I do."

"We're making use of all available resources to keep Gibson where he belongs."

"I'm counting on that. Well, the press is looking to take a piece out of me, and you know how I hate to keep them waiting."

The chief laughed. "Allow me to have your back," he said, gesturing for the door.

As always, Sam was grateful for his unwavering support.

The instant they stepped through the double doors, the reporters pounced.

"Has Senator Lightfeather been arrested for murder?"

"How does he know the dead woman?"

"Were they having an affair?"

"Is he in custody?"

The chief held up his hands to stop the barrage of questions. "If you give Lieutenant Holland the chance to speak, she has a brief statement that should answer some of your questions."

Sam stepped forward, burrowing deeper into her coat. The February day had grown frigid and stormy. "Senator Lightfeather discovered Regina Argueta de Castro dead last night in her Columbia Heights apartment."

"How did he know her?"

"She worked for the company that cleans the Capitol and congressional offices. Throughout the night, the senator cooperated with our efforts to confirm his alibi, which we have now done. He has been released with instructions to remain in the District until we close the case. Ms. Argueta de Castro was from Guatemala and was in the country legally. Her mother and two children in Guatemala survive her, and they have been notified of her death. That is all I'm going to say at this point. We'll keep you informed as developments occur."

"Were they romantically involved?"

"No comment."

"How do you feel about your ex being sprung from prison?"

"Absolutely no comment."

As Chief Farnsworth ushered her back inside, Sam realized if the press knew about Peter it was only a matter of time before Nick would hear about it too.

"I need to make a phone call," she said to the chief.

"Go right ahead."

Sam started to walk away but turned back when he called out to her.

"If he gets sprung," the chief said, "we'll be so far up his ass he won't be able to fart without us knowing about it."

"Thanks." Sam didn't trust herself to say anything more without losing her famous cool. She knew he was trying to comfort her, but the very thought of that monster on the loose again was enough to turn her legs to jelly. He'd tried to *blow her up.* All because she'd reconciled with Nick—six years after Peter had gone to extraordinary lengths to keep them apart.

Back in the detective's pit, she closed the door to her office, sank into her chair and called Nick.

"Hey, babe," he said. "How's it going?"

The smile she heard in his voice went a long way toward soothing her frayed nerves. "I've had better days. You?"

"What's wrong? And don't say it's nothing."

"This time it's not nothing." She told him about Peter's case possibly falling apart.

"You've got to be fucking kidding me."

That he was swearing told her a lot about how upset he was. Nick never swore. That was *her* claim to fame. "I wish I was."

"We've got to do something. What can we do?"

"There will be a hearing, and hopefully the judge has an ounce of sense."

"If they let him go, he'll come at you again."

"Maybe his stint in prison has scared some sense into him."

"You don't believe that any more than I do. He's totally obsessed with you, and now he's even more pissed off than he was before."

"Malone and Farnsworth assured me they're doing everything they can to keep him in jail."

"Does he have a leg to stand on with this hearing?"

"He might," Sam said, hating to admit it. She filled him in on the issue with the warrant. "If they suppress the evidence we found in his apartment, our entire case falls apart. A partial print isn't enough to prosecute."

"This is such *bullshit*! He was caught red-handed!"

"I hate to do this to you when you're so busy. Sorry."

"I'm never too busy for you, babe. And you have nothing to be sorry about. You're the victim in this case."

"We both are." He'd been more severely injured in the bombing, suffering a mild concussion and a cut over his eye that had required stitches and left a scar.

"I'll make a few phone calls," he said. "See what I can find out."

"Don't do anything politically risky, Nick. That'd be playing right into his hand."

"They're phone calls. That's all."

She had no doubt one of those calls would be to the U.S. Attorney himself. Her fiancé was nothing if not well connected in Washington.

"Are you okay?" he asked softly.

"I'll be better when you get home tonight."

"I'll be there as soon as I can break free of the fund-raising thing."

"Good luck with that."

"Thanks. How's Henry?"

"Sprung for now. His wife is on her way here from Arizona."

"Yikes. I don't envy him that confrontation."

"If he'd kept his fly zipped, there'd be nothing to confront him about."

"True," Nick said, chuckling.

"You know I'd have to kill you, don't you?"

"Kill me for what? What've I done now?"

"If you ever cheated," she said in a small voice, instantly regretting going there. She tensed, awaiting his reply.

"Samantha," he said, his tone chastising. "Tell me you didn't just say that."

"I didn't just say that. I know I have nothing to worry about, even when all that senatorial power goes to your head."

"It may go to my head, but it'll never get to my zipper."

Sam laughed. He always knew just what to say to her. "I'll see you when you get home."

"Yes, you will, and we'll have a more in-depth discussion about who gets access to my zipper—and who does not."

"I'll look forward to that, Senator."

"As well you should. Love you, babe. Thanks for calling and giving me a heads-up about Peter."

She'd learned the hard way not to keep things from him and appreciated that he recognized she was making an effort in that area of their relationship. "Love you too. See you soon."

Sam put down the phone and gave herself a moment to decompress before she considered her next move in Regina's case. She was going over the less-than-fruitful reports from the crime scene detectives and the canvas of Regina's building when Freddie stepped into the office, a grim expression on his face.

"What's the matter?"

EIGHT

"NOTHING," FREDDIE SAID, startled by the question. "I just walked in the door. What makes you think something's the matter?"

"I know you, and I can tell just by looking at you that something is wrong. You've been off all morning."

"So on top of all your other formidable skills, now you're psychic too?"

"Sit," she said, pointing to the door and then the chair on the other side of her desk.

Frowning, Freddie pushed the door closed and sat. "What?"

"Tell me what's wrong."

"It's nothing to do with work or the case. Lightfeather is stashed at the Washington Hilton with two guards as directed. No one followed us, and I checked him in under the name of Jim Dalton. Can I get back to work now?"

"Not until you tell me why your shoulders are hunched and you haven't smiled all day."

"I'm tired, and we're working a rape and murder. Am I supposed to be whistling 'Dixie' at the same time? I wasn't aware of that job requirement."

"Despite your sarcasm, you're not walking out that door until you tell me what's bugging you."

"Just because we've talked about stuff in the past doesn't mean I have to share my every thought with you."

Wow, he was really in a mood. Sam raised a brow to let him know he wasn't going to escape her clutches.

"I'm sorry," he muttered, slumping into the chair. "I shouldn't talk to you that way."

"When it's just you and me and the door is closed, you should speak to me any way you see fit." It was as close as she'd ever come to letting him know she valued their friendship as much as their working relationship.

Seeming surprised, he said, "So it's okay to tell you you're being nosy and that you should butt out?"

"Sure, but it doesn't mean I will."

"God, you're a *pain*."

She smiled. Nick often said the same thing about her, and Sam always took it as a compliment. "I prefer *dogged*."

"That too," Freddie said. "Fine! If you must know, my mother is driving me crazy."

Sam hadn't seen that coming. "Over what?"

Freddie gave her a "you know" look.

"Ahhh, Mama Cruz doesn't approve of the girlfriend, huh?"

"No," he said miserably. "And she won't even give Elin a chance. We had a good talk last night and I thought things would be better, but when I went to check on her before work this morning, we got into it again. Not sure if it's the fever or what, but she's making me nuts!"

Sam stood up, clipped her portable radio to her hip and grabbed her car keys. "Let's discuss this on the road."

He stood. "Where're we going?"

"First to talk to Regina's boss and then hopefully to some of her coworkers."

"I'm with you, boss."

Sam waited while he got the trench coat that he claimed made him feel like Colombo and then led the way to her car. After starting the car she gave some considerable thought to Freddie's predicament. "I can understand where Mama is coming from."

"Great," he said, his voice dripping with sarcasm. "Thanks for the support. I really appreciate it."

"Wait. Hear me out. It's just that when I think of you with a woman, I see someone…different…than Elin for you. Someone…softer, I guess."

"What about what *I* see? Doesn't anyone care about what *I* want?"

"Hmm," Sam said. "How to say this delicately?"

"Oh, for crying out loud. Just say it. What do you care about being delicate?"

"It seems…to those of us on the outside looking in… that you may be letting your, um, little brain do the thinking for your big brain."

Out of the corner of her eye, she caught the glare he directed her way. "That's not the case."

"Are you sure of that?"

"I *like* her! Why doesn't anyone believe that's possible?"

"Okay, I'll bite. What do you like about her?"

"She's…fun and nice and sweet."

"Uh huh. What else?"

"What do you mean what else? Isn't that enough?"

"No. Fun and sweet and nice is not enough to build a relationship on."

"It's more than Nick started with. There's nothing nice or sweet about you."

Sam snorted with laughter. "Good one."

"Thank you. I try."

"What do you talk to her about besides 'your place or mine'?"

"We talk about sports and our friends, our work. The usual stuff."

"If you're together three hours, how much of that time is spent talking?"

"I don't know. I hardly keep track of that."

"Guess."

She could see him squirming in the passenger seat. "An hour or so."

"So one hour talking, two hours screwing. Can you see why your mother might be concerned?"

"No! She doesn't know that!"

"Freddie, come on. Of course she knows. You practically pant and drool whenever Elin is around. It's obvious to everyone that you're hot for her."

"I ask again…so *what*? Why does everyone care so much that I'm hot for her?"

"Because it's not like you to be so…preoccupied."

"I waited a long time for this, Sam. I wish everyone would butt the heck out and let me live my own life."

"We're worried about you. That's all."

"Well, don't worry. I'm a big boy, and I can take care of myself. I don't need you and my mother ganging up on me and screwing with my head. I'm happy with Elin. Can't that be enough for you?"

"I'm sure you're very happy when you're in bed with her. It's the rest of the time we're concerned about."

"You don't know what you're talking about, and to be honest, it's none of your business. Or my mother's."

"That's very true. So I will do as you ask and butt out."

"Good."

"Fine."

They rode the rest of the way to the Capitol Cleaning Services headquarters in uneasy—and unusual—silence. Inside, they were ushered into the offices of JoAnn Smithson, the owner of the company.

Mrs. Smithson looked to be in her late fifties or early

sixties, and judging from her haggard appearance, Sam deduced she hadn't slept well the night before.

After giving them permission to record the interview, Mrs. Smithson folded her hands on top of her cluttered desk. "What can I do to help you find the person who did this to Regina?"

"How long had she been in your employ?" Sam asked.

"Just over two years." She retrieved a file from a stack on the desk and handed it to them. "Here's her personnel file. As you can see, she had all the proper paperwork."

Freddie reached for the folder and flipped through the contents.

"If we checked the rest of your files, we'd find that to be true of all your employees?" Sam asked.

Mrs. Smithson stiffened. "We do *not* hire undocumented workers. We work for *Congress*, Lieutenant. How long do you think we'd hold that contract if I had illegal workers traipsing through the Capitol?"

"Not long I'd imagine. How well did you know Regina?"

"Quite well. I make it a point to know all my employees." She sagged into the chair. "Her poor mother and children. Have they been told of her death?"

"Yes. Were you aware of her relationship with Senator Lightfeather?"

Mrs. Smithson sat up straighter. "Relationship? What relationship did she have with a senator? She cleaned his office."

"According to the senator, they were romantically involved."

The color drained from Mrs. Smithson's face. "That's not possible," she sputtered. "We have rules…strict rules about decorum and behavior. She wouldn't have…" She glanced up at Sam and Freddie. Their expressions must have confirmed the truth. Once again she sagged. "I can't believe this."

"How much was she paid?"

"Seventeen dollars an hour, plus benefits."

"We'd like to speak to some of her friends or coworkers, anyone who might've been aware of what was going on between Regina and the senator. We're also looking for some insight into her life outside of work."

"Maria Espanosa," Mrs. Smithson said. "They were close friends."

"Where can we find her?"

Mrs. Smithson wrote down an address, also in Columbia Heights, and handed it to Sam. "She didn't come into work last night, and no one has heard from her. I planned to check on her when I leave the office."

Sam churned with anxiety. "Is it like her to miss work?"

"She's never missed a shift."

Sam glanced at Freddie and sensed they were on the same wavelength.

Mrs. Smithson watched their silent communication. "You don't think…"

"We'll check on her and let you know what we find."

"Will it be all over the media that Regina was messing around with a senator?"

"We haven't confirmed that information to the press yet," Sam said. "But it's only a matter of time before it becomes public."

"Oh God," Mrs. Smithson said, massaging her temples as tears flooded her already-reddened eyes. "God. Everything I've worked for…all these years. We have rules…"

"You might want to look into hiring a firm that specializes in crisis communication," Freddie suggested. "So you can be prepared to deal with the media."

"Yes," Mrs. Smithson said, brightening. "That's a good idea. Thank you."

"We'll be in touch if we need any further information."

"I'd appreciate that," Mrs. Smithson said as she escorted them past the wary glances of several other employees on their way to the main door. "Please let me know when you find Maria."

"We will," Freddie assured her.

"While we're on the Hill," Sam said to Freddie once they were outside, "let's take a look at the senator's office."

He grunted in reply.

Sam stopped and turned to him. "I know you're pissed with me, and that's your prerogative, but try to keep in mind that I only said what I did because I don't want you to end up heartbroken at the end of this. Trust me when I tell you that's no fun at all."

"I heard everything you said. And I've heard everything my mother has had to say. Now I'd really appreciate it if you'd both leave me alone to live my own life."

"Sure thing," she said, even as she wondered how she'd ever stand idly by and watch a woman walk all over his tender heart with stiletto heels. "I don't know about you, but I want to see this famous sofa where the senator boffed the cleaning lady."

Freddie rolled his eyes at her crudeness, and Sam hoped they'd put things back on track.

GONZO SAT PERFECTLY still and tried to stay focused on what the lawyer, Andy, was saying in response to Christina's many questions. Words flew past him: DNA tests, custody hearings, social workers. All he could think about was that dimpled chin. He didn't need a DNA test to tell him he'd met his son earlier that day—and the child's mother hadn't even given him a name.

"He can't breathe in that house," Gonzo said, interrupting them. He felt like he was coming out of his skin as he remembered the conditions in which his son was living. "We have to get him out of there."

"We'll move as quickly as we can to file for custody," Andy assured him. Blond and handsome, he looked every bit the Yale-educated attorney. "Of course, we can't do a thing until we've confirmed paternity."

"He looks like me," Gonzo said. "He has my dimple."

"I'm glad you were able to see a basic resemblance," Andy said, smiling. "That'll help you to feel confident you're doing the right thing pursuing custody."

"I'd want him out of there if he was mine or not. She didn't even give him a name." Gonzo simply couldn't get his head around that.

"I know, Detective," Andy said. "It's inexcusable. I have a baby of my own and can't imagine him living nameless in a smoke-infested environment. However, I have to caution you, custody cases can often be an uphill battle for fathers. Even when the father proves he can provide a better home than the mother, the courts often rule in favor of the mother."

Gonzo couldn't believe what he was hearing. "Even if she's filling his little lungs with smoke?"

"Unfortunately, it often has to be something more than that to get the court's attention—abuse, drugs, criminal activity occurring inside the home. Smoke, on its own, won't be enough."

"I'd bet my badge that smoking isn't the only thing going on there." Gonzo cast a wary glance at Christina. "She was quite the partier when I knew her."

"Any information you happen to 'stumble upon' that

can be used against her in court would be information worth having, if you catch my drift."

Gonzo took in the pointed look Andy directed his way and nodded to show he understood what Andy was telling him.

"I'll do what I can for you, as long as you understand that the odds are stacked against you going in," Andy said. "And these things can get very, very costly."

"I hate to ask this because I'll pay whatever it takes, but, ah, how much are we talking?"

"Tens of thousands."

Gonzo winced. He had some money, but not that much. No matter. He'd find a way to get what he needed to protect his son, including an appeal to his parents if it came to that.

"Don't worry about the money," Christina said, casting an uncomfortable glance his way. Before Gonzo could ask what she meant, she stood and extended her hand to Andy. "Thank you so much for coming into the office on a Sunday."

"Any friend of the senator's is a friend of mine." He shook Gonzo's hand. "I'll call Social Services to get them over there to check on him, and I'll get the ball rolling with the request for DNA from the baby. If she's interested in your money, she's apt to give up the DNA without objection. Give me a day or two, and I'll be in touch."

"Thank you," Gonzo said. "I appreciate your help."

Feeling as if he was outside himself watching someone else navigate the elevator, Gonzo was aware of Christina silently guiding him back to the car. Once there, he turned to her. "What'd you mean in there? About the money?"

She looked up at him. "I have some. If it comes to that."

Shaking his head, he said, "No way. I'm not taking money from you."

"You heard what he said, Tommy," she said, her hands resting on his chest. He wondered if she could feel his heart racing. "This could get really expensive. What if you run out of money before you get custody?"

"I'll borrow it, but I'm not taking it from you."

"I don't just have some," she said haltingly. "I have a lot. My parents…my family is, um, well, we have money. It'd be nothing to me to help you out if you need it."

"I appreciate the offer, but I'm sure it won't come to that." He stepped out of her embrace and opened the car door for her. When she was settled he went around to the driver's side. On the way to her place, Gonzo tried to process everything that had happened.

"Is this going to change everything between us?" she asked after a long period of silence.

"Is what? The baby?"

"The money," she said in a small voice that told him it had changed things for her in the past.

"Why should it?"

"You'd be surprised how it can change things." Rubbing a hand over her jeans, she added, "For what it's worth, I live on what I make. I've never allowed money to be a big deal in my life."

"Easy to do when you've always had plenty of it." The instant the words were out of his mouth, he regretted them. Her shocked expression indicated a direct hit. He reached for her hand. "I'm sorry. I didn't mean that the way it sounded. I appreciate the offer. I really do, but I hope it doesn't come to that."

"I hope not either, but if it does, the offer is on the table."

Gonzo squeezed her hand even as he continued to

buzz with apprehension. The thought of the baby—his son—in that smoke-filled house…And that there might be nothing he could do about it…That made him shudder.

"Come in, Tommy," Christina said when they reached her house. "You shouldn't be alone tonight."

"I'm not fit for company."

"Don't do this. Don't push me away."

"Christina—"

She reached for him and pressed her lips to his.

When he tried to pull back, she sank her fingers into his hair and held him close to her. "Don't go."

"I'm all churned up."

"Then be churned up with me. We'll figure this out. I promise."

He leaned his forehead against hers. "You're sure you want to take all this on? I wouldn't blame you—"

She rested a finger over his lips. "Let's go in."

As Gonzo stepped out of the car and followed her inside, he had to admit he was grateful not have to spend the night alone with his thoughts.

NINE

In Henry Lightfeather's office, Sam studied the array of family photos displayed on the credenza. Like Henry, his wife Annette seemed to have Native American origins. Their five adopted children were ethnically diverse. One was in a wheelchair. They seemed to be a happy, smiling family in the many photographs. In addition to the group shot, there were individual photos of each of the children as well as framed samples of their artwork.

"I would've felt like they were watching," Sam said.

"Watching what?" Freddie asked.

"While I was doing the cleaning lady on the sofa, I'd have felt like my family was watching with all these pictures right here."

Freddie snorted. "I'll bet they were the last thing he was concerned about when he was doing the cleaning lady on the sofa." He opened a door. "We've got a closet full of suits and personal items. Shaving kit, running shoes, sweats."

Sam opened the door to talk to the Capitol Police officer who'd escorted them into the office. "Were you aware that he was living in his office?"

"We know everything that goes on in these buildings."

"Are there rules about members living in their offices?"

"It's frowned upon, but not unheard of. The cost of living in this city is exorbitant. A lot of members have trouble swinging two places."

"So we've heard." Sam took another look around the spacious office. "We're through here for now, but we may be back. Do us a favor and keep people out of here until we give you the okay."

"Does that include the senator?"

"That includes everyone."

He nodded in agreement.

"Thanks for the courtesy," Sam said.

Lindsey McNamara called as they headed for Maria Espanosa's apartment in Columbia Heights. "What've you got, Doc?"

"No match on the second semen sample with anyone in the system," Lindsey said. "And no shock that Lightfeather is a match for the other."

"Well, we knew he would be." Sam smacked the palm of her hand on the steering wheel. "Why couldn't the other guy have been in the system?"

"Because if it was that easy, none of us would have jobs," Lindsey quipped.

"Yeah, yeah. You're running the fetus, right?"

"As we speak. Another point of interest is the skin we found under her nails was a match with the mystery semen. So we can confirm it was the second guy who roughed her up, not the senator."

"At least that's something. She put up a fight."

"Judging from the skin we found, she scratched him good."

"Thanks for the info, Lindsey. Keep me posted on the fetus."

"You got it."

Sam punched the speaker button on the phone to shut it off. "What're you thinking so far?" she asked Freddie.

"I'm trying to picture how a cleaning lady becomes a United States senator's lover."

"Well, if a cop can do it..."

Freddie laughed.

"Sorry, bad joke. Please proceed."

"While it doesn't seem that Lightfeather did the murder, how can her affair with him not be related somehow?"

"I agree. It would've been a huge bombshell for both of them if anyone found out."

"With him having the most to lose."

"Or so we assume. Maybe the stakes were higher for her."

"Her immigration status would be in jeopardy if she lost her job, and her family was counting on her support," Freddie said.

"The stakes were high for both of them."

"You gotta wonder what they were thinking that first time."

"Probably safe to assume not much thinking was involved."

"Imagine afterward though...when the reality sunk in."

"Total freak-out," Sam said. "On both parts."

"What if someone found out? Someone who would've been furious or jealous or threatened."

"Do you think she'd tell anyone?"

"No," Freddie said emphatically. "Absolutely not."

"Not even her closest friends?"

"I wonder if she had close friends here."

"Let's talk to Maria Espanosa and find out," Sam said.

Maria lived in a basement apartment about four blocks from Regina's place. They knocked on the door and waited.

"Something stinks," Freddie said.

"She ain't home," a young voice from the street called down to them.

They turned to face the boy, who Sam gauged to be ten or eleven.

"Any idea where she is?" Sam asked.

The kid shrugged. "Don't know. Haven't seen her in a coupla days."

Sam and Freddie exchanged glances.

"You cops?" the boy asked.

"That's right," Freddie said.

"Cool. Can I watch?"

"Not this time, buddy." Freddie went up the half set of stairs to speak to the boy while Sam called in their location to dispatch.

"Possible DOA," she told the dispatcher. To the kid, she called, "Any idea where we can find the super?"

"Sure. My grandpa. I'll get him for ya."

"Thanks, man," Freddie said. "Tell him to bring his keys."

The kid scampered off, and Freddie came back down to join Sam. "Smell plus gone a few days equals murder."

"Your thinking matches mine."

"Who would have a beef with two members of the Capitol Cleaning Services?"

"Not sure yet, but you can bet we're going to find out."

The super arrived a few minutes later with a fat wad of keys. His grandson trailed behind him.

"You might want to get the kid out of here," Sam said.

"Mario," the old man barked. "Scram!"

"Aw, Gramps, come on!"

"*Scram*, I said!"

"Nothing fun *ever* happens around here, and then when it does…" His mutterings faded as he clomped off.

The old man unlocked the door. "Holy hell, what's that reek?"

"Most likely a dead body," Sam said as she pushed past him.

He startled. "Hey, this ain't that kinda place! I run a clean building."

Sam ignored him as she followed the smell to the bedroom where she found Maria's naked, bloody body on the bed. "Call it in," she said to Freddie as she stepped in for a closer look at the open wound on Maria's neck. A pool of blood between her legs indicated a vicious sexual assault. "Same as Regina."

"Defensive injuries to her hands," Freddie said.

"Looks like she connected with the knife before it found her throat."

He shook his head with dismay. "Poor thing."

"Start a canvas of the neighborhood. See if you can figure out when she was last seen alive."

"Judging from the smell and the condition of the body, I'd guess thirty-six hours or more."

"Agreed. Which means he did her before Regina. That leads me to wonder if there are others waiting to be found."

"I'll get going on that canvas," Freddie said. "I assume you'll want her cell phone dumped?"

Sam nodded. "How much you want to bet it's the same company? Get a subpoena and let them know if they continue to stonewall us, they'll be hearing from the U.S. Attorney himself."

"Got it."

Left alone with the dead woman, Sam studied the framed photographs on the bedside table. Several young children and a shot of Maria with what must've been her parents. Sam wondered if, like Regina, Maria also had children living in another country. The one room apartment where she'd been killed was spartanly furnished with just a bed and dresser. A small television sat on top of the dresser. Sam deduced that Maria did little more than sleep and bathe in this space. There wasn't much room for anything else.

WHILE WAITING FOR crime scene detectives to arrive, Sam went through the papers she found in the bedside table drawer. Along with a passport from Belize, she found papers authorizing Maria to work in the United States as well as cards and letters from her family at home. Drawing a notebook from her back pocket, Sam wrote down the name and return address that appeared most frequently on the letters in anticipation of making another of those dreaded phone calls.

Lindsey McNamara came down the short flight of stairs into the apartment. "What've you got, Sam?"

"Same M.O. as Regina, right down to the rape."

"Someone's gunning for young immigrant women," Lindsey said as she snapped on latex gloves.

"Starting to seem that way. They had that in common along with their jobs, but what's the motive? Could it be that they stumbled upon something in the course of their jobs that someone didn't want them to know?"

"I can't imagine that members of Congress leave sensitive information laying around the offices for the cleaning staff to find."

"Unless they were sent in to look for something specific," Sam speculated.

"I suppose that's possible."

Crime scene detectives soon descended upon the apartment.

"Get me that report ASAP, Doc," Sam said on her way out.

"You got it," Lindsey said.

Sam took the stairs to the street level where a crowd had formed, no doubt hoping for a glimpse of the murdered woman's body. As she took deep gulping breaths to rid her senses of the death smell, Sam doubted they'd be so curious if they saw even a fraction of what she did on any given day.

Freddie jogged down the street to join her. "Last confirmed sighting was yesterday morning," he reported, consulting his notes. "The owner of the coffee shop on the corner said she bought her usual soy latte after her morning run. From what the neighbors said, she worked nights, ran five miles after her shift ended, got her latte and then went home to sleep. Never deviated from the routine. Seven days a week."

"So someone was either watching her or knew her routine and was waiting for her when she got back to her apartment. Maybe took her by surprise or pulled the knife to get her inside."

"No one I've talked to so far recalls a man hanging out in the area."

"Mrs. Smithson said they work five nights a week cleaning the Capitol, right?"

"Uh huh."

"And Lightfeather said Regina spent 'most nights' after work with him, but they argued about where she was the other nights."

"Right."

"I want to know where they were those other two nights too." Sam consulted her watch. Almost seven o'clock. "Let's turn the canvas over to second shift and pick this up in the morning. We'll meet at HQ at seven and bring everyone up to speed on what we have so far. I'll talk to Malone about putting out an alert to immigrant women in the city, just in case this isn't related to where they worked."

"You don't think it's unrelated, though, do you?"

Sam rested her hands on her hips. "I'm leaning toward related, but I've learned not to make assumptions until I know more."

"We'll hit it hard in the morning," Freddie said.

"You bet we will."

She handed him the slip of paper with Maria's family contact information. "Until then, I need you to make a phone call."

Freddie glanced at the paper. "Ugh. Do I have to?"

"Someone does, and just in case they don't speak English, you get the short straw. While you're at it, give JoAnn Smithson a call too. Let her know about Maria."

"Oh gee, lucky me." He snatched the paper from her. "I hate making these calls."

"Don't we all, Detective? Don't we all?"

SAM SPENT AN hour at HQ updating the murder board and making notes about what she knew about the two victims, which wasn't much. Regina was thirty, Maria twenty-eight. Both had been in the country for about two years. Both had applied for permanent citizenship. Sam knew Regina's application had been denied, but Maria's status was unclear. She wondered if Senator Lightfeather would know and decided to pay him a visit on the way home.

After consulting with Captain Malone, she issued an alert to the media to warn young immigrant women living in the city to be vigilant in and around their places of residence. She didn't mention the similarities between the two murders, lest she set off hysteria in the city. Hopefully, they could apprehend the perpetrator before that became necessary.

On her way to the Washington Hilton on Connecticut Avenue, she received a call from Darren Tabor.

"No comment," she said as she activated the speaker on her phone.

"I haven't asked the question yet."

"Just because Nick and I gave you one exclusive doesn't mean you can randomly call me any time you want." Sam had reluctantly agreed to sit for a joint interview with Nick after their engagement. They'd granted the interview to Tabor because he'd given them a heads-up that the *Reporter* tabloid planned to run a story about Sam's long-ago near-abortion and figured they owed him one. Now they were even—at least as far as Sam was concerned.

"I made you look really good in that article," Tabor said.

Sam snorted. "I don't need your help to look really good."

Laughing, Tabor said, "You might want to work on your self-esteem, Lieutenant. I hate to see you so down on yourself."

Sam choked back a chuckle. She wouldn't give him the satisfaction.

"Just saw your alert to immigrant women," Tabor said. "What else can you tell me?"

"Nothing yet."

"Do you have a second victim?"

"Maybe. Maybe not."

"You must if you saw fit to issue the alert."

"Don't you dare report that, Darren. I'm not confirming anything."

"That's okay. I can check the logs. They'll tell me what you're not."

"I'll leave you to make your own conclusions."

"What's Lightfeather's status?"

"I told you all earlier—he's been cleared on any involvement in the murder of Regina Argueta de Castro."

"You can't do your favorite reporter a favor and confirm they were involved?"

"Give it a rest, Darren. I'm outta here." She shut off the phone and pulled up to the Washington Hilton a few minutes later. Flashing her badge to the bellhop who met her, Sam said, "I'll be just a few minutes."

"The person you no doubt wish to see is on the seventh floor."

"Thank you." Now why couldn't everyone be that cooperative toward the police?

Sam took the elevator to the seventh floor and made her way to the room at the end of the hallway where two of her colleagues stood watch outside the door. "How goes it?" she asked them.

"Pretty quiet, Lieutenant."

"Is the wife here yet?"

"Arrived about thirty minutes ago."

"Any fireworks?"

The two young men smirked.

"That's one way to describe it. She is *not* happy with him."

"With good reason," Sam said as she knocked on the door.

Annette Lightfeather opened the door and blanched at the sight of Sam's badge. "Yes?"

"Mrs. Lightfeather, I'm Detective Lieutenant Sam Holland. I'd like to speak to your husband, please."

"I understood that he'd been cleared of any involvement in the…the—"

"Murder of Regina Argueta de Castro."

The attractive woman swallowed hard. "Yes." Her

eyes were red and raw, as if she'd cried her way across the country. Sam couldn't blame her. In her place, Sam would probably never stop crying.

"I have some follow-up questions I'd like to ask him."

Annette gestured for her to come in.

Henry sat on the sofa, head in his hands.

"Senator," Sam said.

His head shot up, and his eyes widened when he saw her there. "Lieutenant. Have you found the person who killed Regina?"

Annette's lips tightened into an expression of supreme dismay. Her attractive face was totally transformed by rage.

"I'm afraid not," Sam said. "In fact, there's been a second murder. Were you acquainted with Regina's friend Maria Espanosa?"

Henry gasped and his mouth fell open in apparent shock. "Not Maria too!"

"Were you also sleeping with her?" Annette's voice was one note shy of a shriek.

"Of course not," Henry said haltingly. "She was a close friend of Regina's."

"What was Maria's immigration status?"

He glanced at his wife and then at Sam. "Like Regina, she'd applied for permanent residency but had been denied."

"Did you intervene on her behalf as well?" Sam asked.

As Annette watched the proceedings, her expression shifted from dismay to disbelief. "You went to CIS for her?" she asked.

"I made some phone calls," Henry said. "That's all it was. Phone calls."

"For your *lover*," Annette spat back at him. "Did she make you feel like the big powerful man?"

"Mrs. Lightfeather." Sam wished the floor would open

up and swallow her. She'd rather be anywhere else on earth than in the midst of their marital meltdown. "I understand you're upset—"

"*Upset?* You think I'm *upset*? While I'm at home raising our *five* children, he's here banging the cleaning lady *in his office*? I'm not upset, Lieutenant. I'm *livid*."

"Annette—"

"Shut up, Henry. Just shut up." She stormed from the suite's living room and slammed the bedroom door.

Sam let an uncomfortable minute pass before she ventured a glance at Henry. The guy looked awful. Under most circumstances, Sam had sympathy for someone who'd lost a loved one in a violent manner. In this case, however, she was having trouble working up the usual level of sympathy.

"I, um, I know this is a difficult time for you, Senator, but I wondered if you might be willing to answer a few more questions."

Sighing, he gestured for her to go ahead.

Sam sat in a high-backed chair facing him. "How well did you know Maria?"

"I'd met her a few times. When Regina and I took a break from our relationship, Maria cleaned my office. I just don't understand why anyone would want to hurt them. They were hard-working women who only wanted to better themselves and their families. What could anyone have against them?"

"I don't know yet, but we're going to find out. What was Maria's immigration status?"

"It was similar to Regina's. She'd been denied permanent residency, and we'd appealed it."

"Did Regina ask you to do that?"

He nodded. "Once again, I had to be careful not to get too involved because neither of them was my constituent.

However, I did make a few calls to see if there was anything that could be done. Last I heard, both applications were under review. We were hopeful for a positive outcome."

"I know you told your wife you weren't involved with Maria." She cleared her throat. "Too. Is that the truth?"

Henry gaped at her. "Yes! I swear to God, it was only Regina."

"Have you assisted any of Regina's other friends with their immigration status?"

He shook his head. "Just Maria."

"Did Maria have any friends, boyfriends, anyone in the city she was close to that you know of?"

"I think it was just Regina. They relied on each other, kept to themselves for the most part."

Having gotten what she came for, Sam stood. "I appreciate the additional information. I have to remind you to stay put until we close the case."

"The media's caught wind of the affair. Believe me, I'm not going anywhere." He walked Sam to the door. "I know what you must think of me, Lieutenant."

Sam turned to him. "What I think of you has no bearing on the fact that I'm going to do my job and get justice for two women who were killed in my city."

"I'm not a bad person. I just made a bad mistake."

"So you've decided that falling in love with Regina was a mistake?" For some reason, Sam took perverse pleasure in picking at the scab. "That's not what you said last night."

He glanced over his shoulder, as if to gauge whether his wife might be able to hear him. "I *loved* her," he said in a hoarse whisper. "And I don't regret that. I *do* regret the pain my mistake in judgment is causing my wife and family. I deeply regret that."

"I'm sure you do," Sam said. "I'll be in touch."

TEN

SAM ARRIVED AT home just as Nick's driver was dropping him off. From inside her car, she watched him emerge from the Town Car, still wearing the tuxedo from the fund-raiser. He leaned into the car to say something to the driver, and as he closed the door, he glanced over to find her watching him. A smile lit up his face.

Sam got out of her car and met him on the sidewalk.

He was carrying his overcoat, a garment bag and briefcase but still managed to slide an arm around her and kiss her forehead.

Sam leaned into his embrace, breathing in the clean fresh scent of home.

"Long day, huh?" he asked.

"For both of us."

He guided her into the house and hung their coats in the closet. Tugging off the bow tie and releasing the top button on his shirt, he went into the kitchen. "How about a glass of wine?"

Sam sat on the sofa and put her feet up on the coffee table. "Yes, please."

"Coming right up." He returned a few minutes later with two glasses of pinot grigio and put them on the table. "First things first." Sitting next to her, he reached for her and kissed her gently. "There," he said against her lips. "That's what I've been needing for hours now."

Sam ran her fingers over the stubble on his jaw and urged him into another kiss. He stretched out on top of her as one kiss became two and then three. Sam's fingers were buried in his soft hair as his lips moved from her mouth to her face and then her neck.

"I missed you today," he whispered, sending sensation darting through her.

She raised her hips and pressed against his erection, drawing a gasp from him. "So I can tell."

"I didn't plan to jump you the minute we walked in the door."

"You didn't. You were just saying hello."

That smile of his was so potent. She wondered if he had any idea what it did to her.

"Exactly," he said. "Now how about that wine?" He helped her sit up and handed a glass to her.

Sam curled her legs under her and watched the play of muscles in his chest and arms as he removed the tuxedo jacket and reached for his own glass. "How'd the fund-raiser go?"

"One-point-five million. Judson seemed happy," he said, referring to the chairman of the Virginia Democratic Party.

"*Whoa*. That's amazing!"

"You should've seen the people who turned out for the rally at VCU. They had to move it outside to Monroe Park. Even though it was freezing, we still filled the place up."

"You're on fire, Senator. I'm so proud."

He shrugged off the compliment. "How's the case?"

"Doubly complicated. We've got a second vic. Same M.O. Worked with Regina."

"Who was it?"

"Maria Espanosa."

"Oh, no! Not Maria." He sagged into the sofa. "She's so sweet. She cleans our office."

Sam winced at his reaction. "Did you know her well?"

"Just to say hello to. She was very quiet, kept to herself, but she did a great job. How anyone could harm her...it's just hard to believe."

And even though she was hardly a friend, it was another loss on top of so many others he'd sustained recently. Sam caressed his face. "I'm sorry to just drop it on you that way. I wasn't thinking that you might know her."

"It's really sad."

"Talk to me about anchor babies."

Startled, he said, "What about them?"

"Regina was pregnant."

His eyes went wide. "Was it Henry's?"

"He says it was."

"Damn. What a mess."

"Freddie introduced the anchor baby concept to me earlier. I hadn't heard about it before."

"It's a major issue. The numbers have exploded in the last few years. Lots of immigrant women have resorted to getting pregnant to stay in the country. Babies born on U.S. soil are automatically citizens and 'anchor' their mothers to the U.S."

"I see."

"The law can't be changed without amending the Constitution. There was some talk about closing that loophole in the 14th Amendment when we were pushing O'Connor-Martin through, but nothing came of it."

"So Regina's baby would've kept her in the country?"

"Most likely. The CIS isn't out to separate babies from their mothers. The country has no appetite for that kind of enforcement."

"I'll bet she got pregnant on purpose. She told Henry she was on the pill, and he said he saw them in her purse, but I wonder if she was taking them."

"So you think he was duped?"

"Hard to say. The emotion could've been real, but no doubt she got exactly what she wanted from him on that sofa."

"Jeez. What was he thinking?"

"Not much I suppose." She took a closer look at him and saw the fatigue and weariness he worked so hard to hide from her. "You need some sleep, Senator."

"Are we going to talk about it?"

"About what?"

He raised an eyebrow.

"Oh. Peter." For a while there, she'd almost forgotten about it. Almost. Sam wanted to reassure Nick. She wanted to tell him they had nothing to worry about. That's what she would've done a few weeks ago. But she'd been working on not keeping things from him, and that included her own worries.

"Talk to me, Sam. You have to be spun up about it."

"I'm trying not to think about it until I have to."

"How does he even have a case for dismissal? He tried to *kill* you."

"No one's questioning that. They're questioning the evidence gathering." Sam fiddled with her fingers. "If this comes to pass, it'll kill Cruz, Gonzo and Arnold. If they jumped the gun, it was only because he came at me."

He reached for her hand and laced his fingers through hers. "I don't want you to worry. If it happens, we'll deal with it together."

"And that makes it bearable." She leaned her head on his shoulder. "It does kind of freak me out to think of him on the streets again. Stalking me—and you."

"He won't get anywhere near you." A shudder rippled through his big frame. "God, just the thought of him on the loose makes me crazy. I'll do everything I can to make sure it doesn't happen."

"I said it before, but please don't do anything foolish on my behalf."

"Who else would I do foolish things for?"

"Don't make jokes."

"I'm not joking, Sam. I know you can more than take care of yourself, but you can't expect me to sit idly by and let that maniac come after you again."

Just the thought of it made Sam sick. "Let's talk about something else—anything else."

After taking a sip of his wine, he put the glass on the table and turned to her. "I met a really neat kid today." He told her about Scotty and the instant bond he'd felt with him.

"Why does talking about him make you look so sad?"

"Does it?" he asked, seeming surprised.

She nodded.

Nick hesitated for a moment. "Meeting him brought back a lot of memories." He combed his fingers through the long hair he released from the clip she wore to work. "Not all of them good."

His difficult childhood was something he didn't often speak of.

Sam put down her wineglass and reached for him, cradling his head against her chest.

"Would you mind too terribly if I became friends with a twelve-year-old? I know our lives are so chaotic, and there's so much going on, but now that I've met him, there's no way I can just forget about him."

"Of course I wouldn't mind. He sounds like a terrific kid."

"He really is. I want you to meet him."

"I'd like that." She smoothed her hand over his hair

and kissed his forehead. "What do you say we get some sleep?"

"Mmm."

"Upstairs."

"Mmm hmm."

"Nick…"

"Coupla minutes, babe. Just give me a coupla minutes right here."

Since he had so much trouble sleeping, she tightened her hold on him and gave him what he needed.

SAM WOKE UP as Nick carried her upstairs. "What time is it?"

"Three-thirty."

"Put me down. I'm too heavy."

"No, you're not."

She glanced up at him. "Did you sleep?"

"Like a rock."

"Will you be able to go back to sleep?"

In the bedroom, he set her down and turned on the bedside lamp. "Hope so." When she started to take off her sweater, he stopped her. "Let me."

Sam forced herself to stand still while he removed her clothes and pressed strategic kisses to each bit of skin as he uncovered it. "My turn?" she asked when he was finished.

"Sure," he said, reaching for her. "Since you're the *only* one with access to my zipper, have at it."

She swatted his hands away and quickly divested him of the remnants of the tuxedo. "I shouldn't have said that before. It's not something I worry about. It was just the case and this situation with Henry…"

With his fingers on her chin, he tilted her face up to

meet his gaze. "It's not something you'll *ever* have to worry about. I promise you that."

She looped her arms around his neck and went up on tiptoes to kiss him. "I know."

"Come here," he said, leading her into bed.

Sam moved into his embrace.

"Mmm, perfect," he said when he had her arranged on top of him. His fingers kneaded the tension from her shoulders and back.

"You need to sleep," she reminded him as she sank into the massage.

"I am sleeping."

"One part of you is most definitely *not* sleeping."

"As long as he's awake..." He raised his hips and cupped her ass.

"He's always awake."

"Only when you're naked in bed with me. Or if you're in the same room. Or in the shower. Or in the car. Or—"

Laughing, she silenced him with a kiss. "Since I want you to sleep, I'd better deal with him."

"That's probably for the best," he said with a grave expression that made her laugh again.

Pushing herself up, she straddled him and slid her damp heat over his length.

Nick groaned and clutched her hips, encouraging her to take him in.

Sam continued to tease him, enjoying the fierce look on his face as she denied him what he wanted.

Suddenly, he turned them over and entered her in one deep thrust.

Sam cried out and arched into him as he withdrew and then slid into her again.

He gazed down at her and brushed his lips over hers.

"Nick..."

"What, babe?" He flexed his hips, and Sam exploded. Holding her tight against him, Nick went with her.

"God," she whispered. "Where'd that come from?"

He laughed and kissed her once more before he rolled off her, bringing her with him. "I love you, Samantha."

She reached over him to turn off the light. "Love you too."

"When are you going to officially move in with me?"

"I sleep here every night. Isn't that official enough?"

"Not as long as your stuff still lives down the street."

"You're sure you're ready for all that comes with me?"

"I'm very sure."

"Remember that when your anal-retentive freakazoidal self is tripping over my crap and you're swearing at me."

"I'll never swear at you."

She could feel him relaxing into sleep. "You say that now...have I mentioned the other fifty pairs of shoes I have in storage?"

"Doesn't scare me."

Kissing his chest, she smiled. He had no idea. No idea at all.

SAM STROLLED UP the ramp to her father's house, three doors down Ninth Street from Nick's place. Standing on the front stoop, she debated for a minute before she knocked on the door.

Celia opened the door, and her smile became perplexed when she saw Sam standing there. "Why are you knocking?" she asked as she waved her stepdaughter inside.

"You crazy kids are still on your honeymoon. I didn't want to intrude."

Celia's heart-shaped face turned bright red. "Don't

be ridiculous. And don't ever knock on that door again. You hear me?"

"Yes, ma'am." Sam appreciated the warm welcome from her new stepmother. She'd suspected little would change between them now that Skip's longtime nurse had become his wife. Sam had been shocked to learn a few months ago that Celia and her dad had been secretly dating at the time of his shooting. Celia had immediately volunteered to oversee his home care and had quickly become indispensible to the family she was now a part of. "How's the groom?"

"Doing well. He was a little tired yesterday but seems better today. We're planning to have a quiet day. How are you?"

"Caught a murder during the wedding. Sorry we had to leave early."

"When duty calls, you have to go. We know that."

"Duty has been calling a little too often lately." She swallowed hard, hoping she could pull this off. "It was a, ah, nice wedding."

"Aww, thanks, honey. That's sweet of you to say." Celia's green eyes turned mischievous. "So tell me, was the senator involved with the cleaning lady?"

Sam followed Celia into the kitchen. "I can neither confirm nor deny..."

"*I knew it!* His poor wife at home in Arizona with all those kids."

"Don't breathe a word of that," Sam said. "We've yet to confirm the affair to the media."

"My lips are sealed," Celia said.

"Got yourself another hot one, Lieutenant," retired Metro Deputy Chief Skip Holland said. His wheelchair was positioned at the kitchen table where Celia had set him up to peruse the *Washington Post*. His brown and silver hair was still damp from an earlier washing, and his sharp blue eyes were focused on his youngest daughter.

Sam kissed his cheek, sat at the table and accepted the cup of coffee Celia handed her, even though she'd much prefer the diet cola her body still craved in the morning. Dr. Harry had recently broken the news to her that the carbonation in the soda was eating a hole in her stomach. The guy was a killjoy. "It's hot and getting hotter," Sam said of the case.

She told him about Regina being pregnant with Lightfeather's baby as well as the discovery of Maria Espanosa's dead body and the fear that a killer was targeting young immigrant women in the city. "They don't have anything in common, that we can find, other than their place of employment."

"You'll want to talk to some of their other coworkers," Skip said. "Maybe there was something else that tied them to each other."

"That's on the docket for today." She fiddled with her mug for a moment before she glanced over at him again. "I heard yesterday that it's possible Peter could get sprung."

Her father and Celia gasped.

"You can't be serious," Celia said.

Sam told them what she knew, even though she hated to upset them. It was all part of her new effort to be more forthright with the people she loved. "Nick's going to talk to Forrester," she said, referring to the U.S. Attorney. "But I told him not to stick his neck too far out. He needs to be thinking about his campaign."

"He needs to be making phone calls," Skip said emphatically. "Maybe he can do something to stop this insanity."

"Since when do you believe in taking advantage of

friends in high places?" Sam asked in an attempt to lighten the mood.

"Since the monster who tried to murder my little girl might get sprung from jail."

"Let's try not to think about it until we have to," Sam said, touched by his fiercely spoken words. "That's what I'm trying to do."

Celia patted her shoulder. "Probably easier said than done, honey."

"I'm sure Farnsworth and Malone are doing all they can from their end," Skip said.

"They are." Anxious to end the discussion about one of her least favorite subjects, Sam stood up and bent to kiss her dad's forehead. "I gotta hit it."

"Let me know if I can help."

"I'll probably be back later to run through it with you. Don't know enough yet."

"I'll be here."

Sam smiled. "Counting on that." She glanced around at the homey kitchen and was swamped with relief at knowing her gravely injured father had someone who genuinely loved him overseeing his care. It freed Sam to dare to have a life of her own. For the first time in the two years since he was shot by an unknown assailant during a routine traffic stop gone bad, Sam was able to stop worrying constantly about him. "So Nick's making noise about me officially moving down the street."

"Probably time," Skip said.

"I guess so. Especially since we've set a wedding date." Sam still couldn't believe she'd agreed to this.

"Is that so?" Celia said, clapping her hands together with glee. "When?"

"Um, March 26."

"*This year?*" Skip and Celia said in stereo.

"It's all his idea. He's convinced it's no big deal."

"Oh my goodness!" Celia said. "We have to get going right away!"

"Nick said something about hiring someone to deal with all the details." Sam hoped her bold-faced lie wouldn't be obvious to them. As much as Sam loved her new stepmother, no way was Celia getting her hands on this wedding. *No way.* "We'll probably go that route." No doubt he knew someone who could make it all go away for them. She wondered why they hadn't thought of it sooner. "Well, I'm off. See you later."

"Let us know how we can help with the wedding," Celia called after her.

"You'll be the first to know," Sam said, scooting out the front door and taking her guilty conscience with her.

ELEVEN

SAM SCANNED THE faces of the detectives gathered in the conference room to go over the facts of the de Castro and Espanosa cases. Some of them looked like they had Monday morning-itis, especially Cruz, who was yawning his head off, and Gonzales, who seemed totally preoccupied. She hated that she was going to have to tell three of her loyal detectives about the situation with Peter Gibson, but she couldn't let them hear about it through a grapevine that was no doubt already buzzing with the news.

After she ran through what they knew so far on the current cases, Sam handed out assignments and sent the others on their way. "Detectives Cruz, Gonzales and Arnold," she said. "A minute of your time, please?"

They stopped and waited until the others left the room.

"Shut the door," Sam said.

They exchanged nervous glances.

"What's up, L.T.?" Cruz asked.

"Yesterday I received word that Peter Gibson's attorney has requested a hearing to determine whether the evidence collected at Gibson's apartment was fruit of the poisonous tree because you went in without a warrant."

As she expected, they erupted in protest.

Sam held up her hands to stop them. "I know exactly how it went down, and I would've done it the same way. We had every reason to believe he was involved."

"Except at that time we only had suspicion," Gonzo said. "Not solid proof."

"Yes." Sam was not at all surprised that he was the first to figure out what Gibson's attorney was using to force the hearing. "I want to be clear on this—no matter what happens, I don't blame you, and I don't want you to blame yourselves. We were all operating on adrenaline and high emotion that day. I appreciate how fast you all worked to find him and bring him in."

"It sounds like we worked *too* fast," Cruz mumbled, clearly undone by the news.

"Maybe so, but let's wait to see what the judge has to say before we jump to any conclusions. In the meantime, we have two vics who need our full attention right now, so let's keep our focus where it needs to be."

With muttered agreements, they headed for the door, shoulders stooped and heads down. Sam hated to see them like that. "Detective Gonzales, one more minute, please?"

After Cruz and Arnold stepped out, Sam took another long look at Gonzo's face, concerned by the unusual pallor. "Are you feeling better today?"

"Yeah. Sorry about yesterday. Something came up that I had to deal with."

"And everything's all right now?"

He hesitated. "It will be. I hope."

"Anything I can do?"

Once again he hesitated, and she realized he was tormented over something. "Gonzo, what is it? What's going on?" She really, *really* hoped he wasn't going to say that things weren't going well with Christina. Sam truly did not want to hear the details of their romance. She already had her hands full enough with Cruz's romantic troubles.

Gonzo looked so tortured that Sam experienced a pang of fear. "Sit." She gestured to a chair and took the one next to him. "Talk."

He dropped into the chair and released a deep sigh. "It seems that I have a son."

She stared at him. "*Whoa.*"

"That's what I said too." He filled her in on what he knew as well as the steps he was taking to confirm paternity and file for custody. "I hope it's okay that Christina set me up with Nick's lawyer friend Andy. He specializes in family law. I know I should have called you first."

"Of course it's okay," Sam said. "That's exactly what you should've done. What do we know about the mother and her boyfriend?"

"Nothing about him, except he looks like a biker dude. Tattoos everywhere. Leather, the works. Doesn't make him a criminal, but I caught a bad vibe from him."

"If I'm you, my first order of business is to get a last name on him and run them both to see if they have priors."

"Except I'm not supposed to use department resources for personal matters."

"Of course your superior officer never made this suggestion and you never told her you planned to use department resources for personal matters."

"Of course." A hint of a smile graced his face. "I won't let this affect my work. Don't worry."

"Never crossed my mind that you would. Let me know what I can do to help."

"Thanks. I'd appreciate you keeping this between us for now. Until I know for sure he's mine…"

"I understand."

He got up, seeming somewhat relieved to have shared his burden. "Thanks, L.T."

"Any time."

"This thing with Gibson…if he gets sprung, it's on me. I should've known better—"

"Don't," Sam said. She had expected nothing less from him as the most senior detective on the scene that night at Gibson's apartment. "Don't take this on. There were three of you there, and I knew what you were going there to do. Even my dad and Malone were aware of it. Any of us could've stopped you just as easily as you could have stopped it. We can't rewrite history. We can only go forward from here."

"How are you staying so calm about this?"

"Compartmentalization. You oughta try it."

"I suppose that's as good a plan as any. I still can't believe everything that's happened this weekend."

"Hang in there, and let me know what I can do to help you."

"Thanks."

On the way to reinterview JoAnn Smithson, Sam called Nick. "So color me crazy," she said when he answered. "But I had what might be my most brilliant idea ever this morning."

He snickered. "Can't wait to hear this one."

"You won't be laughing when you hear my idea. You'll be basking in my brilliance."

In the passenger seat, Freddie made barfing noises.

Sam shot him a glare.

"I'm breathless with anticipation," Nick said.

"Good. I like you that way. What do you say we hire someone to make all this wedding crap go away?"

"Hire someone? To plan *our* wedding?"

"Yes, exactly. They can figure out the where, the what, the how. We'll do the who and the clothes and the personal stuff."

"I don't know, Sam. How do we turn something that important and personal over to a total stranger?"

"How about we turn over the most important day of our lives to a trained professional who can tell us exactly what to do so we can just show up and get married without all the stress and aggravation of trying to plan it ourselves?"

"When you put it that way...do you know any of these people who magically make weddings happen?"

"No, but I'm sure you do."

"I can assure you that I don't. You'll recall that this is my first rodeo."

"Oh, come on. With that network of yours, someone knows someone who knows someone. Put the word out, and you'll have a dozen people clamoring for the job by the end of the day."

"You aren't seriously suggesting I make use of our newfound notoriety, are you?"

"Maybe I am. For once it might actually benefit us."

"All right. If you're sure you want to go that route, I'll look into it."

"Good. Thank you. I promise this will keep us from losing our minds over the next six weeks."

"Speaking of losing our minds, I just got off the phone with Forrester."

At the reference to the U.S. Attorney, Sam's good mood dissipated. "And?"

"After he chastised me for abusing my office, he let me know that he wasn't inclined to do the police any favors."

"Isn't he a Republican?"

"Gee, how'd you guess?"

"Well, thanks for trying."

"I've got a few other irons in the fire."

"Seriously, Nick, don't set yourself up for trouble over this. He's not worth it."

"Don't worry about me, Samantha."

"I *am* worried about you doing something on my behalf that causes you political trouble. We don't need that on top of everything else."

"I hear ya, babe, but I've got to run. Committee meeting in ten."

"Talk to you later."

"Be careful out there."

"Always am." Sam pulled into the parking lot at the Capitol Cleaning Services' office and cut the engine.

"Good idea on the wedding planner," Freddie said.

"I'm glad you approve. I have another brilliant idea I wanted to run by you."

"And what's that?"

"Have a dinner party for your mother and Elin. Give them a chance to spend time together in a relaxed setting."

"Are you really helping me with this problem when I've caused such a huge problem for you?"

"How do you figure? What problem did you cause for me?"

"Hello? Gibson? I can't *freaking believe* he might get sprung."

"I'll tell you the same thing I told Gonzo—it's not your fault. I was aware of what you were doing, my dad and Malone were aware of it. None of us stopped you."

"We should've waited for the warrant."

"Maybe so, but you had good reason to believe he had bomb-making supplies in there. I can't say I would've waited either."

"Sam, if he gets out—"

She held up her hand to stop him. "*If* he gets out, I'll deal with it then. I don't have to deal with it now."

"I'm sorry," he said, his expression rife with regret

and dismay. "I feel so awful about this. I wanted to nail him so badly."

"We all did. So let's talk about this dinner party you're going to have."

She watched him make an attempt to rally past his worries about Gibson getting sprung. "I thought you didn't approve of her any more than my mother does."

"I don't disapprove of her. I just wonder if she's right for you."

"But you're still offering me advice?"

"You say she is what *you* want. I'm trying to respect that." Sam got out of the car. "Take or leave the dinner idea."

"It's not a *bad* idea."

"Gee, thanks."

"We're in the middle of a case. When do you propose I have this dinner?"

"Today's Monday," Sam said, thinking it out. "Aim for Friday. We should have this wrapped up by then."

He followed her into the office building. "And if we don't?"

"Then I'll still give you the night off."

"And the night before to get ready?"

Sam scowled at him. "The night before too."

"In that case, I accept your idea and the time off."

"How did that just backfire on me?" Sam asked.

Freddie laughed. "I've learned from the best."

In JoAnn Smithson's outer office, Sam and Freddie found the older woman huddled with several colleagues. They were all in tears.

"Oh," Mrs. Smithson said when she saw them. "Detectives! Someone is killing my employees! I don't understand."

"Try to calm down, Mrs. Smithson," Sam said. "We're

doing everything we can to find the person who killed them." Leading her away from the other women, Sam said, "I need a list of all your employees—their names, addresses, immigration status and anything else about them you can tell us that might be relevant."

"I can't give you personal information about my employees."

"Do you want it on your conscience when another of them ends up dead?"

Mrs. Smithson wiped tears from her cheeks. "Of course not."

"Then cooperate with our investigation so we can make sure no one else gets hurt."

"I'll need a few minutes to print the list for you."

"We'll wait."

She scurried off.

"I was thinking," Freddie said, "that we might also want to match up that list to the offices they cleaned and see if there are any patterns."

"That's good thinking. Tell Mrs. Smithson to add that to the info she's getting for us."

"You got it, boss."

Since she had a few minutes to kill, Sam called Lindsey. "What've you got, Doc?"

"Another pregnant victim."

"You don't say."

"Fifteen weeks."

"Jesus. What the hell is going on here?"

"I have no idea," Lindsey said. "But I have full confidence that you'll figure it out."

"What else did you find?"

"Semen from only one man this time. You know, it occurs to me that this guy must be one arrogant SOB."

"Why do you say that?"

"Indulge me for a minute here."

Sam glanced over at the office full of women hard at work on her request. Freddie was overseeing them. "I've got a minute."

"So if I'm a guy who's going to rape and murder women, I think I'd take the time to suit up so I wouldn't leave my calling card behind. My guess is we're looking for someone who never thinks for *one second* that he's ever going to get caught. Like he's above such menial things such as criminal justice."

"It's a good theory," Sam acknowledged. "What I need from you now is confirmation that the DNA from Maria matches guy number two from Regina."

"Running it now. I'll get back to you as soon as I know for sure."

"Great, thanks." Sam ended the call as Freddie rejoined her with the list she'd requested from Mrs. Smithson. "Let's stop at City Hall and figure out who Regina was married to. After we talk to him, we'll start with the immigrants and go from there. For whatever reason, he's targeting them."

"I'm with you, boss."

SAM WAITED IMPATIENTLY for the City Hall clerk to pull Regina's marriage license. "You'd think they'd have all this crap on computers by now," she muttered to Freddie.

"You'd think."

The clerk returned a few minutes later, carrying a binder. "Here we go." She put the book down on the counter and turned it so Sam and Freddie could read the copy of the license.

"Aidan O'Hurley," Freddie said as he wrote down the name.

"Call it in. Let's see if he's in the system." While he was on the phone, they returned to the car.

"Got a hit," he said. "A B&E charge from four years ago. He's on probation."

"Finally, a break," Sam said. A call to O'Hurley's probation officer yielded his place of business, a restaurant on Massachusetts Avenue. "Let's go."

They double-parked outside the restaurant and showed their badges inside. One of the waitresses pointed to the kitchen where they found Aidan working the grill. Medium height and build, he had red hair and blue eyes.

"Oh, Jesus," he said when they flashed their badges. "What now? I talked to my PO yesterday. Whatever it is, I didn't do it."

"When was the last time you saw Regina?" Sam asked.

"Who?"

"Your ex-wife, asshole."

"Shit, that bitch?" As he spoke, he flipped burgers and sautéed onions. "Been more than a year since I laid eyes on her. Biggest mistake I ever made. All she wanted from me was a green card. Totally played me."

"Why do you say that?"

"Because the second she got it she was out the door. I thought she was home visiting her mother until I got served with divorce papers. Too bad for her that she set off CIS alarms when she filed for divorce."

"They rescinded the green card?"

He nodded. "She was able to get a work visa, but that was temporary."

"You never saw her again?"

"Nope. She didn't need me anymore, and I certainly had nothing to say to her."

"How long were you married?"

"About fifteen months all told. Together about ten of them."

"All that time, you had no inkling that she was playing you?" Freddie asked.

"I made the mistake of falling for her." For a moment, he seemed lost in his memories, but then he seemed to remember the hurt. "What's this all about? Is she in some kind of trouble? Wouldn't surprise me."

"She was killed Saturday night," Sam said.

He froze mid-burger-flip. "*Killed?* What happened?"

"She was murdered in her apartment."

"God, I can't believe that."

"Where were you Saturday night?"

His eyes bugged. "You don't think…I hated her for what she did to me, but I'd never *hurt* her."

"Where were you?"

"Right here. Two to midnight."

"You didn't leave at all."

"Not until the end of my shift."

"And someone here can attest to that?"

"Sure, the manager. He's out front."

After confirming Aidan's alibi, Sam and Freddie left the restaurant.

"Another dead end," she said.

GONZO KNOCKED ON the door of the apartment upstairs from Maria's and waited impatiently. He'd told Sam that his personal crisis wouldn't affect his work, but that was proving much easier said than done. His body hummed with tension while he waited to hear something—*anything*—from Andy.

The door opened, and a middle-aged woman greeted him and his badge with a grunt. "This about Maria?" she asked.

"Detective Gonzales, Metro Police. May I have a moment of your time?"

She gave him a good once-over before admitting him into her apartment.

"Do you mind if I ask your name?"

"Debbie Hopkins."

"Have you lived here long?"

"Six years."

"What about Maria?"

"Coupla years, I guess. I didn't know her very well."

"If you could tell me anything you did know about her, that would help."

"She never had much to say but wasn't unfriendly. Just quiet."

"Was she seeing anyone?"

"Not that I ever noticed, but she wasn't around much. She worked a lot."

"Did she work for just the cleaning service?"

"I don't know. It seemed that she worked every night. I heard her shower go on in the mornings because the pipes would clang."

Gonzo's cell phone rang. "Excuse me. I have to take this."

She gestured for him to proceed.

His heart stuttered when he saw Lori's number on the caller ID. "Hello?"

"You had to send fucking *social workers* over here? *Are you fucking kidding me?*"

"Wait a minute—"

"No, *you* wait a minute. I'm sorry I ever called you. You can keep your money and your social workers and your DNA tests. Just stay the fuck away from us."

"I'm not staying away from my son, Lori. I don't care about the money or anything else. I want my kid."

"Then I'll see you in court, because you're not getting anywhere near my son if I have anything to say about it!"

Before he could form an answer to that, the line went dead. His hands shook as he returned the phone to his pocket. He took a moment to collect himself before he turned back to finish the interview. "Sorry about the interruption," he said, forcing a calm tone to his voice when he wanted to shriek with frustration. Withdrawing his card from his pocket, he handed it to Debbie. "If you think of anything else that might be helpful to the investigation, please give me a call."

"You might want to talk to Mrs. Ellison in 4B. I think they were friendly."

"Thank you," Gonzo said, grateful to leave the airless apartment.

Once outside, he sat on the stoop, taking deep breaths of cool fresh air. When he managed to calm down, he reached for his phone again to call Andy.

The moment the lawyer came on the line, Gonzo said, "We've got a problem."

SAM KNOCKED ON the door of Selina Rameriz's apartment. They had turned the non-immigrant portion of the employee list over to McBride and Tyrone. "Miss Rameriz," Sam called when she knocked. "Metro Police. We need to speak to you about Regina and Maria."

"I have nothing to say," came a small voice from inside the apartment. Her English was smooth but accented. Mrs. Smithson had told them Selina was Columbian.

"Miss Rameriz, please open the door. We just want to talk to you. You're not in any trouble."

"Show your badges."

Sam and Freddie held them up to the peephole.

Another minute passed before they heard the sound of

locks being disengaged. The door opened to reveal a tiny young woman with dark hair and skin. She wrapped her arms around herself protectively. “What do you want?” Her eyes, which were rimmed with red, darted between them and then past them to the hallway.

“Have you been threatened, Miss Rameriz?” Sam asked.

She shook her head. “Someone is killing the people I work with. I’m frightened.”

“Did you know of anyone that either of them was involved with who might’ve wanted to harm them?”

Again, she shook her head.

“Did you spend time with either of them away from work?”

“No.”

“Can you tell us anything about who some of their other friends might’ve been? Any men they were seeing?”

“No, I’m sorry. I know none of that.”

Sam glanced at Freddie.

He handed Selina his card. “If you think of anything that might be helpful to the investigation or if you feel threatened in any way, please call me.”

She took the card, shut the door and engaged a series of locks. “The poor girl is terrified,” Freddie said once they were outside.

“I can’t help but think she knows more than she’s saying.”

“I agree. If she barely knew them, why did she look like she’d been crying all night?”

“Good point. Let’s keep her on our list to talk to again if we don’t get anywhere with the others. Maybe if we take her downtown we’ll get somewhere with her. Who’s next?”

TWELVE

AFTER INTERVIEWING FIVE other Capitol Cleaning Services employees with similar results, Sam and Freddie returned to HQ at the end of their shift. Frustrated by the stonewalling from the women they'd spoken to, Sam gathered the other detectives working the case into the conference room for updates.

"Someone please tell me you have something we can work with," Sam said. "This case is starting to piss me off."

"I found one thing kind of interesting," Jeannie McBride said.

"Where'd you come from?" Sam asked the third-shift detective. "Shouldn't you be sleeping?"

Jeannie flashed a sheepish grin. "Couldn't sleep so I came back to work."

"Hear that boys?" Sam said. "Look at that dedication." Enjoying the dirty looks from the male detectives and a bright smile from Jeannie, Sam waved at her to proceed.

"I dug a little deeper on the financials for Regina and Maria. Both recently wired large sums of money to their families at home. Maria sent seventy-five hundred and Regina five thousand."

Sam released a low whistle. "Where do cleaning ladies making seventeen bucks an hour get that kind of money?"

"They had something going on the side—drugs, gambling, prostitution," Freddie said. "Something that pays big."

"Would they take a chance like that when they were desperately trying to stay in this country?" Gonzo asked. "They get caught and they're looking at automatic deportation."

"They take the chance if they—and their families—desperately needed the money," Jeannie said.

"And the babies are insurance policies to keep them here if all else fails," Sam said, hearing the click of pieces coming together. "I'd really like to know who fathered Maria's baby."

"Her neighbor, Mrs. Ellison, was friendly with Maria," Gonzo reported. "But she said she never saw her with a man or heard her talk about being involved with one."

"Check her travel status," Sam said to Cruz. "See if she's been back home recently. The father could be someone there. Follow up with the family to see if she had a significant other there who might be the father."

Cruz nodded and made a note of her instructions.

"I'd also like to know from both families where they were told the money came from. They'll be lies, but I want to know how they explained away that kind of money."

Freddie added that to his list.

"Did we get anywhere with matching them up with the offices they cleaned?" Sam asked.

"They both worked in the Hart Building," Detective Arnold reported. "In addition to Lightfeather, Regina cleaned Ackerman's and Cook's offices."

"Ahh, our old friend Senator Cook," Sam said, glancing at Freddie. Thanks to some inflammatory statements the senior senator from Virginia made to Nick about Julian Sinclair, Sam and Freddie had interviewed Cook after the Supreme Court nominee had been murdered.

To say that Cook had been less than hospitable would be putting it mildly.

"Maria cleaned Lewis's, Cappuano's, Trent's and Stenhouse's," Arnold continued, casting a nervous glance her way as he mumbled Nick's name.

"Another blast from the past," Sam said. Senate Majority Leader William Stenhouse was a bitter enemy of former Senator Graham O'Connor, John O'Connor's father. Sam had interviewed Stenhouse during the investigation into John O'Connor's murder, and like his colleague Cook, Stenhouse had been indignant and outraged by the implication that he might've had something to do with a murder. "Very interesting. In the interest of full disclosure, Nick mentioned that he knew Maria and that she cleaned his offices."

Her comment was met with muttered acknowledgments. She hated when her two worlds collided this way.

"I want someone on Selina for a day or so," Sam decided. "She was hiding something today when we talked to her. I want to know what it is."

"Tyrone and I will take the first shift on her tonight," Jeannie said.

"Excellent," Sam said. "Have patrol show their photos around at the local shops, markets, restaurants again. Let's find some of their other acquaintances. Get me some threads to pull."

"You got it," Jeannie said.

"I'll see the rest of you in the morning," Sam said.

AS THEY FILED out of the conference room, Gonzo gestured for Cruz to follow him down the hallway.

"What's up, man?" Cruz asked when they were alone.

"This thing with Gibson..."

Cruz groaned. "*I can't deal.* We totally screwed up, and if he gets sprung…"

"I hear ya. It's eating me up too."

"I keep going over it and over it in my mind. Why didn't we wait for the warrant?"

"Because we knew we had him, and we wanted to nail that son of a bitch for what he did to Sam."

"Yeah," Cruz said, regretfully. "Wish we had it to do over."

"Well, we don't, but the way I see it, we owe her one."

"No kidding."

"So let's get serious about finding the former tenant at Reese's house. No doubt the people who lived there before Reese know something about her father's shooting. I don't care what we have to do…"

"I'm with you. Whatever it takes."

"Let me think about the next step, and I'll get back with you."

"I'll give it some thought too."

"Good."

"Everything okay with you?" Freddie asked. "You've seemed preoccupied today."

"Yeah," Gonzo said, startled by the question. Despite his best efforts, he was apparently wearing his personal turmoil for everyone to see. "Everything's fine. I'll see you tomorrow."

"Later."

After Cruz walked away, Gonzo reached for his cell phone to call Christina. "Can you break free yet?" he asked when she answered.

"Just about. Why? What's up?"

"Bad day. I need you."

No doubt surprised by his stark admission, Christina said, "I'm here. What can I do?"

"Meet me at my place in an hour?"

"I'll be there."

"Thanks."

"You don't have to thank me. There's nowhere else I'd rather be."

Overwhelmed by the rush of emotion, Gonzo closed his eyes and leaned his head back against the wall. "Same here."

As he ended the call, he took a moment to marvel at the recent changes in his life. He couldn't recall ever saying the words "I need you" to a woman before nor had he imagined rearranging his life for a baby he hadn't even known about three days ago. But the truth was, he did need Christina more than he'd ever needed anyone, and there was nothing he wouldn't do to gain custody of his son.

With that in mind, he made another phone call, to the friend who'd introduced him to Lori.

"Dude," his buddy Mark said when he answered. "Long time, no see."

"Too long. How are you?"

"Hanging in there. You?"

"I've got a little problem I was hoping you could help me with."

"What's up?"

"Remember Lori Phillips?"

"Sure. What about her?"

"You know the baby she had recently?"

"I heard a rumor about that. What about it?"

"She says the kid is mine."

"Holy shit! For real?"

"I saw him yesterday. Looks like me. He's got my chin dimple."

"Wow. I didn't think you guys were all that involved."

"We weren't. Really. But apparently, it doesn't take much."

Mark released a nervous laugh. "So I hear."

"The thing is, I'm not digging the scene where they're living. Do you know anything about that guy Rex she's seeing?"

Mark released a low whistle. "Rex Connolly?"

Bingo. Gonzo made a note of the name. "I don't know his last name."

"Lots of tats? Rough-looking dude?"

"That's the guy. What's his story?"

"I'm not really sure, but Sara said Lori is pretty serious with him." Mark's sister Sara was a close friend of Lori's. "I figured the kid was his."

"So they've been together a while then?"

"About a year maybe. What about the kid? What're you going to do?"

"I'm considering my options," Gonzo said, purposely evasive. He'd played in a softball league with Mark years ago and considered him a friend, but he didn't want it to get back to Lori that he planned to seek custody. "Do me a favor and don't mention to Sara or Lori that you talked to me?"

"No problem. Let me know if you need anything."

"I will." He had what he needed. "Thanks."

Gonzo ended the call and returned to the detectives' pit just as Sam was leaving her office.

"You're still here?" she asked.

Gonzo glanced at the crowded pit where shift change was still under way. "Would you mind if I borrowed your office for a minute?"

She studied him for a long moment. "Sure. Lock up when you're done."

"Will do. Thanks."

"See you tomorrow."

Gonzo was relieved when she left without asking any questions. He went into her office and shut the door. While he waited for her computer to boot up, he thought about Andy telling him to get anything they could use in court to prove the baby would be better off with him than with his mother. In the meantime, Andy had filed the motion to demand a DNA test.

Gonzo typed in Rex's name and was surprised to find five Rex Connollys in the system. He scanned through the mug shots, half hoping he'd find one he recognized and half hoping he wouldn't. The fifth photo was his guy. As his heart thudded, Gonzo clicked on the link to his rap sheet.

Multiple arrests on drug charges—possession and dealing—a breaking and entering charge that was later dropped and a sealed juvenile record. Feeling sick and riddled with anxiety, Gonzo printed the sheet. As long as he was committing acts that could get him fired, he also ran Lori's name through the system and was shocked to find a recent drug charge on her sheet too. The possession charge had been adjudicated six months prior, and she'd been placed on five years' probation.

"Bull's-eye," he whispered as he printed both records.

As his final act of things that could get him fired, Gonzo faxed the information to Andy's office and stood watch over the fax machine until all seven pages had transmitted. He collected them and turned to leave.

"Working late, Detective?" Lt. Stahl asked.

Gonzo almost jumped out of his skin. "Just finishing some paperwork, Lieutenant."

"You're awfully jumpy."

"Am I?" Gonzo just wanted to get the hell out of there, and there was no one he cared to speak with less than the unpleasant man who used to be his boss. "I wasn't expecting anyone to sneak up on me."

"I didn't sneak up on you," Stahl huffed, his multiple chins jiggling with indignation.

"Is there something I can help you with, Lieutenant?"

"Nope."

"Then I'll be on my way," Gonzo said. Feeling Stahl's beady-eyed stare burning a hole in his back, Gonzo tucked the rap sheets under his arm, grabbed his coat and headed out while the getting was still good. Not until he was in his SUV and headed for home, did he manage to take a deep breath. Right before he pulled up to his building, he called Sam.

"What's up?" she asked.

"Just thought you should know that Stahl was skulking around the pit tonight."

"What was he after?"

"Wouldn't say, but as usual, he was acting weird. Just thought I should mention it."

"Thanks for the heads-up," she muttered. "I wish he would stay in the rat squad where he belongs." Stahl had been transferred to the department's internal affairs division after Sam had been given his old command.

"Wouldn't that be nice?"

"I'm betting he had something to do with this situation with Gibson."

"You really think so?" Gonzo asked.

"Wouldn't put it past him."

"He's freaking evil. Why can't they get rid of him?"

"I'm sure they're trying. Did you get anywhere with your situation?"

"I got what I needed."

"Good."

"Thanks for the help."

"Sure thing."

Gonzo ended the call and rested his head on the steering wheel, forcing himself to breathe through the anxiety that cycled through him. His entire life was spinning out of control, and he felt powerless to stop or control it. A tap on his window interrupted his thoughts. Gonzo looked up to find Christina waiting for him.

He reached for his keys and got out of the car.

She held out her hand to him.

Gonzo linked his fingers with hers, and just like that, his world stopped spinning. He stared at her, dazzled and breathless. "I love you," he whispered.

She gasped. "You…you…"

He realized he was doing this badly. Pocketing his keys, he raised his hands, cupped her face and brushed his lips gently over hers. "I love you."

Tears flooded her blue eyes. "You do?"

Nodding, he kissed her again. "Surprised the hell out of me too."

Christina laughed through her tears and leaned into his embrace as he escorted her into his town house. He had no idea if he'd left the place a mess, but he suspected she wouldn't care.

Inside, she turned to him and gripped his hands. Looking up at him with a shy smile gracing her gorgeous mouth, she said, "I love you too."

It was exactly what he needed to hear and exactly what he'd never expected to find. Gonzo leaned his forehead against hers.

"What happened today?" she asked.

He eased the coat from her shoulders and let it fall to

the floor. “Later,” he said, kissing her with more intent. “I’ll tell you later.”

She looped her arms around his neck and fell into the kiss.

THIRTEEN

IN NEED OF a top-notch wedding planner, Nick went to the one source he could always count on—his adopted mother, Laine O'Connor.

"Senator!" she said when she answered the phone. "What a lovely, *lovely* surprise."

Nick smiled at the effusive greeting. From the first time John brought him home from Harvard freshman year, Laine and her husband, Graham, had made Nick a part of their family. After John's death, they had gone out of their way to let Nick know that nothing would change—he would always be an honorary O'Connor.

"How are you, honey?" she asked.

"I'm good. How about you?"

"Oh, you know," she said with a sigh. "Good days. Bad days."

The pain he heard in her voice made Nick ache for her, for all of them. "I miss him. Sometimes I forget he's gone, and then it all comes rushing back..."

"He'd be so proud of you, Nick. I saw the VCU rally on the news. The people of the Old Dominion love you!"

"I'm not sure what I ever did to deserve such an outpouring."

"You stepped in when they needed you." Her voice caught. "You stepped in when *we* needed you."

"Well now I need *you*," he said, steering the conversation in a lighter direction before his emotions got the better of him. He still found it difficult to talk about his best friend's violent death, and he knew she felt the same.

"What can I do for you?"

"Sam and I are looking for a wedding planner. Someone who knows Washington, knows how to deal with the million details, someone who can make it all go away for us. Do you know anyone?"

"You need Shelby Faircloth."

"Who?"

"Lizbeth's friend from Georgetown," she said, referring to her daughter. "She's the go-to person for Washington weddings."

"You think she'd be interested in taking on ours?"

Laine chortled with laughter. "Are you *serious*? You two are the *it* couple of the decade. She'd *kill* for the chance to put together your wedding."

"I don't want her to kill anyone. I'm trying to get Sam a full day off, and the last thing she needs is another body to contend with." Nick winced, realizing it was too soon to be cavalier about murder, especially with John's mother. "I'm sorry. I shouldn't have said that."

"Don't apologize for making a joke, honey. We could all use a little more levity in our lives these days. Do you want me to get in touch with Shelby for you?"

"That'd be great. Ask her to come by the house at nine."

"Tonight?"

"If she wants the job, tell her she has thirty minutes to convince us to hire her."

"I'll give her the message."

"And save March 26th."

"*This year?*"

"Why does everyone keep saying that? Including the bride?"

Once again, Laine chortled with laughter. "If anyone can make it happen, Nick Cappuano, you can."

"I guess we'll find out. So how's Graham?"

"Oh, honey, some days I wonder if he'll ever be the same. The double-whammy of John's death followed so closely by Julian…I don't know."

"I need to get out to see him."

"He'd enjoy that. Why don't you and Sam come for dinner on Sunday?"

Pulling up his calendar, Nick was already figuring how he could rearrange his schedule to make it to the family's weekly Sunday dinner. He hadn't made it to a single one since the campaign began. "I can do it, but I'm not sure she can. She's caught up in another hot case."

"The business with Henry, I'm sure."

"Yes."

"What could he have been thinking? And poor Annette."

"Do you know her well?"

"We've been friends for years. She has to be beside herself. They're speculating on the news that he's going to resign. Have you heard anything?"

"Nothing definitive, but there've been some rumblings on the Hill."

"Might be for the best—for Annette and the children."

"Maybe so."

"I'm sure you'll be hearing from him, but Terry is due home this week. I think the additional two weeks were what he really needed. It was good of you to hold the job for him."

"I'm looking forward to working with him." Nick had offered the deputy chief of staff job in his office to John's older brother Terry, provided he spend at least thirty days attending in-patient alcohol rehab. On his own, Terry had tacked on two extra weeks, which Nick had taken as a good indication of Terry's determination to stay sober. "Well, I won't keep you. Thanks for the info about the wedding planner."

"Happy to help. Let me know if there's anything else I can do."

"I certainly will. Give Graham my love. I'll be there Sunday."

"We'll see you then."

Nick put down the phone, and reached for the framed picture of him and John that he kept on the credenza. Blond, handsome and utterly charming, John O'Connor had had it all until his twenty-year-old son murdered him in a fit of rage. As Nick stared at the brother of his heart, he realized John's death had left him without something else he'd soon need: a best man.

SAM SPENT THE evening online reviewing the websites of senators whose offices were cleaned by the dead women. Lightfeather, Ackerman, Stenhouse, Trent, Lewis, Cook and finally Cappuano. Sam hadn't visited Nick's site since he took office and was immediately captivated by the photo of him. "Wow," she said. "Will you look at that?" Tall, handsome and distinguished, wearing a dark suit and a serious smile, he projected an aura of quiet authority that stirred her.

"Whatcha looking at?" Nick asked as he came into the room.

Embarrassed to be gawking at her fiancé's photo, Sam spun around in the chair. "You, as a matter of fact."

His brows knitted with confusion. "What about me?"

Sam turned back around so he could see the computer screen. "I *love* that picture."

"Do you? I thought it was kind of dorky."

"Um, no. Definitely not dorky."

"Is that so?"

"No wonder the women of the commonwealth are filling stadiums to overflowing at your rallies."

"Cut it out," he said, flustered. "What are you doing on my website anyway?"

"Something my dad said earlier. I stopped to talk shop with him after work."

"What did he say?"

"That people only kill 'the help' when they know too much."

"What's that got to do with my site?"

"I was just looking at the sites of every senator they worked for—yours more out of curiosity than anything."

"What're you looking for?"

"Not sure yet. Anything that ties the seven of you together."

"Who are the other six?"

Sam rattled off the names.

Nick sat in one of the other chairs in the comfortable study. "Some heavy hitters on that list."

"What do they have in common?"

"Ackerman, Cook, Lightfeather and myself are all Democrats. Stenhouse, Lewis and Trent are Republicans. Ackerman and Stenhouse are party leaders. Cook and Lewis have more than thirty years in the Senate, but Trent is relatively new. The Oregon governor appointed him after Tornquist flamed out in a scandal, and Trace was later elected. He's still in his first full term."

"A few are on the same committees. Any bad history between any of them like there was between Graham and Stenhouse?"

"I could do some digging into that and let you know."

"Keep it on the down low for now. I don't want any of them to know I'm even looking into them at this point."

"You really think it was one of them?" Nick asked, incredulous.

"The thing is, I have no idea. This investigation is going nowhere fast. We have two dead immigrant women, both of them pregnant, working for a company that provides a service to Congress. One of them was romantically involved with a senator, carrying his child and had an uncertain immigration status. And despite Lightfeather's airtight alibi, I can't help but wonder how it's possible he didn't have something to do with her murder. He had so much to lose."

"But you're not focusing on him, are you?"

"Not at the moment. I just feel like I'm missing something—something huge that's staring me right in the face."

He reached for her hand and drew her out of the chair and into his lap. "What you need," he said, massaging the tension from her shoulders, "is some time away from the case, some TLC and some sleep."

"Mmm," Sam said with a sigh. "You're good at that. If things don't work out for you in the Senate, you might find work as a masseuse."

Nick laughed and pressed a kiss to the top of her head. "Remember how you solved Julian's case? How it all came together while you were sleeping?"

"In the hospital with my head throbbing from a concussion and my hairline on fire with forty stitches." They'd both been injured in a car crash that occurred after gang members shot at them. "Maybe you should knock me over the head rather than giving me a massage."

"The point is you need to step back from it to gain some perspective."

His talented fingers drew a moan from her. "So no knock on the head?"

"Nope."

The doorbell rang, drawing Sam back to reality.

"That'll be your wedding planner," he said.

She moaned again. "I really have to do this right now?"

He nudged her off his lap and stood. "Remember, this was *your* big idea."

"I already hate her."

"I already feel sorry for her."

"Awww, I love you too."

Laughing, he nudged her toward the door.

Standing on their doorstep was the tiniest pixie of a woman Sam had ever seen.

The pixie extended her hand. "Shelby Faircloth, at your service," she said. Her Southern accent was deep and charming. Even though she had to be in her early forties, she could've passed for twenty-five.

Sam always felt like an Amazon next to tiny perfect blondes like Shelby and Christina Billings.

"Come in," Nick said. "Can I get you anything? A glass of wine maybe?"

"Oh, I'd love that," Shelby said. "It's been a *really* long day."

While he went to get the wine, Sam took a moment to study Tinker Bell. She wore a pink suit and sky-high pink stiletto heels that reminded Sam of those favored by Assistant U.S. Attorney Charity Miller. On another woman, the abundance of pink might've looked ridiculous. On Shelby Faircloth, it just worked.

"I can't believe we've never met before," Nick said as he handed Shelby a glass of pinot grigio.

"I don't get out to the farm very often," she said, referring to the O'Connor's Leesburg home. "But I see Lizbeth and Royce socially and occasionally have the pleasure of running into her parents. I know there's nothing I can say to ease your grief, but I was so very saddened by John's death."

"Thank you," Nick said. "It was a terrible loss for all of us."

"I can't imagine." Shelby took another sip of her wine and then put the glass on the table. "Well, you only gave me thirty minutes to convince you to hire me, so I'd better not waste any time. Now if I had my druthers and could do anything I wanted for you two, I'd have the service at St. John's, the Church of the Presidents, with a reception immediately following at the newly renovated Hay-Adams. I can picture you, hand in hand, dashing across H Street with the White House in the background." She sat back in her chair and sighed, caught up in her own vision. "Old Washington, classic, timeless. Just like the two of you."

Sam and Nick exchanged glances. While she wanted to barf at Shelby's description of them, she had to admit she could see the wedding just the way Shelby described it and the vision wasn't totally repulsive.

"What do you think?" Shelby asked.

"I'm intrigued," Nick said. "You can make this classic, timeless wedding happen in six weeks' time?"

"Oh, absolutely. The whole town will be clamoring for a piece of this one."

"And you'd keep all that clamoring far, *far* away from us?" Sam asked.

"As far away as humanly possible. That's what you'd be hiring me to do."

"How much would we be paying you to run interference for us?" Sam asked.

"It doesn't matter," Nick said. "Whatever it takes to make it as stress-free and perfect as possible, I'll pay it."

Sam wondered if he had lost his mind. "Wait a minute—"

He leaned over to kiss the words right off her lips. "We'll fight about that later."

"Aww," Shelby said, "you two are even cuter than you seem on TV."

That earned her a glare from Sam.

"Mentioning our cuteness will not gain you favor with the bride," Nick said with a smile.

Shelby made a poor attempt to curb her grin and stood up. "Duly noted. I don't want to outstay my welcome. Shall I send y'all an estimate along with ideas for flowers and some of the other details I have in mind? In the meantime, you can check out my website for photos from other weddings I've done, testimonials, references, the works."

She and Nick exchanged cards.

"Sounds good," he said. "Thank you."

"Are both the venues you suggested handicapped accessible?" Sam asked.

"Absolutely. I never would've proposed them otherwise."

"Will you mind if I call you Tinker Bell?"

Shelby laughed. "No problem at all. I like to think of myself as a magician of sorts."

"That's exactly what we need right now."

Shelby shook hands with Sam and Nick. "It was so great to meet you both. I promise if you hire me, you'll have a wedding they'll talk about for years to come."

Sam wasn't at all sure how she felt about that.

Nick saw her out and joined Sam on the sofa. "So? What'd you think?"

"I still can't believe you got Tinker Bell to plan our wedding."

Nick cuffed her jaw. "How about St. John's and the Hay?"

"You don't want to get married in a Catholic church?" She'd been surprised to note at John's funeral that Nick had obviously spent a lot of time in church.

"With you not being Catholic, St. John's would be less complicated," he said. "I can't picture you going through the marriage retreat the Catholics would want us to do."

Sam made a face at that. "I bet even the Catholics would make an exception for the dashing Senator Cappuano."

"Maybe, but I'm fine with St. John's. Episcopal is close enough."

"I'm worried about a media circus."

"We can handle that. I'm sure Shelby is an expert at such things."

"I liked what she said about the church and hotel being handicapped accessible. Shows she did her homework."

"I thought the same thing, but we don't have to decide anything right away. We can meet with a couple of other wedding planners before we pick one."

"We have *six weeks*, Nick. How much of that time do you suggest we spend interviewing wedding planners?"

"So we should just go with her?"

"I want to see the estimate first."

"I don't care about what it costs. I don't want you to worry about that."

"You're not paying for this whole thing. We're splitting it."

"I *am* paying for it, and we're not splitting anything."

"Whoa, Caveman Joe! Hold on just a minute!"

"John left me all that money," he said, referring to the two-million-dollar life insurance policy he'd been shocked to learn John had directed his way. "I can't imagine any better use for some of it than buying my best girl a bang-up wedding that'll make her forget she was ever married before."

All the wind puffed out of Sam's sails. "I don't know how you do it."

"Do what?"

"I'm spoiling for a fight and then you go and say something like that and all I want to do is kiss you."

His smug grin should've made her mad, but she just loved him so damned much. "Don't let me stop you."

She leaned in and set out to blow his mind with a kiss he'd never forget.

FOURTEEN

HIS HEART POUNDING and his lungs burning from exertion, Freddie flopped onto his back and reached for Elin to bring her with him. He wiped a bead of sweat from his brow.

"It's official," he said when he could speak again.

She nudged his nipple with the tip of her finger. "What is?"

"I'm officially addicted to you." He rolled on his side and cupped her breast, watching in fascination as her pierced nipple hardened. "Can't get enough." In truth, having sex with her was becoming a borderline obsession that had him worried—thanks to his mother and Sam who had planted all kinds of doubts in his head. Maybe they were right. When he tried to remember how he used to pass his time before he started spending every night burning up the sheets with Elin he came up totally empty.

"I must be addicted to you too, because I can't get enough either," she said, kissing her way from his chest to his belly.

Freddie sucked in a sharp deep breath when he realized her intent. A minute ago he would've guessed they were done for the night, but his recently satisfied libido roared back to life when she wrapped her talented lips around his shaft.

He clutched the sheet and gave himself over to her. She applied just the right amount of suction and tongue. Then she squeezed his balls and almost sent him into yet another climax. She surprised him when she suddenly straddled him and took him in.

Whereas the last time had been fast and frantic, this time she took it slow, teasing and tormenting him until he was on the verge of begging. He gripped her hips, held her still and surged into her, coming with a roar.

She slumped down on top of him, and he wrapped his arms around her.

All night long, he'd been nervous about broaching the subject of the dinner party. Now that he could feel her starting to inch toward sleep, he couldn't put it off any longer. "I was thinking…"

"About?"

"Getting you and my mom together so you can get to know each other better."

He felt her stiffen in his arms the instant before she shifted off him.

"What?" he asked.

She drew the sheet up and over her. "Let's not do that."

"Why not?"

"Why can't we just be about this?" She gestured to the bed.

"About what? Sex, sex and more sex?"

"What's *wrong* with that? Aren't we having a good time together? Why does it have to involve other people?"

"Because. She's my mother, and you're my…well, girlfriend. I want you two to get along."

"I'm hardly your girlfriend, Freddie."

"Yes, you are." Once again his heart beat faster, but this time it was due to the odd bolt of fear that traveled through him. "Why would you say that?"

"Um, maybe because ever since we started fucking, we haven't been anywhere or done anything—except fuck, that is. I'd say that makes me your fuck buddy rather than your girlfriend."

Put off by her crude language, he sat up in bed. "That's not true! I took you to Skip's wedding. I offered to take you to dinner—"

She rested a finger over his lips. "We're both doing exactly what we want to be doing. Just don't make it into something it's not."

Disentangling himself from her, he got up and went to find his jeans.

"Where're you going?"

Trying to control his anger, he pulled on his pants and zipped them, not bothering with the button.

"Freddie, come on. Don't go."

"I don't want a fuck buddy," he said, making an effort to keep his tone even. "I want a girlfriend. I want a *real* girlfriend. I want this too." He gestured to the bed. "But that's not all I want. So unless you're up for more than this, I'm done." As he said the words, he had the presence of mind to wonder if he could really do without the sex. He was, after all, addicted.

"You don't mean that."

He swallowed hard. "Yes, I do."

Looking over at her as he tugged on his shirt, he said, "I'm making dinner on Friday night, and I've already invited my mother. If you're interested in a real relationship, come to dinner. If you're not, well, then it's been nice, but it's over."

Her blue eyes flashed with anger. "So you're giving me an ultimatum? Have dinner with your mother or we're done?"

He sat on the bed, reached for her hand and linked his fingers with hers. "It's not about my mother, Elin. It's about me wanting more than a sex-only relationship.

Maybe that works for you, but it's just not who I am." As he said the words, Freddie realized this was exactly what his mother and Sam had been trying to tell him.

"They've gotten to you," she said, tuning into his thoughts. "That's what this is really about."

Shaking his head, he leaned in to kiss her. "I care about you. I enjoy being with you, but I need more than this."

"You can't just change the rules midstream. That's hardly fair to me."

"It's terribly unfair. I agree." With one last squeeze, he released her hand and got up to find his boots. "I hope I see you Friday night—any time after seven."

"I won't be there."

He ached with regret, but he had no doubt he was doing the right thing for himself. "That's your choice, but I really hope you'll come. I'd miss you if I never saw you again."

"You'd miss the sex," she muttered.

"I'd miss everything," he said as he donned his coat. With one last long look at her, he left her pouting in bed and walked out of her apartment—maybe for the last time. Every guy he knew would call him ten kinds of crazy for walking away from a woman like her who wanted a sex-only relationship. But Freddie wasn't most guys and he never had been. That much he knew for sure.

How would he live without the sex he'd come to crave? Well, that was another matter altogether.

THE WORDS, ONCE he started, kept coming and coming. For more than an hour, the normally reticent Tommy Gonzales talked to Christina about Peter Gibson, about his role in the search that yielded enough evidence to put the guy away for life, about his memories of the day his friend and colleague had nearly been murdered by her ex-husband, about his great fear that Gibson would be released from jail to come at Sam again, and about how he and Detective Cruz planned to redouble their efforts to find the person who shot Sam's father. He talked about his baby son, who he would name Alejandro, after the baby's grandfather, but would call him Alex. A child growing up in America should have an American name.

Lying next to him in bed, holding his hand between both of hers, Christina listened without interruption.

Finally, he seemed to run out of words. He turned his head so he could see her, his expression sheepish and adorable. "I'm talking your ear off."

"I don't mind." His earlier profession of love was still settling with her. She wanted to pinch herself to make sure this was really happening. For years, she'd pined after John O'Connor who hadn't even known she was alive—as anything other than a good friend and dedicated employee, that is.

And now this…. Despite the differences in their backgrounds, despite the baby who might be entering his life, despite their busy, unpredictable jobs, she and Tommy had each other, and Christina had never felt more lucky or certain that she had found the one for her.

His beautiful brown eyes were so somber, so serious. Before the call from Lori, Christina had never seen them that way before. "What're you thinking?"

"I have to fight for him, you know?"

"Of course you do."

"I just keep worrying about what I'll do if I win."

She pushed herself up on one elbow. "What do you mean?"

"When I say I know nothing about babies, I mean *nothing*. Maybe he's better off with her."

"You know that's not true." She combed her fingers through his hair. "And just like any new parent, you'll figure out what you need to know when you need to know it."

"But what if I break him or something? Yesterday when she handed him to me…?"

Her lips quivering, Christina nodded.

"That was the first time I've held a baby since my nephew was born, and that was *years ago*."

Trying to suppress the urge to laugh, Christina placed her hands on his face. "Tommy, honey, you won't break him." She brushed a kiss over his lips. "You'll be great with him. I promise."

"What if I never get the chance? She's so pissed about social services showing up at her house."

"You're his father. You have rights, just like she does."

"What if I'm not really his father? Until we get the DNA test results back, I won't know for sure."

Christina touched her finger to the dimple on his chin, following with a kiss. "The proof is in the dimple."

He drew her down so she rested on top of him. "I'm doing the right thing, aren't I?"

The vulnerability she heard in his voice and saw on his face touched her heart. "I wouldn't expect you to do anything else."

Sifting his fingers through her hair, he studied her intently. "I couldn't deal with this without you."

"Yes, you could."

"I'm glad I don't have to."

Christina rested her head on his chest and listened to the strong beat of his heart, thrilled to know he'd given it to her.

His hands traveled from her shoulders to her back to her bottom.

Her entire body tingled with awareness. No one had ever made her feel the way he did. “Tommy,” she whispered.

“Hmm?”

“You really love me?”

His arms tightened around her. “I really do. You really love me?”

“Yes.”

“You’re the best thing to happen to me in a really long time. Maybe ever…”

Christina sighed. “Me too.”

He tilted her chin and kissed her.

She’d been on her way to sleep, but within seconds was wide awake again. “You have to work in the morning.”

“I know,” he said.

His lips went to work on her neck, raising goose bumps over her entire body. “*Tommy!*”

Laughing, he kept up the mischief until their laughter faded to moans.

FOR THE FIRST morning since she’d given up her diet cola addiction, Sam didn’t feel like she was slugging through quicksand. That, she supposed, was progress. At HQ, she arrived to utter chaos in the pit.

“Whoa,” she said to the noisy group of detectives gathered outside her office. “*Whoa!*”

All eyes turned to her.

“What the heck is going on?”

“McBride is missing,” Freddie said quietly.

A quick look at his face confirmed that what he’d said was true.

As a surge of fear and adrenaline zipped through her, Sam zeroed in on Detective William Tyrone, McBride’s partner. “Define missing.”

Tyrone swallowed hard. His usual composure had given way to panic, which added to Sam's growing anxiety. "We did like you said—we followed Selina last night. She went to work, came home and that's it. Nothing really happened. So me and Jeannie… I mean, Detective McBride, we parted ways. I told her I'd do the report from home and send it in. When I got home, I had a question I needed to ask her so I tried to call her, but there was no answer."

"Maybe she's asleep?"

He shook his head. "She always takes my calls. Always. Even when she's asleep or with Michael." Sam understood that. She and Cruz had a similar arrangement.

"Did you go to her place?"

Tyrone nodded. "And Michael's. That's when I started to get worried. She goes over there every morning after the nights she's on duty to see him before he leaves for work. She never showed up, and he's been trying to call her too. No way she'd ignore calls from both of us. That's just not her. Something's happened, L.T., I know it."

Sam's stomach ached with the sharp pains she hadn't experienced since she quit soda. The others were looking to her for direction. She bit back her own surge of panic, and tried to focus. "Recall second and third shifts. Put out an APB for her and her car. I want all available department resources directed toward finding her."

As the others scattered to follow her orders, Sam stepped into her office and reached for the phone to let Captain Malone and Chief Farnsworth know what was going on. Both arrived in the pit within minutes.

"What do you know?" Farnsworth asked, his gray eyes flat with concern and stress. Once Sam had updated him, he demanded that Tyrone go through his story once more. By the time he was done, Sam could tell the young detective was coming unraveled.

"Cruz," she said, "take Tyrone to the cafeteria. Get him something to eat."

"I can't eat, L.T. I just can't. Give me something to do. Anything."

Sam thought for a moment. "Dump her cell phone. And the boyfriend's."

"He didn't have anything to do with this," Tyrone said emphatically. "He's crazy about her."

"Just do it, Detective."

"Yes, ma'am," he muttered as he walked away.

"What can I do?" Freddie asked.

"Go with Gonzo and Arnold and get over to Columbia Heights. That's where she was last seen. Take pictures of her with you and start a canvas."

"Do you think it's related to our case?" he asked hesitantly.

Sam thought about Maria and Regina and the bloody crime scenes at their homes. Then she thought of Jeannie—beautiful, smart, funny Jeannie. Her stomach ached. "I sure as hell hope not."

"But?"

"Is it coincidental that she might've been snatched after watching one of their friends all night?"

Freddie released an unsteady breath as the possibilities settled on him.

"Go start the canvas, and report in every half hour."

Nodding, he hurried off.

The chief stepped into the office.

"I authorized all department resources be devoted to finding McBride," Sam said. "But I realized I don't have the authority—"

"In a case like this you do. You absolutely do."

"I know I'm supposed to stay calm and take command..." If only her hands would quit shaking.

"Give yourself a minute and then do just that."

"If anything happens to her..."

"Things happen on this job, Lieutenant. You know that as well as anyone."

His words were the splash of cold water she'd needed. "I'll set up a command post in the conference room and keep you informed of every development."

"Malone and I will run the command post. You're more effective on the streets."

"That's where I'd rather be." She reached for a portable radio. "I'll report in as soon as I have anything."

"Lieutenant," Gonzo said from the doorway. "Jeannie's boyfriend is here."

"Show him in."

Gonzo led a tall, black man dressed in a sharp-looking suit into the office. Sam could see how he and the tall, gorgeous Jeannie would make for a striking couple.

"Thanks," she said, dismissing Gonzo. "I'll see you out there shortly."

"Michael Wilkinson," the other man said, extending a hand.

She shook his hand. "Sam Holland. I've heard a lot about you."

"Likewise. Can you tell me what's being done to find Jeannie?" His voice was calm but Sam could hear the hysteria lurking just below the surface.

"We have every member of the department assigned to the search. When did you first realize something was wrong?"

"Just after seven. Whenever she works at night, she always comes by as soon as her shift ends so we can spend some time together before I have to leave for work around nine. We work opposite schedules, so we grab the time when we can. If she's ever detained, she always calls. So when she didn't come and didn't call and wasn't answering her phone, I started to get worried. But I know how things can be with her job, so I didn't think too much of it at first. Then Will showed up. I could tell something was wrong because he seemed kind of freaked-out and that's not like him."

Sam was getting a better understanding of the dynamics between McBride and Tyrone. He did the reports so she could steal an hour with her boyfriend. Knowing McBride, she picked up the slack elsewhere when she could to pay him back for the courtesy.

"Mr. Wilkinson, I have to ask where you were during the night."

His eyes flashed with surprise and then flattened with shock. "You can't be serious."

"I have to ask."

Hands on his hips, frustration radiating from him, he said, "Since Jeannie came back here early yesterday, I worked late, grabbed dinner on the way home and was home by nine. I have an alarm system in my house that I set after I got home if you want to check."

"I appreciate your candor, and I'm sorry I had to ask."

"I love her, Lieutenant," he said softly. "She's *it* for me. I could never harm her. In fact, I was planning to propose this weekend." He withdrew a small box from his suit pocket and showed her the ring.

"It's beautiful," Sam said sincerely. "She'll love it."

"We have to find her," he said. "We have to."

"We will." Sam's mind raced as the possible scenarios ran through her mind like a horror movie. "We'll find her."

FIFTEEN

THEY LOOKED FOR her all day. A few minutes after seven that night, Sam stood on a sidewalk in Columbia Heights and fielded another call from Jeannie's frantic mother. She did what she could to calm and reassure the woman while wishing someone would do the same for her. Just as she had the thought, Nick called.

"Hey," Sam said.

"Any sign of her?"

"Just her car. We found it down by the Capitol Mall an hour ago. Crime scene is on it, but so far nothing that'll help us find her."

"Shit."

"Yeah."

"What can I do for you, babe? I'll do anything, just name it."

"I can't think of another thing we could be doing. Malone called in the FBI an hour ago." Under normal circumstances, Sam would resent federal agents butting into one of her cases, but in *this* case, she'd take all the help she could get.

"How're you holding up?"

The tender tone of his voice brought tears to her eyes. Sam blinked them back. If she gave into them she might never stop. "I've had better days."

"Babe," he said, sounding agonized. "I wish there was something I could do for you."

"It helps to hear your voice," she said. "I've gotta go."

"I'm here if you need me. For anything."

"I know."

"Hang in there, and please be careful."

"I will." She ended the call and gripped the phone for a long time, as if to hold on to him and his strength. Clearing the emotion from her throat, she turned to head back down the block and ran smack into Lt. Stahl—the very last person she wished to see just then.

"Having trouble keeping track of your people, Lieutenant?" he asked. The smirk on his face took her over an edge she'd been hovering at for hours.

"Are you *enjoying* this? *What the hell is wrong with you?* A decorated officer is missing and you have time to needle me? Get your fat ass out of my face, and go *look* for her!"

She left him sputtering in her wake as she stalked off to find Cruz and Gonzo. Half a block later, she happened upon Captain Malone who'd left the command center in Chief Farnsworth's hands an hour earlier to come out and check on their progress.

"Anything?" Malone asked, his face tight with tension and fatigue.

She shook her head. Her stomach continued to ache and the adrenaline that had fueled her all day had begun to give way to bone-deep fatigue. "What else could we be doing? There has to be something."

"We're doing all we can."

She checked her watch. "We need to release some people to go home and sleep."

"You can release them, but they won't go."

"Is it all over the news?"

He nodded.

"We may as well have put out the word that today

would be a really good day to commit that crime you've been planning in the District."

"No kidding."

Their radios suddenly crackled with activity. They stopped walking to listen to the dispatcher relay a 911 call that was received about a naked black female found in an alley six blocks from where Sam and Malone were standing. Sam set off running and heard the captain following close behind her.

"Is she alive?" Sam screamed into the radio. Her heartbeat rang through her ears like thunder, making it difficult to hear anything over her own heavy breathing.

"The victim's condition is unknown," the dispatcher replied. "Paramedics are en route."

Detectives Arnold and Gonzales reported in from the scene a moment later that the woman in question was in fact Detective McBride and she was alive but unconscious, badly beaten and bleeding.

The relief nearly caused Sam's knees to buckle, and she faltered for a moment before regaining her stride.

"Thank God," she heard Malone say.

They watched an ambulance come around the corner, practically on two wheels with lights flashing and sirens blaring. Sam and Malone arrived on the scene seconds before the ambulance.

Gonzo had covered her with his coat so Sam couldn't fully assess her injuries, but her pretty face was bruised and battered, almost beyond recognition. Sam suppressed a gasp when she noticed the cut across her throat. "Jesus."

When Cruz and Gonzo looked up at her, their expressions were grim.

They all stood back when the paramedics pushed through the crowd that had gathered in the alley.

"Get these people out of here," Sam said. "I'll stay with her. Call Tyrone, have him update her family."

Cruz and Gonzo cleared the spectators out of the alley. Malone answered a cell phone call and followed them.

Sam crouched down by Jeannie's head as the paramedics worked frantically to stabilize her for transport.

"Do you know her blood type?" one of them asked Sam.

"No, but it'll be in her record." She called dispatch and requested the information as the paramedics transferred her onto a stretcher and covered her. "What've you got?" Sam asked them, fighting to retain her professional composure when she wanted to beat the shit out of something or someone.

The words flew at her in a blur as she chased after the paramedics. "Lost a lot of blood from the cut to her neck—even though it was a surface cut—probable sexual assault, possible fractured wrist, abrasions and contusions."

"Will she make it?" Sam asked, choking on a surge of nausea when she imagined what her friend and colleague had endured.

One of the paramedics looked up at her. "Heart rate is steady, BP is low, but not dangerously so."

She knew he couldn't give her any assurances, but it sounded like Jeannie's condition, while grave, could be worse. Sam gestured to Freddie and Gonzo. "Get crime scene down here and go through every inch of this alley. Start a canvas. Someone saw him dump her here. Get me something."

As they took off, the dispatcher called back with Jeannie's blood type. "AB positive."

Sam conveyed the information to the paramedics as she climbed into the ambulance to ride along with Jeannie, who was still unconscious. Sam was grateful Jeannie's body had given her a respite from having to relive the trauma—for now, anyway. The respite didn't last for long, however. Halfway to the hospital Jeannie began to moan.

Sam reached over to place a hand Jeannie's shoulder. "Shh," she said. "You're okay. You'll be okay."

When tears leaked from Jeannie's eyes, Sam wiped them away. "Hurts," Jeannie whispered.

"Can you give her something for the pain?" Sam asked the paramedic.

He nodded and called ahead to the E.R. for instructions.

Jeannie licked her badly swollen lips and winced. "Drugged me. Something pricked my neck."

So that's how they'd gotten to her.

"Just relax." Sam resisted the urge to go into interrogation mode. "We can talk about what happened later, when you feel better."

"I fought him." A sob erupted from her throat. "Hard as I could."

"I know. You did good, Jeannie."

"Never saw him coming. I was going to Michael's." Her eyes flipped up to meet Sam's. "Don't let him see me like this. Please."

"He's out of his mind with worry."

Her tears descended into whimpers that broke Sam's heart. "Keep him away."

"Whatever you want. Just relax and focus on getting better."

"He said…" Her swollen eyes fluttered shut.

"What? What did he say, Jeannie?"

"To tell you to back off or you'll be next."

Sam choked back a gasp as the implication registered.

The man they were looking for had grabbed Jeannie, tortured and raped her and sent her back with a message. That was why he'd let her live. She patted Jeannie's shoulder. "We'll get him. For you and Maria and Regina and every other woman this sick bastard has attacked." She had no doubt there were more women who probably hadn't come forward.

"Lieutenant," the paramedic said. "We're just about there."

Sam sat back on the bench so she wouldn't be in the way as they unloaded the stretcher. She followed them into the Washington Hospital Center Emergency Room where most of the HQ detectives were waiting.

In the instant after Jeannie was whisked into a trauma room Sam was bombarded with questions. She held up her hands to stop them. "She's awake and talking but lost a lot of blood. I know she appreciates you being here, but I need you all to go home and get some sleep so we can hit it hard in the morning. Everyone, please, go home. You did good work today."

After a lot of mumbling and grumbling, most of the detectives left. Cruz, Gonzo, Arnold, Tyrone and Malone remained.

"I thought you were handling the canvas," she said to Cruz and Gonzo.

"Second shift insisted on taking over because they know she's our friend," Cruz said.

Sam nodded. "Okay."

A nurse emerged through the swinging double doors. "Lieutenant Holland? Detective McBride is asking for you."

To Malone, Sam said, "Don't leave. I need to talk to you." She followed the nurse through the corridors to

Jeannie's room where a team of doctors worked feverishly on her.

A lump settled in Sam's throat. She had no idea what to say so she reached for Jeannie's hand and just held on while the plastic surgeon stitched the nasty gash on her throat.

"They'll do a rape kit," Jeannie said, her eyes shining with unshed tears. She looked up at Sam. "Will you stay with me?"

"Of course, but wouldn't you rather have your mother—"

"No!"

"Okay," Sam said, taken aback by her vehemence. "Whatever you want. I need to update the others, but I'll be right back."

Sam returned to the waiting room and signaled to Cruz and Gonzo. "There's nothing more you can do tonight, so go on home. I want everyone well rested for tomorrow."

"Call if you need anything," Gonzo said. "I'll come back."

"Me too," Cruz said.

Sam promised she would and sent them on their way. She turned to Malone and relayed the message the perpetrator had sent.

"Christ." Hands on his hips, he studied her. "I don't suppose you'd allow me to assign a couple of officers to escort you until this is over."

"Get real."

"This guy's good, Sam. He snatched a veteran officer right off the street in broad daylight. Don't tell me it can't happen to you too."

"He won't get to me."

"Um, I hate to remind you of what happened recently with Reese." Clarence Reese had caught Sam off guard by jumping into the backseat of her car and holding her at gunpoint.

"That was a fluke. I was off my game. I assure you I'm fully on my game right now."

"You're exhausted and pissed. We all are. I don't need another of my officers snatched by this guy."

"He won't do it again," Sam said.

"You're awfully certain of that."

"He snatched Jeannie to send a message. We're getting too close in the investigation."

"He's been awfully brazen. Leaving DNA all over the place, as if he thinks he's above the law ever catching up to him."

"Lindsey said the same thing. What do you think would happen if I demanded DNA samples from the senators the two dead women worked for?"

Malone uttered a harsh chuckle. "Best of luck with that."

"Based on the profile, I'm starting to think it's one of them—well, one of five. We know it's not Lightfeather, and we know it's not Nick."

"You're seriously asking me for authorization to request DNA samples from five United States senators?"

"Yeah," Sam said as the idea took hold. "I guess I am."

"You'll be the death of me, Holland. The living breathing death."

For the first time all day, she smiled. "Run it up the pole and get back to me."

"Yeah, I'll get right on that."

"You're the best."

Muttering, he stalked out the door.

Sam turned to Tyrone, the only remaining detective. "You should go home, Will. There's nothing more you can do for her today."

"If it's just the same to you, L.T., I'd rather stay."

Sam could see there was no point in arguing with him. "I know you're beating yourself up, but there was nothing you could've done to prevent this."

"I keep telling myself that, but still…"

Michael Wilkinson rushed in, arm in arm with an older woman who had to be Jeannie's mother. The two of them looked like they'd been to hell and back.

"Lieutenant!" Michael cried as Jeannie's mother hugged Tyrone. "Where is she? I want to see her. Will they let us see her?"

"She's banged up pretty badly," Sam said, "but she's awake and alert. She can't have any visitors for the time being." She had no idea how she'd tell him what had happened to Jeannie or that she didn't want to see him.

"Someone should be with her," he said.

"I'm going back now to talk to her about what happened," Sam said. "I'll be out as soon as I know anything." She also needed to talk to Jeannie to find out what she wanted them to know about the attack.

"Tell her we're here and we love her," Mrs. McBride said.

"I will."

When Sam returned to the trauma room, a nurse was explaining the need for an HIV test and preventative drugs as well as the morning-after contraception pill. Jeannie sobbed as she signed the consent form.

"Your mom and Michael are in the waiting room," Sam told her. "They said to tell you they love you. I told them the docs said no visitors for now."

"Thank you." Jeannie winced as she wiped tears from her swollen face.

"They really want to see you, Jeannie."

"I can't," she whispered. "I just can't."

A portable X-ray machine was wheeled in to take a film of her wrist.

Sam tried to stay out of the way while remaining close to Jeannie as doctors and nurses filtered in and out over the next half hour. A nurse-practitioner schooled on rape kits and evidence retrieval explained the process to Jeannie, even though the detective had worked many a sexual assault case and was well aware of the procedure.

Sam stood by her shoulder and whispered words of comfort as the nurse took photographs of Jeannie's injuries, including the rope burns on her wrists and ankles. The nurse clipped her fingernails, retrieved hair from Jeannie's head and pubic region, identified and collected semen from her legs and vagina, swabbed her for DNA and conducted a pelvic exam. The entire process took about three hours but Sam never left her side, and Jeannie never stopped crying.

When it was over, Sam felt like she too had been beaten up. She couldn't imagine how Jeannie must feel. An orthopedic doctor appeared next and got to work on setting Jeannie's broken wrist, another agonizing ordeal. A short time later, as they were finally ready to settle her in a room upstairs, Sam noticed that Jeannie had stopped crying.

"Is there anything I can get for you?" Sam asked.

"No. Thank you so much for staying with me. I really appreciate it, but you're probably anxious to get home." Her new eerily calm state was almost harder to deal with than the crying. That, at least, was understandable.

"I don't mind staying with you. They're sending up a rape crisis counselor to check in with you."

"That won't be necessary."

"Jeannie, you need to talk to someone—"

"Please tell them not to send the counselor. I need to sleep, not talk."

"What do you want me to tell your mother and Michael?"

"You can send them up to the room after they get me settled."

"Are you sure you're up for seeing them?"

She nodded. "I want no mention of the rape to them. Do you understand?"

"Of course." Sam hesitated before she said, "You'll have to tell them eventually…"

"It doesn't have to be now."

"Okay. I'll get them and bring them up to your room."

"Then I want you to go home. I'll be all right, and you need to sleep so you can get busy catching the monster who did this to me and Regina and Maria. We need you, Lieutenant."

After hours of tears, Sam couldn't figure out where this calm, collected Jeannie had come from. Sam squeezed the hand that wasn't encased in plaster. "You have me. I'll give it all I've got."

"I have no doubt about that." She looked up at Sam, her normally animated eyes dull and flat. "I'll never forget what you did for me today."

"I just did my job."

"You did much more than that and I won't forget it."

"I wish it could've been more, that we could've found you before…"

Jeannie shook her head. "What's done is done. Let's not rehash it."

"We'll need to get into the details tomorrow. What you remember, where he took you…"

"I understand."

"I'll get your mom and Michael and see you upstairs."

SIXTEEN

NICK RETURNED FROM yet another fund-raising dinner and hated coming home to an empty house, especially knowing Sam was at the hospital with Jeannie. He'd been so relieved to get the cryptic text from Sam, indicating McBride had been found injured but alive. Rather than spend the rest of the evening pacing the floor waiting to hear from Sam, he took advantage of the quiet to go through the thirty-eight messages that had collected on his voice mail. Number twenty-four was from Scotty.

"Um, ah, Senator Cappuano, this is Scotty Dunlap." Nick smiled at the way the boy stammered through the message. "Mrs. Littlefield told me it was okay to call you to say I really love the jersey you sent me. That was the nicest thing anyone has done for me in a long time. If you, um, want to call me back, I can get calls until nine." He rattled off the number. "Ok, um, bye."

Nick checked his watch. Twenty minutes to nine. He dialed the number Scotty had given him, asked for the boy and waited while the woman who answered went to find him.

"Hello," Scotty said a few minutes later, sounding breathless.

"Hi there, it's Nick Cappuano."

"Oh. Senator."

"You can call me Nick if you'd like to."

"Really?"

"Sure. I get tired of everyone calling me senator. It's not like that's my name or anything."

Scotty giggled.

"So you liked the jersey?"

"I *loved* it. All the other guys were so jealous."

"Maybe I should get jerseys for them too."

"Nah, let 'em be jealous."

Nick laughed. "So there's this family dinner thing on Sunday. I was wondering if you might want to come along with me."

"To *your* family?"

"My adopted family."

"You're adopted?"

"Well not officially. Their son John was my best friend, and when he took me home when we were in college, his parents made me part of their family."

"What about your own family?"

"I don't have a lot of family."

"Just like me."

"Right."

"You said he *was* your best friend. Isn't he anymore?"

The burst of pain caught Nick off guard. He ought to be used to it by now. "He died a couple of months ago."

"I'm sorry. You must've been really sad."

"Yeah. I still am."

"It took a long time after my grandpa and my mom died before I stopped being sad every day."

Nick cleared the huge lump from his throat. "Is that so? How long did it take?"

"A year or so. Maybe a little longer."

"That must've been hard on you all by yourself."

"It was, but you're not alone, are you?"

"No, buddy. I've got my fiancée and lots of good friends and John's family. They're helping me through it."

"You're lucky."

"I know."

"Mrs. Littlefield told me your fiancée is a police officer."

"She is—a detective, in fact."

"That's *really* cool."

"Cooler than being a senator?"

"Ah...*duh.* Yeah!"

Nick's smile faded as he thought about her desperate search for Jeannie McBride. "Some days it is. Other days it's really stressful. I told her about you, and she's looking forward to meeting you."

"She is?"

Nick laughed. "She sure is. So what do you think? Dinner on Sunday?"

"How would I get there?"

"I have a campaign thing in the morning. Afterward, I'll drive down to Richmond to pick you up. Then we'll head up to the farm."

"They live on a *farm*?"

"A working horse farm."

"That's awesome!"

Nick smiled at Scotty's enthusiasm. "Have you ever ridden a horse?"

"Nope."

"Maybe we can give it a whirl on Sunday?"

"I'd like that."

"I'll be there to get you about noon, okay?"

"What should I wear?"

"Jeans and a nice shirt. Sound good?"

"I can do that."

"Then I'll look forward to seeing you Sunday."

"Me too. I mean I'll look forward to it too. Thank you so much for taking me."

He was so sweet and mature and thankful. "I have a feeling it'll be my pleasure. See you soon."

Nick closed the phone and sat back against the sofa. He'd spend most of the day on the road, but that was okay. He couldn't wait to see Scotty again.

DISMAYED BY JEANNIE'S sudden calm, Sam headed for the waiting room. While she was glad that Jeannie had stopped crying and settled down, the calm was worrisome in light of what Jeannie had endured that day. When Sam entered the waiting room, Michael jumped to his feet.

"Lieutenant, how is she? Can we see her yet?"

"They're moving her upstairs, and I'll take you up. But you should know that her face is swollen and bruised."

A nerve in his cheek pulsed with tension, and he looked like he could kill someone. Sam understood. She'd felt the same way most of the day. Mrs. McBride wept softly as she listened to their exchange.

"I'll take you up now," Sam said.

Detective Tyrone followed along as they took the elevator to the fourth floor. Sam led them to the room number she'd been given and stepped aside to let them go in ahead of her. Michael and Tyrone hung back as Jeannie's mother rushed to her daughter's bedside.

Jeannie hugged her sobbing mother, assured her she was just fine and held the older woman until she got herself together. Tyrone stepped up next, gave his partner a hug and brushed a hand over her hair.

"Scared the shit out of me," he said.

"Sorry."

"You've got nothing to be sorry about. We're going to nail the bastard."

Jeannie nodded. "I know you will. Go on home now and get some sleep. I'll be okay."

"Are you sure?"

Jeannie worked up a smile for him. "Positive."

"I'll be with her," Michael assured Tyrone.

The detective joined Sam in the doorway. "I'll be in early."

"Take some time if you need it," Sam said.

He shook his head. "I want to help."

"I'll see you in the morning then."

Tyrone left, and Sam tuned back into the scene unfolding in Jeannie's room. Michael enveloped Jeannie in a big hug, his broad shoulders shaking as he finally broke down.

"Thought I'd never see you again, baby," he said between sobs.

"I'm here." She ran a hand up and down his back. "I'm right here."

The emotional exchange was almost too much for Sam to handle after the grueling day. Over Michael's shoulder she made eye contact with Jeannie and was startled by the flat expression on the detective's face. Something inside her had broken, and Sam wondered if her friend would ever be the same. She turned to leave the room to give them some privacy but Jeannie called her back.

"You must be anxious to get home to Nick," Jeannie said.

"I can stay as long as you need me."

"I'll be with her," Michael said.

"Go on home, L.T.," Jeannie said. "I'll be okay."

"I need to talk to you more in-depth in the morning."

Her face set in a resigned expression, Jeannie nodded. "I know."

"I'll see you then."

"Sam?"

Sam turned to her.

"I'm sorry, I should say, Lieutenant… Thank you. For everything."

Sam nodded and left her colleague in the hands of her devoted boyfriend. Trudging out of the hospital, every bone in Sam's body ached and exhaustion clung to her like a wet blanket. Outside, the fresh cold air was like a wake-up call, snapping her out of the fog she'd been in for hours. The suppressed fear, emotion and horror of the long day caught up to her all at once, and her hands began to shake so violently she wondered how she would drive home. Then she remembered her car was somewhere in Columbia Heights, so she called Nick.

"Hey, babe," he said, sounding sleepy. "How is she?"

"As well as can be expected." Sam glanced up at the clear, starry sky as her breath came out in white puffs in the cold air. "I hate to do this because it's so late, but do you think you could come get me? I seem to be stranded at the Washington Hospital Center."

"I'll be there in a few minutes."

"Thanks."

While she waited for him, Sam sent a text message to her entire squad, ordering them to a seven o'clock meeting at HQ. Fifteen minutes later, Nick's black BMW turned into the hospital complex. He pulled up to the curb and opened her door from the inside.

Sam scurried in and released a sigh of pleasure when her aching body made contact with the heated seats. "Oh, that feels good." She leaned over to kiss him and smoothed his mussed hair. "I got you out of bed. Sorry."

"I wasn't sleeping." He shifted the car into drive. "I was hoping you'd come home." They drove in silence for a few minutes before he glanced at her. "She's really okay?"

"She will be," Sam said, even though she harbored significant doubts. "Eventually."

"What happened?"

With her head resting against the seat, she turned so she could see him. "Will you hate me if I just can't go through it again? Not tonight anyway."

"That bad, huh?"

"Yeah."

He rested a hand on her leg.

Sam yearned to cover his hand with hers, but she didn't want him to feel how badly her hands were shaking so she kept them tucked into her coat pockets.

At home, Sam headed straight to the shower and stood under the water for a long time, thinking about what had happened, what might've happened, what needed to happen and the threat Jeannie had brought back with her.

Sam had hoped the shower would take care of the trembling, but it only made it worse. Battling her shaking hands, she pulled on sweats and a long-sleeve T-shirt and joined Nick in bed.

"Are you going skiing or something?" he asked as he put his arms around her and drew her in close to him. Like him, she usually slept in as little as possible.

"Freezing," she muttered, hoping he'd accept her explanation for the trembling.

"Let me warm you up."

Sam clung to him and breathed him in, trying to clear her mind of the horror. She knew she needed to tell him about the threat that had been made against her. She'd been working hard to be more open and honest with him, but with her emotions hovering perilously close to th surface, she was afraid to move let alone speak for fear of losing control.

"Why are you still shaking like a leaf?" he asked many minutes later.

"Dunno."

"Samantha." He kissed the top of her head and then her forehead. "I've got you. It's over. She's okay and so are you. Everyone is safe."

Sam would've been fine. She would've survived the bout of trembling if he hadn't figured out exactly what had caused it. His tender words tore a sob from somewhere deep inside her. As if a dam had broken, tears streamed down her face, wetting her hair and his chest.

He held on tight but didn't say anything. His hand moved up and down her back, offering just the right amount of comfort. Once again it occurred to her that before him, before *them*, she never would've let the emotion out. She would have tamped it down and found a way to power through the nightmare. His steady presence reminded her that she didn't have to do that anymore.

Nick wiped the tears from her face and combed his fingers through her hair.

After a while, Sam noticed the trembling had stopped. She released a deep sigh of relief. The crisis had passed.

"Feel better?" he asked.

Suddenly embarrassed by the outburst, she tried to pull away from him. "Yeah."

"Don't, Sam."

"Don't what?"

"Don't be ashamed of being as human as the rest of us mere mortals."

For whatever reason, that made her laugh. She looked up at him, not even caring that he would see her tear-ravaged face. "You are exactly perfect for me, and I love you."

"Well," he said, clearly caught off guard, "that works out well because you're exactly perfect for me too, and I love you."

She snuggled back into his chest. "We ought to get married or something."

"Or something."

"Did you hear from Tinker Bell today?"

"She sent over her estimate."

"And?"

He rattled off a number that made Sam sit up and gasp. "You gotta be freaking *kidding* me."

"That's for everything—her, the reception at the Hay, the church, the flowers, the cars, the cake. Everything except dresses and tuxes."

"That's outrageous! We could sponsor a third world nation for a year with that much money!"

"We can always elope—fly to Vegas and be done with the whole thing."

As much as that idea appealed to her, she couldn't deny him the wedding she knew he wanted, even if he'd skip it to spare her. "We're not flying to Vegas." She sounded sulky, even to herself.

"Are you sure?"

She realized this was her last chance to beg off the big white wedding. Once they signed the contract with Tinker Bell, it would be out of her hands. "Yeah, I'm sure."

He arranged her under him and gazed down at her. "I'm not convinced."

Sam studied his handsome face as a new swell of emotion reminded her that there was absolutely nothing she wouldn't do to make him happy. She lifted her arms to encircle his neck. "It's *so* much money."

He bent his head and gave her a sweet kiss. "Don't worry about that. I've got it covered. I have some of my own money too." She knew he meant in addition to what John had left him. "Back in the day, all I did was work. The money tends to add up when you're all work and no play."

"You're *sure* this is how you want to spend it?"

His sexy mouth twisted into a sinful smile. "I'm very sure, but only if it's what you want too."

"I'll allow it on one condition."

"I can't wait to hear this."

"I get to pay for the honeymoon."

"You don't have to—"

Sam tugged his head down and kissed him. "That's my final offer."

He leaned his forehead against hers. "You drive a tough bargain, but okay. I'll allow it."

"You'll *allow it? Allow it*?" As Sam started a wrestling match that would no doubt lead to lovemaking, she realized the cloud of sadness and despair had lifted. Since he was the only guy who could've done that for her, she supposed it was the least she could do to give him a day neither of them would ever forget.

SEVENTEEN

FOR A LONG time after Sam finally fell asleep, Nick lay awake watching her. She was always so strong and in control. To see her any other way was disconcerting, even if the breakdown was understandable. The long day of looking for Jeannie, finding her bruised and battered—and God knows what else she'd endured—would make anyone crack under the pressure, even his cool, competent Samantha.

Running his fingers through her long toffee-colored curls, he was glad that she'd let go of it all with him, glad he could be there when she needed him. He wanted to always be there when she needed him. Their wedding couldn't happen soon enough for him. Sam would prefer to run off and elope. He knew that. But Shelby would make sure it was a day they'd remember always, and Nick wanted that for both of them.

His cell phone rang, startling him since his phone wasn't the one that rang in the middle of the night. Nick reached for it, hoping it wouldn't wake Sam. "Hello," he whispered.

"Senator Cappuano? This is Dr. Manchester at Huron Hospital in Cleveland."

Baffled, Nick pulled on gym shorts and left the room, closing the door behind him. "What can I do for you?"

"I wanted to let you know that your mother was brought into the emergency room tonight. She fell down a flight of stairs."

"Is she…is she okay?" Nick wondered why the doctor had called him. He hadn't seen his mother in more than five years.

"She's suffered a number of bumps, bruises and abrasions but no broken bones. We did a CT scan to rule out a head injury, and that came up clear."

"Okay." Nick swallowed hard. "What can I do?"

"She would like you to come, if that's at all possible."

Nick had no idea what to say as he was revisited by the old familiar twinge of hope. It took him right back to countless occasions during his childhood when his mother promised to come see him and then never showed up.

"Senator?"

"She really wants me to come there?" Nick heard the confused ten-year-old he'd once been in the wistful tone of his voice.

"She said she doesn't have anyone else."

Nick bent his head, took a deep breath and wondered what had become of the guy she'd married the last time he saw her. Before he could wrap his head around all the reasons why it was a bad idea, he said, "I'll be there in the morning. Will you let her know?"

"Yes, of course."

He went downstairs to the kitchen, looking for a pen. "Is there a number I can call to check on her before I leave?"

The doctor gave him the number for the nurses' station. "I'll see you tomorrow."

"See you then," Nick said. He ended the call and leaned against the counter for a minute before he went into the study to log on to the computer to buy a plane ticket.

When he returned to the bedroom Sam sat up in

bed and turned on the bedside lamp. "Who was on the phone?"

He was sorry to have woken her. "No one, babe. Go on back to sleep."

"Didn't sound like no one to me."

Still holding the phone, Nick sat on the bed. "My mother fell down the stairs. She's in the hospital."

"Oh. Wow. And she called you?"

"The doctor did. She told him she didn't have anyone else."

Sam shifted so she was behind him, her arms looped around his shoulders and her chin propped on his head. "What're you going to do?"

"I'm going out there tomorrow."

"I don't even know her name—your mother."

"Nicoletta Bernadino. That was her maiden name, anyway. I have no idea what name she's using these days."

"When was the last time you saw her?"

"Five years ago."

"How about talked to her?"

"Two or three."

"Hmm."

"What?"

"Nothing. Let's go back to sleep." She tried to cajole him into bed.

He turned to her. "What do you want to say?"

"Nothing," she said, but he didn't believe it. He could see the questions in her cool blue eyes.

"Samantha…"

"I'm just, you know, finding the timing interesting."

"How so?"

"You recently came into a lot of money. I hope that's not what this is about."

Nick experienced a pang of worry. It certainly wasn't

outside the realm of possibility. His mother's life had been nothing if not a hand-to-mouth existence marked by multiple marriages and an equal number of divorces.

"I'm sorry," Sam said after a long moment of silence. "I shouldn't have said that."

"It's fine." He got back into bed and shut off the light. "It's nothing that hasn't occurred to me too."

"But you're still hopeful that maybe she just wants her son with her when she's in the hospital."

He shrugged. Leave it to Sam to hit the bull's-eye.

Sam shifted so she was on top of him and kissed his chest. "I don't want to see you hurt, Nick. That would hurt me too."

Sighing, he put his arms around her.

"Don't let her hurt you, okay?" she whispered

Easing her down to rest on him, he kissed the top of her head. "I won't." But as he said the words he wondered if, even at thirty-six, he was capable of seeing his mother and not hoping for anything.

SAM DROPPED NICK at Reagan National Airport just after six. He looked so handsome in a black leather jacket and well-worn jeans. In his hazel eyes, Sam saw a hint of anxiety and vulnerability that worried her.

"Call me when you get there," she said, kissing him at the curb.

"I will." He tapped his finger on her nose. "Don't worry about me."

"Too late."

Hugging her, he whispered, "Love you, babe."

"Love you too, Senator."

A flash interrupted the moment.

Sam snarled at the photographer who had taken their picture.

"Where ya headed, Senator?" the photog asked.

Sam noted he was from *The Washington Star*. "None of your business," she said. To Nick, she added, "You'd better go before you witness a murder."

Nick laughed. "Behave yourself. I'll be back tonight."

"I'll be here."

"Be careful today."

Rather than her usual reply, she said, "You too." Filled with trepidation, she watched him go and returned the wave he sent her as he approached the terminal door. She wished she could go with him to protect him from whatever emotional firestorm awaited him in Cleveland.

"What happened with McBride yesterday?" the nosy photographer asked.

Sam had forgotten he was there. "Also none of your business."

"Is it related to the dead immigrants?"

She went around her car to get in. "No comment."

"You're Miss Congeniality today," the photog grumbled.

Sam took great pleasure in flipping him the bird as she drove off, heading for the meeting she'd called at HQ. When she remembered what she needed to tell her detectives about what had happened to their colleague she felt sick.

At seven, she found a somber group gathered in the conference room. Just like breaking news to victims' families, Sam knew that short and to the point was the best course in situations like this. As she geared herself up to begin, Captain Malone and Chief Farnsworth stepped into the back of the room.

Sam nodded to them and returned her focus to the roomful of grim-faced detectives who were looking to her for leadership and answers to questions. They'd get answers for Jeannie and Regina and Maria and every other woman that animal had attacked. Sam had no doubt about that.

"As you all know, Detective Jeannie McBride was abducted in the Eye Street/Foggy Bottom neighborhood sometime between 0700 and 0730 yesterday morning. She was found fourteen hours later in an alley in the Adams Morgan neighborhood. She had been beaten and sexually assaulted."

A gasp went through the room. Detective Tyrone dropped his head into his hands. Freddie placed a comforting hand on his colleague's shoulder.

"She returned with a message from her attacker," Sam continued. "According to Detective McBride, he told her to tell me to back off the case or I'd be next."

She glanced at Malone and Farnsworth, certain they'd be all over her about protection after the meeting.

"I'll be interviewing Detective McBride further about the abduction and attack this morning. It's important to note that she has asked that her boyfriend and family members not be told about the sexual assault until she feels ready to tell them. It goes without saying that no one is to speak to the media or anyone else about the details of Detective McBride's abduction. Except for emergencies, all leave is canceled until we get this guy."

"What can we do, Lieutenant?" Cruz asked, looking fierce and furious.

"Where are we on that cell phone data?"

"I just talked to the phone company," Gonzo replied. "They promised it by ten a.m."

"Let them know that at one minute past ten, I'm going to Forrester," she said. "This is bullshit. We've got two dead women and the cell company is worried about their privacy?" Trying to control her anger, Sam rested her hands on her hips. "Tyrone, check on what the lab found in Jeannie's car and get me a report."

He seemed relieved to have something to do. "Yes, ma'am."

"I want all available personnel on Eye Street by 0900. Let's find a security camera or someone who saw the abduction."

"I'll authorize overtime," Farnsworth said.

"Thank you, Chief. Cruz, give Regina's mother a call," Sam said, her mind racing. "Make it a courtesy call, as if you're checking on how she's doing. See what you can find out about Regina's life here, anything she might've told her mother about men or friends or hobbies. Anything you can get."

"Do you want me to call Maria's family too?" Freddie asked.

Knowing how difficult the calls would be for her sensitive partner, she appreciated his offer. "That'd be great. Let me know what you find out." To the others, she said, "One of our own has been drugged, kidnapped, attacked and beaten. Let's show this son of a bitch the full might of the MPD. That's all."

Their faces tense and determined, the detectives left the room to go do what they did best.

"I KNOW WHAT you're going to say," Sam said as soon as she was alone in the conference room with Malone and Farnsworth. "So don't get going on safe houses and taking me off the street or any other nonsense. One of *my* detectives was snatched. There's no way you're taking me off this case."

"All right." Farnsworth's eyes locked on her and his jaw ticked with tension. "Why don't you tell me how you plan to ensure that this guy, who managed to grab a smart, savvy detective off a city street in broad daylight, won't do the same to you."

"Because I'll be watching for him, and she wasn't."

"Now you have eyes in the back of your head too?" Malone asked.

"One of my many gifts."

"This guy is brazen, Lieutenant," Farnsworth said. "He won't think twice about coming after you if he sees you as a threat to his freedom."

"I'll be vigilant."

"You'll also be tailed while on duty."

"No way! That is *not* happening—"

"It's either that or you're off the case," Farnsworth said.

"I don't need a tail! It's a ridiculous waste of resources."

"They're my resources to waste. Take it or leave it."

Fuming, Sam stared him down for a long moment in which he never blinked. The old guy still had a good bit of scary left in him. "Fine. Whatever. Just tell them to stay the hell out of my way."

"You might want to consider offering them hazardous duty pay, Chief," Malone said with a grin aimed at Sam. "Ever since she was forced off the diet soda she's been a bit…grouchy."

She glared at him.

"Before you hit the streets, you need to meet with the press," Farnsworth said.

"This day just gets better and better," Sam said. What she wouldn't give for a diet cola right about then. Maybe she'd have one in defiance of Dr. Harry's orders. Surely just one couldn't hurt anything, right?

"They're clamoring for information about Detective McBride's abduction."

"I'm not telling them anything."

"You don't have to," Farnsworth said. "You just have to go out there and tell them we're closing in on a suspect. Keep them from storming the building for another few hours."

"We're not even close to a suspect. In fact, we've got zilch on this guy." Frustration gripped her. "Where are we with requesting DNA from the senators Maria and Regina worked for?"

"It's a no-go," Farnsworth said. "I went all the way to the mayor on this one, and he said absolutely not—not without probable cause."

"The probable cause is that the dead women worked for these guys, had regular contact with them and we're working with a profile of a killer who thinks he isn't going to get caught, which leads us to believe he's powerful—or at least caught up in his own presumption of power."

"But we don't have anything *specific* tying any of the senators to the crimes," Farnsworth reminded her. "Until we do, no DNA."

"If it turns out to be one of them we'll have wasted a ton of time while he's out raping and killing women."

"You may be right about that, but we're not conducting a witch hunt on Capitol Hill."

"We'll get him with or without the DNA," Sam said.

"I have no doubt about that," the chief said. "Shall we meet the press?"

"If I have to," Sam grumbled as she followed him from the conference room. After a stop to grab her coat in her office, she met him outside the main door of the public safety building where the media had gathered, waiting to take another piece out of her hide. "We meet again," she said.

Questions flew at her.

"Is Detective McBride's abduction related to the dead cleaning ladies?"

"Was she raped too?"

"Is it the same guy?"

"How did he manage to grab a cop off the street in the middle of the day?"

"How close are you to a suspect?"

Sam held up her hands to stop the flurry. She proceeded to tell them what she knew about the abduction, minus the detail about the sexual assault. Of course they couldn't let that go.

"Was she raped?"

"I will not discuss the details of her abduction at any time during this investigation. If Detective McBride chooses to speak publicly about the incident, that'll be her decision. That is all I'll say about it—now or ever."

"Is it the same guy who killed the other women?" Darren Tabor asked.

"We're waiting on the lab to tell us that."

"So he did leave DNA on the detective?"

"No comment."

"What do you mean no comment? Either he left DNA or he didn't. Which is it?"

Sam turned a frosty stare his way. "No. Comment. Need me to spell that for you, Darren?"

"How close are you to a suspect?" another reporter asked.

"Not as close as I'd like to be, but we're following every lead and one of them will be the one that closes this case. He's got a mob of angry cops looking for him, that's for sure."

"Where did Senator Cappuano fly off to so early this morning?" Tabor asked.

"That's it," Sam said. "We're done."

EIGHTEEN

SAM ENTERED JEANNIE'S room a short time later to find her sleeping. Her face was swollen and the bruises had darkened to a deep purple overnight.

Michael was standing in front of the window, staring outside. When Sam came in, he turned to her, his face a study of exhaustion, worry and sadness.

"How is she?" Sam asked.

"They gave her a sedative a couple of hours ago, and she's been sleeping ever since."

"If you want to get something to eat, I'll be here for a while."

Seeming torn, he glanced at the bed and then at Sam.

"You're no good to her if you get sick," Sam said.

"I'm sensing there was more to this attack than anyone is telling me."

Sam worked at keeping her expression neutral. "What matters right now is getting her back on her feet and out of here."

"Would you tell me? If there was more to it than a kidnapping and beating?"

"No."

He took a moment to absorb that. "I guess I can understand that." Looking at Jeannie, he said, "I hope she knows I love her, and I'd do anything for her."

"I have no doubt that'll make all the difference to her. Go on and get something to eat. I'll sit with her."

"She speaks so highly of you. I can see why."

"Thanks," Sam said, taken aback by the compliment. "That's nice to hear."

"I'll be back. Shortly."

"I'll be here."

Michael leaned over to kiss Jeannie's forehead before he left the room.

Sam stepped up to her bedside.

"Thanks," Jeannie whispered, her eyes still closed. "For not telling him."

"Not my place to tell him anything. That's up to you."

Tears leaked from Jeannie's closed eyes. "I can't imagine telling him. Telling anyone…"

"You don't have to think about that right now." Sam placed a comforting hand over Jeannie's. "Can I do anything for you?"

"I'd love some water."

Sam poured some from the pitcher on the bedside table and held the straw up to Jeannie's cracked lips.

She winced as she took a sip. "Everything hurts today."

"I can only imagine."

"You need to know what happened. That's why you're here."

"That's not the only reason I'm here."

"You need to know. For the case."

"Only if you feel up to talking about it."

Jeannie's face tightened with pain as she tried to sit up. Pressing the button on the hospital bed took Sam right back to the grim days following her father's shooting and all the hours she'd spent by his bedside. "Is that okay?"

"Yeah," Jeannie said. Grimacing, she reached for a device tied to the bed rail and pressed the big red button. "Pain meds."

"We can do this later if you want."

"I'd rather get it over with."

Sam tried to be subtle when she reached for the notebook in her back pocket. "You said the last thing you remembered was a prick to your neck?"

"Yes. I was about two blocks from Michael's house." She gave Sam the Foggy Bottom address. "There's never anywhere to park near Eye Street, so I usually walk a short distance."

"Do you remember anything about who was on the street with you?"

Jeannie shook her head. "I was in a rush because Michael only has so much time before he has to be at work. I wasn't paying much attention, to be honest. I was thinking about seeing him."

"I can understand that. He seems quite devoted to you."

"He is," she said softly. "Although after this..."

"Jeannie, he loves you. This won't change anything for him."

New tears rolled down Jeannie's cheeks. "I guess we'll see, won't we?" She carefully wiped her sore face and seemed to be summoning the fortitude to continue her story. "The last thing I remember is someone bumping into me from behind and then the needle in my neck. Everything went dark."

"And when you came to? Can you describe where you were?"

Jeannie closed her eyes. "In a room with just a bed. The walls were yellow and there was a small window. They had...he had...my clothes. They were gone and I was tied to the bed. I was shaking so hard, and I remember I had to pee desperately. I started screaming. I screamed until my throat hurt, but no one came for the longest time."

Sam wondered if her abductor had been out moving

her car from Foggy Bottom to the Capitol Mall area. "How long do you think you were awake before he returned?"

"An hour. Maybe two. It was really cold in the room, and I was freezing with no clothes. Between that and the fear, I was shaking like a leaf."

Sam had taken a lot of victim statements in the course of her twelve-year career, but this had to be one of the more excruciating. She forced herself to stay focused on Jeannie and getting her through this as quickly as possible. "What happened then?"

"I heard a key in the door."

"Did it sound like a padlock or a dead bolt or something else?"

"A dead bolt. Definitely. He…" She took a deep breath. "He came into the room wearing a ski mask over his face, but I could see his eyes." Shuddering from the memory, Jeannie began to breath faster. "They were dark and mean. I could see there were some lines at the corners, so I don't think he was young."

"Can you describe his build?"

"Tall. Six feet, maybe a little more. Broad shoulders. Bulky muscles, like he spent a lot of time at the gym."

"How about race?"

"White."

"Did he say anything?"

"No," Jeannie whispered. "He just started taking off his clothes. I was crying and begging him to let me go, but he never said a word as he took off everything but the ski mask."

"Can you describe his body at all? Any scars, tattoos, distinguishing marks?"

"He had a lot of gray in his chest hair and some

scratches on his neck, but I can't say I noticed anything else."

"What happened next?"

Blinded by tears, Jeannie used her free hand to wipe them away. "He…he got on the bed." Sobs wracked Jeannie's body.

Sam started to get up, but Jeannie held up her hand to stop her. She took a moment to get herself together. "I asked him why he was doing this. What had I done to him? He just laughed." Sniffing and wiping her face frantically, she focused on a point on the far wall. "And then he…he started to rape me. I screamed for him to stop and he hit me in the face. Twice. I think I blacked out for a short time. When I came to he was…inside me. I tried to fight him off, but I couldn't move because I was tied to the bed. I bit his shoulder, and he hit me again."

"Take a minute," Sam said, her own hands shaking.

"After he was…done…he grabbed my throat and started to squeeze. He got really close to my ear and said, 'Tell your boss to back off on the dead whores, or she'll be next.'"

A shudder rippled through Sam. This case was rattling her in a way that not many did.

"I really think he meant it, Lieutenant. You have to be careful."

"Don't worry about me. Just focus on what you need right now." Sam tapped her pen against the pad. "Did he have any kind of accent or dialect that stood out to you?"

"Not that I noticed."

"What happened after he said that?"

"He raped me again. It just seemed to go on forever. I was crying and screaming the whole time. I thought it would never end. At some point, I lost consciousness again. He might've given me something."

"But you don't remember him giving you a shot?"

She shook her head. "The next thing I knew I was in the ambulance with you."

"How did you break your wrist?"

"I assume it happened when he dumped me in the alley. It wasn't broken yet when we were in that room."

"How about your throat?"

"I don't know when that happened. I assume it was after I was knocked out because I didn't feel it."

Sam reached up to squeeze her detective's arm. "You did great. You gave me a lot to work with."

"I didn't give you much."

"It could be enough to break this case wide-open."

"What if we never get him? How will I ever walk down a street again without worrying about who is behind me?"

"We'll get him," Sam assured her. "The entire department is out looking for him. I wouldn't want to be him right now."

"He won't care that we're all looking for him," Jeannie said.

"Why do you say that?"

"He thinks he's above the law. That's the only reason he'd be so brazen as to grab and assault a cop."

"Lindsey said the same thing." Sam's cell phone chimed. A text from Gonzo reported the cell phone records were being transmitted. She passed the information along to Jeannie.

"Took them long enough," Jeannie said.

"No kidding. I was hoping it would be Nick. He flew out to Cleveland this morning. I need to know he got there okay."

Against all odds, Jeannie chuckled. "Your fear of flying extends to other people's flights too?"

Chagrined but encouraged by Jeannie's lighthearted reply, Sam smiled at her. "Yep."

"What's in Cleveland?"

"His deadbeat mother. She's in the hospital and somehow didn't have anyone else to call but the son she hasn't seen in five years who recently came into a truckload of money."

Jeannie winced. "Ouch."

"I'm worried this'll go badly for him. After everything with John and Julian…"

"He doesn't need any more right now."

"No," Sam said. "Sorry. I shouldn't be dumping my worries on you."

"Don't be sorry. It's nice to think about something besides my own problems for a minute. And besides, after what we went through together yesterday, I'd like to think that maybe we crossed the threshold from great colleagues to good friends."

Sam leaned over the bed to carefully hug Jeannie. "Definitely," she whispered, caught off guard by a rush of emotion. "Call me if you remember anything else or if you need anything at all. Day or night."

"I will. Thanks."

"We'll get you through this, Jeannie. I promise."

As tears swam in her eyes, Jeannie nodded.

"I'll be back later."

"I'll be here—at least until tomorrow the doctor said."

Sam stepped into the hallway and found Michael leaning against the wall.

He straightened when he saw her. "I figured you two needed a few minutes to be cops."

"We did, thanks."

"I want to know what happened to her, but I'm not sure I can hear it, you know?"

"What she needs right now is to know that you're here, you love her and that no matter what happened to her it won't change anything between the two of you."

"It won't."

"Keep telling her that. It's what she needs to hear."

He nodded. "Thanks." Seeming to fortify himself to be strong for Jeannie, he went back into the room.

As Sam watched him go, she didn't envy the long road they had ahead of them as Jeannie recovered from the trauma of her attack. But Sam was more optimistic today than she'd been last night that Jeannie would bounce back.

Eventually.

THE MINUTE THE plane touched down Nick powered up his phone to send Sam a text, knowing how she worried when anyone she loved was in the air. Before he could finish composing his message to her, the phone beeped with an incoming message.

Tell your girlfriend to back off before she gets hurt.

Nick sat up straighter in the seat and fumbled with the phone, looking for the sender's number, which was unavailable. He immediately called Sam.

"Hey," she said. "Did you get there?"

"Babe," he said, filled with relief at the sound of her voice. "I got a text." He relayed the message.

"Damn it," she muttered. "How did he get your number? Unless it's someone you know who would already have it."

"Sam! I don't *give a shit* how he got my number! What are you going to do about the threat he made against you?"

"I've got a tail assigned to me, so don't worry."

"Which means this isn't the first threat." He gritted his teeth. "You'd better start talking, Lieutenant. Right now."

"You've got enough to deal with today with your mom. I'll tell you about it when you get back."

"Samantha, I'm not ending this call until you tell me what the *hell* is going on."

"McBride came back with a message for me. Similar to the one you received."

Nick closed his eyes and leaned his head back against the seat as the plane taxied to the gate. "I never would've come here if I'd known that."

"There's nothing you can do that's not being done. Farnsworth put a tail on me."

"Which I'm sure you objected to."

"It's ridiculous! I don't need two patrolmen following me around like I can't take care of myself."

"Samantha, I swear to God, you're to do exactly what they tell you to do or you'll answer to me."

"Oh boy," she said. "I love when you get all bossy with me like that. It makes me hot."

"I'm not joking!" he said loudly enough that the people sitting near him on the plane turned to look at him. He lowered his voice. "This isn't funny. He's already abducted and done God knows what to one of your detectives. Don't you dare be so cocky as to think he can't get to you too."

"I'm not being cocky, don't worry."

"Don't worry. Right."

"Can I have permission to dump your cell phone? We might be able to trace the source of the text."

"Whatever you have to do."

"Try not to worry. We're taking every precaution."

His mind immediately went to the recent day when he'd been absolutely certain she'd been shot in Clarence

Reese's house. In fact, it had been Freddie who'd been shot. Shuddering from the memory, he said, "Not *every* precaution. If I had my way you'd be locked up somewhere until this freak is found."

"I'm okay, Nick. I'll continue to be okay. Focus on your mother and what you're there to do today. I'll be waiting for you when you get home."

"Promise?"

"I promise."

"I'm not even going to tell you to be careful."

"I always am. You know that."

"I'm counting on it."

"Let me know how it goes with your mother."

"I'll call you when I'm back at the airport."

"I'll be waiting."

"Don't let anything happen to my fiancée," he said gruffly. "I love her very much."

"She loves you too. I'll talk to you later."

Nick followed the stream of people off the plane. Once inside the terminal, he called Skip Holland. When Celia put him on the phone, Nick said, "I thought you should know that the guy who grabbed McBride threatened Sam."

Sam would be pissed with him for alerting her father, but Nick had no doubt Skip would make sure the cops were doing everything they could to protect her.

NINETEEN

IN THE CAB to the hospital, Nick tried to brace himself to see his mother, to expect that nothing would have changed since the last time, to accept once again that she would never be the mother he'd yearned for all his life. He hated the way thoughts of her took him right back to that tiny apartment he'd shared with a grandmother made bitter by the unwanted responsibility of raising her son's child. His grandmother used to love to remind him of what a good-for-nothing bitch had given birth to him and then saddled *her* with "the kid."

So many times his mother had called to arrange visits that never materialized. As often as she'd disappointed him, though, he never stopped hoping she'd change, even if she'd rarely given him any reason to hope. He'd worked long and hard to build a life for himself that wasn't based on bitterness and disappointment. Seeing his mother set him back like nothing else ever could. It had happened before and would happen again if he wasn't careful.

This time, he was determined not to let her rip him to shreds. He was a grown man, about to marry the love of his life and inherit a family of in-laws he liked and respected. He had great friends and colleagues, was closer to his father than he'd ever been and he still had John's family, which considered him one of their own. Keeping all those positives in mind, Nick stepped into the elevator.

As he approached her room, the doctor stepped out. "Senator Cappuano?"

"Yes," Nick said, extending a hand. "How is she?"

The doctor shook his hand. "Anxious to see you. I told her you were on your way."

Hearing she was anxious to see him put Nick immediately on guard. To his knowledge, she'd ever been anxious to see him in his entire life. At least not that he could recall. Sam's warning echoed through his mind. He'd be wise to keep that guard up.

"When can she go home?" Nick asked.

"We're waiting for the results of several tests. Provided everything checks out, she can leave this afternoon."

"Okay, thank you."

The doctor walked away, and Nick stood outside the door. His stomach was queasy, the way it used to get when he'd sit in his grandmother's window for an entire Saturday waiting for a mother who wasn't coming. Taking a final unsteady breath, he pushed the door open and stepped inside.

"Oh! There he is! Look at him," Nicoletta said to the nurse who was checking her monitors. "My son, the United States *senator*!" She held out her arms. "Come, darling. Give your mother a hug."

Nicoletta had often been compared to Sophia Loren with wavy auburn hair, flawless skin and dazzling smile. However, as Nick approached the bed to hug her, he noticed lines on her face that hadn't been there the last time he saw her.

His mother drew him in tight, and Nick was surrounded by her familiar fragrance. Releasing him from the hug, she framed his face with her hands. "Isn't he so handsome, Roberta? Didn't I tell you?"

"He sure is, and you sure did," the nurse said. "I'll leave you two to visit. Ring the call button if you need anything, Nicoletta."

"Thanks." Turning back to Nick, she said, "Well, look at you. So grown up and *so* handsome. Thank you for coming, sweetheart."

Despite all the warnings he'd given himself before seeing her, Nick glommed on to the compliments and endearment like a starving man who'd just found food. "Um, sure, no problem."

She dropped her hands from his face. "I know how busy you must be. When I heard you'd become a senator, well…I just couldn't believe it!"

"I thought I might hear from you." Nick hated that he sounded like a sad little boy who still sought his mother's approval.

"I had every intention of calling, but one day became two and then three. I didn't want to bother you."

He dropped into the chair next to her bed. "Too bad you didn't call. Maybe you could've come for the swearing-in. The president and first lady were there." Inside, Nick winced at his shameless name-dropping.

"You don't say! I'd love to meet the president. How lucky you are!"

"I've been very lucky lately. I'm not sure if you've heard that I'm engaged."

"I read that in the paper. Congratulations."

"They reported our engagement *out here*?"

"I read the Washington paper on the computer," she said, chagrined. "I was so curious after I heard you'd taken office."

Sam's warnings echoed through his mind, louder than ever. If his mother had read about his engagement, she'd no doubt read about the two-million-dollar life insurance payment too. "Her name is Samantha, but she goes by Sam. She's a homicide detective in Washington."

"And you're happy with her, Nicky?"

The nickname was a shot to the heart. His parents were the only people who'd ever called him that. "I've never been happier in my life."

"I'm glad for you," she said, sounding sincere. "You certainly deserve to be happy."

"I certainly do."

Nicoletta looked down at her hands in her lap and then at him. "I know I have no right to call you here, and it's no thanks to me that you're the kind of man who comes when his mother needs him even if she's never done the same for you."

Nick couldn't deny that, so he said nothing.

"It's just that I've, you know, fallen on some hard times. And now this accident..."

Here it comes, Nick thought. "What happened to Mel?" he asked, referring to the man she'd married the last time Nick saw her—at her third wedding during which she'd refused to introduce him as her son. Nothing like being a walking, talking symbol of someone's youthful indiscretion.

"He's been gone a while now."

"What do you want from me, Nicoletta?" She'd asked him to call her that at the wedding. Apparently, it was easier for her to introduce him as an old friend than the son she'd never wanted.

Right on cue, fat tears began to roll down her flawless face. "When Mel left, he took everything. I had a job for a while, but I got laid off and now my benefits have run out. I didn't know who else to turn to."

"So you thought this would be a good time to hurl yourself down a flight of stairs?"

Her eyes widened with shock at his cold tone. "Don't be ridiculous! I could've been killed! I tripped over the runner on the stairs." She held up her arms so he could see the bruises she'd sustained on the way down. She turned those potent, tearful eyes on him again. "You'll help me, won't you, Nicky?"

Nick schooled his face into what he hoped was a flat, emotionless expression. "How much do you need?"

GONZO SIFTED THROUGH the phone records the cell company had finally produced, highlighting common numbers that appeared on the lists for both Regina and Maria. There were three, which gave Sam some of those threads she liked to pull. He was about to report in to her when his cell phone rang.

"Tommy, it's Andy," his lawyer said. "I just got off the phone with the child protective services representative who did the home inspection."

"And?"

"Apparently, when she went to the house, the conditions were so poor that she immediately removed the baby from the premises."

Gonzo sat up straighter in his seat. "Where is he?"

"At the moment, in foster care, but here's the good news—a family court judge has agreed to hear our petition for custody. Today."

"On what grounds?" Gonzo asked, his heart and mind racing. "We haven't even gotten her to agree to the DNA test to establish my paternity."

"We don't have to," Andy said, sounding ebullient.

"Okay, you've totally lost me here."

"Tommy," Andy said, "she listed you as the father on the baby's birth certificate!"

All the air left Gonzo's body in one long whoosh. "*Seriously?*"

"Yep. Normally, they send written notice of a hearing, but the judge waived the notice."

"Who is it?" Gonzo asked even though he suspected.

"Morton. Do you know him?"

"I caught his sister's killer two years ago. Got the guy put away for life with no chance of parole."

"Well, that explains it. Unless he says something in court, don't mention that. If he's doing you some sort of favor, we don't need to point it out."

"Don't worry, I won't say a word."

"So while the judge will no doubt order formal paternity testing, there should be nothing standing in the way of them awarding you temporary custody today. Can you be in court in an hour?"

Gonzo thought about the case they were working and Sam's declaration that all leave was canceled. Surely, this counted as an emergency, right?

"I'll be there," he said.

"Not to be premature, but I hope to be saying, 'Congratulations, Dad,' before the end of this day. See you soon."

Dad. The word struck every emotion he'd ever experienced. Joy warred with fear as he remembered he didn't know a damned thing about taking care of a baby. He'd figure it out, though. If it meant he got to bring his son home, he'd do whatever it took to make it work. Picking up his phone again, Gonzo called Sam.

"Give me something, give me anything," she said when she answered.

Her familiar line made him smile. He brought her up-to-date on what he'd found on the cell records. "I'll run the common numbers now and see what we get."

"Excellent work. Thank you."

"How's McBride?" When he thought about what had happened to his friend and colleague, Gonzo saw red.

He wanted to be right in the thick of tracking down the monster who'd attacked her, but today he had something else he had to do.

"A little better. It's gonna be a long road."

"Yeah. Listen, Lieutenant...something's come up, and I wondered if I could take some emergency leave."

The request was met with silence.

In a rush of words, he told her about the call from Andy. "I know this is the worst possible time and you canceled all leave, but if I'm awarded custody I need to be there and the judge needs to see that I'm a fit father and—"

"Gonzo! *Gonzo!* Of course you have to be there. No question."

"But the case—"

"We've got it covered. Go take care of your kid."

"Jeannie—"

"Would tell you the same thing."

"Okay," he said, releasing a deep breath he hadn't realized he was holding. "Sam..."

"Yeah?"

"What the hell do I do with a baby? My parents are in Arizona for the winter, my sisters are hours from here. *What the hell do I do?*"

Laughing, she said, "I'll call my sisters. They'll set you up with everything you need. Leave it to them."

"I can't ask that of you—or them."

"You didn't ask. I offered them up, and trust me, they love to butt into other people's business. They'll have you fixed up in no time."

"Wow, thanks. I mean that. Really."

"I'm not doing it for you. I'm doing it for the poor kid."

Gonzo laughed. "And for that he will be eternally grateful."

"What's his name, Tommy?" she asked softly.

"It's going to be Alejandro, after my father. But we'll call him Alex."

"That's a beautiful name."

After a long pause he said, "You really think I can do this?"

"Absolutely. I have no doubt that you'll be great. Let me know how you make out in court. I'll call my sisters and give them your number."

"Thank you so much—for that and the flexibility."

"Go take care of your family. Keep me posted."

His family. The whole thing blew his mind. "I will." He ended the call with her and called Christina to bring her up to speed. "Can you come to court? I'm totally freaking out over here."

"*I can't*," she said in a protracted wail. "Nick got called away on a family emergency today, and I'm scrambling to shift all his appointments and meetings to tomorrow. The office is insane, and I'm *still* waiting for my deputy to show up after his stint in rehab. I can't believe I'll miss it!"

Gonzo couldn't believe he had to get through it without her by his side. "I wish you could be there."

"I do too," she said with a whimper. "I'll be *dying* over here waiting to hear something."

"I'll call you as soon as I can."

"I love you, Tommy. I'm so happy for you."

The words were still so new that they caught him by surprise. "I love you too. Thank you for all the support. I couldn't have gotten through this without you."

"That's nice of you to say, but getting custody might turn out to be the easy part," she said with a laugh.

"No kidding. I'll call you."

"Good luck!"

As soon as Sam ended the call with Gonzo, her dad's number beeped in. "Hey, Skippy, what's up?" She pictured him in the kitchen wearing the headset that allowed him to use the telephone.

"Just checking on my daughter who's been threatened once again."

"How do you know about that?" Neither Malone nor Farnsworth would've wanted to worry him, which left... "Nick. Ugh, I'll shoot him."

"He's worried, Sam, and rightfully so. If this guy could grab McBride the way he did, what's to stop him—"

"I hear you. Farnsworth put a tail on me. They're right here." She glanced at the two young officers, who waved at her. When she scowled at them, they had the good sense to look elsewhere. Coupla probies, right out of the academy, no doubt, but at least they were armed.

"If I hear you dodged them or did anything other than exactly what your superior officers tell you to do, you'll answer to me. Am I clear?"

"You did get the memo that I'm thirty-four now and don't have to do what you tell me anymore, didn't you?"

"You'll do what I tell you for as long as I draw a breath on this earth, missy."

Sam laughed. "Did you really just call me 'missy'? I haven't heard that one since middle school."

"You drove me to it with your insolence."

"I apologize for my insolence, and I promise to do what I'm told. Happy now?"

"I'll be happy when you catch this bastard."

"So will I," Sam said with a sigh. "Believe me."

"Come see me if I can help."

"Freddie and I will be by later to run a few things past you."

"I'll be here."

"Counting on it."

"Right back atcha. Be careful."

GONZO SAT IN the courtroom wishing he'd had time to go home and change. In a room full of suits, he felt woefully underdressed in the jeans and pullover sweater he'd worn to work. Even though the room was warm, he kept his black leather jacket on because it made him feel more dressed up. He had, however, unzipped the jacket so the gold shield clipped to his belt was visible. That had to count for something, right?

Looking harried, Andy rushed into the courtroom and joined Gonzo in the gallery's front row. Lori and Rex walked in a minute later and the glare she directed his way was sharp enough to cut glass. After noting that Rex had dressed up for court by removing his bandana, Gonzo looked away from them. She wasn't his problem. No; the baby who arrived in the arms of a woman wearing a suit had Gonzo's full attention. Under the woman's arm was a manila file folder. A yellow diaper bag hung from her shoulder.

Lori cried out when she saw the baby, and Rex held her back as she dissolved into tears.

Gonzo rubbed his sweaty palms on his jeans.

A few minutes later the judge entered the chambers and court was called to order. Feeling like he was watching a movie rather than a scene from his own life, Gonzo observed the proceedings with an odd sense of detachment. Surely all this talk about competency and best interests of the child and other legalese was making sense to someone because a lot of it was lost on him. The judge thoroughly quizzed the social worker about the condition of Lori's home as well as her criminal record and Rex's.

Lori's attorney stood up. "Your honor, may I please address the court?"

"No. Sit down."

Andy surged to his feet. "Your honor, Andrew Simone, representing Detective Thomas Gonzales, the child's father."

"Detective, please approach the bench." The judge gave no indication they had ever met before.

Andy nodded at him to go ahead and followed him to the front of the courtroom.

"Is it my understanding," the judge said, "that you had no knowledge of the child until this past weekend?"

"Yes, Your Honor."

The judge glanced at Lori, who was quietly weeping as Rex kept an arm around her.

"And you believe you could provide a loving home for the child?"

"I do, Your Honor."

"Do you have a crib, car seat and other necessary equipment?"

"It's being procured for me as we speak by two experienced mothers. One of them will deliver the car seat here momentarily."

"Have you ever cared for an infant before?"

Gonzo swallowed hard. "No, Your Honor. But I'm a fast learner, and I have friends who can show me what I need to know. My parents will come too. There's nothing I wouldn't do to ensure he has a safe, clean, comfortable home."

The judge cast a distasteful look at Lori. "And will you see fit to give him a name?"

"Yes, Your Honor. His name would be Alejandro, after my father. Alex for short."

The judge seemed satisfied with his answer. "I'm granting temporary custody to Detective Gonzales. Miss Avery," he said, referring to the social worker. "Please conduct weekly visits with Detective Gonzales and report to the court. We'll reconvene in thirty days to determine how the arrangement is working out."

As the judge's words registered, Gonzo couldn't believe this was actually happening. Any moment now, he was going to wake up and discover he'd dreamed the whole thing.

Lori's attorney once again stood up. "Your Honor, if I may, will his mother be permitted to see the baby?"

"Two hours a week, supervised," the judge said. "Work out a schedule that suits Detective Gonzales and Miss Avery."

"You can't do this!" Lori screamed. "He's *my* baby! You're only giving him to his father because he's a cop!"

The judge's eyes narrowed with displeasure. "Unless you'd care to spend a few nights in the city jail, I'd suggest you contain your outbursts in my courtroom. Do you understand me?"

Through her sobs, Lori managed a nod.

"I'm giving him to his father because your home is a pigsty and frequented by criminals."

Rex pulled her back down to her seat.

"Two hours a week. Take it or leave it." The judge banged his gavel. "Next case."

Just like that, it was over, and Miss Avery was handing him his son. The baby's big eyes, so wide and trusting, gazed up at him, his lips forming that adorable pucker that Gonzo remembered from the other time he'd seen him. He held the tiny body against him, struck by just how small he was. Had he been that tiny the other day? Or did the baby seem smaller because it was now up to Gonzo to keep him safe? The enormity of the moment came down on him all at once.

Oh my God, he thought. *How in the world am I going to do this?*

TWENTY

"WHAT'D YOU GET from the mothers?" she asked Freddie by phone once she'd gotten her team started on the canvas in the Foggy Bottom neighborhood where Jeannie was abducted.

"Not much, unfortunately. Neither of the women talked to their mothers about anything other than their families, their work and their immigration status when they called home."

"Damn it," Sam said. "How did they explain the money?"

"Regina's mother said she had been saving up her pay from the cleaning company—or at least that's what Regina told her."

"No way a seventeen-dollar-an-hour cleaning lady has an extra five grand lying around—not living in this city. What did Maria's mother say about the money?"

"She said she didn't know where it came from and didn't think to ask because everyone is rich in the U.S., or so she seems to think. So what's next?"

"Gonzo was running the phone numbers that appeared on both Regina's and Maria's phones. Did you get that report?"

"Not yet. The computer geeks are backed up. They promised it by the end of the day."

Sam wanted to shout with frustration. *Didn't these people realize she was running a homicide investiga-*

tion? "I wish to hell Farnsworth would let me test the senators for DNA."

"That'll never happen," Freddie said. "Not without probable cause."

"Then let's get it."

"Define 'get it.'"

"Time to do some digging into senatorial closets."

"Do I have to?"

"Yes, you have to. Let's go run this one by Skip. Maybe he can help us figure out a way to do this without ending up unemployed afterward."

"That'd be preferred. I'll meet you there."

"Anything yet on Nick's phone?"

"Not yet."

"You put a rush on it?"

"Sure did."

Sam sighed. More delays. "Alright, I'll see you at Skip's."

On the way to her father's house, she debated whether to call Nick. She wanted so badly to know how things were going in Cleveland—and to give him a piece of her mind for calling her father about the threat. But every time she imagined Nick's mother wanting nothing from him but his money, she ached for him. How she hoped she was wrong about that, but her gut was telling her to be worried. In the end, she decided not to call him. She'd wait to hear about it when he got home, even if the waiting was killing her.

Ignoring the patrol car that followed her, she parked on Ninth Street and took the ramp to her father's house. With a quick knock she entered the living room to find Skip and Celia sitting in front of the TV.

"What did I tell you about knocking?" Celia asked without removing her eyes from the screen.

"I'll do better next time," Sam said. "What's going on?"

"Senator Lightfeather is resigning from the Senate," Skip said.

"Oh man," Sam said.

"...and so I've decided," Lightfeather was saying, "that I need to spend as much time as I can with my family, to repair the damage I have caused." Next to him, his wife stood with a tight-lipped frown. The dais sported a Washington Hilton logo, so at least he hadn't left the building where Sam had told him to stay. "As such, today I announce my resignation from the United States Senate. I have treasured every moment of the years I spent representing the people of the great state of Arizona. I thank the citizens for the faith they had in me, and I will work for the rest of my life to once again be worthy of that faith. I ask that you respect my family's need for privacy at this difficult time."

The moment he stepped off the stage, the network's anchor and political analyst began speculating about Lightfeather's association with two Capitol Cleaning Services employees who'd been murdered. "A well-placed police source tells Capitol News that Regina Argueta de Castro was expecting Lightfeather's baby," the analyst said.

Sam let out a shriek. "*How the hell do they know that? Goddamn it!*" She reached for her phone and called HQ. "It's Lieutenant Holland. Put me through to the chief immediately." When told he was in a meeting, she said, "Interrupt it."

The chief came on the line a minute later. "Lieutenant."

"Sorry to interrupt your meeting, but we have a leak." She told him what she'd heard the reporter say. "I will guarantee you none of my people breathed a word of that to the media, so I want to know who this 'well-placed' source is."

"So do I."

"You might want to start with Stahl."

"He may have it in for you personally, but he'd never squeal to the press."

"And you're *sure* of that?"

"Not as sure as I'd like to be. Have you seen Detective McBride today?"

"Yes. She's hanging in there."

"I wanted to see her or send her something, but I wasn't sure if I should go there…"

It was so unlike him to be uncertain. "In this case, it might be best to send some flowers. A visit from the chief might be more than she can handle."

"Then that's what I'll do. Keep me posted on the investigation."

"Find that mole," Sam said.

"On it."

Returning the phone to her coat pocket, Sam turned to her father and stepmother.

"How's Jeannie?" Celia asked, her pretty face etched with worry.

"As well as can be expected."

"Did he…?"

They knew she couldn't give them details and would never ask her to. Her silence spoke for her.

"Oh, God," Celia said. "I was so hoping…"

"Me too."

"What's the status of the investigation?" Skip asked, his voice gruff. Sam had no doubt he was deeply affected by what had happened to McBride. Even as a disabled retiree, he was still one of them. Sam made sure of that, as did Farnsworth, Malone and Skip's many other friends within the department.

"Stalled," Sam said, falling onto the sofa. "I'm convinced we're probably looking for a senator or someone equally powerful, but Farnsworth won't let me request DNA without probable cause."

"So you're going to get it," Skip said.

"That's the plan."

"You gotta be *really* careful."

"That much I know. How do you suggest I approach it?"

Before he could answer, Sam's cell phone rang again. She didn't recognize the 202 number, but took the call anyway.

"Holland."

"Darren Tabor."

Sam suppressed a groan. "I'm *busy*, Darren."

"I saw Detective Gonzales coming out of the courthouse with a baby in his arms. I didn't think he had kids, so I'm smelling a story."

While Sam was thrilled for Gonzo, who'd apparently prevailed in court, the fact that Darren knew about it wasn't good news. "Don't go there, Darren. Please. I'm asking you to do this for me as a personal favor."

"That'll mean you owe me one."

Sam grimaced. "What do you want?"

"Tell me there's a connection between McBride's abduction and the dead cleaning ladies."

"There's a connection, but I can't say more than that right now."

"And when you can?"

"I'll keep you in mind."

"Excellent."

"And you'll forget about the thing with Gonzales?"

"What thing?"

Sam released a sigh of relief. "Thanks. While I have you, maybe you could do me another favor."

"That'd put you pretty deep in the hole to me," he said, but she could hear the laughter in his voice.

"It'd be worth owing you if you can find out where the leak about the father of Regina's baby came from."

"Is it true? It's Lightfeather's?"

"Maybe, maybe not. Either way, I'd like to know how the media got that tidbit."

"I'll do some sniffing around. See what I can find out."

"Keep it down low that you're doing it for me."

"Lieutenant, I am nothing if not the *soul* of discretion."

"Sure you are," she said, chuckling. "Let me know what you hear."

"Maybe you should program my number into your phone so you'll have it when you need me in the future."

"Hanging up now."

"Where did Nick go today?" Darren asked.

Sam slapped the phone closed.

"If I didn't know better," Skip said, "I might think you enjoy sparring with that boy."

"He's not as bad as some of them."

"He was tough on you after Johnson."

Sam shuddered at the reminder of the child who had died in a shoot-out she'd ordered at a crack house. "He gave us a heads-up when the *Reporter* was getting ready to trash me," she reminded her father.

"That's true," Skip said.

Sam hated remembering that the entire city knew about her near-abortion—the one she'd planned to have in college before she miscarried. An employee of the women's clinic that had treated her had decided to cash in on Sam's newfound notoriety. But they'd taken care of her and ensured she'd be tied up in a legal web for many years to come.

"So you want to talk about how to get those guys in high places to talk?" Skip asked.

Anxious to think of anything other than the long-ago nightmare that she believed had led to her current fertility issues, Sam nodded. "Yeah. Tell me what you'd do."

SAM AND FREDDIE took over the dining room at Nick's place, using laptops to search the internet for every detail they could find about the lives of the five senators who'd had regular contact with Regina and Maria. The daylong canvas in Foggy Bottom had yielded two security cameras that had caught only shadowy images and not a single witness who reported seeing the abduction. They'd also gotten nothing helpful from a thorough investigation of the alley where Jeannie had been dumped. Sam was about to tear her hair out in frustration.

"Get this," Freddie said, his eyes dancing over the screen. "Trent was in a car accident his senior year of high school."

"Fatalities?"

"Two—both girls. He was driving, and his pants were unzipped when the cops cut him out of the car."

"Drunk?"

"High. They found marijuana in the car."

"Whoa. How'd the press never get ahold of this?"

"They did." He spun the laptop around so she could see the video Freddie had found of Trent's interview on Oprah in which he'd taken full credit for what he called a "youthful mistake." The Montana voters had bought his story and sent him to Washington ten years earlier, as an appointee to finish out the term of a senator who was forced to resign after a scandal. He'd won the seat on his own in the last election.

"Once again, the little woman stands staunchly by her husband's side while he admits to being a scumbag," Sam said of the Oprah video that featured Trent and his wife.

"You've got a real beef with that, huh?"

"I just don't get these women who think so little of themselves that they blindly stand by these guys."

"What would you do if the press found out about something stupid that Nick had done as a kid? You wouldn't stand by him if it turned into a media circus?"

"Nick doesn't do stupid things."

"Everyone does stupid things at some point in their lives."

"Nick never did." Sam chewed on her pen as she wondered once again how things were going with his mother. "He had an odd upbringing. Not a lot of time for foolishness." She was quite certain, in fact, that he'd been so focused on hockey and school and his goal of going to Harvard on an academic scholarship that he never had time for youthful stupidity.

"Why do you have that worried look on your face?"

"Do I?"

Freddie nodded.

Sam told him about where Nick was and who he was dealing with as well as her worries that his mother might be after his money.

"Damn," Freddie said. "I can't imagine having a mother like that."

"Speaking of mothers, is the dinner party on?"

"I don't know if I should do it. With the case and McBride…"

"You need to get this issue resolved once and for all.

You can't be caught in the middle between your mother and Elin the way you are now."

"We'll see what Friday brings. I asked them both to save the night, but I'm not sure Elin will show. She wasn't too happy about the idea. If she does come, I might take them out to eat rather than cooking. I figure if we're in public, they can't claw each other's eyes out."

"True." Turning back to the case, she tapped a pen against the table as she mulled over the thoughts swirling around in her mind.

"What're you thinking?"

"Something Jeannie said today keeps nagging at me."

"What's that?"

"The message he told her to give me—'Tell your boss to back off on the dead whores, or she'll be next.'"

"What about it?"

"He called them whores."

"So?"

"So nothing in our investigation has led to any kind of promiscuity. Even though both were pregnant and Regina was involved with Lightfeather, we haven't found a single other man linked to either of them."

"Figure of speech?"

"Could be," Sam said. "But I keep going back to the money they were sending home. Where would they get that? You said drugs, gambling or prostitution. Remember?"

"Yeah, so you think they were hooking on the side?"

"Gonzo spoke to Maria's neighbor who said her routine was exactly the same seven days a week. She came home from work and took a shower. The woman upstairs heard the pipes clanging every morning."

"Okay..."

"JoAnn Smithson told us they work five nights a week,

Monday through Friday nights. So what was Maria doing the other two nights?"

"Good question."

"One to ask her friend Selina. We can follow up with Lightfeather again about Regina's weekend schedule. In the meantime, let's finish the research on the senators. I'd love to find some skeletons in the closets of Stenhouse or Cook."

"If they've got 'em, we'll find 'em."

BY ELEVEN, SAM and Freddie had read every word they could find about their five senators, but hadn't found any other bombshells. "I guess we'll start with Trent in the morning," she said.

"Sounds like a plan. Should I meet you there?"

"Let's go to HQ first to see if third shift got anywhere tonight. I also want to know if we've got DNA results from Maria. Will you check to see if there's a report on Nick's cell yet?"

"Logging in right now." He scrolled through his emails. "Not yet."

"What the hell is taking so long? Everything on this case is taking forever!"

"A couple of dead cleaning ladies certainly don't inspire the same sense of urgency as a dead senator or Supreme Court nominee. That's for sure."

"They're just as urgent to me."

"Which is why you're a rare and special woman, Lieutenant."

She made a face at him even though she was amused, as always, by his sucking up.

At the sound of the front door opening and closing, Freddie gathered up his laptop and shoved it into his backpack. "I'll see you at HQ in the a.m."

Filled with anxiety, Sam followed Freddie into the living room where Nick was hanging his coat in the closet. One look at his handsome exhausted face and Sam could tell it hadn't been a good day.

Freddie said a quick hello to Nick and showed himself out.

Sam went to Nick and slipped her arms around him, snuggling into his chest. At first he was rigid, but then his arms encircled her and the starch left his spine.

"You were right," he said after a long period of silence.

Sam closed her eyes tight, aching from the hurt she heard in his voice. "I'm sorry." While she wanted to know how much the day trip had cost him, she didn't ask because it would embarrass him.

"I should've known," he said in a bitter tone that was so unlike him. "People like her don't change."

Sam looked up at him and raised her hands to frame his face. "We don't need her. *You* don't need her."

He nodded in agreement.

"It's her loss, Nick. She'll never know the wonderful, kind, loving, generous man that I know, because she's too selfish to be bothered."

With his hands on her hips, he held her close to him. "I couldn't wait to get home to you. All day, I stayed focused on that, and it got me through. *You* got me through."

"I felt so helpless, wanting to do something for you," she said, hugging him again.

"You did, babe. By being here waiting for me, you helped." He bent to kiss her. "I've had enough of this day. Let's go to bed."

TWENTY-ONE

GONZO STOOD OVER the crib and watched his son sleep. In the course of one amazing evening, he'd learned how to feed, change and bathe him, how to properly hold him, how to console him and he'd been told that at this young age, smiles usually mean gas. Sam's sisters, Angela and Tracy, had spent hours turning his empty second bedroom into a fully outfitted nursery and teaching him everything he needed to know to care for little Alex.

Now the rise and fall of his tiny chest held Gonzo mesmerized. He had his hands thrown over his head, and when Gonzo touched one of them it squeezed shut around his finger in a surprisingly tight grip. Gonzo's heart contracted just as tightly. Ever since Ms. Avery placed the baby in his arms, Gonzo's every emotion had hovered close to the surface.

Christina came up behind him and slipped her arms around his waist. "You should sleep when he sleeps," she whispered. "He'll be awake and hungry in a few hours."

"I'm afraid to leave him. What if he stops breathing or something?"

"He won't," she said. "I promise."

Gonzo gazed at the baby for another minute before he extricated his finger from Alex's grip and let Christina lead him from the room.

Even though his bedroom was right across the hall, Gonzo still checked to make sure the baby monitor Tracy had set up was working properly. He turned to find Christina watching him, amusement dancing in her eyes.

"Are all new parents this much of a mess?" he asked as he tugged the T-shirt over his head.

"Probably, but most of them have nine months to prepare for it. You've only had a few days."

"What do you think about Angela offering to watch him for me while I'm at work?"

"It sounds ideal to me. She's someone you trust who certainly knows what she's doing."

He sat next to her on the bed and reached for her hand. "I can't believe how it all worked out. A week ago, I didn't even know he existed. And now…"

Christina leaned her head on his shoulder. "Now you can't imagine your life without him."

"Yes. Exactly." He squeezed her hand, appreciating that she seemed to understand how he was feeling. "I have to find a way to tell my parents about this—soon."

"I'm sure they'll be very excited for you and on the first plane back from Arizona."

"I hope they won't be disappointed about how it happened. Not my finest hour."

"But look what it got you—an adorable son."

"True."

"They might be upset at first by how it happened, but once they see him and that dimpled chin of his, they'll fall in love too."

"I hope you're right."

"Come on." She tugged his hand to urge him into bed. "You need to sleep."

"Shouldn't I check on him one more time?"

She laughed. "He's fine, Tommy."

Reluctantly, he let her draw him into bed. If she hadn't been there, he probably would've stood watch by the crib all night long. After she shut off the light, he reached for her. When she was settled in her usual spot with her head on his chest, her arm across his belly and her leg intertwined with his, he exhaled a long deep breath. So this was what it felt like to have a family of his own, he thought. A woman who'd become indispensible to him and a baby he'd fallen for at first sight.

It hadn't happened the conventional way his mother probably would've preferred, but somehow it had happened.

"What're you thinking about?" she asked.

"That I like this—having you here with me and him sleeping in the next room."

"You sound surprised."

"I guess I am a little. I never saw my life turning out this way."

"And what way is it turning out?"

"Settled."

"Is that bad?"

He heard vulnerability in her question and wanted to reassure her. Kissing the top of her head, he said, "It's good—very, very good. I know it's a lot for you to take on, Christina. You didn't sign on for a guy with a baby..."

"I signed on for you, and Alex comes with the package now. I get that, Tommy, so please don't worry about me." She rested her fingers on his lips. "Shut it all off for a while and get some sleep. You're going to need it."

He tried to close down his whirling mind because he knew she was right. The baby would be up before the night was out, and he needed to sleep while he could. For a long time after she drifted off, he stared into the darkness. When he was sure she was asleep, he extricated himself from her embrace, got up, tugged on a pair of boxers and went across the hall—just to make sure his son was still breathing.

SAM WOKE UP to find Nick studying the ceiling. She shifted to her side and rested her hand on his chest. "Did you sleep?"

"Some."

Which meant not much. "Want to talk about it?"

"Nope." He surprised her when he abruptly got up and headed for the shower.

"Hmm," Sam said to the empty room. Not sure how to play this one, she lay there for a few minutes mulling over her options. Then she got up and went into the bathroom. She opened the shower door. "Want some company?"

"Sure."

The one-word answers were driving her nuts, but she kept her mouth shut and got busy washing her hair. Usually, he liked to do that for her, but today he didn't offer, and she didn't ask. In the aftermath of Julian Sinclair's murder, she'd learned to give him space to let him deal with things his own way. But Sam worried about him bouncing back from yet another setback when he was still grieving his lost friends.

"I wonder how Gonzo is making out with the baby," Sam said, deciding that he'd prefer to talk about anything other than the elephant in the room.

"He got custody?" Nick asked.

At least he was up to three words. That was progress. "Yes." Sam filled him in on what had happened the day before.

"Wow. That's amazing. Good for him."

"Tough timing right in the middle of the case."

"I can imagine."

Under normal circumstances, Sam might try to talk

to him about the odd feelings pinging around inside of her since hearing that Gonzo won custody of the son he hadn't even known he had until a few days ago. Here she was, desperately wanting a baby she probably couldn't have, and one had landed in her friend's arms. While she was genuinely happy for Gonzo, she couldn't help being a little jealous too. But with Nick nursing his own hurts, she didn't think this was the time to mention hers.

They went through the motions of getting dressed and eating breakfast, and still Nick remained quiet and withdrawn.

Sam put her cereal bowl in the dishwasher and turned to study him. He seemed to be absorbed in the *Washington Post*, but she wondered if he was really reading or using the newspaper to avoid talking to her. She went to him and rested her hands on his shoulders, bending to press a kiss to his smooth cheek. "May I say something?"

Reluctantly—or so it seemed to her—he nodded.

"I get that you're used to dealing with this stuff on your own because you didn't have anyone else to share it with, but now you do. You don't have to go through this or anything else by yourself anymore."

He reached up to take her hand and brought it to his lips. "I appreciate that you want to help, babe, and as soon as I figure out what I need, you'll be the first to know, okay?"

"Fair enough. I can't stand to see you suffering in silence, Nick."

He shifted the chair and brought her down to sit on his lap, wrapping his strong arms around her. They sat there for a long time, until Sam pulled back to caress his face and kiss him. "I love you. I wish I had time to go to Cleveland and tell her what I think of her."

That drew a short laugh from him. "She wouldn't know what hit her."

"Might be just what she needs."

"No doubt, but it won't change anything. It is what it is."

"Will you be okay today?"

He nodded. "I've got another long day and dinner with Richard and Judson at the Old Ebbitt after work," he said, referring to the Virginia Democratic Party leadership.

Recalling that John O'Connor had spent his last night alive doing the exact same thing, Sam shuddered.

"What?"

"That was how John spent his last night."

"Yeah."

The sadness she saw on his face made her sorry she'd mentioned it, especially right now when he had something else making him sad.

"Life goes on," he said. "Even when we think it won't."

The statement reminded her of the aftermath of the ectopic pregnancy during her marriage to Peter that had nearly taken her life and her sanity. "I'm here if you need me today." She got up from his lap. "Don't hesitate to call. I'm never too busy for you."

"You're being extra careful, right?"

"I'm being tailed." She frowned as she checked her watch. "In fact, my posse should be arriving any second." As if on cue, the doorbell rang. Sam forced a smile. "Right on time."

He stood up to hug her. "I know you hate it, but remember, it's temporary. The faster you find this guy, the faster you lose the tail."

"I know, I know. I just wonder if they'd insist on a tail if he'd threatened a male cop."

"They probably would."

"*Right…*"

"I haven't forgotten that I offered to do some digging on the senators Maria and Regina cleaned for. I'll do that today."

"Thanks. While you're at it, see if Christina gave your cell number to anyone new this week."

"Be careful today, Sam."

"I always am." She cradled his face in her hands and left him with one last kiss. "Hang in there, Senator."

"I always do."

"TELL ME YOU have *something*," Sam said to Lindsey McNamara.

"Just stuff you already suspected—the DNA from Maria matched guy number two from Regina, and he's not in the system. Regina's fetus was definitely Lightfeather's."

"Okay," Sam said. "I needed the confirmation even though we already knew, so thanks for that. How soon until you can confirm that guy number two grabbed Jeannie?"

"I'm running her rape kit now." Lindsey's green eyes went soft with compassion. "How is she?"

"Not good," Sam said. "Not that all rapes aren't vicious, but this one was particularly so. Probably because she's a cop."

Dismayed, Lindsey shook her head. "Unbelievable. Let me know if I can do anything else to help catch this asshole."

"You got it, Doc. Thanks."

Malone came in as Lindsey was leaving.

"What's up?" Sam asked him.

"No luck from our end figuring out who your mole is."

"You talked to Stahl?"

"Denied it vehemently and was 'offended' you suggested it could be him."

"Whatever."

"They've set a date for Peter's hearing."

Sam braced herself. "When?"

"Tomorrow."

"I can't believe they're really going through with this."

"Neither can I or anyone else around here, but you need to prepare yourself, Sam."

"How do I prepare myself to have the ex-husband who tried to kill me and my fiancé back on the streets?"

"If he screwed up once, he'll do it again, and next time we'll nail him."

"Will that be before or after he kills me—or Nick?" Remembering that day—the huge explosion, being propelled through the air into the bushes outside Nick's former home in Virginia, the smells, the blood on his face, the shattered glass, the ringing in her ears… A shudder rippled through her.

"We'll be watching him, Lieutenant. Count on that."

"Well, since my life—and Nick's—probably depends on it, I'll count on you to make sure we have eyes and ears on him." She glanced up at him. "You really think he'll get sprung."

He gave a short nod. "Unfortunately."

"Sometimes our justice system really sucks."

"Yes, it does, but it's the only one we have. We'll get him next time, Sam. I promise."

"I just hope I'm alive to see it."

Malone winced. "I'm sorry about all of this. I feel like we failed you so profoundly."

Sam shook her head. "No, you didn't. I was as responsible as anyone for what happened that night. I should've known better."

"Will you attend the hearing tomorrow?"

Sam thought about that for a minute. "No, I don't think I will. Why should I give him the satisfaction of thinking he's that important to me? You'll be there, right?"

Malone nodded. "You bet I will."

"Just make sure he comes out with a big fat restraining order keeping him as far away from me, Nick and my family as we can get him. I want every member of my family named in the order."

"That much I can do," he said on his way out.

Just the thought of Peter back on the streets was enough to make her sick, so Sam took a moment to clear her mind and refocus.

Freddie came in a few minutes later.

"Grand Central Station around here this morning," Sam said.

"What's the matter with you? You're pale as a ghost."

"Peter's hearing is tomorrow."

"Crap."

"Yeah," she said, shaking it off. Time to get back to work. She refused to give that asshole one more ounce of her energy. She'd already given him far too much. "What's up?"

"Someone here to see you, boss."

"Who is it?"

"Patricia Donaldson," he whispered.

Sam's eyes widened. She was the mother of John O'Connor's son—the son who had murdered his father and several other people. "What does she want?"

"To talk to you. That's all she would say."

"Ugh," Sam said. "Like I need this today. While I'm with her, get me the names and addresses of the numbers that showed up on both Regina's and Maria's phones. Also, tell Archie he has thirty minutes to get me the dump on Lightfeather's phone and Nick's," she said, referring to Lt. Archelotta, who ran the IT squad. "I don't care what he has to do."

"I was just going to tell you—the phone company wants a subpoena for Nick's phone."

"Tell them to *call him*. He'll authorize it, for Christ's sake."

Freddie scowled at her use of the Lord's name. "Should I show Patricia in?"

Sam moaned. "If you must..."

A well-dressed blonde came through the door a minute later, looking nervous and out of place. "Thank you so much for seeing me, Lieutenant."

"Of course. Please, have a seat."

She perched on the chair on the other side of Sam's desk. "I understand you were the detective in charge of John's case."

"I was, yes."

"I wanted to thank you for moving so quickly to get justice for him, even if I wish justice had led in a direction other than my son."

"Ms. Donaldson..."

She fiddled with a tissue she produced from her purse. "It's just, I wondered...you're absolutely certain that it was my Thomas who killed his father?"

Oh God, Sam thought. *God, God, God.*

"They were always so close, and I'm having trouble imagining that my son could've done these horrible things he's accused of. I figured you'd tell me the truth. I don't know who to believe anymore."

"I'm absolutely certain it was Thomas," Sam said. "I'm sorry if that's not what you want to hear, but the evidence is irrefutable. In addition to the evidence, he confessed in front of me as well as Senators O'Connor and Cappuano. I'm afraid the case against him is solid."

Her eyes filled with tears. "He must've had some sort of breakdown and didn't know what he was doing. The boy I raised would never hurt anyone, let alone his father or those other people he didn't even know." Two of his father's ex-lovers and the husband of one of them had been among Thomas's victims.

"I'm sure his attorney will take that under consideration," Sam said, desperately wanting to end this excruciating interview. "Hearing that his father had been unfaithful to you did something to him."

"They're considering an insanity plea, as you must already know."

"I've heard that."

"I'm sorry to have taken up your time. I was just looking for some answers."

"I wish I could've been more helpful." As she said the words, another thought occurred to Sam. "I know someone you could talk to who might understand what you're going through."

Patricia's eyes brightened with hope. "Who?"

"Laine O'Connor."

Patricia's hope was quickly replaced by despair. "She won't want to talk to me. They think I ruined John's life by getting pregnant. I'm sure they blame me for his death too."

"They don't," Sam assured her. "If anything, they blame themselves for forcing John to live a double life. I've come to know them quite well in the last few months, and I'm fairly confident Laine would welcome the chance to make amends with you." At least Sam hoped so. She was dabbling in areas she probably had no business butting into. The bad blood between the O'Connors and Patricia went back decades. “Would you like me to call her for you?”

“If you’re sure she won’t mind,” Patricia said.

“I’m sure she won’t.”

TWENTY-TWO

"THAT WAS A good thing you did back there," Freddie said when they were in the car.

"Huh?"

"Hooking Patricia up with Laine—two grieving mothers, two women who loved John O'Connor. It was a good thing."

"I hope so," Sam said. "I'm half expecting a 'what the hell were you thinking' phone call from Nick."

"Nah." Freddie bit into one of the three cream donuts he'd bought from the roach coach outside HQ. "He'll approve. In fact, I hate to say it, L.T., but you're becoming sensitive in your old age. Being in love has softened you."

"Screw you."

He chortled with laughter and then downed a second donut.

Sam's mouth watered at the smell of sugar and cream. "If you're done stuffing your face, tell me what we know about Bradford Tillinghast."

"He's a lobbyist with the firm Tillinghast-Young. They represent oil company interests to Congress."

"And what was his number doing on the cell phone records for both our dead cleaning ladies?"

"A very good question indeed."

Sam smiled. "I have a feeling this interview is gonna make my day." Sensitive. Whatever. She loved nothing more than watching smug, powerful people—or people who *thought* they were powerful—come unglued when they became the subject of a murder investigation.

"What about our plan to talk to Senator Trent first thing?" Freddie asked.

"We'll get to him. Eventually. Gonna be a long-ass day."

At the well-appointed K Street offices of Tillinghast-Young, Sam and Freddie were told that Mr. Tillinghast was in a meeting and couldn't be disturbed.

"I love that answer," Sam said to Freddie. "Don't you love that answer?"

"It's one of my favorites," he said.

The pretty receptionist's eyes darted between them, and Sam noticed the slight tremble of a manicured hand.

Sam leaned on the reception desk and brought her face in close to the other woman's. "Here's the deal—go tell Mr. Tillinghast that two homicide detectives from the MPD are here to see him. Tell him we can either do this here in the comfort of his office, or we can arrest him and do it downtown where the interrogation rooms are not nearly as comfortable. Got me?"

The receptionist scurried down a long hallway as if her pants were on fire.

"Mean and scary," Freddie said.

"Sensitive, my ass."

"Is your ass sensitive? Hmm, I wouldn't have thought that."

Sam glowered at him. "You'd better shut up before you find out how sensitive my fist is."

"Yes, ma'am," he said, but she caught the smirk he directed her way.

"You're in a good mood for a guy who isn't getting any."

The smirk was replaced by a frown. "I'll be back in the saddle after tomorrow night."

"You're certain she's going to show, huh?"

"Of course she will. She's into more than just the sex."

"Sure about that?"

"Yes," he said, but he didn't sound sure. "She'll show."

"Hmm, hope so."

"Do you? Do you really hope so?"

Before Sam could reply, the receptionist returned and gestured for them to follow her.

"This is the kind of cooperation that goes a long way toward earning the favor of the MPD," Sam said to Freddie who rolled his eyes at her.

Bradford Tillinghast was exactly what Sam expected him to be: tall, blond, built like a former college football player and dressed in a navy pinstripe suit that had been cut just for him. The luxurious office completed the picture of an all-American success story.

"What can I do for y'all?" he asked in a drawl that sounded like Texas.

"You can tell us how you know Regina Argueta de Castro and Maria Espanosa."

For a brief instant his eyes widened before his expression became impassive. But Sam caught the flash of fear.

"Who?"

"Don't screw with us, Mr. Tillinghast. We've got your number on both their cell phones. So unless you'd like to move this interview downtown, you have five seconds to tell me how you know them."

She watched his Adam's apple bob up and down.

"I'd like to speak to my lawyer."

"Great," Sam said. "Have him meet you at MPD Headquarters." She nodded to Freddie who pulled out his handcuffs.

"Wait." Tillinghast glanced warily at the coworkers who were pretending to not watch the goings-on behind his glass-walled office. "Are the handcuffs really necessary?"

"We don't transport anyone uncuffed. Department policy."

As he ran a trembling hand through his well-coifed hair, Sam caught the glint of a wedding ring.

"What's it going to be?" she asked. "Here or there?"

He took a deep breath and released it. Hands on hips, he fixated on the wall displaying his trophies and framed awards. Life had been good to Bradford Tillinghast. Until today.

"I paid them for sex," he said in a rush of words. "I didn't know their last names or anything else about them. And I only met with each of them twice."

Buzzing from the first big break in the case, Sam said, "Where did you meet for these encounters?"

"The Ambassador," he said, naming a four-star hotel in the heart of downtown Washington.

"How did you make contact with them?"

Hesitating, he shifted his gaze to the window. "I'd really like to speak to my lawyer now."

Apparently, he was far more concerned about giving up the information on how he found Regina and Maria than he was about being paraded through his office in handcuffs. Interesting. She gestured for Freddie to cuff him.

Freddie slapped the cuffs on Tillinghast's wrists and read him the Miranda warning. Tillinghast kept his head down as they walked him past his shocked colleagues.

Sam tried not to be judgmental, but she figured the walk of shame was the least of what a married guy deserved for paying for sex four times—or so he said—

with other women. She wondered how long it would take for official Washington to be set abuzz by Tillinghast's arrest.

Just as she had the thought, her cell phone rang. A quick glance at the LCD showed Nick's number. She hoped he wasn't annoyed at her for asking Laine to see Patricia.

"Hey," she said.

"Did you really just arrest Brad Tillinghast?"

"Christ have mercy. That didn't take long. How did you hear?"

"Trevor saw it on Twitter," he said, referring to his communications director.

"Fabulous." Tillinghast's coworkers hadn't wasted any time spreading the word.

"You are one *ballsy* chick, Holland. What'd he do?"

"Stonewalling. That's all I can say right now."

"The news has set the Hill on fire."

"Wait 'til you hear the rest of the story."

"I'll look forward to that."

"So, um, you might be hearing from Laine today."

"Already did."

"Is she pissed? The idea was out of my mouth before I took the time to consider—"

"She thinks it's a great idea, babe. As she said, if she'd done it years ago, maybe her son would still be alive."

"Oh, well, I'm glad she's not mad. I just figured, you know, they both loved John. Maybe they could help each other."

"You did good, Samantha."

Shrugging off the praise, she said, "How are you?"

"I'm okay."

Sam stood on the K Street sidewalk and watched Freddie load Tillinghast into the back of her car. "Really? Or are you just saying that?"

"It usually takes a week or two to bounce back from seeing her." He released a bitter-sounding chuckle. "You'd think I would've learned by now not to get my hopes up."

Sam closed her eyes. The pain she heard in his voice was unbearable. "I don't want you to see her anymore. At some point you have to say enough already."

"I think maybe I've reached that point this time."

"Good," she said. "Well, not good, but you know what I mean."

"Yes, babe, I know what you mean."

"We have each other now. We don't need people who bring us down." She thought of Peter being released from jail—possibly tomorrow—and knew she needed to tell him. "I hate to pile on, but I heard Peter's hearing is tomorrow. Malone made it sound like there's almost no way he won't get sprung."

"Goddamn it," Nick muttered. "I know I've said this before, but you've just gotta be fucking kidding me. He tried to *kill* us!"

"I know, babe. Believe me, I know." She hated to hear him so upset on top of what he was already dealing with. "We'll be on him like white on rice. He won't be stupid enough to pull another stunt like the bombs."

"You hope."

"I hate to say it, but I've got to go."

"You're not trying to dodge the tail, are you?"

The thought had occurred to her—more than once—but she'd never admit that to him. "I've been on my best behavior."

That drew a short laugh from him. "That'll be the day. Talk to you later. Be careful out there."

"Always." As Sam ended the call and got into the car, she experienced a pang of fear about what he might do to keep Peter in jail.

"THIS IS SENATOR Nick Cappuano for Mr. Forrester."

"One moment please, Senator."

Even though Nick knew this phone call was not a good idea from a personal *or* political standpoint, there was no way he could sit idly by and not make one last effort to keep that scumbag Gibson in jail where he belonged.

"Senator," Forrester said in his nasally New York accent. "What can I do for you or do I already know?"

"You can tell me you're doing everything in your power to keep that bastard Gibson in jail."

The U.S. Attorney cleared his throat. "As I mentioned the last time we spoke on this subject, I don't have the evidence to retain Mr. Gibson."

"That's bullshit, and you know it."

"Senator, this conversation is so far outside the realm of appropriate that it may be of interest to the Senate Ethics Committee."

"Go ahead and report me. But if I were you, I'd be far more concerned about releasing a murderer who will no doubt come after my future wife again."

"I'll remind you that Mr. Gibson was only charged with *attempted* murder. Your future wife and her team failed to follow procedure, Senator, and that's the only reason we're having this conversation. If they can get me something else that ties Gibson to the items found in his apartment, I'll certainly entertain new charges. Until then, we have nothing to talk about."

"If something happens to her, Forrester, I hope you'll be able to live with it."

"My conscience, Senator, is crystal clear. Your fiancée

and her team had Gibson by the short hairs. All they had to do was wait for the warrant. They chose not to do that, and there's not a damned thing I can do about it now."

"You could find a way to delay his release to give them time to gather more evidence."

"If there was more evidence to be gotten, I'd have it by now. You know that as well as I do."

"There has to be something you can do—"

"I have to get back to work, and I'm sure you do too. Have a good day, Senator."

Before Nick could reply, the line went dead. Furious, he threw his BlackBerry across the room and watched with satisfaction as it hit the wall and shattered into pieces.

Christina stepped into the office, surveyed the remnants of the phone and then turned to him. "Everything all right in here, Senator?"

"No." He reached for his suit coat and headed for the door. "Everything is *not* all right."

Nick stalked out of his office in the Hart Building and hustled through the underground tunnels that led into the Capitol building. In one of the hallways a network news reporter was interviewing one of his colleagues. He waited until they were finished and then flagged down the reporter and cameraman. "I have a statement I'd like to make."

Since Nick rarely gave interviews despite frequent requests, the reporter's eyes lit up with anticipation.

When the cameraman was in place, Nick tried not to think about the political fallout that might occur in the aftermath of his statement. "As many of you know, Peter Gibson, the ex-husband of my fiancée, Lieutenant Sam Holland, affixed bombs to her car and mine in December. When the device attached to her car detonated, we were both injured. Later that night, believing Gibson had dangerous bomb-making materials in his apartment, officers entered the dwelling prior to obtaining a search warrant. Once inside they discovered items that could've leveled his building as well as several others nearby. Even though a partial fingerprint ties Gibson to the bomb that was attached to my car, the charges against Gibson may be dropped tomorrow because the officers entered his apartment without a warrant. U.S. Attorney Forrester tells me there's nothing he can do to stop this from occurring. This time tomorrow, Peter Gibson may once again be free to resume his bomb-making activities. I thought it was important that the citizens of the District were aware of this so they can be vigilant. That's all I have to say."

The stunned reporter and cameraman stared at him.

Nick turned away from them and found Christina and his communications director, Trevor Donnolly, also staring at him.

"*You called Forrester about this?*" Christina's voice was an octave higher than usual.

"You're goddamned right I did. Gibson tried to *murder* us. You really think he ought to be let out of jail?"

"I just, um… Wow."

"Forget it," Nick said, needing to get out of there. "I'm going to the gym. Tell Richard and Judson I can't meet them tonight. I'll see you tomorrow." He left his overcoat and belongings in the office and exited through the south entrance to the Capitol. On the way out, several other reporters tried to stop him, but he waved them off. He had nothing left to say.

TWENTY-THREE

When Sam and Freddie entered the interrogation room, Bradford Tillinghast sat up straighter in his chair. His attorney, an older man with snow-white hair, sat next to him.

"May I please make a phone call?" Tillinghast asked.

"Eventually," Sam said.

"I need to talk to my wife. Before she hears about this from someone else."

Judging by how quickly Nick had heard, Sam guessed that ship had already sailed, but she wasn't about to tell Tillinghast that. Funny how he was thinking of his wife *now*.

"May we have your permission to record this interview?" she asked.

The lawyer acquiesced. "What about the phone call?" he asked.

"Later."

Tillinghast released a tortured sigh, as it seemed to settle in on him that his wife would probably hear about his arrest from someone other than him.

"I'd like to know how you made contact with Regina and Maria," Sam said.

"I don't wish to disclose that information," Tillinghast said, his face suddenly red and flushed.

Sam cast a glance at the lawyer, who'd no doubt provided the line, and then back at Tillinghast. "Will you disclose the details of the various encounters with the women?"

His eyes darted to the lawyer, who nodded.

A bead of sweat ran down Tillinghast's face. "I, um… I met Maria first. We…I ah…have 'appetites' that my wife finds offensive." He'd no sooner swiped away one drop of sweat when another appeared.

"And what about Maria? Did she find your 'appetites' offensive?"

"If she did, she never said so to me."

"How much did you pay her to satisfy your perversions?"

His eyes flashed with outrage. "I'm not perverted! I just like certain things…"

"How much?"

"Two thousand."

"And that bought you how much time to satisfy your 'appetites'?"

"Four hours," he mumbled.

"So you saw her twice?"

He nodded.

"I'd like the dates of these encounters."

Tillinghast looked again to his lawyer.

"Do you know the dates?" the lawyer asked him.

"Not off the top of my head."

"Where would they be?" Sam asked.

"On my calendar at work."

How stupid could he be? Sam wondered. "Which is where?"

"In my top desk drawer."

Sam looked to Freddie, who nodded with understanding. He briefly left the room to find someone to go get the calendar and returned a minute later with a consent to search form that Tillinghast signed, granting them permission to retrieve the calendar and place it into evidence.

"Did you contact them outside of the organization they worked for?"

He looked down at his hands.

"Mr. Tillinghast?"

"I offered them twice what the service paid—in cash—to meet with me the second time."

"That's how you came to have their cell numbers."

"Yes."

Sam wondered if their "freelancing" was a motive for murder. "Where were you last Friday and Saturday?"

"At a family wedding in Long Island. My wife and children can attest to that as well as scores of other family members who were there and saw me."

"Is there any chance you got Maria pregnant?" Sam asked.

At that, Tillinghast's face went from red and flushed to chalky white. "*Pregnant?*" he squeaked.

"You heard me."

"No. There's no chance."

"And you know that how?"

"Because I used condoms."

"Provided by you or her?"

The question seemed to catch him off guard. "Her," he said. "She insisted."

Sam trained a steely stare on him, waiting for the realization to set in.

"Oh my God," he said softly, so softly she wondered if the recording would capture it. "Are you saying...?"

"I'm saying she was pregnant at the time of her death."

"And you think it was *mine*?"

"I have no idea who the father is." Sam wondered if even Maria knew, but this hunk of successful all-

American manhood would no doubt have made an attractive candidate to a woman looking to anchor her place in America. "Would you be willing to submit to a DNA test?"

Frantic, Tillinghast turned to his lawyer, his expression beseeching.

"If my client's DNA matches that of Maria's fetus, what would he be charged with?"

"Nothing—unless it also matches the DNA of the man who raped and murdered her."

"I did not murder her!" Tillinghast cried. "I saw her twice. We had sex, I paid her and I left. I never saw her again! I wasn't even in town when she was killed!"

"If that's the case, I'd think you would welcome a DNA test."

After a charged moment of silence, the lawyer said, "We'll submit."

"Detective Cruz, please ask Dr. McNamara to join us." After Freddie left the room, Sam said, "How soon after your liaisons with Maria did you meet up with Regina?"

"A couple of weeks."

"Why the switch to a different woman?"

"Maria refused to see me again after the second time."

"Why was that?"

"Do we really have to get into the details?"

"Yeah, we really do."

Sighing, he tightened his crossed hands until his knuckles went white. "She said I was too rough."

"But Regina didn't mind that?"

"After the second time, she wouldn't see me either."

"You're a prince among men, Mr. Tillinghast."

"Look, I can't help—"

"Save it. Were there any others?"

"Just one."

"Her name?"

"I don't know her last name."

"What was her first name?"

"Selina."

Sam suppressed a gasp. "When was the last time you saw her?"

"Last night," he muttered.

Hearing that lovely buzz of pieces falling together, Sam said, "I'm going to need to know how you initially found these women."

"I'm not willing to tell you that." His earlier bravado had been replaced by what looked like fear to Sam.

"What were you told would happen to you if you ended up in this situation?"

"I'm not willing to tell you that."

"Until you're willing, you'll be our guest in the city jail."

He launched out of his chair. "You can't do that! I didn't kill those women. I have an alibi!"

"You have information pertaining to a homicide investigation that you are not willing to divulge. That makes you an accessory to murder."

Tillinghast appealed to his lawyer. "*Do something!*"

"Tell him," Sam said to the lawyer. "There's nothing you can do."

"There's nothing I can do," the lawyer said, tugging his client's arm to get him to sit back down.

Tillinghast slumped in his chair. His robust complexion had gone pale and pasty under the fluorescent lights at HQ.

Sam smiled. "See? Told you."

Freddie returned with Lindsey McNamara.

"He's all yours, Doc." Sam called Detective Arnold from the pit. "When Dr. McNamara is done with Mr.

Tillinghast, take him to central booking. Cruz, you're with me."

"Where're we going Lieutenant?"

"To pick up our old friend Selina Rameriz. Our new friend Tillinghast hooked up with her last night."

"No way."

"Yep." Because she was concerned that the word was out about Tillinghast's arrest, Sam used her radio to order patrol officers to Selina's apartment as quickly as possible. In her car, Sam flipped on the lights and siren and made quick work of getting to Columbia Heights.

Two department cruisers were parked outside Selina's building. Sam was filled with anxiety as she wondered whether she'd find a witness or a victim waiting for her. A quick look at Freddie's tense face told her he was worried about the same thing.

Sam was relieved when she saw Selina emerge from the building, escorted by two patrol officers. The young woman was crying and resisting their attempts to escort her to the street, but she was alive. Taking a good look around at the crowd gathered on the street to watch the proceedings, Sam had no doubt that if they hadn't gotten to her when they did, their killer would have. After they talked to her downtown, Sam planned to arrange a safe house for her until they caught this guy.

Despite Tillinghast having had contact with both dead women, Sam believed him when he said he didn't kill them. Besides, his eyes were blue, and Jeannie had described her attacker's eyes as dark and mean-looking. The proof would be in the DNA and in the alibi, which she asked Freddie to confirm with Tillinghast's wife.

"Why are you arresting me?" Selina cried. "I haven't done anything!"

Sam stepped up to the handcuffed woman. “Solicitation and prostitution. Ringing any bells, Ms. Rameriz?”

“I don’t know what you’re talking about,” Selina said even as her face drained of color.

“You know exactly what I’m talking about.” She gestured to Freddie. “Let’s get her downtown.”

“Please,” Selina said as tears cascaded down her face. “Please don’t do this. I needed the money. I was desperate.”

“If you cooperate with our investigation into the murders of your colleagues, I might be willing to talk to the assistant U.S. attorney about immunity for you.”

“What do I have to do?” she asked, her expression wary.

“Let’s talk about it downtown.”

AT HQ, SAM was met by the usual pack of reporters. The questions flew at her.

“Lieutenant, what do you think of the senator’s statement to the media?”

“Did you put him up to calling Forrester about Gibson?”

“Why did you arrest Brad Tillinghast?”

Sam pushed past them and directed Freddie to take Selina to interrogation. She headed for her office where Captain Malone greeted her.

“What has Nick done?” she asked.

“He went to Forrester and the media about Gibson. Made quite a statement.”

“Shit,” Sam muttered. “He shouldn’t have done that.”

“It seems to have touched a chord in the city. We’ve been bombarded with calls.”

“Fabulous,” Sam said, wondering what Nick had been thinking.

"They've been calling Forrester too," Malone continued, "and he is *not* pleased."

"It won't stop them from releasing Gibson, and Nick has probably created a boatload of political trouble for himself." This was exactly the type of thing she'd been concerned about when the Virginia Democrats first approached him about finishing out the last year of John O'Connor's term—her crap landing on his crap and causing him deep shit.

"That's on him, Sam. You certainly didn't ask him to call Forrester for you." Malone hesitated. "Did you?"

"No! You know I hate that good old boy network bullshit that goes on in this town." Frustrated, Sam released the clip that held her long hair and let it fall past her shoulders. "He had a run-in with his deadbeat mother yesterday. He's not in a good place today. I don't know why he'd make that kind of statement. He has to know the media will jump all over both of us."

"Maybe it'll help."

"I guess we'll see," Sam said even though she doubted it would do anything more than cause him a great deal of political heartburn. It would probably also please Peter to see Nick so spun up over his release, but Sam refused to care about what Peter thought of anything.

Before she joined Freddie in the interrogation room, she tried to call Nick, but his phone went right to voicemail. She wondered if he'd shut it off to dodge the deluge of calls from the media or to avoid the call he knew would be coming from her.

When Sam entered the interrogation room, Selina startled and wiped the tears from her face—a pointless gesture, since they kept right on coming.

"Are you going to report me to CIS?" she asked. Her English was slightly accented but fluent nonetheless.

"That depends on whether or not you cooperate with our investigation."

"What do you want to know?" Her eyes darted between Sam and Freddie.

"May I have your permission to record this interview?" Sam asked.

Selina stared at the recorder for a long moment before she nodded.

"Tell us how you came to be involved in providing sex for money," Sam said.

"You have to understand, if I hadn't been desperate, I never, *ever* would've gotten involved in something like this."

"We're not here to pass judgment, Ms. Rameriz," Sam said. "We're trying to figure out who killed your coworkers. How did you become involved?"

"It was on a break at work," she said softly. "I mentioned that my mother needed an operation and we didn't have the money. Regina said she might be able to help me."

Questions cycled through Sam's mind, but she stayed quiet and gave Selina the chance to collect her thoughts.

"Regina said she knew someone who helped girls like us who needed fast money."

"Who was this person she referred to?"

"I don't know," Selina said. "Regina gave me a phone number and told me to call if I was interested. She said I could make thousands of dollars in a single night."

"Did you know what you'd have to do when you made that call?"

Selina shook her head. "I was led to believe that we provided escorts—literally—to men who needed dates for events. I thought that's all it was. Apparently, if another of their girls refers you, she gets a bonus. I found that out later."

"What kind of information did they want from you before they took you on?"

"I had to send a photo, a health screening, background. That kind of stuff."

Sam couldn't believe the health screening hadn't been a giveaway for what the men were really after. "How did you find out it was more than dates to parties?"

"The first time I called, the woman I talked to was really nice. She said a man had requested a date for a black-tie gala and was willing to pay for a beautiful woman. All I had to do, she said, was dress formally and meet the man at the event."

"Which was held where?"

"At the Reagan Building downtown. I was told to enter the building on the 14th Street side and to wait for him inside security."

"And this was when?"

"January 18."

"Did your contact give you the name of the man you were meeting?"

She shook her head. "I was told he'd know to look for me. A short time after I arrived, he came through security and walked right over to me."

"What did he look like?"

"Older, balding, overweight." A shudder rippled through Selina's petite frame.

"He never gave you his name?"

"He said his name was John and asked me not to speak to anyone we met other than to exchange greetings."

Sam wanted to laugh at the absurdity of the guy using the name John. "So you went to the event?"

"We made a brief appearance, said hello to a few

people, but it was obvious he didn't want to be there. I couldn't understand why he'd gone to so much trouble and expense to hire me if he didn't want to go to the party. For what it's worth, I think he was someone important—people were very…solicitous toward him." She took a drink of the glass of water Freddie had gotten for her.

"How long were you at the party?"

"Less than an hour."

"What happened when you left there?"

Sam noted Selina's hands were trembling so badly that the water in the glass threatened to spill over. "He had a car waiting, and he said he'd take me home except once we were inside, the car headed away from the address I had given him. I asked him where we were going, but he wouldn't answer me. While we were in the car, he started touching me." Her voice had gotten so soft it was almost a whisper.

"What did you do?"

"I asked him to stop. I said that wasn't what I'd agreed to, but he just laughed. He said he loved it when girls played hard to get. We were in the car for a while before it stopped at a hotel outside the city. I wasn't sure where we were. That's when I started to get really scared. I couldn't believe Regina had done this to me." She took another drink of water. "He told me if I didn't want to get hurt, I'd be very quiet and do exactly what I was told. Then he dismissed the driver and all but dragged me into the hotel."

"Did he check into the hotel?"

She shook her head. "He already had a room key."

"Did you have to go through a lobby or were the rooms outside?"

"Outside."

He'd chosen the place with that in mind, Sam thought,

so no one would see him dragging an unwilling woman into a room.

"What happened once you were inside the room?"

Selina looked at Freddie and then beseechingly at Sam.

"Detective Cruz," Sam said. "Would you mind giving me a few minutes alone with Ms. Rameriz?"

"Not at all," Freddie said.

On her pad Sam wrote: Get the info on the Jan. 18 event @ Reagan. Video. Witnesses that put her there with bald guy.

He nodded, got up and left the room.

"What happened at the hotel, Selina?"

"He…he ordered me to take off my clothes. I begged him not to touch me. I told him he could have his money back, that I'd never tell anyone if he'd let me go. He laughed at me, and when I bolted for the door he dragged me back and slapped me so hard I saw stars. After that I was kind of out of it, but I was aware of him undressing me and touching me." Her voice caught on a sob. "I kept pleading with him to stop, but he wouldn't. He said he'd paid for sex and that he wasn't leaving until he'd gotten what he'd paid for." By now she was crying so hard she could hardly speak.

Sam gave her a couple of minutes to regain her composure. "Did you have sex with him, Selina?"

She nodded. "He hurt me. I was screaming and crying, so he put his hand over my mouth. I couldn't breathe. I think I blacked out for a time. When I came to…He was…I was facedown on the bed and he was…Oh God, *the pain*. I've never felt pain like that."

Sam reached across the table for her hand. "He raped you, Selina. He raped and sodomized you. No matter what he paid for, the moment you said no, it became a rape."

"I was so stupid," she said between sobs. "How could I have been so naive? Of course that's what he wanted. No one pays thousands of dollars for a date to a party."

"How long were you in the room with him?"

"All night," she whispered. "It went on and on. I was in and out of consciousness. Every time I came to, he was on top of me, inside me. I thought it would never end." She wiped away tears. "Finally, I woke up and he was gone."

"You never saw him again?"

She shook her head. "I took the longest shower and got dressed before I ran out of there and hailed a cab to take me home."

"You have no idea where you were? You didn't notice any landmarks or anything that stood out to you?"

"No. Wherever it was, I'd never been there before. I was so anxious to get out of there that I didn't pay much attention to anything but finding a cab."

"Do you still have the dress you wore that night?"

Selina glanced up at her, startled. "It's in the back of my closet in a suitcase with the other things I wore that night."

Sam wanted to jump up and down with glee. "What compelled you to keep it?"

"I remembered that intern who slept with the president... No one believed her until she produced the dress. I figured I should keep it just in case I ever had a chance to punish him for what he did to me."

"That was very good thinking. May we have your permission to retrieve it?"

"Yes, of course." Selina folded her hands on the table, but Sam noticed they were still trembling.

Sam got up and went to the door to find someone to

get the suitcase from Selina's apartment. "Take it to the lab right away," she said to the officer after Selina signed a consent to search form. Returning to the table, she encouraged Selina to continue her story.

"The next day, three thousand dollars was deposited to my checking account. It was enough for a down payment on the surgery my mother needed."

"Did you seek out medical attention?" Sam asked, knowing the answer before she asked the question.

She shook her head. "I don't have insurance, and I wired all the money to my family."

"Were you injured enough to need medical attention?"

"Probably. Everything…down there…hurt. I had bruises all over. I could barely move for days. I had to call in sick to the cleaning company for the first time since I worked there."

"What did you say to Regina the next time you saw her?"

"I asked her how she could've led me to believe it was just a date. She seemed shocked that I didn't know what 'date' meant when thousands of dollars were involved. She apologized profusely and said that what had happened to me had never happened to her. I think she reported the guy."

"To whom?"

"To the people who run the service."

"And who is that?"

"I don't know. I was just given a number to call to arrange the initial date."

"Do you still have that number?"

"It changes all the time."

"How do you get word of the change?"

"I receive a text message from an unavailable number."

"How did you end up going on another 'date'?"

Selina's shoulders sagged. "I needed more money. My mother's surgery cost forty thousand dollars."

"I find it hard to believe that you were able to bring yourself to do this again after what happened the first time."

"I was terrified. But I was far more terrified of the cancer killing my mother before she could have a surgery that doctors said would save her life."

"You were able to um…perform, despite being terrified?"

Selina looked down at the table and then back up at Sam. "The fear seemed to…you know…turn them on. I've since learned that fear is a fetish."

Sam fought back a shudder. Just when she thought she'd heard everything on this job… "How many other guys were there?"

"Eighteen," Selina said, chagrined. "As of last night, I have the money I need. I'm all done."

So Brad Tillinghast had been the last, Sam thought. "Walking away is an option?"

Selina seemed taken aback by the question. "What do you mean?"

"The people who run this…operation. They allow women to say 'no more'?"

"Of course they do. Why wouldn't they?"

"I'm wondering if Regina and Maria tried to quit."

Selina's eyes went wide. "They were *killed* because they wanted to quit?"

"It's a possibility."

Selina's hand landed on her chest over her heart. "Oh my God."

"Did you tell anyone you were done after last night?"

"Not yet."

That may have saved her life, Sam thought. "What were you told about confidentiality?"

"Just that it was imperative I never speak of these liaisons with anyone. Not that I would have anyway." She pinched her lips as if to hold back a sob. "I was so ashamed. If my parents had any idea where the money was coming from…"

"Where do they think you're getting it?"

"I told them I'd met a lovely man who was well-off, and he gave me the money."

"They believed that?"

Selina nodded. "She's very ill."

"There was no other way for your family to raise the money?"

"We tried everything, even selling the family home in Santa Elena, but we couldn't find a buyer, and she was just getting sicker. We needed money, and we needed it fast."

"I need the details of every encounter you had. Names, ages, description, where the liaisons took place, what kind of sex you had with them and anything distinctive about them you remember."

Selina stared at her, eyes agog. "You can't be serious."

"I'm dead serious. If you want me to catch this guy before he makes you his next victim, you'll tell me everything you know about these men and the outfit that connected you to them."

"But I told you! I don't know anything about the business other than the most recent phone number."

"Then we'll start with that."

"What if I refuse to cooperate?"

"Then I'll release you."

Selina brightened at that possibility.

"I hope you've got your affairs in order since you probably won't have long to live once you walk out of here."

"You're just trying to scare me into cooperating."

"You should be scared. This guy has already brutally raped and murdered two of your 'colleagues' as well as kidnapped and raped one of my detectives. If you think you'll be spared after spending a couple of hours with me, you're more naive than I thought."

"But you could protect me! You could assign officers to watch me!"

"Why should I do that when you won't help me?"

"I've told you everything I know!"

"No, you haven't, and until you do, I'm afraid there's nothing I can do to help you." Sam hoped and prayed the bluff would work. No way would she let Selina walk out of HQ—with or without an escort—but Selina didn't know that.

"I don't know their names. They have numbers. That's all I'm given. Most of them give me a name to call them when we're together, but I know they're not their real names."

"I'll take whatever you can give me—including the most recent phone number."

Selina stared at the wall for a long moment, no doubt weighing her options and finding all of them less than appealing.

"What's it going to be?" Sam asked.

After another long stretch of silence, Selina looked at Sam. "Could I have some paper and a pen?"

TWENTY-FOUR

"TONIGHT, I'M BUYING you a hooker," Sam announced to Freddie as she met him in front of the murder board that he'd updated while she was with Selina.

He wondered if she had finally lost her mind. "I'm not that desperate. Yet."

Sam laughed and waved a piece of paper in front of his face. "The phone number Selina uses to get in contact with the call girl ring."

"Let me guess—I'm going to call that number and arrange a date."

"You got it. Archie is setting us up with a secure line. The goal is to stay on the line long enough to get a trace. You're going to have a long list of fetishes that need to be satisfied."

An awful thought occurred to him. "I'm not expected to actually have sex with this woman, am I?"

"Now, Freddie, would I do that to you?"

"I'm not entirely sure."

She made a face at him. "All you have to do is arrange the meeting and keep the appointment. We'll take care of the rest. I figure if we can nab another of the women, we can start to narrow in on the johns. They'll lead us to the organization."

"Or so you hope."

"So I hope."

"What about your crooked senator angle?"

"I'm still almost certain that one or more of them is

involved. Think about it—they had access to all three of these women. All of the women were financially insecure, their long-term immigration status was in question and they had people depending on them at home. Someone recruited them knowing they'd be easy marks. That someone is going to turn out to be one of Nick's colleagues. Mark my words. If we can't go at them directly, we'll get them through the women."

"Have you spoken to Nick? Since he gave the statement?"

"He's not answering his phone."

Her phone chimed with a new text. "Maybe that's him now." She glanced at the screen, which said, *Back off bitch or you're dead.* "Not him," she said, showing the text to Freddie.

"How would they have gotten your number?"

"That's a very good question."

"Want me to have Archie put a trace on it?"

"You can try, but I'll bet my last dollar it'll be another throwaway phone."

"Maybe we'll get a ping on a cell tower."

"Worth a shot. I also want to arrange for computer renderings of some of the johns. Can you get Officer Jackson in here ASAP to do that? I like his work."

"Yep."

"While you're doing that, I'm going to talk to Tillinghast again. Hopefully, I can get him to tell me if there's a code or anything he has to give when he calls in to request a 'date.'"

"Good luck with that."

"Your evening plans depend on my success."

Freddie watched her go, not sure whether he should wish for or against her getting the information from Tillinghast. Maybe if his mother heard he was arranging for an evening with a call girl, Elin would start to look more appealing to her. As he laughed at the outrageous thought, his cell rang. Freddie took the call from Gonzo.

"Hey, man, what's up?" In the background Freddie heard crying. "Is that a baby?" What the hell?

"That'd be my son, Alex," Gonzo said.

"*Your son?* What're you talking about?"

"I'm talking about the son I never knew I had until last weekend."

"And now he's *living* with you?"

"For the time being. I'm hoping it'll be permanent."

"Wow. I don't know what to say."

"Congratulations works."

"Of course. Yes. Congratulations! No wonder you've been on leave."

"Believe me, this is the only thing that could've kept me away after what happened to McBride. I'll be back on Monday. I just needed a couple of days to get him settled before I came back to work. But the reason I'm calling is I spent the morning on the phone trying to get some more info on who owns Reese's house."

"Did you get anywhere?"

"I got a name. Not sure if it's the right name, but it's a start. Can you run it for me? I don't have my laptop."

"Absolutely."

"Gerald Price."

As Freddie typed the name into the system, his heart raced with hope and anticipation. Could this be the guy they'd been looking for since a bullet rendered Skip Holland a quadriplegic two years ago? "Okay, here we go." Freddie scanned the screen that detailed a Price's extensive criminal history. "Fifty-six years old, long list of priors. He's doing time in Jessup," Freddie said, referring to the state prison in Maryland. "Mostly drug stuff."

"How long has he been in?"

"Fourteen months, six to go, which puts him on the streets at the time of the shooting."

"Damn it," Gonzo said. "I can't get up there right now."

"Neither can I. Sam has me arranging dates with hookers."

"What?"

"You heard me."

"Wow, I picked the wrong week to become a dad."

"I couldn't agree more. You'd be much better at this than I am."

Gonzo snorted with laughter. "Not sure if I should take that as an insult or a compliment."

"Both probably."

"As soon as we close this one, what do you say about a field trip to Jessup?"

"I'm in."

"Tell Sam I called to check in, but let's keep Price between us until we know more."

"Agreed. Did you hear that Gibson's hearing is tomorrow? Malone told Sam there's almost no way he won't get sprung."

"God, we fucked that up, didn't we?"

"Big time."

"I can't even think about it without wanting to rip someone's head off."

"I hear ya. I feel the same way."

"Maybe we can make it right if this thing with Price leads somewhere."

"God, I'd love to solve Skip's case—for her as much as him."

"Me too. Good luck with the hookers. I'll see you Monday."

"Congratulations on the baby, Gonzo. Seriously."

"Thanks, man."

AT THE CITY jail, Sam asked the officer at the desk to put Tillinghast in a room for her.

"Right away, Lieutenant."

When Sam was ushered in a few minutes later, she encountered an entirely different Bradford Tillinghast than the K Street star he'd been a few hours ago. This one wore a jumpsuit rather than a hand-sewn business suit. His expensive gold watch and wedding ring were gone. In prison orange, he looked like any other average white guy.

"They fucking strip-searched me! They treated me like a fucking criminal!"

"Accessory to murder is a felony, Mr. Tillinghast."

"I had nothing to do with those murders, and you know it."

"You have information that could lead to an arrest. Are you still unwilling to share that information?"

His jaw shifted from side to side. "Yes."

"What did they threaten you with? Did they say they'd harm your wife and children if you ever got caught?"

Eyes widening, he gasped.

"That's it, isn't it?"

"I can't let them hurt my family. I can't take that chance."

"I'll put them in protective custody." Sam would do that with or without his cooperation. As long as he was here, his family was in danger. "Tell me who they are, Brad. I can't help you if you don't help me."

He shook his head. "I won't risk it."

"You had to know what you were risking the first time you made a call to this service."

"I had no idea," he said, before he seemed to catch himself. The unguarded moment passed as quickly as it had come.

"When you order up a woman, how does it work? Can you tell me that much?"

He hesitated for a minute and then got up to pace the room. "Will you take care of my family? I tried to reach my wife, but she won't take my calls. I need to know they're safe."

"I'll take care of your family."

"I have two girls, five and seven. I can't let anything happen to them."

"I'll do everything I can, but the longer I'm in here with you, the more danger they're in. News of your arrest is all over town. No doubt the very people you're worried about know full well where you are right now."

He ran his fingers roughly through his blond hair. "God, *what was I thinking?* I never should've—"

Sam slapped her hand on the table. "Brad! Tell me what I need to know so I can go take care of your family!"

He startled and stared at her for an instant before he started to talk. "When I call, I punch in my number—18262. They have a database of men and their interests that matches them to compatible women. I punch in the date I wish to meet the woman and the zip code where I want the meeting to take place. They do everything else."

"So you never talk to a person?"

He shook his head.

"Do you know who's behind the operation?"

"I've heard rumors."

"And these people are powerful?"

"Extremely."

"How did you first hear about the service?"

"From a colleague. He swore it was totally safe and completely anonymous. Safe and anonymous, my ass."

"How do you pay?"

"I have a separate credit card just for this."

"Do you know the number?"

Sighing deeply, he rattled it off.

Sam headed for the door. "Keep talking and I might see fit to drop the charges."

"Lieutenant."

She turned back.

"You need to be very careful. If the rumors are true, this touches the very highest level of the federal government. Do you understand what I'm telling you?"

Sam's heart began to pound. "By highest levels are we talking legislative, executive or judicial?"

"All of the above." He turned his back on her. "That's all I'm saying until you can prove to me that my family is safe."

"I'll be back."

SAM RETURNED TO the detectives' pit, tore the page out of her notebook that contained Brad Tillinghast's credit card number and handed it to Freddie. "He uses this card to pay for the call girls. Do a run and see what you can find. Before that, though, send the U.S. Marshals to Tillinghast's home in Potomac. I want his wife and daughters put into protective custody immediately."

"Got it. Gonzo called to check in. He said he'll be back on Monday."

"Okay, good." She checked her watch. Almost six o'clock and no word from Nick.

"Um, so you knew about Gonzo's baby?"

"He told me when he requested the emergency leave."

"Why didn't you tell me?"

"Not my news to tell. I've got to make a phone call, and then I'm going back to talk to Lightfeather again."

"What about?"

"Something Tillinghast just said. I'm wondering if this call girl ring is one of Washington's worst-kept secrets." She'd love to know if Nick had ever heard rumblings about it—if only he'd answer his damned phone.

"So Tillinghast was a little more forthcoming this time around?"

"The strip search and jumpsuit seemed to have changed his attitude a bit."

"They tend to have that effect."

"Let me know what the card shows." Sam went into her office and closed the door to call Gonzo. "Hey," she said when he answered. "How's it going?"

"I'm getting the hang of it, slowly but surely. Cruz told you I called?"

"Yeah, thanks for checking in. Listen, I need a favor." She pinched the bridge of her nose, hoping to hold back a headache she felt forming. "Is Christina there by any chance?"

"Yeah, why?"

"I can't reach Nick, and I'm starting to get a little worried. It's not like him to be out of touch for hours. And after his 'performance' this afternoon, I'm doubly concerned."

"Let me get her for you."

Christina came on the line a minute later. "Hi, Sam."

"Hi there." Sam paced the office, hating that she'd had to call his chief of staff like a clingy, nagging girlfriend. "So, um, Gonzo told you I'm trying to reach Nick?"

"His phone is broken." She told Sam about the incident in the office. "After that, he stalked out and went to find the reporter. I guess you know the rest."

Sam sighed. "I can't believe he went off in front of a camera like that."

"Or that he called Forrester. He'll be lucky if the Senate Ethics Committee doesn't take issue with that."

"Damn it. What was he thinking?"

"I guess he was thinking about the guy who tried to kill you both being released from jail."

"Do you have any idea where he might be?"

"He said he was going to the gym. I bet he ran into some friends there, played some basketball and probably went out for a few beers. He might even be home by now."

They'd never bothered to install a landline on Ninth Street since they both had cell phones, so Sam couldn't call him. She could, however, call her stepmother and ask her to go check to see if he was home. "Thanks for the info, Christina. I appreciate it."

"I hope he's okay. He was really spun up today."

"I'm sure he's fine. I'll talk to you later." She ended that call and found Celia on speed dial. After explaining what was going on, she asked Celia to run up the street to see if Nick was at home.

"I'm going right now, honey. Did you see him on TV earlier? I've never seen him looking so furious."

"I didn't see it. I heard about it, though." The headache between her eyes was taking hold despite her efforts to will it away.

"The house is dark, and he's not answering the door."

"He must not be home yet. I'll be there after a while. Thanks for checking, Celia."

"You're worried, Sam. I can hear it in your voice."

"It's not like him to be out of touch all day."

"How did things go with his mother yesterday?"

"About like I expected. She wanted his money, not him."

Celia sighed. “Poor guy. Between that and Peter possibly getting out of jail…”

“Yeah. No good.”

“Let me know if you need anything tonight, honey. I’ll be here.”

And that, Sam realized, brought comfort. “I will. Thanks.”

TWENTY-FIVE

As she was ending the call with Celia, Lt. Archelotta knocked on her door.

"Hey, Archie. You got the secure phone?" Sam glanced at the tall, handsome, dark-haired officer and tried to forget that she'd once seen him naked. They'd had a brief fling after her split with Peter, and like she did every time she ran into him, she wondered if he imagined her naked whenever he saw her.

He handed the phone to her. "Let me know when you're ready to make the call, and we'll set up the trace."

"Can we do it now?"

"Sure." He reached for his own phone and called down to his department. "Lt. Holland is ready to make the call. Everything in place?" He paused and nodded. "Good. Standby." To Sam, he said, "You're good to go. The best we can do is attempt to intercept the pings on the cell tower to narrow it down to a neighborhood."

"I'll take whatever you can get." Since Tillinghast had told her the system was automated, Sam made the call herself, typing in Brad's access code. "Good evening, sir," the recording stated. "Thank you for your call. Please enter the date for which you require services." Sam punched in today's date. "Please enter your zip code." Sam entered the code for downtown. "Thank you. Your date will meet you at 9:00 p.m. at The Ambassador Hotel, room 482. Your key will be waiting for you at the front desk. Shall I charge the credit card on file? If yes, press the pound key. If you wish to enter a different card number, press the star key." Sam pressed pound. "Do you require any special services this evening? If so, please press pound for our menu."

Sam glanced at Archie, who was watching her with a barely disguised gleam in his eye. "This is so gross," she said.

"Never arranged for a call girl before, Lieutenant?"

She rolled her eyes at him and pressed pound, bracing herself for the menu.

"For domination, please press one. For restraint, please press two. For animals, please press three."

"Oh my God," Sam whispered. "I'm going to be ill."

Archie snickered.

"For anal intercourse, please press four. For autoerotic asphyxiation, please press five. For whips, chains and S and M, please press six."

Sam decided she'd heard more than enough and pressed the number one.

"Thank you for your selection. Your date will be prepared to fulfill your every fantasy. Please call again soon. Goodbye."

Sam closed the phone and glanced at Archie. "I need a shower."

He laughed and took the phone from her. "Who's the lucky john?"

"Cruz. He can barely contain his excitement."

"What've you got planned for him?"

"Just some domination. I figured animals might be too much for him."

Grimacing, he said, "Ugh. Disgusting."

"Totally."

"I'll go see what we were able to get from the cell towers."

"Thanks."

"Hey, Sam, this thing with Gibson…sucks."

"It is what it is. I'll deal with it."

"I hope you know every cop in this city will be keeping tabs on him. He wouldn't dare step out of line again."

"Yes, he probably will, and when we nail him next time, we'll do it right."

"You bet we will."

"Appreciate the support."

"I haven't had a chance to say congrats on the engagement, either. Seems like you got a good guy there."

She smiled. "Thanks, I like him."

"You deserve to be happy after all you've been through."

Sam remembered that in a weak moment she'd told him about the miscarriages she'd suffered while married to Peter. "Thanks."

"I'll get back to you with what we got from the call." He left with a wave, and Sam watched him go. He was the only fellow cop she'd ever dated, and no one they worked with had ever known they were together. She was relieved that they were now able to be good colleagues without the "we used to sleep together" baggage.

Sam grabbed the portable radio off her desk and her coat. In the pit, she found Freddie on the phone. When he hung up, she said, "Nine o'clock at the Ambassador. Tell all of second shift I want them on backup."

"What'd you order for me, or do I not want to know?"

"Probably better if you don't know. How's Selina making out with Jackson?"

"Slow going. He's having trouble getting her to focus."

"When you have a picture, text me. Nick knows everyone in this town. He might be able to ID the guy."

"Have you heard from him?"

"Not yet. I'm off to see Lightfeather. See you around eight-thirty in The Ambassador lobby."

"I'll be there."

"Call me if anything comes up between now and then."

"Sam?"

She turned back.

"Are you going to court tomorrow? For Peter's hearing?"

"Hell no."

"Why not?"

"I won't give him the satisfaction of thinking that I care enough to waste part of my day on him." She would've told Nick the same thing if he'd consulted her before he lost his mind on TV.

"I've been worried about how you'll deal with this."

"He tried to run my life for four long years. I'm not giving him one more minute."

"It might help Nick to hear you say that."

"You're probably right. I'll tell him if I can find him."

"If you need help with that, you know where I am. Otherwise, see you in a couple of hours."

On the way to see Lightfeather, she thought about what Freddie had said. She wished she knew where Nick was just then. If she knew, she'd go find him as soon as she finished with Henry. Hopefully, Nick would be home by then.

Sam's cell phone rang, and hoping it was him, she put the phone on speaker. "Holland."

"Sam, it's Shelby Faircloth. Have I caught you at a bad time?"

"Tinker Bell," she said, "it's always a bad time in my world. That's why I need you."

Shelby's girlish giggle made Sam smile. "I'm at your service. I received a phone call today from Vera Wang."

"The *actual* Vera Wang?"

"The one and only. She saw some photos of you wearing her at the White House and asked about the possibility of doing your dress."

Sam had to suppress her own urge to giggle like a girl. "Vera Wang—*the Vera Wang*—wants to do *my* dress?"

"You heard me. I thought you might approve, so she's sending several options for you via overnight express. Could I bring them by after work tomorrow?"

"Sure, but I'm in the middle of a murder investigation. I can't promise to be there by a certain time."

"That's all right. I'll start with a fitting for your sisters and the girls for their dresses, and we'll work up to the main event once you break free. Is seven-thirty okay?"

"I'll make sure they're there, and I'll get there as soon as I can."

"You might also want to make sure the groom has other plans."

"Ohhh, good thought."

"See you then."

After indulging in a most un-cop-like squeal, Sam called her sisters to share the news. Angela and Tracy, after some major squealing of their own, agreed to meet Shelby at Nick's place. Tracy promised to bring her daughters Brooke and Abby, who were Sam's junior bridesmaids. She couldn't wait to tell Nick that she'd actually managed to handle some wedding business during the long workday.

ON THE HOTEL'S seventh floor, she found the same two police officers guarding Lightfeather's door. "Anything going on?" she asked.

"They've been fighting," one of them said.

"Been going at it all day," the other said. "How much longer do you think we'll need to be here?"

"Hopefully, not much longer." Sam knocked on the door.

"Thank God," the younger of the two officers muttered.

Annette Lightfeather answered the door, grimacing once again at the sight of Sam and her badge. "What now?"

"May I please speak to your husband?"

Annette stepped aside to admit Sam. A suitcase sat inside the door.

"Going somewhere?" Sam asked.

"Home to my children."

"Lieutenant," Henry said. "What can I do for you?"

He looked like he hadn't slept in days. Wearing a polo shirt and wrinkled khaki pants, his eyes were rimmed with red, and he seemed to have given up on shaving.

As Sam crossed the room to him, she heard Annette's suitcase roll over the tile foyer. The hotel room door opened and snapped closed behind her.

"Well," Henry said. "I guess that's that."

"Sir?"

"She asked for a divorce."

"I'm sorry."

"No job, no wife and probably no kids either, since she vowed to fight me for custody. Best part is I have no one but myself to blame."

Since Sam had no idea what to say to that, she sat down in the same chair she'd occupied the last time they met. "I'm afraid I have some news that's going to add to your dismay." She watched him brace himself for further disaster. "Regina was involved in a call girl ring."

His mouth fell open and then closed. "That can't be true."

Sam had learned to stay quiet at times like this. People needed to reach their own conclusions in their own time. Saying it a second time didn't help it go down any easier.

"You're sure?" he asked softly.

"Yes."

Henry got up and went over to the window. Hands in his pockets, his shoulders were hunched. "This entire week, as my life unraveled around me, do you know what has kept me sane?" He turned to face her. "Knowing that she loved me. She *loved me*."

"She needed money. That doesn't mean she didn't love you."

He picked up a glass and rolled it between his hands. Suddenly, he whipped his arm back and sent the glass hurling across the room. It smashed on contact with the wall. Sam wondered if Nick had looked as fierce when he threw his phone across his office.

"I gave up *everything* for her, and she was screwing other guys the same time she was screwing me?"

Sam held her tongue and gave him a chance to absorb the blow.

Another thought seemed to occur to him. "The baby..."

"Was yours. The DNA confirmed that."

His eyes, which had been fixed on a spot on the wall, shifted to her. "Why are you telling me this?"

"I believe there's a major, high-level prostitution organization ring at work in the city, and everyone knows about it but those of us in law enforcement."

Returning to the sofa, he sat. "I don't know about it."

"You've never heard rumors, innuendo, talk, *anything*?"

"I'm known on the Hill—or I *was* known—as a family man. My colleagues would hardly discuss hookers around me."

"We believe Regina, Maria and their colleague Selina Rameriz were recruited into the organization by one of your colleagues."

Lightfeather stared at her. "One of my *Senate* colleagues?"

Sam nodded. "Someone whose office is in the Hart Building. All three of the women worked there."

"A lot of people work in the Hart Building. Some of the senior staff wield as much power behind the scenes as the senators themselves."

"We'll be investigating everyone who works in that building, but I'd bet my badge it's not going to be a staffer. Anything you can tell me would help us to find the person who murdered Regina."

"After hearing she was sleeping around, I'm supposed to still care about who killed her?"

"The sooner we find the killer, the sooner we'll release you from this hotel room. Maybe then you can attempt to put your life back together."

Lightfeather ran his fingers through his hair. "Talk to Bob Cook," he said, referring to the senior senator from Virginia. "Nothing happens on the Hill that he doesn't know about."

"What about Trent?" Sam asked.

"Other than the car accident in high school, he's squeaky clean. As far as I know anyway." He released a short laugh. "A week ago, people would've said the same about me."

Sam stood up. "I appreciate your candor, Senator."

"I'm not a senator anymore."

"I still appreciate your candor. Let me know if you think of anything else that might help our investigation."

TWENTY-SIX

FREDDIE CALLED AS Sam was heading home. "Tillinghast's wife is refusing protective custody."

"Oh for Christ's sake. Have the marshals call me so I can talk to her."

"On it."

Sam closed her phone and waited for the callback. When it came, she said, "Put her on."

"Here she is, Lieutenant."

"I know what you're going to say, but—"

"Shut up and listen to me," Sam said in her best cop growl. "The man we're protecting you and your daughters from has viciously raped and murdered two women as well as kidnapping and raping one of my officers. Now, I want you to pack your bags and *get into the goddamned car with the marshals.* Do I make myself clear?"

"Yes," she said, sounding more subdued now. "Fine. What about my low-life husband?"

"He's probably safer in jail than he'd be with you."

"No question about that."

"Cooperate with the marshals so we can keep you and your girls safe. No screwing around."

"For how long?"

"As long as it takes. Don't tell anyone where you've gone."

"Anywhere is better than here. Media trucks are lining my street."

"Then get the hell out of there."

When Sam parked on Ninth Street a short time later, she was distressed to see their place still dark and Nick's car nowhere in sight. "*Where is he?*" For a brief, horrifying moment, she wondered if the sicko she was hunting down had nabbed him to get at her. "No," she whispered, refusing to entertain the possibility. He was out with his friends, and he knew she was busy with the case so he wasn't worried about getting home.

Since she had ninety minutes until she was due to meet Freddie and the others at The Ambassador, she took her radio and went inside, hoping Nick would come home before she had to leave again. In the kitchen, she contemplated making something to eat, but her stomach turned at the idea of food. As the possibility of something untoward happening to Nick took hold, Sam paced the living room. "Maybe I should be out there looking for him," she said to herself. But where to even begin? She didn't even know what gym he frequented.

Just as she was about to call Freddie to see if he thought they should be looking for Nick, the doorbell rang. Sam ran for the door, threw it open and was relieved to find Nick and his doctor friend Harry on the stoop. After the thorough examination she'd recently withstood at Harry's hands, it was all Sam could do to make eye contact.

"I understand this belongs to you," Harry said. His sinfully handsome face became even more so when he smiled.

Nick stepped into the light, and Sam gasped at the bruise under his right eye. "What happened? Did you get into a fight?" She was so damned glad to see him that she didn't even care if he'd been fighting.

"Nothing so dramatic, babe," he said, a slight slur infecting his words. “An elbow to the face on the basketball court.”

Sam stepped aside so Harry could escort Nick to the sofa. Once there, Nick put his head back against the cushions and closed his eyes. His white dress shirt was dirty and his loosened tie was crooked. She’d never seen him even slightly buzzed, so drunk and disheveled was unexpected, to say the least.

“I joined them after happy hour,” Harry whispered to Sam. “Never did manage to catch up.”

“Did anyone see him like this?” Sam asked, wondering what kind of media coverage he was in for the next day in addition to losing his cool on TV.

“Only his close friends. We take care of our own, Lieutenant.”

Since Nick seemed to be asleep, Sam said, “He’s had a rough couple of days.”

“He mentioned that he saw his mother yesterday, but we sort of suspected since that’s the only time he really hits the bottle.”

“So this has happened before?”

“Couple of times over the years. After her last wedding, he was drunk for a week. We found out later that she refused to introduce him as her son because she didn’t want the new husband to think she was lying about her age. You probably already know this latest encounter cost him twenty-five grand. Now that she knows he has money, no doubt she’ll be back for more.”

“What a bitch.” Sam had suspected he’d given his mother money, but not that much. “I’d like two minutes alone with her to tell her what a piece of shit she is.”

“You and everyone else who loves him. He told me once, years ago in a weak moment, that the scent of her perfume undoes him. I think he said it’s Chanel No. 5 or some knockoff version. Every time he catches a whiff of that stuff he goes into a tailspin. He said when he was little, he use to be able to smell her for days after she visited until his grandmother forced him to take a bath."

Sam's heart broke in half for the little boy who'd craved his mother's love and attention—and never got either. "Will he be okay?"

"Usually takes him a week or two to shake it off, but with your ex-husband about to get sprung, might take longer this time. He's taking that really hard too."

Listening to his friend, Sam realized she still had a lot to learn about the man she loved. "Thanks for bringing him home, Harry."

"No problem." He headed for the door. "You and I are overdue for a little chat."

"We are?"

"Don't play dumb with me, Lieutenant."

Sam smiled, remembering how much she'd enjoyed his wit the first time they met—over an exam table in his office.

"How's the soda famine going?" he asked.

"I'm cranky as hell but my stomach is better."

"Shocking! Maybe it was that gallon of diet cola you were drinking every day that was giving you crippling stomach pain. What an incredible coincidence!"

"Do they teach sarcasm in medical school?"

"I come by that naturally. What about the other thing we talked about?"

Sam's smile faded, and her heart raced.

"Given it any thought?"

Sam gave him a withering look. "What do you think?"

"And?"

"I'm late...I think." She hadn't been able to even ponder the possibility that had been hovering in her subconscious, let alone say it out loud.

Harry's eyebrows came together in an expression that took him from carefree friend to concerned doctor in an instant. "Define late."

"A week. Maybe two. I don't really keep track because my periods are so erratic, but I probably should've had one." She cleared her throat. "By now."

"I told you if you had all your parts that it was possible..."

Sam gripped his arm. "I can't be pregnant, Harry. *I just can't.*"

Laughing, he eased her into a chair and squatted down in front of her. "Of course you can."

Sam shook her head. "I can't go through that again. I can't lose another one." She'd rather stare down the barrel of a loaded shotgun than go through that hell again.

"I'll tell you what—I'm off tomorrow, so come into the office on Monday. We'll do a quick test and see what's what, okay?"

"It's not okay." No other subject had the ability to render her so powerless against the overwhelming array of emotions.

He reached for her hands and held on tight. "It will be. I promise. If you are..." He seemed to know better than to use the "p" word just then. "I have a friend who's an amazing OB/GYN who I'll refer you to." Flashing a sheepish grin, he added, "Well, to be honest, I've been seeing her for a while now, but I haven't told the guys yet. Keep my secret?"

"If you keep mine. Until we know for sure...Nick has had enough with his mother and everything."

"My lips are sealed. Let me see your phone."

"What the hell for?"

"Hand it over."

Confused, she drew it out of her pocket, put it into his outstretched hand and watched him program his number into her address book. "If anything comes up, anything at all, call me. Night or day."

"That's nice of you. Thanks."

He stood and helped her up, giving her a quick hug and a kiss on the cheek. "Take good care of my buddy," he said, looking over at Nick.

"Always."

"And try not to worry, Sam. Everything will be okay."

"I hope you're right."

He flashed that charming dimpled smile that made him so adorable. "I was right about the soda, wasn't I?"

"Oh *brother*. Am I ever going to hear the end of that?"

"Not in this lifetime. Sleep tight."

After she showed Harry out, she turned to study her fiancé. The idea of him being in so much pain that he'd felt the need to drink excessively was shocking to her. The Nick she knew and loved was *always* in control. Except, it seemed, when his loser mother turned his world upside down. She couldn't add to that right now by sharing the possibility that she *might* be pregnant—might being the operative word. Resting her back against the closed front door, Sam reached for her phone to call Freddie.

"What's up, boss?"

"Something's come up, and I can't be there tonight. Can you all handle it on your own? You know the drill—arrest the girl for solicitation and prostitution. Offer her a deal if she'll give up what she knows about the operation. Cue Malone in too." She should've done that herself but hadn't gotten to it.

"We can handle it. I just heard from Archie that the trace came up empty. The signals were all blocked."

"Son of a bitch. Another dead end."

"The text to your phone came from a throwaway, as we suspected. We're trying to track it down."

"We can't catch a break on this one."

"I know. Is everything okay? Did you find Nick?"

"I found him, but I can't leave him right now." She had no doubt that he'd never leave her in the same condition. Nothing, not even her all-consuming job, was more important to her than he was. If ever there'd been a timc to prove that, it was now. "I'll tell you about it tomorrow. Call me after it goes down?"

"You got it."

"Go in with backup, and be careful."

"We will."

Sam closed the phone, stashed it in her pocket, sent the two officers who were tailing her home for the evening and went to sit with Nick.

"WHAT TIME IS it?" Nick mumbled.

Sam put aside her laptop and turned to him. "Almost nine."

"How'd I get here?"

"You don't remember? Harry brought you home."

"Oh, yeah. Right." He ran his hand over his face and winced when he came into contact with the bruise under his eye. "Andy's elbow. Did you know he's been helping Gonzo with the baby?"

"I'd heard that."

"Sorry you had to see me like this. Won't happen again."

Sam reached out to caress his face. "Don't apologize. You needed to blow off some steam, and I'm glad your friends were there to help you do it."

"I blew off some steam on TV earlier too."

"So I heard."

"Are you pissed?"

She shook her head. "I've never had anyone to defend me against Peter. I used to have to deal with him and his games all on my own. So it's rather nice to have someone in my corner."

He reached for the hand on his face and brought it to his lips. "I'll always be in your corner, babe. You don't have to deal with anything alone anymore."

"Neither do you." She rested her head on his shoulder.

"Seeing her screws me up. Always has. You'd think after all these years I'd be better equipped to deal with it, but I never have gotten the hang of it."

"I wish there was something I could do for you."

"You're doing it. Just by being here. I want to take a shower. I must smell like the inside of a whiskey bottle."

"I could use one too. Come on, I'll go with you."

They walked up the stairs together. In the bathroom, she helped him out of his clothes and into the shower before she followed him. He reached for her, brought her in tight against him and held her while the warm water beat down on them.

"This goes a long way toward fixing what ails me," he said, sighing with what sounded like contentment.

"Good." Sam closed her eyes and held on to him, thankful that she'd chosen to stay home with him rather than go back to work. After a while, she reached for his bottle of shampoo and washed his hair. When she was done, he returned the favor.

He filled his hands with liquid soap and ran them reverently over her.

Sam watched him, wondering what he was thinking.

"I gave her twenty-five thousand," he said.

"Harry told me."

He looked at her, his beautiful eyes filled with pain. "Are you horrified?"

Sam combed the wet hair off his forehead. "Of course not. You did what you felt you needed to."

"She'll probably be back for more when that's gone."

"Probably." Sam turned off the water and reached for their towels. "But we'll be ready for her next time."

A hint of a smile graced his face. "Will we?"

"Next time," she said, kissing him, "she'll deal with me."

He chuckled. "I almost feel sorry for her."

Sam secured a towel around his waist and then wrapped another around herself. "Don't bother feeling sorry for her. She isn't worth your time. Neither is Peter, for that matter."

"That's different."

"It's really not, Nick. We can't give these people power over us. The minute we do, they win."

"So I'm not supposed to be concerned about what he might do to you once he's out of jail?"

"We'll take every possible precaution, but there's no need for us to give him the satisfaction of knowing that we care in the least about him."

"If that's how you feel, you have to be pissed about what I did today."

"I'm concerned about political fallout for you, but I'm not mad at you for doing it. From now on, though, how about we deny him the satisfaction?"

"Won't that infuriate him?"

"He's already infuriated. Nothing we do or don't do will change that. We don't care, remember?"

"I'll care if he comes at my wife. I'll definitely care about that."

Sam rested her hands on his chest. "She's very capable of taking care of herself. You need to keep that in mind."

He put his arms around her. "As capable as she is, even she didn't think he'd strap bombs to our cars."

"She knows better now. She'll be looking for the first chance to nail his ass—but she'll *never* let him know that."

"You're sure this is the best way to handle it?"

"Making a lot of noise hasn't gotten us anywhere, has it? They're still going to let him out."

"So we just say nothing and let it happen?"

"We don't have any choice. How about we let our happiness be our revenge? He wants what he can never have again. Sooner or later, he'll figure that out."

"I'm still worried about him trying to hurt you."

"And I'm worried about him trying to hurt *you*. In his mind, you're the only thing standing in the way of what he wants. I'm sure he's forgotten all about the year we were divorced before you and I got back together. To him, you're the root of all evil, so you'll need to be careful too."

"Hopefully, his stint in jail will have scared him straight and he'll leave us alone."

"Hopefully."

"You don't think so, though, do you?"

"Who knows? I guess we'll find out soon enough." She glanced up at him. "Can we please change the subject?"

"Absolutely."

Following him into the bedroom, Sam told him about the call from Shelby and the appointment for the following evening. "You'll have to make yourself scarce so you don't see the dress."

"I never pictured you as the superstitious type," he said.

"I'm not usually. But I've got one failed marriage behind me. I'm not inviting any bad mojo into this one."

He sat on the bed and reached out a hand to her. "This one won't be anything like the first one."

Taking his hand, Sam sat next to him. "No, it won't, but you're still not seeing the dress until March 26." She leaned over to kiss him. "Nice try, though."

Hooking an arm around her, he anchored her for another kiss. "Did you get to eat?"

"Wasn't hungry. You?"

"I had some pizza with the guys." He nuzzled her neck, nibbled on her earlobe and tugged on her towel. "Wanna go to bed?"

"In a little bit. I'm waiting to hear from Freddie. We've got something going down tonight."

Nick raised his head to meet her eyes. "Shouldn't you be there?"

She shrugged. "I let them deal with it."

"Samantha..."

"What? It's no big deal. I chose to stay here with you."

His face softened, and he stole another kiss. "Thank you."

"It's nothing you wouldn't have done for me."

Hugging her, he said, "I love you. I don't think I've told you that today."

"Don't start slacking off before we're even married," she said with a teasing grin.

"No chance of that," he said, bringing his lips down on hers for a kiss that sucked every other thought right out of her head.

HEARING THAT SHE had stayed home to take care of him set off a powerful swell of emotion inside Nick. No one had ever loved him the way she did, and her love went a long way toward soothing the hurt he'd carried with him for as long as he could remember.

He wished he had the words to tell her what she meant to him. If he lived forever, he'd probably never find the perfect words.

Cupping her breast, he teased her nipple with his tongue and teeth.

Sam gasped and pushed at him.

"What?" he asked, surprised. She usually loved that.

"Nothing," she said, but the almost panicked look in her eyes caught his immediate attention.

"What, honey? What's the matter?" He watched, shocked as she blinked back tears. There was only one issue that could be guaranteed to bring his fearless, gutsy cop to tears every time. "Samantha?"

She looked up at him with those eyes that saw right through him. "I can't be," she said as tears rolled down her cheeks. "I just can't."

"Sweetheart, you're scaring me. What're you talking about?"

She crossed her arms over her breasts. "The only time they're that sensitive…"

The realization hit him all at once, and all the air whooshed from his lungs. "Sam…"

"I don't know! Don't look at me like that! They told me I can't…" She broke down into tears and hiccuping sobs. "They said I couldn't have any more. They told me that. I believed them!"

Overwhelmed with joy and excitement and trepidation, Nick put his arms around her. "How long have you known?" he asked after several quiet minutes.

"I *don't* know. Not for sure. I've just noticed some… signs. And just now, when you did that…"

"This?" He kissed his way from her neck to her breast and twirled his tongue around her nipple before sucking hard on it.

She cried out, her fingers gripping his hair. "*Nick*..."

"Hmmm?"

"I can't do it. I can't."

"Oh, honey, sure you can. I have no doubt." He kissed a path from oversensitive breasts to belly. Just the *possibility* that she could be carrying his child had him blinking back his own tears.

"I can't be terrified for nine months. How will I work or do anything but be afraid?"

He rested his face on her belly and wrapped his arms around her. Looking up at her, he said, "You'll just do what you always do and let the rest take care of itself."

"What if I am...and then...what if..."

"If the worst happens, we'll deal with it together and we'll try again. We'll never stop trying until we get it right."

"I'm so scared. I've noticed a few signs, but I've been afraid to even consider the possibility. The other times, my breasts...They were so sensitive. That's the only time they've ever been like that. It's almost like confirmation..."

He kissed his way back up her body, from her belly to her lips. "We need to get you in to see Harry."

"Monday." Raising her hands to his face, she brought him down for a soft, sweet kiss that shattered his remaining defenses. She owned him. There was nothing he wouldn't do for her, nothing he wouldn't give her, nothing he wouldn't do to protect her, even if she didn't want his protection. And now, maybe, a baby too...

"Samantha," he whispered against her lips as he entered her, "I love you so much."

"Mmm, me too." She wrapped her arms and legs around him, holding him tight against her, and gazed up at him with eyes still shiny with tears but also full of love—for him.

Before she returned to his life, he'd had no idea what he'd been missing. Now she was so much a part of him that he couldn't imagine a life without her at the center of it. Knowing what she liked, he wanted to pick up the pace, but held back, afraid to do anything to hurt her or the baby.

"Nick…

"What, babe?"

"Faster."

"We have to be careful, just in case."

"It's okay." She slid her hands down his back. "Really."

Gripping her hips to hold her still, he pumped into her, giving her what she wanted. His heart raced from exertion and emotion until he thought it would burst from his chest.

As Sam cried out, he felt her nails score his back, which sent him surging into her one last time in a release that seemed ripped from his very soul. Afterward, he fought to catch his breath as her hands soothed his back.

"I can't believe I scratched you," she said, laughing.

He rested carefully on top of her, his lips pressed to her neck. "I don't care."

"Good thing you're required to wear a shirt to work."

"I've given them enough to talk about for a while."

Her fingers combed through his hair, a loving gesture of hers that never failed to stir him. She had given him exactly what he'd needed most, and he hadn't known he needed it. She just knew.

"Will you do something for me?" she asked.

"Anything. Name it."

"I have to give this case my full attention until we close it. Can we not talk about the *other thing* until after that? If I let myself get all nutty about it, I won't be able to focus on anything else. I've become an expert at compartmentalizing this stuff so I can function at work."

"Of course. I understand."

She released a deep, contented sigh. "You always do."

He tightened his hold on her and kissed her forehead. "I try."

Bon Jovi interrupted the peaceful moment when "Livin' on a Prayer" sounded through the room.

"I need to get that," she said. "It's probably Freddie."

Nick rolled to his side and reached for her phone on the bedside table, handing it to her.

As she took the call, she linked her fingers with his, letting him know she was still right there with him.

Touched by the gesture, he shifted to his side so he could see her.

"How'd it go?" she asked.

Nick watched her process what Freddie was telling her.

"What?" she said, laughing. "They asked for your preferences. I figured you'd *love* a dominatrix. Was I wrong?"

Nick chuckled, imagining Freddie's indignation.

"She wouldn't give you *anything* on the organization?" Sam paused, listening. "We'll let her cool her heels in jail for the night since we've still got her on solicitation and prostitution. Maybe she'll be more forthcoming in the morning. Good work, thanks."

"Do I even want to know?" Nick asked when she'd ended the call.

"Have you ever heard any references to a high-level call girl ring in the city? We're talking *highest* level."

"I've heard rumors over the years, but nothing concrete."

"What kind of rumors?"

"Just that it exists but no specifics."

She shot him a coy look. "Were you ever tempted to dial up a girl?"

He cringed. "*No.*"

Sam laughed at his indignation. "That's right—you didn't have to. According to your buddy Harry, you were the ultimate chick magnet."

Rolling his eyes, he said, "Whatever."

"You never talk about them, you know."

"Who? My friends?"

"The women."

"What women? You're the only one who's ever mattered. You know that."

"So you were a monk for the six years between when we first met and when we got back together?"

"Absolutely. I sat at home and thought about you."

She poked his ribs. "You're so full of crap." Looking over at him, she said, "I was really hoping you'd have the lowdown on the call girls."

"I'm sorry to disappoint you, but I can't believe you thought I'd know about that. I should probably be insulted."

"You never heard *anyone* talk about it? I thought guys loved to share the dirty details."

"Guys talk about a lot of things, but they don't talk about hookers, especially not in this town where the word 'hooker' has the power to end careers."

"I guess I'll have to talk to Cook tomorrow. I was hoping to avoid that after our last friendly encounter."

"What the hell does Cook have to do with it?" Nick asked, his eyes widening. He'd had his own run-CIS with the senior senator from Virginia.

"Tillinghast said if anyone would have the skinny,

Cook would. He said Cook knows everything that happens on the Hill."

Nick reached for his phone.

Sam yawned. "Who're you calling?"

"Someone who knows even more than Cook does about what happens on the Hill."

TWENTY-SEVEN

"YOU'RE SURE THEY won't care if we show up there this late?" Sam asked as they approached the Leesburg home of Nick's adopted parents, retired Senator Graham O'Connor and his wife Laine.

"I'm positive. They're night owls."

"This sure is a nicer ride than mine," she said of Nick's BMW, which she was driving for the first time.

"I should hope so."

She made a face at him. "You're such a snob."

"Only about cars—and hookers. Only the best will do."

"Very funny."

"Connect the dots for me. What does the call girl ring have to do with your case?"

"Regina and Maria were involved as well as another woman from the Capital Cleaning Services, Selina Rameriz. There could be more, but we've confirmed those three so far."

"Wow," Nick said, "I can't picture Maria as a call girl. She was so quiet and unassuming."

"It was all about the money. They sent every dime home." Sam pulled into the O'Connor's driveway. "Our theory is they knew they might not have much time here, so they had to make it any way they could before they were sent home. In Selina's case, she needed the money for her mother's surgery." Sam's phone chimed to indicate a message. "Check that for me, will you?" She handed the phone to Nick.

"Why are you guys drawing pictures of Jack Bartholomew?"

"Who's that?"

"Chief of staff to the vice president."

Sam released a low whistle. "When Tillinghast said the top levels of government, he wasn't kidding."

"Are you saying *Bartholomew* has something to do with the call girl ring?"

"At the very least, he's a customer. He attacked and raped Selina Rameriz."

"You've got the wrong guy, Sam. There's no way he has anything to do with this."

"Not according to Selina. She worked with the computer artist all afternoon."

Nick sat back in the seat. "I can't believe it. This could rock the entire administration."

Her mind racing, she brought the car to a stop in front of the garage. "How well do you know Bartholomew?"

"Not all that well, but I've seen a lot more of him since I took office. The vice president is leading the president's new accountability and transparency effort, and Bartholomew is the VP's point man. He's been in a number of meetings I've attended over the last few weeks."

"If Selina's account is true, he's one sick bastard."

"You think he could be killing these women to shut them up?"

"He fits the profile. All along we've said it's going to be someone who thinks he's above being caught. He's left DNA all over the place, so if it is him, we've got him nailed."

"What're you going to do?"

Sam thought about it for a moment before she opened

her phone and called Freddie. "Jack Bartholomew," she said, "chief of staff to Gooding."

"Whoa. How do you know?"

"Nick recognizes him. Do a run on him, and get me an address."

"We're going to talk to him at home?"

"We're going to *arrest* him at home."

"Holy shit," Nick said.

Sometimes Sam really loved this job. "I don't care who he is, if he's running a prostitution ring in my city and murdering women to gain their silence, I'm taking him down."

"Right there with you, boss."

"Put someone on Bartholomew for tonight until we can get subpoenas for his DNA and phone records. I don't want him killing someone else in the meantime. Meet me at HQ at six-thirty. We'll go together."

"Got it."

"Is Selina still working with Jackson to ID some of the other johns?"

"He's giving it another hour. They're both running out of steam. I've got a house set up for her as soon as they're done."

"After that, go home. We've got another long one ahead of us tomorrow, and you've got a very important evening to prepare for."

"Thanks for reminding me," he mumbled.

"See you in the morning." To Nick she said, "Let's see what your buddy Graham knows."

GRAHAM AND LAINE ushered them into the family room of their comfortable farmhouse where a blazing fire cast an amber glow over the cozy room.

Sam was surprised to see Terry O'Connor jump up

from the sofa. "Senator," he said, adding almost begrudgingly, "Lieutenant."

The two men shook hands.

"You look great, Terry," Nick said.

Dressed in sweats and a Georgetown T-shirt, Terry appeared to have lost at least twenty pounds since Sam last saw him, and his eyes seemed clearer than she'd ever seen them—not that he looked at her. Ever since she'd interrogated him as a suspect in his brother's murder, things had been tense between them. But he was going to be Nick's deputy chief of staff, so Sam decided to at least make an effort to be cordial. "You really do look terrific," she said.

"Thanks," Terry said with only the slightest of glances her way. He ran his fingers through his prematurely gray hair almost as if he needed something to do with his hands.

"What brings you out our way this time of night?" Graham asked.

"Sam's working on a case I thought you might be able to help her with," Nick said.

"Whatever I can do—anytime," Graham said, gesturing for them to sit on the love seat.

"I appreciate that," Sam said. "Tell me what you know about high-end call girls in Washington."

Laine gasped, and Terry snickered.

"Well, I ah..." Graham said, sputtering.

"I'm probably better versed on that subject than my dear old dad," Terry said, looking chagrined.

Laine cast a disparaging glance at her eldest child. "Honestly, Terry."

"I'm not proud of the way I used to live, Mother, but the truth is, I've met my share of call girls."

Sam handed him a slip of paper. “Have you ever seen this phone number before?”

“No, but that doesn’t mean anything. If it’s the same outfit I think it is, the number changes all the time.”

“How do customers keep up?”

“Text messages.”

“Do you have any idea who runs the organization?”

“Not specifically, but there’re always rumors and speculation.”

“Humor me.”

“I’ve heard Gooding’s name,” he said, referring to the vice president. And Daniels.”

“The *speaker of the House*?” Nick said, incredulous.

A burst of adrenaline had Sam’s heart pumping hard.

“I’ve also heard Cook’s name in the mix,” Graham said.

The other three stared at him.

“You gotta be kidding me,” Nick said.

Graham shrugged. “I always chalked it up to rumors started by the Republicans.”

“If what you’re telling me is true,” Sam said, “the Republicans are squeaky-clean compared to the Democrats.”

“That’s just what we want to hear,” Graham said, glancing at Nick. “This could be a freaking nightmare for us.”

Sam got a kick out of the way Graham always stuck to the present tense when speaking about politics, as if he still had an oar in the race. She supposed he did with his protégé Nick now holding the office that had once been his.

“I just can’t believe Bob Cook would be involved with call girls,” Laine said. “Millie will kill him.”

"I believe it," Graham said. "He's a money-hungry pig."

"Graham!" Laine said, shocked. "He's our good friend. How can you say such a thing?"

"Because it's true, Mother," Terry said. "With the tight reins the Senate puts on members' outside income, it wouldn't surprise me at all that Cook had something like this going on the side."

"Something that could ruin his career and his marriage?" Laine asked.

"Millie enjoys the lifestyle he provides," Graham said. "And just because he's running the ring, doesn't mean he's sleeping with the employees."

"*Right*," Terry said, dripping with sarcasm. "As if he could resist that kind of temptation."

"This is so shocking," Laine said.

"I know I don't have to tell you that it's vital to my investigation that none of you repeat a word of this to anyone," Sam said.

"Of course we wouldn't, honey," Laine said. "We'd never do that to a member of our family."

Nick smiled at Laine who reached over to squeeze his hand.

"Well, you've given me a lot to think about," Sam said.

"Be careful, Sam," Terry said, surprising her. "If this is true, there's nothing they won't do to protect their cash cow *and* their reputations."

"They've already resorted to murder," she reminded him.

"Which is why they'd think nothing of gunning for a cop. What else do they have to lose?"

"I appreciate the warning, but I can take care of myself."

"I hear that a lot," Nick said, grinning. "She thinks she's bulletproof."

They spent another half hour talking about wedding plans and catching up on O'Connor family news.

As Sam and Nick got up to leave, Terry stood to shake hands with Nick.

"You ready to start on Monday?" Nick asked.

"I'll be there." Terry hesitated, as if there was something else he wanted to say. "I just want you to know… Thinking about the opportunity you've given me got me through rehab. It gave me something to look forward to. I haven't had that in a long time." His DUI weeks before he'd been due to declare his candidacy for his father's office had derailed his promising political career, clearing the way for his younger brother John to run for an office he'd never wanted. Terry's spiral had continued unabated ever since—until recently.

"I'm looking forward to having you on my team," Nick said. "In fact, I know Christina would love for you to take over the campaign, especially now that she and Tommy have a baby to contend with."

"She's having a *baby*?"

"No," Nick said, laughing, bringing Terry up to speed on how Gonzo came to have a son.

"That's amazing," Laine said. "He had no idea about the child?"

"None at all," Sam said.

"We're going to stay at the cabin tonight," Nick said. "Give us a call if you think of anything else that might help the investigation."

"We will," Graham said as he and Laine walked them out.

"You'll be here for dinner on Sunday, right?" Laine asked.

"Wouldn't miss it," Nick said, kissing her cheek. "I hope it's okay that I invited a friend. Don't worry, though, he won't eat much. He's only twelve."

Laine chuckled. "You know you can invite anyone you want. Any friend of yours is a friend of ours." She hugged him and kissed his cheek. "When I see you on Sunday, you can tell me what has you looking so troubled, young man."

"Yes, ma'am," he muttered, clearly taken aback by her insight.

Laine turned to Sam. "I want to thank you for putting Patricia in touch with me. We had a lovely visit, and we both felt better afterward."

"I'm glad to hear that. I wasn't sure I was doing the right thing."

Laine reached out to squeeze Sam's arm. "It was the exact right thing, and I appreciate it."

"It was nothing," Sam mumbled.

"We'll see you on Sunday," Graham said, hugging them both.

SAM COULDN'T STOP yawning on the short ride to the cabin John had left to Nick.

"Aren't you glad now that I made you pack a bag?" Nick asked from the passenger seat.

"Yes, dear."

"You ought to get used to saying that. I plan to be right most of the time."

She rolled her eyes at him. "Whatever." Reaching for her cell phone, she pressed speed dial number four.

"Sleeping," Malone answered, his voice gravely.

"I need you," Sam said.

"Are you going to take years off my life again?"

"Well, if requesting subpoenas for personal cell

records and DNA for the vice president, his chief of staff, the speaker of the House of Representatives and the senior senator from Virginia doesn't give you heartburn, I'm not sure what will."

Malone uttered a tortured moan. "You're screwing with me again, Holland."

"I wish I was."

"Speak."

Sam told him what she knew.

"Because Rameriz identified him, we can justify asking for Bartholomew's records and DNA, but not the rest," Malone said. "We're not going after the vice president, the speaker and a senior senator without more than rumors. Bring Bartholomew in. Maybe you can get him to roll on the others if you make it seem like he'd be going down alone."

"I guess I'll take what I can get. Wait until after seven to request the subpoena. I don't want to tip him off."

"Is there anything else I can do for you, Lieutenant?"

"We took a suitcase to the lab today. Inside are the clothes Selina Rameriz was wearing when Jack Bartholomew raped her. I need you to put a rush on that report."

"Consider it done."

"That's it for now, Captain. Sleep tight."

"The death of me, Holland. The living, breathing death."

Laughing, Sam ended the call. As they were pulling up to the cabin, her phone chimed with a new text. *You don't do what you're told. Time to teach you a lesson.* Sam swallowed hard and slapped the phone closed.

"What?" Nick asked.

"Nothing." Following him into the cabin, Sam was

suddenly glad that no one, other than the O'Connors, knew where they were just then.

Nick flipped on a light, illuminating a comfortable living room filled with John O'Connor's belongings. "I probably need to get around to packing up John's stuff for his parents."

"When you're ready. There's no rush."

He picked up a picture of John with his young niece and nephew. "He sure did love those kids." After studying the photo for a moment, he returned it to the shelf and held out a hand to her. "Let's go to bed."

Curling up to him a short time later, Sam thought about the first night she'd spent at the cabin, in the midst of the O'Connor investigation.

With his arm around her, he brushed his lips over her forehead. "What are you thinking about?"

"The first night we spent here."

"In separate bedrooms."

"That was back when I was trying to do the right thing by resisting you."

"Which of course was the exact wrong thing."

Sam laughed and pressed her lips to his chest and breathed in his endlessly appealing scent. "Very wrong."

"You still think that even though you got suspended for hooking up with me in the middle of the investigation?"

"I've learned it's not wise to resist that which is meant to be."

"That's very profound, Samantha."

"And very true."

"Very true indeed." His arms tightened around her, and Sam drifted into sleep. What seemed like minutes later, her ringing cell phone woke her up. A glance at the digital clock on the bedside table told her it was just after three. Clearing her throat, Sam reached for the phone.

"Holland."

"Oh, Sam!" Celia sounded frantic. "Thank God I reached you."

Sam sat straight up in bed. "Is it Dad?"

"There's a fire at your place! You need to get out of there!"

"Celia, we're in Leesburg. What do you mean there's a fire?"

Now Nick was also awake and sitting up.

"Thank goodness you're not there." Sam heard Celia telling her father they weren't home. "Your place up the street," Celia said. "The fire engines woke us up."

"Oh my God." To Nick, Sam said, "The place on Ninth is on fire."

"Shit," he said, leaping from the bed and pulling on jeans as Sam did the same.

"We're on our way," Sam told Celia. As she recalled the text threat from earlier, her stomach took a nosedive.

Minutes later, they left the cabin with Nick driving as fast as he dared.

"This is my fault," Sam said after several tense minutes of silence.

"How do you figure?"

"I got a text earlier. They said because I didn't back off the investigation like they told me to it was time to teach me a lesson."

He took his eyes off the road long enough to look over at her. "Why didn't you say anything?"

"After the day you'd had, I didn't want you to worry."

"If we'd been in the house, Sam, we could've been killed!"

"I realize that."

"Who're you calling?"

"Malone. He needs to know about this."

"But I didn't?" He shook his head. "Just when I think we're really getting somewhere you go back to keeping things from me."

After Sam had reported in to her superior officers, she turned to Nick. "I was going to tell you in the morning—after you got a good night's sleep."

"It's a good thing I was sleeping in Leesburg and not on Ninth Street."

"I'm sorry about the house," she said.

He smacked the heel of his hand on the wheel, startling her. "I don't *give a shit about the house, Sam*! It's insured. Anything in there can be replaced. That's not what you need to be apologizing about!"

"I'm trying." After years of living with passive-aggressive Peter, Sam had become a pro at keeping things from her significant other. "I can't completely change who I am overnight. I'm doing the best I can."

"You need to do better."

"Pardon me for thinking you'd had enough for one day."

"You should've told me."

Sam bit back a retort that would've escalated the disagreement to a full-blown argument, and they passed the rest of the ride in tense silence.

EMERGENCY VEHICLES BARRICADED the entire block around their home. Nick grabbed the first spot he could find on the next block and took off running with Sam right behind him.

She flashed her badge to one of the firefighters. "Lieutenant Holland, MPD. This is my place. What've you got?"

"You got lucky, L.T. Someone called it in, and we got here before it got past the front room. You'll have some smoke and water damage on the first floor as well as a broken window and front door, but that's about it."

"How'd it start?" Nick asked.

Looking from Nick to Sam and then back to Nick, the young firefighter's eyes bugged. "Oh, Senator. Um, ah, let me grab my captain."

"It doesn't look too bad," Sam said, staring at the house where smoke billowed from the broken window.

Keeping his eyes fixed on the house, Nick said nothing.

"Senator, Lieutenant, I'm Captain Grayson. Our investigator will be here shortly. Looks like something went through the window and ignited the carpet inside, but I'll let the fire marshal give you the official findings."

"So the window was broken from the outside?" Sam asked.

"That's how it appears to us. You're welcome to take a look."

They followed him through the maze of police and firefighters and curious neighbors who were braving the cold to watch the proceedings. The exploding flash of a camera blinded Nick.

"Goddamn it," he muttered. No doubt the vultures were loving this new story on top of his rant earlier in the day.

The stench of smoke and puddles of water greeted them inside the house where the floors, walls and ceiling closest to the front were damaged. He watched Sam zero in on the window as well as the smashed, fire-blackened glass on the floor.

"Some of the glass is too thick to be window glass," she said. "Looks like some kind of bottle."

"My guess," the captain said, "is there will be traces of gas or some sort of accelerant in the bottle glass." He turned to Sam. "Any idea who might've tossed a Molotov cocktail through your window?"

"I'm in the midst of a hot case, and I've been receiving threatening texts."

"I've gotten one too," Nick said.

"When was the most recent one?" the captain asked.

"A couple of hours ago. It inferred that it might be time to 'teach me a lesson.'"

"Well, this certainly does make a statement," a new voice said.

Sam and Nick turned to find Chief Farnsworth in the doorway.

"Are you both all right?" he asked.

"Yes, sir," Sam said. "We weren't here."

"What's this about threats?" he asked, giving Sam a stern-faced stare.

"I've reported them," she said, clearing her throat. "Most of them. Sir."

"Where's your detail?"

"I sent them home for the night because I was staying in."

"And yet you weren't here when a fire broke out in your home." Stepping further into the room, the chief bent to take a closer look at the glass on the floor. "I haven't been a detective in years, Lieutenant, but if you weren't here when the fire started then I have to deduce that you went somewhere." He glanced up at Sam. "Without the detail your superior officers assigned to you until you close your current case. Is that possible?"

Apparently sensing trouble brewing, Captain Grayson headed for the door. "I'll wait outside for the inspector."

"I didn't plan to go anywhere," Sam said to the chief.

"But Nick thought Senator O'Connor might be able to help with the case, so we went to Leesburg. Since we were there, we stayed at Nick's place rather than drive all the way back to the city. Turned out to be a good thing we weren't here."

"That's true, and I do appreciate your after-hours dedication. However, if you go *anywhere* again without your detail—until I say otherwise—I'll have your badge. Am I clear?"

"Yes." She cleared her throat again. "Sir."

"You'll need to vacate the premises until the inspector finishes his work. I assume you'll be at your father's place?"

"Yes, sir."

"I'll have your detail meet you there in the morning."

"Thank you, sir."

As they followed the chief out of the house, Sam grimaced, and Nick choked back a laugh. After what she'd kept from him earlier, he'd rather enjoyed watching the chief take her to task—not that he'd ever admit that to her.

Leaving the fire scene to the experts, Farnsworth escorted Sam and Nick to Skip's house. He and Celia were waiting in the living room.

"Everyone all right?" Skip asked.

"We're fine." Sam bent to kiss her father's forehead. "The damage to the house isn't too bad."

"That true, Joe?" Skip asked his old friend the chief.

"That's how it looked to me."

"Celia wouldn't let me out to see for myself," Skip said, glaring at his wife.

"It's too cold out," she said. "Not good for your lungs."

Skip rolled his eyes at her.

"I'm going home," Farnsworth said. To Sam, he added, "I'll see you in the morning—with your detail."

"Yes, sir."

"Good to see you newlyweds."

"You too, Joe," Skip said. "Thanks for coming."

"Anytime."

Sam turned on her father after the chief left. "*You called him?* What the hell for?"

"If someone's throwing fire through my daughter's window when she's in the middle of a case, then he needs to know."

"Thanks to you I got a major chewing out for being out without my detail."

"Good," Skip said. "You had no business leaving without them."

Watching the exchange, Nick suspected that Sam had never given her detail a thought before they left for Leesburg. Neither of them had.

"What were you doing in Leesburg?" Celia asked.

"We went to see Senator O'Connor for background on the case," Sam said. "We decided to stay at the cabin."

"Thank goodness for that," Celia said.

"Anything else you want to tell me?" Skip's sharp eyes zeroed in on his daughter.

"The case is getting hot," Sam said. "We've uncovered a call girl ring operating at the highest levels of the government. We're arresting the vice president's chief of staff in the morning."

"You don't say," Skip said. "What'd he do?"

"We know he raped one woman, and we suspect he may be one of the organizers of the ring. If that turns out to be true, it certainly gives us a motive for murder."

"I wonder what he'd be more interested in protecting," Skip said. "The ring or his reputation."

"A very good question," Sam said. "One I hope to have answered by this time tomorrow."

"Sounds like you two kids could use a place to sleep for a few hours," Skip said. "Your old room is available."

"Thanks," Nick said.

"I'll get you some towels," Celia said, hustling up the stairs.

Sam consulted her watch. "I've got about two hours."

"Go shut your eyes while you can," Skip said. "Sounds like tomorrow is going to be one hell of a day."

TWENTY-EIGHT

EVEN THOUGH SHE badly needed the sleep, Sam lay awake in her old bedroom staring at the ceiling, thinking over every aspect of the case. This one had felt disjointed from the very beginning, with an early suspect in Lightfeather who'd ended up having an airtight alibi. Since then, they hadn't had so much as a person of interest. Judging by the lengths the perp (or perps) had gone to by making personal attacks on two cops, however, it was clear someone was watching their every move.

"Why aren't you sleeping?" Nick asked.

Sam turned to him. "Why aren't you?"

"Someone threw fire in my window after threatening my fiancée. Stuff like that tends to make me a bit… anxious."

"Are you still mad at me?"

"Yes," he said, but she could tell by his tone that the true mad had passed.

She sighed. "I didn't think you needed any more bad news."

He looked over at her. "Don't keep things from me, Sam. Please don't."

"Even when it might be what's best for you?"

Reaching for her hand, he laced his fingers through hers. "What's best for me is knowing what's going on with you. Even the hard-to-hear stuff."

"I'm trying really hard to be more forthcoming with

you. I meant what I said earlier about not being able to change who I am overnight."

"I'd never want to change who you are. I just want you to change this one little annoying habit..."

"*Annoying?*"

"Very. But luckily for you—and for me—you're also annoyingly cute, distractingly sexy, and perfectly imperfect."

Sam smiled. "Perfectly imperfect. I like that." Rolling to her side, she kissed his chest and then his lips. "Try to get some sleep."

"Where're you going?"

"Sleep isn't happening, so I'm going to get an early start."

"With your detail."

"Yes, dear."

"I do so love the way you say that."

Sam laughed as she pulled on jeans and a sweater. "Before this day is over, I may have to arrest the freaking speaker of the House—or better yet, the vice president. Not your typical day at the office."

"Are any of your days at the office typical?"

Sam pretended to think about that for a minute. "Um, no, but I wouldn't have it any other way." She leaned over the bed to kiss him one last time.

He gripped a handful of her hair. "Be careful out there."

"Always."

"More so than usual today."

"I promise." She kissed him again. "Gotta go."

NICK WENT TO survey the damage at the house, hoping he could get in to get clothes for work. The crime scene tape had been removed, and all that remained was the charred exterior and broken front door. A lone police officer stood watch outside.

"Am I allowed in?" Nick asked the officer.

"Yes, sir, Senator. The fire inspector has cleared the scene. They asked me to keep an eye on things because the door was broken and because of the threat the lieutenant received."

"Thanks for that." A few of their favorite reporters would no doubt love to gain access to their house if given an easy opportunity.

"Looks like quite a mess you've got there, Senator."

Nick turned to find a man he'd seen around the neighborhood. He was young with dark blond hair that could use a cut and a friendly, engaging smile.

"Craig Lawton," he said, extending his hand.

"Nick Cappuano. Nice to meet you."

"Likewise. What happened?"

"Molotov cocktail, or so I'm told."

"You gotta hate when that happens."

Nick laughed. "This kind of thing happens far too often in our lives."

"So I've read. Not sure if it would help, but I'm a contractor. I'd be happy to squeeze you in."

"That'd be great. Are you sure you have time?"

Craig shot him a sly grin. "Landing this job will put me on the map. I think I can make some time."

Amused, Nick said, "Let me show you what needs to be done."

Craig followed him inside and marveled—as most visitors did—at the size of the double townhouse. As they inspected the damage and discussed the work that needed to be done, Craig whipped out his measuring tape and made notes in a pad he pulled from his pocket.

"Is this related to one of your fiancée's cases?"

"Unfortunately, yes."

"I've seen her around. Her dad is the one that's paralyzed, right?"

"Yes." Nick contemplated the damaged doorway. "Let me run something by you..."

"Sure."

"How hard would it be to install a ramp? I've been thinking that Sam will want to have her father over at some point."

"Shouldn't be too difficult. A buddy of mine works in the city's permitting office. I could run it by him for you, but I'm sure it won't be a problem when I tell him about her dad."

"Would he be doing a special favor because, you know, of who we are?" Such things still made Nick uncomfortable, and he knew how Sam felt about special favors too. In this case, however, she'd probably make an exception.

"Maybe a little. But Skip Holland is a hero in this city. They'd do anything for him." Craig gestured to the door. "The whole frame and stoop will need to be replaced anyway, so it's the perfect time to demo the stairs and do the ramp."

"Absolutely." Nick shook his hand. "Do it. As soon as possible."

"Pending building inspection approval, I can have the stairs mostly out by the end of the day. You'll have to use the back door for a while."

"That's no problem."

"Do you need to wait for the insurance company?"

Nick shook his head. "Just do it. I'll pay whatever. I'd like to forget this ever happened."

"You got it, Senator. I'm on it."

SAM INDULGED IN a rare cup of coffee to give her a badly needed jolt after the nearly sleepless night. She logged into her email, looking for a report on Selina's clothes from the lab. "Crap," she said. "Nothing yet. That's all right, Jack." She called up the computer rendering of Jack Bartholomew. "I've got you on a victim ID. We'll do a lineup, and then we'll have you nailed. But I have a feeling Selina is just the tip of the iceberg."

"Talking to yourself, Lieutenant?"

Sam looked up to find Lieutenant Stahl standing in the doorway. "What do you want?"

"Heard you had some excitement at your place last night."

"How'd you hear that? Were you there?"

His eyes narrowed at the insinuation. "You'd love that wouldn't you?"

"To have you out of my life forever? Sure, throw a cocktail through my window. By all means."

"I'd never give you the satisfaction."

"I'll get it some other way. Eventually."

"Doesn't look like you're going to get it with Gibson."

"I'll get him too. Assholes like the two of you always end up where they belong."

Stahl's rotund face turned the unhealthy shade of purple that so often colored his conversations with Sam. "You can have the last word. I've already gotten what I want today."

What the hell did that mean? "Good for you. Unlike those of you in the rat squad, I have real work to do, so if you don't mind…"

"Have a great day, Lieutenant." He left her with a creepy smile that made her crave a shower.

"Dick," she whispered. She'd suspected he'd had something to do with Peter's pending release. Now she was all but sure of it. Once she had a minute to call her own, she'd look into what role her nemesis had played.

Until then, she had a murdering rapist to catch. With that in mind, she printed out photos of the vice president, the speaker of the House, Senator Robert Cook and three other members of Congress who were not involved in the investigation. To ensure that her photo array held up in court, six was the magic number. She took the photos with her to the safe house where Freddie had stashed Selina.

On her way out, she ran into Freddie. "You're here early."

"Couldn't sleep."

Sam knew the feeling.

"I'm glad I caught you," he said. "Crime scene found something in Regina's stuff that you'll want to see." He produced a plastic bag with a Valentine card opened to the inside. In it, Regina had written the message in Spanish.

Freddie translated for her, "My darling Henry, how did I ever get so lucky to find you? I love you so much and I can't wait to meet our baby. Forever yours, Regina."

Sam thought of how despondent Henry had been upon hearing of Regina's involvement in the call girl ring. She was oddly relieved to know that Henry's entire life hadn't blown up in his face just so Regina might be able to stay in the country after her baby was born.

"What do you want me to do with it?" Freddie asked.

"Take it to him."

"Keep it as evidence?"

Sam shook her head. "I'm going to talk to Selina again. I'll catch up to you after."

"Sounds good."

At 5:20 in the morning, the city's streets were all but deserted, but Sam still kept a close eye on the rearview mirror to make sure she wasn't being followed by anyone other than the two officers in the unmarked sedan behind her—as if that wasn't a dead giveaway to anyone who might be watching her.

Outside the house, two officers stood watch. Even though she knew them, Sam still showed them her badge and gave them a moment to thoroughly study it, as they were required to do.

"Go ahead, Lieutenant."

"Thanks."

Sam found Selina on the sofa in the living room, curled up under a blanket nursing a cup of tea.

"You couldn't sleep either?" Selina asked.

"Someone tossed a Molotov cocktail through the window at my house last night. Do you know what that is?"

Eyes wide with fear, Selina nodded. "Was anyone hurt?"

Sam took a seat across from her. "Fortunately, my fiancé and I weren't home at the time."

"That's good."

"Do you know why I told you that?"

Selina shook her head.

"Because I want you to know that these people aren't above throwing fire into the home of a high-ranking police officer and a United States senator. Did I mention my fiancé is a senator?"

Selina swallowed hard and shook her head again.

Sam placed the six photos she'd brought on the coffee table. "Have you ever provided sexual services for any of these men?"

A tear rolled down Selina's cheek. Judging by the raw redness of her eyes, it wasn't the first she'd shed during that long night. "Him," she said, pointing to the speaker. A shudder rippled through her petite frame. "And him." Grimacing, she gestured to Cook.

"What about him?"

"No. I haven't had sex with the vice president of the United States."

"Well," Sam said. "That's a relief. The speaker of the House of Representatives and the senior senator from Virginia will be enough for one morning."

Selina gasped. "*Oh, my God!* I didn't know! *I didn't know who they were!*"

"I know that, Selina, and they knew it too. In fact, that's exactly why they recruited immigrant women." Sam heard the click of the final pieces fitting into place. "It was *because* you wouldn't recognize them. They were counting on that. Even though some of you worked on Capitol Hill, you probably didn't pay much attention to politics."

"What's going to happen to me?"

"I need you to testify."

"I can't do that! I can't have my family find out how I really got the money. I could never live with the shame of that."

"Could you live with another woman being murdered or raped because you didn't help me stop these bastards?"

Tears streamed down the young woman's face. "How can this be happening? I just wanted to save my mother... I didn't know what else to do."

"I can help you, Selina, but I need to know I can count on your testimony before I arrest Bartholomew." Sam paused to let her words sink in before she went for the jugular. "You'll have to pick him out of a lineup of men and then testify against him in court. You'll have to recount—in detail—what he did to you."

Hand to mouth to muffle her sobs, Selina shook her head.

"If you refuse to testify, Selina, my case against Bartholomew will hinge on whether he left any DNA on your clothing the night of the attack. And even if he did, the assistant U.S. attorney may refuse to prosecute without your testimony. That means he goes free to do this to someone else. He continues to get away with victimizing women while holding a lofty government job."

Selina's muffled sobs echoed through the silent room.

"I need you, Selina. Regina and Maria need you."

"*Regina can go to the devil!* This is all her fault."

"Maybe so, but she helped you find a way to pay for your mother's surgery. And trust me when I tell you that no one deserves what was done to her. No one."

Sam sat very still and let Selina think it through as she continued to weep bitterly.

"I went to college, you know? In Belize. I got a degree in business, and I came here hoping to make something of myself." She swiped at her face with the sleeve of her shirt. "But when I got here, it was so bad. No one would hire me because I wasn't a citizen or because they had someone better. I was lucky to get the job with the cleaning company."

"I'm sure you worked very hard," Sam said, trying to be patient.

"I worked until my hands ached and my fingers were blistered and sore. I worked overtime and weekends, but it wasn't enough. If only my mother hadn't gotten sick. None of this would be happening."

"My father was shot two years ago," Sam said. "He was a police officer doing a routine traffic stop and was shot by the driver. He's paralyzed and in a wheelchair. We still don't know who did it, and sometimes when I think that whoever shot him is out there going on with his or her life while he's stuck in that chair..." Sam's throat tightened with emotion. "I understand that you'd do anything you could for your mother. I get that."

"Even something illegal?"

"Whatever you had to do."

"Will I be charged?"

"I'll talk to the assistant U.S. attorney about immunity for you as soon as I leave here. But first I need to know if I can count on you to testify. That'll be her first question."

"How do I go into a public court and tell people what that animal did to me? How do I do that?"

"We'll get someone to help you through every step of the process. We have rape counselors specially trained to assist victims and prepare them for court. I'll get you all the help and support I have at my disposal."

"And how will you keep me alive long enough to testify?"

"Our entire case hinges on you. We'll take good care of you. You have my word on that."

After another endless stretch of silence, Sam leaned forward, elbows on knees. "Will you help me, Selina? Shall I go arrest Jack Bartholomew so he can pay for what he did to you and probably other women too?"

"Will the others come forward so your case doesn't hinge only on me?"

"We can hope for that, but in the meantime, it all comes down to you."

"If I testify, do you promise it won't be for nothing? He's a powerful man. I don't want to see him go free."

"I'll do everything in my power to make sure he gets what's coming to him." She thought of Peter being released from prison and remembered that even her powers had limits. "But I won't make you a promise I may not be able to keep. We'll do our very best. That's all I can do."

"Will you arrest the other men too? The speaker and the senator?"

"I don't know that yet, but we'll be pursuing charges against anyone who was involved with running the organization, anyone who provided the services and anyone who sought them out. If that includes the speaker and the senator, so be it."

Selina sat very still as she thought it over.

Sam's heart beat hard and fast. This was it. The whole thing hung on one tiny woman who was in way, *way* over her head.

"Since I need you to keep me alive as much as you need me to testify, I guess we both need each other."

"Yes, we do."

"Okay," Selina said, seeming resigned now to her fate. "I'll do it."

Sam reached over and clutched Selina's hand. "Thank you."

SAM FELT LIKE she'd expended a day's worth of energy on the half hour she'd spent with Selina. But she'd gotten what she needed, and that's what mattered. Before going to HQ to meet Freddie, she headed for the Washington Hospital Center. Even thought it was still early, she hoped to find Jeannie McBride awake.

Michael was coming out of Jeannie's room as Sam approached the door.

"How is she?" Sam asked.

"Seems a little better today. They're going to release her later on."

"That's good."

He shrugged.

"Are you okay?"

"She refuses to talk to me about what happened. I'm

trying not to push her, but it's just…it's hard. Not knowing…"

Sam rested a hand on his arm. "Try not to push. She'll tell you if and when she feels able to. Until then, you just have to be patient and supportive. That's what she needs from you right now."

"I know."

"Hang in there. It's only been a few days."

He nodded. "You're right. It's all about her and what she needs."

"Did she talk to the counselor?"

Shaking his head, he said, "Sent her away. Said she didn't need it."

Sam hated to hear that. "I hope she'll consider it at some point. You might want to, as well. Can't hurt anything."

"I'll think about it. She's awake if you want to go in. I'll give you a few minutes."

"Thanks." Sam pushed open the door to find Jeannie sitting up in bed. "Hey there. How're you feeling?"

"A little better. Did you see Michael?"

"In the hallway. He seems like a really nice guy, Jeannie."

"He is," she said, sighing. "He wants me to tell him what happened…"

"There's no rush. You don't have to talk about it until you feel ready."

"What if I never feel ready?"

"Well, you may have to testify…"

Jeannie shook her head, as if the very idea of it was too overwhelming to imagine.

"You're sure you won't consider talking to the counselor?"

"I'm sure. At least the HIV test came back negative—for now. I have to be tested again in three months."

"That's a huge relief."

"It's something. Right about now, I'll take it."

"I hate to ask you this, but do you feel up to looking at a few photos?"

Jeannie cast a wary glance at Sam. "Of what?"

"Possible suspects."

Jeannie gripped the blanket so tightly her knuckles turned white. "Do I have to?"

"I could really use your help. We have a pretty good case for rape against one of them, but I can't pin the murders on him. At least not yet."

"I only saw his eyes…"

"Then that's what I'll show you. Okay?"

Gritting her teeth, Jeannie nodded.

Sam took a moment to fold the six sheets of paper so just the eyes of the men were showing. And then she lined them up on the bed next to each other. "Take your time." She watched Jeannie force herself to look at the first one. And then her eyes darted across the array.

"No. None of them."

"You're sure?"

"I'll never forget those eyes. Ever."

"I appreciate you taking a look. I know it was hard for you."

"I know you'll need my help and my testimony. I just have to find a way to tell Michael first."

Sam reached for Jeannie's hand. "May I offer a suggestion?"

Jeannie nodded. "Of course."

"It seems to me that worrying about telling him is causing you grief that you hardly need on top of everything else. Maybe if you just tell him and get it over with, you'll have one less thing to worry about."

"That's not a *bad* suggestion."

Sam smiled at her. "Gee, thanks."

Jeannie thought about it for a moment. "I'm going to tell him and get it over with. Then I'll let him tell my mother. I *really* couldn't deal with that."

"It always helps to have a plan. Just remember he loves you—all he's thinking about is you and what you need."

Jeannie bit her lip and nodded. "He's been amazing." She blinked back tears. "He's hardly left my side since it happened."

"Where will you go when they release you?"

"His house has a security system, so I guess I'll go there even though it's in the same neighborhood where it…happened."

"The security system is a good idea—especially until we catch this guy." Sam checked her watch. "I'm sorry, but I have to run. We're arresting the chief of staff to the vice president this morning."

"Wow! Wish I could be there for that."

The spark of interest she saw in Jeannie's soft brown eyes reassured Sam. "You'll be back with us before you know it. Until then, focus on recovering from your injuries and anything that makes you feel better."

"I'll feel better when you find the guy who did this to me—and the others."

"I'll find him, and I'll make him pay."

"I'm counting on that."

Sam hugged her detective. "I'll check in with you tomorrow."

"Thanks. If you see Michael out there, will you tell him I need to talk to him?"

"Sure." Sam left the room and found Michael in the

waiting room at the end of the long hallway. “I think she might be ready to talk…”

He jumped to his feet. “Really?”

“I have to warn you…I’ve heard a lot of hideous crap in twelve years on this job, but what happened to her… it’s bad. You need to prepare yourself.”

A tick of tension pulsed in his tightly clenched jaw. “I appreciate the warning.”

“If either of you need me for anything, she has my number.”

“Thanks for everything.”

“No problem.”

TWENTY-NINE

SAM'S NEXT ORDER of business was a phone call to the U.S. Attorney's office as she drove back to HQ to meet Freddie.

"What've you got, Lieutenant?" asked Assistant U.S. Attorney Faith Miller.

Sam laid out her case against Jack Bartholomew. "I'll need a warrant for his DNA, which will hopefully be a match for DNA that may or may not be on the clothes Selina was wearing the night of the attack. But even without the DNA, she's willing to do a lineup and she'll testify. I'm hoping other victims will come forward after we arrest him. We've got him on rape and soliciting a prostitute."

Faith was silent for a long time. "Did she seek medical attention?"

Sam had been expecting that question. "She couldn't afford it. She sent all the money she made home to her family, but she took several days off of work after it happened. I can get the owner of the cleaning company to testify to that."

"She didn't tell anyone what had happened?"

"No."

Faith went silent again.

"Come on, Faith, you're killing me here! You know we've got enough."

"I don't want to see another case fall apart before we get to trial."

"That's a dig on Gibson, right?"

"Forrester isn't happy with how that case fell apart. He's warned us to be more careful in the future that all our ducks are in a row before we move forward."

"So where does that leave me with Bartholomew?"

"Call me when you hear from the lab. Until then, hold off."

"You gotta be kidding me—"

"Sam, I'm not budging on this. You're talking about the top aide to the vice president of the United States. I want an airtight case before you go near him."

"Fine. You want airtight, I'll get you airtight."

"Excellent. I'll be here when you're ready."

Sam ended the call and let out a growl of frustration. Opening the phone, she called the chief. His administrative assistant put her right through.

"Good morning, Lieutenant."

"I need your help with the lab." She explained the urgency of the situation to the chief. "Can you lean on them for me?"

"I'll do what I can."

"He's the key. I have a feeling if I can get him in here and lean hard on him I can get him to roll on the others. He won't want to go down alone. All I need to know from the lab right now is that there's male DNA on the clothes. We can test it against a sample from him after we have him in custody."

"I'll make the call. Where's your detail?"

Sam glanced in her rearview mirror. "Right up my ass where they belong."

"That sounds rather...uncomfortable."

"You said it."

Snorting with laughter, the chief hung up.

Now all she could do was wait—and hope the killer didn't strike again while they were waiting on the lab.

NICK AND CHRISTINA were in a meeting with other key campaign staff going over the next week's schedule when one of the administrative assistants interrupted them.

"I'm sorry to disturb you, Senator, but Judson Knott is here with Mitchell Sanborn."

Startled, Nick glanced at Christina.

Looking equally surprised, she shrugged.

"Send them in," Nick said. To the others in the room, he added, "Would you please excuse us for a moment?"

The staffers collected their belongings and passed Knott and Sanborn on their way out.

"Gentlemen." Nick shook hands with both men and invited them to sit across from him and Christina. "This is a nice surprise." The last time Nick had seen Sanborn, chairman of the Democratic National Committee, he'd mentioned the party's potential interest in Nick making a run for the White House in four years. Nick still had trouble believing he'd actually been part of that conversation. "What can I do for you?"

"We've been hearing some disturbing rumblings on the Hill," Sanborn said in his deep Kentuckian accent. The former governor of the Bluegrass state had sandy brown hair shot through with silver and intense dark eyes. "Things that have us quite…worried."

Pretending to be baffled, Nick glanced at Judson, the chair of the Virginia Democratic Committee. "What kind of rumblings?" he asked.

Sanborn's eyes narrowed. "That your girlfriend—"

"Fiancée," Nick said.

"My apologies," Sanborn said. "Your *fiancée* is investigating members of our own party for consorting with call girls. I don't have to tell you what that kind of scandal would do to the party, especially with the midterm elections just a few short months away."

Nick decided the best way to play this was the dumb way. "I'm afraid you gentlemen have me at a disadvantage. This is the first I'm hearing of it." In hindsight, he realized he should've expected this visit. If they'd had any idea who exactly Sam was targeting, they'd be too busy having apoplexies to be bothering him.

"Senator, I'd like to think we're all one big happy family in the Democratic Party," Sanborn said with a charming smiling lighting up his handsome face. "Wouldn't you?"

"I suppose."

"And a family takes care of one another, am I right?"

Not my family, Nick wanted to say but didn't. "Mitchell, why don't you save us all a lot of time and trouble and tell me what is you want from me?"

"Let's talk first about what I want *for* you, Senator, shall we? I believe you'll recall our last conversation in which I mentioned the very high aspirations the party has for you as our brightest new star."

Starting to get a feel for where this was heading, Nick said, "You'll recall that I told you I wasn't ready to have that particular conversation."

"Indeed. However, I'd like to think that when you *are* ready, your party will be standing by, willing to lend you the support and encouragement you would need."

"In exchange for what?"

Sanborn's face once again lost its amiable expression. "Tell your fiancée to back off."

"Wait a minute," Knott said, practically levitating out of his chair. "You never said you were going to say that to him!" To Nick, Knott added, "I didn't condone this.

He asked me to come with him to see you, but he never said he planned to do that!"

Nick put up a hand. "Easy does it, Judson. Let me make this real simple for all of us."

"That'd be preferred," Sanborn said.

"Get out of my office."

Sanborn sputtered, and his face turned very red. "You can't…I won't…"

Nick stood up to his full six-foot-four-inch height. "Get. The. Hell. Out. *Now.*"

Sanborn stood up slowly, smoothing his hands over his suit. "You're making yourself a powerful enemy, young man."

"That's *senator* to you, and by the time I'm through telling the party leadership what you came in here asking me to do, you won't have much power left, so enjoy it while it lasts."

"Judson," Sanborn said. "Let's go."

"You go on ahead. I'm not going anywhere with you."

Sanborn turned on his heel and stalked out of the room.

"There goes my chance to be president," Nick muttered with a chuckle intended to defuse the tension in the room.

"I'm so sorry, Senator," Judson said. "I had no idea…"

Nick rested a hand on the older man's shoulder. "Don't worry about it." Judson and the rest of the Virginia Democratic Party had been nothing but supportive of Nick and his staff since John O'Connor's sudden death turned their lives upside down.

"If he had told me what he planned to do," Judson said, "I would've told him it was a waste of time."

"What did he tell you he wanted with me?"

"To talk about the campaign and check in with you."

"Well, he checked in."

"And checked out," Christina said.

"They must be really scared," Nick said as another thought occurred to him. He drew his new BlackBerry from his pocket. "Would you mind giving me a minute?"

"Of course, Senator," Judson said. He and Christina quietly left the room, closing the door behind them.

The moment he was alone, Nick dialed Sam's number. "Hey, babe."

"Hey."

"What's wrong?"

"How can you tell something is wrong with one word?"

"Because I know you."

"The AUSA won't let me go after Bartholomew until we have more than Selina's testimony. I'm waiting on the freaking lab, and it's taking them *all* goddamned day! Tell me things are going better over there."

"They were going well until a few minutes ago." He told her about Sanborn's visit and how infuriated the party chairman had been by Nick's refusal to interfere with the investigation.

"And you just handed me a new suspect."

"That's what I was thinking too."

"Have I mentioned lately that I love you?"

He smiled. "I'll take it whenever I can get it."

"I'm sorry you were put in that position."

"It's certainly not your fault."

"I told you so," she said.

"What did you tell me?"

"That my shit was going to bang up against your shit and cause you trouble."

"I *love* when your shit bangs up against my shit."

"That's so gross. I'm trying to be serious here."

"And I'm trying to say that I don't *care* if your shit bangs up against my shit. I'm doing the best possible job I can for the people of Virginia. If Election Day comes and they're not happy with me, so be it. I refuse to let this job take over my entire life."

"You're very evolved. How did you get so evolved?"

"Thanks to you and the murders of two of my good friends, I've figured out what really matters in life, and I absolutely refuse to let people like Sanborn think I'm for sale."

"I'm seriously turned on right now."

Nick laughed. "For all the good that does me."

"Luckily for you, it'll keep until I see you."

"Mmm, can't wait."

"Thanks for the new lead and for standing up to Sanborn. For what it's worth, I'm proud of you."

"It's worth a lot," he said. "It's worth everything."

"I'll see you when I see you."

For a moment, he debated telling her about the ramp at the house but then decided he'd rather it be a surprise. "Be careful with my fiancée. I love her more than life itself."

"Nick...You make me all fluttery. No one has *ever* made me fluttery. How do you do that?"

Ridiculously pleased, he smiled. "What can I say? It's magic. Take care, babe."

WHILE SHE WAITED for the results from the lab, Sam did a run on Mitchell Sanborn. As his photo popped up on the screen, her skin tingled with goose bumps. Those eyes... Remembering Jeannie's description of her attacker's eyes, Sam sat riveted, staring at the screen. She read through his impressive biography, which detailed his Ivy League education and meteoric rise through the ranks of the Democratic Party. But she kept returning to that photo and those eyes…

She printed it—along with five other random men—and grabbed her radio. "Cruz!"

He popped up in his cubicle, a dollop of cream clinging to his bottom lip. "Right here, boss."

"Let's go."

Grabbing his trench coat, Freddie scrambled after her. "Where to?"

"First to see Jeannie and then, hopefully, to start arresting evil bastards."

"Oh, I *love* when we get to arrest evil bastards!"

"Will you please finish that donut so I don't have to smell it?"

"Want some?"

"Yes, but my ass is growing at such an alarming rate that my wedding dress will have to be sewn by a tentmaker rather than Vera Wang. Keep it away from me."

"Your ass is not that big. Not that I've looked or anything…"

Sam shot him her most withering look.

He swallowed the last bite of donut. "Is Vera Wang really making your dress? Even I've heard of her."

"Apparently so. That reminds me…" Reaching for her phone, she texted Shelby and her sisters, moving the evening's appointment to her father's house since hers was fire damaged at the moment.

"Everything okay with Nick? I assume he eventually showed up last night."

"Yeah. He's kind of a mess after seeing his deadbeat mother this week. She shook him down for twenty-five grand."

Freddie released a low whistle. "Poor guy. He's had enough lately."

"I couldn't agree more. What about you? All ready for tonight?"

His mood changed in an instant. "I guess."

"Any word from Elin?"

Dejected, he shook his head. "Not since I told her to show up tonight or else."

"Are you regretting the ultimatum?"

"Kind of. I like her. I don't want it to be over."

"You don't think she's going to show?"

"No."

"Maybe you're not giving her enough credit."

He shrugged. "Why should she have to put up with the cold shoulder from my mother? She can have any guy she wants."

"Seems to me she wants you."

"I guess we'll see, won't we?"

Over the top of her car, Sam said, "There're a lot of women out there, Freddie. If things don't work out with this one, there are plenty of other fish in the sea."

"Took me twenty-nine years to reel this one in. I'm not ready to throw her back yet."

Inside the car, Sam started it and gave it a minute to warm up. Her cell phone rang, and she took the call from Captain Malone.

"Tell me you've got news from the lab," Sam said.

"We'll get to that. But first I wanted to let you know that Peter Gibson was just released from custody."

Sam had known it was coming but hearing confirmation sent her stomach into a tailspin. Resting a hand over her churning belly, she said, "Okay."

"I'm sorry, Sam."

"Not your fault." A knot of fear settled in her throat, threatening her legendary composure. "What've you heard from the lab?"

"Semen was found on the clothing."

"Thank you, Jesus."

"You're to tread lightly with Bartholomew until we know the DNA is his."

"We know it's his."

"We know that a call girl told us it was. Until the *lab* tells us, you're to consider him a person of interest not a suspect. That's right from Farnsworth and Forrester."

"Semantics," she said, scoffing. "Did you get me the warrant for his DNA?"

"Signed, sealed and delivered."

"Cruz and I are heading out now. I need to see McBride for a moment, and then we'll track down Mr. Bartholomew."

"What're you up to with McBride?"

"Not sure yet. Could be something, could be nothing."

"Let me know if it's something."

"I will."

"Where's your tail?"

Realizing she had once again forgotten all about the two police officers following her, she glanced in the mirror. "Right where they belong."

"Excellent. Keep me posted."

Closing the phone and dropping it into her pocket, she took a moment to absorb the news that Peter Gibson was once again walking the streets. Sam gripped the wheel but didn't put the car into Drive.

"Gibson?" Freddie asked.

She nodded.

He let out a curse that was so wildly out of character for him that Sam couldn't help but laugh.

"He'll screw up again, and when he does, we'll be ready," Freddie vowed.

"I have no doubt."

"I'm sorry, Sam."

"Not your fault. We all screwed this up, and now we have to live with it. The best thing we can do now is to get justice for our current victims. They're counting on us."

"I admire the way you're rolling with it."

"What choice do I have?"

"None I suppose."

"I had a somewhat major revelation while talking to Selina Rameriz this morning," Sam said to Freddie as they pulled out of the HQ lot.

"And that was?"

"The reason they recruited immigrant women for the call girl ring—so they wouldn't recognize the schmucks paying for their services. Sure, they might recognize the president and vice president, but how many Americans can pick out the speaker of the House let alone one of the senators from Virginia?"

"Well, everyone in America would know Nick."

"Luckily, he has no need for call girls," Sam said dryly.

"Cook is a pretty big name in American politics."

"People new to the country wouldn't recognize it."

"True."

"So it's rather brilliant of them to recruit beautiful young immigrant women who'd have no idea who they were servicing," Sam said.

"And who wouldn't raise much suspicion if they suddenly turned up dead."

"The person who killed them certainly wasn't counting on a senator being in love with one of them."

"He also wasn't counting on us," Freddie said. "They probably thought the MPD wouldn't care much about a couple of dead cleaning ladies."

"They thought wrong."

"You bet your ass they did."

"Such language, Lieutenant," he said, frowning.

Sam gave him the finger.

"I'm offended."

"You'll survive."

"What're we seeing McBride about?"

"I have a picture I want to show her. Just a hunch."

"Your hunches are usually spot-on."

"If this one is, we've got our killer."

THIRTY

JUDGING BY JEANNIE'S visceral and almost violent reaction to one of the six photos Sam showed her, they'd found their man.

As she pushed the picture away, Jeannie began to sob.

Michael, whose haggard face and red eyes told the story of how he'd taken the news about the rape, crawled right into the bed with her and wrapped his arms around her.

"Who is he?" Jeannie whispered.

Sam folded the photo and jammed it into her coat pocket. "Mitchell Sanborn, chairman of the Democratic National Committee."

"Oh God, it'll be all over the news."

"Yes."

"Will you arrest him right away?"

"I'm going for him as soon as I leave here." Sam hesitated but only for a second before she reached for Jeannie's hand. "If there's anyone who should hear about what happened from you, the time to tell them is now."

"My mother," Jeannie said, turning frantic eyes on Michael. "My family."

"It's okay, honey," Michael said. "I called your mom. She's bringing your sister over. I'll talk to them."

"It's not enough that this had to happen, but now it'll be blasted all over the news too," Jeannie said as her tears turned to anger.

"We'll get you through this," Sam said, gripping Jeannie's hand. "I had an idea, and it might not seem to make any sense..."

"What idea?" Jeannie asked.

"Remember when *The Reporter* was getting ready to publish the story about my near-abortion years ago?"

Jeannie nodded.

"Nick encouraged me to get ahead of the story—to tell it my way before they could tell the incorrect version."

"You're not suggesting I actually talk to the media..."

"I'm saying you might want to consider talking to *one* reporter, and tell him you're all right, you survived, you're on the mend. Show him—and the rest of the world—that this guy didn't ruin you."

"I'm still not sure he didn't."

"People don't need to know that."

"If I did this, wouldn't it hurt the case?"

"Only if you gave away things that only you and he would know. I'm suggesting a very high-level interview that puts the story in your words but doesn't jeopardize the case. You know what you can say and what you can't."

Jeannie glanced at Michael. "What do you think?"

"It's entirely up to you, of course, but I agree with Sam that it's worth considering."

"I can't imagine telling a stranger..." Her voice faded to a whisper, and her eyes filled with new tears.

"Exposing your personal pain to strangers is difficult," Sam said. "But Nick was right in my case. Once we put out the statement, the lies *The Reporter* printed lost some of their power over me. I don't think I would've gotten through that episode as well as I did if I hadn't gotten the chance to tell the story my way."

"Do you know someone? A reporter I could talk to?"

"I have just the guy. He'll do right by you. Darren

Tabor from the *Star*. He did the joint interview with Nick and me."

"I loved that interview. He did a beautiful job."

"It was okay," Sam said begrudgingly. Talking to reporters about her personal life would never sit well with her, but she'd done it for Nick and his campaign.

"Would you be there with me?" Jeannie asked Michael.

"Always. For as long as you need me, I'm right here."

Jeannie sent him a small but grateful smile and tightened her hold on his hand. "Okay," she said. "I'll do it."

"I'll make the call and have Darren meet you at Michael's house later this afternoon. That way you'll have time to get home and settled first."

"Thank you, Sam. I feel better just knowing who did this and that you're going to get him."

"I'm going to nail his ass to the wall," Sam vowed. "For you and the others."

"I'm counting on that."

GONZO AWOKE AND sat up quickly, his heart racing. Alex had been crying relentlessly for hours. Finally, the baby had worn himself out and drifted into restless sleep a little over an hour ago. Gonzo and Christina had fallen into bed to sleep while they could. Through the baby monitor Gonzo could hear the little coos the baby made in his sleep, and was reassured. Sam's sisters had told him the panic receded eventually. He certainly hoped so. Living in a perpetual state of terror was draining, to say the least.

Gonzo glanced over at Christina. He wanted so badly to kiss her, but he hated to disturb her after she'd been up most of the night helping with the baby. He shifted onto his side, put an arm around her and drew her in closer to him. As much as he loved having the baby in his life, he missed the uninterrupted time with her.

She murmured in her sleep, and he kissed the top of her head, breathing in the sweet fragrance of her hair.

"Tommy," she whispered.

"Hmm?"

"Why aren't you sleeping?"

"I woke up and couldn't hear him. I got worried."

"He's fine. You're fine. We're all fine."

"Are we?"

She looked up at him, smiling. "Of course we are.

"I love you so much, Christina. I spent my whole life trying to avoid this kind of committed relationship. Now that I have it, I can't imagine why I was so eager to avoid it. And I'm not just saying that because you're helping me with the baby."

"I know." She caressed his face. "I love you too. I can't believe how fast everything happened and how content I feel."

He curled his hand around her neck and pressed his lips to hers. Sinking into the kiss, Gonzo's heart beat harder as he understood with a clarity he'd never experienced quite so vividly before that she was *it* for him—the one he'd been waiting for without even knowing he'd been waiting.

Shifting on top of her, he reveled in the feel of her soft skin.

Her hands moved on his back, soothing and arousing. She raised her hips in invitation, and he entered her in one swift stroke. No other woman had ever affected him the way she did. When they were first together, he'd expected to grow tired of her the way he had all the others. But the more time he spent with her, the more he wanted her. He was beginning to realize he would never get enough. That was certainly unprecedented.

Resting on his elbows, he brushed the hair back from her face and touched his lips to hers. "So beautiful. Such a lady."

"Not always," she said with a coy grin. Her hands cruised down his back to grip his ass, tearing a groan from deep inside him.

She triggered something primal in him, something possessive and altogether new as he made fierce love to her.

Afterward, he rested carefully on top of her, worried as always about how much bigger than her he was. Her fingers sifted through his hair as she ran her foot up and down his leg.

Gonzo breathed her in, wanting her again, wanting her forever. "Marry me," he said. The words were out of his mouth before he had a second to consider the implications.

She gasped. "Tommy..."

"I'm sorry. I didn't mean to just blurt that out. I don't have a ring, and a classy woman like you deserves a romantic proposal..." At the sight of her tears and the sound of her laughter, he stopped. "What?"

"If you don't stop talking you'll ruin the most romantic moment of my life."

She staggered him. "Yeah?"

Nodding, she reached for him and brought him down for a kiss that made his head spin.

"Let me try this again...Christina Billings, I love you. Will you please marry me?"

"Yes," she said, laughing through her tears. "Yes, I'll marry you, Tommy Gonzales."

"I'll get you a ring. As soon as I can."

"I don't need one." She hugged him tight against her. "I have everything I need right here."

Alex chose that moment to let out a lusty wail.

"And then some," Christina whispered, smiling as she kissed him.

SAM AND FREDDIE sat in the car outside the headquarters of the Democratic National Committee on South Capitol Street.

"How's this gonna go?" Freddie asked.

"We're going in there and arresting Sanborn for Jeannie's kidnapping and rape. Once we get him to HQ, we'll hammer him on the rest."

"What about Bartholomew?"

"He's next."

"Isn't that Sanborn over there?" Freddie pointed to where two men were having a heated discussion.

"It is! And that's Daniels with him," she said, referring to the speaker of the House. "He was third on my list. Gee, wonder what they're fighting about."

"How about we go see?"

They emerged from the car, and with Sam's detail following them, made their way toward the two men who never saw them coming until they were nearly upon them.

Sanborn looked up, saw Sam and blanched. Then he took off running. Daniels bolted in the other direction. "Get him," she called to Freddie as she took off after Sanborn. "One of you go with him," she said to her two-officer detail. To the cop who followed her she said, "Stay out of this and leave it to me."

"Yes, ma'am."

Sanborn ran down South Capitol Street, darting in and around pedestrians. Sam's legs and lungs burned with exertion, but when she thought about what this monster had done to Jeannie, a new burst of adrenaline brought her within an arm's length of her prey. Worried about him managing to slip through her fingers, she sprung at him from behind and took him down hard on the pavement. The impact briefly knocked the wind out of both of them. As she struggled to cuff him, he fought her off, and his elbow caught her hard in the abdomen.

"Let me go, you fucking bitch. You have no idea who you're screwing with."

The shot to her gut had left her seeing stars and fighting for every breath. "I know exactly who I'm screwing with—and your days of raping and murdering women are over."

"You've got the wrong guy, and I'll have your job for this."

"We'll let the DNA tell the story."

That seemed to shut him up. Choking back a surge of nausea, she pressed her knee to his back and managed to get the cuffs on him. She left him lying facedown on the sidewalk and stood to call for backup. A sharp pain in her belly had her bending in half, hands on knees as she tried to breathe through it the way she used to do before she gave up the soda that had caused crippling stomachaches. This pain, however, felt different…

"Are you okay, Lieutenant?" her detail officer asked.

"Fine. Just need a minute."

"That was an awesome tackle."

"Thanks." A second, sharper pain ripped through her when she tried to stand up. Son of a bitch…When she tried to stand up straight another pain ripped through her.

"You don't look too good, Lieutenant."

"I'm okay," Sam managed to say.

Within minutes the street was swarming with MPD

officers and cars. Sam ordered that Sanborn be taken to HQ and held in an interrogation room until she arrived.

"I think Lieutenant Holland needs medical attention," the young detail officer said.

Sam looked daggers at him. "I do *not.* I told you I'm fine."

"You don't look fine."

Sam stalked off in the direction of where they'd parked, hoping Freddie had managed to grab Daniels. She was aware of the young officer scurrying after her, but all her focus remained on breathing her way through the pains that continued to come fast and furious.

Of course she recognized the pains for what they were. After all, she'd been through this three times before. This time, though… This time… If she allowed herself to acknowledge what was happening, she'd never be able to finish the job on behalf of Regina, Maria and Jeannie. So she kept breathing, kept walking, kept functioning when inside her heart was shattering.

Outside the DNC building, Freddie jogged up to her. "Did you get him?"

"Yep. You?"

"In custody and on the way to HQ."

"Let's go pick up Bartholomew."

"Are you okay?" he asked, following her to the car.

"Fine."

"Then why are you pale as a ghost, sweating and breathing funny?"

"Took an elbow to the gut. Hurt."

"Maybe we should hit the ER."

She dug out her phone to update Malone. "The only place we're hitting is the vice president's office and then HQ to nail these bastards."

"With you, boss."

SAM AND FREDDIE had to surrender their firearms to get through security at the Eisenhower Executive Office Building, located adjacent to the White House. Being without her weapon always made her twitchy, but when added to the growing discomfort in her abdomen, she was downright anxious.

They were escorted to the vice president's suite where they were told that Mr. Bartholomew was in a meeting.

Sam and Freddie exchanged glances.

She leaned on the reception desk to bring her face down close to the nervous-looking man. "Go get him," she said in her lowest, most sinister tone.

The young man scooted back from his desk and disappeared into the office.

Another sharp pain stole Sam's breath.

"Sam..."

"It's nothing."

"It's not nothing."

"Um," the receptionist said when he returned, "right this way."

Sam and Freddie followed him to a large office that was filled with pictures and political memorabilia—yet another shrine to a long, successful career.

Bartholomew stood as they entered the room. He was tall, heavy and bald. Sam tried to imagine poor Selina Rameriz trying to fight him off. She'd never stood a chance.

"What can I do for you?"

"Jack Bartholomew?" Freddie asked.

"Yes."

Freddie flashed his badge. "We need you to accompany us to MPD Headquarters for a conversation about Selina Rameriz."

"*Who?*"

"The call girl you raped and sodomized?" Sam said. "Remember her?"

Bartholomew blanched. "I did no such thing! I don't know what you're talking about!"

"You know *exactly* what I'm talking about."

"You've got the wrong guy!"

Sam had to laugh at how they all said that. "If that's the case, then you won't mind coming with us, giving us a sample of your DNA and clearing this whole thing up. Will you?"

At that, a bead of sweat appeared on his forehead.

Sam nodded to her partner.

Freddie approached the other man and recited the Miranda warning.

"This is an outrage!" Bartholomew said as he resisted Freddie's attempts to cuff him.

"What's going on in here?" another voice asked from the doorway.

Sam turned to find the vice president himself watching the proceedings.

"Mr. Bartholomew is a person of interest in an aggravated sexual assault case," Sam said.

Gooding's mouth fell open for a second before he quickly recovered his composure.

"Mr. Vice President," Bartholomew said. "You have to believe me. I swear to God. I didn't do this."

"You shouldn't swear to God," Freddie said. "You'll go to hell."

Gooding studied his aide, but his expression remained unreadable. Handsome with snow-white hair and piercing blue eyes, Gooding was taller than he appeared on TV.

"Bill," Bartholomew said, pleading as Freddie directed him to the door. "Help me. Please."

As Freddie took Bartholomew out, Sam hung back.

"If I may say so, sir, you don't seem as shocked as I'd expect you to be after seeing your top aide arrested for aggravated sexual assault."

Gooding finally blinked. "Of course I'm shocked. I've known Jack Bartholomew for twenty-five years."

"And never had any reason to believe he was capable of attacking women?"

"Absolutely not," he said, but Sam noted that his words lacked the conviction she'd expect from someone who'd just watched a close colleague be arrested. "Is this going to be on the news?"

"That the vice president's chief of staff is a person of interest in a rape? That he and other high-level government officials ran and patronized a call girl ring that was Washington's best-kept secret? I'd guess it'll probably make the news."

At that, Gooding finally looked a bit concerned. "I have things…I need to do."

Sam gestured for him to go on ahead. The moment she was alone, she grasped the back of a chair and held on through another sharp pain. As soon as she was able to she left Bartholomew's office and ducked into the first ladies' room she found in the vast office building.

Inside the stall, her hands shook as she unzipped her jeans. "Oh my God," she whispered at the sight of blood—a lot of blood. "No, no, *no*…" She pulled herself together enough to purchase a couple of pads from the vending machine on the wall. Her hands shook as she tried to clean herself up and deal with the pads.

Sweating and nauseous, she closed her eyes and gave herself a moment—just one moment to absorb the shock and pain. Her ringing phone ended the moment. Fumbling with the phone, she flipped it open and then dropped it on the floor. It skidded out of her reach. She managed to button her jeans and leave the stall to retrieve her phone.

"Yeah?" she said, breathing through the cramps.

"Sam?" Freddie said. "I've been waiting down here for twenty minutes. What the hell is taking so long?"

Twenty minutes? "Sorry."

"Did Gooding hassle you?"

"What? No."

"Then what's taking so long?"

"Nothing. I'm coming."

"You okay?"

"Yeah." Sam ended the call and scrolled through her contacts, looking for the number Harry had programmed into her phone. She wanted to call Nick. She *needed* to call Nick. But she had to close the case before she could allow herself to fall apart. If she heard his voice, she'd fall apart.

"This is Sam Holland," she said when Harry answered.

"Hey, Sam. What's up?"

"I'm sorry to bother you on your day off, but I, um…I think I might be miscarrying."

"Oh, no. What's going on?"

"I took a hard hit to the belly, and the cramps started almost right away. Now I'm bleeding too."

"Is it more than a regular period?"

Swallowing the hard lump of emotion that had formed in her throat, she said, "Yeah."

"Can you get yourself to an E.R.? I could meet you."

"I'm about two hours from closing a big case. I'm just wondering…" Her eyes burned with tears. "If I went to the E.R. right now, they wouldn't be able to stop it or anything, would they?"

"How far apart are the cramps?"

"Every minute or so."

Harry sighed. "That coupled with the bleeding…I doubt it could be stopped. I'm sorry, Sam."

"S'okay. Not like I haven't been down this road before."

"I know you might not be able to see it as such right now, but this is actually very good news."

"How in the hell is this good news?"

"It proves you *can* get pregnant."

"That's not good news if it's going to end like this every time."

"It may not. You took a hard hit. The follicle was probably not fully attached to the uterine wall yet, so it didn't take much to dislodge it."

"This is the shit that happens in my job. I take hard hits. You can't exactly wrap me in foam for nine months and expect me to do my job."

"Wanna bet?"

"Listen—"

"Call me when you get home, and I'll bring Maggie over to take a look at you."

"Is she the girlfriend?"

"Yep. She's slipping me a note right now that says until she can see you, if you feel faint or nauseous, the pain becomes sharp and/or constant, or the bleeding becomes profuse get to an E.R. right away. Otherwise, it should be like a bad period with cramps and bleeding. Okay?"

"Yeah."

"I'm sorry this is happening to you again."

"So am I. Thanks for the help."

"Anytime."

She closed the phone and put it in her coat pocket, determined to close this case before she had her fourth miscarriage.

THIRTY-ONE

SAM TURNED THE keys over to Freddie.

"You're sure you're okay, boss?"

"Just drive."

"I sent Bartholomew with patrol. He'll be waiting for us in interrogation. I also called Faith Miller and asked her to meet us there."

"Good. Thanks."

"What did the vice president say?"

Sam put her head back against the seat and fought off the array of emotions storming around inside of her. So much to absorb and no time to do it. "He was concerned about the media catching wind of his chief of staff's arrest."

"Always a politician." Freddie navigated the car through rush hour traffic. "So what's the plan for when we go at them?"

"We'll let them stew for a bit and then tell each one that the others rolled on him."

Freddie nodded. "I like it. None of them will want to go down alone."

"That's the idea."

After a long moment of silence, he took his eyes off the road to look over at her. "I get that you don't want to tell me what's wrong, but I can see you're upset. You have to be thinking about Peter..."

"Yeah." Sam watched the blur of lights and buildings. When tears threatened, she quickly closed her eyes and fought them off. Once she started, she might never stop. "Hard to believe he's out there somewhere."

"He won't be for long."

"I hope you're right." When they arrived at HQ, she went straight to her office where she downed three of the pain pills she kept in her top drawer for emergencies. This certainly counted. "Let's get this sewed up," she said when she rejoined Freddie in the pit. "You've got somewhere to be."

"I'm here 'til we're done. My plans will keep."

Captain Malone and Chief Farnsworth joined them.

"Lieutenant," the chief said. "You've got some high-profile guests taking up space in my interrogation rooms."

"Yes, sir."

Farnsworth tipped his head as he studied her. "What's wrong with you?"

"Nothing." To Malone she said, "Did you get DNA samples?"

"On their way to the lab as we speak."

"Good."

Assistant U.S. Attorney Faith Miller entered the pit. "What've you got?" she asked Sam. The Miller triplets were three of the most stunning women Sam had ever met. They had soft brown hair that each sister wore in a different style, green eyes and figures more often seen on supermodels than lawyers.

"Sanborn is the kingpin," Sam said. "McBride identified him as her attacker. I believe the DNA will also show him to be responsible for the murders of Regina Argueta de Castro and Maria Espanosa. I want to use Daniels and Bartholomew to set up Sanborn. Immunity for both of them on the call girl ring, but if the DNA on Selina Rameriz's clothes matches Bartholomew's, I'll charge him with aggravated sexual assault. Selina worked with Jackson on a composite sketch that's a perfect match for Bartholomew. I can also get her employer to testify that she was out of work for several days after the attack and that she'd never missed a day of work before then. I can get her coworkers to testify to the bruises on her face and arms."

"We've also got several people who attended the gala at the Reagan Building who will testify that they saw Bartholomew with Selina that night," Freddie said. "And we've got videotape showing them there together."

Faith nodded. "With the DNA, that's enough to charge him."

"The lab is rushing the results through," Farnsworth said.

"Glad something can get them to rush," Sam muttered.

"What've you got on Daniels?" Faith asked.

"Involvement in the call girl ring as well as solicitation and prostitution. If I can offer him immunity, I might be able to get him to tell me what he knows. From what I know about him, losing his political career will be significant punishment."

Faith nodded in agreement. "Do it." She zeroed in on Sam. "Are you feeling all right?"

"Cramps," Sam whispered so the men wouldn't hear.

"Ouch."

Gesturing to Freddie, Sam headed toward the interrogation rooms. "Let's talk to Daniels first." On the way, she stopped to remove several photos from her murder board.

When they entered the room, the speaker of the House of Representatives leaped to his feet. "I don't know why I'm here. What did I do?"

"Mr. Speaker, I need to remind you that you have the

right to remain silent." Sam reviewed the Miranda warning and received his permission to record the interview. Freddie remained by the door. "Do you understand your rights in this matter?"

"I haven't done anything! I don't know what 'matter' you're referring to!"

"If you didn't do anything, why'd you bolt when you saw us coming earlier?" Sam asked.

"Because Sanborn did. I didn't know what was going on."

"Pardon me if I find that hard to believe." Sam put Selina Rameriz's photo down on the table.

Daniels, who was short and stocky with dark hair and the starting of jowls, went perfectly still as he stared at the picture.

"Know her, Mr. Speaker?"

"I've never seen her before in my life."

"Would you be willing to take a polygraph to confirm that?"

Daniels tore his eyes off the photo and began to pace. "You don't understand…"

Sam pulled a chair out from the table and lowered herself gingerly. "What don't I understand?"

"It was one time."

Sam laughed. "Sure it was. If I ask Ms. Rameriz, will she corroborate your story?

"Maybe it was twice, but the point is, it wasn't any big deal."

"It's against the law," Sam reminded him. "Especially when you start killing the women to keep them quiet."

Daniels stopped pacing and turned to her. "*Killing?* I've never killed anyone! Give me a polygraph on that."

Sam shrugged. "Funny, that's not what Sanborn said. He claims the whole thing was your idea."

Daniel's complexion got very red. "That son of a bitch. He's lying! If anyone was pulling the strings, it was him!"

Sam leaned forward, elbows on the table. "I want to know what you know about the call girl ring, and I want it now. If the information you give me is credible, I may speak to the AUSA about immunity for you."

"I'd have to testify against the others?"

"Yes." Sam watched him absorb the fact that his political career was probably over.

His face twisted into an ugly snarl. "How can you do this to people in your future husband's own party?"

Sam laughed. "You think I care about that? You think *he* cares about that? We both want justice for the two women who were murdered by one of you. *That's* what we care about."

"He won't have much of a career if he doesn't learn how to manage his woman," Daniels said.

Sam treated him to her most intimidating cop stare. "Keep up that crap and the deal's off the table." She glanced at her watch. "You've got one minute. Do we have a deal?"

"I want to talk to my lawyer."

Ignoring the cramps seizing her midsection, Sam stood. "Then no deal. I need the information, and I need it now. Your choice."

As he stood with his hands on his hips pondering his limited options, Sam watched the starch go out of his spine. "It was all Sanborn's idea."

"What was?"

"A service...For us, by us. Our jobs are stressful, and we needed a way to let off steam and relax. We figured if we had control then we could determine who was allowed to patronize it and keep it secret. We could choose the women..."

"Immigrants who wouldn't recognize most of you."

Daniels sighed and dropped into a chair. "Yes."

"How long has the organization been in business?"

"Twelve years."

Sam couldn't believe they'd never caught wind of it in all that time. "So why did Regina and Maria have to die?"

"I honestly don't know. I had nothing to do with that. I swear to God."

"But you know who did."

"I have my suspicions."

"Is that what you were arguing with Sanborn about?"

"I wanted him to tell me what he knew about it and why there were cops sniffing around the Hill. I also wanted to know what he knew about the police officer who was kidnapped."

"What did he say?"

"He told me it was none of my business and that I needed to keep my mouth shut and stay out of it."

"How did it work? The service?"

"We hired a woman. She works out of her home and manages the administrative aspects."

"Who else besides yourself and Sanborn are behind the organization?"

"Bartholomew and Cook." Sam couldn't wait to arrest that bastard Cook. "We wouldn't even be here right now if Cook hadn't gotten greedy and pushed us to open the service up to anyone who called. We told him it was a mistake. The more people who knew..."

"What's Gooding's involvement?" she asked, referring to the vice president.

"Nothing that I know of, but he and Bartholomew are tight. I wouldn't be surprised if he knows the ring exists, but I don't think he's ever been a patron."

"You don't know for sure."

"No. The only person who knows all the who, what, when, where and how is the woman who runs the organization."

Sam pushed a pad and pen across the table. "Her name and address."

"She's an innocent party—a wife and mother just trying to make a living."

"Running a call girl ring for pampered politicians? Hardly innocent."

Daniels put down the pen. "Tell me you'll protect her, or I'm not giving you her name."

"Give me her name or our deal is off."

"I gave you what you asked for!"

"I told you the deal was only good if you were entirely forthcoming."

Daniels glared at her.

Sam glared back.

He grabbed the pen and wrote the name and address and shoved the pad back at her.

"That wasn't so hard, now was it?" Sam eased herself up. "Sit tight. I'll be back."

"When? I need to get out of here before my wife hears about this."

"It's probably safe to assume she already knows," Sam said.

Moaning, he dropped his head to folded arms.

Malone was waiting for her and Freddie outside the interrogation room.

"Anything from the lab yet?" Sam asked.

He shook his head. "They said it would be tomorrow at the earliest.

"Goddamn it."

"Lieutenant," Freddie said, frowning at her language.

"It occurred to me that your suspects don't know how

long it takes to get DNA results," Malone said. He handed her two sheets of official-looking paper.

Sam studied them and smirked. "Traffic tribunal, huh?"

"Put them in this." He produced a manila folder. "That makes it *very* official. They know it's their DNA, so why wait for the lab to confirm it when they can do it for us?"

"I like the way you think, Captain."

"I still have a few working brain cells after riding the desk all these years."

"This is just what I needed to nail those bastards."

"What's the plan?"

"Bartholomew first and then Sanborn. Depending on how it goes with Bartholomew, I might need you to have someone bring Selina over here for a lineup of fat, balding middle-aged guys. Her ID will put a bow on top of the aggravated sexual assault charge. Can you set that up if I can't get him to roll?"

"Absolutely. Let's wrap this up, people."

If only she didn't feel so shitty, Sam would be salivating in anticipation of toppling two powerful scumbags from their lofty pedestals.

"You sure you're all right, Holland?" Malone asked.

"Girl trouble," she said, knowing he'd drop it once he heard that.

He cleared his throat. "Um, very well then. Carry on."

"I UNDERSTAND YOU'VE been running a call girl ring in Washington for twelve years," Sam said without preamble. She'd witnessed Freddie reading Bartholomew his rights earlier, so she didn't repeat the Miranda warning.

Bartholomew attempted to surge to his feet, but with his girth, the surge was more like a lumber. "Who the hell told you that?"

"Doesn't matter. Is it true?"

"It most certainly is not. I had nothing to do with any call girls. I work for the vice president of the United States. Why would I jeopardize my position, my career, my *reputation* to dally with call girls?"

"That's a very good question. Isn't it, Detective Cruz?"

"Indeed," Freddie said. "Personally, I think it's all about money—and the sex, of course."

"I've never had sex with a call girl," Bartholomew huffed. "I don't need to pay for it."

Sam took a long measuring look at the unattractive man. "If you say so." She produced the folder she'd kept behind her back. "You're sure you've never met Selina Rameriz?"

He eyed the folder warily. "Positive."

"Then how do you explain the fact that you were seen with her at a gala on January 18 at the Ronald Reagan Building?" She turned to Freddie. "Detective Cruz, do you have several witnesses prepared to testify that Mr. Bartholomew accompanied Ms. Rameriz to the gala?"

"I do," Freddie said. "We've also obtained the security videotape from the Reagan Building where you're seen with her at the event."

Sam directed her gaze from Freddie back to Bartholomew. "Still certain you've never met her?"

"So I hired her to go to a party with me. That doesn't make me a rapist."

Sam withdrew one of the traffic tribunal forms. "No, but your semen on her clothes sure does."

Watching his face drain of color was among one of the more satisfying moments in Sam's career.

"That can't be right," he stammered.

"The beautiful thing about DNA is that, unlike people, it never lies."

His round face was suddenly shiny with sweat. "Okay so maybe I had sex with her. That also doesn't make me a rapist."

"Detective Cruz, when we talked to Ms. Rameriz, did she leave you with the impression that the sex she'd had with Mr. Bartholomew was in any way consensual?"

"No, ma'am."

"And is the owner of the Capitol Cleaning Services company willing to testify that the only time Ms. Rameriz has ever missed work in more than two years was on the nineteenth, twentieth and twenty-first of January?"

"Yes, ma'am."

"And will Ms. Rameriz's coworkers testify that when she returned to work on the twenty-second, her face and arms were still bruised from what was obviously a vicious assault?"

"They will."

Sam returned her attention to Bartholomew. "That, along with the identification Ms. Rameriz will soon make as well as her very compelling and very *believable* story, gives you a rather significant problem, Mr. Bartholomew."

"I'd like to see my lawyer."

"We can arrange for that. Once your lawyer is here, however, I won't be able to offer you any sort of deal on the prostitution charges—money laundering, racketeering, solicitation of prostitution." She'd let the Feds look into the money trail after she'd nailed them on the more serious counts. "When you add those charges to the aggravated sexual assault charges, you're looking at spending the rest of your life in prison."

"What sort of deal?"

"Plead guilty to the sexual assault charge, sparing Ms. Rameriz from having to testify against you, and tell me everything you know about Sanborn's involvement in the call girl ring."

"In exchange for what?"

"Immunity on all the prostitution-related charges."

"And leniency on the assault charge?"

"No way. You'll do the full ride on that one."

"How long do I have to think about it?"

She glanced at her watch. "Two minutes."

His eyes almost popped out of his fat face. "*Two minutes?*"

"One minute, forty-five seconds…"

Bartholomew ran a hand over his mouth and began to pace the small room.

"One minute, fifteen seconds…" Watching him, Sam tried to focus on the time and not on the cramps still rolling through her belly. Was it hot in there or was it her? "What's it going to be, Mr. Bartholomew? Do we have a deal?"

He stopped and turned to her, his expression grim, as if it had just registered with him that life as he knew it—pampered, privileged, successful—was over. "Yes," he said. "We have a deal."

"Tell me something—why did Sanborn kill Regina and Maria?"

"I have no idea."

"None at all?"

"I had nothing to do with what happened to those girls," he said emphatically.

Hands on hips, Sam waited for him to say more.

He rubbed the back of his neck. "They were supposed to take care of birth control. They weren't supposed to get pregnant. It was stipulated in the contract they signed."

"At least now we know why," Sam said on her way out.

Freddie followed Sam from the room. "That was awesome," he said. "Totally *awesome*."

"Suck up."

"The way you got him to cop to the rape *and* to roll on Sanborn. I aspire to be that smooth."

"Why thank you. Even though you're totally sucking up, I do appreciate the sentiment behind the sucking."

He rubbed his belly. "All this nailing of scumbags is making me hungry."

"What *doesn't* make you hungry?" she shot over her shoulder as she pushed open the door to the room where Sanborn cooled his heels.

"Finally," he muttered. "I demand to know what this is all about. I'm a busy man with important people, including the president of the United States, depending on me."

"You're busy, we're busy," Sam said, taking note of healing scratches on his neck, "so let's cut to the chase. Your friends Daniels and Bartholomew claim you're the mastermind behind the prostitution ring."

His mouth fell open. "They wouldn't dare."

"The threat of long prison sentences does funny things to people, Mr. Sanborn. Shockingly, your friends were more concerned with saving their own skins than they were with saving yours." Sam paused to let that sink in. "Doesn't matter, though." She produced the file folder. "DNA links you to the rapes and murders of Regina Argueta de Castro and Maria Espanosa as well as the kidnapping and rape of Detective Jeannie McBride."

His face set into a mulish expression, he said, "I want my lawyer."

When Sam thought about what this man had done to Jeannie, it took every ounce of self-control she possessed to resist plowing her fist into his sanctimonious face. "Great. Just let me know who I should call for you."

"That's it?"

"Yeah," Sam said. "That's it."

"You don't have any questions for me?"

"Nope. Bartholomew and Daniels connected all the dots for me. I'm good."

He seemed to understand all of a sudden that she wasn't going to deal. "But wait—I need to get out of here. We've got a major fund-raiser tomorrow evening. I have to be there!"

This is for you, Jeannie, Sam thought, as she leaned forward, hands on the table. "Mr. Sanborn, I hate to be the bearer of bad news, but you're not going anywhere for a long, *long* time."

Leaving him to ponder his fate, Sam gestured for Freddie to follow her out of the room.

"You don't hate to be the bearer of bad news all the time," Freddie said with a droll smile.

"Some bad news is actually good news."

Faith Miller stepped out of the observation room. "Get a hold of his lawyer and take him to central booking. You can also book Daniels and Bartholomew."

"I'll take care of that," Malone said. "I'll make sure every I is dotted."

"I'll see what I can do to get Daniels arraigned and released," Faith said. "The other two will be staying a while."

"I've got two more to pick up," Sam said.

"Go get 'em," Malone said.

THIRTY-TWO

"You can head home," Sam said to Freddie as she went to retrieve her coat. "I'll take care of sewing this up."

"I want to be there when you arrest Cook."

"I'll tell you all about it tomorrow."

"But—"

"Freddie, you have plans. *Important* plans. Go."

"What about the reports?"

He usually handled them because of her dyslexia. "I'll take care of them this time. All I need is for you to call Regina's and Maria's parents and let them know we got the guy who killed their daughters. Then you're done."

"But—"

"No buts. I promised you a night off, so get to it."

"I don't feel right about leaving before we're finished."

"We *are* finished. I'm going to arrest Cook and Cheri, the call girl ring's administrative assistant. I'll send them back with patrol to be booked, and then I'm going home too. I'll do the paperwork in the morning."

"All right," he said, frowning. "If you insist."

"I insist." She rested a hand on his arm. "I hope it all goes your way tonight. I really do."

"Thanks. I hope so too. I'll be here in the morning to help with the reports."

"Sleep in. I'll see you at ten." She left him in his cubicle and headed out to the parking lot, her detail in tow. "I'm going to have you transport two people back to HQ for me, and then you're released from babysitting duty. Case closed."

"Yes, ma'am, Lieutenant."

Sam studied the two eager young faces. "Thanks," she said begrudgingly. "For keeping an eye on me the last few days."

"Our pleasure," one of them said with a cheeky grin. Sam smiled. Apparently, she still could turn a head or two. It was small solace in the midst of the physical and emotional pain of losing another baby.

On the way to Capitol Hill, Nick called. Sam saw his number on the caller ID and decided to wait to take his call until after she'd arrested Cook. He was better off not knowing what was happening until it was over and done with. She didn't want anyone questioning him later about what he knew and when he knew it. Her phone dinged to indicate a voicemail message from him, which she would retrieve later. At the moment, it took all she had to focus on the task at hand while enduring the regular waves of pain cycling through her gut.

The police cruiser following her slid into the next parking space in a lot adjacent to the Hart Office Building. Sam noticed that the space reserved for Nick was empty. Hit with a blast of nerves over the grim news she'd have to share with him when she saw him later, she wondered if he had a campaign event that evening. She hoped not. She wanted to go home and feel his strong arms around her.

A black Cadillac Coup de Ville occupied the spot next to Nick's, which was reserved for the senior senator from Virginia.

Sam made her way to Cook's office, which was twice the size of that occupied by his junior counterpart. Having been there before, she knew the layout and strolled straight past Cook's startled receptionist on her way to the senator's vast corner office. She barged past numerous staffers and straight into Cook's inner sanctum. He was in a meeting with three other men and two women.

"What's the meaning of this?" he said, startling when he realized who'd come to call.

"Senator Robert Cook, you're under arrest for solicitation of prostitution, running a prostitution ring and racketeering. I'm sure that once we dig a little deeper, we'll be adding money laundering and other charges to the list."

"You can't come in here and accuse me of these egregious charges without an ounce of proof to back up your claims."

"Oh, I've got proof." She stepped around his massive desk to cuff him. "You have the right to remain silent." He struggled against the cuffs as she recited the Miranda warning. The other people in the room watched the proceedings in stunned silence.

"What proof do you have?"

"Your good friends Daniels and Bartholomew are fully prepared to testify against you, as is one of the women you paid for sex."

"*What about them?*" he cried. "Daniels and Bartholomew—and Sanborn? They're in it up to their necks too!"

"Daniels and Bartholomew have agreed to testify against you and Sanborn."

"*In exchange for what?*"

"Immunity on the prostitution charges."

"And I don't get the same courtesy?"

Sam thought of the way he'd threatened Nick during the Sinclair investigation. It gave her tremendous pleasure to say, "Sorry, but I don't need you. I've already got enough to put Sanborn away for life."

"You fucking bitch," he said, seething. "*You mother-fucking whore.*"

"You've got some nerve calling me a whore, Senator. Or should I call you *Mr.* Cook? Convicted felons can't serve in the United States Senate, can they?" She turned to her audience of shocked staffers. "Anyone know the answer to that? Been a while since high school social studies for me."

"You're enjoying this," Cook said through gritted teeth.

Sam leaned in close to him. "You bet your ass I am." She marched him out of the Hart Building, past startled congressional staffers and one thrilled news photographer, and stowed him in the backseat of the patrol car. "Follow me," she said to the two officers, who appeared as stunned as the staffers when they recognized their passenger. "When we get to Seventh Street, one of you stay with him and the other come with me."

"Yes, ma'am."

Back in her car, Sam absorbed a particularly painful cramp before she started the engine and headed for Cheri Anderson's house, a few blocks from Nick's place and far too close for comfort to the apartment Peter Gibson had rented after their divorce. The thought of running into him only added to the sick feeling in her belly.

Sensing Cook glaring at her from the car, Sam climbed the steps and rang the doorbell. The patrol officer hung back at the foot of the stairs.

The door swung open. An attractive woman in her early forties took in Sam's badge as well as the officer standing on the sidewalk and released a deep sigh. "Come in. I've been expecting you."

Sam gestured for the other officer to wait outside and followed the woman into a comfortable home. Dressed in khakis and a Catholic University T-shirt, Cheri Anderson looked like a typical suburban mom. That the Catholic U grad was running a prostitution ring out of her home would've struck Sam as almost comical if it wasn't for what had happened to Regina, Maria and Jeannie as a result of the criminal activity.

"When I heard on the news that Daniels, Bartholomew and Sanborn had been arrested, I figured it was only a matter of time before they blamed the whole thing on me and sent you here."

"For what it's worth, Daniels didn't give up your name easily. I tied it to his immunity deal."

Blue eyes flashed with rage. "So he gets immunity, and I go down for the whole thing?"

"I want Sanborn. He's the one who murdered two women and kidnapped and raped a police officer."

"He's an evil son of a bitch. I've always known that. When I heard Regina and Maria had been murdered…I knew it was him. He was so furious when I told him they were pregnant. They were no longer any use to him, and he feared they'd be tempted to venture into blackmail since their immigration status was so tenuous. When I heard they were dead…"

"You knew it was him."

"Yes." She glanced up at Sam, eyes bright with tears. "To be honest, I've been worried about my own safety. Two days ago, I bought a gun." She gestured to the artwork decorating her refrigerator. "Having a gun in a house where my children live terrifies me, but I couldn't let him get me too."

"How did they recruit you?"

"I worked for Sanborn at the DNC for a couple of years before I had my son. My husband and I, we had a plan—he'd work and I'd stay home with the kids. Then he got laid off just before my son was born. I'd already resigned from the DNC, so we were in a bad place financially. Sanborn must've heard about that from one of my former colleagues. He called me, asked if I'd be interested in a business opportunity, and of course I snapped it up, even though I was mortified when I realized what I'd be doing." She shrugged. "We needed the money."

"What did you tell your husband?"

"That the DNC had asked me to do some work for them from home."

"And he never questioned that?"

She shook her head. "I handle all the household money. He has no idea..."

"This might be a good time to tell him."

Nodding, Cheri wiped away tears and reached for a CD case on the counter. "Clients, employees, finances, records—the entire business. I signed a very restrictive confidentiality agreement when I started with them, but I assume that's null and void now that they're all in jail."

Sam took the CD from her. "How many careers and marriages will this ruin?"

"Scores." Folding her arms in a protective stance, Cheri said, "What will happen to me?"

"Are you willing to testify against the four principals?"

"To stay out of jail? You bet."

"Let me talk to the U.S. attorney and see what I can do."

"Are you going to arrest me?"

Sam slipped the CD that cemented her case into her coat pocket. "Not right now. I may be back, though."

Cheri's gaze locked on a photo of her children. "I'll be here."

SAM SENT HER detail to HQ and called Captain Malone to let him know that Senator Cook was on his way. She told him of her decision to hold off on arresting Cheri Anderson for the time being—and why.

"Good call. By the way, DNA came back on Maria's baby—a match for Tillinghast."

"You can let him know that when you spring him and let his family out of protective custody."

"Will do. What else can I do to help you clean up the details? I know you're not feeling well and you probably want to get home."

"You can have Selina Rameriz's detail notify her that we've arrested the four principals, and tell her the information she gave me was critical to closing the case."

"Will do."

"Let her know I'll check in with her in the next few days about the next steps."

"Got it. Good work, Lieutenant—as always."

"Glad to put this one behind me. I'll be in tomorrow to go through the CD Anderson gave me so we can get busy ruining the lives of some other high-ranking scumbags."

His laughter sparked hers. "A lot of times this job truly sucks, but other times, it truly doesn't."

"Eloquently put, Captain."

"Go home and put your feet up. I'll see you in the morning."

"Thanks for handling Cook."

"My pleasure."

Sam hung up with him and called Jeannie McBride's cell number. Michael answered.

"This is Lieutenant Holland. How's Jeannie?"

"Settled in at my place and sleeping. The trip home seemed to wear her out."

"Do me a favor when she wakes up, and tell her we got the bastard."

"Oh God, that's such a relief," he said, sounding jubilant. "She'll be so glad to hear that."

"Tell her I'll be by to check on her in the next day or two."

"I will. Thank you so much for everything you've done for us."

"No problem." Before she stashed the phone in her coat pocket, Sam sent a text to Shelby and her sisters to postpone the dress plans. She couldn't deal with that tonight. Leaning against her car, she took a moment in the fading daylight to breathe in the cold February air and absorb the satisfaction of another case successfully closed.

"Fancy meeting you here."

Shocked out of her reverie, she spun around to find Peter Gibson giving her the once-over. Before he'd affixed crude bombs to her car and Nick's, Sam had never thought to be afraid of her ex-husband. Antagonistic? Absolutely. But afraid? Never. However, when she remembered the bomb-making materials, the photos of her on the job and the newspaper articles about her they'd found in his apartment…Seeing him now, released from jail on a technicality, Sam experienced true terror for the first time since Clarence Reese carjacked her and held her hostage.

"What do you want?" she asked, trying not to think about the way she'd nailed him in the interrogation room and goaded him about her satisfying sex life with Nick.

"From *you*? Not a damned thing. You gave me everything I needed when you let your officers knock down my door without a warrant. Thanks for that, by the way. I can't tell you how much I appreciated it."

"You're required to stay a thousand feet from me and everyone in my family," Sam reminded him. Since their acrimonious divorce Sam had been hard-pressed to remember what she'd ever seen in him. His sandy-colored hair was now mostly silver, and the face she'd once found handsome was filled with bitterness.

"This is *my* neighborhood," he said. "Maybe I need a restraining order to keep *you* away from *me*."

"Enjoy your freedom. I predict it won't last. In fact, we've got a pool going at HQ as to how long it'll take you to fuck up again."

His expression one of mock horror, he said, "Who picked today? I hope it wasn't you. I'd hate to hand you any easy victories."

"What's that supposed to mean?" she asked, her heart hammering.

"Figure it out. Good to see you, Sam. Hope you're taking good care of your senator. He didn't look too hot the last time I saw him. You have a nice night now."

Nick. Oh God, Nick. Leaving her car, she took off running because it was faster than driving this time of day. In the background, she heard Peter laughing. If he'd done something to Nick, she'd kill him with her own hands. Pulling her phone from her pocket as she ran, her hands shook as she pressed No. 1 on her speed dial. The call went straight to voicemail. "Oh my God. *Please…*"

Ignoring the increasingly sharp pain in her abdomen, Sam ran as fast a she could. Odd dots of light danced before her eyes just as the sign for Ninth Street appeared in the distance. "Please, please, *please*."

She rounded the corner and stumbled as she took in the pile of rubble that used to be their front stairs. "Oh," she whispered. The entire front of the house was in shambles. "No…" Instinctively, she reached for her radio and called for backup, relieved to see no sign of Nick's car on the street. Her eyes fixed on the wreckage outside their home, Sam inched forward, certain she had to be seeing things. Would Peter really be so stupid as to plant another bomb—on the *same day* he'd been released from prison?

Taking a quick look around, she didn't see any of the shattered glass that had marked the area surrounding the bombing the last time. What the hell was going on? And most important of all, where was Nick?

BATTLING HIS WAY through rush hour traffic, Nick was riveted by the news on the radio about the arrests of Senator Cook, Speaker Daniels, Mitch Sanborn and Jack Bartholomew. Washington's political machine was on fire, and Nick was enjoying every minute of it. Even though his party had taken a hard hit, he had no patience for people who took advantage of powerful positions and the public's trust.

He'd been forced to shut off his phone, which had been ringing incessantly for hours as the news ripped through the city. He needed to talk to Sam before he discussed the situation with other members of his party or with the reporters who were clamoring for a statement from the senator whose fiancée had arrested some of the heaviest hitters in town.

All at once it occurred to him that if Cook was forced to resign—and Nick couldn't see how the older man would be able to hold on to his office after helping to run a prostitution ring for twelve years—then Nick would become the senior senator from Virginia, just fifty days after he took office. The thought made Nick's head spin, as it had since the day he'd found John O'Connor dead in his apartment.

Pulling on to Ninth Street, his heart skipped a beat at the sight of flashing lights and emergency vehicles lined up outside his house—again. Sam...Peter... "*No*," he whispered as he bolted from the car. "*Samantha!*" He'd closed half the distance before he saw her talking to another cop, her hands dancing in the air as she gestured to the ruined front stairs. Right in that moment, he realized she hadn't gotten his message about using the back door, and she'd thought Peter had struck again.

They'd probably laugh about this. Someday…

"Samantha!"

She looked up, and the expression of sheer relief on her face reminded him once again that she loved him more than anyone ever had. Since she seemed frozen in place, he ran to her and swept her up. Right there, in front of no fewer than ten other police officers, the gorgeous cop who despised public displays of affection kissed him square on the lips.

"There you are," she whispered, clinging to him.

"Here I am."

"I was so scared. Peter…he said…"

A jolt of shock zipped through Nick. "You *saw* him? *Already*?"

She nodded. "He made it sound like he'd done something to you. He…I was so scared. I couldn't find you."

Nick tightened his hold on her, surprised to feel dampness on her cheeks. "I'm fine, babe. I asked the contractor to put in a ramp so we can have your dad over. He got called away before he could finish. It was supposed to be a surprise. I'm sorry you were scared."

She drew back from him, eyes wide with surprise and emotion. "You're putting in a ramp?"

"I thought he'd like to see our place."

Hugging him again, she said, "Love you so much."

"Love you too, babe."

"Not feeling so good," she said, her eyes closing. "Need to talk to you."

He scooped her up and carried her home.

EPILOGUE

NICK STOOD AT the white split rail fence with Graham O'Connor and watched Graham's daughter Lizbeth lead Scotty around the training ring on a gentle mare. The handsome boy's grin stretched from ear to ear as he adapted to the horse's cadence.

"He's a natural," Graham said. "What an adorable kid."

"He had us laughing all the way from Richmond." They had needed the laughter after the loss they were still struggling to absorb. "I'm totally smitten."

"What're you going to do about that?" Graham asked.

Nick returned Scotty's wave and his big smile. "Haven't decided yet."

"Sure, you have," Graham said. "You've decided you'll do *something*."

"I suppose I will—when the time is right." He kept his eyes on Scotty, riveted by the boy's laughter. "I once knew a kid like him who was lost and lonely until a boisterous family took him into their home and their hearts and changed his life forever."

Graham cleared his throat and rested a hand on Nick's shoulder, squeezing lightly. "And now you want to do the same for another lost and lonely kid."

That he and Sam might be able to have children of their own after all was still settling with him. He watched the boy who rode the horse with such unbridled and infectious joy, and thought again about the many ways he could improve Scotty's circumstances. "There's something about him."

"I know that feeling," Graham said. "There once was a lost and lonely eighteen-year-old who came to spend a weekend in my home and touched me in exactly the same way."

Nick turned to the man who'd been a father to him in every possible way except biology. "I wondered if I could ask a favor."

"Anything, anytime. You know that."

"Would you be my best man?"

Graham's eyes filled, and for a moment he seemed too shocked to speak. "I'd be honored," he said gruffly, "to stand in my late son's place beside the man I love like a son."

Nick hugged him, grateful that he understood exactly why Nick had asked him. "Thank you."

Sam walked up to them. "Sorry to interrupt."

"Hey, babe," Nick held out a hand to her, pleased to see some color returning to cheeks.

"There's the woman who's been single-handedly cleaning house in Washington," Graham said, his smile matching the teasing tone. "What's the tally now? Speaker, senator, VP's chief of staff, DNC chair, EPA administrator, deputy secretary of defense, too many lobbyists to count..."

"The divorce attorneys are sending me engraved thank-you notes," Sam said with a cheeky grin of her own.

Graham barked out a ringing laugh.

"It's a tough job, but someone's gotta do it," she added. "I still can't believe all the other women who came forward claiming Bartholomew and Sanborn had attacked them too. I doubt either of them will ever see the light of day again."

"You think you know people," Graham said, his expression turning pensive. "It's so shocking."

"I imagine it must be. I was sent out to tell you your presence is requested in the kitchen to carve the turkey."

"Ah, duty calls. Give me about fifteen minutes, and then round up the troops."

"We will," Nick said. As Graham walked away, Nick slipped an arm around Sam and returned his attention to Scotty. "He's having a ball."

"He's such a sweetheart."

"I'm glad you think so." He kissed her forehead. "How're you feeling?"

"Still tired and a little achy, but better than yesterday." They'd spent most of the day before curled up to each other, absorbing the loss and sharing the grief. It hadn't exactly been the day off they'd dreamed about.

"Did you talk to Freddie again?"

"Not since this morning. He called to let me know all the reports are done and filed."

"It was good of him to go in and take care of that for you yesterday."

"After Elin didn't show Friday night, he all but begged me for something to do."

"Poor guy."

"He'll recover. In time."

Nick framed her face with his hands and brushed a soft kiss over her lips. "Will you?"

"In time."

Nick held her close for several minutes before he signaled Lizbeth and Scotty to let them know it was dinnertime.

After Lizbeth helped him off the horse, Scotty darted

out of the corral and caught up to Sam and Nick, who kept one arm tight around the love of his life.

"That was the coolest thing—*ever*," Scotty said, his eyes dancing with excitement and his cheeks rosy from the cool air. "Can I ride some more after dinner?"

"I don't see why not." Nick held out his free hand to the boy.

"You looked good out there, buddy," Sam said.

"Thanks, Sam. Will you show me your gun and cuffs after dinner?"

She laughed, and Nick felt his heart settle and lighten. She was going to be okay. *They* were going to be okay.

"It's a date," she said.

* * * * *

Don't miss the other books in the Fatal series by Marie Force, available now from Carina Press!

Join the Fatal Consequences Reader Group at www.facebook.com/groups/FatalConsequences/ and the Fatal Series Reader Group at www.facebook.com/groups/FatalSeries/.

FATAL DESTINY

For Aly and Ronlyn, who planned such an incredible wedding, and all the friends who helped with the details.

Sam Holland
and
Nick Cappuano
request the honor of your presence
as they exchange marriage vows and begin their life together.

Saturday, the twenty-sixth day of March
Two thousand eleven
at four o'clock in the afternoon

St. John's Church
1525 H Street NW
Washington, D.C.

Reception immediately following
The Hay-Adams
16th & H Streets

ONE

NICK STOOD BEFORE the window, looking out over Ninth Street as rain mixed with snow to create a slushy mess on the pavement. The city had been buzzing all day about the late wintry blast and the impact it might have on Washington's fabled cherry blossoms, which were due to bloom any day now.

Hands in pockets, Nick stared intently at the orange glow of the streetlights, not seeing any sign of Sam or her car. *Any minute now*, he thought. *She'll be home any minute.*

Behind him voices, laughter and the distinctive clink of ice meeting crystal echoed through the double-sized townhouse he shared with Sam. The "Jack and Jill" shower had been Shelby's idea. The wedding planner Sam called Tinker Bell had suggested a gathering of their family, close friends and colleagues. Shelby had correctly assumed that Sam would prefer that over the more traditional all-female event. Nick had gone along with it because Sam had liked the idea. Whatever made her happy made him happy.

But now she was late, and he was worried. Not that it was unusual for her to be late—the nature of her job as the lieutenant in charge of the city's homicide detectives' squad made her late more often than not. Since she wasn't in the midst of a hot case at the moment, Nick had expected her home more than an hour ago. Now here it was fifteen minutes after the party started with no sign of her, and her phone had gone straight to voicemail.

His gut twisted with unease. Ever since her ex-husband had been released from jail on a technicality, Nick had found himself obsessing even more than usual about her safety. Peter Gibson had affixed crude bombs to both their cars, injuring them when the device attached to Sam's car exploded in late December. A glitch with evidence collection had been Peter's ticket out of jail, and the stress of waiting for him to come at Sam again had Nick as tightly wound as he'd ever been.

She'd be furious if she knew about the private investigator he'd hired to keep tabs on Gibson. Or he supposed she would. Truth was, she hadn't been herself since the miscarriage she suffered just after Valentine's Day, and more than a month later, Nick was left with nagging doubts about whether she still planned to marry him one week from today.

The signs of something amiss were hard to ignore—rather than spend time together, she'd cleaned up her mess of an office at work and devoted hours she'd normally spend with him organizing the closet he'd had built for her in their new home. The Sam he knew and loved—*his* Sam—would rather be hung upside down by her toes than clean or organize anything. But that was only one sign of trouble. That they hadn't made love since the miscarriage was another hard-to-miss sign of impending doom.

It was his own fault—he'd been so caught up in work as the Senate wound down to the Easter recess with heated budget debates, a flurry of legislation and the relentless pace of his campaign. By the time he'd resurfaced from four of the busiest weeks of his life, Sam had drifted so far from him he had no idea how to bring her back.

He sucked in a sharp deep breath as he finally acknowledged his greatest fear, thoughts he hadn't allowed himself to have before she failed to show up for their shower. Did she still want to marry him? Had he made a huge mistake by pushing for a short engagement? And what would he do if she decided she didn't want to marry him after all? How was he supposed to live without her after the bliss of being with her these last few months?

His queasiness increased as each question added to his overwhelming anxiety. Something was wrong. Something was very wrong.

"Nicky?" The touch of his father's hand on his shoulder roused Nick out of the pensive state he'd slipped into but didn't erase the sense of panic that grew with every minute Sam failed to appear. "You okay?"

He turned to his father. "I can't imagine where Sam is."

"Probably got hung up at work," Leo said.

Nick glanced over his father's shoulder to where Sam's partner Freddie Cruz talked with fellow detective, Tommy "Gonzo" Gonzales, as well as Gonzo's fiancée and Nick's chief of staff, Christina Billings. If something were going on at work, wouldn't Freddie and Gonzo be at HQ too?

"I'm sure that's all it is," Nick said to his father. "Excuse me for a minute, Dad."

"Of course," Leo said. Just fifteen years older than his son, Leo looked more like Nick's older brother than his father. But Nick was grateful to have the father who'd been absent for so much of his childhood by his side for what he hoped would be the most important week of his life—that is if the bride hadn't changed her mind.

On his way to Freddie, Sam's older sisters Tracy and Angela waylaid him.

"*Where is she?*" Tracy asked through gritted teeth.

"Not sure." Nick gestured for Freddie to follow him into the kitchen.

"What's up?" Freddie asked.

Nick noticed that Freddie looked tired. He'd taken the recent breakup with his girlfriend Elin hard. "Have you heard from Sam?"

Freddie stole a canapé off a tray and popped it into his mouth. "Not since earlier. Why? Where is she?"

"I was hoping you could tell me."

Freddie stopped chewing, his eyes widening. "You don't know where she is?"

"I have no idea," Nick said.

"The last I talked her she said she'd see me tonight. That was around four."

"That's about when I last talked to her too."

Freddie glanced around to make sure no one could hear him. "You don't think..."

Knowing where Freddie's thoughts were heading, Nick's chest tightened with a new wave of anxiety. He withdrew his BlackBerry from his pocket and pressed the speed dial number he'd assigned to the guy watching Gibson. With every passing moment, he wished he'd hired someone to follow her too, but he hadn't done that knowing what she would think of it when—not if—she figured it out. At least by putting someone on Gibson, Nick always knew where that scumbag was.

"Senator."

Nick headed into his study, away from the party fray. "Where's Gibson?"

"Been home all day. Haven't seen him."

"You're sure of that?"

"Positive. Why? What's up?"

"Sam is late getting home, and we can't reach her."

"I wish I could help you out, but she hasn't been around here. Not today anyway."

Nick stood up straighter. "What does that mean?"

"She came by the day before yesterday, watched the place for half an hour or so. Never got out of her car or anything."

"Why didn't you tell me this?" Nick asked, working to keep the anger out of his voice.

"Because you're not paying me to watch her. You're paying me to watch *him*."

Nick rested his hand on the top of his head to keep it from blowing off his neck. "If you see her there again, I want to know. Am I clear?"

"Yes, sir. I apologize for not letting you know before now."

"Don't let him out of your sight."

"Me and my people are on it. Don't worry."

Nick ended the call and jammed the BlackBerry in his pocket. "Don't worry," he muttered. "What do I have to worry about?"

"Everything all right?"

Nick spun around to find Skip Holland's wheelchair in the doorway to the study. "I'm not sure." He'd learned to be honest with Sam's dad, who valued that quality above all others—especially from the man his precious daughter slept with.

"Where's Sam?"

"I wish I knew." Hands on his hips, Nick shifted his eyes to meet Skip's steely stare.

"You're not thinking… Gibson…"

Nick could see the fear on the older man's face. "I've got a guy on him."

The half of Skip's face that wasn't paralyzed lifted into a smile. "Of course you do. Does she know?"

"What do you think?"

Skip chuckled. "Hope I'm around to witness the explosion when she finds out."

Nick had no doubt the explosion would be something to see, but he didn't want to talk about that. "Something's not right with her."

"Hasn't been since just after Valentine's Day."

"So I'm not the only one who's noticed?"

"Hardly."

"I don't think she wants to get married—"

"It's not that."

"Then *what*?"

"The baby."

"But we got through that. We talked about it. She said she was okay, that she was coping with it."

Skip used the one working finger on his right hand to roll his chair farther into the study. "It breaks her. Every time it happens, it breaks her a little more than the last time. The pieces never seem to go back together the same way they were before."

"She said—"

"She always says what she thinks we need to hear. That she's okay, feeling better, stronger, but inside… Inside, she bleeds."

Nick wanted to shriek with frustration. "How could I not see this?"

"Because she's become masterful at hiding it from everyone."

"Even from me?"

"Especially from you. She wouldn't want you to know how badly she's suffering."

Nick hung his head. "Why wouldn't she turn to me? Doesn't she know that I've suffered too? That I've suffered *for* her and with her?"

"I suspect that embracing your pain would only make hers worse. She knows how much you want a family of your own."

"Not at this price I don't."

"Don't be too quick to say that. You've had one setback, but just think, she was *sure* she couldn't get pregnant again, so at least there's hope now."

"I guess. I can't even think about any of that until I know she's safe."

"I have an idea of where she might be."

Instantly on alert, Nick said, "Where?"

"You know."

"Oh, God. Lincoln." He wondered why he hadn't thought of it. After all, he'd found her there once before during an earlier crisis. "Is she purposely skipping the shower?"

"Doubt it's even on her radar at the moment."

"Do we need to postpone the wedding?"

"You'll have to play that one by ear."

Nick released a harsh laugh. "It's in *seven days*."

"If she's not ready, she's not ready."

Nick swallowed a new surge of panic. Somehow he knew if they didn't get married next Saturday they never would. "I'm going to find her. Will you hold down the fort here?"

"Absolutely."

"Thanks for the heads-up about what's going on with her."

"You'd have figured it out eventually."

"I wish I was so confident." Just when he thought he really knew her, he discovered he didn't know her at all. The unsettling thought did nothing to calm his rattled nerves. "I'll be back as soon as I can. If for any reason it's not going to happen tonight—"

"Just call. Take care of Sam. We'll take care of things here."

On his way to the door, Nick took a second to squeeze Skip's right hand, which retained sensation more than two years after he was shot on the job and left a quadriplegic.

"She loves you," Skip said. "I'm sure of that."

"I hope you're right." Nick grabbed a coat and went into the kitchen to go out through the back door. No sense alerting everyone that he was leaving. Whatever was going on with Sam was her business—and his.

In the cab he took to the Lincoln Memorial, Skip's words echoed through Nick's mind: *She loves you. I'm sure of that.* Nick had been too. But something had changed in the last few weeks, something fundamental and essential. Whether or not they could get back what they'd once had was anyone's guess.

And the last thing Nick wanted the week before he was due to marry the love of his life was to be guessing about whether she still loved him enough to marry him or if losing his baby had broken her so badly she'd never be the same again.

As he took the steps to the Lincoln Memorial, Nick recalled the last time he'd come here to find her, after she'd met his friend Julian Sinclair, the Supreme Court nominee. She and Julian had sparred over right-to-life issues, which had brought up the painful memory of her first miscarriage years earlier. Nick had learned then that Sam came to Lincoln when she was troubled by something.

Where would he look next if she wasn't there? He had no idea.

Rounding the monument, he headed for the Gettysburg Address, and there she was, knees pulled up to her chin, lost in thought, oblivious to him watching her. Overwhelmed with relief that she was safe, he wondered if he should leave her alone. Or should he remind her that there was somewhere else she was supposed to be?

United States Senator Nick Cappuano, who was rarely at a loss, had no idea what to do.

Just then she shifted her eyes and met his gaze, a look of surprise overtaking her pretty face.

He took a step forward.

"What're you doing here?" she asked.

"I might ask you the same thing."

"I had an errand down this way and decided to pay Mr. Lincoln a visit."

"You must've lost track of time."

"I guess." She shrugged and checked her watch. "Wow, it's getting late."

"Sam, the shower—"

"Oh shit! Shit, shit, *shit*." She scrambled to her feet. "Let's go."

He stopped her when she would've headed for the stairs.

She looked up at him, questioning. "We're late. We have to go."

"Sam..."

"What?"

"Is everything okay?" He hated the weird, needy tone of his voice. But more, he hated that he had to ask.

"Everything's fine. I'm sorry I was late. I lost track of time. Now are we going to go or stand here all night asking questions?"

"It's not just tonight." He reached out to caress her cold face. "You haven't been yourself lately. I'm worried."

"What are you worried about?"

She looked like his Sam. She sounded like his Sam. But her eyes...the clear blue eyes that had always been the gateway to her innermost feelings were shuttered now. Did he dare say it? Did he dare risk opening that door? How could he not?

"Is it the wedding? Is that the problem?"

She stared at him as if he had two heads or were speaking a foreign language. "What about the wedding?"

Nick's heart raced, his mouth went dry and his palms were suddenly damp. "Do you still want—"

"To get married?" she asked, seeming incredulous.

He nodded.

"Do *you*?"

"Yes! You know I do! I just don't know what you want anymore. You won't talk to me! If you've changed your mind or something has happened, I wish you'd tell me. Just tell me. Anything would be better than wondering what's going on with you."

"I don't know what you're talking about. Haven't I been going to dress fittings and meeting with Tinker Bell and doing all the things I need to do?"

He nudged at the marble with the toe of his loafer. "Yeah."

"Why would I be doing that if I didn't want to get married?"

Nick couldn't think of a good answer to that.

"I was late for the shower. I'm sorry about that. But let's not turn it into something it's not, okay?"

Biting his tongue and holding back the desire to shake her until she leveled with him, Nick nodded.

She brushed past him, and he followed her, relieved to have found her but still riddled with worries. She'd said exactly what she thought he needed to hear. But the wall was still up, and he was beginning to wonder if it would ever come down again.

THE GIFTS HAD been opened and properly oohed and ahhed over. She'd eaten and laughed with her sisters and coworkers and even razzed his deputy chief of staff, Terry O'Connor, a man she'd tangled with in the past, about his flirtation with Chief Medical Examiner Lindsey McNamara.

Their guests left with an impression of a happy bride eagerly awaiting her big day. The moment the last guest left, though, Sam mentioned a headache and went upstairs to bed. Before the miscarriage, they'd always gone to bed together. Always. Now, it seemed she couldn't go far enough out of her way to avoid him.

Listening to the soft cadence of her breathing, he remembered something she'd once shared about being lonely with her ex-husband. She'd said that even when Peter was sitting right next to her on the sofa or lying next to her in bed, she was often lonely in the relationship. They'd vowed to never let that happen to them. Yet here in the dark of night with the woman he'd waited so long to find sleeping right next to him, Nick was lonelier than he'd ever been in his life.

TWO

Sam waited impatiently in the exam room. Harry was running late, but she'd forgive him since he snuck her in last-minute on a Monday morning. At least this time he wouldn't have his hands all over her girl parts.

A knock on the door preceded him into the room. "So sorry to keep you waiting, Sam. I had an emergency earlier that's put me behind."

"No problem." Like she did every time she saw Nick's close friend, Sam admired his dark hair, handsome face and adorable dimples.

"Nice shower the other night."

"It really was. My sisters went all out."

"I gotta say, I'm surprised to see you this week," he said. "I figured you'd have far more important things to do than to check in with me."

"I need a favor."

His smile faded and his brows knitted with concern. "Everything okay with you and Nick?"

"Yeah, sure. Everything's fine. It's just that…um…"

"Sam," he said, smiling. "Spit it out. Whatever it is, we'll figure it out."

"I want something for birth control," she said in a burst of words. "Something that works right away."

"I'm surprised to hear that. I was under the impression you were anxious to start a family."

"I've decided I need some more time before that happens. Nick and I haven't been together that long. We could use some time alone before we take the next step."

"Hmm."

Sam studied him. "What does that mean—*Hmm*?"

"It's just, you know, you suffered a miscarriage a few weeks ago, and now you've totally changed direction on how you feel about having a baby. I wouldn't be doing my job if I didn't ask how you're doing up here." He tapped his head.

"I'm fine," Sam said, annoyed. She wanted a shot, and she wanted to get out of there. What was so hard about that? "Look, Harry, I appreciate the concerned friend routine. I really do. I'm not looking to get my tubes tied. I want something short-term that will buy me a little time to get used to being married before I add a baby to the picture. That's all there is to it."

"While I'm honored that you consider me a friend, I'm actually coming at this as a doctor more than a friend. I know how much you wanted that baby, Sam."

Goddamn him. Goddamn him and the softly spoken words that had her swallowing frantically to deal with the emotion that closed her throat. "I wanted the baby. I won't deny that. And I won't deny I'm not ready to try again."

"So why not go with condoms until you are?"

Good old Harry was too damned perceptive for his own good. "Not that you probably want to hear this, but if I'm covered, then we can be spontaneous, which makes for a much better honeymoon, right?" Sam made a big show of checking her watch. "Are you going to help me out, or should I go somewhere else?"

Harry studied her for a long, *long* moment.

It was all Sam could do not to squirm under the heat of his stare.

"Stay here," he finally said. "I'll be right back."

He left the room, and Sam released a long deep breath. She hated being evasive with Nick's friend, but she had to do something. She couldn't continue to avoid sex forever, and there was no way she was putting herself through another pregnancy. No way. So short of having to endure the emotional firestorm of that conversation with Nick the week of their wedding, she'd chosen to buy herself some time until she felt more ready to go there.

If her research were to be believed, the birth-control shot would give her twelve weeks. By then, hopefully, she would be able to talk to Nick about it. Hopefully.

Harry returned a few minutes later with his girlfriend, Dr. Maggie Tyndall, an OB/GYN in his practice. Sam had met her after the miscarriage when Harry and Maggie had come by the house to check on her.

"Oh jeez," Sam said. "Are you guys ganging up on me or something?"

Maggie, who was tall and lanky with long dark hair and bright blue eyes, laughed. "No ganging. You've ventured out of Harry's area of expertise, so he called me in to consult. He tells me you're interested in short-term birth control?"

Nodding, Sam said, "I read about the shot that lasts twelve weeks. That would work for me."

"When was the first day of your last period?"

"Yesterday."

"Then it would be effective within twenty-four hours."

Sam sighed with relief. "Good. That's good." Thinking about their upcoming wedding night had filled Sam with anxiety. You could avoid sex a lot of nights, but not that night.

"The shot isn't the only option, you know."

"Believe me, I know. After I got pregnant in college, I tried just about everything else. The pill made me eat everything that wasn't nailed down until I was twenty-five pounds heavier. The patch gave me a rash, the IUD caused a weird—and scary—infection, and I never had the diaphragm with me when I needed it." She remembered the night six years ago that she first met Nick and looking for a place they could buy condoms at midnight while her diaphragm was stashed across town in her bedside table. "Funny, isn't it, that I went through all that to keep from getting pregnant, and then look at what happens when I *do* get pregnant."

Maggie pulled up a stool. "I'm worried about depression."

"What about it?" Sam asked, confounded.

"You've recently been through a traumatic event. It would be entirely natural, especially having had three prior miscarriages, to be a bit depressed."

"I'm not depressed." Sam glanced at Harry, who was watching her intently, and beat back a swell of panic. She wasn't sure what she'd do if they refused to give her something to prevent pregnancy. Well, that wasn't entirely true. She knew exactly what she'd do—she'd go somewhere else where no one knew her and tell whatever lies necessary to get what she needed.

"If you're at all depressed, the shot can make it worse," Maggie said.

"Well, I'm not, so no worries there. Anything else?"

"It can take longer—sometimes nine to twelve months longer—for women who've had the shot to get pregnant after the dose wears off."

"That's fine. We're in no rush."

"You've certainly changed your tune," Harry said, studying her again with those intense eyes that made Sam feel like she was six years old and in the principal's office.

"A woman's prerogative." Sam flashed him what she

hoped was a convincing grin. "Come on, guys. I'm fine, really. I'm about to get married to a guy I've been with three months. I love him more than anything, but don't we deserve a little time to ourselves before we have kids? Now that I know all the plumbing works, I want to be sure I'm ready before we go there. That's all it is. I swear."

Maggie and Harry exchanged a look before Maggie withdrew a syringe from her lab coat pocket and handed it to him. "She's all yours. I'll see you at the rehearsal, Sam." Harry was one of Nick's groomsmen.

"Thanks, Maggie."

After she left the room, Harry said, "Take off your sweater and roll up your sleeve."

Sam's stomach heaved over the idea of a shot, but she did as directed.

"Why are you suddenly shaking like a leaf?"

"Needles and I don't get along too well."

He rubbed alcohol on her arm. "You're sure about this, Sam?"

She'd never been more certain about anything. "Very sure. Let's just get it over with." The sting of the needle and the burn of the injection drew a gasp from her, but then it was over, and she had one less thing to worry about for the next twelve weeks. "You won't say anything about this to Nick, will you?"

Harry seemed taken aback by the question. "Of course not. That's not something you ever need to worry about with me."

"I'll see you Friday. Thanks for your help." Ignoring his disappointed expression, Sam made her escape before he could make her feel any worse than she already did.

SAM ARRIVED AT her HQ office, determined to put the episode with Harry behind her. *What's done is done*, she thought, hanging up her coat and taking in her unusually orderly office. She wasn't sure what had gotten into her lately, but she was beginning to worry that Nick's anal-retentive neatness was wearing off on her. It wasn't like her to be concerned about cleaning up her office or closet or anywhere else for that matter.

When she realized there was nothing left to clean, nothing left to organize, she felt panicked. What the hell was wrong with her? Her emotions were all over the freaking place the last few weeks. Had to be the wedding and all the associated craziness. Once they got past next weekend, things would calm down. Or so she hoped.

What she really needed was a grisly murder to get things back on track. Ever since she'd closed the case of the murdered call girls, things had been freakishly slow. That had to be contributing to her odd mojo lately. Sam was always happier when she was in the midst of a complex case. All this idleness left her with too much time to brood.

Sinking into her office chair, she took a moment, just one moment to think about what might've been… Oh how she'd wanted that baby! For so long she'd been convinced she couldn't get pregnant again, and she'd begun to make peace with that. After three miscarriages, one of them an ectopic pregnancy that had nearly taken her life, Sam had been told the likelihood of ever conceiving again was practically nonexistent. Certain she was infertile, the use of birth control had never occurred to her when she and Nick started burning up the sheets.

Leave it to him to prove the doctors wrong, she thought with a laugh that quickly became an ache when she remembered the joy of those few days last month after she realized she was carrying his baby. Recalling his reaction when he'd figured out what had her so freaked out and emotional... He'd been *so* excited. They'd barely had a chance to celebrate beating the odds when a violent confrontation with a perp led to the miscarriage.

"No sense dwelling," Sam muttered, trying as she had over the last month to let it go, to move on, to do what she always did when the one thing she wanted more than just about anything was once again snatched away from her.

A knock on the office door startled her out of the morose thoughts, and Sam looked up, grateful for the interruption.

Her partner, Detective Freddie Cruz, and Detective Tommy "Gonzo" Gonzales stood in the doorway.

"Got a minute, L.T.?" Cruz asked.

"Sure. Come in." The two men exchanged glances that put her immediately on alert. "What's up?"

"We've been working on something—on our own time," Gonzo said.

"Oh yeah? What's that?"

"The guy who owns Reece's house," Cruz said.

Sam's heart slowed to a crawl. She'd been meaning to get back to that, but she'd been so preoccupied that it had been hard to focus on anything. A while back they'd found items relating to her father's unsolved shooting at the rented home of Clarence Reece, a man who'd murdered his entire family and then later carjacked Sam before taking his own life. Tracking down the owner of the house had turned into an exercise in futility.

"What've you got?" she asked.

"Gerald Price," Cruz said, placing an open file folder on Sam's desk.

Sam devoured the info on Price, including the long rap sheet of petty crimes that had escalated to breaking and entering and a series of drug charges that landed him in jail. She reached for her portable radio. "I need to get up to Jessup to talk to this guy," she said, referring to the state prison in Maryland.

"Already done," Gonzo said.

"You've been to see him? And you never said anything?"

"We know you've had a lot going on with the wedding and everything," Cruz said. "We thought if we could, you know, save you some time, it might help you out."

"Plus," Gonzo added. "We owe you."

Touched by their efforts on behalf of her father's case, she looked at Gonzo. "Owe me? What the hell are you talking about?"

"If we'd waited for the warrant, Gibson would still be in jail," Gonzo said, his face tight with tension and fatigue. He had a new baby son at home who was keeping him up half the night. Sam had made a huge effort not to be jealous of her friend who'd recently learned that an ex-girlfriend had borne him a son, but it wasn't easy.

"That's not on you," Sam said. "I've told you that a hundred times. I knew what you were doing at his place, my dad knew, Captain Malone knew. We all screwed up by not waiting on the warrant. You need to get over it."

They shrugged her off as they had for weeks since her ex-husband was released on a procedural technicality. The evidence they'd found all over Peter's apartment had cemented their case against him in the bombing of Sam's car. Gonzo, Cruz and their colleague, Detective Arnold, blamed themselves for not waiting on the warrant before entering the apartment.

Knowing the dwelling contained bomb-making materials that could clear a city block, Sam wouldn't have done it any differently herself, but she'd had no luck convincing them of that. They'd probably never get over it.

"So what did Price have to say?" she asked.

"Two years ago, he rented the place to a guy named Trace Simmons." Gonzo handed Simmons's rap sheet to Sam, who skimmed the long list of priors that involved significant gang activity. "Price said the place was like a Do-Drop-Inn. Simmons had a bunch of people living there with him, brothers, cousins, fellow gangbangers."

"All those people in that tiny space?" Sam asked.

"Exactly," Cruz said. "Price got sick of the complaints from the neighbors and started eviction proceedings. Around that same time, which was about three weeks before your dad's shooting, one of the cousins, Darius Gardner, was accused of raping a woman in the house."

"Why didn't that come up during the Reece investigation?" Sam asked.

"Very good question," Gonzo said. "We did some digging and found that the case against Gardner never went anywhere. It made it as far as the U.S. attorney and then the charges mysteriously disappeared."

"No idea why?" Sam asked.

The two detectives exchanged glances. "We figured that was a question for you to ask," Cruz said. "We took it this far and decided it was time to bring you in. This is your case. We didn't want to step on toes. We just wanted to give you one of those threads you love to pull."

Overwhelmed by what they'd done for her—and her dad—Sam stood and stepped around her desk to address two men who ranked among her closest friends, not that she'd ever tell them that. Didn't matter. They knew. "You gave me far more than one thread, and I can't thank you enough. You have no idea how badly I needed this right now."

"Oh, well, no problem," Cruz said, clearly flustered by her appreciation.

"Means a lot to me," she added. "I won't forget it."

"Let's hope it leads somewhere this time," Gonzo said. He handed her another sheet of paper with the last known addresses for Simmons and Gardner as well as the bagged newspaper clippings about her father's shooting that they'd found in Reece's house.

"Yes," Sam said. "Let's hope." She wasn't sure she could withstand another disappointment just then.

THREE

"I WANT TO see Roberto first," Sam decided.

"Been a while," Freddie rcplied.

Sam didn't like to think about the six months she'd spent undercover with the Johnson family. The investigation into a far-reaching drug ring in the city, a special assignment she'd been handpicked for, ended so badly she still had nightmares about the hail of gunfire that took young Quentin Johnson's life.

Intellectually, Sam knew it hadn't been her fault. Yes, she'd ordered her officers to return fire, but how could she have known that Marquis Johnson would be stupid enough to bring his young son to a crack house? In all the months she'd been undercover with the Johnsons, she had never once seen Quentin in that house. She was still struggling with the outcome more than nine months later.

"Don't go there, Sam," Freddic said, knowing how she'd suffered in the aftermath of that calamitous night.

"Hard not to." For months after the incident, she had repeatedly woken in a sweat, after hearing Marquis's tortured screams in her sleep. Sam shuddered. Only to close her father's baffling case would she take a step back in time to the lowest point in her career.

"What do you think Roberto knows?"

"Everything that goes on in Washington Highlands. I should've thought to ask him about Reece's house before now."

"Don't feel bad—I didn't think of him, either."

They arrived at a public housing complex on Southern Avenue. As Sam and Freddie made their way from the parking lot to a first-floor unit, they caught the attention of those gathered outside. The residents of the crime-riddled neighborhood knew cops when they saw them. Before Sam could knock on Roberto's door, a gorgeous young woman with long dark hair and eyes opened it. She eyed Sam suspiciously.

"What do you want?" she asked. "We got no trouble around here."

"I'm not looking for any trouble," Sam said. "Is Roberto around?"

She looked Sam up and down. "Who wants to know?"

Sam showed her badge. "Lieutenant Holland. MPD."

"Let her in, Angel," came a voice from inside the apartment.

Giving Sam a glare, she stepped aside to let Sam pass but put up a hand to stop Freddie. "He said *her*."

"She doesn't go in there without me," Freddie said.

Sam turned to see Freddie and Angel locked in a battle of wills. Just as she was about to tell him to wait in the hallway, Angel backed down and let him by. He gave Sam a satisfied grin.

"Long time no see," Roberto said. He held up a closed fist to Sam.

Sam returned the fist bump, looking down at the good-looking young man in the wheelchair whom she had befriended during the Johnson investigation. As one of the lower-ranking members of the Johnson organization, Roberto hadn't much registered on Marquis Johnson's radar, which is how Sam had been able to get close to him. He had short dark hair and world-weary eyes. He'd seen far too much far too soon. "How goes it, Roberto?"

He shrugged. “Good days, bad days. Today’s been a good day. You ain’t gonna change that, are ya?”

“Nope. I’m wondering what you know about Trace Simmons and Darius Gardner.”

Roberto let out a low whistle. “What’s a nice girl like you asking about a couple hard-core bangers like them for?”

Sam smiled at him. The shootout in the crack house had changed his life too—in some ways for the better. While the bullet wound had stolen his legs, it had also given him a way out of a life that was going nowhere fast. Sam had helped him get a job as a clerk with the city.

Sam filled him in on what’d happened at Reece’s house and the possible connection to Simmons and Gardner.

“I read about that dude taking you hostage. You like to keep it real, huh?”

Sam rolled her eyes. “A little *too* real lately.”

“For what it’s worth, I ain’t never heard either of them brag about shooting no cop—and those two? They woulda talked.”

Sam kept her expression neutral to hide the rush of disappointment. She knew she should be used to it by now after so many dashed leads, but the letdown never got easier to take.

“That don’t mean they didn’t do it, though,” he quickly added. “They both got long sheets, and doing a cop would put ’em away for a long stretch. They mighta kept it on the down low cuza that.”

“What do you know about them?”

“Simmons busted outta the foster system a million times ’til they finally gave up on him and let him go. He’s been on the streets since he was a kid. Rotten little bastard. Takes care of number one. Gardner’s a total douche bag. That girl who said he raped her?”

Sam nodded.

"She's my second cousin. I saw her right after it happened. No doubt he did it."

"Why'd it get squashed?"

"No fuckin' clue. The U.S. attorney tossed it and never told us why."

Something stunk to high heaven there, and Sam planned to find out what.

"You can't go from me to them," he said, looking like a fearful kid. "You'll get me iced."

"You're not tied up in that shit any more. Are you?"

"Hell, no. That don't mean nothin' to them though. They hear I'm squealing to a cop, and my life ain't worth shit. You know that."

"Don't worry. I'll be careful."

Roberto studied her for a long moment. "You still dream about it? That night?"

Sam nodded. "Not as often as I used to, but when I do…"

"It's bad," he said, his tone full of understanding. "I hear Quentin…"

"I do too. That's the part I can't forget."

"Such a cute kid with two assholes for parents. Worst thing I ever did getting mixed up with Marquis Johnson."

"At least you figured that out before you ended up in jail or dead."

"Came damn close to dead," he said, his hands resting on useless legs.

"How've you been adapting?"

"As well as anyone ever does, I guess." He glanced at Angel. "Thank God for my girl. She's got my back."

"I'd like to get you together with my dad some time."

"He's in a chair too, right?"

"Yeah. C3-C4."

Roberto winced. "That blows."

"Big time."

"If you want me to meet him, I'm down with that."

"We'll set it up. After the wedding."

His face was transformed by the innocent smile. Not that long ago he'd been living a life of crime, and Sam couldn't be more proud of the changes he'd made. "I've been reading all 'bout you and your senator." He let out a low whistle. "Fancy, fancy."

Embarrassed, Sam rolled her eyes. "Not all that fancy."

"Whatever you say, lady cop. I watch the news. I see the way that guy looks at you. He's diggin' you big."

Roberto's teasing words sent a twinge of discomfort through Sam. She had to stop holding Nick at arm's length and find a way to reconnect with him before the wedding. Now that she had taken the chance of pregnancy off the table, maybe it wouldn't be so damned hard to look into his amazing eyes and not see the pain he tried to keep hidden from her.

Losing their baby had hit him hard too. He had grown up without a family of his own. More than anything, Sam had wanted to fill that void for him with a house full of kids. But now… She just couldn't go there anymore. Not even for him.

"Hey, yo," Roberto said. "Where'd you zone out to?"

"Sorry."

"Didn't mean to bum you out."

"You didn't. Thanks for the info." She lifted her fist to him. "It was good to see you."

Rather than fist bump her, he curled his hand around hers in a gesture that touched her. "Don't be a stranger."

"I won't."

He released her hand. "Have a nice wedding, Sam. You deserve to be happy."

"So do you."

"I'm getting there."

"Keep up the good work. Make me proud." Following Freddie out of the apartment, Sam ignored the glare she received from Angel. Outside, she took deep breaths of the unseasonably cool air.

"He seems good," Freddie said. He'd worked behind the scenes to support Sam while she was undercover and knew better than anyone what she'd been through during that difficult assignment.

"Better than the last time I saw him. That's for sure." Seeing Roberto took Sam right back to the horrible days that followed the crack house shooting. She'd snuck into the hospital under the cover of darkness to check on the young man who'd become one of her only friends among the Johnson crowd.

At first Roberto had been furious to learn her true identity, but when Sam offered to find him a way out of his life of crime, he'd come around and let her help him. Knowing he was just a kid who'd been sucked into something way bigger than he'd ever bargained for, Sam stepped up for him with the U.S. attorney. As a result, they'd declined to prosecute him as one of Marquis Johnson's group of drug runners.

Sam figured the permanent loss of his legs was punishment enough for the petty crimes Roberto had committed to earn favor with Marquis.

"You did a good thing for him, Sam," Freddie said when they were in the car. "He's gotten his life back on track."

"So it seems." Who, she wondered, was going to help get hers back on track?

"What's next?" Freddie asked.

"Let's go see Faith Miller. I want to know why that rape charge got quashed."

"So do I."

SAM AND FREDDIE waited twenty minutes in the U.S. attorney's reception area for Faith to return from court.

"Ah," she said, lighting up when she saw them waiting. "Here comes the bride!"

"Very funny," Sam said. "Thank God it's almost here so I can be done with all the bride jokes."

"Just FYI," Freddie said, "I'd planned on another six to eight months of jokes."

Sam rewarded him with her sweetest smile. "Not if you expect to continue carrying a gold shield, Detective."

Faith laughed at their banter and showed them into her office. She was one of the identical triplets who served the District as assistant U.S. attorneys. While Sam had also worked closely with Hope and Charity, she was friendliest with Faith.

"What can I do for you?" Faith asked.

"Darius Gardner," Sam said.

All the color drained from Faith's face, and she sat perfectly still behind her file-laden desk. "What about him?"

Sam watched Faith closely. "You remember the case?"

The AUSA shrugged. "Rape accusation a few years back. Didn't go anywhere." She affected a casual tone of voice, but Sam caught the slight tremble of her hand. Glancing at Freddie, she saw that he'd noticed it too.

"What the hell is going on here, Faith?" Sam asked.

"I don't know what you mean. You asked about a case, and I answered you. What more do you want?"

"I want the truth!"

"Why do you care about an old rape case that never made it to court?"

"Why do you *remember* an old rape case that never made it to court?"

The two women stared at each other.

"I asked first," Faith said.

"Fine. The place where he 'allegedly' raped that girl is the same house where Clarence Reece lived."

"The guy who killed his family and carjacked you."

"Right. Cruz, the clippings?"

Freddie handed her the plastic bag containing the clippings about her father's shooting.

Sam placed the bag on the desk in front of Faith. "This was found in Reece's place. Before he offed himself the day he carjacked me, he told me the stuff belonged to a former tenant who'd left it there and never come back to claim it."

"And you think that's Gardner?"

"I don't know. He was one of several people who lived there before Reece moved in."

"Who are the other people?"

"Trace Simmons is one of them."

"I know the name. Gangbanger."

Sam nodded in agreement. "Are you going to tell me why hearing Gardner's name freaks you out so badly?"

Faith's eyes shifted to Freddie and then back to Sam.

"Give us a minute, will you, Cruz?" Sam said.

"Of course." He got up and left the room, closing the door behind him.

Sam waited patiently, giving the other woman a moment to collect herself. "What happened, Faith?" she finally asked.

"This stays between us."

"I need to hear what's staying between us before I agree to anything."

Faith gripped a pen with both hands.

Sam had never seen the usually cool, unflappable prosecutor so undone.

"I want to help you find the person who shot your father, Sam, but I'm not talking about Gardner."

"Then I'll go to Forrester," Sam said, referring to the U.S. attorney. "I'll ask him why a slam dunk rape case was thrown out by one of his AUSAs before it ever got to court."

"Don't."

"Tell me why I shouldn't."

"For Christ sake, Sam! Just leave it the hell alone! You're wading into something you can't even *begin* to understand."

"You're seriously saying that to *me*? What the fuck, Faith? What waters do you think I won't understand after twelve years on this goddamned job?" The other woman's hands were now visibly shaking. "Whatever it is, you can trust me with it. You know that."

When Faith looked up at her there was none of the hard-nosed prosecutor Sam had come to know and respect. Rather, she looked into the eyes of a very frightened woman. In a low, soft tone, Faith said, "He threatened to have my baby niece Molly killed if I didn't drop the case."

Sam tried to digest that. "And you believed him? Surely you've been threatened before."

"Not like this. There's something truly evil about this guy, Sam. You bet your ass I believed him."

"Who knows about this?"

"You and me. Hope had just had Molly. I couldn't exactly share this with her or Charity. If Forrester ever found out, it would end my career—and theirs, if they knew. I never told anyone why we declined to prosecute."

"What did you tell Forrester?"

"That I didn't think we could win. He's a politician.

He wants wins. It didn't take much to convince him to dismiss the charges."

"How about the special victims detectives?" She could only imagine what her police colleagues had thought about their solid case being tossed.

"Gardner claimed the sex was entirely consensual. I told the SVU detectives it would turn into a he said, she said in court."

"And you knew that wasn't true."

"The pictures from the victim's rape kit haunt me," she said with a defeated sigh. "Nothing about that encounter was consensual. I have no doubt I could've gotten a conviction."

"*Why didn't you come to me?*"

Faith's green eyes flooded with tears. "They said they'd chop up the baby and send her back to us in pieces."

Fury, hot and potent, streaked through Sam. "Start at the beginning. Don't leave anything out."

"Sam, *please*. I'm asking you as a colleague and a friend—leave it alone."

Sam rested her elbows on Faith's desk and leaned in. "I'm going to nail his ass to the wall, and you're going to help me."

Faith shook her head and wiped the tears from her face. "Molly is almost three now. How can you ask me to risk that beautiful child—my *sister's* child?"

"How can you sleep knowing you've let a violent rapist roam free all this time?"

"I haven't gotten a full night of sleep in years."

"Faith, come on! You took an *oath*!"

"Don't you dare talk to me about oaths! She's my *niece*! Tell me how well I'd sleep if I go after this sleezeball and something happens to her!"

"You need to talk to Hope about this. She'll tell you the same thing I'm telling you."

Faith snorted with disdain. "She'll *agree* with me. We're talking about her *child*. Don't you have nieces and nephews, Sam?"

"Four," Sam muttered. "Fifth one on the way."

"Put yourself in my place—what would you do if someone threatened to chop one of them up and mail him or her back to you in pieces?"

Sam couldn't even get her head around the idea of it, so she didn't try. "How did he get to you?"

"One of his buddies conveyed the message along with up-close photos of the baby with a gun pointed to her head. I have no idea how they got that close to her, but it certainly got my attention. The next day, Gardner and I came face-to-face in the courthouse. He smiled at me..." A shudder rippled through her willowy frame, and her face lost every bit of remaining color. "The evil... Just pure evil. I knew, right in that moment, that he'd have Molly killed if I pursued prosecution."

"I have to ask you... Has anything like this ever happened before?"

"If you're asking if I've been threatened before, the answer is yes. Almost weekly. But I've never before or since backed away from a prosecution because of a threat. This one was different."

Sam sat back in her chair, frustrated and furious. "I wish you'd come to me."

"I wish I'd felt that was an option."

"You need to tell Hope about this."

Faith shook her head. "Never."

"I'm going to get him, Faith. I'll dig and dig and dig until I find something I can bury him with. If he didn't shoot my dad, I'll find something else. And then I'll take my case right to Forrester himself so Gardner won't have any reason to come at you or your family."

"What about *your* family?"

"I'll take care of them."

"Don't underestimate him, Sam. I've seen a lot of evil in my time in this office, but I've never gotten the vibe from anyone else that I got from him. I can't even describe it."

"Leave it to me. I'll take care of him. And when I'm done with him, he won't be threatening anyone, let alone an assistant U.S. attorney."

"Be careful. Be very, very careful."

Sam flashed a cocky grin. "Always am."

"Keep me posted."

"Not this time. If I leave you out of it entirely, there's no way it can come back on you."

"Thanks, Sam."

"You can thank me after we throw the book at this guy."

"Believe me, I will."

"See you at the wedding?"

"I'll be there."

Sam left Faith's office and found Freddie flipping through a magazine in the reception area. "Cruz, let's hit it."

Startled by her sudden reappearance, Freddie leaped to his feet, and the magazine went flying. He stopped to retrieve it, tossed it on a table and hustled after her. "Where're we going, boss?"

"To nail a scumbag."

"One of my favorite things."

FOUR

"ARE YOU GOING to tell me what happened in there?" Freddie asked as Sam drove them back to HQ.

Sam took a moment to think it over. "I'm going to tell you and Captain Malone and no one else."

"Okay."

She conveyed what Faith had told her.

"Holy shit," Freddie muttered. The rare curse told Sam how affected he was by the story. "What's the plan?"

"We're going to nail his ass—for Faith and the woman he raped." Sam swallowed hard, thinking of her colleague, Detective Jeannie McBride, who'd been abducted and brutally raped during a recent investigation. Jeannie said she planned to attend the wedding, but Sam would believe it when she saw it. Jeannie had barely left her boyfriend Michael's home since being released from the hospital.

"What's the first step?"

"I'm going to see Ramsey—the SVU detective who handled the rape case. While I'm there, I want you to pull every single thing you can find on Gardner. No detail is too small."

"Got it."

"Keep a lid on this, Cruz. I mean it. Faith would lose her job if this ever came to light, not to mention what the bar association might have to say about it."

"I get that the stakes are high."

"I know I can trust you or I wouldn't have told you."

Sam's cell phone chimed with the tune of "When You Wish Upon a Star." She withdrew it from her coat pocket and flipped it open, groaning. "Goddamn it."

Freddie scowled at her. He hated when she took the Lord's name in vain. "What's wrong?"

"Freaking Tinker Bell, reminding me I have my final dress fitting at six." She glanced at her watch. Just after five. Where the hell had this day gone? "I'm going to hit SVU before I head out of here. You're on the rest?"

"Yep."

"Shoot me a report at home. I'll authorize overtime."

"For what?" asked a voice behind her.

Sam spun around to find her captain and mentor standing with his hands on his hips, his silver eyebrows knitted.

"Has there been a murder I don't know about?"

Pressed for time, Sam glanced at Freddie. "Will you please fill in the captain?"

"You got it."

"Dress fitting," Sam said sheepishly.

Malone grinned. "Will you take video so we can laugh at you later?"

The phrase "bite me" was on the tip of her tongue.

"She has something she's dying to say," Freddie said, sharing a laugh with the captain.

God, she couldn't *wait* to get the wedding behind her. "Get to work, Cruz."

He choked back a grin and said, "Yes, ma'am."

Sam forced a phony smile for her boss. "Captain."

"Lieutenant." He tapped his watch. "Don't be late now."

"Bite me," she muttered under her breath and felt better even as laughter followed her out. Navigating her way through HQ, she took the elevator to the third floor where the special victims unit resided. Sam asked the department's admin assistant for Detective Ramsey.

"One minute, Lieutenant. Let me see if he's available."

While she waited, Sam made a quick call to her sister Tracy to let her know she hadn't forgotten about the fitting and would be there shortly. She knew she'd been a bit of a handful as a distracted bride. That was why Shelby, the wedding planner she called "Tinker Bell," had programmed reminders into her cell phone. Without them, Sam would've been even more of a disaster. She had no doubt it would be a wonderful, beautiful, memorable day. But she was ready for the hoopla to be over and life to return to normal.

That thought made her laugh to herself. Since reconnecting with Nick six years after a memorable one-night stand, her life had been anything but "normal," and she wouldn't have it any other way. Suddenly, she was anxious to see him, to be with him, to feel the way she did just being in the same room with him. She'd missed him, and it was time to get things back on track between them.

"Lieutenant?" the admin said. "Detective Ramsey will see you in the conference room. Right this way."

Sam followed the young woman through a maze of cubicles so recently renovated that the new-carpet smell was overpowering. When, she wondered, would her own beleaguered pit get a much-needed face-lift? She made a mental note to take that up with Chief Farnsworth. After she'd closed three high-profile murder cases in short order, he owed her a few favors.

Detective Ramsey was in his mid-fifties with a salt-and-pepper crew cut and a no-nonsense demeanor. "What can I do for you, Lieutenant?"

"I'm interested in an old case of yours, a sexual assault. Darius Gardner was charged but never tried."

His no-nonsense expression became stormy. "Because AUSA Faith Miller totally screwed me over. And then my vic refused to testify. I've always suspected Miller said something to her."

That part was news to Sam. Faith had never mentioned advising the victim not to testify. In light of what Faith had told her, Sam surmised that it was far more likely that Garner had threatened his victim. "Would it be possible to get your file and notes on the case?"

"For what purpose?"

"I'm looking into a cold case, and his name came up."

He thought it over. "Give me a minute."

"That's about all I have. Should I come back tomorrow?"

"I have it handy. I'll be right back." He returned and handed her the file. "You'll get it back to me?"

"Absolutely. Appreciate the courtesy."

"If you wouldn't mind, keep me in the loop. What happened with this one…it stays with you, you know?"

Sam thought of Quentin Johnson. "I do know, and I'll be happy to keep you informed."

"You're quite the little star around here."

Taken aback by his tone, Sam weighed her words carefully. "If you say so."

"Must be nice."

Okay, there was no denying the snide that time. "Something on your mind, Detective?"

"No, ma'am."

Sam made a mental note to look into Ramsey's career trajectory—or lack thereof. She was easily twenty years younger and outranked him by two grades, which she suspected was one reason for his derision.

"Congratulations," he said, seeming to make an effort to be more conciliatory. "On your wedding."

"Thank you. Speaking of that, I'm late. Thanks again for the information."

He nodded, and she felt his eyes—and those of everyone in the division—on her as she made her way through the maze of cubicles.

Well, that was pleasant. If there was one thing about her new life with Nick that Sam couldn't bear it was all the press scrutiny of their relationship. It was relentless and had brought her far more attention than she wanted or needed as a cop. She put up with it because she knew it furthered Nick's campaign and career, but it didn't do much for hers.

On the way to Tinker Bell's fashionable Georgetown storefront, Sam made an effort to shake off the unsettling day and slip into bride mode. Even though she'd had the big white wedding once before and would've been perfectly satisfied to fly off to Vegas and elope, this would be Nick's first marriage. In the six weeks since she'd lost a bet with him and let him set their wedding date, she'd often had to remind herself that she was doing all this for him.

Sam hustled into the store at ten after the hour. Waiting for her were her sisters Tracy and Angela, who was round with her second pregnancy, as well as Tracy's daughters, fifteen-year-old Brooke and seven-year-old Abby, who were serving as Sam's junior bridesmaids. As usual lately, Brooke looked put out by the whole thing while Abby glowed with excitement. She came running when she saw Sam.

"Sam! You're here!"

"Hey, doll face." Sam scooped up the little girl and twirled her around, her heart clutching when she remembered the conversation with Faith. While she'd like to think she knew exactly what she would've done in the same situation, Abby's chubby arms around her neck and the scent of strawberry shampoo clinging to her blond curls gave Sam pause. Was there anything she wouldn't do to protect this child? To protect any of the four children she loved with all her heart?

No, there wasn't. As Abby clung to her, Sam understood why Faith had done what she did.

"Oh, there you are, honey." Sam's stepmother Celia stepped out from a back room wearing the lavender mother-of-the-bride gown they'd chosen weeks earlier.

"Looks fantastic, Celia." Sam put Abby down to take a measuring look at the woman who'd married her father on Valentine's Day. Celia had auburn hair, green eyes and a heart-shaped face that was flushed with excitement at the moment.

"I love it too."

Shelby Faircloth came into the room, dressed in yet another of her endless supply of pink power suits and sky-high heels. Even with the heels, the petite blonde barely reached Sam's shoulder. "Oh yay," she said, clapping when she saw Sam. "Everyone's here. Let's get started."

"Oh yay," Brooke said with a sneer for Shelby.

Since she was bringing up the rear, Sam witnessed the smack upside the head Tracy gave her oldest daughter. "Snap out of it," Tracy said in a low tone. "Despite what you think, it's not all about you this week."

"Fuck off," Brooke said.

Sam mouth fell open. When had her adorable niece turned into such a brat?

Tracy hung back. "Sorry about that."

"What the hell, Trace?"

"She's a pain in my ass."

"You let her talk to you like that?"

"*Let her?*" Tracy snorted. "How do you suggest I stop her?"

"Take her phone. Take everything."

"Done it. A hundred times. She doesn't give a shit."

Angela came back for them. "Are you guys coming?"

"Yeah," Tracy said.

Sam nodded to Angela who went back to rejoin the others. To Tracy, she said, "If there's anything I can do…"

"Don't worry about us. This is your week."

"But still—"

"Let's get this bride into her dress," Tracy said, dragging Sam along with her. "I don't know about you guys, but I can't wait to see her."

SAM DROVE HOME thinking about the ugly scene with Brooke, which had overshadowed the thrill of seeing her wedding ensemble finally and fully fitted to her. After Sam wore one of her dresses at a White House State Dinner, Vera Wang herself had contacted Tinker Bell about designing Sam's dress. The ivory silk dress was strapless and formfitting on top, flaring into a full, embroidered skirt with no train. Sam *loved* it and had a feeling Nick would too.

She cringed when she remembered Shelby flipping out about the bruise the birth control shot had left on her arm. It had never occurred to Sam that it would leave such a big mark. Post flip-out, Shelby had assured her they could cover the bruise with makeup on Saturday. Sam was far more concerned about explaining it to Nick who kept a running inventory of her injuries.

She hated keeping things from him, but she didn't want to upset him the week of their wedding by getting into an emotional discussion about the baby they'd lost. Sam simply couldn't talk about that subject without coming unglued, and her emotions were already raw enough without tearing off that scab during this of all weeks. She'd tell him when they were on their honeymoon, when they were relaxed and removed from the stress of work and wedding planning.

That was the best plan. Hopefully, once she got around to telling him, he'd understand why she'd gotten the shot and why she'd kept it from him. Pulling up in front of their townhouse on Ninth Street, Sam debated stopping over to see her dad before going home. Since she'd moved in with Nick, she tried to see her dad every day, but right now she wanted Nick. She decided to go by her dad's house before work in the morning.

Grabbing the Gardner file, she stood outside their place, taking a moment to appreciate the ramp Nick had had installed as a surprise for her so they could have her dad over. When she'd first seen the wreckage of their front stairs, she'd mistakenly thought her newly freed ex-husband had planted another bomb. The sight had given her a few rough moments before Nick arrived and set her straight. That he'd opened their home to her paralyzed father meant the world to her. There was no denying that her fiancé was one of a kind.

Anxious to see him, Sam hustled up the ramp and used her key in the door. Inside she was greeted by the smell of something mouthwatering and candlelight flickering in the dining room. He emerged from the kitchen wiping his hands on a towel with his BlackBerry tucked into his shoulder.

"You're sure you're okay with staying with Sam's sister Angela and her family Saturday night?" He paused to listen. "Right, Jack's parents. You met them at the dinner at Sam's dad's house. They'll drive you home on Sunday."

Nick laughed and winked at Sam. "I'll be there at noon on Friday. See you then, buddy. Okay. Bye."

"How's Scotty?" Sam asked.

"All kinds of excited about me signing him out of school on Friday." Nick had met the twelve-year-old at a state home for children in Richmond, and the two had formed a fast friendship based initially on their shared love of the Boston Red Sox. The boy had spent a recent weekend with Sam and Nick, and hadn't seemed to mind following Nick around on the campaign trail. Sam suspected there was nowhere the boy wouldn't go if it meant he got to spend more time with Nick, something she could certainly understand.

"Did you remember to order his tux?" she asked.

"All taken care of."

"Of course it is. Do you ever screw anything up? Forget something? Ever act like a *normal* person who occasionally drops one of the seventy-five thousand balls he has in the air at one time?"

Smiling, he said, "Once in a while."

"Will you let me know the next time it happens? I'd really like to savor the moment."

"You got it." He planted a kiss on her forehead and took her coat, hanging it as he always did in the front closet. Sam would've tossed it over the sofa. Why hang it up when she'd just need it again in the morning?

"How was the fitting?" he asked.

"It was great, and the best part? It was the *last* one."

He chuckled. "How's it looking?"

Sam made a face and shrugged. "Eh. You know. A dress is a dress."

"Are you trying to lower my expectations?"

"I'd really hate for you to be disappointed."

With his fingers on her chin he tilted her face to meet

his intense gaze. "You could wear a burlap sack, and I wouldn't be disappointed—as long as you're in it, and as long as I get to take it off you afterward." He punctuated the statement with a sweet kiss.

Whenever he looked at her in that particular way, she positively melted. "Now you tell me! You couldn't have saved me all those damned fittings by telling me that six weeks ago!"

That smile of his… *Whoa*, so potent.

"Are you hungry?" he asked.

"Starved. What's for dinner?"

"Roast chicken, mashed potatoes and vegetables."

"When did you have time to roast a chicken?"

"The grocery store did the roasting. I just bought it and brought it home."

"Which is the most important part of the equation. Smells great."

He led her to the dining room, held her chair and poured her a glass of wine.

Sam couldn't remember the last time one of them had cooked a meal at home. Lately they'd been grabbing meals here and there on the fly. There'd been none of the quality time she'd grown accustomed to since they'd been together.

The meal he'd prepared was tasty and filling, and they lingered over the bottle of white wine.

"Didn't you have a campaign event tonight?"

"I postponed it. Told them I felt the flu coming on."

"Why?"

"Because I had more important things to do tonight."

"What things?"

"Dinner with you, for one."

"Nick," she said, touched by the gesture. "You're in

the middle of a campaign. You can't be skipping important events."

"If one missed cocktail party costs me the election, then it was never mine to begin with." He reached for her hand and brought it to his lips, a gesture so uniquely his that it never failed to set her heart to racing. "I've missed you. Things have been so hectic that we've barely seen each other. I hate that."

"I've missed you too." She linked their fingers. "It's my fault." Swallowing hard to fight back the swell of emotion that threatened to derail her, Sam forced herself to look at him, to *face* him. "I have this bad habit of retreating into myself after… You know."

"It's not entirely your fault, babe. I buried myself in work so I wouldn't have time to think about it."

"I hate that you're hurting. And I hate that I couldn't give you—"

"Don't. Please don't say that." He tugged on her hand and drew her onto his lap, wrapping his arms around her. "You've given me so much, Samantha." He released the clip that held her hair for work and let it rain down around them. "So, so much. More than I ever dreamed of having."

She rested her head on his shoulder, surrounded by the clean, fresh scent of him. "I know how much you want a family of your own."

"You're the family I've never had. You're far more than enough. I've told you that."

"Still…"

"I'm worried about you, babe. I know it rocked you, and I should've been there for you rather than caught up in how it affected me. I'm sorry I wasn't there the way I should've been."

Tears filled her eyes. Whatever had she done to deserve this kind, wonderful man? Hearing that he'd ditched an important campaign event to spend the evening with her filled Sam with guilt over what she'd kept from him, and she knew she had to level with him.

"I did something today. Something I should've talked to you about before I did it." The words were out before she could stop them—so much for her short-lived plan to wait until their honeymoon to talk to him about this.

Under her, his body went rigid. "What?"

"I saw Harry."

"About?"

She lifted her head off his shoulder so she could see his face. "Birth control."

His expression was so impassive that Sam couldn't get a read on what he was thinking. "And?"

"He gave me a shot that lasts three months."

Nick didn't say anything for the longest time. "Oh," he finally said. "I thought you wanted, I mean, I thought *we* wanted..."

"I do. *We* do. But I need to be stronger before we go there again. I was feeling desperate, and I went to him before I came to you, which was wrong. I know it was. I just... I need some time, Nick."

"Did you think I wouldn't understand that?"

"I was afraid you'd be disappointed, and I couldn't bear that. Not again."

"Sam, honey, when are you ever going to learn that you can't possibly disappoint me? The only time you even come close is when you keep stuff from me. Important stuff that we should decide together." The last part he said in a stern tone that got her attention, but when she ventured a glance at him, he was looking at her with nothing but love and concern.

"I'm working on that. I swear I am."

He sighed, hugged her tighter and pressed his lips to her forehead. "I can't even imagine what you've been through with four miscarriages. One about killed me."

Hearing that and seeing the raw pain on his face made Sam wince. "Sometimes I wonder if it just isn't in the cards for me."

"If that's the case, we have other options, and I've told you before I'm fine with adopting or hiring a surrogate. Whatever you want. We'll figure it out when we're ready."

"I'm not sure I have it in me to try again."

"Nothing has to be decided today."

Sam took a moment, chose her words carefully and fought to keep her emotions out of the mix. "I want you to really understand, before you say 'I do' on Saturday, that it's very possible I won't want to try again to have a baby."

"You might feel differently—"

Sam rested a finger over his lips. "And I might not. I need to know you're okay with that. Discovering the plumbing actually works changes everything."

"No, it doesn't. I've told you all along that we'll play this any way you want to play it."

"You need to be sure."

"I'm very sure that I love you, that I can't possibly live without you and I'll take you any way I can get you, even if we never have a baby the old-fashioned way."

"You're not mad about the shot?"

"I wish you'd talked to me about it first, but I understand why you did it. Just remember—whatever is going on, we can always find a way to work it out. Look at everything we've already gotten through together."

"Our life can't always be as wild as it's been lately, can it?"

"Jesus, I hope not."

Sam laughed and realized she felt lighter since she'd told him the truth. She should've known he would get it. Didn't he always? "I love you," she said. "I love you more than anything in this world."

"I love you too, and I can't wait until you're my wife."

"Only four more days—still time to change your mind," she said with a teasing smile.

"Not happening." He kissed her then with all the pent-up passion and desire that had been put on hold the last few weeks. "Let's make another deal," he said when they resurfaced.

"What other deal?"

"The next time something happens—something bad or upsetting—let's go through it together. Let's not do it alone like we did this time."

She nodded. "Deal."

"How about a soak in the Jacuzzi?"

"Oh, yes," she said, sighing at the thought of it. "Please."

FIVE

EVEN THOUGH SHE'D intended to spend the evening with the Gardner file, Sam couldn't seem to work up the energy to get out of the tub. The combination of the warm water, the wine, the company and the clearing of the air with Nick had left her more relaxed than she'd been in weeks.

His finger tracing a circle on her arm drew her out of the languid state she'd drifted into. "What happened here?" he asked of the bruise.

"The shot."

He winced. "Ouch," he said, gently pressing his lips to the mark.

"All better."

"You must've been truly desperate to subject yourself to a shot."

Remembering the needle, Sam shuddered. "Truly."

His lips continued to move on her arm, leaving goose bumps in their wake. "I'm sorry you let it get to that point. I wish you'd told me."

She combed her fingers through his hair. "I know I should have. But to be honest, I was afraid you'd charm me out of it."

"I might've tried."

"I want so badly to give you a family, Nick."

"A family doesn't necessarily mean a baby."

"What do you mean?"

He raised his eyes to meet hers, and the vulnerability

she saw on his face touched her deeply. "I've been thinking... about Scotty."

"So have I."

"Really?"

She nodded. "You're spending a lot of time driving back and forth to Richmond."

Shrugging, Nick said, "I don't mind. I love being with him."

"I do too. He's such a sweet kid."

"I love how grateful he is for even the smallest kindness. He reminds me..."

"He reminds you of yourself, doesn't he?"

Nodding, he said, "I know what it's like to be alone in the world. Even though I had my grandmother, she didn't want me around. I always knew that."

Sam's heart ached imagining Nick as a lonely little boy. "We could do so much for him."

Nick took her hand and linked their fingers. "I think about that all the time. I can't explain it, but the moment I met him I felt like I knew him."

"What're we going to do about that?"

"I have no idea. We barely have time for each other. Just because I'd love to swoop in and change his life, we have to be realistic. He could end up lonelier with us than he is now."

"That wouldn't happen."

"How do you know?"

"Because he wouldn't have just us. He'd have my dad and Celia and Ang and Spence and Jack and Tracy and Mike and their kids. Then there're the O'Connors, your dad, his family. He'd be surrounded by our entire village."

Nick sat up a little straighter. "Are you saying what I think you're saying?"

"I'm saying we should absolutely talk about it and be sure we'd be doing the right thing for all of us."

"Once again, you surprise me, Samantha."

She laughed. "Because I'm thinking the same thing you are? Why is that so surprising?"

"I was pretty sure you wouldn't be all that into the idea."

"From the first time I saw you with him, I knew he was going to be a part of us. I didn't know how or what or when, but I could see that you love him."

Nick reached out to caress her face and leaned in to kiss her. "Thank you for understanding."

"We'll do something about it." She leaned into his embrace. "After the wedding. We'll do something."

"Ready to get out?"

"If we have to."

"It's getting late." He got out first and reached for towels, wrapping one around his waist and holding the other for her. As he draped it around her, he brought her in close to him and held her for a long time.

"Thanks for staying home tonight," she said.

"My pleasure."

Smiling up at him, Sam ran her hands over his muscular chest. "Speaking of your pleasure..."

His cell phone rang in the bedroom, drawing a tortured groan from him. "That's Christina."

"How do you know?"

"She programmed in a special ring tone so I'd know it was her."

Laughing, Sam said, "That's clever of her. I should do that too."

"You don't need it." He kissed her nose and then her lips. "I *always* take your calls. Don't go anywhere. I'll be right back."

"I'll be here." Sam toweled off, combed her hair and brushed her teeth before she ventured into the bedroom and helped herself to one of Nick's T-shirts. She grabbed her own phone and got in bed while Nick paced the room discussing the next day's campaign stops with Christina.

Sam took advantage of him being occupied to text Harry: *I told him, so quit looking at me that way.* Smiling, she pressed Send and awaited his reply.

Predictably, he fired right back. *What way am I looking at you?*

The make-me-feel-guilty way.

Don't blame me for your guilty conscience. What'd he say?

All the right things. As usual.

Good.

Sam was so glad Nick had friends like Harry to help fill the terrible void John O'Connor's death had left in his life.

Any ill effects from the shot?

Just a bruise the wedding planner is freaking about. Thanks for helping me out.

Any time. Get some sleep. Nothing worse than a bride with suitcases under her eyes.

Very funny. See you Friday.

Can't wait.

"What's got you all smiles?" Nick asked as he got in bed.

"Your buddy Harry. He's quite the comedian."

"Are you stepping out on me already? We're not even married yet."

"I like him. He's a pain in my ass, but I like him anyway."

"Everyone likes him. He's a good guy."

"How'd you meet him?"

"In the emergency room of all places."

"Really?"

"About seven years ago, I broke my wrist playing hockey in a rec league. He was doing his ER rotation. We hit it off, and we've been friends ever since. I met Andy through him too," he said of his lawyer friend who was also in their wedding party.

"Only you could break a bone and make a friend."

"Two friends."

"Which wrist did you break?"

He held up his left arm. "This one, thank God. I could still write and drive for the four months it was in a cast."

"Four *months?*"

"Yep. I played years of high school and college hockey with only bumps and bruises. Then I join a league here just for fun. Roughest sons of bitches I ever played with. Happened in my second game with them."

Sam took his left hand and studied his arm. "Is that where you got this?" She traced a finger over a faint scar.

"Uh huh. They had to pin it back together. Hurt like a mother."

Sam planted a trail of kisses over the scar. "Do you still play?"

"Once in a while, but not in that league. I never played with them again."

"I'd like to see you play."

He smiled. "Yeah?"

"I bet you look hot out there."

Drawing her in closer to him, he said, "You think so, huh?"

"I know so." Sam rested her head against his chest, breathing him in. "I've really missed you."

"I've missed *us*. You're essential to me, Samantha."

With the tip of his finger he tipped her chin up and kissed her. "So very essential."

Sam slipped her arms around his neck and fell into the kiss as all the worries of the day disappeared. As he held her tight against him, his tongue caressed hers, teasing and tempting until Sam was out of her mind with desire.

"Nick," she said, gasping. "I want you."

"I was thinking," he said, his lips busy on her neck, "that since it's been a while, maybe we should wait… until our wedding night."

Her hand, which had been cruising down his chest, came to a stop on his belly. "You aren't serious."

"It's been this long, what's a few more days?"

She tilted her hips into his erection. "An eternity?"

He released a choppy laugh that told her how much this show of restraint was costing him.

Sam shifted her hand lower and wrapped it around him, stroking him.

His head fell back on the pillow, and his eyes drifted shut.

"You're sure you want to wait?" she asked, kissing her way down his chest.

"Imagine how good our wedding night will be."

"It'll be good no matter what." She bent her head and took him into her mouth.

"Oh, *God*, Sam."

"Mmmm." She took him deep and loved how he grew harder when she lashed him with her tongue.

"Babe," he said, sounding desperate as his fingers tunneled into her hair. "Sam…"

"Relax," she whispered. "Let it happen."

All the oxygen seemed to leave his body in one long exhale. Sam smiled as she returned to the task at hand. She could tell from the tremble that rippled through him that he was close, so she stroked him harder and sucked him in.

He took in a sharp deep breath and broke out in a sweat. As she felt him reach the point of no return, she backed off and then took him up again.

"Payback is a bitch," he said through gritted teeth.

Sam laughed and decided she'd tortured him enough. This time, she took him deep and right over, reveling in the cry of completion that seemed to come from his very soul.

"Son of a bitch," he whispered, his chest heaving as Sam crawled on top of him. His arms encircled her, and his lips found her forehead. "Give me a minute to recover, and then I'm *so* getting you back for that."

"Promises, promises."

"That fresh mouth of yours…"

"You love my fresh mouth."

He ran his fingers through her hair. "I sure do."

"I've never done that for anyone else."

"Done what?"

"The whole thing."

"Samantha," he said with a sigh as he very smoothly turned them so he was on top. He looked down at her with those amazing hazel eyes, and Sam had never felt more loved or cherished in her life. "We are so very lucky to have found each other—twice."

She looped her arms around his neck. "So lucky. Don't ever let me go, okay?"

"No chance of that."

"Promise?"

"I promise. Do you?"

"I do," she said.

He smiled at her choice of words. "Does this mean we're married now?"

"In all the ways that matter." She tilted her hips against his reawakened erection. "So that makes this our wedding night."

"Nice try," he said as he removed her T-shirt and kissed his way to her breasts.

"Nick..."

"Relax, honey," he said, chuckling. "Let it happen."

EVEN THOUGH SHE was always consciously aware that the nightmare had returned, she was never able to pull herself out of it in time to keep from hearing the screams or seeing the blood. Every time her subconscious forced her to relive one of the worst nights of her life, Sam tried to change the outcome.

If I can get to Quentin before he's hit, maybe, maybe I can get him out of there, she would think as she ran through the decrepit house where Marquis Johnson kept his crack stash. Sam ran as fast as she could, calling for Quentin. The rest of her team was behind her, and she heard them yelling for her to wait for them.

"Don't shoot," she cried. "Hold your fire!" Now, with the benefit of hindsight, she knew how it would end. This time, she could change everything by not allowing her officers to return fire. She could go back and rewrite history to make it come out the way it should have the first time.

"Marquis!" Sam said. "Get Quentin out of here!" Her command was met with silence. Sam inched along the hallway toward the bedroom where all hell had broken loose that fateful night. "Marquis, please. Let him go before he gets hurt."

A muffled cry stopped her heart. Oh, God, it was happening again. She couldn't bear to see that adorable, innocent little boy covered in blood as his shrieking father held his lifeless body.

Rounding the final corner before the back bedroom, Sam gripped her weapon with both hands and extended it in front of her. She should wait for Freddie and the others to catch up to her, but a second muffled cry had her rushing into the room where Darius Gardner had Nick in a chokehold, a gun pressed to his temple. Duct tape covered Nick's mouth. His arms and legs were bound.

Nick's eyes met hers, and Sam faltered. She could see and smell his fear. Blood ran down the side of his face, forcing him to blink to keep it out of his eye. "Darius," she said, her voice little more than a whisper. "Please. Let him go."

"Faith told you not to butt into my life." He drove the gun harder into Nick's head, drawing a moan from Nick that tore at Sam. "You should've listened to her."

"Don't hurt him," Sam said. "I'm the one you want. Let him go, and take me."

Nick let out a low growl and fought against Darius's hold.

It all happened so fast. One minute Sam was pleading with Darius. In the next instant, the gun fired and Nick went down. She ran for him, screaming his name, but something held her back, keeping her from him. Sam struggled against the arms that held her tight.

"Babe, wake up. You're dreaming." His lips moved on her face as sobs shook her body.

The sheer, overwhelming relief at realizing it had been a terrible dream left her weak and clinging to him.

"Shhh," he said. "It's okay. I'm here."

She breathed in his scent, letting the beat of his heart calm and comfort her.

"Want to talk about it?"

Shaking her head, she drew in another deep breath as the implications spiraled through her mind. In all the months since the crack house shooting, the dream had never changed. Until now. What did it mean?

During the course of her career, she'd been threatened plenty of times. Never once had a threat caused her to back down from an investigation. But she'd never had quite so much to lose. What if someone seriously threatened Nick's life? What would she do?

Nick combed his fingers through her hair.

She nuzzled his chest and kissed his throat. The images from the dream kept running through her mind, making her shudder.

As he tightened his arms around her, Sam realized there was absolutely nothing she wouldn't do to ensure his safety—including back off an investigation if it came to that.

"Just a dream, babe," he said, massaging her shoulders.

"Yeah." *Except*, she thought, *it wasn't just a dream. It was her greatest nightmare.*

"Will you be able to go back to sleep?"

She nodded, telling him what he needed to hear so he would get some sleep. His insomnia had been bad lately as the campaign and wedding compounded his stress.

"Sure you don't want to tell me about it?"

"Same old dream. You know the one."

"Hasn't happened in a while. What brought that on?"

"We were talking about the Johnson case today. Probably stirred it up."

"I'm sorry you have to carry that horrible memory with you."

Sam shrugged. "Goes with the territory." Anxious to

change the subject, she tilted her head back and kissed him. "Sorry I woke you."

"I wasn't asleep."

"Nick… Will you take a pill? Please? You can't go another night without sleep."

"I'm okay."

She ran her hand from her chest to his belly. "I need you *very* well rested for this weekend."

Laughing softly, he stopped her hand before it could go any lower. "And I need *you* well rested." He linked their fingers and brought their joined hands to his chest.

"I will if you will."

He rolled to his side and drew her in closer to him. "You got it."

Sam took a deep breath and closed her eyes tight against the image of Gardner holding that gun to Nick's head. A tremble rippled through her body. She blinked back tears, knowing if she broke down he'd never get the sleep he so desperately needed.

"I hate how you suffer over that job."

"I'm all right, Nick. Really. I want you to sleep."

"And I love how you care more about me than you do about yourself."

Sam gripped his hand. "Always will." Lying there in the dark, Sam vowed to nail Darius Gardner to the wall. She would get him before he could harm anyone else. And once she had him, she'd make sure he never saw the light of day again.

SIX

SAM DIDN'T GO back to sleep. She waited until she was sure she wouldn't wake Nick before she eased herself out of his embrace and got up. Glancing at the clock, she saw it was just after three. *Great*, she thought. *Just what I need this week—a sleepless night.* She went across the hall to her closet and found a pair of sweats and pulled them on along with warm socks.

In the far back corner of the closet, she took the top off a shoebox and withdrew one of the six cans of diet cola she'd stashed there for emergencies. A sleepless night the week of her wedding certainly counted as a caffeine emergency.

She went downstairs, got a glass of ice and took Gardner's file into the study to fire up Nick's computer. While she waited for it to boot up, she took pleasure in rearranging the perfectly placed items on his desk. It made her smile to imagine him finding her calling card the next time he sat there.

Sam reached for a framed photo she hadn't seen there before—the picture of them that had run with their interview in the *Washington Star*. When had he gotten that? Nick sat behind her, with his arms around her. Sam traced a finger over the photo, wishing for one for her own desk. She'd have to ask Nick how he'd come to have it.

She cracked open the diet cola and poured it over the ice, practically drooling in anticipation. Since Dr. Harry identified it as the cause of her crippling stomach pain, she hadn't had so much as a sip of soda. One can wouldn't hurt anything, she decided as she took the first sip. The carbonation zipped through her system, giving her a much-needed boost.

"Ah, hello, old friend," she said, taking a second drink. "Oh, how I've missed you."

Resisting the urge to guzzle, she put the glass aside and reached for the file folder. Inside she found the photos that haunted Faith. "Sadistic son of a bitch," Sam muttered as she sifted through them. The woman Gardner attacked hadn't been more than a teenager at the time. Her bruised and battered face told the story of a vicious assault.

She withdrew the victim's statement and tried to read it, blinking when the words jumbled into an unreadable mess. "Goddamn it," she muttered, frustrated by the dyslexia that plagued her at times of stress or exhaustion. Closing her eyes, she took a deep, calming breath and tried again. No good.

Then she remembered Nick had showed her how the computer could read for her. She scanned the document and sat back to listen to the techno-sounding narration.

Sam forced herself to focus on the report given by Gardner's traumatized victim and was chilled by the monotone recitation of what had been an emotionally devastating event. Once again her thoughts drifted to her detective and friend, Jeannie McBride, who'd recently survived an equally horrific attack.

As an officer charged with keeping people safe in the District of Columbia, Sam was infuriated on behalf of Gardner's victim and Jeannie. At least they'd gotten the bastard who attacked Jeannie.

Remembering the elbow that had connected with her abdomen during his arrest had Sam resting a hand on her belly. Because of him, she'd lost the baby she and Nick had wanted so badly. She'd never forgive that son of a bitch for what he'd taken from them—and from Jeannie and his other victims. But he was locked up where he belonged, and after hearing the report from Gardner's victim, she was determined to lock him up too.

Nick's hands landed on her shoulders, startling her. "What're you doing up?" he asked. "And *why* must you mess with my desk *every* time?"

"So you'll know I was here." Smiling, she looked up at him, noting the fatigue that clung to him during particularly intense bouts of insomnia.

"As if I could ever forget you're here." He scowled when he saw the glass on the desk. "I thought you gave that up."

"Just one. I needed a boost. What're *you* doing up?"

"Couldn't sleep without you."

"I'm sorry." Sam gathered up the papers on the desk. "Come on, let's go back to bed." The pile slipped from her fingers and scattered on the floor.

Nick bent to retrieve the photos, wincing at the images of Gardner's victim. "What happened to her?"

"Beaten and raped."

"Is she related to a new case of yours?"

Sam shook her head. "Possible new lead in my dad's case. But it'll keep until tomorrow. You need sleep."

"And you don't?"

"It wasn't happening, so I figured I'd get some work done."

He pulled up the other chair and dropped into it. Sam let her eyes take a lazy journey over broad shoulders, well-defined pectorals and washboard abs. He had just the right amount of dark chest hair trailing into the sweatpants he'd put on.

He waved a hand to get her attention. "Hello?"

Sam realized she was staring at him. "Sorry, just enjoying the view."

Grinning, he said, "You can enjoy it all you want next week."

"Can't wait. That's the part I'm most looking forward to."

"Me, too." Gesturing to the pictures, he raised an eyebrow.

Sam filled him in on what Gonzo and Freddie had uncovered about the former tenants at the house where Clarence Reece murdered his family.

"How does she fit in?" Nick asked, gesturing to the photo of the battered woman.

"Gardner was accused of raping her in the house shortly before my father was shot."

"So he's locked up?"

"I wish. The case got tossed."

"How come?"

"Procedural stuff. Anyway, it's probably another dead end on my dad's shooting."

"What aren't you telling me?"

"What do you mean?"

"Don't play coy with me, Samantha. Spill it."

Unnerved by the way he read her so easily, she studied his handsome face for a long moment. "You can't tell anyone. Ever."

"Understood."

"Faith Miller could lose her job."

"The AUSA?"

Sam nodded. "Gardner threatened her. One of his minions told her he'd chop up her baby niece and return her to her parents in pieces."

Nick blanched. "And she believed him?"

"She had a face-to-face with him the next day in court. The way he looked at her, she had no doubt he'd do it."

Nick picked up a picture of the victim and studied it intently. "Now you've made her yours, and you're going after him."

"I can't let him get away with that! He *threatened* a federal prosecutor."

"Who chose to back off. That was her call."

"So I should sit back and allow a violent criminal to walk the streets? Maybe if Faith hadn't backed down, my dad never would've been shot."

"You have no way to know that."

"I can find out."

He put down the photo, leaned his arms on his knees and looked at her. "I want you to do something for me."

She'd never seen that particular expression on his face before and was taken aback by it. "What?"

"Let this one go. It's not your fight."

"How can you say that? He might've shot my father!"

Pointing to the woman in the photo, he said, "Her fight is not yours. Not this week. *Not* this week."

"Because of the wedding."

He took her hands and linked their fingers. "We're so close to having it all, Samantha. I've never wanted anything more than to have you as my wife. Please don't take this on. Not this week."

"You're not being fair. This is my *job*."

"This time it's personal, and you know it."

"Because of Jeannie."

"That and your dad and a lot of other things."

"You can't make a habit of this."

"I won't."

While the cop in her wanted to rant and rage, the fiancée understood him well enough to know he wouldn't make a habit of it. "All right."

"All right what?"

"All right, I won't go after Gardner for the rape. Not this week."

"Thank you."

"Now can we go to bed?"

He stood, helped her up and drew her in tight against him. "So close, Samantha."

Resting her head against his chest, she closed her eyes. The image of Gardner pressing the gun to Nick's head made her shudder. She would get him. Maybe not the way she'd planned to. But she *would* get him.

SAM WAS STRAPPING on her shoulder harness and turning up her nose at the oatmeal Nick had made for breakfast when her phone rang. She took the call from her stepmother. "Hey, Celia, what's up?"

"Are you coming by on your way out this morning?"

"I was planning to. Why?"

"I don't want to worry you, but your dad has seemed a little…off this week."

Sam was immediately on alert. "How so?"

"Quiet and kind of morose. I can't seem to cajole him out of it. He was just to the doctor yesterday, so I know it's nothing physical."

Celia sounded dejected, which wasn't at all like her.

"I was hoping you might talk to him," Celia added.

"I'll be right over."

"Thanks, Sam. I know you're so busy this week—"

"I'm never too busy for him. Or you."

"That's sweet of you, honey. I'll see you soon."

"What's up?" Nick asked after she ended the call.

"Not sure. Celia says my dad is in a funk."

"When you think about it, it's amazing he's not in a funk more often."

"True." Sam downed the last half of a glass of orange juice, wishing it was a diet cola. "I'm going to head over there and see what's up."

"Want me to go with you?"

She bent to kiss him. "No need, but thanks for offering."

Nick raised a hand to her face and kissed her more intently. "Four more days."

She leaned her forehead against his. "Mmm. Five more days until beach and sun."

"Can't wait. Let me know what's up with your dad."

"I will."

"Be careful out there today, Samantha."

"Always am."

Sam walked to her father's house with a growing sense of dread. Since he was shot more than two years ago, Skip had done such an amazing job of staying upbeat and positive despite having every reason to not be either. His attitude had gone a long way toward helping those who loved him to accept his new reality.

She had feared the day might come when he just couldn't stay positive anymore. And like Nick had said it was amazing it hadn't happened sooner. "Not this week, Skippy," she whispered as she took the ramp to her father's front door. "Please not this week."

Inside, she found Celia waiting for her in the living room and gave her stepmother a quick hug.

"Look," Celia whispered, gesturing to the kitchen where Skip sat in his chair with the *Washington Post* loaded into his reading device—just like every other morning. However, rather than peruse the paper the way he normally did, Skip stared out the window. "He's been like that for a couple of days now. No interest in anything."

"I'll talk to him."

"Thanks, Sam. If anyone can snap him out of it, you can."

Sam swallowed hard. No pressure or anything. "I'll do my best." She patted Celia's arm and went to the kitchen.

"Hey, Skippy." She dropped a kiss on his freshly shaven cheek. "How goes it?"

"Oh, hey. Where'd you come from?"

"Three doors down the street."

That earned her a weak smile. "How are things at wedding central?"

"Not too bad." Sam helped herself to a bottle of water from the fridge and cracked it open. "Shelby is doing a good job of keeping the madness far, far away from us."

"Earning her keep anyway."

Sam sat at the table. "For what Nick is paying her, it's the least she can do." She studied him for a moment and noticed he looked tired and wan. A stab of fear caught her off guard. While she'd always known it would've been so much better for him in many ways if the bullet had killed him, she was eternally grateful that it hadn't. "How are you?"

"Good."

"Anything new or exciting?"

He glanced at her, suspicious. "What's with the small talk?"

She shrugged. "Just checking on my dear old dad. Any objection to that?"

"If you've got something on your mind, Sam, spill it."

"Gonzo and Cruz tracked down the guy who owns Reece's place. We're following some leads. Might be something. Might not." In two years of hunting her father's shooter, Sam had learned to not get her hopes up—or his.

"You'll keep me posted."

"Absolutely." She found it odd that he didn't want the details on the leads. "Something bothering you, Skippy?"

"Why do you ask?"

"You seem a little, I don't know…off…maybe."

He looked away from her. "I'm fine. You've got plenty to think about this week without fretting about me."

Sam reached out to squeeze his right hand, the one spot that retained sensation. "I *always* fret about you, and you know that. Tell me what's on your mind—and don't say it's nothing. You can pull that shit with everyone else, but not with me."

He grunted out a laugh. "The chip off my old block."

"Exactly."

"I've been thinking a lot about you this week."

Not at all sure she was prepared for the direction this conversation was taking, Sam continued to hold his hand. "What about me?"

"I don't know if I say it enough or if I've ever said it, but you know I'm so proud of you, don't you?"

Definitely not prepared. She cleared her throat. "Of course I know that."

"And that you've found the perfect guy for you. I couldn't have picked anyone better for my little girl."

"I'm so glad you like him. Means a lot to me."

"I'm just sorry that I can't…you know…"

She really didn't know. "What?"

His sharp blue eyes were filled with despair that broke Sam's heart. "I never told you how much I hated giving you away to Peter. I couldn't stand him. But Nick…I sure do wish I could give you away to him. I'm sorry I can't."

"What are you talking about? Of course you're giving me away. Who else would do it?"

"But I can't—"

"Yes, you can. I have a whole plan worked out." And it dawned on her that she probably should've shared it with him. "I was thinking I'd put my hand on your shoulder, and we'll go in like that. If that's okay with you."

"If you're sure that's what you want."

"Dad…Come on, I can't do this without you. It's exactly what I want."

Right before her eyes he seemed to brighten. "Okay then."

"I wish you had talked to me about this rather than stewing in silence."

"I didn't want to bother you."

Sam got up and rested her head on his shoulder. "Just because it seems like everything is changing, some things will never change. You got me?"

"Yeah," he said gruffly. "I got ya. Love you, Sam Holland."

"Love you too."

"Could I ask you something else?"

She rested her hands on his shoulders. "Anything."

"Is your mother coming?"

"Not this time."

"Did you invite her?"

Sam shook her head. "I wanted you to be able to enjoy yourself."

"And after the scene I made at your first wedding—"

"That had nothing to do with why I didn't invite her this time. I don't want her there."

"I hate that you girls never see her."

"That was her choice, not ours. She should've thought

of us before she cheated on you." She kissed his forehead. "I'll see you tomorrow if not before."

"I'll be here."

"You'd better be." She left him with a smile and went into the living room where Celia was wiping up tears.

"I should've known it had something to do with the wedding," she whispered.

Sam hugged her. "It never occurred to me that he'd be worried about giving me away. I should've talked to him about it sooner."

"Your plan is perfect, honey."

"I'm glad you think so. Nick will drop off Dad's tux on Friday."

"Sounds good. Thanks for coming by."

"Like I told him—nothing is changing. I'm right up the street any time you need me. My future husband saw to that."

"Which is just one of the many reasons we love him."

SEVEN

DRAINED FROM THE conversation with her father and beating herself up for not talking to him sooner about the wedding, Sam arrived at her HQ office to find Shelby Faircloth waiting for her. "Did we have an appointment, Tinker Bell?"

"Nope, just a few last-minute details that I need to pin you down on, and since I can't get Mohammad to come to the mountain…"

Sam grinned at her. She'd been fully prepared to hate whatever wedding planner they hired, but Shelby was damned hard to hate. "Mohammad is at your service. Fire away."

Shelby withdrew a pink portfolio from a pink briefcase.

"Don't you ever get sick of all the pink?" Sam asked.

Shelby recoiled. "Sick of pink? Never! It's my signature color."

"No! *Really?*"

Grinning at Sam's sarcasm, Shelby withdrew a three-panel brochure containing the groupings of flowers she'd given Sam to choose from. "This is it. You *have* to decide. What's it going to be? Orchids, calla lilies or tulips?"

Sam moaned and put her head down on the desk. "I can't decide! I like them all!"

"I've got the florist and the cake lady so far up my kazoo I can't take a deep breath without hearing from one of them. You can't put it off any longer."

"Which one would you pick?"

"It's not my wedding."

"*Shelby!*"

"Most brides would've made this decision weeks ago. It's only because all these people are so thrilled to be affiliated with your wedding that they've let you slide this long."

"Eeny, meany, miney, mo..."

Shelby dissolved into laughter. "I should've gone to Nick with this."

"Why didn't you?"

"I figured *something* had to be your choice."

Sam scowled at her. "Fine. Go with the orchids. That's it. A decision. Are you happy?"

"I'm thrilled!" Shelby fired off a text message from her BlackBerry. "Now, let's talk about your hair."

"What about it?"

"Up and sleek, down and smooth, up and messy." Shelby placed photos of each style in front of Sam.

"What will best hide this?" Sam pointed to the still-healing scar at her hairline from the car accident she and Nick had been in.

"Don't worry about that. My makeup girl will make it disappear."

"What makeup girl?"

"The one I hired to do your makeup."

"I'll do my own."

"Can you make that scar disappear? How about those bags under your eyes?"

"Now you're just being mean."

"I'm keeping it real, sister. You need her."

"I want Nick to recognize me when I walk in there."

Shelby rolled her eyes. "Puleeze. Would I hire someone who'd make you look freakish?"

"To pay me back for being a pain in your ass? Yes."

Snorting with laughter, Shelby said, "Then stop being a pain in my ass and *decide*." She tapped on the photos to refocus Sam's attention. Even Shelby's fingernails were painted pink.

"That one." Sam pointed to the sleek updo with the flower tucked in. "Nick prefers it long, but he can take it down afterward."

"There's the spirit. Now, about favors. What'd you decide?"

"Instead of favors, we're doing a donation in the name of each guest to the Christopher and Dana Reeve Foundation for spinal cord research."

"I love that idea."

"I'm glad you approve."

"We'll have something printed up and placed on the tables." Shelby withdrew a velvet pouch from her bag. "One more thing." Tugging open the pouch, she dropped three platinum rings on the desk.

"Don't you have enough work to do, Lieutenant?"

The voice coming from the doorway turned her stomach. "Get out of here," she said, refusing to even look at her nemesis Lieutenant Stahl.

"I'll have to talk to your captain about how you're spending your work time."

Sam still didn't look at him as she got up and shut the door in his face. "Now," she said to Shelby, "you were saying?"

Shelby cleared her throat. "We can do this after work if that would be better for you."

"Now is fine." Looking at the rings for Nick, Sam's heart beat faster all of a sudden as it suddenly dawned on her that they were getting *married. Saturday.* "Oh, boy," she said, perusing the choices. "They're all beautiful." Sam picked them up one-by-one and studied them closely. The first was made of brushed platinum with engraved edges. The second had two engraved circles in the middle, and the third was the brightest of the batch, also with engraved edges. "Which one best matches the one he chose for me?"

"Nice try, but you are *not* getting that out of me. They all match yours."

"All right then, which one do you like best for him?"

"I like them all, or I wouldn't have brought them to you."

"Just for the record—you're no help at all."

Shelby giggled. "I beg to differ."

Sam looked the rings over again and kept coming back to the first one—classic and elegant, but not flashy. Just like him. "This one." She held it up for Shelby.

"Excellent. Now what would you like to have engraved inside?"

Sam blanched. "*Engraved?* I have to *engrave* something?"

"Well, it is customary."

"What did he put in mine?"

Shelby rolled her eyes. "Stop asking me that stuff."

Sam rested her hand on her weapon. "I could make you tell me."

"No, you couldn't."

"You're awful ballsy, Tinker Bell. I gotta give you that."

"I have to be to manage you."

A knock on the door interrupted them. "Unless you're Stahl, enter."

Freddie entered. "Definitely not Stahl."

"What's up, Cruz?"

"I can come back when you're not busy."

"Help me out here—what should I have engraved inside Nick's ring?"

"You haven't decided that yet?"

"Thank you," Shelby said. "A man after my own heart."

"You're too old for him," Sam said, earning a glare from Shelby. Returning her attention to Freddie, she handed him the ring she had chosen. "You like this one?"

He took it from her, examined it from every angle and held it up to the light. "Yep. That works."

"So what do I put inside?"

Shelby reached into her bag and withdrew yet another piece of paper. "Here are some suggestions."

Sam scanned the list and passed it to Freddie. "Nothing really jumps out at me."

"Personally, I like 'Someone to watch over me,' because you certainly need that," Freddie said, which got him a scowl from his boss and a snort from Shelby.

"If you don't have anything productive to add, hit the road," Sam said to her partner.

"I need to talk to you about Gardner when you're free."

"Give me five."

"Good ring choice," Freddie said on his way out. "Nick will like it."

Shelby leaned in to whisper to Sam. "He hasn't RSVP'd for the wedding yet."

"Huh?"

Shelby shrugged.

Sam couldn't imagine why Freddie hadn't replied to the invitation. "I'll talk to him."

"Now, about the inscription…"

"I think I know what I want," Sam said, feeling embarrassed. "It's kind of hokey, but it works for us."

Shelby reached for a pen. "Ready when you are."

"How about, 'You're my home. Always, Samantha.'"

Shelby looked up at her, clearly startled.

"What? That's stupid, isn't it?"

"Not at all." Shelby wrote it down. "In fact, I think it's just right. I'll get the ring over to the engraver." She got busy gathering up her belongings. "We should be all set now."

"What about Scotty's gift to Nick? The Fenway Park cake? That's good to go, right?"

"I was over there earlier to check on their progress. It'll be fabulous."

"Scotty is so excited about that."

"With good reason. Nick will love it."

Thinking about the other gift she'd procured for Nick and Scotty made Sam smile. She couldn't wait to give it to them on Friday. "Shelby?"

"Yes, ma'am?"

"You did a great job of keeping the crazy away from me. I appreciate that, and I'm sorry if I was a bit of a handful."

"I meet a lot of brides and grooms, but every so often I get to work with a couple so absolutely perfect together that it's my pleasure to do whatever it takes to ensure their day is every bit as perfect as they are for each other." She leaned in to squeeze Sam's hand. "I'll see you Friday, and don't worry about a thing."

"I won't," Sam said, taken aback by Shelby's compliment.

"Get those vows written," Shelby called over her shoulder as she left in a cloud of pink.

"Oh my God," Sam moaned, dropping her head to her desk once again. "*Vows!*"

"WHAT'VE YOU GOT on Gardner?" Sam asked Freddie.

"I dug into some of his priors, and it seems nothing

ever sticks to him. He's managed to plead his way to probation for charges that should've gotten him locked up for years."

"You're thinking he's pulled this intimidation thing before."

"Seems possible."

"Except we can't exactly go around interviewing former assistant U.S. attorneys about something that could possibly get them disbarred."

"True. So what's the plan?"

"Let's find out where he and his pal Simmons were on December 28th, two years ago."

"With you, boss."

Once they were in the car, Sam tried to find a tactful way to broach the subject of the wedding. She'd been surprised to hear that Freddie hadn't responded. "So, um, are you coming on Saturday?"

"Of course I am. Why?"

"You never sent back the RSVP thingie. Shelby's having vapors over it."

"Oh. Sorry. I was…waiting, but um, I'll get it to you later on."

"No need to worry about the card. I'll tell her you're coming. Unless…Are you bringing someone?"

He looked down and brushed what might've been doughnut powder off his jeans. "I asked Elin."

Sam almost drove off the road. "You *did*? When?"

"A week ago."

"And?"

"She said no."

Sam had no idea what to say.

"It was stupid. I shouldn't have asked her. Nothing's changed, right? My mother still can't stand her, and I'm not interested in a sex-only relationship. So what's the point?"

"There must be a point if you asked her in the first place."

"It's so stupid."

"What is?"

"I only went out with her for a month, but I can't stop thinking about her. I miss her."

"Did you tell her that?"

"Not really. I said I wanted to see her, asked if she wanted to go to the wedding and she said she didn't think it was a good idea. That was it."

He was so dejected that Sam's heart went out to him, even though she hadn't liked Elin for him, either. "Is it possible," Sam said, clearing her throat, "that you might be, you know, in love with her?"

"How would I know? I've never been in love."

"I hate to say that it seems like you could be now if you can't stop thinking about her and you miss her so much."

"What do I *do*?"

"That depends on you. Are you able to get past your mother's disapproval and move forward with Elin or…"

"Or what?"

"Or not," Sam said with a shrug.

Moaning, Freddie banged his head against the headrest. "I can't *deal* with this. I seriously can't."

Sam pulled into a parking space in Washington Heights and cut the engine. "You're almost thirty years old, Freddie. At some point you have to cut the cord with your mother and live your own life."

He looked over at her. "I thought you were glad I wasn't with Elin anymore."

"I'm not glad you're unhappy."

"I want to be the guy who tells off my mother and does whatever the heck I want, but that's so not me."

"Christ, you don't even swear properly."

That drew a short laugh from him. "What've I asked you about taking the Lord's name in vain?"

"Yeah, yeah. I'm going to tell you something, but you have to promise you'll never let on to your mother that I encouraged you to pursue Elin."

Smiling, he said, "Promise."

"I first met Nick six years ago. We spent an incredible night together and connected on every possible level. But then he never called."

"That doesn't sound like him."

"Turns out he *did* call—repeatedly, but douche bag Peter, who was my roommate at the time, never gave me his messages."

"That son of a bitch!"

"*There* it is!" Sam said, laughing.

"I can believe he'd do that!"

"Peter worked my disappointment to his advantage. Wormed his way in by pretending to be my friend. Eventually, Nick gave up on me." She looked over to find Freddie hanging on her every word. "I can't tell you how much I wish I'd tried to call him rather than just accepting he hadn't called me. Can you imagine how different the last six years would've been for me—and him?"

"No bombs, no restraining orders…"

She smiled. "Exactly. When I was married, I'd take these mental vacations and allow myself to remember that one perfect night with Nick. It would get me through, you know? It made me so sad to think he hadn't called."

"Wow, that really sucks."

"Do you understand why I'm telling you this?"

"Ahhh, is it because all this talk of weddings has made you go soft?"

Sam punched his arm lightly. "Don't spend years pining away for the woman you love when all you have to do is pick up the phone."

"I get it, and I appreciate you sharing that with me. I had no idea. I knew you'd met Nick a long time ago, but not all that about Peter. That guy is such a scumbag."

"You won't get any argument from me on that. So you'll think about what I said?"

Freddie nodded. "Thank you."

"Tell you what. I'll let Shelby know you're coming with a guest—just in case."

"But what if—"

Sam rested her hand on his arm. "Either way, it's fine. With or without. It's up to you." She glanced at the dilapidated row houses. "Let's talk to Gardner."

As they approached the house, Sam noticed it was the best-looking place on the run-down block. It boasted a fresh coat of white paint and bushes rather than the trash that collected in front of the neighboring houses.

"Nice place," Freddie said. "For this neighborhood."

"What do you want?"

Sam looked up to the second-floor window where Gardner had a gun trained on them. "Fuck," she muttered. Through the window Gardner had cracked open, Sam heard a baby begin to cry. The sound sent a cold chill down her spine as she reached for her weapon.

"*What do you want?*"

Sam flashed her badge. "We'd like to speak to you about an incident two years ago." Sam made an effort to keep her voice calm. "In late December."

"What incident?"

"Shooting on G Street. A cop was hit."

"I don't know nothing about that."

"You once lived in a house owned by Gerald Price?" Sam rattled off the address.

"Yeah, so?"

The baby's cries were getting louder, which ramped up Sam's anxiety. "We found items in the house referring to the shooting. Newspaper clippings, reports, photos."

"What's that got to do with me?"

"Where werc you on December 28th, two years ago?"

He released a harsh laugh. "You expect me to know that off the top of my head? Fuckin' cops. Get the hell out of here. I got nothing to say to you."

Sam swallowed hard and tried to forget about the threats this man had made toward Faith Miller as well as the pictures of his battered rape victim. "I need you to tell me where you were that day."

"And *I* need *you* to get the fuck off my property before I get pissed."

"We can continue this conversation downtown."

"Sam…"

She waved Freddie off. "What's it going to be Mr. Gardner? Here or downtown?"

A shot rang out. Before Sam could register that he'd actually shot at them, she was flying through the air. She landed under Freddie in the next yard over from Gardner's place. In the second before her head made contact with a large rock, Sam had the wherewithal to realize that Nick was going to be really mad when he heard about this.

Then everything went black.

EIGHT

SAM BATTLED HER way through the fog of pain and confusion to discover she was in the back of an ambulance. "Freddie," she said as the events at Gardner's house came rushing back to her. "Where's Cruz?"

The paramedic put his hands on her shoulders to stop her from sitting up. "Detective Cruz stayed at the scene to deal with the shooter."

Sam's tongue felt too big for her mouth. "Tell me he's not there alone."

"The place is crawling with cops. Don't worry."

"We get Gardner?"

"Your partner was quite the hero. He dragged you to safety and called for backup. SWAT got Gardner."

"Jeez. How long was I out?"

"Twenty-five minutes."

"Shit." The pain radiating from her head suddenly had her full attention. "There was a baby in the house. I heard a baby crying."

"Social services is on it."

"Need my phone." She squirmed on the gurney, trying to get her phone from her coat pocket. Her head pounded and her stomach surged with nausea. "Shit, did I lose it?"

"Lieutenant, you need to stay still. You could have a concussion."

Having suffered a concussion in the car accident a few short weeks ago, Sam could've diagnosed that herself. Nick would be seriously pissed. "I really need a phone.

I swear I won't move if you let me borrow yours." She had once promised Nick she'd call him the minute she could any time something crazy happened at work. Unfortunately, she'd had to keep that promise far more often than either of them liked.

Uttering a sigh, the paramedic produced a touchscreen cell phone.

"I don't know what to do with that. Will you dial a number for me?"

"Maybe after that I can do your nails for you too."

"I do need a manicure for my wedding."

He laughed. "What's the number?"

Sam rattled off Nick's cell number, praying he'd take the call from a number he didn't recognize. "Come on, come on, pick up." When she reached his voicemail, Sam handed the phone back to the paramedic. "Call again. Please."

Frowning at her, the paramedic redialed.

"Come on, Nick. Pick up."

NICK SPENT THE morning in meetings with his campaign team, but couldn't concentrate on work as he thought about the previous evening. Whatever Sam dreamed about had frightened her deeply, and that had rattled him.

And when he thought about that freak Gardner and what he'd done to that poor girl... He shuddered remembering those photos. Asking Sam not to pursue the case against Gardner wasn't something he'd done lightly. He also knew it wasn't something he could do again any time soon.

All morning he'd had a bad feeling nagging at him. She'd promised she wouldn't go after Gardner for the rape of that girl. On the way into the office it had dawned on him that he'd failed to include investigating what role

Gardner might've played in her father's shooting in his wedding week moratorium.

"Senator?"

Startled, he looked up at Christina, his chief of staff. "I'm sorry. What were you saying?"

"We're talking about your latest numbers in southern Virginia. We need to spend more time in Norfolk, Newport News and Virginia Beach after your vacation."

Nick's BlackBerry buzzed in his pocket. "Excuse me." He checked the caller ID, didn't recognize the number and returned the phone to his pocket. "What's the issue in that area?"

"Heavy concentration of military," the head pollster said. "Because you've never served—"

The phone buzzed again. "Sorry," Nick mumbled. "Crazy week." Normally, he'd never bother with his phone during a meeting, but there was that *feeling* he just couldn't shake. He glanced at the caller ID, saw the same number as before and took the call.

"Nick Cappuano."

"Oh thank goodness you answered."

"Samantha?"

"Something happened, but I'm fine."

Nick sat up straighter in his seat. "What happened?"

"Freddie and I got shot at, and I smacked my head. They're taking me in to get it checked." He heard her ask someone which hospital they were taking her to.

"Going to GW," she said to Nick. "It's no biggie. Coupla stitches maybe. Won't show on Saturday."

"Who shot at you?" Nick asked, taking in the stunned expressions on his staffers' faces. Why couldn't he have fallen for an accountant?

"We went to talk to Gardner about my father's shooting, and he was *not* happy to see us. The good news is now we've got him on charges that'll stick. Even he can't wiggle out of shooting at cops."

Nick watched as Christina signaled to the others to step out of the office. When the door shut behind them, he said, "I thought you were going to stay away from him."

"I never mentioned the rape."

"Well, that's good of you. You stuck to the letter of our agreement. I appreciate that."

"You're pissed."

"You knew I would be."

He heard her release a deep sigh. "I needed to ask him about my father's shooting."

"And look at where that got you—yet another trip to the ER, the week of our wedding, no less."

"The last time wasn't my fault. You'll recall that the gang members were gunning for us."

"I don't appreciate you making light of this, Samantha."

"I'm not making light. I have to go. We're almost there. I'll see you at home."

"I'm coming to get you. Don't move from that hospital until I get there." He ended the call before she could put up an argument.

For a long time he sat there, riveted by overwhelming anger and impotence. There wasn't a goddamned thing he could do to keep her safe. He thought he'd accepted that new fact of his life, but apparently he hadn't. Not if the fury he was experiencing at the moment was any indication. The last thing they needed the week of their wedding was a big, fat fight, but as he left the Capitol and headed for the GW Emergency Room, he feared that's exactly what was going to happen.

FREDDIE LEANED IN for a closer look at the cut on Sam's head and winced. "I feel so bad. I never noticed the rock."

"Since you probably saved both our lives, I wouldn't worry about it."

"I saw the gun move and just reacted."

"You did good. I heard you were like a superhero out there."

"Nah," he said, brushing off the compliment. "Nick's gonna be pissed at me for getting you hurt this week."

"I imagine he'll join me in thanking you for making sure I didn't get killed." She looked up at her ashen-faced partner. "Tell me you've got Gardner in custody."

"On his way to HQ as we speak."

"Is Captain Malone here?" Sam asked.

"In the waiting room."

"Go get him for me, will you?"

"Sure." Freddie reached into his coat pocket, withdrew Sam's phone and handed it to her. "Found it after the paramedics carted you away."

"Oh good. I was wondering where it was."

"I'll send Malone in."

Sam closed her eyes and focused on remaining as still as possible to calm the relentless pounding in her head. The doctor had ordered a CT scan to confirm the concussion, which Sam had told him was a waste of time. He'd also indicated the need for five or six staples to close the wound. Fabulous. She wondered if Tinker Bell had ever had a bride with staples in her head before. The thought of asking her would've made Sam want to laugh if her head hadn't been pounding.

Captain Malone stepped into the room. "This is beginning to be a disturbing pattern, Lieutenant. I've heard they're giving you a frequent-flyer card."

"That's very funny. Ha. Ha."

He smiled and leaned in for a closer look at the injury. "At least it won't show in the pictures."

"For which I'm grateful. Listen, I need you to do something for me."

"As always, Lieutenant, I am at your service."

"I have to tell you something that has to be handled with the utmost discretion. The career of a colleague and friend hangs in the balance."

His expression turned serious. "Understood."

She told him about Gardner's threats toward Faith Miller and the rape case that had never been prosecuted. "The victim was nineteen at the time and refused to testify. She's older now, and he's locked up. Someone needs to talk to her, compel her to testify."

"I'll see to it."

"Bring Forrester in on the new charges," she said of the U.S. attorney. "I don't want Gardner sliding through again."

"He took a shot at two cops and just missed you both," Malone said. "He's not getting away with that."

"You'll take it right to Forrester?"

Malone nodded.

"Let's nail him on the whole package this time." As Sam's burst of energy began to fade, she closed her eyes to seek relief from the relentless pounding. "I also want to know where he was on December 28, 2008."

"We'll find out," Malone assured her.

"His buddy Simmons too. Someone left that stuff about my father's shooting in Reece's house. I want to know who."

"You take it easy. We're on it."

Sam looked up at him. "There's something about this Gardner guy. I've never had such a strong feeling about any suspect since my dad was shot."

"If he did it, Sam, we'll get him."

She appreciated the fierce tone of his voice. She wasn't the only one who desperately wanted to catch her father's shooter. He had a police department full of friends who'd like five minutes alone with the person who'd condemned him to life in a wheelchair. "Thanks."

"Get some rest," Malone said. "I'll check on you later."

Sam heard the captain exchange greetings with Nick in the hallway and braced herself to deal with her furious fiancé.

Nick came into the room and stopped short as he took a visual inventory of her and the blood-soaked coat on the chair next to her.

Sam held out a hand to him. "It's not as bad as it looks."

He stepped forward and wrapped his fingers around hers. "I heard it was a very close call."

"Nah, he missed by a mile."

"I'm not finding this funny."

Sam brought his hand to her lips. "I know, babe. I'm sorry."

"If there's any upside, at least you'll be out of work the rest of the week."

"But I still have stuff to do before—"

"On the way over here I had to talk myself out of picking a big, fat fight with you the week of our wedding. But if you so much as *think* about going back to work, there's gonna be a *really* big fight. You got me?"

"I've said it before, and I'm sure I'll say it again, but you're extremely sexy when you're pissed."

He took a deep, rattling breath and looked up at the ceiling, presumably to keep from throttling her.

Sam smiled at his show of restraint. "I didn't get all freaked out when Andy's elbow gave you a black eye," she said in a teasing tone, hoping to coax a grin out of him.

The comment earned her another scowl. "Only you would compare a basketball injury to getting shot at."

"Love you," she said, flashing her cheesiest grin.

Rolling his eyes, he bent to kiss her. "If I have to swaddle you in bubble wrap to get you to that church in one piece, I'll do it."

Sam reached up to comb her fingers through his hair. "I wouldn't miss it for the world. Don't worry."

"Right. Don't worry. What do *I* have to worry about?"

She urged him into another kiss. "Nothing at all. I promise."

"GARDNER LAWYERED UP," Detective Tommy "Gonzo" Gonzales informed Freddie when he arrived at HQ. "Won't say a word."

"Figures. The guilty ones always lawyer up right away. Where is he?"

"Back in holding until they arraign him in the morning."

"What about Simmons?"

"He caught wind of what we wanted to talk to him about and produced travel documents that show he was in New Orleans visiting his family for the holidays when Skip was shot."

"Crap."

"How do we find out where Gardner was?"

"We're running his credit cards now, seeing what we can find out about his activity that week."

"Sam wants us to talk to the woman he raped. She refused to testify when it happened, but Sam thinks because she's older now..." Freddie shrugged. "Worth a shot."

"Let's go."

They found Leticia Nixon working at a daycare center in Washington Heights. Oblivious to their presence, she sang with animated hand gestures as she entertained a classroom full of three-year-olds. Laughing, she looked up and saw them watching her. The smile fled from her face, and the animated young woman transformed into a scared child right before their eyes.

Freddie signaled to her, asking for a minute of her time.

She turned her class over to the second teacher in the room and made her way to the back of the room. "What do you want?"

"I'm Detective Cruz. This is Detective Gonzales. We wondered if we could speak to you outside."

She pushed through the double doors and led them through the foyer to the parking lot out front. "Is this about Gardner?"

"How did you know?" Gonzo asked.

Leticia shrugged. "No other reason cops would want to talk to me. What'd he do this time?"

"He shot at me and my partner this morning," Freddie said.

"Doesn't surprise me."

"We know he threatened you to keep you from testifying," Gonzo said.

Her eyes flashed with anger and then defeat. "You don't know the half of what he did to me."

"We've got him, Leticia," Freddie said. "He'll do hard time for shooting at cops."

"So what do you want with me?"

"This is your chance for justice. This is your chance to see him pay for what he did to you."

She bit her lip and shook her head. "I've got nothing to say."

"You're willing to let him get away with it?" Freddie asked.

She eyed him with disdain. "He's gotten away with it for more than two years. He gets away with it every time I'm afraid to step foot out my front door and every time I refuse to go out with another guy for fear of it happening again. He won the second he took my virginity from me and filled my mind with violent images that are with me every second of every day."

"Let us help you," Gonzo said.

"Thank you, but I'm fine knowing he's off the streets and behind bars. That's enough for me."

"Did you ever hear him brag about shooting a cop?" Freddie asked.

"Not that I can recall."

"You're sure of that?"

"I try not to think about that time in my life."

Freddie handed her his card. "The father of our lieutenant was left a quadriplegic in that shooting. If you remember anything that might help our investigation, please give me a call."

Taking the card, she said, "I need to get back to work." She walked away and disappeared into the cheerful-looking building.

"Well, that was unproductive," Gonzo said.

"You never know. She might come around." Freddie checked his watch. "I have something I need to take care of. I'll meet you back at HQ."

"Want me to drop you somewhere?"

"Nah, I'll take the Metro."

"See you back at the house."

Long after Gonzo drove off, Freddie stood there thinking over what Sam had said that morning. Getting shot at—again—had helped to bring things into perspective for him. Life was too short to spend it wishing for something he could have if he was willing to make some concessions. The thought of seeing Elin, of holding her and making love with her had him jogging for the nearest Metro station. If he got lucky, he'd catch her leaving the gym where she worked to take her lunch hour. She always went at two.

On the train, he thought about what he might say to her and imagined how she might react. He had to play it cool. That much he knew for sure. If he professed his love, she'd run for the hills. No, he needed to start all over again with her and hope for a better outcome this time.

He jogged up 16th Street just as she emerged from the gym wearing his favorite black yoga pants that showed off her amazing ass and a light blue down vest that offset her shockingly blue eyes. The wind caught her white-blonde hair, and she stopped to capture it into a ponytail. That's when she saw him coming toward her.

"What're you doing here?" she asked, clearly taken aback by his presence.

He put an arm around her waist and drew her in close to him.

Her eyes widened, and her lips parted.

"This is what I'm doing here." He dipped his head and captured her mouth in a searing kiss that had him to firing on all cylinders. When her arms encircled his neck and her fingers combed into his hair, his legs went weak with relief. Having her back in his arms was the answer to his every prayer.

Like a famished man who'd just found food, he feasted on her, his tongue dipping into her sweet softness. "Missed you," he whispered when he had no choice but to come up for air. He trailed kisses from her jaw to her neck and nipped at the base of her throat.

"I've missed you too."

He'd never seen her looking more vulnerable than she did at that moment, and that gave him hope. Framing her face with his hands, he kissed her again, softly this time. "Come to Sam's wedding with me. We'll figure out the rest. I promise."

Her hands found his chest under his coat, and he'd never wanted her more. Freddie had to remind himself they were standing on a public street and attracting more than a few curious stares.

"Are you sure this is what you want?" He knew she meant a relationship his pious mother disapproved of.

Leaning his forehead on hers, he said, "I'm not sure of anything except I can't stop thinking about you."

Her hand slid from his chest to his belly, causing Freddie to suck in a sharp deep breath. She smiled up at him. "What time is the wedding?"

"Four."

Elin went up on tiptoes to kiss him. "Pick me up at three-thirty." She patted his cheek and left him standing on the street with his head spinning and his heart racing. She'd said yes. He wanted to dance a jig. She'd said yes!

NINE

By the time Friday rolled around, Sam was out of her mind with boredom. She'd followed doctor's orders and gotten plenty of rest over the last few days and other than a nagging throb from the healing cut, she felt much better. This concussion had been milder than the previous one, and she was itching to get back to work.

Nick came bounding down the stairs looking awfully chipper for a guy who'd been out with his buddies until two in the morning for a bachelor party that supposedly didn't include strippers.

"Where are you going?" he asked.

Sam put on her coat. "I have to go in for a few hours to tie up some loose ends before the trip."

"Get someone to do it for you."

"There is no one else."

"You're not going in there. I already told you that."

"You can't tell me what to do."

He reached for his phone, scrolled through his contacts and found the one he wanted.

"Who are you calling?"

Rather than reply, he gave her the stone-faced expression she'd seen far too much of over the last few days.

"This is Nick Cappuano. Sam tells me she has to go into work today because there's stuff she *needs* to get done before her vacation." He paused to listen. "That's what I thought. Very good, thank you. We'll see you at the wedding." Closing the phone, he gave her a smug smile. "No need to go in today."

"What the hell? Who was that?"

"Captain Malone. He said to tell you they've got everything under control and to enjoy the day off."

"You have him *programmed* into your phone?"

"I have to leave soon to get Scotty, and there's something I want to do on the way. You can come with me."

Sam folded her arms and dug in for the fight that'd been brewing all week. They may as well get it over with before their rehearsal dinner. "I don't want to go." What she really wanted was to interview Darius Gardner to find out what he knew about her father's shooting. Gonzo and Cruz hadn't gotten anywhere with him. Sam wanted her chance.

Nick put his arms around her and snuggled her into his embrace.

As if they had a mind of their own, her hands found their way under his sweater. Even though he'd been driving her crazy with the hovering this week, she couldn't wait for their wedding night. "I don't like this high-handed, alpha-male side of you."

"I'm not too fond of it either.

She poked his side. "I hate when I get all ready to have a big fight with you and then you say something that totally sucks the wind out of my sails."

Laughing, he kissed her. "I know I'm being a pain in your ass, and I know I can't do this to you after we're married unless it's for something really important like your health or safety. It's just that tomorrow is our wedding, and rather than spend today being anxious that something will happen to mess it all up, I'd much rather have you with me."

"You're superstitious. I never would've guessed."

"What? I am not."

"Yes, you are."

"*No*, I'm not."

Sam laughed, loving that she'd flustered him. "Maybe just a little?"

"Fine. Whatever. Come with me?"

"On one condition."

"What condition?"

"Tell me the truth—did Harry have strippers last night?"

Nick laughed. "No comment."

"I'll kill him."

"What's your *real* condition?"

"The minute we're married, you'll go back to normal. No more of this alpha beast business."

"What if this *is* normal for me?"

Sam pulled back. "Then we have a problem."

Nick put his hands on her hips to keep her from getting away from him. "I'll always worry about you. I'll always wish I could do more to keep you safe." He reached up to tuck a strand of hair behind her ear. "But I understand what you're asking."

"So then back to normal after tomorrow?"

He nodded. "If I have to."

"In that case," she said, going up on tiptoes to kiss him, "I'll go to Richmond with you."

NICK SURPRISED HER when he took the exit for Arlington National Cemetery.

He glanced over at her. "I wanted to see John. I hope that's okay."

She rested her hand on his leg. "Sure it is."

They drove along a winding road to a parking lot. They'd come to John's interment three months ago, but it seemed much longer. Nick took her hand to walk up the hill to the O'Connor family plot, which now boasted a headstone with John's name. Graham and Laine would one day be buried with their son.

Nick squatted down and ran a hand over the white stone. "Looks good."

"Yes."

"Sometimes I still can't believe it, you know?"

Sam knelt next to him and leaned her head against his shoulder.

"How can I get married tomorrow without him?"

The pain she heard in his voice made her ache. "He's always with you."

"Not the same."

"No, it isn't."

"Sometimes I wonder how I'm supposed to get through the whole rest of my life without him. I feel like he's going to show up one day and breeze into the office like he's been on vacation and pick up where he left off. Maybe this whole thing was a bad dream."

Sam put an arm around him. "It hasn't been all bad."

"Do you think we ever would've found each other again if he hadn't been killed?"

"I'd like to think so."

"Yeah, me too."

"Might've taken a little longer, though."

"What would you say if I told you I'd been thinking about going to see Thomas?"

Sam stared at him, wondering if she'd heard him right.

"I know it's hard to believe I want to see the person who killed my best friend. But I just keep thinking he's John's son, and what would I want him to do if the roles were reversed?"

"You'd want him to see your boy. To see if he needed

anything. To maybe understand why he'd done what he did."

As his eyes filled, Nick nodded.

Sam squeezed his hand.

"Maybe after we get back." He wrapped his hand around hers and stood. "Thanks for coming with me."

"No problem."

"Let's go get Scotty." Nick took a long last look at his best friend's grave and then turned to walk with her back to the car.

BEING WITH SCOTTY helped to put them in a festive mood. The boy was so excited to be included in the wedding that his excitement fueled hers.

Freddie was waiting outside the house when they returned from Richmond. Sam introduced Scotty to Freddie and told Nick she'd join them inside in a minute.

"What's up?" she asked her partner.

"We've done a thorough run on Gardner's credit cards, bank statements and other receipts, and from what we can tell, he was in town on December 28, 2008."

A buzz of anticipation rippled through her. "Is that so?"

Freddie nodded. "He's not talking, though. Lawyered up big time." Freddie named a prominent local defense attorney. "How do you want us to proceed?"

Sam glanced at the warm light coming from her living room. "It seems I have other things I need to attend to in the next few days, so let's put it on hold for now. Since Gardner isn't going anywhere, I can have a go at him when I get back. In the meantime, if you and Gonzo want to dig into some of his known associates and see what you can find out, that would help."

"Will do, boss." He looked down at the sidewalk and

then at her, seeming chagrinned. "So I um talked to Elin. She's coming tomorrow."

"Good for you."

"Thanks for giving me the push I needed."

"Any time. I'll see you tomorrow?"

"Yes, ma'am."

Sam started up the ramp leading to her front door.

"Hey, Sam."

She turned back to him. "Yeah?"

"Enjoy every minute. You deserve to be happy."

Smiling, she said, "I will. Thanks." Inside, she followed the sound of voices to the study where Scotty was dancing around in front of a wrapped package.

"There you are," he said. "Nick said I couldn't open it until you were here."

Sam glanced at her fiancé. "Is that so?"

"Well, the gift is from both of us to thank him for being in our wedding."

That was news to her.

Nick smiled at her. "Go ahead and open it, buddy," he said.

Scotty tore the paper off the package and let out a shriek over the game system he found inside. "Oh wow!" he said. "This is *awesome*!"

"There're some games in there too. I wasn't sure which ones you'd like, so we can take them back if you'd rather have others."

Scotty dug out baseball and hockey games, and Sam could tell from the boy's expression that Nick had gotten it just right—as always.

"This is so cool," Scotty said, hugging Nick. "Thanks, Nick."

"You're welcome. I figured it would be fun to have it here when you visit."

"Stay there for a second," Sam said. "I have something for you too." Her heart raced with excitement as she went upstairs to retrieve the gift she'd moved heaven and earth to acquire for them. She returned to the study a few minutes later. They were busy setting up the new game system, and Sam took a moment to watch the two of them, dark heads bent together in concentration as they kept up a steady stream of chatter. "Ready for another present?"

Scotty jumped up, his eyes dancing with excitement. "This is better than Christmas!"

Sam held out the envelope to him.

Nick stood and looked over Scotty's shoulder as he opened it.

The boy let out a gasp and his face went flat with shock when he realized what it was. "No way. Oh my God. *Oh my God*!" He hurled himself into Sam's arms, and as she held him close to her, she was caught off guard by a surge of love for the boy who might one day be theirs.

"What've you got?" Nick asked.

When he turned to Nick, Sam noticed tears on the boy's face.

"Red Sox tickets!" Scotty said. "*Fenway Park*."

"Opening Day," Sam added. "Against the Yankees—and Green Monster seats."

"*Wow*, Sam." Nick took a closer look at the tickets. "How'd you pull that off?"

"I'll never tell," she said, thrilled by their reaction.

"This is the best day of my whole life," Scotty said, hugging Sam again. "Thank you so much." Looking up at Nick, he said, "How will we get there?"

Nick ruffled the boy's hair. "I suppose we'll fly."

"I've never been on a plane before."

"First time for everything," Nick said, leaning over Scotty to kiss Sam. "Thank you."

"I racked my brain trying to think of something to get you for a wedding present—"

"Nothing I'd rather have."

"That's what I figured."

"Speaking of gifts," Nick said. "Stay put." He went to his desk, retrieved a small blue box from the top drawer and brought it to her.

Sam's eyes widened when she saw the distinctive Tiffany box.

"I asked your sisters for dibs on the something new," Nick said.

"Open it, Sam," Scotty said.

Her hands trembled with excitement as she opened the box to reveal a diamond-encrusted key on a white-gold chain. "Oh, it's beautiful! I love it."

Nick took the box from her and removed the necklace. Gathering her hair and shifting it out of his way, he fastened the clasp and then kissed her neck. "Let me see."

Sam turned to him.

"Perfect," he said, his eyes warm with love and desire.

"You know," Scotty said gravely, "that's the key to his heart."

Smiling at the boy, she reached up to touch the key. "I promise to take very good care of it."

"Good," Scotty said. "Now let's play some baseball!"

Nick stole a quick kiss from Sam, and went to play ball with his buddy.

NICK'S FATHER, LEO, had insisted on hosting the rehearsal dinner at Trattoria Alberto, an Italian restaurant on Capitol Hill. After a rehearsal at the church that Shelby had likened to "herding cats" thanks to the antics of Sam's two young nephews and Nick's four-year-old twin half brothers, Sam was ready for a big glass of wine. It'd been her idea to include all the kids, and she didn't regret it, but she sure hoped the four boys could find their way down the aisle tomorrow without making a huge scene.

"Thank God for Scotty," Nick said, reading her mind as he signaled the waiter for drinks.

"No kidding," Sam said. "He was the master cat herder."

Nick leaned in to kiss her forehead. "From this point on, whatever happens happens. No worries, okay?"

Sam clinked her glass against his. "You got it." After all, what did she carc if the kids made a scene? She'd still be married to Nick by this time tomorrow, and she didn't give a rat's ass if the whole thing was a freaking spectacle. Her phone vibrating in her purse interrupted her musings. Sam withdrew it and viewed a text from Freddie: *Thought you'd want to know Leticia Nixon came in and made a statement. We've got him this time.*

"*Yes*," Sam said, relieved to know Gardner would be locked up for years to come.

Nick took the phone from her and powered it down.

"Hey!"

He put the phone in her purse and reached for her hands, bringing them to his lips. "I want ten days, Samantha. Ten days when I don't have to share you with your job. Is that too much to ask?"

"No," Sam said softly.

He wrapped his arms around her.

Sam snuggled into him, breathing him in. Right in that moment, she decided to put aside her quest to find her father's shooter for the next ten days. She vowed to enjoy every minute of the time alone with him that she'd craved for months.

As if he sensed her capitulation, Nick tightened his hold on her.

A throat clearing behind them interrupted the moment.

Sam pulled back from Nick and turned to find her sister Tracy waiting for them.

"Ready to eat?" she asked.

Looking down at Sam, Nick said, "We're ready." He put his hand on Sam's back and followed her into dinner.

TEN

NICK'S DAD LEO stood and shushed the boisterous group made up of Sam's sisters and their families, her dad and Celia, Leo's young wife Stacy, Nick's adopted parents Graham and Laine O'Connor, Dr. Harry and his girlfriend Maggie, Nick's lawyer friend Andy and his wife, and a separate table full of kids. Even Sam's sulky niece Brooke seemed to be having fun.

"I want to thank you all for being here tonight," Leo said. His shy smile tugged at Sam, who knew how he and Nick had struggled over the years to maintain a cordial relationship. "I also want to thank Nicky and Sam for including the boys in the wedding party. In case you hadn't noticed, they're a little excited."

Sam glanced at Nick and saw amusement and affection in his expression as he waited to hear what his father had to say. They'd both had complicated relationships with their mothers, so she was grateful their fathers could be with them this weekend.

"Nicky, I was never much of a father to you, but I couldn't be more proud of the man you grew up to be. A United States senator of all things."

Nick's friends led a rousing round of applause that clearly embarrassed him.

"And in Sam," Leo continued, "you've found the perfect mate and partner. I have no doubt you'll be very happy together." He raised his glass. "To Sam and Nick."

While the others were busy toasting, Nick took the opportunity to steal a kiss from Sam.

"Skip," Leo said, gesturing to Sam's dad. "Your turn."

"Thank you, Leo—and Stacy—for hosting us tonight." Skip shifted his gaze to Sam. "After I was shot, I had some dark days when I found out I'd be in this chair the rest of my life. For a while there, I wondered if it would be easier on everyone—hell, easier on *me*—to just give up."

Sam stared at him. She'd never heard him say such things in the two years since the shooting.

Under the table, Nick reached for her hand.

"My girls Tracy and Angela have been happily settled for quite some time, but Sam... She was so unhappy before. If anything kept me going, it was knowing I had to hang around long enough to see her find happiness too. As soon as I met Nick, I knew he was the one for my little girl. Seeing the two of you together, watching you fall hard for each other—that was definitely worth sticking around for. I wish you many, many years of wedded bliss."

Sam's sisters and stepmother wiped up tears as Sam raised her glass to her father. "Thank you," she whispered, blinking back tears of her own.

He winked and the half of his face that wasn't paralyzed lifted into a smile.

When the party broke up a short time later, Angela and Tracy shanghaied Sam.

"Say goodnight," Tracy said, trying to tug Sam away from Nick.

She clung to him. "Don't let them take me."

Nick laughed and kissed her. "You can survive one night without me."

She looked up at him, not wanting to be parted from him for even a few hours. "I'm not sure I can."

He tugged her close to him and kissed her passionately right in front of her sisters. For once, Sam didn't mind the public display of affection. "One more night," he whispered against her lips, "and then we get forever."

Sam buried her fingers in his hair and brought him back for a final kiss intended to make sure he thought of nothing but her until they saw each other again.

"Save it for the honeymoon," Tracy said, taking Sam's arm and leading her away from Nick.

"See you at the church," she said.

"Don't be late."

"Not this time."

Sam let Angela and Tracy lead her to Tracy's car. They were spending the night together at Skip and Celia's where they'd get dressed tomorrow.

Harry, Andy and Scotty were in charge of getting Nick home and delivering him to the church tomorrow. Graham, Nick's best man, was spending the night with his wife at the Hay-Adams.

"Gonna be one hell of a wedding night," Angela teased when they were in the car.

Sam couldn't wait.

AFTER BEING MANICURED and pedicured, and after suffering through a facial and a massage her sisters had thoughtfully arranged, Sam was buzzing with energy when she should've been sleeping. The digital clock read just after two. Sam sighed. Just what she needed the night before her wedding.

She wondered if Nick was faring any better. Maybe she should sneak over there and check on him.

Sam sat up slowly, not wanting to disturb Angela who

was pregnant or Tracy who was asleep on a blow-up mattress on the floor. Reaching for the zip-up sweatshirt she'd left at the foot of the bed, Sam put it on and slid her feet into Tracy's plush slippers.

"Where do you think you're going?" Tracy whispered.

Startled, Sam said, "Downstairs to get some water."

"You're such a liar."

"What're you talking about?"

"You're going to see him."

"I am not!"

"Liar."

"Be quiet before you wake up Ang."

"Too late," Angela muttered.

"She's going to see Nick," Tracy said, sounding scandalized.

"I am not! I just want something to drink. Sheesh, Trace, when did you become such an ass pain?"

"Right around the time Brooke became a teenager."

Angela snickered at that. "Leave her alone, Tracy. If she wants to see him, let her go."

"It's bad luck to see him before the wedding," Tracy reminded her.

"Since we've been together, we've been nearly blown up, shot at, had a few concussions between us, survived a rollover, had broken bones, stitches and staples." She reached up to touch the healing wound in her scalp. "We've used up our share of bad mojo."

"When you put it that way," Tracy said, gesturing for the door.

"Thanks, Mom. Get some sleep, ladies."

"Don't be late for the hair appointment," Tracy said. "She'll be here at eleven."

"Got it. Sleep tight."

"Don't do anything we wouldn't do," Angela added.

Sam laughed and closed the bedroom door behind her. Feeling like a teenager sneaking out of her parents' house in the middle of the night, she crept down the stairs, found her keys and headed out the door. She was halfway to their place when a shadow emerged from the darkness. All at once, Sam remembered why she never stepped foot out the door without her weapon. Figures the one time she did…

"Going somewhere?"

Shit. "What're you doing here, Peter?" At the sight of her ex-husband, her heart beat fast and her breath came out in white, puffy clouds in the cold. She began to shiver.

"I want to talk to you."

"I have nothing to say to you."

"I have something to say to you, and it's high time you listened to me."

"Get out of here before I have your ass thrown back in jail for violating the no-contact order."

She started to push past him, but he grabbed her arm and pulled her tight against him.

"Let go of me, or I swear to God I'll cripple you."

He pushed something hard against her ribs. "Don't make any fast moves, sweetheart, or your family will be attending a funeral rather than a wedding."

Sam cursed herself for being so stupid as to go out unarmed. She glanced up at the second floor of their house where Nick was hopefully sleeping, unaware that she was in grave danger on the eve of their wedding. "What do you want?" she asked through gritted teeth.

"That's more like it." His lips brushed against her hair, and it was all Sam could do not to cringe. "You're making a big mistake marrying that guy."

"Is that so?"

"He doesn't love you the way you deserve to be loved—the way I love you."

Sam swallowed hard. "Peter, please. Let me go and get out of here before someone sees you and carts you back to jail."

"There's nowhere they can take me that's worse than living without you."

Sam swallowed hard. "I'm sorry you feel that way."

"Are you really?"

"Of course I am. I never wanted you to be unhappy."

"Then why did you leave me?"

Sam wanted to shove her elbow into his gut but the press of metal against her ribs kept her still. "I want you to let me go now. You need to find someone who loves you the way you deserve to be loved—"

"I don't want anyone else," he growled in her ear tightening his hold on her to the point of pain. "What about that don't you get?"

The click of a gun engaging sounded next to them.

"Let her go, and step back."

"Who the hell are you?" Peter asked.

"Doesn't matter who I am. You need to let her go right now unless you want me to make road kill out of you."

Out of the corner of her eye, Sam saw the lights go on in their place as she tried unsuccessfully to place the voice of her rescuer.

"This is not over," Peter whispered in her ear. "It'll never be over."

He let her go so abruptly that Sam stumbled for a second before regaining her footing.

She turned to find her savior holding a gun to Peter as a police cruiser rounded the corner, lights flashing. "Who the hell are you?" she asked the dark-haired man with muscles that were evident through his coat.

Nick emerged from their house and ran down the ramp to her. "Thank God you're all right."

"You want to explain to me how you knew about this and who that is hauling my ex-husband off to jail?"

Nick had his eyes glued on the hand-off of Peter to the police officers. "I hired him to keep an eye on Gibson."

"You *hired* someone to watch him?"

"You bet your ass I did." Nick looked down at her, his eyes fierce and furious. "I knew he'd come after you again. It was just a matter of time, and no way was I going to sit back and let that happen."

"Nick—"

He rested a finger on her lips. "We're not fighting about this now—not the night before our wedding. We can fight about it later, but not now."

"I was just going to say thanks."

"Really? You were?"

He looked so surprised and so adorable that she laughed. "I like to think I can take care of myself, but I have a feeling that wasn't going to end well."

He held her so tightly that Sam felt the shudder that rippled through his big frame. "What the hell were you doing out here anyway?"

"Coming to see you."

Pulling back, he smiled down at her. "Is that so?"

"Uh huh."

"Um, excuse me, Lieutenant Holland," one of the officers said. "I understand you have a protective order in place against Mr. Gibson."

Without taking her eyes off Nick, she said, "That's right. He's supposed to stay at least a thousand feet from me and every member of my family." She glanced at the officer. "Was he armed?"

The officer nodded. "Nine millimeter."

Sam released a shaky breath. "Transport him to HQ, and if you could see to it that they delay the arraignment for about forty-eight hours, I'd be indebted to you." She had no doubt Peter would post bail, but she and Nick would be long gone by then.

"I'll do what I can."

"Get Captain Malone involved. He'll take care of it."

"Got it. Um, congratulations to you both."

"Thank you," Sam said.

Nick's guy approached them. "Sorry he got close enough to get his hands on you, ma'am. I figured you'd want me to wait until he did something to get himself arrested. I had just called it in when you came out, and things happened pretty quickly."

"Thanks for the backup," Sam said.

Nick shook his hand. "Take the week off. We'll be back next Sunday."

"Yes sir, Senator. Enjoy your wedding."

"We will. Thank you." Nick put his arm around Sam and guided her up the ramp to their home. The minute they were inside, he pulled her into his arms and held on tight. "This could only happen to us," he said after a long moment of silence. "Only we could have this kind of drama the night before our wedding."

"At least we're never bored."

Grunting out a short laugh, he pressed his lips to her forehead. "There is that. So what did he say to you?"

Sam wanted to forget the entire incident. If she never saw that son of a bitch again, it would be too soon. His last words would haunt her. *This will never be over*. She shuddered. "Doesn't matter."

"Matters to me."

Reluctantly, Sam looked up at him. "He said I'm making a mistake marrying you. That you'll never love me the way he does."

"Thank God for that."

Sam didn't expect to laugh just then, but leave it to Nick.

"Let's go to bed," he said. At the top of the stairs he held up a finger to tell her to wait a second while he looked in on Scotty. "Slept through the whole thing," Nick whispered when he rejoined her.

"Lock the door," Sam said. "Just in case."

"Good idea." Nick turned the lock on the door before he unzipped her sweatshirt and helped her out of the pajamas she'd worn to sleep with her sisters. After he stripped off the T-shirt and gym shorts he'd probably pulled on after his guy called about the altercation in the street he followed her into bed.

Sam snuggled in close to him and released a long sigh. *Nothing* was better than this.

With his hand cupping her face, he kissed her.

She wound her arms around his neck and gave into the wave of desire that overtook her.

His kiss was urgent and ravenous. After a long while, he broke the kiss and shifted his attention to her neck. "Why do people keep trying to take you away from me?"

His softly spoken words went straight to her heart. "It'll take much more than a lunatic with a nine millimeter to take me away from you."

He cupped her breast and teased her nipple with his tongue. "I was expecting you to be pissed that I had a guy watching him."

"I probably should be, but since he saved my ass tonight, I'll give you a pass on this one."

Nick sucked her nipple into his mouth, and Sam cried out.

"Shhh," he said. "Don't forget we've got company."

"If I have to be quiet, don't do that."

He chuckled softly, and gave her other breast the same attention.

Sam bit her lip to hold back the urge to cry out. He knew exactly what she liked best and never failed to give it to her. Running her fingers through his silky dark hair, she arched into him, begging for more. "I thought we were going to wait," she said, breathless with wanting him.

"It *is* our wedding day," he reminded her, nodding to the bedside clock.

"We'll be a couple of wrecks at the wedding."

"No, we won't," he said, kissing his way to her lips. "We're young and hardy, and we've survived sleepless nights before."

"True." Sam wrapped her legs around his hips and urged him into another carnal kiss. "I've missed this."

"Mmm. Me, too. So much."

"We're getting married today."

He smiled down at her. "So I've heard. Are you ready?"

"Never been more ready for anything. You?"

"Same." He kissed her again and entered her slowly, releasing a deep sigh of completion. "In case I forget to tell you later," he said, peppering his words with kisses, "you're the single best thing to ever happen to me, and I can't imagine how I managed to live without you for all those years after we first met."

She ran her hands down his back. "Ditto." Closing her eyes, she rode the wave of love and passion and desire that only he could inspire in her.

"Damn," he muttered, "this is going to be fast."

Sam laughed and urged him on. "We have all week for slow."

His lips found the curve of her neck, and he tightened his arms around her. "Love you, babe. Love you so much."

"Love you too." As he drove them to an explosive finish, Sam had no doubt at all that she was marrying the exact perfect guy for her.

ELEVEN

THE WEDDING DAY preparations passed in a blur of hair and makeup and flowers and children. Sam waited all day for the crash that usually followed a sleepless night, but it never happened. She figured she was running on an extra dose of wedding adrenaline with a sex-induced high thrown in for good measure.

Standing before a full-length mirror in the dress that had been made just for her, Sam had to give Tinker Bell credit. It was pretty safe to say that she'd never looked better in her life. She raised her long skirt and took another admiring look at the *fabulous* Jimmy Choos with the sparkling buckle and let out a giddy squeal of delight.

As promised, her makeup was subtle, yet effective. The scar at her hairline was nowhere in sight. Her hair was swept into a sleek, sophisticated style with an orchid strategically placed above her right ear.

Her entire family was abuzz about the altercation with Peter. Sam was relieved that he was locked up and couldn't do anything to disrupt her wedding day. The incident with him had been a small price to pay for that peace of mind.

Remembering the passionate night she'd spent with Nick, she reached up to touch the diamond key he had given her. After everything with Peter and in the wake of their rancorous divorce, she'd never imagined getting married again. That is until she reconnected with Nick after John O'Connor's murder. Once they were back together, the idea of being remarried had stopped seeming so preposterous. Now she couldn't wait to be his wife and to take, as he'd said in his proposal, the journey of a lifetime together.

She slid the sparkling engagement ring off her finger and transferred it—temporarily—to her right hand to make room for the wedding band he would soon place on her left hand.

Dressed in dark purple tea-length bridesmaid dresses Tracy and Angela stepped into the room.

"*Wow*, Sam," Tracy said with a sigh. "You're stunning."

"Seriously," Angela added.

"Thanks, guys, you look gorgeous too. Is everyone ready to go?"

"Dad and Celia already left with the kids," Angela said, "but we needed a moment alone with the bride.

Tracy handed Sam a jeweler's box. "Since Nick took care of your something new, here's your something old.

"Grandma's diamond earrings! But she gave them to you."

"Which is why they're also your something borrowed," Tracy said with a pointed look.

Sam laughed as she put them on. "Gotcha."

Angela handed Sam a fancy lace garter with blue satin ribbon threaded throughout. "And your something blue.

"Was this yours?" she asked Angela.

"It was originally Mom's," Tracy said. "Angela and I both used it for our weddings."

"But you didn't give it to me last time?" Sam said, fingering the lace.

"We had a feeling that was your starter marriage." Tracy rested her hands on Sam's bare shoulders and went up on tiptoes to kiss her sister's cheek. "This one is for keeps."

"Yes, it certainly is," Sam said softly as her eyes flooded with tears. She frantically blinked them back. "Stop the schmoopy stuff before I have mascara running down my face!"

Tracy smiled and stepped back.

Angela leaned in to kiss Sam's other cheek. "We love you. We love him. And we're so very, *very* happy for you."

"Okay, now you really have to stop it," Sam said, waving her hands in front of her face.

Angela laughed and handed Sam a tissue.

"The limo is downstairs when you're ready," Tracy said. "We can put the garter on in the car."

"As long as we're being schmoopy," Sam said, willing the tears away, "thank you both for seeing me through some rough times. I doubt I'd be standing here in one piece if it wasn't for you guys, and I love you both. Very much."

"Aw, Sam," Angela said, dabbing at her eyes. "Now you've got me going too. Not that it takes much these days."

"Let's get you to the church before we descend all the way to maudlin," Tracy said, her eyes bright with tears too.

SAM STEPPED OUT her father's front door to a warm spring day and a crowd gathered on Ninth Street to watch the proceedings. Police cruisers with lights flashing were positioned in front of and behind the black limo.

"What's with the cops?" she asked Shelby.

"Apparently, Chief Farnsworth ordered an escort for you."

Sam smiled. “That’s sweet of him.” The flash of a camera interrupted the moment, and Sam looked over to find several of the roving pack of photographers who’d dedicated themselves to documenting her and Nick’s every move over the last few months. While her first inclination was to scowl at them the way she normally did, this time she smiled radiantly, refusing to let them ruin her mood.

Shelby shepherded Sam and her sisters smoothly into the limo. As they proceeded through the city to the church at 16th and H Streets, Sam marveled at the people who’d come out apparently hoping for a glimpse of her. That, more than anything else that’d happened in the last few months, told her how popular they’d become in the city. As someone who preferred life well below the radar, it certainly was a jarring realization.

The closer they got to the church, the bigger the crowd seemed to get.

“Damn,” Tracy said. “Look at all the people!”

“William and Kate didn’t get this many people for the royal wedding,” Angela said.

“Shut up,” Sam muttered. “I’m not a princess, and this is just another wedding.”

“Whatever you say, Your Highness,” Ang joked.

From the front seat, Shelby turned to them. “Don’t worry, Sam. We’ve got security all around the church.”

“What if Nick and my dad can’t get in?”

“They’re already there,” Shelby assured her with a comforting smile.

Sam was once again grateful for her presence. At first she had balked at the cost of a wedding planner, but she couldn’t imagine how they would’ve pulled this off without her.

Sam’s stomach, which had been on remarkably good

behavior lately, took a nosedive as she experienced the day's first flutter of nerves.

Tracy reached over to pat Sam's arm. "It's all good. It's just you and Nick and a few thousand of your closest friends."

Sam laughed, which helped with the butterflies.

They managed to get her inside St. John's with a minimal amount of fuss, which Sam appreciated. She was escorted to a holding room at the back of the church where her father waited for her.

"There you are," he said. "Quite a madhouse out there, huh?"

Sam bent to kiss his cheek. "My future husband is too popular for his own good."

"I think his future wife is just as popular. She's certainly beautiful today."

She squeezed his right hand. "Thank you."

Tracy and Angela came in a minute later looking frazzled.

"What's the matter?" Sam asked.

"Small problem," Angela said. "Leo just let us know that Nick's mother is here."

Sam gasped. "No. She can't be! She wasn't invited!"

"That doesn't seem to have stopped her," Tracy said.

Sam's mind churned as she pondered the implications. She turned to Shelby. "Please go get Graham and Harry. And Leo Cappuano. Hurry."

"What do I tell them?"

"Make something up. Some sort of wedding duty you need them for, but don't let Nick know there's something going on."

"I'm on it." Shelby scurried from the room.

"I'm sorry, Sam," Angela said. "I hate to see anything ruin this day for either of you."

"Nothing will ruin this day. Not if I have anything to say about it." All she could think about was how badly Nick had wanted this one perfect day to celebrate their love and begin their life together. No way would she let his witch of a mother ruin it for him.

"As much as I want to see this, the kids are getting restless," Tracy said. "We'll wait for you outside."

As her sisters stepped out, the men came in with Shelby.

"Sam," Graham said. "You look positively gorgeous."

"Radiant," Harry added.

"Beautiful," Leo said.

"Thank you," Sam said, embarrassed by the praise. "We have a problem." She explained about Nick's mother crashing the wedding and watched their smiles fade. Leo looked down at the floor, his face unreadable. "We have to keep her away from Nick. Whatever you have to do no matter how rude you have to be, keep her away from him."

"Don't worry," Graham assured her. "We'll take care of it."

Sam focused on Harry. "It's very important that she not get anywhere near him. You understand why."

Harry nodded somberly. "It won't happen. I'll personally make sure of it."

Sam turned to Shelby. "Do you have a copy of the invitation?"

"Of course." Ever efficient, Shelby crossed the room to her pink leather briefcase and produced the green and lavender invitation Sam had loved on first sight. "Here you go."

"Thanks. Will you please go get Nick's mother? I'd like a word with her."

"Sam," Skip said. "Are you sure about that?"

Ignoring the concern coming from the other men, she nodded. "Go ahead, Shelby."

"I'll point her out to you," Leo said, following Shelby.

While she waited, Sam vibrated with tension. She deeply resented Nick's mother intruding—uninvited—on their special day. But she would take care of it and get on with the wedding with him none the wiser.

Shelby and Leo returned a minute later with a beautifully dressed woman who, as Nick had once said, resembled Sofia Loren. As she came closer, however, Sam saw the hard edges lurking beneath the shiny surface. This woman had nothing on Loren. Nick's parents were just fifteen years older than him, and while Leo remained youthful, Nicoletta appeared worn. She cast a hateful glance at Leo, who looked away from her as if he couldn't stand the sight of her. Sam could relate to that.

"It's so nice to finally meet you," Nicoletta said, extending her hand to Sam.

Sam ignored the proffered hand and held up the invitation. "Did you receive one of these?"

"I did not, but I figured it had to be a mistake. How could I not be invited to my own son's wedding?"

"You were *not* invited," Sam said, "because neither of us wants you here."

Nicoletta's face turned bright red. "How *dare* you speak to me like that minutes before you marry my son?"

"You've done nothing but hurt and disappoint him his entire life. You will *not* do that today. I won't allow it. You may sit *quietly* in the back of the church for the service, after which you will leave—quietly—or security will have you removed. From now on, you will stay far, *far* away from him or you'll deal with me. Do I make myself clear?"

Nicoletta glared at her. "My son is marrying a bitch!"

"Hey now," Skip growled. "Watch yourself, or you won't be watching a wedding."

Nicoletta appealed to Leo. "You have nothing to say about this, you spineless excuse for a man?"

Leo shook his head. "I don't want you here any more than they do."

"I'm about to change my mind and have you removed before the wedding," Sam said, glowering at her. "What's it going to be?"

"I'd like to see my son."

"That's not going to happen."

"You can't decide that for him!"

Sam smirked. After what this woman had put Nick through, Sam was rather enjoying this. "You don't think so?"

With Harry, Graham, Leo and her father united as one behind her, Sam stared down the older woman. "You have one minute to decide because I have no intention of keeping my fiancé waiting. He's waited long enough for a family of his own."

She often used the same time limit with perps when giving them the choice between cooperating with an investigation or going straight to jail. This woman had emotionally abused Nick his entire life. Her crimes were nearly as egregious as those of the criminals Sam dealt with.

"Fine," Nicoletta huffed. "You may think you've won this round, but you haven't seen the last of me."

"Yes, I have. And believe me, you don't want to try me on that."

"God help my poor son," Nicoletta said as she turned and stalked from the room. "He'll need all the help he can get married to a shrew."

Sam let her have the parting shot. She'd made her point.

"I'm so sorry you had to deal with that today of all days, Sam," Shelby said, clearly undone by the whole thing.

"I'm not sorry, so don't you be either. It would've happened eventually." Sam turned to Harry. "Go on back to Nick, and *please* keep her the hell away from him."

"I will, Sam. I promise."

"Graham," Sam said when he started to follow Harry. "What I said about Nick having a family of his own…"

"I understand, honey. We did our best to fill the void, but there's no substitute for the real thing."

"He loves you all very much."

"And we know that. We love him just as much."

Sam nodded, and Graham left so he could be with Nick.

"I probably shouldn't be here either," Leo said morosely. "I didn't do much better by him than she did."

"You've never shaken him down for money or refused to introduce him as your son," Sam said.

Leo stared at her, agog. "She did not."

"She called him a month or so ago. She'd fallen down some stairs and was in the hospital. He went to her and came home twenty-five thousand dollars poorer. The last time she got married, she refused to introduce him as her son because she didn't want the guy she was marrying to think she was lying about her age."

"*Bitch*," Leo said. Sam was surprised by his tone. She'd never seen Leo angry before.

Sam extended her hand to him.

Hesitantly, he took it.

"You've made an effort to right some of the wrongs. You and Stacy have made him part of your family. You've never asked him for anything other than his time and his forgiveness. You have *every* right to be here."

"Thank you, Sam." He embraced her carefully. "For what it's worth, I think my son is a very lucky man."

"It's worth an awful lot coming from you."

"I'll see you out there."

"I'll be right along." When they were alone, Sam turned to her father. "Well, nothing like a little drama to keep things interesting."

"I'm so proud of you, baby girl. I sure wish Nick could've seen that."

"I was just doing for him what he'd do for me."

"What was it exactly that you asked of Harry?"

"When Nick was a kid, she'd promise to come visit and then never show up. He'd wait all day for her only to be disappointed. Then when she would come, he'd be able to smell her perfume on his skin for days afterward. He'd refuse to take a bath until his grandmother made him. To this day, the smell of her perfume sends him off a cliff. It just happened the last time he saw her. Takes him a while to get past it, which is the last thing either of us needs today."

"And Harry knows this?"

Sam nodded. "Nick told him once in a weak moment. He clued me in after Nick saw her in Cleveland. Harry won't let her get close enough to do that to him again."

"It's amazing Nick came through it all as well as he did."

"Isn't it?" Sam glanced at the clock on the wall. Five minutes to four. Feeling euphoric and victorious and ready to marry the love of her life, Sam looked down at her dad. "Well, my friend, you and I have a wedding to get to."

"After you, my love."

TWELVE

As the soloist Shelby had hired sang "At Last," Sam stood next to her dad's chair in the back of the church and watched Nick's brothers, her nephews, nieces and sisters precede her down the aisle. She had yet to allow herself to look at Nick for fear she'd lose her cool if she caught his eye before she was ready.

"I like the song," her dad said gruffly. "Perfect."

"I thought so too. I'm glad you approve." Sam bent at the waist to look him in the eye. "And I'm glad you stuck around so you could give me away today, but don't get any ideas about punching out now that all your girls are happily married."

The right side of his face lifted into a smile. "As it happens, I am too." His Valentine's Day wedding to his faithful nurse Celia had given them all something to celebrate. "Don't worry about me. I've got plenty to live for, and I know it."

Shelby approached them. "Ready?" She handed Sam her bouquet of dark purple orchids.

"Thank you, Shelby. For everything. I truly couldn't have gotten through this without you."

"My pleasure. You have a very handsome senator waiting anxiously for you." Shelby gestured to the doorway. "Whenever you're ready."

Sam placed her hand on her dad's shoulder. "I'm with you, Skippy."

"Let's go then."

When they moved into the doorway, Sam took a deep breath and finally dared to look at Nick. Her throat closed at the sight of him. Tall, handsome and sinfully sexy in a sharp black tuxedo that emphasized his broad shoulders and muscular build. The orchid on his lapel matched her bouquet. Despite the sleepless night, he appeared happy and relaxed and maybe just a tad bit nervous. In fact, he looked so good standing with Graham, Harry, Andy and Scotty that Sam deduced he had no idea his mother was in attendance.

And there was no chance of him noticing now because he never took his eyes off her as she moved with her father down the aisle.

NICK TOLD HIMSELF to keep breathing. *Just a dress*. Right. He'd never seen her looking more beautiful. That wasn't even a good enough word. Breathtaking was more like it. And happy. Her pale blue eyes were bright with excitement, and she positively glowed as she and Skip came toward him. Everyone else in the crowded church faded away, and there was only her.

When they reached the front, Nick stepped forward to squeeze Skip's right hand.

"Take good care of her," Skip said so softly that only Nick could hear him.

"Always," Nick said.

Sam bent to kiss her father's cheek. "Love you."

"Love you too, baby girl. Go be happy now."

Celia stood to help Skip get his chair settled next to the front row. Across the aisle, the kids in the wedding party sat with Nick's father, his stepmother Stacy and Laine O'Connor.

Nick held out his hand to Sam, feasting his eyes on his stunning bride. "That's the best you could do?"

She threw her head back and laughed, and it was all *he* could do to resist the urge to lean in and kiss the spot on her neck that drove her wild. Instead, he tucked her hand into the crook of his arm and escorted her to the altar.

Nick tried to pay attention to the ceremony, but truthfully, he wanted it over with. When he thought about the crazy, wild ride they'd taken to get to this day, he just wanted to hear the words "husband and wife." He tuned back into the proceedings to hear Celia read the passage from the Book of Ruth that he'd chosen. "Where you go I will go, and where you stay I will stay. Your people will be my people and your God my God."

Angela read from the Book of the Corinthians. "Love bears all things, believes all things, endures all things, hopes all things. Love never ends."

He and Sam lit candles, and the pastor spoke to them about love and fidelity and the importance of working every day to make their marriage successful. The pastor led them through the recitation of the traditional vows to love, honor and cherish each other that they'd wanted included in the ceremony.

Finally, he had them turn to each other and join hands.

Sam passed her bouquet to Tracy and reached for his hands, linking their fingers.

The pastor gestured to him. "Nick?"

He squeezed her hands and tried to forget that more than a hundred people were watching them. "This day was six years in the making." Nick hoped he could get through this without embarrassing himself. "From the first instant I ever laid eyes on you, Samantha, I knew you were the one for me. It took far longer to get here than it should have, but all that matters is that we're finally here. Since I already promised all the most important things, I thought I'd throw in a few things that I know are important to you."

Sam's smile warmed his heart and gave him the courage to continue.

"So I promise to be a little less freakishly neat—"

That drew a laugh from his bride.

"—and slightly less obsessed with your safety." He paused for another laugh from her. "You're not supposed to find *all* of this funny."

Sam tried—and failed—to wipe the grin from her face.

"I promise not to let my phone ring more than twice, to do my best not to constantly clean up after you and to let you be you—even when you drive me crazy." He stepped closer and leaned his forehead against hers. "I promise I'll always love you and put you and our family first in my life because there's nowhere else in the world I'd rather be than with you."

Sam looked up at him with bottomless eyes full of tears.

"That works out rather well," she said, "since there's nowhere else I'd rather be than with you. I had the same plan—to offer you a few things I thought you would appreciate."

Smiling, Nick raised his head to give her some space.

"I promise to *try* not to leave my shoes all over the place, to hang my coat in the closet rather than tossing it over the sofa where it belongs, to make the bed once in a while and to stop rearranging your desk every time I sit there."

"I'll believe that when I see it."

Smiling back at him, Sam brought their joined hands to her lips. "I promise to try very hard to not protect you by keeping things from you. And even though it may sometimes seem that my job and the case of the moment are more important to me than you, I promise you they are not. I've loved you for as long as you've loved me, and I always will."

Overwhelmed, Nick took a deep, shuddering breath and accepted the rings from Graham. After they were in place, the pastor uttered the words Nick had often wondered if he would ever hear: "I now pronounce you husband and wife. You may kiss your bride."

"At last," Nick whispered as he drew her in close to him.

Sam linked her arms around his neck and slipped him some tongue, making his blood race.

"Brat," he said against her lips.

She laughed at the face he made at her and reclaimed her bouquet from Tracy.

"Ladies and gentlemen," the pastor said, "it's my pleasure to introduce Senator and Mrs. Nicholas Cappuano."

Nick winced. His Samantha was no one's Mrs., but oh well. For better or worse, she was his.

Finally and forever his.

HAND IN HAND they made their way down the aisle. Sitting behind Sam's family was her Metropolitan Police family, including Chief Farnsworth, Deputy Chief Conklin, Captain Malone and their wives. Freddie and Elin, Gonzo and his fiancée—Nick's chief of staff Christina Billings. Sam was pleased and relieved to see her friend and colleague Detective Jeannie McBride there with her boyfriend Michael.

Nick's side of the church was also filled to overflowing. What he lacked in family he more than made up for in friends. John O'Connor's sister Lizbeth, her husband Royce, and John's brother Terry—Nick's new deputy chief of staff—were there along with most of his staff. Sam recognized the leadership of the Virginia Democratic Party along with Virginia Governor Zorn and his wife Judy. Behind them were a number of Nick's colleagues from the Senate and another of Nick's close friends, White House deputy chief of staff Derek Kavanaugh, and his wife, Victoria.

When Nick seemed to founder all of a sudden, Sam realized he'd spotted his mother waving from the back row. True to their agreement, she was being quiet, but of course she'd had to make sure Nick knew she was there. Sam wished she could wave a magic wand and make the woman disappear.

"Just keep moving, babe," she said to Nick. "Keep moving."

"But...that's—"

Sam tugged him along with her. "I know who she is."

They emerged from the church to an enormous crowd that had grown during the hour-long ceremony. Shelby's security folks shepherded them through the gauntlet so they could cross the street to the Hay-Adams. The photographer had let them know ahead of time that he would be angling for a shot of them crossing H Street with the White House in the background. Shelby's people had cleared the street to allow for the photo.

While Sam sensed the lingering tension in Nick, he played his part to perfection, dashing slightly ahead of her to give the photographer the shot he'd claimed would be the iconic image from their wedding. All Sam cared about was getting a moment alone with her groom to soothe and assure him that his mother wouldn't bother him today.

With the photo taken, they arrived at the hotel where Shelby greeted them.

"We need a moment," Sam said to her.

"Right this way."

They followed Shelby to the elevator, which transported them to the hotel's rooftop where the reception would take place. She showed them into a small salon. "I'll be right outside when you're ready for photos."

"Thank you." Sam closed the door and turned to Nick. "Are you okay?"

He looked confused and undone, which Sam deeply resented. "What's she doing here?"

"She crashed. I took care of it. I said she could stay for the ceremony, but I let her know she wasn't welcome here."

He shook his head, his mouth set with dismay. "I'm sorry you had to deal with that."

"Look at me," Sam said.

In his eyes she saw disbelief and resignation.

"We're not spending our first minutes as husband and wife talking about someone who's not worth our time." As she watched him make a huge effort to shake it off, Sam raised her hands to his face and kissed him softly. "She's not worth our time."

His arms encircled her waist. "Did you rip her to shreds?"

Sam smiled at his attempt at humor. "I made confetti out of her."

"I really wish I could've seen that."

"Someday, I'll tell you all about it, but not today."

"I'll look forward to that."

Sam kissed him again. "Will you be all right?"

"Yeah. Thanks for having my back."

"Always."

He reached for her right hand and removed her engagement ring, placing it on her left hand with the low-key but elegant diamond band. Running his thumb over the two rings, he said, "Do you like your ring?"

"It's beautiful and perfect. And it won't get in the way at work."

"I knew you'd say that."

She captured his left hand. "What do you think of yours?"

"I love it. Very classy."

"Just like you." Sam kissed his ring. "I've always thought there was something so incredibly sexy about a wedding ring on a man's finger. It tells the world he has pledged himself to someone and isn't afraid to say so. Everyone you meet will know you're taken. I like that."

"Then I'll never take it off."

"You have to take it off at least once so you can see the engraving."

"All right, but just this once." He slid the ring from his finger and tipped it into the light so he could read the inscription. She hadn't expected him to laugh. "Take a look at yours."

Sam removed both rings and held up the wedding band so she could see inside. *You're my home. Always, Nick.* She looked up at him, astounded. "No way! No wonder Shelby seemed so surprised by what I'd chosen!"

Nick laughed again, and the sound warmed Sam's heart. Thankfully, he seemed to have rebounded from the shock of seeing his mother. "What a pair we are, huh?"

"A match made in heaven," Sam said, sighing as she kissed him.

For the longest time, they stood there gazing at each other like two lovesick fools.

"I can't believe you're finally my wife," he said softly, reverently.

"And you're finally my husband."

He framed her face, kissing her long and hard before he seemed to remember they had guests waiting for them. "We probably ought to get out there before Shelby thinks we're consummating in here."

Chuckling, Sam looked around the small but elegant room that included an upholstered chaise lounge. "That's not a *bad* idea..."

"Hold that thought for a couple of hours."

She reached up to wipe the lingering lipstick off his mouth. "*That long*?"

"I'll make it *well* worth the wait," he promised with a salacious grin that sent shivers down her spine as he led her out the door to rejoin Shelby.

THE ROOM FAIRLY shimmered in candlelight and the waning glow of daylight. Greens and purples and orchids with painted glass vases full of more flowers on the tables. Sam had seen sketches of Shelby's vision, but nothing could've prepared her for the reality of just how amazing it turned out to be. Through the floor-to-ceiling windows, their city stretched out before them—from the White House to the Washington Monument to Lincoln, Jefferson and the Potomac beyond.

Earlier, word had rippled through the city that the famed cherry trees that lined the tidal basin in front of the Jefferson Memorial had burst into bloom overnight. As the photographer took shots of them on the patio with the monuments in the background, Sam pointed out the sea of cherry blossom pink to Nick.

"The city is giving us its blessing," he said.

She went up on tiptoes to kiss him, hearing the click, click, click of the camera that recorded their every move. "It certainly seems that way, doesn't it?"

Nick never left her side as they received guests, had

dinner, took what seemed like a thousand photos and exchanged an equal number of on-demand kisses. Freddie, Gonzo and the others from the MPD seemed to have placed themselves in charge of regularly clinking silverware against crystal to demand more of the PDA Sam avoided like the plague. She'd get them back when it was their turn to tie the knot.

Freddie seemed thrilled to have Elin with him, and Sam was glad she'd encouraged him to try again with her—even if there'd be hell to pay if Mrs. Cruz ever found out what Sam had done. They'd been united in their dislike of Elin for Freddie, but he was right. It was his life, and he had to live it as he saw fit, even if that meant loving a woman his mother didn't approve of.

"I have a little surprise for you," Sam's husband of two hours whispered in her ear.

Sam looked up at him, caught off guard by how happy and adorable he seemed. She'd never seen him looking happier than he did just then, and vowed in that moment to do whatever it took to make him that happy every day for the rest of their lives. "What's that?"

"Wait 'til you see, Sam," Scotty interjected, fairly busting the buttons of his tuxedo as he jumped from foot to foot.

"You're keeping all kinds of secrets, aren't you?" she asked the boy.

"Uh-huh," he said with a delighted grin.

"So what is it?" Sam asked.

"Look," Nick said, pointing to the small stage where their DJ had set up. They'd gone with a DJ over a live band to make space for more guests in the rooftop reception room.

Sam looked to where Nick pointed, and her mind went totally blank. It couldn't be...Was that...No. No way. *No freaking way!* She let out a most un-coplike shriek. *Jon Bon Jovi at her wedding?* Stop it. Stop it right now! Sam wondered if it was possible for a bride to hyperventilate at her own wedding.

She glanced up at Nick who was thoroughly enjoying her shock. "You call this a *little* surprise?" Her voice was squeaky and high-pitched.

Bowing before her, Nick held out his hand. "May I please have this dance with my wife?"

Sam's heart had never beat faster, even when she was being chased by gun-toting lunatics, than it did as she took Nick's hand and followed him to the dance floor.

"I understand the bride is one of our biggest fans," Bon Jovi said with a charming smile that made Sam want to swoon, "so I'm delighted to be here for Sam and Nick's first dance as Mr. and Mrs."

Jon Bon Jovi himself sang the most beautiful acoustic version of "Thank You for Loving Me" that Sam had ever heard. She had to keep reminding herself to focus on her new husband and not on the rock star she'd admired for so many years.

"How in the world did you pull this off?" she asked Nick.

"The junior senator from New Jersey is a friend of mine."

"Of course he is. Who *isn't* a friend of yours?

He flashed that winning grin that made her knees go weak every damned time. "He knew someone who knew someone." Nick shrugged, like it was no big deal to get one of the music world's biggest stars to come to their wedding. "My only fear was that once you met him, you'd forget all about me and run off with him."

Sam hugged him so hard he gasped. "No chance of that, but is it okay if I ogle him just a little bit? My love affair with him has lasted years and years, and you're still kinda new around here."

Nick tossed his head back and laughed. "Ogle away. Just remember who's taking you home tonight."

"As if I could ever forget." She brought him down for a lingering kiss that generated catcalls from their guests. "And I'll never forget that you did this for me."

"My pleasure, babe."

She loved that about him—how pleasing her was always more important to him than pleasing himself.

Their wedding party joined them for "Make a Memory." Sam was still trying to absorb that Jon Bon Jovi, *the* Jon Bon Jovi, was actually at *her* wedding when he asked her to have a seat next to her dad. In a daze, Sam made her way across the room to her dad and sat with him, her hand joined with his right hand.

"Can you even *stand* this?" she squealed.

Her dad and Celia cracked up laughing.

Bon Jovi sang "I'll Be There for You," which reduced the entire family to tears. He sang four more songs before turning the music back over to the DJ. When Sam and Nick went to thank him, he gave her a big hug and posed for pictures with them before he took his leave.

"Unbelievable," Sam said, still wanting to pinch herself to make sure she hadn't dreamed it. "Seriously."

"I'm so glad you liked my surprise," Nick said.

"*Liked it?* I'll live off that hug for the rest of my life!"

He raised an eyebrow to let her know she was pushing her luck. "Is that so?"

"Well, maybe not the *rest* of my life, but for a little while anyway."

"Better," Nick said with a tolerant grin.

"Sam," Scotty said, tugging at her arm. "What about the *other* surprise?"

"Ah, yes," she said, "is it time for that?"

Radiating excitement, Scotty nodded.

"Go ahead and tell Shelby. She'll get it for you."

Scotty scurried off, and Sam turned to her husband.

"What're you up to, Samantha?"

"Wait until you see. This was all Scotty's idea, so give him the credit."

Nick leaned in to kiss her.

"What did I do to deserve that?"

"You've embraced a child who means a lot to me, and I appreciate it."

"I love him too."

They exchanged a meaningful look, both remembering their talk in the Jacuzzi about making Scotty a part of their family.

"When we get back," Sam said.

Nick smiled and tightened his grip on her hand.

The moment was interrupted when Scotty, supervised by a team of waiters, pushed a table to the middle of the dance floor.

"*Whoa*." Nick's eyes widened in surprise at the sight of the exact replica of Fenway Park, made of cake and icing. "That is the coolest thing I've ever seen!"

Delighted by Nick's reaction, Scotty held up his hand for a high-five from Sam.

"You did this?" Nick asked Scotty.

"With a little help from Sam," he said modestly.

"Thank you so much," Nick said, hugging Scotty.

"Thank *you*," Scotty said. "For being such a good friend to me."

Nick's eyes filled with tears. "Right back atcha, pal," he said gruffly.

They shared a smile that had Sam blinking back tears. She wondered if they had any idea they were slowly becoming father and son. Watching that happen ranked among the greatest thrills of her life.

"While we're on the subject," Shelby said as her team brought out the orchid-laden wedding cake. "What do you say we cut this one too?"

"Tell me I don't have to cut Fenway," Nick said, stricken by the idea of it.

"We took lots of pictures," Shelby assured him, handing him a knife. "Have at it."

"I can't! It would be like bringing another eighty-six-year curse down on the Sox!"

Sam rolled her eyes at Shelby and took the knife from Nick. "Allow me."

"I can't look," he said with a whimper.

"Me either," Scotty added, covering his eyes.

THIRTEEN

SAM AND NICK were enjoying a few minutes off their feet along with some wedding cake when the DJ handed a microphone to Nick's best man and surrogate father, retired senator Graham O'Connor.

The room quieted, and Nick reached for Sam's hand. She enveloped it between both of hers.

"I know I speak for all of you when I say it's been such a thrill to be part of this celebration of love and joy—two things we can never have too much of in this life," Graham said. "I first met Nick when my son John brought him home for a weekend during their freshman year at Harvard. Right away, I was struck by his eagerness and determination to make something of his life. I remember encouraging John, who was somewhat less…*determined*…at that time in his life to spend more time with the oh-so-serious Nick Cappuano."

A soft wave of laughter rippled through the room.

"That turned out to be a good move on my part. I don't like to think about how responsible Nick probably was for getting John through school."

That drew a short laugh from Nick.

"When John later took office, he insisted Nick run the show, and John always said Nick was the brains behind the whole operation. I'm not sure if that's entirely true, but I do know they made for one hell of a team."

Nick bent his head to beat back a flood of emotion as memories of John swamped him.

"Nick has been a part of our family since that firs weekend at the farm. Of course, we all know John shoul be the one making this speech since he and Nick wer each other's best men from the time they were eighteen They stood by each other through life's ups and downs and when John was taken from us so suddenly, Nic stood by my wife and me through the darkest days o our lives."

Sam leaned into Nick and tightened her grip on hi hand.

"When Nick honored me by asking me to be his bes man, I tried to think of what John would've said today. decided he probably would've told a few off-color joke and stories we'd all be better off not hearing."

Nick looked over at his staffers, gathered at three ta bles, and saw Christina dabbing at her eyes even as sh laughed. She'd carried a quiet torch for John for year before he was killed.

"But the most important thing John would've said i that he loved you like a brother, Nick. We all love you and the O'Connors are delighted to welcome Sam int our hearts and our family. I have no doubt she'll take ver good care of our Nick. We wish you both a lifetime of th love and joy we've all experienced here today." He hel up his champagne flute. "To Nick and Sam."

Nick held up his glass to the man he loved like a fa ther and then toasted his bride. "I'll drink to that," h said as he kissed her.

"Hear, hear," she said. "Now, let's dance our asses off.

FREDDIE HELD ELIN as close as he dared in a room full c colleagues and superior officers. As they moved as on on the crowded dance floor, all he could think about wa getting out of there and being alone with her. It'd bee many weeks since they'd last spent a night together, and he hoped he wasn't getting ahead of himself by planning to spend tonight with her. She'd never mentioned sleeping with him when she agreed to go to the wedding.

She had her arms around him, inside his suit coat, and her hands were warm against his back. Despite his best efforts to contain his raging libido, she had him rock-hard and ready with just the brush of her lips against the sensitive skin on his neck.

Freddie slid his hand down her back to better align her with his erection.

"No need to ask what you're thinking about," she said in a teasing tone.

He released a nervous laugh. "Not doing much thinking at the moment."

"That's not true. You're always thinking."

"Which has kind of been our problem, right?"

"You said it, not me."

He looked down at her, mesmerized as always by her piercing blue eyes and cool blonde beauty. She stole the breath from his lungs when she looked at him the way she was right now. "I want to be with you."

She tilted her hips and tore a groan from deep inside him. "So I noticed."

"Not just in bed. I missed *you*."

"I missed you too."

"Only in bed?"

"Everywhere."

A surge of hope made Freddie feel more buoyant than he'd been since the last time he was with her.

"What about your mother?" Elin asked, her smile fading. "I assume nothing's changed on that front."

"I've decided I can't live my life for her. I have to live it for me." *Sam would be proud of me*, Freddie thought, as he scanned the dance floor and found his partner laughing and dancing with her new husband. Seeing her so happy, after all she'd been through, filled him with determination. He returned his attention to Elin. "And what I want more than anything is you."

Elin flashed him a saucy grin. "How badly do you want me?"

"*Bad.*" Freddie bent his head and kissed her right there in front of his coworkers. He didn't care in the least if anyone saw him kiss the woman he loved. "Very, *very* bad."

"How soon can we sneak out of here?"

"Soon," Freddie said. "Very, very soon."

"I WOULD LIKE," Nick said against Sam's ear, "to take my wife upstairs to bed."

Sam quivered at the desire she heard in his voice. "Your wife would encourage you to do whatever it is you wish to do."

"Mmm," he said, capturing an earlobe between his teeth. "I like the sound of that." He drew back from her and extended an arm. "Shall we?"

"I'm with you, Senator."

"Let's make sure Scotty's set to go with Angela."

They found the boy entertaining Sam's nieces and nephews.

"Are you guys leaving now?" he asked.

Sam was touched by the hint of trepidation she saw on his face.

Nick bent to meet Scott's gaze. "We'll only be gone a week, and I'll call you the minute we get back, okay?"

Scotty nodded. "Thanks for letting me be here for this. It was really awesome."

"Aw, buddy." Nick hugged him. "Thank *you* for all your help with the kids."

"You're welcome." Scotty released Nick and reached for Sam.

She hugged him and kissed the top of his head. "Angela and Spence will take good care of you tonight and get you back to Richmond tomorrow. Make sure you hit her up for pancakes in the morning."

Scotty laughed. "I will. Don't worry about me. I'll be okay."

"We'll see you soon," Nick said. "I promise."

Tracy and Angela appeared out of the crowd to hug them, and Angela slipped a reassuring arm around Scotty.

Sam took the hand Nick extended to her. They were nearly to the door when Sam stopped him. "Wait! I forgot to toss my bouquet."

Nick moaned. "We were almost to a clean getaway!"

"One more minute."

"Hurry!"

Sam signaled for Shelby, who had the whole thing organized in under a minute. "One, two, three!" Sam tossed the bouquet over her shoulder and turned just in time to see it land with Freddie's girlfriend Elin. Like a deer caught in headlights, Elin tossed it up in the air, and Gonzo's fiancée Christina Billings caught it the second time.

She let out a delighted squeal and threw herself into Gonzo's arms.

Sam blew a kiss to her sisters and friends and took her husband's outstretched hand. With a last look back at the beautiful room, Sam left with him to begin their new life together.

I HAVE TO confess that you were right about something," Sam said when they arrived in their suite and found their

honeymoon luggage neatly placed in the corner. Someon
had lit candles, left champagne chilling in an ice bucke
and placed more orchids around the sitting room. Th
suite was cozy and elegant, but she didn't give it much at
tention after waiting all day to be alone with her husband

"I love how you say that, as if me being right abou
something is a special occasion. I expect it to be a regu
lar—maybe even *daily*—occurrence in our marriage."

Sam rolled her eyes at him. "Whatever you say, dear.

Nick tugged off his bowtie and released the top but
ton of his shirt. "So what was I right about this time?"

"Shelby. She was worth every single one of the man
thousands of dollars you paid her. She's a freaking mi
acle worker."

"No kidding. Was there anything she didn't think of?"

"Not that I saw."

Sam turned to him and put her arms around him. "
could use some help getting out of this getup. Are yo
game?"

"I suppose I could be convinced to lend a hand."

Sam smiled at him and tilted her head. "You can sta
at the top and work your way down."

Nick slid the orchid from her hair and brought it t
his nose. "That scent will always remind me of the be
day of my life." He trailed the delicate bloom down he
cheek. "I know you would've preferred something les
elaborate—"

"You were right about the wedding too."

"This me-being-right thing is becoming a bit of a pa
tern."

"Don't get used to it. I'm sure we'll be back to norm
in no time." She reached up to caress his face. "The wed
ding was beautiful and everything I hoped it would be fo
you and so much more that I didn't even know I wanted

"I'm glad to hear you say that." He put the orchid on table and reached up to remove the pins from her hair. Are you kidding me?" he asked as he watched her gor-;eous hair spill down over her shoulders. "Three pins vere holding that whole thing together?"

"Apparently, when you put them in the right places, hat's all you need. Who knew?"

Nick buried his fingers in her hair and tilted his head o kiss her. "You were so incredibly beautiful today, amantha. You are every day, but today…you took my reath away."

"When I saw you waiting for me in church, I've never een you look so handsome." She smoothed her hands ver his chest and made quick work of divesting him of he onyx studs that had served as buttons. "I broke a lot f hearts in the Capitol region today by taking you off he market."

"Right," he said, laughing. "So my guy Terry and your irl Lindsey, huh?"

Sam moaned. She too had noticed his deputy chief f staff dancing most of the evening with the District's hief medical examiner. They'd seemed positively smit-n. "*Why* do our two worlds have to keep colliding?"

He kissed her nose. "Because all our friends want to e as happy as we are."

"I guess," she said as she dropped the studs in a pile n a table and turned around. "Unzip me?"

"If I have to," he said with a dramatic sigh that made er giggle. "Is there something under here that'll stop y heart?"

"Perhaps," she said, sending him a coy smile over er shoulder.

His lips found her neck as he slowly unzipped her ress.

"My sisters gave me a frilly thing I'm supposed t wear tonight."

"Is that so?"

She tipped her head to give him better access to h neck. "Uh huh."

"Is it sexier than what I'm finding under this dress?

Sam bit her lip and smiled. "It's not quite as *dirty* a what's under the dress."

He wrapped his arms around her from behind an pulled her in tight against him. "I'm a big fan of dirty.

Laughing, Sam said, "I never would've guessed."

His hands slid up her front and nudged the dress dow to reveal a bustier. "I haven't even seen the whole thin yet, and I already love it."

Sam's laughter faded to a moan as he cupped h breasts through the cups, teasing her nipples until sh was straining against him. "Nick…"

"What, baby?"

"I want you." Her head fell back to rest on his shou der as he kept up the mischief.

"You have me. I'm all yours for the rest of our lives He shifted, ever so slightly, and her dress dropped in a pool of silk at their feet. Nick helped her to step out it but kept her back to him, pressing his arousal again her bottom. "Oh my God, are those *garters*?"

Enjoying the choked tone of his voice, Sam smile raised her arm and linked it around his neck. "Uh huh

"Have I ever mentioned that as far as I'm concern there's *nothing* sexier than garters?" He took advanta of the opportunity to slide his fingers into the top of t bustier to toy with her nipple.

"I don't think you have," she managed to say as h legs went weak.

He tightened the arm he had around her waist. "I've ot you," he whispered.

Sam closed her eyes and floated on a sea of sensa- on as his lips and fingers set her afire. She hadn't ex- ected marriage to change much of anything between em. She hadn't expected their loving to be any hotter an it had been before. As he kissed and caressed her, he realized she'd been wrong on both counts. Every- ing had changed, and she wanted him more than she ver had before.

As if he'd read her mind, he scooped her up and car- ed her through the doorway to the bedroom where more ndles awaited them. He deposited her gently on the bed, nd stood back to slide the shirt from his shoulders. His ndershirt followed as his gaze took a lazy journey from er feet to her breasts.

Raised up on elbows, Sam watched him, feasting her yes on his muscular chest and arms.

"See something you like?" he asked with the grin that elted her.

"I like everything about you."

He raised an eyebrow. "Everything?"

Reaching out to him, she said, "Everything. Some ings more than others."

"Like what?" he asked as he took her hand and retched out next to her.

Sam caressed his chest, which was covered with just e right amount of soft dark hair. One finger followed e trail that led into his pants. "I love your chest."

He released a long deep breath and shifted to his back.

Sam moved so she was over him, her lips following e path her finger had taken. "And your belly." It quiv- ed under her lips. Encouraged, she unbuttoned and un- pped his pants.

"Sam..."

She looked up to find his eyes closed and his face tig with tension that she planned to relieve in the way sh knew he loved best. Pushing his clothes out of the wa she wrapped her hand around his erection and touche her tongue to the tip.

His fingers burrowed into her hair, holding her rig where he wanted her most. "*Babe*," he moaned.

"Mmm," she said as she took him deep, giving him h tongue and a light scraping of teeth that seemed to dri him wild. She kept it up until he broke out in a sweat an drew her away from him.

"First time together," he said through gritted teet He got busy pulling and tugging at hooks until the bus ier flew across the room. From her feet to her knees her thighs, he took his hands on a journey to her cent where he tugged the scrap of silk covering her out of h way and bent to give her his tongue.

Sam arched her back, wanting more, so much mor

He found the tight nub of her desire and sucked it in his mouth just as he pushed two fingers into her. Aft taking her nearly to the brink of release, he kissed h way up the front of her, teasing her nipples with his tee and tongue until she cried out from the overwhelmi sensations.

"Now, Nick," she said, reaching for him to bring hi into her embrace, breathing in his clean, fresh scent.

His lips found hers in a devouring kiss that made h head spin. The sheer intensity of the feelings coursi through her was unlike anything she'd ever experience even with him. His tongue was everywhere, drinking h in like he'd been waiting forever for the chance to sh her just how much he desired her.

Tears pooled in her eyes as she raised her hips, aski

im for what she wanted more than the next breath. He ntered her swiftly, tearing his lips from hers to draw in ragged deep breath. Fierce and sexy and so beautiful in he candlelight, he loved her with everything he had, as if e'd waited until now, until she was his in every way pos-ible, to show her the full scope of his love and adoration.

His hands were under her, holding her tight against im as he pumped into her with total abandon.

Sam reached the first peak faster than she ever had efore, soaring higher than she'd known she could go. he clung to him, asking him without words to anchor er, to never let her go.

His brow was damp with sweat when he once again evoured her mouth in a series of deep, drugging kisses.

She buried her fingers in his silky hair to keep him ere as took her up again, swiftly, until she hovered on e edge of something big and powerful and altogether ut of her control.

Tearing his mouth free, he groaned and buried his face her hair, crying out his own release as Sam followed im in a shower of light and heat and love so deep she ondered if they'd survive the storm.

Afterward, he rested on top of her for a long time, reathing hard. When he finally raised his head to meet er gaze, he looked as stunned as she felt.

"I thought we'd done that pretty well before," he said, but that… that was…"

"Beyond amazing."

"Yes." He kissed her softly, sweetly. "If that's what arried sex is like I can see why Shelby stays so busy."

Still joined with him, Sam laughed and lifted her legs wrap them around his hips. "Ready for round two?" e asked in a teasing tone.

"I'll never survive the honeymoon." He propped his

chin on her chest and looked into her eyes. "Speakin of that, when are you going to tell me where you're tak ing me?"

She'd agreed to let him pay for the wedding, but onl if she could arrange their honeymoon. All she'd told hi was to pack for warm weather. She combed her finge through his hair, smoothing and soothing. "How doe Bora Bora sound?"

His eyes nearly popped out his head. "*For real?* You' actually going to spend twenty something hours on plane? You who hate to fly? I figured we'd go to Be muda or some place close."

She'd been in deep denial about the lengthy flight but once she'd seen the pictures of the remote Tahitia island, she couldn't image them going anywhere els Sam swallowed hard. "It's only thirteen hours."

Laughing, Nick finally withdrew from her and rolle to his back, arranging her head on his chest. "Have mentioned lately that I love you, Samantha Holland?"

"That's Samantha Holland Cappuano, to you, sir."

He sucked in a sharp deep breath, and the hand th had been caressing her back went still. "What did yo say?"

Suddenly filled with shyness that seemed downrig silly after what they'd just done, she looked up at hin "I'm still Sam Holland at work, but at home, with yo I'm Samantha Cappuano."

He cupped her face and kissed her softly. "I didr think I could love you any more than I already did, b you've made me happier today than any man has a rig to be."

"No one deserves to be happy more than you do."

"More than *we* do," he corrected her.

"I'll let you be right again since you're on such a roll onight."

His face lifted into a half smile that was so sexy it nade her want him all over again.

"You wanna see if that married sex thing was a one-me deal?" she asked.

"Give me a minute to recover, and then we'll find out."

She snuggled into him, happier in that moment than he'd ever been in her life. "We've got all the time in ne world."

* * * * *

AUTHOR'S NOTE

View the wedding details chosen by readers a http://mariesullivanforce.blogspot.com under the "Fata Wedding" tag. Thank you to everyone who helped t make all of Sam's decisions. Neither she nor I could'v done it without you.